PECULIAR

A Tale of the Great Transition

By EPES SARGENT

NEW YORK
CARLETON, PUBLISHER, 413 BROADWAY
M DCCC LXIV

UNIVERSITY PRESS:
WELCH, BIGELOW, AND COMPANY,
CAMBRIDGE.

CONTENTS.

PECULIAR.

CHAPTER I.

A GLANCE IN THE MIRROR.

"Wed not for wealth, Emily, without love, — 't is gaudy slavery; nor for love without competence, — 't is twofold misery." — *Colman's Poor Gentleman.*

IT is a small and somewhat faded room in an unpretending brick house in one of the streets that intersect Broadway, somewhere between Canal Street and the Park. A woman sits at a writing-table, with the fingers of her left hand thrust through her hair and supporting her forehead, while in her right hand she holds a pen with which she listlessly draws figures, crosses, circles and triangles, faces and trees, on the blotting-paper that partly covers a letter which she has been inditing.

A window near by is open at the top. March, having come in like a lion, is going out like a lamb. A canary-bird, intoxicated with the ambrosial breath and subduing sunshine of the first mild day of spring, is pouring forth such a *Te Deum laudamus* as Mozart himself would have despaired of rivalling. Yesterday's rain-storm purified the atmosphere, swept clean the streets, and deodorized the open gutters, that in warm weather poison with their effluvium the air of the great American metropolis.

On the wall, in front of the lady at the table, hangs a mirror. Look, now, and you will catch in it the reflection of her face. Forty? Not far from it. Perhaps four or five years on the sunny side. Fair? Many persons would call her still beautiful. The features, though somewhat thin, show their fine

Grecian outline. The hair is of a rich flaxen, the eyes blue and mild, the mouth delicately drawn, showing Cupid's bow in the curve of the upper lip, and disclosing, not too ostentatiously, the whitest teeth.

Her dress is significant of past rather than present familiarity with a fashionable wardrobe. If she ever wore jewels, she has parted with all of them, for there is not even a plain gold ring on her forefinger. Her robe is a simple brown cashmere, not so distended by crinoline as to disguise her natural figure, which is erect, of the average height, and harmoniously rounded. We detect this the better as she rises, looks a moment sorrowfully in the glass, and sighs to herself, " Fading! fading! "

There is a gentle knock at the door, and to her " Come in," an old black man enters.

" Good morning, Toussaint," says the lady; " what have you there? "

" Only a few grapes for Madame. They are Black Hamburgs, and very sweet. I hope Madame will relish them. They will do her good. Will she try some of them now? "

" They are excellent, Toussaint. And what a beautiful basket you have brought them in! You must have paid high for all this fruit, so early in the season. Indeed, you must not run into such extravagances on my account."

" Does Madame find her cough any better? "

" Thank you, Toussaint, I do not notice much change in it as yet. Perhaps a few more mild days like this will benefit me. How is Juliette? "

" *Passablement bien.* Pretty well. May I ask — ahem! Madame will excuse the question — but does her husband treat her with any more consideration now that she is ill? "

" My good Toussaint, I grieve to say that Mr. Charlton is not so much softened as irritated by my illness. It threatens to be expensive, you see."

" Ah! but that is sad, — sad! I wish Madame were in my house. Such care as Juliette and I would take of her! You look so much like your mother, Madame! I knew her before her first marriage. I dressed her hair the day of her wedding. People used to call her proud. But she was always kind to me, — very kind. And you look like her so much! As I grow old I think all the more of my old and early friends, — the first I had when I came to New York from St. Domingo. Most of them are dead, but I find out their children if I can; and if they are sick I amuse myself by carrying them a few grapes or flowers. They are very good to indulge me by accepting such trifles."

"Toussaint, the goodness is all on your side. These grapes are no trifle, and you ought to know it. I thank you for them heartily. Let me give you back the basket."

"No, please don't. Keep it. Good morning, Madame! Be cheerful. *Le bon temps reviendra.* All shall be well. *Bon jour! Au revoir*, Madame!"

He hurries out of the room, but instantly returns, and, taking a leaf of fresh lettuce out of his pocket, reaches up on tiptoe and puts it between the bars of the bird-cage. "I was nigh forgetting the lettuce for the bird," says he. "Madame will excuse my *gaucherie*." And, bowing low, he again disappears.

The story of Emily Bute Charlton may be briefly told. Her mother, Mrs. Danby, was descended from that John Bradshaw who was president of the court which tried Charles the First, and who opposed a spirited resistance to the usurpation of Cromwell in dissolving the Parliament. Mrs. Danby was proud of her family tree. In her twentieth year she was left a widow, beautiful, ambitious, and poor, with one child, a daughter, who afterwards had in Emily a half-sister. This first daughter had been educated carefully, but she had hardly reached her seventeenth year when she accepted the addresses of a poor man, some fifteen years her senior, of the name of Berwick. The mother, with characteristic energy, opposed the match, but it was of no use. The daughter was incurably in love; she married, and the mother cast her off.

Time brought about its revenges. Mr. Berwick had inherited ten acres of land on the island of Manhattan. He tried to sell it, but was so fortunate as to find nobody to buy. So he held on to the land, and by hard scratching managed to pay the taxes on it. In ten years the city had crept up so near to his dirty acres that he sold half of them for a hundred thousand dollars, and became all at once a rich man. Meanwhile his wife's mother, Mrs. Danby, after remaining fourteen years a widow, showed the inconsistency of her opposition to her daughter's marriage by herself making an imprudent match. She married a Mr. Bute, poor and inefficient, but belonging to "one of the first families." By this husband she had one daughter, Emily, the lady at whose reflection in the mirror we have just been looking.

Emily Bute, like her half-sister, Mrs. Berwick, who was many years her senior, inherited beauty, and was quite a belle in her little sphere in Philadelphia, where her family resided. Her mother, who had repelled Berwick as a son-in-law in his adversity, was too proud to try to propitiate him in his prosperity. She concealed her poverty as well as she could from her daughter, Mrs. Berwick, and the latter had often to resort to stratagem in order to send assistance to the family. At last the proud mother died; and six months afterwards her first-born daughter, Mrs. Berwick, died, leaving one child, a son, Henry Berwick.

Years glided on, and Mr. Bute had hard work to keep the wolf from the door. He was one of those persons whose efforts in life are continual failures, from the fact that they cannot adapt themselves to circumstances, — cannot persevere during the day of small things till their occupation, by gradual development, becomes profitable. He would tire of an employment the moment its harvest of gold seemed remote. Forever sanguine and forever unsuccessful, he at last found himself reduced, with his daughter, to a mode of life that bordered on the shabby.

In this state of things, Mr. Berwick, like a timely angel, reappeared, rich, and bearing help. He was charmed with Emily, as he had formerly been with her half-sister. He proposed marriage. Mr. Bute was enchanted. He could not conceive of Emily's hesitating for a moment. Were her affections pre-engaged? No. She had been a little of a flirt, and that perhaps had saved her from a serious passion. Why not, then, accept Mr. Berwick? He was so old! Old? What is a seniority of thirty years? He is rich, — has a house on the Fifth Avenue, and another on the North River. What insanity it would be in a poor girl to allow such a chance to slip by!

Still Emily had her misgivings. Her virginal instincts protested against the sacrifice. She had an ideal of a happy life, which certainly did not lie all in having a freestone house, French furniture, and a carriage. She knew the bitterness of poverty; but was she quite ready to marry without love? Her father's distresses culminated, and drove her to a decision. She became Mrs. Berwick; and Mr. Bute was presented with ten thousand dollars on the wedding-day. He forthwith relieved himself of fifteen hundred in the purchase of a "new patent-spring phaeton" and span. "A great bargain, sir; splendid creatures; spirited, but gentle; a woman can drive them; no more afraid of a locomotive than of a stack of hay; the carriage in prime order; has n't been used a dozen times; will stand any sort of a shock; the property of my friend, Garnett; he would n't part with the horses if he could afford to keep them; his wife is quite broken-hearted at the idea of losing them; such a chance does n't occur once in ten years; you can sell the span at a great advance in the spring."

This urgent recommendation from "a particular friend, entirely disinterested," decided Bute. He bought the "establishment." The next day as he was taking a drive, the shriek of a steam-whistle produced such an effect upon his incomparable span, that they started off at headlong speed, ran against a telegraph-pole, smashed the "new patent-spring phaeton," threw out the driver, and broke his neck against a curbstone; and that was the end of Mr. Bute for this world, if we may judge from appearances.

Emily's marriage did not turn out so poorly as the retributions of romance might demand. But on Mr. Berwick's death she followed her mother's example, and married a second time. She became Mrs. Charlton. Some idea of the consequences of this new alliance may be got from the letter which she has been writing, and which we take the liberty of laying before our readers.

CHAPTER II.

A MATRIMONIAL BLANK.

"Time doth transfix the flourish set on youth,
And delves the parallels in beauty's brow."
Shakespeare.

To HENRY BERWICK, CINCINNATI.

DEAR HENRY: You kindly left word for me to write you. I have little of a cheering nature to say in regard to myself. We have moved from the house in Fourteenth Street into a smaller one nearer to the Park and to Mr. Charlton's business. His complaints of his disappointment in regard to my means have lately grown more bitter. Your allowance, liberal as it is, seems to be lightly esteemed. The other day he twitted me with *setting a snare* for him by pretending to be a rich widow. O Henry, what an aggravation of insult! I knew nothing, and of course said nothing, as to the extent of your father's wealth. I supposed, as every one else did, that he left a large property. His affairs proved to be in such a state that they could not be disentangled by his executors till two years after his death. Before that time I was married to Mr. Charlton.

Had I but taken your warning, and seen through his real feelings! But he made me think he loved me for myself alone, and he artfully excited my distrust of you and your motives. He represented his own means as ample; though for that I did not care or ask. Repeatedly he protested that he would prefer to take me without a cent of dowry. I was simpleton enough to believe him, though he was ten years my junior. I fell foolishly in love, soon, alas! to be rudely roused from my dream!

It seems like a judgment, Henry. You have always been as kind to me as if you were my own son. Your father was so much my senior, that you may well suppose I did not marry him from love. I was quite young. My notions on the subject of matrimony were unformed. My heart was free. My father urged the step upon me as one that would save him from dire and absolute destitution. What could I do, after many misgivings, but yield? What could I *do?* I now well see what a woman of real moral strength and determination could and ought to have done. But it is too late to sigh over the past.

I behaved passably well, did I not? in the capacity of your step-mother. I was loyal, even in thought, to my husband, although I loved him only with the sort of love I might have entertained for my grandfather. You were but two or three years my junior, but you always treated me as if I were a dowager of ninety. As I now look back, I can see how nobly and chivalrously you bore yourself, though at the time I did not quite understand your over-respectful and distant demeanor, or why, when we went out in the carriage, you always preferred the driver's company to mine.

Your father died, and for a year and a half I conducted myself in a manner not unworthy of his widow and your mother. At the end of that period Mr. Charlton appeared at Berwickville. He dressed pretty well, associated with gentlemen, was rather handsome, and professed a sincere attachment for myself. Time had dealt gently with me, and I was not aware of that disparity in years which I afterwards learned existed between me and my suitor. In an unlucky moment I was subdued by his importunities. I consented to become his wife.

The first six months of our marriage glided away smoothly enough. My new husband treated me with all the attention which I supposed a man of business could give. If the vague thought now and then obtruded itself that there was something to me undefined and unsounded in his character, I thrust the thought from me, and found excuses for the deficiency which had suggested it. One trait which I noticed caused me some surprise. He always discouraged my buying new dresses, and grew very economical in providing for the household. I am no epicure, but have been accustomed to the best in articles of food. I soon discovered that everything in the way of provisions brought into the house was of a cheap or deteriorated quality. I remonstrated, and there was a reform.

One bright day in June, two gentlemen, Mr. Ken and Mr. Turner, connected with the management of your father's estate, appeared at Berwickville. They came to inform me that my late husband had died insolvent, and that the house we then occupied belonged to his creditors, and must be sold at once. Mr. Charlton received this intelligence in silence; but I was shocked at the change wrought by it on his face. In that expression disappointment and chagrin of the intensest kind seemed concentrated. Nothing was to be said, however. There were the documents; there were the facts, — the stern, irresistible facts of the law. The house must be given up.

After these bearers of ill-tidings had gone, Mr. Charlton turned to me. But I will not pain you by a recital of what he said. He rudely dispelled the illusions under which I had been laboring in regard to him. I could only weep. I could not utter a word of retaliation. Whilst he was in the midst of his reproaches, a servant brought me a letter. Mr. Charlton snatched it from my hand, opened, and read it. Either it had a pacifying effect upon him, or he had exhausted his stock of objurgations. He threw the letter on the table and quitted the room.

It was your letter of condolence and dutiful regard, promising me an allowance from your own purse of a hundred dollars a month. What coals of fire it heaped on my head! To please Mr. Charlton I had quarrelled with you, — forbidden you to visit or write me, — and here was your return! The communication coming close upon the dropping of my husband's disguise almost unseated my reason. What a night of tears that was! I recalled your warnings, and now saw their truth, — saw how truly disinterested you were in them all. How generous, how noble you appeared to me! How in contrast, alas! with him I had taken for better or worse!

I lay awake all night. Of course I could not think of accepting your offer. In the first place, my past treatment of you forbade it. And then I knew that your own means were narrow, and that you had just entered into an engagement of marriage with a poor girl. But when, the next day, I communicated my resolve to my husband, he calmly replied: "Nonsense! Write Mr. Berwick, thanking him for his offer, and telling him that, small as the sum is, considering your wants, you accept it." What a poor thing you must have thought me, when you got my cold letter of acceptance. Do me the justice to believe me when I affirm that every word of it was dictated by my husband. How I have longed to see you in person, to tell you all that I have endured and felt! But this circumstances have prevented. And now I am possessed with the idea that I never shall see you in this life again. And that is why I make these confessions. Your marriage, your absence in Europe, your recent return, and your hurried departure for the West, have kept me uncertain as to where a message would reach you. Yesterday I got a few affectionate lines from you, telling me a letter, if mailed at once, would reach you in Cincinnati, or, if a week later, in New Orleans. And so I am devoting the forenoon to this review of my past, so painful and sad.

Let me think of your happier lot, and rejoice in it. So your affairs have prospered beyond all hope! Through your wife you are unexpectedly rich in worldly means. Better still, you are rich in affection. Your little Clara is "the brightest, the loveliest, the sunniest little thing in the wide world." So you write me; and I can well believe it from the photograph and the lock of hair you send me. Bless her! What would I give to hug her to my bosom. And you too, Henry, you too I could kiss with a kiss that should be purely maternal, — a benediction, — a kiss your wife would approve, for, after all, you are the only child I have had. Mr. Charlton has always said he would have no children till he was a rich man. He and the female physician he employs have nearly killed me with their terrible drugs. Yes, I am dying, Henry. Even the breath of this sweet spring morning whispers it in my ear. Bless you and yours forever! What a mistake my life has been! And yet, how I craved to love and be loved! You will think kindly of me always, and teach your wife and child to have pleasant associations with my name.

All the rich presents your father made me have been sold by Mr. Charlton; but I have one, that he has not seen, — a costly and beautiful gold casket for jewels, which I reserve as a present for your little Clara. I shall to-morrow pack it up carefully, and take it to a friend, who I know will keep and deliver it safely. That friend, strange as it may sound to you, is the venerable old black hair-dresser, Toussaint, who lives in Franklin Street. Your father used to say he had never met a man he would trust before Toussaint; and I can say as much. Toussaint used to dress my mother's hair; he is now my adviser and friend.

Born a slave in the town of St. Mark in St. Domingo in 1766, Pierre Toussaint was twelve years the junior of that fellow-slave, the celebrated Toussaint l'Ouverture, born on the same river, who converted a mob of undrilled, uneducated Africans into an army with which he successively overthrew the forces of France, England, and Spain. At the beginning of the troubles in the island, in 1801, Pierre was taken by his master, the wealthy Mons. Berard, to New York. Berard, having lost his immense property in St. Domingo, soon died, and Pierre, having learnt the business of a hair-dresser, supported Madame Berard by his labors some eight years till her death, though she had no legal claim upon his service. Bred up, as he was, indulgently, Pierre's is one of those exceptional cases in which slavery has not destroyed the moral sense.

I know of few more truly venerable characters. A pious Catholic, he is one of the stanchest of friends. One of his rules through life has been, never to incur a debt, — to pay on the spot for everything he buys. And yet he is continually giving away large sums in charity. One day I said, "Toussaint, you are rich enough; you have more than you want; why not stop working now?" He answered, "Madame, I have enough for myself, but if I stop work, I have not enough for others!" By the great fire of 1835, Toussaint lost by his investments in insurance companies. The Schuylers and the Livingstons passed around a subscription-paper to repair his losses; but he stopped it, saying he would not take a cent from them, since there were so many who needed help more than he.

An old French gentleman, a white man, once rich, whom Toussaint had known, was reduced to poverty and fell sick. For several months Toussaint and his wife, Juliette, sent him a nicely cooked dinner; but Toussaint would not let him know from whom it came, "because," said the negro, "it might hurt his pride to know it came from a black man." Juliette once called on this invalid to learn if her husband could be of any help. "O no," said the old Monsieur, "I am well known; I have good friends; every day they send me a dinner, served up in French style. To-day I had a charming vol-au-vent, an omelette, and green peas, not to speak of salmon. I am a person of some importance, you see, even in this strange land." And Juliette would go home, and she and Toussaint would have a good laugh over the old man's vauntings.*

But what has possessed me to enter into all these details! I know not, unless it is the desire to escape from less agreeable thoughts.

I have a request to make, Henry. You will think me fanciful, foolish, perhaps fanatical; and yet I am impelled, by an unaccountable impression, to ask you to give up the tickets you tell me you have engaged in the Pontiac, and to take passage for New Orleans in some other boat. If you ask me *why*, the only explanation I can give is, that the thought besets me, but the reason of it I do not know. Do you remember I once capriciously refused to let your father go in the cars to Springfield, although his baggage was on board? Those cars went through the draw-bridge, and many lives were lost. Write me that you will heed my request.

And now, Henry, son, nephew, friend, good by! Tell little Clara she has an aunt or grandmother (which, shall it be?) in New York who loves to think of her and to picture the fair forehead over which the little curl you sent me once fell. By the way, I have examined her photograph with a microscope, and have conceived a fancy that her eyes are of a slightly different color; one perhaps a gray and the other a mixed blue. Am I right? Tell your wife how I grieve to think that circumstances have not allowed us to meet and become personally acquainted. You now know all the influences that have kept us apart, and that have made me seem frigid and ungrateful, even when my heart was overflowing with affection. What more shall I say, except to sum up all my love for you and all my gratitude in the one parting prayer, Heaven bless you and yours!

Your mother, EMILY CHARLTON.

* Having slept under Toussaint's roof, and seen him often, the writer can testify to the accuracy of this sketch of one of the most thorough gentlemen in bearing and in heart that he ever knew.

CHAPTER III.

THE WOLF AND THE LAMB.

"Bitten by rage canine of dying rich;
Guilt's blunder! and the loudest laugh of hell!"
Young.

THE poor little lady! First sold by a needy parent to an old man, and then betrayed by her own uncalculating affections to a young one, whose nature had the torpor without the venerableness of age! Her heart, full of all loving possibilities, had steered by false lights and been wrecked. Brief had been its poor, shattered dream of household joys and domestic amenities!

It was the old, old story of the cheat and the dupe; of credulous innocence overmatched by heartless selfishness and fraud.

The young man "of genteel appearance and address" who last week, as the newspapers tell us, got a supply of dry-goods from Messrs. Raby & Co., under false pretences, has been arrested, and will be duly punished.

But the scoundrel who tricks a confiding woman out of her freedom and her happiness under the false pretences of a disinterested affection and the desire of a loving home, — the swindler who, with the motives of a devil of low degree, affects the fervor and the dispositions of a loyal heart, — for such an impostor the law has no lash, no prison. To play the blackleg and the sharper in a matter of the affections is not penal. Success consecrates the crime; and the victim, when her eyes are at length opened to the extent of the deception and the misery, must continue to submit to a yoke at once hateful and demoralizing; she must submit, unless she is willing to brave the ban of society and the persecutions of the law.

Ralph Charlton, when he gave his wife Berwick's letter the night before, had supposed she would sit down to pen an answer as soon as she was alone. And so the next morning, after visiting his office in Fulton Street, he retraced his steps, and re-entered his house soon after Toussaint had left, and just as Mrs. Charlton had put her signature to the last page of the manuscript, and, bowing her forehead on her palms, was giving vent to sobs of bitter emotion.

Charlton was that prodigy in nature, — a young man in whom an avarice that would have been remarkable in a senile miser had put in subjection all the other passions. Well formed and not ungraceful, his countenance was at first rather prepossessing and propitiatory. It needed a keener eye than that of the ordinary physiognomist to penetrate to the inner nature. It was only when certain expressions flitted over the features that they betrayed him. You must study that countenance and take it at unawares before you could divine what it meant. Age had not yet hardened it in the mould of the predominant bias of the character. Well born and bred, he ought to have been a gentleman, but it is difficult for a man to be that and a miser at the same time. There was little in his style of dress that distinguished him from the mob of young business-men, except that a critical eye would detect that his clothes were well preserved. Few of his old coats were made to do service on the backs of the poor.

Charlton called himself a lawyer, his specialty being conveyancing and real estate transactions. His one purpose in life was to be a rich man. To this end all others must be subordinate. When a boy he had been taught to play on the flute; and his musical taste, if cultivated, might have been a saving element of grace. But finding that in a single year he had spent ten dollars in concert tickets, he indignantly repudiated music, and shut his ears even to the hand-organs in the street. He had inherited a fondness for fine horses. Before he was twenty-five he would not have driven out after Ethan Allen himself, if there had been any toll-gate keepers to pay. His taste in articles of food was nice and discriminating; but he now bought fish and beef of the cheapest, and patronized a milkman whose cows were fed on the refuse of the distilleries.

Charlton was not venturous in speculation. The boldest operation he ever attempted was that of his marriage. Before taking that step he had satisfied himself in regard to the state of the late Mr. Berwick's affairs. They could be disentangled, and made to leave a balance of half a million for the heirs, if a certain lawsuit, involving a large amount of real estate, should be decided the right way. Charlton burrowed and inquired and examined till he came to the conclusion that the suit would go in favor of the estate. On that hint he took time by the forelock, and married the widow. To his consternation matters did not turn out as he had hoped.

As Charlton entered his wife's room, on the morning she had been writing the letter already presented, "What is all this, madam?" he exclaimed, advancing and twitching away the manuscript that lay before her.

The lady thus startled rose and looked at him without speaking, as if struggling to comprehend what he had done. At length a gleam of intelligence flashed from her eyes, and she mildly said, "I will thank you to give me back those papers: they are mine."

"*Mine*, Mrs. Charlton! Where did you learn that word?" said the husband, really surprised at the language of his usually meek and acquiescent helpmate.

"Do you not mean to give them back?"

"Assuredly no. To whom is the letter addressed? Ah! I see. To Mr. Henry Berwick. Highly proper that I should read what my wife writes to a young man."

"Then you do not mean to give the letter back, Charlton?"

Another surprise for the husband! At first she used to speak to him as "Ralph," or "dear"; then as "Mr. Charlton"; then as "Sir"; and now it was plain "Charlton." What did it portend?

The lady held out her hand, as if to receive the papers.

"Pooh!" said the husband, striking it away. "Go and attend to your housework. What a shrill noise your canary is making! That bird must be sold. There was a charge of seventy-five cents for canary-seed in my last grocer's bill! It 's atrocious. The creature is eating us out of house and home. Bird and cage would bring, at least, five dollars."

"The letter, — do you choose to give it back?"

"If, after reading it, I think proper to send it to its address, it shall be sent. Give yourself no further concern about it."

Mrs. Charlton advanced with folded arms, looked him unblênchingly in the face, and gasped forth, with a husky, half-choked utterance, "Beware!"

"Truly, madam," said the astonished husband, "this is a new character for you to appear in, and one for which I am not prepared."

"It is for that reason I say, Beware! Beware when the tame, the submissive, the uncomplaining woman is roused at last. Will you give me that letter?"

"Go to the Devil!"

Mrs. Charlton threw out her hand and clutched at the manuscript, but her husband had anticipated the attempt. As she closed with him in the effort to recover the paper, he threw her off so forcibly that she fell and struck her head against one of the protuberant claws of the legs of her writing-table.

Whatever were the effects of the blow, it did not prevent the lady from rising immediately, and composing her exuberant hair with a gesture of puzzled distress that would have excited pity in the heart of a Thug. But Charlton did not even inquire if she were hurt. After a pause she seemed to recover her recollection, and then threw up her head with a lofty gesture of resolve, and quitted the room.

Her husband sat down and read the letter. His equanimity was unruffled till he came to the passage where the writer alludes to the gold casket she had put aside for little Clara. At that disclosure he started to his feet, and gave utterance to a hearty execration upon the woman who had presumed to circumvent him by withholding any portion of her effects. He opened the door and called, "Wife!" No voice replied to his summons. He sought her in her chamber. She was not there. She had left the house. So Dorcas, the one over-worked domestic of the establishment, assured him.

Charlton saw there was no use in scolding. So he put on his hat and walked down Broadway to his office. Here he wrote a letter which he wished to mail before one o'clock. It was directed to Colonel Delancy Hyde, Philadelphia. Having finished it and put it in the mail-box, Charlton took his way at a brisk pace to the house of old Toussaint.

That veteran himself opened the door. A venerable black

man, reminding one of Ben Franklin in ebony. His wool was gray, his complexion of the blackest, showing an unmixed African descent. He was of middling height, and stooped slightly; was attired in the best black broadcloth, with a white vest and neckcloth, and had the manners of a French marquis of the old school.

"Is my wife here?" asked Charlton.

"Madame is here," replied the old man; "but she suffers, and prays to be not disturbed."

"I must see her. Conduct me to her."

"*Pardonnez.* Monsieur will comprehend as I say the commands of Madame in this house are sacred."

"You insolent old nigger! do you mean to tell me I am not to see my own wife?"

"*Precisement.* Monsieur cannot see Madame Charlton."

"I 'll search the house for her, at any rate. Out of the way, you blasted old ape!"

Here a policeman, provided for the occasion by Toussaint, and who had been smoking in the front room opening on the hall, made his appearance.

"You can't enter this house," said Blake, carelessly knocking the ashes from his cigar. Charlton had a wholesome respect for authority. He drew back on seeing the imperturbable Blake, with the official star on his breast, and said, "I came here, Mr. Blake, to recover a little gold box that I have reason to believe my wife has left with this old nigger."

"Well, she might have left it in worse hands, — eh, Toussaint?" said Blake, resuming his cigar; and then, removing it, he added, "If you call this old man a nigger again, I 'll make a nigger of you with my fist."

Toussaint might have taken for his motto that of the old eating-house near the Park, — "*Semper paratus.*" The gold box having been committed to him to deposit in a place of safety, he had meditated long as to the best disposition he could make of it. As he stood at the window of his house, looking thoughtfully out, he saw coming up the street a gay old man, swinging a cane, humming an opera tune, and followed by a little dog. As the dashing youth drew nearer, Toussaint recognized in him an old acquaintance, and a man not many years his junior, — Mr. Albert Pompilard, stock-broker, Wall Street.

No two men could be more unlike than Toussaint and Pompilard; and yet they were always drawn to each other by some subtle points of attraction. Pompilard was a reckless speculator and spendthrift; Toussaint, a frugal and cautious economist; but he had been indebted for all his best investments to Pompilard. Bold and often audacious in his own operations, Pompilard never would allow Toussaint to stray out of the path of prudence. Not unfrequently Pompilard would founder in his operations on the stock exchange. He would fall, perhaps, to a depth where a few hundred dollars would have been hailed as a rope flung to a drowning man. Toussaint would often come to him at these times and offer a thousand dollars or so as a loan. Pompilard, in order not to hurt the negro's feelings, would take it and pretend to use it; but it would be always put securely aside, out of his reach, or deposited in some bank to Toussaint's credit.

Toussaint stood at his door as Pompilard drew nigh.

"Ha! good morning, my guide, philosopher, and friend!" exclaimed the stock-broker. "What 's in the wind now, Toussaint? Any money to invest?"

"No, Mr. Pompilard; but here 's a box that troubles me."

"A box! Not a pill-box, I hope? Let me look at it. Beautiful! beautiful, exceedingly! It could not be duplicated for twelve hundred dollars. Whose is it? Ah! here 's an inscription, — '*Henry Berwick to Emily.*' Berwick? It was a Henry Berwick who married my wife's niece, Miss Aylesford."

"This box," interposed Toussaint, "was the gift of his late father to his second wife, the present Mrs. Charlton."

"Ah! yes, I remember the connection now."

"Mrs. Charlton wishes me to deposit the box where, in the event of her death, it will reach the daughter of the present Mrs. Berwick. Here is the direction on the envelope."

Pompilard read the words: "For Clara Aylesford Berwick, daughter of Henry Berwick, Esq., to be delivered to her in the event of the death of the undersigned, Emily Charlton."

"I will tell you what to do," said Pompilard. "Here come Isaac Jones of the Chemical and Arthur Schermerhorn. Isaac shall give a receipt for the box and deposit it in the safe of the bank, there to be kept till called for by Miss Clara Berwick or her representative."

"That will do," said Toussaint.

The two gentlemen were called in, and in five minutes the proper paper was drawn up, witnessed, and signed, and Mr. Jones gave a receipt for the box.

Briefly Toussaint now explained to Charlton the manner in which the box had been disposed of. Charlton was nonplussed. It would not do to disgust the officials at the Chemical. It might hurt his credit. A consolatory reflection struck him. "Do you say my wife is suffering?" he asked.

"Madame will need a physician," replied the negro. "I have sent for Dr. Hull."

"Well, look here, old gentleman, I'm responsible for no debts of your contracting on her account. I call Mr. Blake to witness. If you keep her here, it must be at your own expense. Not a cent shall you ever have from *me*."

"That will not import," replied Toussaint, with the hauteur of a prince of the blood.

Felicitating himself on having got rid of a doctor's bill, Charlton took his departure.

"The exceedingly poor cuss!" muttered Blake, tossing after him the stump of a cigar.

"Let me pay you for your trouble, Mr. Blake," said Toussaint.

"Not a copper, Marquis! I have been here only half an hour, and in that time have read the newspaper, smoked one regalia, quality prime, and pocketed another. If that is not pay enough, you shall make it up by curling my hair the next time I go to a ball."

"But take the rest of the cigars."

"There, Marquis, you touch me on my weak point. Thank you. Good by, Toussaint!"

Toussaint closed the door, and called to his wife in a whisper, speaking in French, "How goes it, Juliette?"

"Hist! She sleeps. She wishes you to put this letter in the post-office as soon as possible. If you can get the canary-bird, do it. I hope the doctor will be here soon."

Toussaint left at once to mail the invalid's letter and get possession of her bird.

CHAPTER IV.

A FUGITIVE CHATTEL.

"The providential trust of the South is to perpetuate the institution of domestic slavery as now existing, with freest scope for its natural development. We should at once lift ourselves intelligently to the highest moral ground, and proclaim to all the world that we hold this trust from God, and in its occupancy are prepared to stand or fall." —*Rev. Dr. Palmer of New Orleans*, 1861.

THE next morning Charlton sat in his office, calculating his percentage on a transaction in which he had just acted as mediator between borrower and lender. The aspect of the figures, judging from his own, was cheerful.

The office was a gloomy little den up three flights of stairs. All the furniture was second hand, and the carpet was ragged and dirty. No broom or dusting-cloth had for months molested the ancient, solitary reign of the spiders on the ceiling. A pile of cheap slate-colored boxes with labels stood against the wall opposite the stove. An iron safe served also as a dressing-table between the windows that looked out on the street; and over it hung a small rusty mirror in a mahogany frame with a dirty hair-brush attached. The library of the little room was confined to a few common books useful for immediate reference; a City Directory, a copy of the Revised Statutes, the Clerk's Assistant, and a dozen other volumes, equally recondite.

There was a knock at the door, and Charlton cried out, "Come in!"

The visitor was a negro whose face was of that fuliginous hue that bespeaks an unmixed African descent. He was of medium height, square built, with the shoulders and carriage of an athlete. He seemed to be about thirty years of age. His features, though of the genuine Ethiopian type, were a refinement upon it rather than an exaggeration. The expression was bright, hilarious, intelligent; frank and open, you would add, unless you chanced to detect a certain quick oblique glance which would flash upon you now and then, and vanish before you could well realize what it meant. Across his left cheek was an ugly scar, almost deep enough to be from a cut lass wound.

"Good morning, Peculiar. Take a chair."

"Not that name, if you please, Mr. Charlton," said the negro, closing the door and looking eagerly around to see if there had been a listener. "Remember, you are to call me Jacobs."

"Ah yes, I forgot. Well, Jacobs, I am glad to see you; but you are a few minutes before the time. It is n't yet twelve. Just step into that little closet and wait there till I call you."

The negro did as he was directed, and Charlton closed the door upon him. Five minutes after, the clock of Trinity struck twelve, and there was another knock at the door.

Before we suffer it to be answered, we must go back and describe an interview that took place some seven weeks previously, in the same office, between Charlton and the negro.

A year before that first interview, Charlton had, in some accidental way, been associated with a well-known antislavery counsel, in a case in which certain agents of the law for the rendition of fugitive slaves had been successfully foiled. Though Charlton's services had been unessential and purely mercenary, he had shared in the victor's fame; and the grateful colored men who employed him carried off the illusion that he was a powerful friend of the slave. And so when Mr. Peculiar, *alias* Mr. Jacobs, found himself in New York, a fugitive from bondage, he was recommended, if he had any little misgivings as to his immunity from persecution and seizure, to apply to Mr. Charlton as to a fountain of legal profundity and philanthropic expansiveness. Greater men than our colored brethren have jumped to conclusions equally far from the truth in regard not only to lawyers, but military generals.

Charlton's primary investigations, in his first interview with Peek, had reference to the amount of funds that the negro could raise through his own credit and that of his friends. This amount the lawyer found to be small; and he was about to express his dissatisfaction in emphatic terms, when a new consideration withheld him. Affecting that ruling passion of universal benevolence which the fond imagination of his colored client had attributed to him, he pondered a moment, then spoke as follows:

"You tell me, Jacobs, you are in the delicate position of a fugitive slave. I love the slave. Am I not a friend and a brother, and all that? But if you expect me to serve you, you must be entirely frank, — disguise nothing, — disclose to me your real history, name, and situation, — make a clean breast of it, in short."

"That I will do, sir. I know, if I trust a lawyer at all, I ought to trust him wholly."

There was nothing in the negro's language to indicate the traditional slave of the stage and the novel, who always says "Massa," and speaks a gibberish indicated to the eye by a cheap misspelling of words. A listener who had not seen him would have supposed it was an educated white gentleman who was speaking; for even in the tone of his voice there was an absence of the African peculiarity.

"My friends tell me I may trust you, sir," said Jacobs, advancing and looking Charlton square in the face. Charlton must have blenched for an instant, for the negro, as a slight but significant compression of the lip seemed to portend, drew back from confidence. "Can I trust you?" he continued, as if he were putting the question as much to himself as to Charlton. There was a pause.

Charlton took from his drawer a letter, which he handed to the negro, with the remark, "You know how to read, I suppose."

Without replying, Peek took the letter and glanced over it, — a letter of thanks from a committee of colored citizens in return for Charlton's services in the case already alluded to. Peek was reassured by this document. He returned it, and said, "I will trust you, Mr. Charlton."

"Take a seat then, Jacobs, and I will make such notes of your story as I may think advisable."

Peek did as he was invited; but Charlton seemed interested mainly in dates and names. A more faithful reporter would have presented the memorabilia of the narrative somewhat in this form:

"Was born on Herbert's plantation in Marshall County,

Mississippi. Mother a house-slave. When he was four years old she was sold and taken to Louisiana. His real name not Jacobs. That name he took recently in New York. The name he was christened by was PECULIAR INSTITUTION. It was given to him by one Ewell, a drunken overseer, and was soon shortened to Peek, which name has always stuck to him. Was brought up a body servant till his fourteenth year. Soon found that the way for a slave to get along was to lie, but to lie so as not to be found out. Grew to be so expert a liar, that among his fellows he was called the lawyer. No offence to you, Mr. Charlton.

"As soon as he could carry a plate, was made to wait at table. Used to hear the gentlemen and ladies talk at meals. Could speak their big words before he knew their meaning. Kept his ears and eyes well open. An old Spanish negro, named Alva, taught him by stealth to read and write. When the young ladies took their lessons in music, this child stood by and learnt as much as they did, if not more. Learnt to play so well on the piano that he was often called on to show off before visitors.

"Was whipped twice, and then not badly, at Herbert's: once for stealing some fruit, once for trying to teach a slave to read. Family very pious. Old Herbert used to read prayers every morning. But he did n't mind making a woman give up one husband and take another. Did n't mind separating mother and child. Did n't mind shooting a slave for disobedience. Saw him do it once. Herbert had told Big Sam not to go with a certain metif girl; for Herbert was as particular about matching his niggers as about his horses and sheep. A jealous negro betrayed Sam. Old Herbert found Sam in the metif girl's hut, and shot him dead, without giving him a chance to beg for mercy.* Well, Sam was only a nigger; and did n't Mr. Herbert have family prayers, and go to church twice every Sunday? Who should save his soul alive, if not Mr. Herbert?

"In spite of prayers, however, things did n't go right on the

* A fact. The incident, which occurred literally as related (on Bob Myers's plantation in Alabama), was communicated to the writer by an eye-witness, a respectable citizen of Boston, once resident at the South. The murder, of course, passed not only unpunished, but unnoticed.

plantation. The estate was heavily mortgaged. Finally the creditors took it, and the family was broken up. Peculiar was sold to one Harkman, a speculator, who let him out as an apprentice in New Orleans, in Collins's machine-shop for the repair of steam-engines. But Collins failed, and then Peek became a waiter in the St. Charles Hotel. Here he stayed six years. Cut his eye-teeth during that time. Used to talk freely with Northern visitors about slavery. Studied the big map of the United States that hung in the reading-room. Learnt all about the hotels, North and South. Stretched his ears wide whenever politics were discussed.

"Having waited on the principal actors and singers of the day at the St. Charles, he had a free pass to the theatres. Used often to go behind the scenes. Waited on Blitz, Anderson, and other jugglers. Saw Anderson show up the humbug, as he called it, of spiritual manifestations. Went to church now and then. Heard some bad preachers, and some good. Heard Mr. Clapp preach. Heard Mr. Palmer preach. After hearing the latter on the duties of slaves, tried to run away. Was caught and taken to a new patent whipping-machine, recently introduced by a Yankee. Here was left for a whipping. Bought off the Yankee with five dollars, and taught him how to stain my back so as to imitate the marks of the lash. Thus no discredit was brought on the machine. A week after was sold to a Red River planter, Mr. Carberry Ratcliff.

"Can never speak of this man calmly. He had a slave, a woman white as you are, sir, that he beat, and then tried to make me take and treat as my wife. When he found I had cheated him, he just had me tied up and whipped till three strong men were tired out with the work. It 's a wonder how I survived. My whole back is seamed deep with the scars. This scar over my cheek is from a blow he himself gave me that day with a strip of raw hide. He sold me to Mr. Barnwell in Texas as soon as I could walk, which was n't for some weeks. I left, resolving to come back and kill Ratcliff. I meant to do this so earnestly, that the hope of it almost restored me. Revenge was my one thought, day and night. I felt that I could not be at ease till that man Ratcliff had paid for his barbarity. Even now I sometimes wake full of wrath from my dreams, imagining I have him at my mercy.

"I went to Texas with a bad reputation. Was put among the naughty darkies, and sent to the cotton-field. Braxton, the overseer, had been a terrible fellow in his day, but I happened to be brought to him at the time he was beginning to get scared about his soul. Soon had things my own way. Braxton made me a sort of sub-overseer; and I got more work out of the field-hands by kindness than Braxton had ever got by the lash.

"One day I discovered on a neighboring plantation an old woman who proved to be my mother. She had been brought here from Louisiana. She was on the point of dying. She knew me, first from hearing my name, and then from a cross she had pricked in India ink on my breast. She had n't seen me for sixteen years. Had been having a hard time of it. Her hut was close by a slough, a real fever-hole, and she had been sick most of the time the last three years.

"The old woman flashed up bright on finding me: gave me a long talk; told me little stories of when I was a child; told me how my father had been sold to an Alabama man, and shot dead for trying to break away from a whipping-post. All at once she said she saw angels, drew me down to her, and dropped away quiet as a lamb, so that, though my forehead lay on her breast, I did n't know when she died.

"After this loss, I was pretty serious. Was n't badly treated. My master, an educated gentleman, was absent in New Orleans most of the time. Overseer Braxton, after the big scare he got about his soul, grew to be humane, and left almost everything to me. But I felt sick of life, and wanted to die, though not before I had killed Ratcliff. One day I heard that Corinna, a quadroon girl, a slave on the plantation, had fallen into a strange state, during which she preached as no minister had ever preached before. I had known her as a very ordinary and rather stupid girl. Went to see her in one of her trances. Found that report had fallen short of the real case. Was astonished at what I saw and heard. Saw what no white man would believe, and so felt I was wiser on one point than all the white men. My interviews with Corinna soon made me forget about Ratcliff; and when she died, six weeks after my first visit, felt my mind full of things it would take me a lifetime to think out and settle.

"After Corinna's death, I stayed some months on the plantation, though I had a chance to leave. Stayed because I had an easy time and because I found I could be of use to the slaves; and further, because I had resolved, if ever I got free, it should be by freeing myself. A white man, a Mr. Vance, whose life I had saved, wanted to buy and free me. I made him spend his money so it would show for more than just the freeing of one man. But Braxton, the overseer, who was letting me have pretty much my own way, at last died; and Hawks, his successor, was of opinion that the way to get work out of niggers was to treat them like dogs; and so, one pleasant moonlight night, I made tracks for Galveston. Here, by means of false papers, I managed to get passage to New Orleans, and there hid myself on board a Yankee schooner bound for New London, Connecticut. When she was ten days out, I made my appearance on deck, much to the surprise of the crew. Fifteen days afterwards we arrived in the harbor of New London.

"Old Skinner, the captain, had been playing possum with me all the voyage, — keeping dark, and pretending to be my friend, meaning all the while to have me arrested in port. No sooner had he dropped anchor than he sent on shore for the officers. But the mate tipped me the wink. 'Darkey,' said he, 'do you see that little green fishing-boat yonder? Well, that belongs to old Payson, an all-fired abolitionist and friend of the nigger. Our Captain and crew are all under hatches, and now if you don't want to be a lost nigger, jest you drop down quietly astern, swim off to Payson, and tell him who you are, and that the slave-catchers are after you. If old Payson don't put you through after that, it will be because it is n't old Payson.'

"I did as the mate told me. Reached the fishing-boat. Found old Payson, a gnarled, tough, withered old sea-dog, who comprehended at once what was in the wind, and cried, 'Ha! ha!' like the war-horse that snuffs the battle. Just as I got into the boat, Captain Skinner came up on the schooner's deck, and saw what had taken place. The schooner's small boat had been sent ashore for the officers whose business it was to carry out the Fugitive-Slave Law. What could Skinner do? Visions of honors and testimonials and rewards and dinners from Texan slaveholders, because of his loyalty to the *institution* in returning a runaway nigger, suddenly vanished. He paced the deck in a rage. To add to his fury, old Payson, while I stood at the bows, dripping and grinning, came sailing up before a stiff breeze, and passed within easy speaking distance, Payson pouring in such a volley of words that Skinner was dumbfounded. 'I 'll make New London too hot for you, you blasted old skinflint!' cried Payson. 'You 'd sell your own sister just as soon as you 'd sell this nigger, you would! Let me catch you ashore, and I 'll give you the blastedest thrashing you ever got yet, you infernal doughface, you! Go and lick the boots of slaveholders. It 's jest what you was born for.'

"And the little sail-boat passed on out of hearing. Payson got in the track of one of the spacious steamboats that ply between the cities of Long Island Sound and New York, and managed to throw a line, so as to be drawn up to the side. We then got on board. In six hours, we were in New York. Payson put me in the proper hands, bade me good by, returned to his sail-boat, and made the best speed he could back to New London, fired with hopes of pitching into that 'meanest of all mean skippers, old Skinner.'

"This was three years ago. The despatch agents of the underground railroad hurried me off to Canada. As soon as I judged it safe, I returned to New York. Here I got a good situation as head-waiter at Bunker's. Am married. Have a boy, named Sterling, a year old. Am very happy with my wife and child and my hired piano. But now and then I and my wife have an alarm lest I shall be seized and carried back to slavery."

Here Mr. Institution finished his story, which we have condensed, generally using, however, his own words. Charlton did not subject him to much cross-questioning. He asked, *first*, what was the name of the schooner in which Peek had escaped from Texas. It was the Albatross. Charlton made a note. *Second*, did Mr. Barnwell, Peek's late master, have an agent in New Orleans? Yes; Peek had often seen the name on packages: P. Herman & Co. And, *third*, did Peek marry his wife in Canada? Yes. Then she, too, is a fugitive slave, eh?

Peek seemed reluctant to answer this question, and flashed a quick, distrustful glance on Charlton. The latter assumed an air of indifference, and said, "Perhaps you had better not answer that question; it is immaterial."

Again Peek's mind was relieved.

"That is enough for the present, Mr. Jacobs," continued Charlton. "If I have occasion to see you, I can always find you at Bunker's, I suppose."

"Yes, Mr. Charlton. Inquire for John Jacobs. Keep a bright lookout for me, and you sha'n't be the loser. Will five dollars pay you?"

Charlton wavered between the temptation to clutch more at the moment, and the prospect of making his new client available in other ways. At length taking the money he replied, "I will make it do for the present. Good morning."

CHAPTER V.

A RETROSPECT.

"Any slave refusing obedience to any command may be flogged till he submits or dies. Not by occasional abuses alone, but by the universal law of the Southern Confederacy, the existing system of slavery violates all the moral laws of Christianity." — *Rev. Newman Hall.*

BEFORE removing Peculiar from the closet which at Charlton's bidding he has entered, we must go back to the time when he was a slave, and amplify and illustrate certain parts of his abridged narrative. His life, up to the period when he comes upon our little stage, divides itself into three eras, all marked by their separate moral experiences. In the *first*, he felt the slave's crowning curse, — the absence of that sense of personal responsibility which freedom alone can give; and he fell into the demoralization which is the inherent consequence of the slave's condition. In the *second* era, he encountered his mother, and then the frozen fountain of his affections was unsealed and melted. In the *third*, he met Corinna, and for the first time looked on life with the eyes of belief.

It will seem idle to many advanced minds in this nineteenth century to use words to show the wrong of slavery. Why not as well spend breath in denouncing burglary or murder? But slavery is still a power in the world. We are daily told it is the proper *status* for the colored man in this country; that he ought to covet slavery as much as a white man ought to covet freedom. Besides, since Peek has confessed himself at one time of his life a liar, we must show why he ought logically to have been one.

To blame a slave for lying and stealing, is about as fair as it would be to blame a man for using strategy in escaping from an assassin. For the slaveholder, if not the assassin of the slave's life, is the assassin of his liberty, his manhood, his moral dignity.

Mr. Pugh of Ohio, Vallandigham's associate on the gubernatorial ticket for 1863, presents his thesis thus: "When the slaves are fit for freedom, they will be free."

The profundity of this oracular proposition is only equalled in the remark of the careful grandmother, who declared she would never let a boy go into the water till he knew how to swim.

"*When* the slaves are fit!" As if the road were clear for them to achieve their fitness! Why, the slave is not only robbed of his labor, but of his very chances as a thinking being. Yes, with a charming consistency, the slavery barons, the Hammonds and the Davises, while they tell us the negro is unfitted for mental cultivation, institute the severest penal laws against all attempts to teach the slave to read!

The first natural instinct of the slave, black or white, towards his master is, to cheat and baffle that armed embodiment of wrong, who stands to him in the relation of a thief and a tyrant. Thus, from his earliest years, lying and fraud become legitimate and praiseworthy in the slave's eyes; for slavery, except under rare conditions, crushes out the moral life in the victim.

Any conscience he may have, being subordinate to the conscience of his master, is kept stunted or perverted. The slave may wish to be true to his wife; but his master may compel him to repudiate her and take another. He may object to being the agent of an injustice; but the snap of the whip or the revolver may be the reply to any conscientious scruples he may offer against obedience.

In the first stage of his slave-life, Peculiar probably gave little thought to the moral bearings of his lot; although old Alva, his instructor, who was something of a casuist, had offered him not a few hard nuts to crack in the way of knotty questions. But Peculiar did precisely what you or I would have done under similar circumstances: he taxed his ingenuity to find how he could most safely shirk the tasks that were put upon him. Knowing that his taskmasters had no right to his labor, that they were, in fact, robbing him of what was his own, he did what he could to fool and circumvent them. Thus he grew to be, by a necessity of his condition, the most consummate of hypocrites and the most intrepid and successful of liars. At eighteen he was a match for Talleyrand in using speech to conceal his thoughts.

He saw that, if slaves were well treated, it was because the prudent master believed that good treatment would pay. Humanity was gauged by considerations of cotton. Thus the very kindnesses of a master had the taint of an intense selfishness; and Peculiar, while readily availing himself of all indulgences, correctly appreciated the spirit in which they were granted.

The devotional element seems to be especially active in the negro; but it has little chance for rational development, dwarfed and kept from the light as the intellect is. The uneducated slave, like the Italian brigand, — indeed, like many worthy people who go to church, — thinks it an impertinence to mix up morality with religion. He agrees fully with the distinguished American divine, who the other Sunday began his sermon with these words, "Brethren, I am not here to teach you morality, but to save your souls." As if a saving faith could exist allied to a corrupt morality!

Peculiar could not come in contact with a sham, however solemn and pretentious, without applying to it the puncture of his skeptical analysis. He saw his master, Herbert, go to church on a Sunday and kneel in prayer, and on a Monday shoot down Big Sam for attaching himself to the wrong woman. He saw the Rev. Mr. Bloom take the murderer by the hand, as if nothing had happened more tragical than the shooting of a raccoon.

And then Peculiar cogitated, wondering what religion could be, if its professors made such slight account of robbery and murder. Was it the observance of certain forms for the propitiation of an arbitrary, capricious, and unamiable Power, who smiled on injustice and barbarity? The more he thought of it, the more inexplicable grew the puzzle. Herbert evidently regarded himself as one of the elect; and Mr. Bloom encouraged him in his security. If heaven was to be won by such kind of service as theirs, Peculiar concluded that he would prefer taking his chances in hell; and so he became a scoffer.

His residence in New Orleans, in enlarging the sphere of his experiences, did not bring him the light that could quicken the devotional part of his nature. Dwelling most of the time in a hotel which frequently contained three or four hundred inmates, he was thrown among white men of all grades, intellectual and moral. He instinctively felt his superiority both ways to not a few of these. It was therefore a swindling lie to say that the blacks were born to be the thrall of the whites, that slavery was the proper *status* of the black in this or any country. If it were true that *stupid* blacks ought to be slaves, so must it be true of the same order of whites.

He heard preachers stand up in their pulpits, and, like the Rev. Dr. Palmer, blaspheme God by calling slavery a Divine institution. "Would it have been tolerated so long, if it were not?" they asked, with the confidence of a conjurer when he means to hocus you. To which Peek might have answered, "Would theft and murder have been tolerated so long, if they were not equally Divine?" The Northern clergymen he encountered held usually South-side views of the subject, and so his prejudices against the cloth grew to be somewhat too sweeping and indiscriminate. Judged of by its relations to slavery, religion seemed to him an audacious system of impositions, raised to fortify a lie and a wrong by claiming a Divine sanction for merely human creeds and inventions.

This persuasion was deepened when he found there were intelligent white men utterly incredulous as to a future state, and that the people who went to church were many of them practically, and many of them speculatively, infidels. The remaining fraction might be, for all he knew, not only devout, but good and just. Indeed, he had met some such, but they could be almost counted on his ten fingers.

One day at the St. Charles he overheard a discussion between Mr. James Sterling, an English traveller, and the Rev. Dr. Manners of Virginia. Slaves are good listeners; and Peculiar had sharpened his sense of hearing by the frequent exercise of it under difficulties. He was an amateur in keyholes. On this occasion he had only to open a ventilating window at the top of a partition, and all that the disputants might say would be for his benefit.

"Will you deny, sir," asked the reverend Doctor, "that slavery has the sanction of Scripture?"

"I exclude that inquiry as impertinent at present," said Sterling. "If Scripture authorized murder, then it would not be murder that would be right, but Scripture that would be wrong. And so in regard to slavery. On that particular point Scripture must not be admitted as authoritative. It cannot override the enlightened human conscience. It cannot render null the deductions of science and of reason on a question that manifestly comes within their sphere."

"Ah! if you reject Scripture, then I have nothing more to say," retorted the Doctor. But, after a pause, he added, "Have you not generally found the slaves well treated and contented?"

"A system under which they are well treated and made content," replied Sterling, "is really the most to be deplored and condemned. If slavery could so brutalize men's minds as to make them hug their chains and glory in degradation, it would be, in my eyes, doubly cursed. But it is not so; the slaves are not happy, and I thank God for it. There is manhood enough left in them to make them at least unhappy." *

"You assume the equality of the races," interposed the Doctor.

"It is unnecessary for my argument to make any such assumption," said Sterling. "I have found that many black men are superior to many white men, and some of those white men slaveholders. I do not *assume* this. I know it. I have seen it. But even if the black men were inferior, I hold, that man, as man, is an end unto himself, and that to use him as a brute means to the ends of other men is to outrage the laws of God. I take my stand far above the question of happiness or unhappiness. Have you noticed the young black man, called Peek, who waits behind my chair at table?"

"Yes, a bright-looking lad. He anticipates your wants well. You have feed him, I suppose?"

"I have given him nothing. I have put a few questions to him, that is all; and what I have to say is, that he is superior in respect to brains to nine tenths of the white youth who suck juleps in your bar-rooms or kill time at your billiard-tables."

* See James Sterling's "Letters from the Slave States."

"As soon as the Abolitionists will stop their infatuated clamor," replied the Doctor, "the condition of the slave will be gradually improved, and we shall give more and more care to his religious education."

"So long as the negro is ruled by force," returned Mr. Sterling, "no forty-parson power of preaching can elevate his character. It is a savage mockery to prate of *duty* to one in whom we have emasculated all power of will. We cannot make a moral intelligence of a being we use as a mere muscular force."

"All that the South wants," exclaimed the Doctor, "is to be let alone in the matter of slavery. If there are any alleviations in the system which can be safely applied, be sure they will not be lacking as soon as we are let alone by the fanatics of the North. Leave the solution of the problem to the intelligence and humanity of the South."

"Not while new cotton-lands pay so well! Be sure, reverend sir, if the South cannot quickly find a solution of this slave problem, God will find one for them, and that, trust me, will be a violent one. American civilization and American slavery can no longer exist together. One or the other must be destroyed. For my part, I can't believe it to be the Divine purpose that a remnant of barbarism shall overthrow the civilization of a new world. Slavery must succumb." *

"I recommend you, Mr. Sterling, not to raise your voice quite so high when you touch upon these dangerous topics here at the South. I will bid you good evening, sir."

* This last paragraph embodies the actual words of Mr. Sterling, published in 1856.

CHAPTER VI.

PIN-HOLES IN THE CURTAIN.

"The reader will here be led into the great, ill-famed land of the marvellous."
Ennemoser.

THE conversation between the English traveller and the Virginia Doctor of Divinity was brought to a close, and Peek jumped down from the table on which he had been listening, refreshed and inspired by the eloquent words he had taken in.

A week afterwards he made a second attempt to escape from bondage. He was caught and sold to Mr. Carberry Ratcliff, who had an estate on the Red River. Here, failing in obedience to an atrocious order, he received a punishment, the scars of which always remained to show the degree of its barbarity. He was soon after sent to Texas, where he became the slave of Mr. Barnwell.

Here he was at first put to the roughest work in the cotton-field. It tasked all his ingenuity to slight or dodge it. Luckily for him, about the time of his arrival he found an opportunity to make profitable use of the ecclesiastical knowledge he had derived from the Rev. Messrs. Bloom and Palmer.

Braxton, the overseer, had been frightened into a concern for his soul. He had a heart-complaint which the doctor told him might carry him off any day in a flash. A travelling preacher completed the work of terror by satisfying him he was in a fair way of being damned. The prospect did not seem cheerful to Braxton. He had found exhilaration and comfort in whipping intractable niggers. The amusement now began to pall. Besides, the doctor had told him to shun excitement.

In this state of things, enter Mr. Peculiar Institution. That gentleman soon learnt what was the matter; and he contrived that the overseer, seemingly by accident, should overhear him at prayers. Braxton had heard praying, but never any that had the unction of Peek's. From that time forth Peek had him completely under his control.

Peek did not abuse his authority. He ruled wisely, though despotically. At last the accidental encounter with his dying mother introduced a new world of thoughts and emotions. Short as was his opportunity for acquaintance with her, such a wealth of tenderness and love as she lavished upon him developed a hitherto inactive and undreamed-of force in his soul. The affectional part of his nature was touched. She told him of the delight his father used to take in playing with him, an infant; and when he thought of that father's fate, shot down for resisting the lash, he felt as if he could tear the first upholder of slavery he might meet limb from limb, in his rage.

The mother died, and then all seemed worthless and insipid to Peek. Having seen how little heed was paid to the feelings of slaves in separating those of opposite sex who had become attached to each other, he early in life resolved to shun all sexual intimacies, till he should be free. He saw that in slavery the distinction between licit and illicit connections was a playful mockery. The thought of being the father of a slave was horrible to him; and neither threats of the lash nor coaxings from masters and overseers could induce him to enter into those temporary alliances which Mr. Herbert used pleasantly to call "the holy bonds of matrimony." His resolution grew to be a passion stronger even than desire.

Thus the affections were undeveloped in him till he encountered his mother. He knew of no relative on earth, after her, to love, — no one to be loved by. Life stretched before him flat, dull, and unprofitable; and death, — what was that but the plunge into nothingness?

True, Mr. Herbert and the clergyman who drank claret with Mr. Herbert after the latter had shot down Big Sam talked of a life beyond the grave; but could such humbugs as they were be believed? Could the stories be trustworthy, which were based mainly on the truth of a book which all the preachers (so he supposed) declared was the all-sufficient authority for slavery? Well might Peek distrust the promise that was said to rest only on writings that were made to supply the apology of injustice and bloody wrong!

While in this state of mind, he heard of Corinna, the quadroon girl. Unattractive in person, slow of apprehension, and rarely uttering a word, she had hitherto excited only his pity. But now she fell into trances during which she seemed to be a new and entirely different being. At his first interview with her when she fell into one of these inexplicable states, she seized his hand, and imitating the look, actions, and very tone of his dying mother, poured forth such a flood of exhortations, comfortings, warnings, and encouragements, that he was bewildered and confounded.

What could it all mean? The power that spoke through Corinna claimed to be his mother, and seemed to identify itself, as far as revelations to the understanding could go. It recalled the little incidents that had passed between them in the presence of no other witness. It pierced to his inmost secrets, — secrets which he well knew he had communicated to no human being.

And yet Peek saw upon reflection that, though a preternatural faculty was plainly at work, — a faculty that took possession of his mind as a photographer does of all the stones, flaws, and stains in the wall of a building, — there was no sufficient identification of that faculty with the individual he knew as his mother. Little that might not already have been in his own mind, long hidden, perhaps, and forgotten, was revealed to him.

He also concluded that the intelligence, whatever it might be, was a fallible one, and that it would be folly to give up to its guidance his own free judgment.

He renewed his interviews daily as long as the quadroon girl lived. Skeptical, cautious, and meditative, he must test all these phenomena over and over again. And he did test them. He established conditions. He made records on the spot. He removed all possibilities of collusion and deception. And still the same phenomena!

Nor were they confined to the imperfect wonders of clairvoyance and prophecy. Once in the broad daylight, when he was alone with the invalid girl in her hut, and no other human being within a distance of a quarter of a mile, she was lifted horizontally before his eyes into the air, and kept there swaying about at least a third of a minute, while the drapery of her dress clung to her person as if held by an invisible hand.*

A bandore — a stringed musical instrument the name of which has been converted by the negroes into *banjo* — hung on a nail in the wall. One moonlight evening, when no third person was present, this African lute was detached by some invisible force and carried by it through the room from one end to the other! It would touch Peek on the head, then float away through the air, visible to sight, and sending forth from its chords, smitten by no mortal fingers, delectable strains. The same invisible power would tune the instrument, tightening the strings and trying them with a delicate skill; and then it would hang the banjo on its nail.

After this improvised concert, Peek felt all at once a warm living hand upon his forehead, first lovingly patting it and then passing round his cheek, under his chin, and up on the other side of his face. He grasped the hand, and it returned his pressure. It was a hand much larger than Corinna's, and she lay on her back several feet from him, too far to touch him with any part of her person. Plainly in the moonlight he could see it, — a perfect hand, resembling his mother's! It shaded off into vacuity above the wrist, and, even while he held it solid and flesh-like, melted all at once, like an impalpable ether, in his grasp.†

* Similar occurrences are related by Cotton Mather to have taken place in Boston in 1693. Six witnesses, whose affidavits he gives, namely, Samuel Aves, Robert Earle, John Wilkins, Dan Williams, Thomas Thornton, and William Hudson, testify to having repeatedly seen Margaret Rule lifted from her bed up near to the ceiling by an invisible force. It is a cheap way of getting rid of such testimony to say that the witnesses were false or incompetent. The present writer could name at least six witnesses of his own acquaintance now living, gentlemen of character, intelligence, sound senses and sound judgment, who will testify to having seen similar occurrences. The other phenomena, related as witnessed by Peek, are such as hundreds of intelligent men and women in the United States will confirm by their testimony. Indeed, the number of believers in these phenomena may be now fairly reckoned at more than three million.

† There are thousands of intelligent persons in the United States who will testify to the fact of spirit touch. The writer has on several occasions *felt*, though he has not *seen*, a live hand, guided by intelligence, that he was fully convinced belonged to no mortal person present. The conditions were such as to debar trick or deception. There are several trustworthy witnesses, whom the writer could name, who have both *seen* and *felt* the phenomenon, and tested it as thoroughly as Peek is represented to have done.

These phenomena, with continual variations, were repeated day after day and night after night. Flowers would drop from the ceiling into his hands, delicious odors of fruits would diffuse themselves through the room. A music like that of the Swiss bell-ringers would break upon the silence, continuing for a minute or more. A pen would start up from the table and write an intelligible sentence. A castanet would be played on and dashed about furiously, as if by some invisible Bacchante. A clatter, as of the hammering of a hundred carpenters, would suddenly make itself heard. A voice would speak intelligible sentences, sometimes using a tin trumpet for the purpose. Articles of furniture would pass about the room and cross each other with a swiftness and precision that no mortal could imitate. The noise of dancers, using their feet, and keeping time, would be heard on the floor.

Once Corinna asked him to leave his watch with her. He did so. When he was several rods from the house she called to him, "You are sure you have n't your watch?" "Yes, sure," replied Peek. He hurried home, a distance of two miles, without meeting a human being. On undressing to go to bed, he found his watch in his vest pocket.

These physical thaumaturgies produced upon Peek a more astounding effect than all the evidences of mind-reading and clairvoyance. In the communications made to him by the "power," there was generally something unsatisfying or incomplete. He would, for instance, think of some departed friend, — a white man, perhaps, — and, without uttering or writing a word, would desire some manifestation from that friend. Immediately Corinna would strip from her arm the drapery, and show on her skin, written in clear crimson letters, some brief message signed by the right name. And then the supposed bearer of that name (speaking through Corinna) would correctly recall incidents of his acquaintance with Peek.*

* The phenomenon of *stigmata* appearing on the flesh of impressible mediums is one of the most common of the manifestations of modern Spiritualism. Sometimes written words and sometimes outline representations of objects appear, under circumstances that make deception impossible. The writer has often witnessed them. St. Francis, and many other saints of the Catholic Church, were the subjects of similar phenomena. The late Earl of Shrewsbury, a Catholic nobleman, has published a long account of their occurrence during the present century. The Catholic Church has been always true to the doctrine of the miraculous.

Thus much was amazing and satisfactory; but when Peek analyzed it all in thought, he found that no sufficient proof of identification had been given. A "power," able to probe his own mind, might get from it all that was spoken relative to the individual claiming identity; might even know how to imitate that individual's handwriting. Peek concluded that one must be himself in a spiritual state in order to identify a spirit. The so-called "communications" he found, for the most part, monotonous. They were, some of them, above Corinna's capacity, but not above his own. Erroneous answers were not unfrequently given, especially in reply to questions upon matters of worldly concern. He was repeatedly told of places where he could find silver and gold, and never truly.

He concluded that to surrender one's faith implicitly to the word of a spirit *out* of the flesh, either on moral or on secular questions, was about as unwise as it would be to give one's self up to the control of a spirit *in* the flesh, — a mere mortal like himself. He was satisfied by his experience that it was not in the power of spirits to impair his own freedom of will and independence of thought, so long as he exercised them manfully. And this assurance was to his mind not only a guaranty of his own spiritual relationship, but it pointed to a supreme, omniscient Spirit, the gracious Father of all. If the words that came through Corinna had proved, in every instance, infallible, what would Peek have become but a passive, unreasoning recipient, as sluggish in thought as Corinna herself!

We have said that the "communications" were generally on a level with Peek's own mind. There was once an exception. Said a very learned spirit (learned, as to him it seemed) one night, speaking through Corinna: —

"Attend, even if you do not understand all that I may utter. The great purpose of creation is to exercise and develop independent, individual thought, and through that, a will in harmony with the Supreme Wisdom. Men are subjected to the discipline of the earth-sphere, not to be happy there, but to qualify themselves for happiness, — to deserve happiness.

"What would all created wonders be without thought to appreciate and admire them? Study is worship. Admiration is worship. Of what account would be the starry heavens, if there were not *mind* to study and to wonder at creation, and thus to fit itself for adoration of the Creator?

"My friend Lessing, when he was on your earth, once said, that, if God would *give* him truth, he would decline the gift, and prefer the labor of seeking it for himself. But most men are mentally so inert, they would rather believe than examine; and so they flatter themselves that their loose, unreasoning acquiescence is a saving belief. Pernicious error! All the mistakes and transgressions of men arise either from feeble, imperfect thinking, or from not thinking at all.

"The heart is much, — is principal; but men must not hope to rise until they do their own thinking. They cannot think by proxy. They must exercise the mind on all that pertains to their moral and mental growth. You may perhaps sometimes wish that you too, like this poor, torpid, parasitical creature, Corinna, might be a medium for outside spirits to influence and speak through. But beware! You know not what you wish. Learn to prize your individuality. The wisdom Corinna may utter does not become hers by appropriation. In her mind it falls on barren soil.

"We all are more or less mediums; but the innocent man is he who resists and overcomes temptation, not he who never felt its power; and the wise man is he who, at once recipient and repellent, seeks to appropriate and assimilate with his being whatever of good he can get from all the instrumentalities of nature, divine and human, angelic and demoniac."

Peek derived an indefinable but awakening impression from these words, and asked, "Is the Bible true?"

The reply was: "It is true only to him who construes it aright. If you find in it the justification of American slavery, then to you it is not true. All the theologies which would impose, as essentials of faith, speculative dogmas or historical declarations which do not pertain to the practice of the highest human morality and goodness, as taught in the words and the example of Christ, are, in this respect at least, irreverent, mischievous, and untrue."

"How do I know," asked Peek, "that you are not a devil?"

"I am aware of no way," was the reply, "by which, in your present state, you can know absolutely that I am not a devil,

— even Beelzebub, the prince of devils. Each man's measure of truth must be the reason God has given him. But of this you may rest assured: it is a great point gained to be able to believe really even in a devil. Given a devil, you will one day work yourself so far into the light as to believe in an angel."

"Is there a God?" asked the slave.

"God is," said the spirit, "and says to thee, as once to Pascal, '**Be consoled! Thou wouldst not seek me, if thou hadst not found me.**'"

These were almost the only words Peek ever received through Corinna that struck him by their superiority to what he himself could have imagined; and he was impressed by them accordingly. Though they were above his comprehension at the moment, he thought he might grow up to them, and he caused them to be repeated slowly while he wrote them down.

Corinna died, and Peek kept on thinking.

What rapture in thought now! What a new meaning in life! What a new universe for the heart was there in love! Henceforth the burden and the mystery of "all this unintelligible world" was lightened if not dissolved; for death was but the step to a higher plane of life. The old, trite emblem of the chrysalis was no mere barren fancy. Continuous life was now to his mind a *certainty;* arrived at, too, by the deductions of experience, sense, and reason, as well as intimated by the eager thirst of the heart.

The process by which he made the phenomena he had witnessed conduce to this conclusion was briefly this. An invisible, intelligent *force* had lifted heavy articles before his eyes, played on musical instruments, written sentences, and spoken words. This *force* claimed to be a human spirit in a human form, of tissues too fine to be visible to our grosser senses. It could pass, like heat and electricity, through what might seem material impediments. It had a plastic power to reincarnate itself at will, and imitate human forms and colors, under certain circumstances, and it gave partial proof of this by showing a hand, an arm, or a foot undistinguishable from one of flesh and blood. On one occasion the human form entire had been displayed, been touched, and had then dissolved into invisibility and intangibility before him.

Now he must either take the word of this intelligent "force," that it was an independent spiritual entity, or he must account for its acts by some other supposition. The "force," in its communications to his mind, had shown it was not infallible; it had erred in some of its predictions, although in others it had been wonderfully correct. If its explanation of itself was untrue, — if no outside intelligent force were operating, — the other supposition was, that the phenomena were a proceeding either from himself, the spectator, or from Corinna. And here, without knowing it, Peek found himself speculating on the theory of Count Gasparin,* who has had the candor to brave the laugh of modern science (a very different thing from *scientia*) by recounting as facts what Professor Faraday and our Cambridge *savans* denounce as impositions or delusions.

Peek was therefore reduced to these two explanations: either the "force" was a spirit (call it, if you please, an outside power), as it claimed to be, or it was a faculty unconsciously exerted by the mortals present. In either case, it supplied an assurance of spirit and immortality; for it might fairly be presumed that such wonderful powers would not be wrapt up in the human organism except for a purpose; and that purpose, what could it be but the future development of those powers under suitable conditions? So either of Peek's hypotheses led to the same precious and ineffable conviction of continuous life, — of the soul's immortality!

On one occasion a Northern Professor, who had given his days to the positive sciences, and who believed in matter and motion, and nothing else, passed a week, while visiting the South for his health, with his old friend and classmate, Mr. Barnwell; and Peek overheard the following conversation.

"How do you get rid of all this testimony on the subject?" asked Mr. Barnwell.

"Stuff and nonsense!" exclaimed the Professor. "That a poor benighted nigger should believe this trash is n't surprising. That poets, like Willis and Mrs. Browning, should give in to it may be tolerated, for they are privileged. In them the imaginative faculty is irregularly developed. But that sane and

* Author of "The Uprising of a Great People," "America before Europe," &c.; also of two large volumes on Modern Spiritualism.

intelligent white men like Edmonds, and Tallmadge, and Bowditch, and Brownson, and Bishop Clark of Rhode Island, and Howitt, and Chambers, and Coleman, and Dr. Gray, and Wilkinson, and Mountford, and Robert Dale Owen, should gravely swallow these idiotic stories, is lamentable indeed. The spectacle becomes humiliating, and I sigh, 'Poor human nature!'"

"But Peek is far from being a benighted nigger," replied Barnwell; "he can read and write as well as you can; he is the best shot in the county; he is a good mechanic; for a time he waited on one of the great jugglers at the St. Charles; he can explain or cleverly imitate all the tricks of all the conjurers; he is not a man to be humbugged, especially by a poor sick girl in a hut with no cellar, no apparatus, no rooms where any coadjutor could hide. It has been the greatest puzzle of my life to know how to explain Peek's stories."

"Half that is extraordinary in them," said the Professor, "is probably a lie, and the other half is delusion. Not one man in fifty is competent to test such occurrences. Men's senses have not been scientifically trained; their love of the marvellous blinds them to the simplest solutions of a mystery. *How to observe* is one of the most difficult of arts; and one must undergo rigid scientific culture in the practical branches before he can observe properly."

"Under your theory, Professor, ninety-eight men out of every hundred ought to be excluded as witnesses from our courts of justice. It strikes me that a fellow like Peek — with his senses always in good working trim, who never misses his aim, who can hit a mark by moonlight at forty paces, and shoot a bird on the wing in bright noonday, who can detect a tread or a flutter of wings when to your ear all is silence — is as competent to see straight and judge of sights and sounds as any blinkard from a college, even though he wear spectacles and call himself professor of mathematics. Remember, Peek is not a superstitious nigger. He will feel personally obliged to any ghost who will show himself. He shrinks from no haunted room, no solitude, no darkness."

"Truly, Horace, you speak as if you half believed these absurdities."

"No, — I wish I could. Peek once said to me, that he would n't have believed these things on *my* testimony, and could n't expect me to believe them on *his*."

"Our business," said the Professor, "is with the life before us. I agree with Comte, that we ought to confine ourselves to positive, demonstrable facts; with Humboldt, that 'there is not much to boast of after our dissolution,' and that 'the blue regions on the other side of the grave' * are probably a poet's dream. Let us not trouble ourselves about the inexplicable or the uncertain."

"But you do not consider, Professor, that Peek's facts *are* positive to his experience. Besides, to say, with Comte, that a fact is inexplicable, and that we can't go beyond it, is not to demonstrate that the fact has its cause in itself; it is merely to confess the mystery of a cause unknown." †

"Well, Horace, I'm sleepy, and must retire. I'll find an opportunity to cross-examine Peek before I go, and you shall see how he will contradict and stultify himself."

Before the opportunity was found, the Professor had *passed on*. Less modest than Rabelais was in his last moments, he did not condescend to say, "I go to inquire into a great possibility." The physician in attendance, who was a young man, and had recently "experienced religion," asked the Professor if he had found the Lord Jesus. To which the Professor, making a wry face, replied, "Jargon!" "Have you no regard for your soul?" asked the well-meaning doctor. "Can you prove to me, young man, that I *have* a soul?" returned the Professor, trying to raise himself on his pillow, in an argumentative posture. "Don't you believe in a future state?" asked the doctor. "I believe what can be proved," said the Professor; "and there are two things, and only two, that can be proved, — though Berkeley thinks we can't prove even those, — matter and motion. ‡ All phenomena are reducible to matter and motion, — matter and motion, — matter and mo-o-o— "

* See Alexander Humboldt's Letters to Varnhagen.

† See Edouard Laboulaye, "De la Personnalité Divine."

‡ Tertullian, a devout Christian, when he wrote the following, would seem to have believed there could be no spirit independent of substance and form: "Nihil enim, si non corpus. Omne quod est, corpus est sui generis;

The effort was too much for the moribund Professor. He did not complete the utterance of his formula, at least on this side of the great curtain. Probably when he awoke in the next life, conscious of his identity, he felt very much in the mood of that other man of science, who, on being told that the microscope would confute an elaborate theory he had raised, refused to look through the impertinent instrument.

For several months Peek retained his place under Braxton. But even overseers, whip in hand, cannot frighten off Death. Braxton disappeared through the common portal. His successor, Hawks, had a theory that the true mode of managing niggers was to overawe them by extreme severity at the start, and then taper off into clemency. He had been lord of the lash a week or two, when he was asked by Mr. Barnwell how he got along with Peek.

"Capitally!" replied Hawks. "I took care to put him through his paces at our first meeting, — took the starch right out of him. He 'd score his own mother now if I told him to. He 's a thorough nigger — is Peek. A nigger must fear a white man before he can like him. Peek would go through fire and water for me now. He has behaved so well, I have given him a pass to visit his sister at Carter's."

"I never knew before that Peek had a sister," said Barnwell.

Peek did not come back from that visit.

nihil est incorporale, nisi quod non est. Quis enim negabit Deum corpus esse, etsi Deus spiritus est? Spiritus enim corpus sui generis, sua effigie;" — "For there is nothing, if not body. All that is, is body after its kind; nothing is incorporeal except what is *not*. For who will deny God to be body, albeit God is spirit? For spirit is body of its proper kind, in its proper effigy." These views are not inconsistent with those entertained by many modern Spiritualists.

CHAPTER VII.

AN UNCONSCIOUS HEIRESS.

"She is coming, my dove, my dear;
She is coming, my life, my fate;
The red rose cries, 'She is near, she is near';
And the white rose weeps, 'She is late';
The larkspur listens, 'I hear, I hear';
And the lily whispers, 'I wait.'"
Tennyson.

WE left Peek (known in New York as Jacobs) in the little closet opening from the apartment where Charlton sat at his papers. The knock at the outer door was succeeded by the entrance of a person of rather imposing presence.

Mr. Albert Pompilard stood upwards of six feet in his polished shoes and variegated silk stockings. He was bulky, and could not conceal, by any art of dress, an incipient paunch. But whether he was a youth of twenty-five or a man of fifty it was very difficult to judge on a hasty inspection. He was in reality sixty-nine. He affected an extravagantly juvenile and jaunty style of dress, and was never twenty-four hours behind the extreme fashions of Young America.

On this occasion Mr. Pompilard was dressed in a light-colored sack or pea-jacket, with gaping pockets and enormous buttons, the cloth being a sort of shaggy, woollen stuff, coarse enough for a mat. His pantaloons and vest were of the same astounding fabric. He wore a new black hat, just ironed and brushed by Leary; a neckerchief of a striped red-and-black silk, loosely tied; immaculate linen; and a diamond on his little finger. A thick gold chain passed round his neck, and entered his vest pocket. He swung a gold-headed switch, and was followed by a little terrier dog of a breed new to Broadway.

Mr. Pompilard's complexion was somewhat florid, and presented few marks of age. He wore his own teeth, which were still sound and white, and his own hair, including whiskers, although the hue was rather too black to be natural.

"I believe I have the honor of addressing Mr. Charlton," said Pompilard, with the air of one who is graciously bestowing a condescension.

"That's my name, sir. What's your business?" replied Charlton, in the curt, dry manner of one who gives his information grudgingly.

"My name, sir, is Pompilard. You may not be aware that there is a sort of family connection between us."

"Ah! yes; I remember," said Charlton, looking inquiringly at his visitor, but not asking him to sit down.

Pompilard returned his gaze, as if waiting for something; then, seeing that nothing came, he lifted a chair, replaced it with emphasis on the floor, and sat down. If it was a rebuke, Charlton did not take it, though the terrier seemed to comprehend it fully, for he began to bark, and made a reconnoissance of Charlton's legs that plainly meant mischief.

Pompilard refreshed himself for a moment with the lawyer's alarm, then ordered Grip to lie down under the table, which he did with a quavering whine of expostulation.

"I see," said Pompilard, "you almost forget the precise nature of the connection to which I allude. Let me explain: the lady who has the honor to be your wife is the step-mother, I believe, of Mr. Henry Berwick."

"Both the step-mother and aunt," interposed Charlton, somewhat mollified by the language of his visitor.

"Yes, she was half-sister to his own mother," resumed Pompilard. "Well, the wife of Mr. Henry Berwick was Miss Aylesford of Chicago, and is the niece of my present wife."

"I understand all that," said Charlton; and then, as the thought occurred to him that he might make the connection useful, he rose, and, offering his hand, said, "I am happy to make your acquaintance, Mr. Pompilard." That gentleman rose and exchanged salutations; and Grip, under the table, gave a smothered howl, subsiding into a whine, as if he felt personally aggrieved by the concession, and would like to put his teeth in the calf of a certain leg.

"My object in calling," said Pompilard, "is merely to inquire if you can give me the present address of Mrs. Henry Berwick. My wife wishes to communicate with her."

Charlton generally either evaded a direct question or answered it by a lie. He never received a request for information, even in regard to the time of day, that he did not cast about in his mind to see how he could gain by the withholding or profit by the giving. He took it for granted that every man was trying to get the advantage of him; and he resolved to take the initiative in that game. And so, to Pompilard's inquiry, Charlton replied:

"I really cannot say whether Mr. Berwick is in the country or not. The last I heard of him he was in Paris."

"Then your intelligence of him is not so late as mine. He arrived in Boston some days since, but left immediately for the West by the way of Albany. I thought your wife might be in communication with him."

"They seldom correspond."

"I must inquire about him at the Union Club," said Pompilard, musingly. "By the way, Mr. Charlton, you deal in real estate securities, do you not?"

"Occasionally. There are some old-fashioned persons who consult me in regard to investments."

"Do you want any good mortgages?" asked Pompilard.

"Just at present, money is very scarce and high," replied Charlton.

"That 's the very reason why I want it," said his visitor. "Could you negotiate a thirty thousand dollar mortgage for me?"

"But that 's a very large sum."

"Another reason why I want it," returned Pompilard. "Supposing the security were satisfactory, what bonus should you require for getting me the money? Please give me your lowest terms, and at once, for I have an engagement in five minutes on 'Change."

"Well, sir," said Charlton, in the tone of a man to whom it is an ordinary act to drive the knife in deep, "I think in these times five per cent would be about right."

"Pooh! I 'll bid you good morning, Mr. Charlton," said Pompilard, with an air of unspeakable contempt. "Come, Grip."

And Mr. Pompilard bowed and turned to leave, just as another knock was heard at the door. He opened it, encountering four men, one of whom kicked the unoffending terrier; an indignity which Pompilard resented by switching the aggressor smartly twice round the legs, and then passed on. He had not descended five steps when a bullet from a pistol grazed his whiskers. "Not a bad shot that, my Southern friend!" said the old man, deliberately continuing his descent.

Before losing sight of Pompilard we must explain why he was desirous that his wife should communicate with Mrs. Berwick.

Inheriting a fortune from his mother, Albert Pompilard had managed to squander it in princely expenditures before he was twenty-five years old. The vulgar dissipations of sensualists he despised. He abstained from wine and strong drink at a time when to abstain was to be laughed at. With the costliest viands and liquors on his table for guests, he himself ate sparingly and drank cold water. Had he been as scrupulously moral in the management of his soul as he was of his body, he would have been a saint. But he was a spendthrift and a gambler on a large scale.

Having ruined himself financially, he married. A little money which his wife brought him was staked entire on a stock operation, and won. Thence a new fortune larger than the first. At thirty-five he was worth half a million. He took his wife, two daughters, and a son to Paris, gave entertainments that made even royalty envious, and in ten years returned to New York a bankrupt. His wife died, and Pompilard appeared once more at the stock board. Ill-luck now pursued him with remorseless pertinacity, but never succeeded in disturbing his equanimity. He was frightfully in debt, but the consideration never for a moment marred his digestion nor his slumbers. The complacency of a man contented with himself and the world shed its beams over his features always.

At fifty, a widower, with three children, he carried off and married Miss Aylesford, who at the time was on a visit to New York, — a girl of eighteen, handsome, accomplished, and worth half a million. In vain had her brother tried to open her eyes to Pompilard's character as an inveterate fortune-hunter and spendthrift. The wilful young lady would have her way. Pompilard took possession, paid his debts with interest, and, with less than one third of his wife 's property left, once more tried his fortune in Wall Street. This time he won. At sixty he was richer than ever. He became the owner of a domain of three hundred acres on the Hudson,— built palatial residences, — one in the country, and one on the favored avenue that leads to Murray Hill, — bought a steamboat to transport his guests to and from the city, — gave a series of *fêtes*, and kept open houses.

But soon one of those panics in the money-market which take place periodically to baffle the calculations and paralyze the efforts of large holders of stocks, occurred to confound Pompilard. In trying to *hold* his stocks, he was compelled to make heavy sacrifices, and then, in trying to *hedge*, he heaped loss on loss. He had to sell his acres on the Hudson, — then his town house, — finally his horses; and at sixty-nine we find him trying to get a mortgage for thirty thousand dollars on five or six poor little houses, the last remnant from the wreck of his wife 's property. In the hope of effecting this he had persuaded his wife to communicate with her niece, Mrs. Berwick.

The brother of Mrs. Pompilard, Robert Aylesford, had inherited a large estate, which he had increased by judicious investments in land on the site of Chicago, some years before that wonderful city had risen like an exhalation in a night from the marsh on which it stands. His wife had died in child-birth, leaving a daughter whom he named after her, Leonora. His own health was subsequently impaired by a malignant fever, caught in humane attendance on a Mr. Carteret, a stranger whom he had accidentally met at Cairo in Southern Illinois.

Deeply chagrined at his sister's imprudent marriage, and feeling that his own health was failing, Aylesford conceived a somewhat romantic project in regard to his only child, Leonora. During a winter he had passed in Italy he had become acquainted with the Ridgways, a refined and intelligent family from Western Massachusetts. One of the members, a lady, kept a boarding-school of deserved celebrity in the town of Lenbridge.

To this lady Aylesford took his little girl, then only two years old, and said: "I wish you to bring her up under the name of Leonora Lockhart, her mother's maiden name, and her own, though not all of it. When she is married, let her know that the rest of it is *Aylesford*. She is so young she will not remember much of her father. Keep both her and the world in ignorance of the fact that she is born to a fortune. My wish is that she shall not be the victim of a fortune-hunter in marriage; and you will take all needful steps to carry out my wish. I leave you the address of my man of business, Mr. Keep, in New York, who will supply you with a thousand dollars a year as your compensation for supporting and educating her. Neither she nor any one else must know that even this allotment is on her account. My physician orders me to pass the winter in Cuba, and I may not return. Should that be my lot, I look to you to be in the place of a parent to my child. Her relations may suppose her dead. I shall not undeceive them. Her nearest relative is her aunt, my sister, Mrs. Pompilard, who, in the event of my death, will be legally satisfied that such a disposition is made of my property that it cannot directly or indirectly fall into the hands of that irreclaimable spendthrift, her husband. As I have lived for the last twenty years at the West, I do not think you will have any difficulty in keeping my secret."

Subsequently he said: "On the day of Leonora's marriage, should she have passed her eighteenth year, the trustees of my property will have directions to hand over to her the income. Till that it is done, your lips must be sealed in regard to her prospects. In the event of her remaining single, I have made provisions which Mr. Keep will explain to you. I am resolved that my daughter shall not have to buy a husband."

Mrs. Ridgway accepted the trust in the same frank spirit in which it was offered. Mr. Aylesford took leave of his little girl, and before the next spring she was fatherless. Her eighteenth birthday found her developed into a young lady of singular grace and beauty, with accomplishments which showed that the body had not been neglected in adorning the mind. But the mystery that surrounded her family and origin produced a shyness that kept her aloof from social intimacies.

Vainly did her attentive friends try to overcome her fondness for solitary musings and rides. She was possessed with the idea that she was an illegitimate child, though to this suspicion she never gave utterance till candor seemed to compel it.

On a charming morning in June, as a young man, just escaped from a law-office in New York for a week's recreation among the hills of Lenbridge, was entering "the cathedral road," as it was called, overarched as it was by forest-trees, and spread with an elastic mat of pine-leaves, he saw a young lady riding a spirited horse, a bright-colored bay, exquisitely formed, and showing high blood in every step. The sagacious creature evidently felt the exhilaration of the fresh, balsamic air, for he played the most amusing antics, dancing and curvetting as if for the entertainment of a circus of spectators; starting lightly and feigning fright at little shining puddles of water, leaping over fallen stumps, but with such elastic ease and precision as not to stir his rider in her seat, — and frolicking much like a pet kitten when the ball of yarn is on the floor.

His mistress evidently understood his ways, and he hers, for she talked to him and patted his glossy neck and seemed to encourage him in his tricks. At last she said, "Come, now, Hamlet, enough of this, — behave yourself!" and then he walked on quite demurely. He traversed a cross-road newly repaired with broken stones, and entered on the forest avenue. But all at once Hamlet seemed to go lame, and the lady dismounted, and, lifting one of his fore-feet, tried to extract a stone that had got locked in the hollow of his sole. Her strength was unequal to the task. The pedestrian who had been watching her movements approached, bowed, and offered his assistance. The lady thanked him, and resigned into his hand the hoof of the gentle animal, who plainly understood that something for his benefit was going on.

"The stone is wedged in so tightly, I fear it will require a chisel to pry it out," said the new acquaintance, whose name was Henry Berwick. Then, after a pause, he added, "But perhaps I can hammer it out with another stone."

"Let me find one for you," said Leonora, running here and there, and searching as she held up her riding-habit.

Henry looked after her with an interest he had never felt

before for any one in the form of a young lady. How bewitchingly that black beaver with its ostrich plumes sat on her head, but failed to hide those luxuriant curls, — luxuriant by the grace of nature and not of the hair-dresser! And then that face, — how full of life and tenderness and mind! And how admirably did its red and white contrast with the surrounding blackness of its frame! And that figure, — how were its harmonious perfections brought out by the simple, closely fitting nankeen riding-habit trimmed with green!

While she was engaged in her search, Mr. Henry Berwick dishonestly did his best to loosen the shoe. All at once, in the most innocent manner, he exclaimed, "This shoe is loose, — it has come off, — look here!"

And he held it up, just as Leonora handed him a stone.

He took the stone, and with one blow knocked out the fragment that lay wedged in the hollow of the sole.

"Thank you, sir," said Leonora.

"You are one of Mrs. Ridgway's young ladies, I presume," said Henry.

"Yes, I shall not be back in time for my music-lesson, if I do not hurry."

"There is a blacksmith not a quarter of a mile from here. My advice to you is to stop and have this shoe refitted. Remember, you have a mile of a newly macadamized road to travel before you get home, and over that you will have to walk your horse slowly unless you restore him his shoe."

Leonora seemed struck by these considerations. "I will take your advice," she said, putting herself in the saddle with a movement so quick and easy that Berwick could not interpose to help her. But the horse limped so badly that she once more dismounted.

"Let me lead him for you," said Berwick, "I shall not have to go a step out of my way."

"You are very obliging," replied the lady.

And the young man led the horse, while the young lady walked by his side.

The quarter of a mile was a remarkably long one. It was a full hour before the blacksmith's shed was reached, and then Berwick, secretly giving the man of the anvil a dollar, winked at him, and said aloud, "Call us as soon as you have fitted the shoe"; and then added, in an *aside*, "Be an hour or so about it."

The new acquaintances strolled together to a beautiful pond within sight among the hills.

O that exquisite June morning, with its fresh foliage, its clear sky, its pine odors, its wild-flowers, and its songs of birds! How imperishable in the memories of both it became! How much happier were they ever afterwards for the happiness of that swift-gliding moment!

Leonora spied some harebells in the crevices of the slaty rocks of a steep declivity, and pointed them out as the first of the season.

"I must get them for you," cried Berwick.

"No, no! It is a dangerous place," said Leonora.

"They shall be your harebells," said Berwick, swinging himself, by the aid of a birch-tree that grew almost horizontally out of the cleft of a rock, over the precipice, and snatching the flowers. Leonora treasured them for years, pressed between the leaves of Shelley's Poems.

Thus began a courtship which, three weeks afterwards, was followed by an offer of marriage. Early in the acquaintance, foreseeing the drift of Berwick's eager attentions, Leonora had frankly communicated by letter her suspicions in regard to her own birth.

In his reply Berwick had written: "I almost wish it may be as you imagine, in order that I may the better prove to you the strength of my attachment; for I do not underrate the desirableness of an honorable genealogy. No one can prize more than I an unspotted lineage. But I would not marry the woman who I did not think could in herself compensate me for the absence of all advantages of family position and wealth; and whose society could not more than make up for the loss of all social attractions that could be offered outside of the home her presence would sanctify. You are the one my heart points to as able to do all this; and so, Leonora, whether it be the bar sinister or the ducal coronet that ought to be in your coat of arms, it matters not to me. No herald's pen can make you less charming in my eyes. Under any cloud that could be thrown over your origin, to me you would always be, as Portia was to Brutus, a fair and honorable wife; —

'As dear to me as are the ruddy drops
That visit this sad heart.'

And yet not sad, if you were mine! So do not think that any future development in regard to the antecedents of yourself or of your parents can detract from an affection based on those qualities which are of the soul and heart, and the worth of which no mortal disaster can impair."

To all which the imprudent young lady returned this answer: "Do not think to outdo me in generosity. You judge me independently of all social considerations and advantages; I will do the same by you; for I know as little of you as you do of me."

They met the next morning, and Berwick said: "Is not this a very dangerous precedent we are setting for romantic young people? What if I should turn out to be a swindler or a bigamist?"

"My heart would have prescience of it much sooner than my head," replied Leonora. "Women are not so often misled into uncongenial alliances by their affections as by their passions or their calculations. The lamb, before he has ever known a wolf, is instinctively aware of an enemy's presence, even while the wolf is yet unseen. If the lamb stopped to reason with himself, he would be very apt to say, 'Nonsense! it is no doubt a very respectable beast who is approaching. Why should I imagine he wants to harm me?'"

"But what if I am a wolf disguised as a lamb?" asked Berwick.

"I am so good a judge of tune," replied Leonora, "that I should detect the sham the moment you tried to cry *baa*. Nay, a repugnant nature makes itself felt to me by its very presence. There are some persons the very touch of whose hand produces an impression, I generally find to be true, of their character."

"An ingenious plea!" said Berwick with an affectation of sarcasm. "But it does not palliate your indiscretion."

"Very well, sir," replied Leonora, "since you disapprove my precipitancy, we will—"

Berwick interrupted the speech at the very portal of her mouth, by surprising its warders, the lips.

And so it was a betrothal.

How admirably had Mrs. Ridgway behaved through it all! How scrupulous she had been in withholding all intimations of Leonora's prospective wealth! There were young men among the Ridgways, handsome, accomplished, just entering the hard paths of commercial or professional toil. How easy it would have been to have hinted to some of them, "Secure this young lady, and your fortune is made. Let a hint suffice." But Mrs. Ridgway was too loyal to her trust to even blindly convey by her demeanor towards Leonora a suspicion that the child was aught more than the dowerless orphan she appeared.

Berwick took a small house in Brooklyn, and prepared for his marriage. Clients were as yet few and poor, but he did not shrink from living on twelve hundred a year with the woman he loved. He was not quite sure that his betrothed was even rich enough to refurnish her own wardrobe. So he delicately broached the question to Mrs. Ridgway. That lady mischievously told him that if he could let Leonora have fifty dollars, it might be convenient. The next day Berwick sent a check for ten times that amount.

But after the wedding, an elderly gentleman, named Keep, to whom Berwick had been introduced a few days before, took him and the bride aside, and delivered to him a schedule of the title-deeds of an estate worth a million, the bequest of the bride's father, and the income of which was to be subject to her order.

"But this deranges all our little plans!" exclaimed the bride, with delightful *naïveté*.

"Well, my children, you must put up with it as well as you can," said Mr. Keep.

Berwick took the surprise gravely and thoughtfully. With this great enlargement of his means and opportunities, were not his responsibilities proportionably increased?

CHAPTER VIII.

A DESCENDANT OF THE CAVALIERS.

"Pride of race, pride in an ancestry of gentlemen, pride in all those habitudes and instincts which separated us so immeasurably from the peddling and swindling Yankee nation, — all this pride has been openly cherished and avowed in all simplicity and good faith." — *Richmond (Va.) Enquirer.*

PEEK sat in the little closet which opened into Charlton's office. Suddenly he heard the crack of a pistol, followed by a volley of ferocious oaths. Efforts seemed to be made to pacify the utterer, who was with difficulty withheld by his companions from following the person who had offended him. At these sounds Peek felt a cold, creeping sensation down his back, and a tightness in his throat, as if it were grasped by a hand. The pistol-shot and the nature of the oaths brought before him the figure of the overseer with his broad-brimmed hat, his whip, and his revolver.

All the negro's senses were now concentrated in the one faculty of hearing. He judged that five persons had entered the room. The angry man had cooled down, and the voices were not raised above a whisper.

"Is he here?" asked one.

No answer was heard in reply. Probably a gesture had sufficed.

"Will he resist?"

"Possibly. These fugitives usually go armed."

"What shall we do if he threatens to fire?"

Here an altercation ensued, during which Peek could understand little of what was uttered. But he had heard enough. His thoughts first reverted to his wife and his infant boy, and he pictured to himself their destitute condition in the event of his being taken away. Then the treachery of Charlton glared upon him in all its deformity, and he instinctively drew from the sheath in an inside pocket of his vest a sharp, glittering dagger-like knife. He looked rapidly around, but there was nothing to suggest a mode of escape. The only window in the closet was one over the door communicating with the office.

Suddenly it occurred to him that, if he were to be hemmed in in this closet, his chances of escape would be small. It would be better for him to be in the larger room, whether he chose to adopt a defensive or an offensive policy. Seeing an old rope in a corner of the closet, he seized it with the avidity a drowning man might show in grasping at a straw.

He listened intently once more to the whisperers. A low susurration, accompanied with a whistling sound, he indentified at once as coming from Skinner, the captain of the schooner in which he had made his escape. Then some one sneezed. Peek would have recognized that sneeze in Abyssinia. It must have proceeded from Colonel Delancy Hyde.

Standing on tiptoe on a coal-box, the negro now looked through a hole in the green-paper curtain covering the glass over the door, and surveyed the whole party. He found he was right in his conjectures. The captain was there with one of his sailors, — an old inebriate by the name of Biggs, both doubtless ready to swear to the slave's identity. And the Colonel was there as natural as when he appeared on the plantation, strolling round to take a look at the "smart niggers," so as to be able to recognize them in case of need. Two policemen, armed with bludgeons, and probably with revolvers; and Charlton, with a paper tied with red tape in his hand, formed the other half of this agreeable company. Peek marked well their positions, put his knife between his teeth, and descended from the box.

Colonel Delancy Hyde is a personage of too much importance to be kept waiting while we describe the movements of a slave. Colonel Delancy Hyde must be attended to first. Tall, lank, and gaunt in figure, round-shouldered and stooping, he carried his head very much after the fashion of a bloodhound on the scent. Beard and moustache of a reddish, sandy hue, coarse and wiry, concealed much of the lower part of a face which would have been pale but for the floridity which bad whiskey had imparted. The features were rather leonine than wolfish in outline (if we may believe Mr. Livingstone, the lion is a less respectable beast than the wolf). But the small brownish eyes, generally half closed and obliquely glancing, had a haughty expression of penetration or of scorn, as if the person on whom they fell would be too much honored by a full, entire regard from those sublime orbs.

The Colonel wore a loosely fitting frock-coat and pantaloons, evidently bought ready made. They were of a grayish nondescript material which he used to boast was manufactured in Georgia. He generally carried his hands in his pockets, and bestowed his tobacco-juice impartially on all sides with the *abandon* of a free and independent citizen who has not been used to carpets.

There were two things of which Colonel Delancy Hyde was proud: one, his name, the other, his Virginia birth. It is interesting to trace back the genealogy of heroes; and we have it in our power to do this justice to the Colonel.

In the year 1618 there resided in London a stable-keeper of doubtful reputation, and connected with gentlemen of the turf who frequented Hyde Park and Newmarket in the early days of that important British institution, the horse-race. This man's name was Hyde. He had a patron in Sir Arthur Delancy, a dissipated nobleman, whom he admired, naming after him a son who was early initiated in all the mysteries of jockeyship and gambling.

Unfortunately for the youth, he did not have the wit to keep out of the clutches of the law. Twice he was arrested and imprisoned for swindling. A third offence of a graver character, consisting in the theft of a pocket-book containing thirteen shillings, led to his arraignment for grand larceny, a crime then punishable with death. The gallows began to loom in the not remote distance with a sharpness of outline not pictorially pleasant to the ambition of the Hyde family.

About that time the "London Company," whose colony in Virginia was in a languishing condition, petitioned the Crown to make them a present of "vagabonds and condemned men" to be sent out to enforced labor. The senior Hyde applied to Sir Arthur Delancy to save his namesake; and that nobleman laid the case before his friend, Sir Edward Sandys, treasurer of the company aforesaid. By their joint influence the Hydes were spared the disgrace of seeing their eldest hung; and King

James having graciously granted the London Company's petition for a consignment of "vagabonds and condemned men," a hundred were sent out (a mere fraction of the numbers of similar gentry who had preceded them), and of this precious lot the younger Hyde made one.* Just a year afterwards, namely, in 1620, a Dutch trading-vessel anchored in James River with twenty negroes, and this was the beginning of African slavery in North America.

Neither threats nor lashes could induce young Mr. Hyde, this "founder of one of the first families," to work. Soon after his arrival on the banks of the Chickahominy he stole a gun, and thenceforth got a precarious living by shooting, fishing, and pilfering. He took to himself a female partner, and faithfully transmitted to his descendants the traits by which he was distinguished.

Not one of them, except now and then a female of the stock, was ever known to get an honest living; and even if the poor creatures had desired to do so, the state of society where their lot was cast was such as to deter them from learning any mechanical craft or working methodically at any manual employment.

Slavery had thrown its ban and its slime over white labor, branding it with disrepute. To get bread, not by the sweat of your own brow, but by somebody else's sweat, became the one test of manhood and high spirit. To be a gentleman, you must begin with robbery.

The Hydes were hardly an educated race. There was a tradition in the family that one of them had been to school, but if he had, the fruits of culture did not appear. They seemed to have shared the benediction of Sir William Berkeley, once Governor of Virginia, who wrote: "I thank God there are no free schools nor printing, and I hope we shall not have them these hundred years."

It is true that our Colonel Delancy Hyde could read and write, although indifferently. The labor of acquiring this ability had

* In a work published in London by De Foe, in 1722, one of his characters speaks of the Virginia immigration as being composed either of "first, such as were brought over by masters of ships, to be sold as servants; or, second, such as are transported, after having been found guilty of crimes punishable with death."

been enormous and repugnant; but before his eighteenth year he had achieved it; and thenceforth he was a prodigy in the eyes of the rest of his kin. He got his title of Colonel from once receiving a letter so addressed from Senator Mason, who had employed him to buy a horse. Among the Colonel's acquaintances who could read, this brevet was considered authoritative and sufficient.

Not being of a thrifty and forehanded habit, the Colonel's father never rose to the possession of more than three slaves at a time; but he made up for his deficiency in this respect by beating these three all the more frequently. They were a miserable set, and, to tell the truth, deserved many of the whippings they got. The owner was out of pocket by them, year after year, but was too shiftless a manager to provide against the loss, and was too proud to get rid of the encumbrances altogether. He and his children and his neighbors were kept poor, squalid, and degraded by a system that in effect made them the serfs of a few rich proprietors, who, by discrediting white labor, were able to buy up at a trifling cost the available lands, and then impoverish them by the exhausting crops wrung from the generous soil by large gangs of slaves under the rule of superior capital and intelligence.

And yet no lord of a thousand "niggers" could be a more bigoted upholder than the Hydes of "our institutions, sir." (Living by jugglery, Slavery usually speaks of *the* institution as our *institutions*.) They would foam at the mouth in speaking of those men of the North who dared to question the divinity and immutability of slavery. To deny its right to unlimited extension was the one kind of profanity not to be pardoned. It was worse than atheism to say that slavery was sectional and freedom national.

To the Colonel's not very clear geographical conceptions the white Americans south of Mason and Dixon's line were, with hardly an exception, descendants of noblemen and gentlemen; while all north were, to borrow the words of Mr. Jefferson Davis, either the "scum of Europe" or "a people whose ancestors Cromwell had gathered from the bogs and fens of Ireland and Scotland." *

* These passages are from a speech of President Davis at Jackson, Miss.,

Colonel Delancy Hyde revelled in those genealogical invectives of a similar tenor by a Richmond editor, whose fatuous and frantic iterations that the Yankees were the descendants of low-born peasants and blackguards, while the Southern Americans are the progeny of the English cavaliers, betrayed a ludicrous desire to strengthen his own feeble belief in the asseveration by loud and incessant clamor; for he had faith in Sala's witty saying, that, if a man has strong lungs, and will keep bawling day after day that he is a genius or a gentleman, the public will at last believe him.

The Colonel never tired of denouncing the Puritans:—"A canting, hyppercritical set of cusses, sir; but they had some little fight in 'em, though they could n't stahnd up agin the caval'yers,—no sir-r-r!—the caval'yers gev 'em particular hell; but the Yankee spawn of these cusses,—they hev lost the little pluck the Puritans wonst had, and air cowards, every mother's son on 'em. One high-tone Southern gemmleman—one descendant of the caval'yers—can clare out any five on 'em in a fair fight."

December, 1862. When he gets in a passion, Mr. Davis repudiates the truth even as he would State debts. Notorious facts of history are set aside in his blind wrath. The colonists of New England, he well knows, were the friends and compatriots of Cromwell and his Parliament; and the few prisoners of war Cromwell sent over from Ireland and England as slaves did not constitute an appreciable part of the then resident population of the North. It is a well-known fact, which no genealogist will dispute, that not Virginia, nor any other American State, can show such a purely English ancestry as Massachusetts. The writer of a paper in the New York Continental Monthly for July, 1863, under the title of "The Cavalier Theory Refuted," proves this statistically. "Let it be avowed," he says, "that Puritanic New England could always display a greater array of *gentlemen by birth* than Virginia, or even the entire South. This is said deliberately, because we know whereof we speak." He gives figures and names. And yet even so judicious a writer as John Stuart Mill has fallen into the error of supposing that the South had the advantage of the North in this respect. The anxious and persistent clamor of the Secessionists on this point, in the hope to enlist the sympathy of the British aristocracy, has not been wholly without effect. We would only remark, in conclusion, that Davis and his brethren, in their over-anxiety to prove that *their* ancestors were gentlemen, and *ours* clodhoppers, show the genuine spirit of the upstart and the *parvenu*. The true gentleman is content to have his gentility appear in his acts.

Mr. Clay of the Confederate Congress has introduced a resolution proposing that the coat of arms of the Slave Confederacy shall be *the figure of a cavalier!* Would not a beggar on horseback, riding in a certain familiar direction, be more appropriate?

By a fair fight for a descendant of the cavaliers, the Colonel meant one of two things: either a six-barrelled revolver against an unarmed antagonist, or an ambush in which the aforesaid descendant could hit, but be secure against being hit in return. One of the Colonel's maxims was, "Never fire unless you can take your man at a disadvantage."

His sire having been unluckily cast in a petty lawsuit, "by a low-born Yankee judge, sir," Colonel Delancy Hyde drifted off to the Southwest, and gradually emerged into the special vocation for which the unfortunate habits of life, which the Southern system had driven him to, seemed to qualify him. He became a sort of agent for the recovery of runaway slaves, and in this capacity had the freedom of the different plantations, and was frequently applied to for help by bereaved masters. Every man is said to have his specialty: the Colonel had at last found *his*.

In the survey which Peculiar took of the assemblage in Charlton's office, he saw that Charlton himself was separated from the rest in being behind a small semicircular counter, an old piece of furniture, bought cheap at a street auction. By getting in the lawyer's place the negro would have a sort of barrier, protecting him in front and on two sides against his assailants. Behind him would be the stove.

Stealthily throwing open the closet-door he glided out, and before any one could intercept him, he had fastened Charlton's arms in a noose, and was standing over him with upraised knife. So rapid, so sudden, so unexpected had been the movement, that it was all completed before even an exclamation was uttered. The first one to break the silence was Charlton, who in a paroxysm of terror cried out, "Mercy! Save me, officers! save me!"

Iverson, one of the policemen, started forward and drew a revolver; but Peek made a shield of the body of the lawyer, who now found himself threatened with a pistol on one side and a knife on the other, much to his mortal dismay.

"Put down your pistol, Iverson!" he stammered. "Don't attempt to do anything, any of you. This g-g-gentleman does n't mean to do any harm. He will listen to reason. The gentleman will listen to reason."

"Gentleman be damned!" exclaimed Colonel Delancy Hyde. "Officer, put down your pistol. This piece of property must n't be damaged. I 'm responsible for it. Peek, you imperdent black cuss, drop that rib-tickler, — drop it right smart, or yer 'll ketch hell."

The Colonel advanced, and Peek brought down his knife so as to inflict on Charlton's shoulder a gentle puncture, which drew from him a cry of pain, followed by the exclamation, in trembling tones: "Keep off, keep off, Colonel! Peek does n't mean any harm."

Iverson made an attempt to get in the negro's rear, but a shriek of remonstrance from Charlton drove the officer back.

Finding now that he was master of the situation, Peek let his right arm fall gradually to his side, and, still holding Charlton in his grasp, said: "Gentlemen, there are just five chairs before you. Be seated, and hear what I have to say."

The company looked hesitatingly at one another, till Blake, one of the policemen, said, "Why not?" and took a seat. The rest followed his example.

And then Peek, crowding back the rage and anguish of his heart, spoke as follows: "My name is Peculiar Institution. I came to this lawyer some seven weeks ago for advice. I paid him money. He got me to tell him my story. He pretended to be my friend; but thinking he could make a few dollars more out of the slaveholder than he could out of me, he sends on word to the man who calls himself my master; — in short, betrays me. You see I have him in my power. What would you do with him if you were in my place?"

"I 'd cut off his dirty ears!" exclaimed Blake, carried beyond all the discretion of a policeman by his indignation.

"What do you say, Colonel Hyde?" asked Peek.

"Wall, Peek, I don't car' what yer do ter him, providin' yer' don't damage yerself; but I reckon yer 'd better drop that knife dam quick, and give in. It 's no use tryin' to git off. We 've three witnesses here to swar you 're the right man. The Yankees put through the Fugitive Law right smart now. Yer stand no chance."

"That 's all true, Colonel," replied Peek, speaking as if arguing aloud to himself. "The law was executed in Boston last week, where there was n't half the proof you have. To do it they had to call out the whole police force, but they *did* it; and if such things are done in Boston, we can't expect much better in New York. But you see, Colonel, with this knife in my hand, I can now do one of two things: I can either kill this man, or kill myself. In either case you lose. The law hangs me if I kill him, and if I kill myself the sexton puts all of me he can lay hold of under the ground. Now, Colonel, if you refuse my terms, I'm fully resolved to do one of these two things, — probably the first, for I have scruples about the second."

"The cussed nigger talks as ef he was readin' from a book!" exclaimed Hyde, in astonishment. "Wall, Peek, what tairms do yer mean?"

"You must promise that, on my letting this man go, you'll allow me to walk freely out of this room, and go where I please unattended, on condition that I'll return at five o'clock this afternoon and deliver myself up to you to go South with you of my own accord, without any trial or bother of any kind."

The Colonel gave a furtive wink at the policeman Iverson, and replied: "Wall, Peek, that's no more nor fair, seein' as you're sich a smart respectible nigger. But I reckon yer'll go and stir up the cussed abolitioners."

"I'll promise," returned Peek, "not to tell any one what's going on."

Hyde whispered in Iverson's ear, and the latter nodded assent.

"Wall, Peek," said Colonel Hyde, "if yer'll swar, so help yer Gawd, yer'll do as yer say, we'll let yer go."

"Please write down my words, sir," said Peek, addressing Blake.

The policeman took pen and paper, and wrote, after Peek's dictation, as follows: —

"We the undersigned swear, on our part, so help us God, we will allow Peculiar Institution to quit this room free and unfollowed, on his promise that he will return and give himself up at five o'clock this P. M. And I, Peculiar Institution, swear, on my part, so help me God, I will, if these terms are carried out, fulfil the above-named promise."

"Sign that, you five gentlemen, and then I'll sign," said Peek.

The five signed. The paper and pen were then handed to Peek, and he added his name in a good legible hand, and gave the paper to Blake.

Having done this, he pulled the rope from Charlton's arms, and threw it on the floor, then returned his knife to the sheath, and picked up his cap.

But as he started for the door, Colonel Hyde drew his revolver, stood in his way, and said: "Now, nigger, no more damn nonsense! Did yer think Delancy Hyde was such a simple cuss as to trust yer? Officers, seize this nigger."

"Iverson stepped forward to obey, but Blake, with the assured gesture of one whose superiority has been felt and admitted, motioned him aside, and said to Hyde, "I'll take your revolver."

The Colonel, either thrown off his guard by Blake's cool air of authority, or supposing he wanted the weapon for the purpose of overawing the negro, gave it up. Blake then walked to the door, threw it open, and said: "Peculiar Institution, I fulfil my part of the contract. Now go and fulfil yours; and see you don't come the lawyer over me by breaking your word."

Before Colonel Delancy Hyde could recover from the amazement and wrath into which he was put by this act, Peculiar had disappeared from the room, and Blake, closing the door after him, had locked it, and taken out the key and thrust it in his pocket.

"May I be shot," exclaimed the Colonel, "but this is the damdest mean Yankee swindle I ever had put on me yit, — damned if it ain't! Here I've been to a hunderd dollars expense to git back that ar nigger, and now I'm tricked out of my property by the very man I hired to help me git it. This is Yankee all through, — damned if it ain't!"

Charlton, still pale and trembling from his recent shock, had yet strength to put in these words: "I must say, Mr. Blake, your conduct has been unprofessional and unhandsome. There is n't another officer in the whole corps that would have committed such a blunder. I shall report you to your superiors."

Blake shook his finger at him, and replied, "Open your lips again, you beggarly hound, and I 'll slap your face."

Charlton collapsed into silence. Blake took a chair and said, "Amuse yourselves five minutes, gentlemen, and then I 'll open the door."

"A hell of a feller fur an officer!" muttered the Colonel. "To let the nigger slide in that ar way, afore I 'd ever a chance to take from him his money and watch, which in course owt to go to payin' my expenses. Cuss me if I—"

"Silence!" exclaimed Blake in a voice of thunder.

Cowed by the force of a reckless and impulsive will, all present now kept quiet. Colonel Hyde, who, deprived of his revolver, felt his imbecility keenly, went to the window and looked out. Iverson, who was a coward, tried to smile, and then, seeing the expression on Blake's face, looked suddenly grave. Captain Skinner gave way to melancholy forebodings. His companion, Biggs, refreshed himself with a quid of tobacco, and stood straddling and bracing himself on his feet as if he thought a storm was brewing, and expected a lurch to leeward to take him off his legs. As for Charlton, he drew a slip of paper toward him, and appeared to be carelessly figuring on it; although, when he thought Blake was not looking, his manner changed to an eager and anxious consideration of the matter before him.

The five minutes had nearly expired when Blake rose, turned his back to Charlton, and seemed to be lost in reverie. Charlton took this opportunity to hastily finish what he had been writing. He then enclosed it in an envelope, and directed it. This done, he motioned to Iverson, and held up the letter. The latter nodded, and pointed with a motion of the thumb to a newspaper on the table. Charlton placed the letter under it, coughed, and turned to warm himself at the stove. Iverson sidled toward the newspaper, but before he could reach it, Blake turned and dashed his fist on it, took up the letter, and whispered menacingly to Charlton, "Utter a single word, and I 'll choke you."

Then unlocking and opening the door, he said to the other persons in the room, "Go! you can return, if you choose, at five o'clock."

"Give me my revolver," demanded the Colonel.

"Say two words, and I'll have you arrested for trying to shoot an unarmed man," replied Blake.

The Colonel swallowed his rage and left the room, followed by Iverson and the two witnesses. Blake again locked the door and took the key.

"What's the meaning of all this?" asked Charlton, seriously alarmed.

"It means that if you open that traitor's mouth of yours till I tell you to, you'll come to grief."

Charlton subsided and was silent.

Blake unfolded the paper he had seized, and read as follows: "You will probably find Peek, either at Bunker's in Broadway, or at his rooms in Greenwich Street, the side nearest the river, third or fourth house from the corner of Dey Street."

Blake thrust the paper back into his pocket, and, wholly regardless of Charlton's presence, began pacing the floor.

CHAPTER IX.

THE UPPER AND THE LOWER LAW.

"There is a law above all the enactments of human codes, — the same throughout the world, the same in all times: it is the law written by the finger of God on the heart of man; and by that law, unchangeable and eternal, while men despise fraud and loathe rapine and abhor bloodshed, they will reject with indignation the wild and guilty fantasy than man can hold property in man." — *Lord Brougham.*

THE policeman, Blake, was a Vermonter whose grandsire had been one of the eighty men under Ethan Allen at the capture of Fort Ticonderoga. The traditions of the Revolution were therefore something more than barren legends in Blake's mind. They had inspired him with an enthusiastic admiration of the republic and its institutions. His patriotism was a sentiment which all the political and moral corruption, with which a New York policeman is inevitably brought in contact, could not corrode or enfeeble.

Even slavery, being tolerated by the Constitution of the United States, was, in his view, not to be spoken of lightly. He shut his eyes and his ears to all that could be said in its condemnation; he opened them to all its palliating features and facts. Did not statistics prove that the blacks, in a state of slavery, increase in double the proportion they do in a state of freedom, surrounded by whites? This comforting argument was eagerly seized by Blake as a moral sedative.

The Fugitive-Slave Law he was satisfied was strictly in accordance with both the spirit and the letter of the Constitution of the United States. Therefore it must be honestly enforced. The Abolitionists, who were striving to defeat the execution of the law, were almost as bad as Mississippi repudiators who were swindling their foreign creditors. So long as we were enjoying the benefits of the Constitution, was it not mean and dastardly to undertake to jockey the South out of the obvious protection of that clause in it which has reference to the "person held to service or labor," which we all knew to mean the slave?

Considerations like these had made Blake one of the most earnest advocates of the enforcement of the law among his brethren of the police; and when at last he was called on to carry it out in the case of Peek, he felt that obedience was a duty which it would be poltroonery to evade. He went forth, therefore, with alacrity that morning, resolved to allow no mawkish sensibility to interfere with his obligations as an officer and a citizen.

Accompanied by Iverson, he waited on Colonel Delancy Hyde at the New York Hotel. They found that worthy in the smoking-room, seated at a small marble table, with a cigar in his mouth and an emptied tumbler, which smelt strongly of undiluted whiskey, before him. The Colonel graciously asked the officers to "liquor." Iverson assented, but Blake declined.

A refusal to "liquor," the Colonel had been bred to regard as a personal indignity; and so, turning to Blake, he said: "Look here, stranger! I 'm Colonel Delancy Hyde. Virginia-born, be Gawd! From one of the oldest families in the State! None of yer interloping Yankee scum! No Puritan blood in *me!* My ahncestor was one of the cavalyers. My father was one of the largest slave-owners in the State. Now if yer want to put an affront on me, I 'd jest have yer understand fust who yer 've got to deal with."

"Bah!" said Blake, turning on his heel, and walking to the window.

Iverson, who dreaded a scene, smoothed over the affront with a lie. "The fact is, Colonel," whispered he, "Blake would n't be fit for duty if he were to drink with us. A spoonful upsets him; but he 's ashamed to confess it. A weak head! You understand?"

The explanation pacified the Colonel. Indeed, his sympathies were at once wakened for the unhappy man who could n't drink. This representative of the interests of slavery certainly did not prepossess Blake in favor of his mission; but justice must be done, notwithstanding the character of the claimant.

An addition was now made to the circle. Captain Skinner and Biggs, the sailor already mentioned, — a short, thick-set stump of a man, with only one eye, and that black and overarched by a bushy, gray eyebrow, — a very wicked-looking old fellow, — entered and made themselves known to the Colonel. They had come up from New London, to serve as witnesses. As a matter of policy, the Colonel could not do less than ask them to join in the raid on the whiskey decanter; and this they did so effectually that the last drop disappeared in Biggs's capacious tumbler.

As it was not yet time for the appointment at Charlton's office, the party, all but Blake, took chairs and lighted cigars, and the Colonel asked Captain Skinner to narrate the circumstances of Peek's appearance on board the Albatross.

"Well, you see, Colonel," said Skinner, "we had been ten days out, when one night the second mate, as he was poking about between decks, caught a strange nigger creeping into a cotton-bale just for'ard of the store-room. We ordered the nigger out, and he came into the cabin, and pretended to be a free nigger, and said he 'd pay his passage as soon as he could git work in New York. In course I knew he was lyin', but I did n't let on that I suspected him. I played smooth; and cuss me, if the nigger did n't play smooth too; for he made as if he believed me; and so when we got to New London, afore I could git the officers on board, he jumped into the water and swam to old Payson's boat, and Payson he got him on board one of the Sound steamers, and had him put through to New York that same night. The next day Payson attakted me in the street, knocked me down, and stamped on me, and afore I could have him tuk up, he was on board that infernal boat of his, and off out of sight. There 's the scar of the gash Payson left on my skull."

Blake, at these words, left the window, and came and looked at the scar with evident satisfaction. Colonel Hyde, with a lordly air of patronage, held out his hand to Skinner, and said: "Capting, the scar is an honor. Capting, yer hand. I love to meet a high-tone gemmleman, and you 're one. Capting, allow me to shake yer hand."

"With pleasure," said Biggs, taking the Colonel's hand and shaking it in his own big, coarsely-seamed flipper, before the Captain had a chance to reach out. The Colonel smiled grimly at Biggs's playfulness, but said nothing.

"Come! it's time to go," exclaimed Iverson, looking at his watch. The party rose, and proceeded down Broadway to Charlton's office. We have already seen what transpired on their arrival. Our business is now with what happened after their departure.

Three o'clock struck. The small hand on the dial of Trinity was fast moving toward four; and still Blake paced the floor in Charlton's office. Every now and then there would be a knock at the door, and Blake, with a menacing shake of his head, would impose silence on the conveyancer, till the applicant for admission, tired of knocking, would go away.

Blake's thoughts were in the condition of a chopping sea where wind and tide are opposing each other. Reflections that reached to the very foundation of human society — questions of abstract right and wrong — were combating old notions adopted on the authority of others, and as yet untested in the cupel of his own conscience.

Brought for the first time face to face with the law for the rendition of fugitive slaves, — encountering it in its practical operation, — he found in it a barbarous necessity from which his heart recoiled with horror and disgust. Must he disregard that pleading cry of conscience, that voice of God and Christ in his soul, calling on him to do in righteousness unto others as he would have them do unto him? Could any human enactment exempt him from that paramount obedience?

How had he felt dwarfed in another's presence that day! He had seen a man, and that man a negro, putting forth his manhood in the best way he could to parry the arm of a savage oppression, doubly fiendish in its mockery, coming as it did under the respectable escort of the law. Surely the negro showed himself better worthy of freedom than any white man among his hunters.

Would the fellow keep his pledge? Would he come back? Blake now earnestly hoped he would not. Was not any stratagem justifiable in such a case? Should we mind resorting to deception in order to rescue ourselves or another from a madman or a murderer? Why, then, might not Peek violate his written promise, made as it was to men who were trying to rob him of a freedom more precious than life to such a soul as his?

But had not he himself — he, Blake — made use of his poor show of generosity to impress it on Peek that he must prove worthy the trust reposed in him? This recollection brought bitter regret to the policeman. Instead of encouraging the negro to escape, he had put scruples of conscience or of generosity in his way, which might induce him to return. Would Blake have done so to his own brother, under similar circumstances? Would he not have bidden him cheat his persecutors, and make good his flight? Assuredly yes! And yet to the poor negro he had practically said, Return!

These reflections wrought powerfully upon Blake. Why not run and urge the negro to escape? It was still more than an hour to five o'clock. Yes, he would do it!

Then came a consideration to check the impulse. He, a sworn officer of the law, should he lend himself to the defeat of the very law he had taken it upon himself to execute? Was there not something intensely dishonest in such a course?

Well, he could do one thing at least: he could resign his office, and then try to undo the mischief he had perhaps done the negro by his injunction. Yes, he would do that.

Impulsive in all his movements, Blake looked at his watch, and found he would have just an hour in which to crowd all the action he proposed to himself. Turning to Charlton, he said: "Your conduct to this runaway slave will make your life insecure if I choose to go to certain men in this city and tell them what I can with truth. What you now are intending to do is to have the slave intercepted. I don't ask you to promise, simply because you will lie if you think it safe; but I say this to you: If I find that any measures are taken before five o'clock to catch the slave, I shall hold you responsible for them, and shall expose you to parties who will see you are paid back for your rascality. Take no step for an arrest, and I hold my tongue."

Glad of such a compromise, Charlton replied: "I 'm agreed. Up to five o'clock I'll do nothing, directly or indirectly, to intercept the nigger."

Blake was speedily in the street after this. He hurried to the City Hall, found the Chief of Police, gave in his resignation, deposited Colonel Hyde's pistol among the curiosities of the room, and said that another man must be found to attend to the case at Charlton's office. Having in this way eased his conscience, Blake ran as far as Broadway, and jumped into an omnibus. But the omnibus was too slow, so he jumped out and ran down Broadway to Bunker's. How the precious time flew by! Before he could be satisfied at Bunker's that Peek was not there, the clock indicated five minutes of five. He rushed out in the direction of the slave's lodgings. An old woman with wrinkled face, and bent form, and carrying a broom, was showing the apartments to an applicant who thought of moving from the story below. Where were the negro and his wife? Gone! How long ago? More than two hours! The clock struck five.

Wholly disheartened, Blake ran back to Charlton's office. He found it locked. No one answered to his knock. Raising his foot he kicked open the door with a single effort. The office was deserted. No one there! He ran to the Jersey City ferry-boat that carries passengers for the Philadelphia cars; it had left the wharf some twenty minutes before. Baffled in all directions, he took his way to the police-station to find Iverson; but that officer was on duty, nobody knew where. After waiting at the station till nearly midnight, Blake at last, worn out with discouragement and fatigue, went home.

What had become of Peek all this time?

Anticipating that he and his wife might at any moment find it prudent to leave for Canada at half an hour's notice, Peek had always kept his affairs in a state to enable him to do this conveniently. He had hired his rooms, furniture, and piano-forte by the week, paying for them in advance. Two small trunks were sufficient to contain all his movable property; and these might be packed in five minutes.

Flora, his wife, who like Peek was of unmixed blood, had been lady's maid in a family in Vicksburg. Here she had become an expert in washing and doing up muslins and other fine articles of female attire. But the lady she served died, and Flora became the property of Mr. Penfield, a planter, who, looking on her with the eyes that a cattle-breeder might turn on a Durham cow, ordered her to marry one Bully Bill, a lusty African with a neck like the cylinder of a steam-engine. Flora objected, and learning that her objections would not be respected, she ran away, and after various fortunes settled at Montreal. Here she married Peek, who taught her to read and write. She had been bred a pious Catholic, and Peek, finding that they agreed in the essentials of a devout and believing heart, never undertook to disturb her faith.

They moved to New York, and Peek with his wages as waiter, and Flora with the money she got for doing up muslins, earned jointly an income which placed them far above want in the region of absolute comfort and partial refinement. Few more happy and loyal couples could have been found even in freestone palaces on the Fifth Avenue.

"Well, Flora, how long will it take you to get ready?" said Peek, entering the neat little kitchen, where she was at work at her ironing-board, while little Sterling sat amusing himself on the floor in building a house with small wooden bricks.

Flora, at once comprehending the intent of the question, replied, "I sha'n't want more 'n half an hour."

"Well, a boat leaves for Albany at five," said Peek, taking the Sun newspaper, and cutting out an advertisement. "We 'd better quit here, and go on board just as soon as we can."

"Le 'm me see," said Flora, meditatively. "The grocer at the corner will send round these muslins, 'specially if we pay him for it. My customers owe me twenty dollars, — how shall we collek that?"

"You can write to them from Montreal."

"Lor! so I can, Peek. Who 'd have thought of it but you?"

"Come, then! Be lively. Tumble the things into the trunks. We 'll give poor old Petticum the odds and ends we leave behind; and she 'll notify the landlord, and take care of the rooms."

In less than an hour's time they had made all their preparations, and were all three in a coach with their luggage, rattling up Greenwich Street towards one of the Twenties. Here they went on board an old steamer, recently taken from the regular line for freighting purposes, and carrying only a few passengers. Having seen Flora and Sterling safely bestowed with the luggage, and given the former his watch and all his money, except a dollar in change, Peek said: "Now, Flora, I 've got to go ashore on business. If I should n't be here when the boat starts, do you keep straight on to Montreal without me. Go to the post-office regularly twice a week to see if there 's a letter for you."

"What is it, Peek? Tell me all about it," said Flora, who painfully felt there was a secret which her husband did not choose to disclose.

"Now, Flora, don't be silly," replied Peek, wiping the tears from her face with his handkerchief. "I tell you, I may be aboard again before you start, — have n't made up my mind yet, — only, if you should n't see me, never you mind, but just keep on. Find out your old customers in Montreal, and wait patiently till I join you. So don't cry about it. The Lord will take care of it all. Here 's a handbill that tells you the best way to get to Montreal. Look out for pickpockets. I should n't leave you if I did n't have to, Flora. I 'll tell you everything about it when we meet. So good by."

Having no suspicion of the actual cause of Peek's leaving her, and confident, through faith in him, that it must be for a right purpose, Flora cheered up, and said: "Well, Peek, I 'spec you 've got some little debts to pay; but do come back to-day if you can; and keep clar' of the hounds, Peek, — keep clar' of the hounds."

And so, kissing wife and child, with an overflowing heart Peek quitted the boat. He did not at once leave the vicinity. There was a pile of fresh lumber not far off. Dodging out of sight behind it, and then sitting down in a little enclosure formed by the boards, where he could see the boat and not be seen, he tried to orient his conscience as to his duty under the extraordinary circumstances in which he found himself.

Go back to the life of a slave? Leave wife and child, and return to bondage, degradation, subordination to another's will? He looked out on the beautiful river, flashing in the warm spring sunshine; to the opposite shore of Hoboken, where he and Flora used to stroll on Sundays last summer, dragging Sterling in his little carriage. Was there to be no more of that pleasant independent life?

A slave? Liable to be kicked, cuffed, spit on, fettered, scourged by such a creature as Colonel Delancy Hyde? No!

To escape the pursuing fiends who would force such a lot on an innocent human being, surely any subterfuge, any stratagem, any lie, would be justifiable!

And Peek thought of the joy that Flora would feel at seeing him return, and he rose to go back to the boat.

A single thought drew him back to his covert. "So help me God." Had he not pledged himself, — pledged himself in sincerity at the moment in those words? Had he not by his act promised Blake, who had befriended him, that he would return, and might not Blake lose his situation if the promise were broken?

As Peek found conscience getting the better of inclination in the dispute, he bowed his head in his hands, and wept sobbingly like a child. Such anguish was there in the thought of a surrender! Then, extending himself prostrate on the boards, his face down, and resting on his arms, he strove to shut out all except the voice of God in his soul. He uttered no word, but he felt the mastery of a great desire, and that was for guidance from above. Tender thoughtt of the sufferings and wants of the poor slaves he had left on Barnwell's plantation stole back to him. Would he not like to see them and be of service to them once more? What if he should be whipped, imprisoned? Could he not brave all such risks, for the satisfaction of keeping a pledge made to a man who had shown him kindness? And he recalled the words, once spoken through Corinna, "Not to be happy, but to deserve happiness."

Besides, might he not again escape? Yes! He would go back to Charlton's office. He would surrender himself as he had promised. The words which Colonel Hyde had conceived to be of no more binding force than a wreath of tobacco-smoke were the chain stronger than steel that drew the negro back to the fulfilment of his pledge. "So help me God!" Could he profane those words, and ever look up again to Heaven for succor?

And so he rose, took one despairing look at the boat, where he could see Flora pointing out to her little boy the wonders of the river, and then rushed away in the direction of Broadway. There was no lack of omnibuses, but no friendly driver would give him a seat on top, and he was excluded by social prejudice from the inside. It was twenty minutes to five when he reached Union Park. Thence running all the way in the middle of the street with the carriages, he reached Charlton's office before the clock had finished striking the hour.

There had been wrangling and high words just before his entrance. Colonel Delancy Hyde was ejecting his wrath against the universal Yankee nation in the choicest terms of vituperation that his limited vocabulary could supply. The loss of both his nigger and his revolver had been too much for his equanimity. Captain Skinner and his companion, Biggs, were sturdily demanding their fees, which did not seem to be forthcoming. Charlton, in abject grief of heart, was silently lamenting the loss of his fifty dollars, forfeited by the non-delivery of the slave; and Iverson, the policeman, was delicately insinuating in the ear of the lawyer that he should look to him for his pay.

Peek, entering in this knotty condition of affairs, was the *Deus ex machina* to disentangle the complication and set the wheels smoothly in motion. No one believed he would come back, and there issued from the lips of all an exclamation of surprise, not unseasoned with oaths to suit the several tastes.

"Cuss me if here ain't the nigger himself come back!" exclaimed the Colonel. "Wall, Peek, I did n't reckon you was gwine to keep yer word, and it made me swar some to see how I'd been chiselled fust out of my revolver and then out of my nigger, by a damned Yankee policeman. But here you air, and we'll fix things right off, so's to be ready for the next Philadelphy train, if so be yer'll go without any fuss."

"Yes, I'll go, Colonel," said Peek, "but you'll have an officer to see I don't escape from the cars."

"Thar's seventy-five dollars expense, blast yer!" exclaimed the Colonel. "Yes, be Gawd! I've got to pay this man for goin' to Cincinnati and back. O, but old Hawks will take your damned hide off when we git you back in Texas, — sure!"

Peek, to serve some purpose of his own, here dropped his dignity entirely, and assumed the manner and language of the careless, rollicking plantation nigger. "Yah! yah!" laughed he. "Wall, look a-he-ah, Kunnle Delancy Hyde. Les make a trade, — we two, — and git rid of the policeman altogedder. I can sabe yer fifty dollars, shoo-er-r-r, Kunnle Delancy Hyde, if you 'll do as how dis nigger tells yer to."

"How 'll yer do it, Peek?" asked the Colonel, much pacified by the slave's repetition of his entire name and title.

"I 'll promise to be a good nigger all the way to Cincinnati, and not try to run away, — no, not wunst, — if you 'll pay me twenty-five dollars."

"Will yer sign to that, Peek, and put in, 'So help me Gawd'?" asked the Colonel.

Peek started, and looked sharply at Hyde; and then quietly replied, "Yes, I 'll do it, if you 'll gib me the money to do with as I choose; but you must agree to le 'm me write a letter, and put it in the post-office afore we leeb."

The Colonel considered the matter a moment, then turned to Charlton, and said, "Draw up an agreement, and let the nigger sign it, and be sure and put in, 'So help me Gawd.'"

The arrangement was speedily concluded. The witnesses and the officers were paid off. Charlton received his fifty dollars and Peek his twenty-five. The slave then asked for pen, ink, and paper, and placed five cents on the table as payment. In two minutes he finished a letter to Flora, and enclosed it with the money in an envelope, on which he wrote an address. Charlton tried hard to get a sight of it, but Peek did not give him a chance to do this.

The Colonel and Peek then walked to the post-office, where the slave deposited his letter; after which they passed over to Jersey City in the ferry-boat, and took the train to Philadelphia.

As for Charlton, no sooner had his company left him, than he seized his hat, locked up his office, and hurried to Greenwich Street, where he proceeded to examine the lodgings vacated by Peek. He found Mrs. Petticum engaged in collecting into baskets the various articles abandoned to her by the negroes, — old dusters, a hod of charcoal, kindling-wood, loaves of bread, and small collections of groceries, sufficient for the family for a week. Mrs. Petticum appeared to have been weeping, for she raised her apron and wiped her eyes as Charlton came in.

"Well, have they gone?" asked he.

"Yes, sir, and the wuss for me!" said the old woman.

Charlton took his cue at once, and replied: "They were excellent people, and I'm sorry they've gone. What was the matter? Were the slave-catchers after them?"

"I don't know," sighed Petticum; "I should n't wonder. Poor Flora! That was all she worried about. I'd like to have got my hands in the hair of the man that would have carried her off. Where 'll you find the white folks better and decenter than they was?"

"Not in New York, ma'am," said Charlton, stealthily looking about the room, examining every article of furniture, and opening the drawers.

"The furniture belongs to Mr. Craig; but all in the drawers is mine," said the old woman, not favorably impressed by Charlton's inquisitiveness.

"O, it's all right," replied Charlton; "I did n't know but I could be of some help. You've no idea where they went to?"

"They did n't tell me, and if I knowed, I should n't tell you, without I knowed they wanted me to."

"O, it's no sort of consequence. I'm a particular friend, that's all," said Charlton. "Did you notice the carriage they went off in?"

"Yes, I did."

"Could you tell me the number?"

"No, I could n't."

Seeing an old handkerchief in one of the baskets, Charlton took it out, and looked at the mark. He could get nothing from that; so he threw it back. An old shoe lay swept in a corner. He took it up. Stamped on the inner sole were the words, "J. Darling, Ladies' Shoes, Vicksburg." Charlton copied the inscription in his memorandum-book before putting the shoe back where he had found it. The Sun newspaper lay on the floor. Taking it up, he found that an advertisement had been cut out. Selecting an opportunity when Mrs. Petticum was not looking, he thrust the paper in his pocket.

And then, after examining an old stove-funnel, he went out.

"He's no gentleman, anyhow," said Mrs. Petticum; "and I don't believe he ever was a friend of the Jacobses."

CHAPTER X.

GROUPS ON THE DECK.

"Incredulity is but Credulity seen from behind, bowing and nodding assent to the Habitual and the Fashionable." — *Coleridge.*

THE Pontiac had passed New Madrid on the Mississippi. She was advertised as a first-class high-pressure boat, bound to beat any other on the river in the long run, but with a captain and officers who were "teetotalers," and never raced.

The weather had been stormy for several days; but it was now a delightful April forenoon. The sun-bright atmosphere was at once fresh and soft, exhilarating and luxurious, in a combination one rarely enjoys so fully as on a Western prairie. The delicate spring tracery of the foliage was fast expanding into a richer exuberance on either bank of the great river. The dogwood, with its blossoms of an alabaster whiteness, here and there gleamed forth amid the tender green of the surrounding trees, — maples, sycamores, and oaks. All at once a magnolia sent forth a gush of fragrance from its snowy flowers. With every mile southward the verdure grew thicker and the blossoms larger.

Two miles in the rear of the Pontiac, ploughing up the tawny waters with her sharp and pointed beak, came the Champion, a new boat, and destined, as many believed, to prove the fastest on the river. Whatever her capacities, she had thus far shown herself inferior to the Pontiac in speed. She kept within two or three miles, but failed to get much nearer. Captain Crane of the Pontiac, a small, thin, wiry man, who had acquired a great reputation for sagacity by always holding his tongue, kept puffing away at a cigar, looking now and then anxiously at his rival, but evidently happy in the assurance of victory.

The passengers of the Pontiac were distributed in groups about different parts of the boat. Some were in the cabin playing at euchre or brag. Some, regardless of the delicious atmosphere which they could drink in without money and without price, were imbibing fiery liquors at the bar, or puffing away at bad cigars on the forward part of the lower deck. A few were reading, and here and there a lady might be seen busy with her needle.

On the hurricane deck were those who had come up for conversation or a promenade. Smokers were requested to keep below. The groups here were rather more select and less numerous than on the main deck. They were mostly gathered aft, so that the few promenaders could have a clear space.

Among these last were a lady and two gentlemen, one on either side of her; the younger, a man apparently about thirty-two, of middle height, finely formed, handsome, and with the quiet, unarrogating air of one whose nobility is a part of his nature, not a question of convention. (The snob's nonchalance is always spurious. He hopes to make you think he is unconscious of your existence, and all the while is anxiously trying to dazzle or stun you by his appearance.)

The other gentleman was also one to whom that much-abused name would be unhesitatingly applied. He seemed to be about fifty-five, with a person approaching the portly, dignified, gray-haired, and his face indicating benevolence and self-control.

The lady, who appeared to be the wife of the younger man, was half a head shorter than he, and a model of delicate beauty in union with high health. Personally of a figure and carriage which Art and Grace could hardly improve, she was dressed in a simple gray travelling-habit, with a velvet hat and ostrich-plumes of the same color. But she had the rare skill of making simplicity a charm. Flounces, jewels, and laces would have been an impertinence. While she conversed, she seemed to take a special interest in a group that occupied two "patent life-preserving stools" near the centre of the deck. A young boy held in his lap a little girl, seemingly not more than two years old, and pointed out pictures to her from a book, while a mulatto woman, addressed as Hattie, who appeared to have the infant in charge, joined in their juvenile prattle, and placed her arm so as to assist the boy in securing his hold.

"Your son seems to know how to fascinate children," said the lady, addressing the elder gentleman; "he has evidently won the heart of my little Clara."

"He has a sister just about her age in Texas," replied the father; "he is glad to find in your little girl a substitute for Emily."

"You live in Texas then?" asked the younger gentleman.

"Yes; let me introduce myself, since I was the first to broach conversation. My name is John Onslow, and my home is in Southwestern Texas, though I was born in Mississippi, whence I removed some six or seven years ago. My family consists of a wife, two sons, and a daughter. The younger of my sons, Robert, sits yonder. The elder, William Temple, is a student at Yale. I inherited several hundred slaves. I have gradually liberated them all. In Texas I am trying the experiment of free labor; but it is regarded with dislike by my slave-holding neighbors, and they do not scruple, behind my back, to call me an Abolitionist. I have been North to buy farming implements, and to offer inducements to German immigrants. There, sir, you have my story; and if you are a Yankee, you will appreciate my candor."

"And requite it, I suppose you think," returned the younger gentleman, laughing. "It strikes me that it is you, Mr. Onslow, who are playing the Yankee. You have been talking, sir, with one Henry Berwick, New-Yorker by birth, retired lawyer by profession, and now on his way to New Orleans to attend to some real estate belonging to his wife. That little girl is his daughter. This lady is his wife. My dear, this is our fellow-passenger, Mr. Onslow. Allow me to introduce him to your better acquaintance."

The lady courtesied, flashing upon the stranger a smile that said as eloquently as smile could say, "I need no vouchers; I flatter myself I can distinguish a gentleman."

As she turned aside her glance it met that of a third person, till then unnoticed. He was pacing the deck and held an opera-glass in his hand, with which he looked at places on either bank. He was slightly above the middle height, compactly built, yet rather slender than stout, erect, square-shouldered, neatly limbed. He might be anywhere between thirty and thirty-five years of age. His hair was here and there threaded with gray, and his cheeks were somewhat sunken, although there was nothing to suggest the lassitude of ill-health in his appearance. His complexion was that of a man who leads an active out-of-door life; but his hands were small and unmarked by toil. He wore his beard neatly trimmed. His finely curved Roman features and small expressive mouth spoke refinement and strength of will, not untempered with tenderness; while his dark gray eyes seemed to penetrate without a pause straight to their object. A sagacious physiognomist would have said of him, "That man has a story to tell; life has been to him no holiday frolic." In the expression of his eyes Mrs. Berwick was reminded of Sir Joshua's fine picture of "The Banished Lord." This stranger, as he passed by, looked at her gravely but intently, as if struck either by her beauty or by a fancied resemblance to some one he had known. There was that in his glance which so drew her attention, she said to her husband, "Who is that man?"

"I have not seen him before," replied Mr. Berwick. "Probably he came on board at New Madrid."

They walked to the extent of their promenade forward, and turning saw this stranger leaning against the bulwarks. His low-crowned hat of a delicate, pliable felt, with its brims half curled up, his well-cut pantaloons of a coarse but unspotted fabric, and his thin overcoat of a light gray, showed that the Broadway fashions of the hour were not unfamiliar to the wearer. This time he did not look up as the three passed. His gaze seemed intent on the children; and the soft smile on his lips and the dewy suffusion in his eyes betrayed emotion and tender meditation.

"Well, Leonora, what is your judgment? Is he, too, a gentleman?" asked Mr. Berwick of his wife.

"Yes; I will stake my reputation as a sibyl on it," she replied.

"Ah! you vain mother!" said Berwick, laughing. "You say that, because he seems lost in admiration of our little Clara. Is n't her weakness transparent, Mr. Onslow? What think *you* of this new-comer?"

"He certainly has the air of a gentleman," said Onslow;

"and yet he looks to me very much like a fellow I once had up before me for horse-stealing. Was he too much interested in looking at your wife, or did he purposely abstain from letting me catch his eye? I should n't wonder if he were either a steamboat gambler or a horse-thief!"

"Atrocious!" exclaimed Mrs. Berwick. "I don't believe a word of it. That man a horse-thief! Impossible!"

"On closer examination, I think I must be mistaken," rejoined Mr. Onslow. "If I remember aright, the fellow with whom I confound him had red hair."

"There! I knew you must be either joking or in error," said the lady.

"And now," continued Mr. Onslow, "I have a vague recollection of meeting him at the hotel where I stopped in Chicago last week."

"Ah! if he is a Chicago man, I must be right in my estimate of him," said Mrs. Berwick.

"Why so? Why should you be partial to Chicago?"

"Because my father was one of the first residents of the place."

"What was his name?"

"Robert Aylesford."

As she uttered this word they repassed the stranger. To their surprise he repeated, in a tone of astonishment, "Aylesford!" then seemed to fall into a fit of musing. Before they again reached the spot, he had walked away, and taken a seat in an arm-chair aft, where he occupied himself in wiping the opera-glass with his handkerchief. If he had recognized Onslow, he had not betrayed it.

Here the attention of all on the upper deck was arrested by an explosion of wrathful oaths.

A tall, gaunt, round-shouldered man, dressed in an ill-fitting suit of some coarse, home-made cloth, had ascended the stairs with a lighted cigar in his mouth. One of the waiters of the boat, a bright-looking mulatto, followed him, calling, "Mister! Mister!"

The tall man paid no heed to the call, and the mulatto touched him on the shoulder, and said, "We don't allow smoking on this deck," whereupon the tall man angrily turned on him, and, with eyes blazing with savage fire, exclaimed: "What in hell air yer at, nigger? Ask my pardon, blast yer, or I 'll smash in yer ugly profile, sure!"

"Ask your pardon for what?"

"For darrin' to put yer black hand on me, confound yer!"

The mulatto replied with spirit: "You don't bully this child, Mister. I merely did my duty."

"Duty be damned! I 'll stick yer, sure, if yer don't apologize right off, damned lively!" And the tall man unsheathed a monstrous bowie-knife.

Mr. Onslow approached, and mildly interposed with the remark, "It was natural for the waiter to touch you, since he could n't make you hear."

"Who the hell air you, sir?" said the tall man. "I reckon I kn settle with the nigger without no help of yourn."

"Yes," said another voice; "if the gentleman demands it, the nigger must ask his pardon."

Mr. Onslow turned, and to his surprise beheld the stranger with the opera-glass.

"Really, sir," said Mr. Onslow, "I hope you do not wish to see a man degrade himself merely because he is n't white like ourselves."

"The point can't be argued, sir," said the stranger, putting his glass in his pocket. Then seizing the mulatto by the throat, he thrust him on his knees. "Down, you black hound, and ask this gentleman's pardon."

To everybody's surprise, the mulatto's whole manner changed the minute he saw the stranger; and, sinking on his knees, he crossed his arms on his breast, and, with downcast eyes, said, addressing the tall man, "I ask pardon, sir, for putting my hand on you."

"Wall, that 's enough, nigger! I pardon yer," said the mollified tall man, returning his bowie-knife to its sheath. "Niggers mus' know thar places, — that 's all. Ef a nigger knows his place, I 'd no more harm him nor I 'd harm a val'able hoss."

The mulatto rose and walked away; but with no such show of chagrin as a keen observer might have expected; and the tall man, turning to him of the opera-glass, said, "Sir, ye 'r a high-tone gemmleman; an' cuss me but I 'm proud of yer acquaint. Who mowt it be I kn call yer, sir?"

"Vance of New Orleans," was the reply.

"Mr. Vance, I'm yourn. I know'd yer mus' be from the South. Yer mus' liquor with me, Mr. Vance. Sir, ye'r a high-tone gemmleman. I'm Kunnle Hyde, — Kunnle Delancy Hyde. Virginia-born, be Gawd! An' I'm not ashamed ter say it! My ahnces'tors cum over with the caval'yers in King James's time, — yes, sir-r-r! My father was one of the largest slave-owners in the hull State of Virginia, — yes, sir-r-r! Lost his proputty, every damned cent of it, sir, through a low-lived Yankee judge, sir!"

"I could have sworn, Colonel Hyde, there was no Puritan blood in your veins."

"That's a fak!" said the Colonel, grimly smiling his gratification. Then, throwing his cigar overboard, he remarked: "The Champion 's nowhar, I reckon, by this time. She ain't in sight no longer. What say yer to a brandy-smash? Or sh'l it be a julep?"

"The bar is crowded just now; let's wait awhile," replied Vance.

Here Mr. Onslow turned away in disgust, and, rejoining the Berwicks, remarked to the lady, "What think you of your gentleman now?"

"I shall keep my thoughts respecting him to myself for the present," she replied.

"My wife piques herself on her skill in judging of character by the physiognomy," said Mr. Berwick, apologetically; "and I see you can't make her believe she is wrong in this case. She sometimes gets impressions from the very handwriting of a person, and they often turn out wonderfully correct."

"Has Mrs. Berwick the gift of second-sight? Is she a seeress?"

"Her faculty does not often show itself in soothsaying," said Berwick. "But I have a step-mother who now and then has premonitions."

"Do they ever find a fulfilment?"

"One time in a hundred, perhaps," said Berwick. "If I believed in them largely, I should not be on board this boat."

"Why so?" inquired Onslow.

"She predicts disaster to it."

"But why did you not tell me that before?" asked Mrs. Berwick.

"Simply, my dear, because you are inclined to be superstitious."

"Hear him, Mr. Onslow!" said Mrs. Berwick. "He calls me superstitious because I believe in spirits, whereas it is that belief which has cured me of superstition."

"I can readily suppose it," replied Onslow. "The superstitious man is the *un*believer, — he who thinks that all these phenomena can be produced by the blind, unintelligent forces of nature, by a mechanical or chemical necessity."

"I may believe in spirits in their proper places," said Berwick, "and not believe in their visiting this earth."

"But what if their condition is such that they are independent of those restrictions of space or place which are such impediments to us poor mortals?"

"Do you, too, then, believe in ghosts?" asked Berwick.

"Yes; I am a ghost myself," said Onslow.

Berwick started at the abruptness of the announcement, then smiled, and replied, "Prove it."

"That I will, both etymologically and chemically," rejoined Onslow. "The words *ghost* and *gas* are set down by a majority of the philologists as from the same root, whether Gothic, Saxon, or Sanscrit, implying vapor, spirit. The fermenting *yeast*, the steaming *geyser*, are allied to it. Now modern science has established (and Professor Henry will confirm what I say) that man begins his earthly existence as a microscopic vesicle of almost pure and transparent water. It is not true that he is made of dust. He consists principally of solidified air. The ashes which remain after combustion are the only ingredient of an earthy character that enters into the composition of his body. All the other parts of it were originally in the atmosphere. Nay, a more advanced science will probably show that even his ashes, in their last analysis, are an invisible, gaseous substance. Nine tenths of a man's body, we can even now prove, are water; and water, we all know, may be decomposed into invisible gases, and then made to reappear as a visible liquid. Science tells me, dear madam, that as to my body I am nothing but forty or fifty pounds of carbon and nitrogen, diluted by five and a half pailfuls of water. Put me under hydraulic pressure, and you can prove it. So I do seriously maintain, that I am as much entitled to the appellation of a ghost (that is, a gaseous body) as was the buried majesty of Denmark, otherwise known as Hamlet's father."

"And I assert that Mr. Onslow has proved his point admirably," said Mrs. Berwick, clapping her little hands.

"I confess I never before considered the subject in that light," rejoined her husband.

"If science can prove," continued Mr. Onslow, "that nine tenths of my present body may be changed to a gaseous, invisible substance (invisible to mortal eyes), with power to permeate what we call matter, like electricity, is it so very difficult to imagine that a spirit in a spiritual body may be standing here by our side without our knowing it?"

"I see you have n't the fear of Sir David Brewster and the North British Review before your eyes, Mr. Onslow."

"No, for I do not regard them as infallible either in questions of physical or of metaphysical science. Rather, with John Wesley, the founder of Methodism, would I say, 'With my latest breath will I bear testimony against giving up to infidels one great proof of the invisible world, that, namely, of witchcraft and apparitions, confirmed by the testimony of all ages.'"

While this discussion was proceeding, Colonel Hyde and his new acquaintance were pacing the larboard side of the deck, pausing now and then at the railing forward of the wheel-house and looking down on the lower deck, where, seated upon a coil of cables, were four negroes, one of them, and he the most intelligent-looking of the lot, being handcuffed.

"How are niggers now?" asked Mr. Vance.

"Niggers air bringin' fust-rate prices jest now," replied the Colonel; "and Gov'nor Wise he reckons ef we fix Californy and Kahnsas all right, a prime article of a nigger will fotch twenty-five hunderd dollars, sure."

"What 's the prospect of doing that?"

"Good. The South ain't sleeping, — no, not by a damned sight. Californy 's bound to be ourn, an' the Missouri boys will take car' of Kahnsas."

"I see the North are threatening to send in armed immigrants," said Vance; "and one John Brown swears Kansas shall be free soil."

"John Brown be damned!" replied the Colonel. "One common Suthun man is more'n a match fur five of thar best Yankees, any day. Kahnsas must be ourn, ef we hev to shoot every white squatter in the hull terrertory. By the way, that's a likely yuller gal, sittin' thar with the bebby. That gal ud bring sixteen hunderd dollars *sure* in Noo Orleenz."

"Whose niggers are those I see forward there, on the cables?" asked Vance.

"Them niggers, Mr. Vance, air under my car', an' I'm takin' 'em to Texas fur Kunnle Barnwell. The feller yer see han'cuffed thar an' sleepin', run away three or four yars ago. At last the Kunnle heerd, through Hermin & Co., that Peek (that's his name) was in New York; an' so the Kunnle gits me ter go on fur him; an' cuss me ef I did n't ketch him easy. The other three niggers air a lot the Kunnle's agent in St. Louis bowt fur him last week."

"How did you dodge the Abolitionists in New York?" inquired Vance. "You went before the United States Commissioner, I suppose, and proved your claim to the article."

"Damned ef I did! Arter I'd kotched Peek, he said, ef as how I'd let him go home, an' settle up, he'd return, so help him Gawd, an' give hisself up without no fuss or trial. Wall, I'm a judge of niggers, — kn see right through 'em, — kn ollerz tell whan a nigger's lying. I seed Peek was in airnest, and so I let him go; and may I be shot but he cum back jest at the hour he said he would."

"Very extraordinary!" said Vance, musingly. "You must be a great judge of character, Colonel Hyde."

"Wall, what's extrordinerer still," continued the Colonel, "is this: Peek wanted money ter send ter his wife, and cuss me ef he did n't offer ter go the hull way ter Cincinnati without no officers ter guard him, ef I'd give him twenty-five dollars. In coorse I done it, seein' as how I saved fifty dollars by the operation. The minute he got on board this 'ere boat I hahd him han'cuffed, fur I knowed his promise wah n't good no longer, anyhow."

"Colonel, what's your address?" asked Mr. Vance. "If

ever I lose a nigger, you 're the man I must send for to help me find him."

The Colonel drew forth from his vest pocket a dirty card, and presented it to Mr. Vance. It contained these words: "Colonel Delancy Hyde, Agent for the Recovery of Escaped Slaves. Address him, care of J. Breckenridge, St. Louis; Hermin & Co., New Orleans."

"Shall be proud to do yer business, Mr. Vance," said the Colonel.

"I must have a talk with that handcuffed fellow of yours by and by," remarked Vance.

"Do!" returned the Colonel. "Yer 'll find him a right knowin' nigger. He kn read an' write, an' that air 's more 'n we kn say of some white folks in our part of the kintry."

"Do the owners hereabouts lose many slaves now-a-days?"

"Not sence old Gashface was killed last autumn."

"Who 's Gashface? Is it a real name?" asked Vance.

"Nobody ever knowed his raal name," returned the Colonel; "an' so we called him Gashface, seein' as he 'd a bad gash over his left cheek. He was a half mulatto, with woolly hair, an' so short-sighted he weared specs. Wall, that bloody cuss hahz run off more niggers nor all the abolitioners in the Northwest, — damned ef he haint! Two millions of dollars would n't pay fur all the slaves he 's helped across the line. He guv his hull time ter the work, an' was crazy mad on that one pint. Last yar the planters clubbed together an' made up a pus of five thousand dollars fur the man that 'ud shoot the cuss. Two gemmlemen from Vicksburg went inter the job, treed him, shot him dead, an' tuk the five thousand dollars. An almighty good day's work!" *

"How did the planters know they had got the right man?" asked Vance.

"Wall, there wah n't much doubt about that, yer see," said the Colonel. "Them as shot him war' high-tone gemmlemen,

* It afterwards appeared that the Vicksburg "gentlemen," impatient at their want of success, selected a man who came nearest to the description of Gashface, shot him, and then marked his body in a way to satisfy the expectations of those who had formed an imaginative idea of the personal peculiarities that would identify the celebrated liberator, so long the terror of masters on the Mississippi.

both on 'em, an' knowed the cuss well. So did I, an' they paid me a cool hunderd, — damned if they did n't! — to come on an' swar ter the body."

"Let 's go and have a talk with your smart nigger," interrupted Vance.

"Agreed!" replied the Colonel with an oath; and the two descended a short ladder, and stood on the lower deck in front of Peek, who was leaning against a green sliding box of stones, used for keeping the boat rightly trimmed.

"Wake up here, Peek," said Hyde, kicking him not very gently; "here 's my friend, Mr. Vance, come ter see yer."

The slave started, and his eyes had a lurid glitter as they turned on Hyde; but they opened with a wild and pleased surprise as they caught the quick, intelligible glance of Vance, whose right hand was pointing to an inner pocket of his coat. The change of expression in the slave was, however, too subtle and evanescent for any one except Vance himself to recognize it; and he was not moved by it to take other notice of the negro than to imitate the Colonel's example by pushing Peek with his foot, at the same time saying, "I wish I had you on a sugar-plantation down in Louisiana, my fine fellow! I 'd teach you to run away! You would n't try it more than once, I 'm thinking."

"Look he-ah, stranger," exclaimed Peek, rising to his feet, with a look of savage irritation, and clenching his fists, in spite of the irons on his wrists, "you jes' put yer foot on me agin, and I 'll come at yer, shoo-ar!"

"You 'll do that, will you," said Vance, laying both hands on the slave's throat, shaking him, and muttering words audible to him only.

Peek, seeming to struggle, thrust his fettered hands into the bosom of his antagonist, as if to knock him down; but Vance pushed him up against the bulwarks of the boat, and held him there, with his grasp on his throat, till the slave begged humbly for mercy. Vance then let him go, and turning to Colonel Hyde, with perfect coolness, said, "That 's the way to let a nigger know you 're master." To which the Colonel, unable to repress his admiration, replied: "I see as how yer understand 'em, from hide to innards, clar' through. A nigger 's a nigger, all the world over. Now let 's liquor."

They went to the bar, around which a motley group of smokers and drinkers were standing. The bar-keeper was a black man, and between him and Vance there passed a flash of intelligence.

"What shall it be, Mr. Vance?" asked the Colonel.

"Gin for me," was the reply.

"Make me a whiskey nose-tickler," said the Colonel, who seemed to be not unfamiliar with the fancy nomenclature of the bar-room.

The bar-keeper, with that nimbleness and dexterity which high art alone could have inspired, compounded a preparation of whiskey, lemon, and sugar with bitters, crushed ice, and a sprig of mint, and handed it to the Colonel, at the same time placing a decanter labelled "GIN" before Vance. The latter poured out two thirds of a tumbler of what seemed to be the raw spirit, and, adding neither water nor sugar, touched glasses with the Colonel, and swallowed it off as if it had been a spoonful of *eau sucré*. So overpowered with admiration at the feat was the Colonel, that he paused a full quarter of a minute before doing entire justice to the "nose-tickler" which had been brewed for him.

Some of the loungers now drew round the Colonel, and asked him to join them in a game of euchre. He looked inquiringly at Vance, and the latter said, "Go and play, Colonel; I'll rejoin you by and by." Then, in a confidential whisper, he added, "I must find out about that yellow girl,—whether she's for sale."

The Colonel winked, and answered, "All right," and Vance walked away.

"Who's that?" asked Mr. Leonidas Quattles, a long-haired, swarthy youth, who looked as if he might be half Indian.

"That's Mr. Vance of Noo Orleenz," replied the Colonel; "he's my partik'lar friend, an' a perfek high-tone gemmleman, I don't car' whar' the other is."

"How stands the Champion now?" said another of the party.

"Three miles astern, and thar she'll stick," exclaimed Quattles.

As Vance reascended to the upper deck, he encountered the

children at play. Little Clara Berwick, in high glee, was running as fast as her infantile feet could carry her, pursued by Master Onslow, while Hattie, the mulatto woman in attendance, held out the child's bonnet, and begged her to come and have it on. But Clara, with her light-brown ringlets flying on the breeze, was bent on trying her speed, and the boy, fearful that she would fall, was trying to arrest her. Before he could do this, his fears were realized. Clara tripped and fell, striking her forehead. Vance caught her up, and her parents, with Mr. Onslow and Hattie, gathered round her, while the boy looked on in speechless distress.

The little girl was so stunned by the blow, that for nearly a minute she could neither cry nor speak. Then opening her eyes on Mr. Vance, who, seating himself, held her in his lap, she began to grieve in a low, subdued whimper.

"The dear little creature! How she tries to restrain her tears!" said Vance. "Cry, darling, cry!" he added, while the moisture began to suffuse his own eyes.

Then, taking from his pocket a small morocco case, he said to Mrs. Berwick, "I have some diluted arnica here, madam, the best lotion in the world for a bruise. With your permission I will apply it."

"Do so," said the mother. "I know the remedy."

And, pulling from a side pocket of his coat a fresh handkerchief of the finest linen, he wet it with the liquid, and applied it tenderly to the bruise, all the while engaging the child's attention with prattle suited to her comprehension, and telling her what a brave good little girl she was.

"What is your name?" he asked.

She tried to utter it, but, failing to make herself understood, the mother helped her to say, "Clara Aylesford Berwick."

"Aylesford!" said Vance, thoughtfully. Then, gazing in the child's face, he rejoined: "How strange! Her eyes are dissimilar. One is a decided gray, the other a blue."

"Yes," said Berwick; "she gets the handsome eye from me; the other from her mamma."

"Conceited man! cease your trifling!" interposed the lady.

Vance picked up from the deck a little sleeve-button of gold and coral. It had been dropped in the child's fall.

"This must belong to Miss Clara," said Vance, "for it bears the initials C. A. B."

The mother took it and fixed it in the little dimity pelisse which the child wore.

Hattie now offered to receive Miss Clara from Vance's arms; but, with an utterance and gesture of remonstrance, the child signified she did not choose to be parted without a kiss; so he bent down and kissed her, while she threw her little arms about his neck. Then seeing the boy, who felt like a culprit for chasing her, she called him to her and gave him absolution by the same token. Thanking Vance for his service, Mr. Berwick walked away with Leonora.

"That's a noble boy of yours, sir," said Vance, addressing himself to Mr. Onslow.

All the father's displeasure vanished with the compliment, and he replied, "Yes, Robert *is* a noble boy; that's the true word for him."

"I fear," resumed Vance, "I gave you some cause just now to form a bad opinion of me because of my conduct to one of the waiters."

"To be frank," replied Onslow, "I *did* feel surprise that you should take not only the strong side, but the wrong one."

"Mr. Onslow, did you ever read Parnell's poem of the 'Hermit'?"

"Yes, it was one of the favorites of my youth."

"And do you remember how many things seemed wrong to the hermit that he afterwards found to be right?"

"I perceive the drift of your allusion, sir," returned Onslow; "but I am puzzled, nevertheless."

"Perhaps one of these days you will be enlightened." Then, changing the subject, Vance remarked, "How do you succeed in Texas in your attempt to substitute free labor for that of slaves?"

"My success has been all I could have hoped; but the more successful I am, the more imminent is my failure."

"Why so? That sounds like a paradox."

"The rich slave-owners look with fear and dislike on my experiment."

"What else could you expect, Mr. Onslow? Take a case,

publicly vouched for as true. Not long since a New York capitalist purchased mineral lands in Virginia, with a view to working them. He went on the ground and hired some of the white inhabitants of the neighborhood as laborers. All promised well, when lo! a committee of slaveholders, headed by one Jenkins,* waited on him, and told him he must discharge his hands and hire *slaves*. The white laborers offered to work at reduced wages rather than give up their employment, but they were overawed, and their employer was compelled by the slave despots to abandon his undertaking and return to a State where white laborers have rights."

"And yet," said Onslow, "there are politicians who try to persuade the people that the enslaving of a black man removes him from competition with white labor; whereas the direct effect of slavery is to give to slaveholders the monopoly and control of the most desirable kinds of labor, and to enable them to degrade and impoverish the white laboring man!"

Here the furious ringing of a bell called the gentlemen to dinner.

* Afterwards the notorious proslavery guerilla leader in Virginia.

CHAPTER XI.

MR. ONSLOW SPEAKS HIS MIND.

"How faint through din of merchandise
And count of gain
Has seemed to us the captive's cries!
How far away the tears and sighs
Of souls in pain!"
Whittier.

AN opportunity for resuming the conversation did not occur till long after sundown, and when many of the passengers were retiring to bed.

"I have heard, Mr. Onslow," said Vance, "that since your removal to Texas you have liberated your slaves."

"You have been rightly informed," replied Onslow.

"And how did they succeed as freedmen?"

"Two thirds of them poorly, the remaining third well."

"Does not such a fact rather bear against emancipation, and in favor of slavery?"

"Quite the contrary. I am aware that the enthusiastic Mr. Ruskin maintains that slavery is 'not a political institution at all, but an inherent, natural, and eternal inheritance of a large portion of the human race.' But as his theory would involve the enslaving of white men as well as black, I think we may dismiss it as the sportive extravagance of one better qualified to dogmatize than argue."

"But is he not right in the application of his theory to the black race?"

"Far from it. Look at the white men you and I knew some twenty-five years ago. How many of them have turned out sots, gluttons, thieves, incapables! Shall the thrifty and wise, therefore, enslave the imprudent and foolish? Assuredly not, whatever such clever men as Mr. Ruskin and Mr. Thomas Carlyle may say in extenuation of such a proceeding."

"Do not escaped or emancipated negroes often voluntarily return to slavery?"

"Not often, but occasionally; and so occasionally a white man commits an offence in order that he may be put in the penitentiary. A poor negro is emancipated or escapes. He goes to Philadelphia or New York, and has a hard time getting his grub. In a year or two he drifts back to his old master's plantation, anxious to be received again by one who can insure to him his rations of mush; and so he declares there 's no place like 'old Virginny for a nigger.' Then what pæans go up in behalf of the patriarchal system! What a conclusive argument this that 'niggers will be niggers,' and that slavery is right and holy! Slave-drivers catch at the instance to stiffen up their consciences, and to stifle that inner voice that is perpetually telling them (in spite of the assurances of bishops, clergymen, and literary *dilettanti* to the contrary) that slavery is a violation of justice and of that law of God written on the heart and formulized by Christ, that we must do unto others as we would have them do unto us, and that therefore liberty is the God-given right of every innocent and able-minded man. Instances like that I have supposed, instead of being a palliation of slavery, are to my mind new evidences of its utter sinfulness. A system that can so degrade humanity as to make a man covet repression or extinction for his manhood must be devilish indeed."

"But, Mr. Onslow, do not statistics prove that the blacks increase and multiply much more in a state of slavery than in any other? Is not that a proof they are well treated and happy?"

"That is the most hideous argument yet in favor of the system. In slavery women are stimulated by the beastly ambition of contending which shall bear 'the most little nigs for massa'! Among these poor creatures the diseases consequent upon too frequent child-bearing are dreadfully prevalent. Surely the welfare of a people must be measured, not by the mere amount of animal contentment or of rapid breeding with which they can be credited, but by the sum of manly acting and thinking they can show. A whole race of human beings is not created merely to eat mush, hoe in cotton-fields, and procreate slaves. The example of one such escaped slave as Frederick Douglas shows that the blacks are capable of as high a civilization as the whites."

"Do they not seem to you rather feeble in the moral faculty?"

"No more feeble than any race would be, treated as they have been. The other day there fell into my hands a volume of sermons for pious slaveholders to preach to their slaves. It is from the pen of the excellent Bishop Meade of Virginia. The Bishop says to poor Cuffee: 'Your bodies, you know, are not your own; they are at the disposal of those you belong to; *but your precious souls are still your own.'* What impious cajolery is this? The master has an unlimited, irresponsible power over the slave, from childhood up, — can force him to act as he wills, however conscience may protest! The slave may be compelled to commit crimes or to reconcile himself to wrongs, familiarity with which may render his soul, like his body, the mere unreasoning, impassive tool of his master. And yet a bishop is found to try to cozen Cuffee out of the little common sense slavery may have left him, by telling him he is responsible for that soul, which may be stunted, soiled, perverted in any way avarice or power may choose."

"Well, Mr. Onslow, will you deny that slavery has an ennobling effect in educating a chivalrous, brave, hospitable aristocracy of whites, untainted by those meannesses which are engendered by the greed of gain in trading communities?"

"I will not deny," replied Onslow, "that the habit of irresponsible command may develop certain qualities, sometimes good, sometimes bad, in the slave-driver; and so the exercise of the lash by the overseer may develop the extensor muscles of the arm; but the evils to the whites from slavery far, far outbalance the benefits. First, there are the five millions of mean, non-slaveholding whites. These the system has reduced to a condition below that of the slave himself, in many cases. Slavery becomes at once their curse and their infatuation. It fascinates while it crushes them; it drugs and stupefies while it robs and degrades."

"But may we not claim advantages from the system for the few, — for the upper three hundred thousand?"

"That depends on what you may esteem advantages. Can an injustice be an advantage to the perpetrator? The man who betrays a moneyed trust, and removes to Europe with his family, may in one sense derive an advantage from the operation. He may procure the means of educating and amusing himself and his children. So the slaveholder, by depriving other men of their inherent rights, may get the means of benefiting himself and those he cares for. But if he is content with such advantages, it must be because of a torpid, uneducated, or perverted conscience. Patrick Henry was right when he said, 'Slavery is inconsistent with the religion of Christ.' O'Connell was right when he declared, 'No constitutional law can create or sanction slavery.' I have often thought that Mississippians would never have been reconciled to that stupendous public swindle, politely called repudiation, if slavery had not first prepared their minds for it by the robbery of labor. And yet we have men like Jefferson Davis,* who not only palliate, but approve the cheat. O the atrocity! O the shame! With what face can a repudiating community punish thieves?"

"Shall we not," asked Vance, "at least grant the slaveholder the one quality he so anxiously claims, — that which he expresses in the word *chivalry?*"

Mr. Onslow shrugged his shoulders, and replied: "Put before the chivalrous slaveholder a poor fanatic of an Abolitionist, caught in the act of tampering with slaves, and then ask this representative of the chivalry to be magnanimous. No! the mean instincts of what he deems self-interest will make him a fiend in cruelty. He looks upon the Abolitionist very much as a gunpowder manufacturer would look upon the wandering Celt who should approach his establishment with a lighted pipe in his mouth; and he cheerfully sees the culprit handed over to the tender mercies of a mob of ignorant white barbarians."

"Do you, then, deny that slavery develops any high qualities in the master?"

"And if it did, what right have I to develop my high qualities at another's expense? Yes! Jefferson is right when he says: 'The whole commerce between master and slave is a perpetual exercise of the most boisterous passions; the most unremitting despotism on the one part and degrading submissions

* The dishonesty of Mr. John Slidell's attempt to expunge from Davis's history the reproach of repudiation is thoroughly and irrefutably exposed by Mr. Robert J. Walker in the Continental Monthly, 1863.

on the other. The man must be a prodigy who can retain his manners and his morals undepraved by such circumstances.'"

Mr. Onslow paced the deck for a moment, and then, returning, exclaimed: "O the unspeakable crimes, barbarities, and deviltries to which the system has educated men here at the South during the last thirty years! Educated not merely the poor and ignorant, but the rich and refined! The North knows hardly a tithe of the actual horrors. Worse than the wildest religious fanaticism, slavery sees men tortured, hung, mutilated, subjected to every conceivable indignity, cruelty, agony, simply because the victim is unsound, or suspected to be unsound, on the one supreme question. I myself have been often threatened, and sometimes the presentiment is strong upon me that my end will be a bloody one. I should not long be safe, were it not that in our region there are brave men who, like me, begin to question the divinity of the obscene old hag."

Mr. Onslow again walked away, and then, coming close up to Vance, said in low tones: "But retribution must come, — as sure as God lives, retribution must come, and that speedily! Slavery must die, in order that Freedom and Civilization may live. I see it in all the signs of the times, in all the straws that drift by me on the current of events. Retribution must come, — come with bloodshed, anguish, and desolation to both North and South, — to Slavery, with spasms of diabolical cruelty, violence, and unholy wrath, and to Freedom with trials long and doubtful, but awaking the persistent energy which a righteous cause will inspire, and leading ultimately to permanent triumph and to the annihilation on this continent of the foul power which has ruled us so long, and which shall dare to close in deadly combat with the young genius of universal Liberty."

Vance grasped Onslow by the hand, but seemed too excited to speak. Then, as if half ashamed of his emotion, he said, "Will there be men at the South, think you, to array themselves on the side of freedom, in the event of a collision?"

"There will be such men, but, until the slave-power shall be annihilated forever, they will be a helpless minority. A few rich leaders control the masses which Slavery has herself first imbruted. Crush out slavery, and there will be regenerators of the land who will spring up by thousands to welcome their brethren of the North, whose interests, like theirs, lie in universal freedom and justice."

"You do not, then, believe those who tell us there is an eternal incompatibility between the people of the slaveholding and non-slaveholding States?"

"Bah! These exaggerations, the rhetoric of feeble spirits, and the logic of false, are stuff and rubbish to any true student of human nature. There is no incompatibility between North and South, except what slavery engenders and strives to intensify. Strike away slavery, and the people gravitate to each other by laws higher than the bad passions of your Rhetts, Yanceys, and Maurys. The small-beer orators and forcible-feeble writers of the South, who are eternally raving about the mean, low-born Yankees, and laboring to excite alienation and prejudice, are merely the tools of a few plotting oligarchs who hope to be the chiefs of a Southern Confederacy."

"And must civil war necessarily follow from a separation?"

"As surely as thunder follows from the lightning-rent! Yes, Webster is undoubtedly right: there can be no such thing as peaceable secession, and I rejoice that there cannot be."

"But would not a civil war render inevitable that alienation which these Richmond scribblers are trying to antedate?"

"No. Enmity would be kept up long enough for the slave-power to be scotched and killed, and then the people of both sections would see that there was nothing to keep them apart, that their interests are identical. The true people of the South would soon realize that the three hundred thousand slaveholders are even more *their* enemies than enemies of the North. A reaction against our upstart aristocracy (an aristocracy resting on tobacco-casks and cotton-bales) would ensue, and the South would be republicanized, — a consummation which slavery has thus far prevented. South Carolina was Tory in the Revolution, just as she is now. Abolish slavery, and we should be United States in fact as well as in name. Abolish slavery, and you abolish sectionalism with it. Abolish slavery, and you let the masses North and South see that their welfare lies in the preservation of the republic, one and indivisible."

"And do you anticipate civil war?"

"Yes, such a civil war as the world has never witnessed.* The devil of slavery must go out of us, and as it is the worst of all the devils that ever afflicted mankind, it can go out only through unprecedented convulsions and tearings and agonies. The North must suffer as well as the South, for the North shares in the guilt of slavery, and there are thousands of men there who shut their eyes to its enormities. Believe me, their are high spiritual laws underlying national offences; and the Nemesis that must punish ours is near at hand. Slavery must be destroyed, and war is the only instrumentality that I can conceive of energetic enough to do it. Through war, then, must slavery be destroyed."

"And I care not how soon!" said Vance. Then, lowering his tone, he remarked: "Have you not been imprudent in confiding your views to a stranger, who could have you lynched at the next landing-place by reporting them?"

"Perhaps. But I bide the risk; you have not been so shrewd an actor, sir, that I have not seen behind the mask."

Vance started at the word *actor*, then said, looking up at the stars: "What a beautiful night! Does not the Champion seem to be gaining on us?"

"I have been thinking so for some minutes," replied Onslow. "Good night, Mr. —— Excuse me. I have n't the pleasure of knowing your name."

"And yet we have met before, Mr. Onslow, and under circumstances that ought to make me remembered."

"To what do you allude?"

"I was once brought before you for horse-stealing, and, what is more, you found me guilty of the charge, and rightly."

"Then my recollection was not at fault, after all!" exclaimed Onslow, astonished. "But were you indeed guilty?"

"I certainly took a horse, but it was a case of necessity. A friend of mine, a colored man, in defence of his liberty, had wounded his master, so called, and was flying for life. To save him I robbed the robber, — took his horse and gave it to his victim, enabling the latter to get off safely. The fact of

* This prediction was merely one among many hundred such which every reader of newspapers will remember.

my taking the horse was clearly proved, but my motive was not discovered. If it had been, Judge Lynch would surely have relieved you of the care of me. You, as justice of the peace, remanded me to prison for trial. That night I escaped. In an outer room of the jail I found a knife and half of a slaughtered calf. The knife I put in my pocket. The carcass I threw over my shoulder, and ran. In the morning I found five valuable bloodhounds on my track. I climbed a tree, and when they came under it, I fed them till they were all tame, and allowed me to descend; and then I cut their throats, lest they should be used to hunt down fugitives from slavery. Two days afterwards I was safe on board a steamboat, on my way North."

"Who, then, *are* you, sir?" asked Onslow.

Vance whispered a word in reply.

Mr. Onslow seemed agitated for a moment, and then exclaimed, "But I thought he was dead!"

"The report originated with those who took the reward offered for his head. Mr. Onslow, I have repaid your frankness with a similar frankness of my own. To-morrow morning, at ten o'clock, meet me here, and you shall hear more of my story. Good night."

The gentlemen parted, each retiring to his state-room for repose.

CHAPTER XII.

THE STORY OF ESTELLE.

"Tears, idle tears, I know not what they mean,
Tears from the depth of some divine despair,
Rise in the heart, and gather to the eyes,
In looking on the happy autumn-fields
And thinking of the days that are no more."

Tennyson.

BALMY, bright, and beautiful broke the succeeding morning. Every passenger as he came on deck looked astern to see what had become of the Champion. She still kept her usual distance, dogging the Pontiac with the persistency of a fate. Captain Crane said nothing, but it was noticeable that he puffed away at his cigar with increased vigor.

Mr. Vance encountered the Berwicks once more on the hurricane deck and interchanged greetings. Little Clara recognized her friend of the day before, and, jumping from Hattie's lap, ran and pulled his coat, looking up in his face, and pouting her lips for a kiss.

"I fancy I see two marked traits in your little girl, already," said Vance to the mother, after he had saluted the child; "she is strong in the affections, and has a will-power that shows itself in self-control."

"You are right," replied the mother; "I have known her to bite her lips till the blood came, in her effort to keep from crying."

"Such is her individuality," continued Vance. "I doubt if circumstances of education could do much to misshape her moral being."

"Ah! that is a fearful consideration," said the lady; "we cannot say how far the best of us would have been perverted if our early training had been unpropitious."

"I knew your father, Mrs. Berwick. He found me, a stranger stricken down by fever, forsaken and untended, in a miserable shanty called a tavern, in Southern Illinois, in the sickly season. He devoted himself to me till I was convalescent. I shall never forget his kindness. Will you allow me to look at that little seal on your watch-chain? It ought to bear the letters 'W. C. to R. A.' Thank you. Yes, there they are! I sent him the seal as a memento. The cutting is my own."

"I shall regard it with a new interest," said Mrs. Berwick, as she took it back.

Mr. Onslow here appeared and bade the party good morning.

"I feel that I am among friends," said Vance. "I last night promised Mr. Onslow a story. Did you ever hear of the redoubtable Gashface, Mr. Berwick?"

"Yes, and I warn you, sir, that I am quite enough of an Abolitionist to hold his memory in a sort of respect."

"Bold words to utter on the Southern Mississippi! But do not be under concern: I myself am Gashface. Yes. The report of his being killed is a lie. Are you in a mood to hear his story, Mrs. Berwick?"

"I shall esteem it a privilege, sir."

"The last time I told it was to your father. Be seated, and try and be as patient as he was in listening."

The party arranged themselves in chairs; and Mr. Vance was about to take up his parable, when the figure of Colonel Delancy Hyde was seen emerging from the stairs leading from the lower deck.

"Hah! Mr. Vance, I'm yourn," exclaimed the Colonel, with effusion. "Been lookin' fur yer all over the boat. Introduce yer friends ter me."

Vance took from his pocket the Colonel's card, and read aloud the contents of it.

"From Virginia, ma'am," supplemented the Colonel, who was already redolent of Bourbon; "the name of Delancy Hyde hahz been in the family more 'n five hunderd yarz. Fak, ma'am! My father owned more slaves nor he could count. Ef it hahd n't been fur a damned Yankee judge, we sh'd hahv held more land nor you could ride over in a day. Them low-born Yankees, ma'am, air jes' fit to fetch an' carry for us as air the master race; to larn our childern thar letters an' make our shoes, as the Greeks done fur the Romans, ma'am. Ever read the Richmond newspapers, ma'am? John Randolph wunst said he 'd go out of his way to kick a sheep. I 'd go out of my way, ma'am, to kick a Yankee."

"If you 're disposed to listen to a story, Colonel," said Vance, "take a chair." And he pointed to one the furthest from Mrs. Berwick. "I am about to read an autobiography of the fellow Gashface, of whom you have heard."

And Vance drew from his pocket a small visiting card crowded close with stenographic characters in manuscript.

"An' that 's an auter — what d' yer call it, — is it?" asked the Colonel. "Cur'ous!"

The Colonel reinforced himself with a plug of tobacco, and Vance began to recite what he called, for the occasion, "The Autobiography of Gashface." But we prefer to name it

The Story of Estelle.

I was born in New Orleans, and am the son of William Carteret. He was a Virginian by birth, the younger son of a planter, whose forefather, a poor Yorkshire gentleman, came over from England with Sir Thomas Dale in the year 1611. You might think me false to my father's native State if I did not vindicate my claim to a descent from one of the first Virginia families. You must be aware that all the gentle blood that flowed from Europe to this continent sought Virginia as its congenial reservoir. It would be difficult to find a low-born white man in the whole eastern section of the State.

["That 's a fak!" interposed the Colonel.]

My grandfather died in 1820, leaving all his property to his eldest son, Albert. (Virginia then had her laws of primogeniture.) Albert generously offered to provide for my father, but the latter, finding that Albert could not do this without reducing the provision for his sisters, resolved to seek fortune at the North. He went to New York, where he studied medicine. But here he encountered Miss Peyton, a beautiful girl from Virginia, nobly supporting herself by giving instruction in music. He married her, and they consoled themselves for their poverty by their fidelity and devotion to each other. The loss of their first child, in consequence, as my father believed, of the unhealthy location of his house, induced him to make extraordinary efforts to earn money.

After various fruitless attempts to establish himself in some lucrative employment, he made his *début*, under an assumed name, at the Park Theatre, in the character of Douglas, in Home's once famous tragedy of that name. My father's choice of this part is suggestive of the moderate but respectable character of his success. He played to the judicious few; but their verdict in his favor was not sufficiently potent to make him a popular actor. He soon had to give up the high starring parts, and to content himself with playing the gentleman of comedies or the second part in tragedies. In this humbler line he gained a reputation which has not yet died out in theatrical circles. He could always command good engagements for the theatrical season in respectable stock-companies. He was fulfilling one of these engagements in New Orleans when I was born.

A month afterwards he ended his career in a manner that sent a thrill through the public heart. He was one evening playing Othello for his own benefit. Grateful for a crowded house, he was putting forth his best powers, and with extraordinary success. Never had such plaudits greeted and inspired him. The property-man, whose duty it is to furnish all the articles needed by the actor, had given him at rehearsal a blunted dagger, so contrived with a spring that it seemed to pierce the breast when thrust against it. At night this false dagger was mislaid, and the property-man handed him a real one, omitting in the hurry of the moment to inform him of the change. In uttering the closing words of his part,—

> "I took by the throat the circumci-sed dog,
> And smote him *thus*," —

my father inflicted upon himself, not a mimic, but a real stab, so forcible that he did not survive it ten minutes.

Great was my mother's anguish at her loss. She was not left utterly destitute. My father had not fallen into the besetting sins of the profession. He saw in it a way to competence, if he would but lead a pure and thrifty life. In the seven years he had been on the stage he had laid up seven thousand dollars. Pride would not let him allow my mother to labor for her support. But now she gladly accepted from the manager an offer of twenty-five dollars a week as "walking lady."

On this sum she contrived for seventeen years to live decently and educate her son liberally.

At last sickness obliged her to give up her theatrical engagement. She had invested her seven thousand dollars in bonds of the Planters' Bank of Mississippi, to the redemption of which the faith of that State was pledged. The repudiation of the bonds by the State authorities, under the instigation of Mr. Jefferson Davis, deprived her of her last resource. Impoverished in means, broken in health, and unable to labor, she fell into a decline and died.

The humane manager gave me a situation in his company. I became an actor, and for seven years played the part of second young gentleman in comedies and melodramas; also such parts as Horatio in "Hamlet" or Macduff in "Macbeth." But my heart was not in my vocation. It had chagrins which I could not stomach.

One evening I was playing the part of a lover. The *dramatis persona* of whom I was supposed to be enamored was represented by Miss B——, rather a showy, voluptuous figure, but whom I secretly disliked for qualities the reverse of those of Cæsar's wife. Instead of allowing my aversion to appear, I played with the appropriate ardor. In performing the "business" of the part, I was about to *kiss* her, when I heard a loud, solitary hiss from a person in an orchestra box. He was a man of a full face, very fair red-and-white complexion, and thick black whiskers, — precisely what a coarse feminine taste would call "a handsome fellow." Folding my arms, I walked towards the foot-lights, and asked what he wanted. "None of your business, you damned stroller!" replied he; "I have a right to hiss, I suppose." "And I have a right to pronounce you a blackguard, I suppose," returned I. The audience applauded my rebuke, and laughed at the handsome man, who, with scarlet cheeks, rose and left the house. I learned he was a Mr. Ratcliff, a rich planter, and an admirer of Miss B——.

Soon after this adventure I quitted the profession, and for some time gave myself up to study. My tastes were rather musical than histrionic; and having from boyhood been a proficient on the piano-forte, I at last, when all my money was exhausted, offered my services to the public as a teacher.

My first pupil was Henri Dufour, the only son of the widow of a French physician. It was soon agreed that, for the greater convenience of Henri, and in payment for his tuition, I should become a member of the family, which was small, consisting only of himself, his mother, Jane, a black slave, and Estelle, a white girl who occupied the position of a humble companion of the widow.

[At this point in the narrative, Mr. Quattles appeared at the head of the stairs, and, with his forefinger placed on the side of his long nose, winked expressively at Colonel Hyde. The latter rose, and said, " Sorry to go, Mr. Vance; but the fak is, I 'm in fur a hahnd at euchre, an' jest cum up ter see ef you 'd jine us."

" You 're too gallant a man, Colonel Delancy Hyde," replied Vance, " not to agree with me, when I say, Duty to ladies first."

" Yer may bet yer pile on that, Mr. Vance; the ladies fust ollerz; but Madame will 'scuze *me*, I reckon. Hahd a high old time, ma'am, last night, an' an almighty bahd streak of luck. Must make up fur it somehow."

" Business before pleasure, Colonel," said Vance. " We 'll excuse you."

And the Colonel, with a lordly sweep of his arm, by way of a bow, joined his companion, Quattles, to whom he remarked, " A high-tone Suthun gemmleman that, and one as does credit to his raisin'." The companions having disappeared, Vance proceeded with his story.]

Let me call up before you, if I can, the image of Estelle. In person about three inches shorter than I (and I am five feet six), slender, lithe, and willowy, yet compactly rounded, straight, and singularly graceful in every movement; a neck and bust that might have served Powers for a model when the Greek Slave was taking form in his brain; a head admirably proportioned to all these symmetries; a face rather Grecian than Roman, and which always reminded me of that portrait of Beatrice Cenci by Guido, made so familiar to us through copies and engravings; a portrait tragic as the fate of the original in its serene yet mournful expression. But Estelle's hair differed from that of Beatrice in not being auburn, but of a rare and beautiful olive tint, almost like the bark of the laburnum-tree, and exquisitely fine and thick. In complexion she could not be called either a blonde or a brunette; although her dark blue eyes seemed to attach her rather to the former classification. She was one of the few beautiful women I have seen, whose beauty was not marred by a besetting self-consciousness of beauty, betrayed in every look and movement, and even in the tones of the voice. In respect to her personal charms Estelle was as unconscious as a moss-rose.

Mrs. Dufour was an invalid, selfish, parsimonious, and exacting; but Estelle, in devotion to that lady's service and in adaptation to her caprices, showed a patience and a tact so admirable that it was difficult to guess whether they were the result of sincere affection or of a simple sense of duty.

Henri, my pupil in music, was a youth of sixteen, who inherited not only his mother's morbid constitution, but her ungenerous qualities of heart and temper. Arrogant and vain, he seemed to regard me in the light of a menial, and I could not find in him intellect enough to make him sensible of his folly.

I spent my last twenty dollars in advertising; but no new pupil appeared in answer to my insinuating appeal. My wardrobe began to get impaired; my broadcloth to lose its nap, and my linen to give evidence of premeditated poverty. One day I marvelled at finding in my drawer a shirt completely renovated, with new wristbands, bosom, and collar. The next week the miracle was repeated. Had Mrs. Dufour opened her heart and her purse? Impossible! Had Jane, my washerwoman, slyly performed the service? She honestly denied it. I pursued my investigations no further.

The next Sunday, in putting on my best pantaloons, I found in the right pocket two gold quarter-eagles. Yes! There could now be no doubt. I had misjudged Mrs. Dufour. Her stinginess was all a pretence. Touched with gratitude, yet humiliated, I went to return the gold. It was plain that Madame knew nothing about it. I looked at Estelle, who sat at a window mending a muslin collar.

"Can you explain, Mademoiselle?" I asked.

"Explain what?" she inquired, as if she had been too absorbed in her own thoughts to hear a word of the conversation.

"Can you explain how those gold pieces came into my pocket?"

Without the least sign of guilt, she replied, "I cannot explain, sir."

Was she deceiving me? I thought not. Though we had met twice a day at meals for weeks, her demeanor towards me had been always distant and reserved.

It was my habit daily, after giving a morning lesson to my pupil, to walk a couple of hours on the Levee. One forenoon, on account of the heat of the weather, I returned home an hour earlier than usual. Henri and his mother were out riding. As I entered the house I heard the sound of the piano, and stopped in the hall to listen. It was Estelle at the instrument.

I had left on the music-stand a rough score of my arrangement of that remarkable composition, then newly published in Europe, the music and words of which Colonel Pestal wrote with a link of his fetters on his prison-wall the day before his execution. I had translated the original song, and written it on the same page with the music. What was my astonishment to hear the whole piece, — this new *De Profundis*, this mortal cry from the depths of a proud, indignant heart, — a cry condensed by music into tones the most apt and fervid, — now reproduced by Estelle with such passionate power, such reality of emotion, that I was struck at once with admiration and with horror.

They were not, then, for Pestal so much as for Estelle, — those utterances of holy wrath and angelic defiance! The words by themselves are simple, — commonplace, if you will.*

* We subjoin one of the various translations: —

"Yes, it comes at last!
  And from a troubled dream awaking,
 Death will soon be past,
  And brighter day around me breaking!
Hark! methinks I hear celestial voices say,
Soon thou shalt be free, child of misery, —
Rest and perfect joy in heaven are waiting thee;
Spirit, plume thy wings and flee!

"Yes! the strife is o'er,
  With all its pangs, with all its sorrow;
 Hope shall droop no more,
  For heavenly day will dawn to-morrow!
Proud Oppression, vain thy utmost tyranny!
Come and thou shalt see, I can smile at thee!
Mine shall be the triumph, mine the victory, —
Death but sets the captive free!"

But, conveyed to the ear through Pestal's music and Estelle's voice, they seemed vivid with the very lightning of the soul. As she sang, the victim towered above the oppressor like an archangel above a fiend. The prison-walls fell outward, and the welcoming heavens opened to the triumphant captive.

I entered the room. She turned suddenly. Her face had not yet recovered from the expression of those emotions which the song had called up. She rose with the air of an avenging goddess. Then, seeing me, she drew up her clasped hands to her bosom with a gesture full of grace and eloquent with deprecation, and said, "Forgive me if I have disturbed your papers."

"Estelle!" I began. Then, seeing her look of surprise, I said, "Excuse me if the address is too familiar; but I know you by no other name."

"Estelle is all sufficient," she replied.

"Well, then, Estelle, you have moved me by your singing as I was never moved before,—so terribly in earnest did you seem! What does it mean?"

"It means," she replied, "that you have adapted the music to a faithful translation of the words."

"I have heard you play," said I, "but why have you kept me in ignorance of your powers as a singer?"

"My powers, such as they are," she said, "have been rarely used since I left the convent. I can give little time now to music. Indeed, the hour I have given to it this morning was stolen, and I must make up for it. So good by."

"Stay, Estelle," said I, seizing her hand. "There is a mystery which hangs over you like a cloud. Tell me what it is. Your eyes look as if a storm of unshed tears were brooding behind them. Your expression is always sad. Can I in any way help you? Can I render a true brother's service?"

She stood, looking me in the face, and it was plain, from a certain convulsed effort at deglutition, that she was striving to swallow back the big grief that heaved itself up from her heart. She wavered as if half inclined to reveal something. There was the noise of a carriage at the door; and, pressing my hand gently, she said, with an effort at a smile that should have been a sob, "Thank you; you cannot—help me; my mistress is at the door; good by." And dropping my hand, she glided out of the room.

I can never forget her as she then appeared in her virginal, spring-like beauty, with her profuse silky hair parted plainly in front, and folded in a classic knot behind, with her dress of a light gauze-like material, and an unworked muslin collar about her neck having a simple blue ribbon passing under it and fastened in front with a little cross of gold. How unpretending and unadorned, — and yet what a charm was lent to her whole attire by her consummate grace of person and of action!

Mrs. Dufour entered, and I did not see Estelle again that day.

It was that fearful summer when the fever seemed to be indiscriminate in its ravages. Not only transient visitors in the city, but old residents long acclimated, natives of the city, physicians and nurses, were smitten down. Many fled from the pest-ridden precincts. Whole blocks of houses were deserted. There were few doors at which Death did not knock for one or more of the inmates.

My pupil, Henri Dufour, was taken ill on a Saturday, and on Wednesday his mortal remains were conveyed to the cemetery. I had tended him day and night, and was much worn down by watchings and anxiety. Jane, a hired black domestic, was wanted by her owner, and left us. All the work of our diminished household now fell on Estelle. As for Madame Dufour, she lived in a hysterical fear lest the inevitable summoner should visit her next. She was continually imagining that the symptoms were upon her. One day she fell into an unusual state of alarm. I was alone with her in the house. Estelle had gone out without asking permission, — an extraordinary event. I did what I could for the invalid, and, by her direction, called in a physician whose carriage she had seen standing at a neighboring door.

The poor little doctor seemed flurried and overworked, and an odor of brandy came from his breath. He assured Mrs. Dufour that her symptoms were wholly of the imagination, and that if she would keep tranquil, all danger would speedily pass.

He administered a dose of laudanum. It afterwards occurred to me that he had given three times the usual quantity. He received his fee and departed; and I sat down behind the curtain of an alcove so as to be within call.

Three minutes had not elapsed when Estelle burst into the room, and in a voice low and husky, as if with overpowering agitation, exclaimed: "You have deceived me, Madame! Mr. Semmes tells me you never gave him any orders about a will. Do you mean to cheat me? Beware! Tell me this instant! tell me! Will you do it? Will you do it?"

"Estelle! how can you?" whined Mrs. Dufour. "At such a time, when the slightest agitation may bring on the fever, how can you trouble me on such a subject?"

"No evasion!" exclaimed Estelle, in imperious tones. "I demand it, — I exact it, — now — this instant! You shall — you shall perform it!"

Madame had some vague superstitious notion connected with the signing of a will, and she murmured: "I shall do nothing at present; I'm not in a state to sign my name. The doctor said I must be tranquil. How can you be so selfish, Estelle? Do you imagine I'm going to die, that you are so urgent just now?"

"You told me three months ago," replied Estelle, "that the will had been regularly signed and witnessed. You lied! If you now refuse to make amends, do not hope for peace either in this world or the next. No priest shall attend you here, and my curses shall pursue you down to hell to double the damnation your sin deserves! Will you sign, if I bring the notary?"

Mrs. Dufour began to moan, and complain of her symptoms, while I could hear Estelle pacing the room like a caged tigress. Suddenly she stood still, and cried, "Do you still refuse?"

The moaning of the invalid had been succeeded by a stertorous breathing, as if she had been suddenly overcome by sleep.

"She is stone, — stone! She sleeps! — she has no heart!" groaned Estelle.

I now left the alcove. Estelle knelt weeping with her face on the sofa. I touched her on the head, and she started up alarmed. She saw tears of sympathy on my cheek. I drew her away with my arm about her waist, and said, "Come! come and tell me all."

She let me lead her down-stairs into the parlor. I placed her in an arm-chair, and sat on a low ottoman at her feet. "Tell me all, Estelle," I repeated. "What does it mean?"

I then drew from her these facts. Her mother, though undistinguishable from a white woman, had been a slave belonging to a Mr. Huger, a sugar-planter. She was *reputed* to be the daughter of what the Creoles call a *meamelouc*, that is, the offspring of a white man and a metif mother, a metif being the offspring of a white and a quarteron. This account of the genealogy of Estelle's mother I never had occasion to doubt till years afterwards. The father of Estelle was Albert Grandeau, a young Parisian of good family. Being suddenly called home from Louisiana to France by the death of his parents, he left America, promising to return the following winter, and purchase the prospective mother of his child and take her to Paris. This he honestly intended to do; but alas for good *intentions!* It is good *deeds* only that are secure against the caprices of Fate. The vessel in which Grandeau sailed foundered at sea, and he was among the lost. Estelle's mother died in child-birth.

And then Estelle, — on the well-known principle of Southern law, "*proles sequitur ventrem,*" — in spite of her fair complexion, was a slave. Mr. Huger dying, she fell to the portion of his unmarried daughter, Louise, who was a member of the newly established Convent of St. Vivia. She took Estelle, then a mere child, with her to bring up. Fortunately for Estelle, there were highly accomplished ladies in the convent, to whom it was at once a delight and a duty to instruct the little girl. French, English, and Italian were soon all equally familiar to her, and before she was seventeen she surpassed, in needlework and music, even her teachers. But the convent of St. Vivia had been cheated in the title of its estate; and through failure of funds, it was at length broken up. Soon afterwards, Louise Huger, whose health had always been feeble, died suddenly, leaving Estelle to her sister, Mrs. Dufour, with the request that measures should be at once taken to secure the maiden's freedom, in the contingency of Mrs. Dufour's demise. It was the failure of the latter to take the proper steps for Estelle's manumission that now roused her anger and anxiety.

These disclosures on the part of Estelle awoke in me conflicting emotions.

Shall I confess it? Such was the influence of education, of inherited prejudice, and of social proscription, that when she told me she was a slave, I shuddered as a high-caste Brahmin might when he finds that the man he has taken by the hand is a Pariah. Estelle was too keen of penetration not to detect it; and she drew her robe away from my touch, and moved her chair back a little.

My ancestors, with the exception of my father, had been slaveholders ever since 1625. I had lived all my life in a community where slavery was held a righteous and a necessary institution. I had never allowed myself to question its policy or its justice. Skepticism as to a God or a future state was venial, nay, rather fashionable; but woe to the youth who should play the Pyrrhonist in the matter of slavery!

Yet it was not fear, it was not self-interest, that made me acquiesce; it was simply a failure to exercise my proper powers of thought. I took the word of others, — of interested parties, of social charlatans, of sordid, self-stultified fanatics, — that the system was the best possible one that could be conceived of, both for blacks and whites. From the false social atmosphere in which I had grown up I had derived the accretions that went to build up and solidify my moral being.

And so if St. Paul or Fenelon, Shakespeare or Newton, had come to me with ebonized faces, I should have refused them the privileges of an equal. To such folly are we shaped by what we passively receive from society! To such outrages on justice and common sense are we reconciled simply by the inertness of our brains, not to speak of the hollowness of our hearts!

Estelle paused, and almost despaired, when she saw the effect upon me of her confession. But I pressed her to a conclusion of her story, and then asked, "Who has any claim upon you, in the event of Madame Dufour's dying intestate?"

"Nearly all her property," replied Estelle, "is mortgaged to her nephew, Carberry Ratcliff, and he is her only heir."

"Give me some account of him."

"He is a South Carolinian by birth. Some years ago he

married a Creole lady, by whom he got a fine cotton-plantation on the Red River, stocked with several hundred slaves. He has a house and garden in Lafayette, but lives most of the time on his plantation at Loraine."

"Have you ever seen him?"

"Yes; the first time only ten days ago, and he has been here four times since to call on Madame Dufour, though he rarely used to visit her oftener than twice a year."

As Estelle spoke, her eyes flashed, and her breast heaved.

"How did he behave to you, Estelle?"

"How should the lord of a plantation behave to a comely female slave? Of course he insulted me both with looks and words. What more could you expect of such a connoisseur in flesh and blood as the planter who recruits his gangs at slave-auctions? Do not ask me how he behaved."

I rose, deeply agitated, and paced the room.

"What sort of a looking man is this Mr. Ratcliff?"

She went to an *étagère* in a corner, opened a little box, and took from it a daguerrotype, which she placed in my hand.

Looking at the likeness, I recognized the man who once insulted me at the theatre.

"I must go and attend to Madame Dufour," said Estelle.

"Let me accompany you," said I.

She made no objection. We went together into the chamber. Estelle rushed to the bedside, — shook the invalid, — called her aloud by name, — put her ear down to learn if she breathed, — put her hand on the breast to find if the heart beat, — then turned to me, and shrieked, "She is dead!"

What was to be done?

I led Estelle into the parlor. She sat down. Her face was of a frightful pallor; but there was not the trace of a tear in her eyes. The expression was that of blank, unmitigated despair.

"Poor, poor child!" I murmured. "What can I do for her? Estelle, you must be saved, — but how?"

My words and my look seemed to inspire her with a hope. She rose, sank upon both knees before me, lifted up her clasped hands, and said: "O sir! O Mr. Carteret! as you are a man, as you reverence the recollection of your mother, save me, — save me from the consequences of this death! I am now the slave of Mr. Ratcliff; and what that involves to me you can guess, but I, without a new agony, cannot explain. Save me, dear sir! Good sir, kind sir, for God's love, save me!" And then, with a wild cry of despair, she added: "I will be yours, — body and soul, I will be yours, if you will only save me! I will be your slave, — your *anything*, — only let me belong to one I can love and respect. Do not, do not cast me off!"

"Cast you off, dear child? Never!" said I, and, raising her to her feet, I kissed her forehead.

That first kiss! How shall I analyze it? It was pure and tender as a mother's, notwithstanding the utter abandonment signified in the maiden's words. That very self-surrender was her security. Had she been shy, I might have been less cold. But her look of disappointment showed she attributed that coldness to some less flattering cause, — plainly to indifference, if not to personal dislike. She could not detect in me the first symptom of what she instinctively knew would be a guaranty of my protection, stronger than duty.

Like all the slaves and descendants of slaves in Louisiana, of all grades of color, she had been bred up to a knowledge that it was a consequence of her condition that there could be no marriage union between her and a respectable white man. Impressed with this conviction, she had pleaded to be allowed to remain in some convent, though it were but as a servant, for the remainder of her life. The selfishness of her mistress and owner, Miss Huger, put it out of her power to make this choice effectual. Her kind-hearted Catholic instructors consoled her, as well as they could, by the assurance that, being a slave, the sin of any mode of life to which she might be forced would be attended with absolution. But she had the horror which every pure nature, strong in the affections, must feel, under like circumstances, at the prospect of constraint. Since her life was to be that of a slave, O that her master might be one she could love, and who could love her! The first part of the dream would be realized if I could buy her. What misery to think that the latter part must remain unfulfilled!

I led her to a chair. She sat down and burst into a passion

of tears. In vain I tried to console her by words. Supporting her head with one hand, I then with the other smoothed back the beautiful hair from her forehead. Gradually she became calm. I knelt beside her, and said: "Estelle, compose yourself. I promise you I will risk everything, life itself, to save you from the fate you abhor. Now summon your best faculties, and let us together devise some plan of proceeding."

She lifted my hand to her lips in gratitude, made me take a seat by her side, and said: "Mr. Ratcliff or his agent may be here any minute, and then you would be powerless. The first step is to leave this house, and seek concealment."

"Do you know any place of refuge?"

"Yes; I know a mulatto woman, named Mallet, who has a little stall on Poydras Street for the sale of baskets. She occupies a small tenement near by, and has two spare rooms. I think we can trust her, for I once tended one of her children who died; and she does not know that I am a slave."

"But, Estelle, I grieve to say it, — I am poor, almost destitute. My friends are chiefly theatrical people, poor like myself, and most of them are North at this season."

"Do not let that distress you," she said; "I am the owner of a gold watch, for which we can get at least fifty dollars."

"And mine will bring another fifty," returned I. "Let us go, then, at once, since here you are in danger."

An old negro, well known to the family, and who carried round oranges for sale, at this moment stopped at the door. I gave him a dollar, on condition that he would occupy and guard the house till some one should come to relieve him. I then, at Estelle's suggestion, sent a letter to the Superintendent of Burials, announcing Madame Dufour's death, and requesting him to attend to the interment. I also enclosed the address of Mr. Ratcliff and Mr. Semmes as the persons who would see all expenses paid. To this I signed my real name.

It was agreed that Estelle should leave at once. She gave me written directions for finding our place of rendezvous. There was before it an old magnolia-tree which I was particularly to note. I was to follow soon with such articles of attire, belonging to her and to myself, as I could bring, and I was to return for more if necessary. We parted, and I think she must have read something not sinister in the expression of my face, for her own suddenly brightened, and, with a smile ineffably sweet in its thankfulness, she said, "*Au revoir!*"

Our plans were all successfully carried out. The wardrobe of neither of us was extensive. Two visits to the house enabled me to remove all that we required. My letter to the Superintendent of Burials I had dropped into his box, and that afternoon I saw him enter the house, so that I knew the proper attentions to the dead would not be wanting.

Mrs. Mallet gladly received us on our own terms. Estelle had appropriated for me the better of the two little rooms, and had arranged and decked it so as to wear an appearance of neatness and comfort, if not of luxury. I expostulated, but she would not listen to my occupying the inferior apartment. Her own preferences must rule.

Ever dear to memory must be that first evening in our new abode! There was one old fauteuil in her room, and, placing Estelle in that, I sat on a low trunk by her side, where I could lean my elbow on the arm of the chair. It was a warm, but not oppressive July evening, with a bright moon. The window was open, and in the little area upon which it looked a lemon-tree rustled as the breeze swelled, now and then, to a whisper.

We were alone. I asked a thousand questions. I extorted the secret of my mended clothes and the mysterious gold pieces. That air of depression which had always been so marked in Estelle had vanished. She spoke and looked like a new being. I put a question in French, and she answered in that language with a fluency and a purity of accent that put me to the blush for my own lingual shortcomings. I spoke of books, and was surprised to find in her a bold, detective taste in recognizing the peculiarities, and penetrating to the spiritual life, of the higher class of thinkers and literary artists, whether French, English, or American.

I asked her to sing. In subdued tones, but with an exquisite accuracy, she sang some of the favorite airs by Mozart, Bellini, and Donizetti, using the Italian as if it were her native tongue.

And there, in that atmosphere of death, while the surrounding population were being decimated by the terrible pestilence, I drank in my first draughts of an imperishable love.

I looked at my watch. It was half an hour after midnight. How had the hours slipped by! We must part.

"Estelle!" I exclaimed with emotion; but I could not put into words what I had intended to say. Then, taking her hand, I added, "You have given me the most delightful evening of my life."

No light was burning in the room, but by the moonbeams I could see her face all luminous with joy and triumph. My second kiss was bestowed; but this time it was on her lips, — brief, but impassioned. "Good night, Estelle!" I whispered; and, forcing myself instantly away, I closed the door.

I entered my apartment, and went to bed, but not to sleep. Tears that I could not repress gushed forth. A strange rapture possessed me. Nature had proved itself stronger than convention. The impulsive heart was more than a match for the calculating head. For the first time in my life I saw the new heavens and the new earth which love brings in. Estelle now seemed all the dearer to me for her very helplessness, — for the degradation and isolation in which slavery had placed her. Were she a princess, could I love her half as well? But she shall be treated with all the consideration due to a princess! Passion shall take no advantage of her friendlessness and self-abandonment.

Then came thoughts of the danger she was in, — of what I should do for her rescue; and it was not till light dawned in the east that I fell into a slumber.

We gave up nearly the whole of the next day to the discussion of plans. In pursuance of that on which we finally fixed, Estelle wrote a letter to Mr. Ratcliff in these words: —

"To Carberry Ratcliff, Esq.: — Sir: By the time this letter reaches you I shall be out of your power, and with my freedom assured. Still I desire to be at liberty to return to New Orleans, if I should so elect, and therefore I request you to name the sum in consideration of which you will give me free papers. A friend will negotiate with you. Let that friend have your answer, if you please, in the form of an advertisement in the Picayune, addressed to Estelle."

Two days afterwards we found the following answer in the newspaper named: —

"To ESTELLE: For fifty dollars, I will give you the papers you desire. C. R."

Long and anxiously we meditated on this reply. I dreaded a trap. Was it not most likely that Ratcliff, in naming so low a figure, hoped to secure some clew to the whereabouts of Estelle?

While I was puzzling myself with the question, Estelle suggested an expedient. The answer to the advertisement undoubtedly came from Ratcliff, and we had a right to regard it as valid. Why not address a letter, with fifty dollars, to Ratcliff, and have it legally registered at the post-office?

"Admirable!" exclaimed I, delighted at her quickness.

"No, it is not admirable," she replied. "An objection suggests itself. Some one will have to go to the post-office to register the letter, and he may be known or tracked."

I reflected a moment, and then said: "I think I can guard against such a danger. Having been an actor, I am expert at disguises. I will go as an old man."

The plan was approved and put into effect. The two watches were disposed of at a jeweller's for a hundred and ten dollars. In an altered hand I wrote Ratcliff a letter, enclosed in it a fifty-dollar bill, and bade him direct his answer simply to Estelle Grandeau, Cincinnati, Ohio. I added one dollar for the purpose of covering any expense he might be at for postage. Then, at the shop of a theatrical costumer, I disguised myself as a man of seventy, and went to the post-office. There I had the letter and its contents of money duly registered.

As I was returning home in my disguise, I saw the old negro I had left in charge at Mrs. Dufour's. He did not recognize me, and was not surprised at my questions. From him I learned, that before he left the house a gentleman (undoubtedly Ratcliff) had called, and had seemed to be in a terrible fury on finding that Estelle had gone away some hours before; but his rage had redoubled when he further ascertained that a young man was her attendant.

The interesting question now was, Had Ratcliff any clew to

my identity? My true name, William Carteret, under which I had been known at Mrs. Dufour's, was not the name I had gone by on the stage. Here was one security. Still it was obvious the utmost precaution must be used.

My plans were speedily laid. Not having money enough to pay the passage of both Estelle and myself up the Mississippi, I decided that Estelle should go alone, disguised as an old woman. I engaged a state-room, and paid for it in advance. I had much difficulty in persuading her to accede to the arrangement, so painful was the prospect of a separation; but she finally consented. At my friend the costumer's I fitted her out in a plain, Quaker-like dress. She was to be Mrs. Carver, a schoolmistress, going North. The next morning I covered her beautiful hair with a grayish wig; and then, by the aid of a hare's foot and some pigments, added wrinkles and a complexion suitable to a maiden lady of fifty. With a veil over her face, she would not be suspected.

The hour of parting came. I put a plain gold ring on her finger. "Be constant," I said. "Forever!" she solemnly replied, pressing the ring to her lips with tears of delight. The carriage was at the door. The farewell kiss was exchanged. Her little trunk was put on the driver's foot-board. Mrs. Mallet entered and took a seat, and Estelle was about to follow, when suddenly a faintness seized me. She detected it at once, turned back, and exclaimed in alarm: "You are not well. What is the matter?"

"Nothing, that a glass of wine will not cure," I replied. "There! It is over already. Do not delay. Your time is limited. Driver! Fast, but steady! Here 's a dollar for you! There! Step in, Estelle."

She looked at me hesitatingly. I summoned all my will to check my increasing faintness. Urging her into the carriage, I closed the door, and the horses started. Estelle watched me from the window, till an angle in the street hid me from her view. Then, staggering into the house, I crawled up-stairs to my chamber, and sank upon the bed.

The next ten days were a blank to consciousness. Fever

and delirium had the mastery of my brain. On the eleventh morning I seemed to wake gradually, as if from some anxious dream. I lay twining my hands feebly one over the other. Then suddenly a speck in the ceiling fixed my attention. Raising myself on the pillow, I looked around. Very gently and slowly recollection came back. The appearance of Mrs. Mallet soon seemed a natural sequence. She smiled, gave an affirmative shake of the head, as if to tell me all was well, and at her bidding, I lay down and slept. The following day I was strong enough to inquire after Estelle.

"Be good, and you shall see her," was the reply.

"What! Did she not take passage in the boat?"

"There! Do not be alarmed; she will explain it all."

And as she spoke, Estelle glided in, held up her forefinger by way of warning, and, smiling through her tears, kissed my forehead. I felt a shock of joy, followed by anxiety. "Why did you not go?" I asked.

"I found I could dispose of my state-room, and I did it, for I was too much concerned about your health to go in peace. It was fortunate I returned. You have had the fever, but the danger is over."

"How long have I lain thus?"

"This is the twelfth day."

"Have I had a physician?"

"No one but Estelle; but then she is an expert; she once walked the hospitals with the Sisters of Charity."

My convalescence was rapid. By the first of September I was well enough to take long strolls in the evening with Estelle. On the fifth of that month, early one starlit night, I said to her, "Come, Estelle, put on your bonnet and shawl for a walk."

She brought them into my room, and placed them on the bed.

"Where shall we go?" she inquired.

"To the Rev. Mr. Fulton's," I replied; "that is, if you will consent to be —"

"To be what?" she asked, not dreaming of my drift.

"To be married to me, Estelle!"

The expressions that flitted over her face, — expressions of doubtful rapture, pettish incredulity, and childlike eagerness,— come back vividly to my remembrance.

"You do not mean it!" at length she murmured, reproachfully.

"From my inmost heart I mean it, and I desire it above all earthly desires," I replied.

She sank to the floor, and, clasping my knees with her arms, bowed her head upon them, and wept. Then, starting up, she said: "What! Your wife? Really your wife? Mistress and wife in one? Me,—a slave? Can it be, William, you desire it?"

It was the first time she had called me by my first name.

"Have you considered it well?" she continued. "O, I fear it would be ungenerous in me to consent. Such an alliance might jeopard all your future. You are young, well-connected, and can one day command all that the best society of the country can offer. No, William, not for me,—not for me the position of your wife!"

I replied to these misgivings by putting on her shawl, then her bonnet, the tying of which I accompanied with a kiss that brought the roses to her cheeks.

"Estelle," I said, "unless we are very different from what we believe, the step is one we shall not regret. I must be degenerate indeed, if I can ever find anything in life more precious than the love you give and inspire. But perhaps you shrink from so binding a tie."

"Shrink from it?" she repeated, in a tone of abandonment to all that was rapturous and delightful in her conceptions, though the tears gushed from her eyes. "O, generous beyond my dreams! Would I might prove to you of what my love is capable, and how you have deepened its unfathomable depths by this last proof of your affection!"

We went forth under the stars that beautiful evening to the well-known minister's house. He received us kindly, asked us several questions, and, having satisfied himself of our intelligence and sincerity, united us in marriage. We gave him our real names,—William Carteret and Estelle Grandeau,—and he promised to keep the secret.

Six weeks flew by, how swiftly! The pressure which circumstances had put upon Estelle's buoyancy of character being taken away, she moved the very embodiment of joy. It was as if she was making up for the past repression of her cheerfulness by an overflow, constant, yet gentle as the superflux of a fountain. Her very voice grew more childlike in its tones. A touching gratitude that never wearied of making itself felt seemed added to an abounding tenderness towards me.

She had a quick sense of the humorous which made hers an atmosphere of smiles. She would make me laugh by the odd and childish, yet charming pet phrases she would lavish upon me. She would amuse me by her anxiety in catering for me at meal-time, and making her humble fare seem sumptuous by her devices of speech, as well as by her culinary arts. The good nuns with whom she had lived had made her a thorough housekeeper, and a paragon of neatness. She wanted further to be my valet, my very slave, anticipating my wants, and forestalling every little effort which I might put forth.

My object now was to raise the sum necessary for our departure from the city. I took pupils in music among the humblest classes, — among the free blacks and even the slaves. I would be absent from nine o'clock in the morning till five in the afternoon. Estelle aided me in my purpose. She learned from Mrs. Mallet the art of making baskets, and contrived some of a new pattern which met a ready sale. We began to lay up five, sometimes six dollars a day.

Once I met Mr. Ratcliff in Carondelet Street. He evidently recognized me, for he turned on me a glance full of arrogance and hate. The encounter made me uneasy, but, thinking the mention of it might produce needless anxiety, I said nothing about it to Estelle. We were sitting that very evening in our little room. Estelle, always childlike, was in my lap, questioning me closely about all the incidents of the day, — what streets I had walked through; what persons I had seen; if I had been thinking of her, &c. I answered all her questions but one, and she seemed content; and then whispered in my ears the intelligence that she was likely to be the mother of my child. Delightful announcement! And yet with the thrill of satisfaction came a pang of solicitude.

"Do you believe," prattled Estelle, "there ever were two people so happy? I can't help recalling those words you read me the other night from your dear father's last part, 'If it were now to die, 't were now to be most happy.' It seems to me as if the felicity of a long life had been concentrated into these few weeks, and as if we were cheating our mortal lot in allowing ourselves to be quite so happy."

Was this the sigh of her presaging heart?

I resolved on immediate action. The next day (a Wednesday) I passed upon the Levee. After many inquiries, I found a ship laden with cotton that would sail the following Sunday for Boston. The captain agreed to give up his best state-room for a hundred dollars. It should be ready for our occupancy on Saturday. I closed with his offer at once. Estelle rejoiced at the arrangement.

"What has happened to-day?" I asked her.

"Nothing of moment," she replied. "Two men called to get names for a Directory."

"What did you tell them?"

"That if they wanted my husband's name, they must get it from him personally."

"You did well. Were they polite?"

"Very, and seemed to seek excuses for lingering; but, getting no encouragement, they left."

Could it be they were spies? The question occurred to me, but I soon dismissed it as improbable.

And yet they were creatures employed by Carberry Ratcliff to find out what they could about the man who had offended him.

Ratcliff was the type of a class that spring from slavery as naturally as certain weeds spring from a certain quality of manure. He was such a man as only slavery could engender. The son of a South Carolina planter, he was bred to believe that his little State — little in respect to its white population — was yet the master State of the Union, and that his family was the master family of the State. The conclusion that he was the master man of his family, and consequently of the Union, was not distant or illogical. As soon as he could lift a pistol he was taught to fire at a mark, and to make believe it was an Abolitionist. Before he was twelve years old he had fired at and wounded a free negro, who had playfully answered an imperious order by mimicking the boy's strut. Of this achievement the father was rather proud.

Accustomed to regard the lives and persons of slaves as subject to his irresponsible will, or to the caprices of his untrained and impure passions, he soon transferred to the laboring white man and woman the contempt he felt for the negro. We cannot have the moral sense impaired in one direction without having it warped and corrupted throughout.

Wrong feeling must, by an inexorable law, breed wrong thinking. And so Ratcliff looked upon all persons, whether white or black, who had to earn their bread by manual labor, as (in the memorable words of his friend Mr. Hammond, United States Senator from South Carolina) "Mudsills and slaves." For the thrifty Yankee his contempt was supreme, bitter, almost frantic.

By mismanagement and extravagance his family estate was squandered, and, the father having fallen in a duel with a political adversary, Ratcliff found himself at twenty-one with expensive tastes and no money. He borrowed a few hundred dollars, went to Louisiana, and there married a woman of large property, but personally unattractive. Revengeful and unforgetting as a savage where his pride was touched, and more cruel than a wolf in his instincts, Ratcliff had always meant to requite me for the humiliation I had made him experience. He had lost trace of me soon after the incident at the theatre. No sooner had I passed him in Carondelet Street than he put detectives on my track, and my place of abode was discovered. He received such a report of my wife's beauty as roused him to the hope of an exquisite revenge. Doubtless he found an opportunity of seeing Estelle without being seen; and on discovering in her his slave, his surprise and fury reached an ungovernable height.

Let me not dwell on the horrors of the next few days. We had made all our arrangements for departure that Saturday morning.

Estelle, in her simple habit, never looked so lovely. A little cherry-colored scarf which I had presented her was about her neck, and contrasted with the neutral tint of her robe. The carriage for our conveyance to the ship was at the door. Our light amount of luggage was put on behind. We bade our kind hostess good by. Estelle stepped in, and I was about to follow, when two policemen, each with a revolver in his hand, approached from a concealment near by, shut the carriage door, and, laying hands upon me, drew me back. At the same moment, from the opposite side of the street, Ratcliff, with two men wearing official badges, came, and, opening the opposite door of the coach, entered and took seats. So sudden were these movements, that they were over before either Estelle or I could offer any resistance.

The coachman at once drove off. An imploring shriek from Estelle was followed by a frantic effort on her part to thrust open the door of the coach. I saw her struggling in the arms of the officers, her face wild with terror, indignation, rage. Ratcliff, who had taken the seat opposite to her, put his head out of the coach, and bowed to me mockingly.

One of my stalwart captors held a pistol to my head, and cautioned me to be "asy." For half a minute I made no resistance. I was calculating how I could best rescue Estelle. All the while I kept my eyes intently on the departing carriage.

My captors held me as if they were prepared for any struggle. But I had not been seven years on the stage without learning something of the tricks of the wrestler and the gymnast. Suddenly both policemen found their legs knocked from under them, and their heads in contact with the pavement. A pistol went off as they fell, and a bullet passed through the crown of my hat; but before they could recover their footing, I had put an eighth of a mile between us.

Where was the carriage? The street into which it had turned was intersected by another which curved on either side like the horns of a crescent. To my dismay, when I reached this curve, the carriage was not to be seen. It had turned into the street either on the right or on the left, and the curve hid it from view. Which way? I could judge nothing from the sound, for other vehicles were passing. I stopped a man, and eagerly questioned him. He did not speak English. I put my question in French. He stopped to consider,—believed the carriage had taken the left turning, but was not quite certain. I ran leftward with all my speed. Carriages were to be seen, but not one with the little trunk and valise strapped on behind. I then turned and ran down the right turning. Baffled! At fault! In the network of streets it was all conjecture. Still on I ran in the desperate hope of seeing the carriage at some cross street. But my efforts were fruitless.

Panting and exhausted, I sought rest in a "magasin" for the sale of cigars. A little back parlor offered itself for smokers. I entered. A waiter brought in three cigars, and I threw a quarter of a dollar on the table. But I was no lover of the weed. The tobacco remained untouched. I wanted an opportunity for summoning my best thoughts.

Even if I had caught the coach, would not the chances have been against me? Clearly, yes. Further search for it, then, could be of no avail. Undoubtedly Ratcliff would take Estelle at once to his plantation, for there he could have her most completely in his power. Let that calculation be my starting-point.

How stood it in regard to myself? Did not my seizure by the policemen show that legal authority for my arrest had been procured? Probably. If imprisoned, should I not be wholly powerless to help Estelle? Obviously. Perhaps the morning newspapers would have something to say of the affair? Nothing more likely. Was it not, then, my safest course to keep still and concealed for the present? Alas, yes! Could I not trust Estelle to protect her own honor? Ay, she would protect it with her life; but the pang was in the thought that her life might be sacrificed in the work of protection.

The "magasin" was kept by Gustave Leroux, an old Frenchman, who had been a captain under Napoleon, and was in the grand army in its retreat from Moscow. A bullet had gone through his cheeks, and another had taken off part of his nose.

I must have sat with the untouched cigars before me nearly three hours. At last, supposing I was alone, I bowed my forehead on my hand, and wept. Suddenly I looked up. The old Frenchman, with his nose and cheek covered with large black patches, was standing with both hands on the table, gazing wistfully and tenderly upon me.

"What is it, my brave?" he asked in French, while tears began to fill his own eyes. I looked up. There was no resisting the benignity of that old battered face. I took the two hands which he held out to me in my own. He sat down by my side, and I told him my story.

After I had finished, he sat stroking his gray moustache with forefinger and thumb, and for ten minutes did not speak. Then he said: "I have seen this Mr. Ratcliff. A bad physiognomy! And yet what Mademoiselle Millefleurs would call a pretty fellow! Let us see. He will carry the girl to Lorain, and have her well guarded in his own house. As he has no faith in women, his policy will be to win her by fine presents, jewels, dresses, and sumptuous living. He will try that game for a full month at least. I think, if the girl is what you tell me she is, we may feel quite secure for a month. That will give us time to plan a campaign. Meanwhile you shall occupy a little room in my house, and keep as calm as you can. My dinner will be ready in ten minutes. You must try to coax an appetite, for you will want all your health and strength. *Courage, mon brave!*"

This old soldier, in his seventieth year, had done the most courageous act of his life. Out of pure charity he had married Madame Ponsard, five years his elder, an anti-Bonapartist, and who had been left a widow, destitute, and with six young parentless grandchildren. Fifty years back he had danced with her when she was a belle in Paris, and that fact was an offset for all her senile vanity and querulousness. It reconciled him, not only to receiving the lady herself, large, obese, and rubicund, and, worst of all, anti-Bonapartist, but to take her encumbrances, four girls and two boys, all with fearful appetites and sound lungs. But the old Captain was a sentimentalist; and the young life about him had rejuvenated his own. After all, there was a selfish calculation in his lovely charities; for he knew that to give was to receive in larger measure.

I accepted his offer of a shelter. The next morning he brought me a copy of the Delta. It contained this paragraph:

"We regret to learn that Mr. Julian Talbot, formerly an actor, and well known in theatrical circles, was yesterday arrested in the atrocious act of abducting a female slave of great personal beauty, belonging to the Hon. Carberry Ratcliff. The slave was recovered, but Talbot managed to escape. The officers are on his track. It is time an example was made of these sneaking Abolitionists."

"O insupportable, O heavy hour!" I tried to reconcile myself to delay. I stayed a whole fortnight with Leroux. At last I procured the dress of a laboring Celt, and tied up in a bundle a cheap dress that would serve for a boy. I then stuck a pipe through my hat-band, and put a shillelah under my arm. A mop-like red wig concealed a portion of my face. Lamp-black and ochre did the rest. Leroux told me I was premature in my movements, but, without heeding his expostulations, I took an affectionate leave of him and of Madame, whose heart I had won by talking French with her, and listening to her long stories of the ancient *régime*.

I went on board a Red River boat. One of the policemen who arrested me was present on the watch; but I stared him stupidly in the face, and passed on unsuspected.

Ratcliff was having a canal dug at Lorain for increasing the facilities of transporting cotton; and as the work was unhealthy, he engaged Irishmen for it. The killing an Irishman was no loss, but the death of a slave would be a thousand dollars out of the master's pocket. I easily got a situation among the diggers. How my heart bounded when I first saw Ratcliff! He came in company with his superintendent, Van Buskirk, and stood near me some minutes while I handled the spade.

For hours, every night during the week, I watched the house to discover the room occupied by Estelle. On Sunday I went in the daytime. From the window of a room in the uppermost story a little cherry-colored scarf was flaunting in the breeze. I at once recognized its meaning. Some negroes were near by under a tree. I approached, and asked an ancient black fellow, who was playing on an old cracked banjo, what he would take for the instrument.

"Look yere, Paddy," said he, "if yer tink to fool dis chile, yer 'll fine it air n't to be did. So wood up, and put off ter wunst, or yer 'll kotch it, shoo-ah."

"But, Daddy, I 'm in right earnest," replied I. "If you 'll sell that banjo at any price within reason, I 'll buy it."

"It 'll take a heap more 'n you kn raise ter buy dis yere banjo; so, Paddy, make tracks, and jes' you mine how yer guv dis yere ole nigger any more ob yer sarss."

"I 'll pay you two dollars for that banjo, Daddy. Will you take it?" said I, holding out the silver.

The old fellow looked at me incredulously; then seized the silver and thrust the banjo into my hand, uttering at the same time such an expressive "Wheugh!" as only a negro can. Then, unable to restrain himself, he broke forth: "Yah, yah, yah! Paddy 's got a bargain dis time, shoo-ah. Yah, yah, yah! Look yere, Paddy. Dat am de most sooperfinest banjo in dese parts; can't fine de match ob it in all Noo Orleenz. Jes' you hole on ter dem air strings, so dey won't break in two places ter wonst, and den fire away, and yer 'll 'stonish de natives, shoo-ah. Yah, yah, yah! Takes dis ole nigg to sell a banjo. Yah! yah!"

Every man who achieves success finds his penalty in a train of parasites; and Daddy's case was not exceptional. As he started in a bee line for his cabin, to boast of his acuteness in trade to an admiring circle, he was followed by his whole gang of witnesses.

All this time I could see Ratcliff with a party of gentlemen on his piazza. They were smoking cigars; and, judging from the noise they made, had been dining and drinking. I slipped away with the banjo under my arm.

That night I returned and played the air of "Pestal" as near to the house as I deemed it prudent to venture. I would play a minute, and then pause. I had not done this three times, when I heard Estelle's voice from her chamber, humming these words in low but audible tones:

"Hark! methinks I hear celestial voices sing,
Soon thou shalt be free, child of misery, —
Rest and perfect joy in heaven are waiting thee;
Spirit, plume thy wings and flee!"

I struck a few notes, by way of acknowledgment, and left.

The next night I merely whistled the remembered air in token of my presence. A light appeared for a moment at the window, and then was removed. I crept up close to the house. On that side of it where Estelle was confined there were no piazzas. I had not waited two minutes when something touched my head and bobbed before my eyes. It was a little roll of paper. I detached it from the string to which it was tied; and then, taking from my pocket an old envelope, I wrote on it in the dark these words: "To-morrow night at ten o'clock down the string. If prevented, then any night after at the same hour. Love shall find a way. Forever."

The letter which I found folded in the paper lies yet in my pocket-book, but I need not look at it in order to repeat it entire. It is in these words: —

"What shall I call thee? Dearest? But that word implies a comparative; and whom shall I compare with thee? Most precious and most beloved? O, that is not a tithe of it! Idol? Darling? Sweet? Pretty words, but insufficient. Ah! life of my life, there are no superlatives in language that can interpret to thee the unspeakable affection which swells in my heart and moistens my eyes as I commence this letter! Can we by words give an idea of a melody? No more can I put on paper what my heart would be whispering to thine. Forgive the effort and the failure.

"I have the freedom of the upper story of the house, and my room is where you saw the scarf. Two strong negro women, with sinister faces, and employed as seamstresses, watch me every time I cross the threshold. At night I am locked in. The windows, as you may see, are always secured by iron bars.

"Ratcliff hopes to subdue me by slow approaches. O, the unutterable loathing which he inspires! He has placed impure books in my way. He sends me the daintiest food and wines. I confine myself to bread, vegetables, and cream. He cannot drug me without my knowledge. Twice and sometimes three times a day he visits me, and, finding me firm in my resolve, retires with a self-satisfied air which maddens me. He evidently believes in my final submission. No! Sooner, death! on my knees I swear it.

"Yesterday he sent splendid dresses, laces, jewels, diamonds. He offers me a carriage, an establishment, and to settle on me enough to make me secure for the future. How he magnifies my hate by all these despicable baits!

"Sweet, be very prudent. While steadily maintaining towards this wretch, whom the law calls my master, the demeanor that may best assure him of my steadfast resolve, I take care not to arouse his anger; for I know what you want is opportunity. He may any time be called off suddenly to New Orleans. Be wary. Tell me what you propose. A string shall be let down from my window to-morrow night at ten by stealth, for I am watched. God keep thee, my husband, my beloved! How I shudder at thought of all thy dangers! Be sure, O William, tender and true, my heart will hold eternally one only image. Adieu! ESTELLE."

The next night I put her in possession of a rope and a boy's dress, also of two files, with directions for filing apart the iron bars. I saw it would not be difficult to enable her to get out of the house. The dreadful question was, How shall we escape the search which will at once be made? For a week we exchanged letters. At last she wrote me that Ratcliff would the next day leave for New Orleans for his wife. I wrote to Estelle to be ready the ensuing night, and on a signal from me to let herself down by the rope.

These plans were successfully carried out. Disguised as a laboring boy, Estelle let herself down to the ground. Once more we clasped each other heart to heart. I had selected a moonless night for the escape. In order to baffle the scent of the bloodhounds that would be put on our track, I took to the river. In a canoe I paddled down stream some fifteen miles till daylight. There, at a little bend called La Coude, we stopped. It now occurred to me that our safest plan would be to take the next boat up the river, and return on our course instead of keeping on to the Mississippi. Our pursuers would probably look for us in any direction but that.

The Rigolette was the first boat that stopped. We went on board, and the first person we encountered was Ratcliff! He was returning, having learnt at the outset of his journey that his wife had left New Orleans the day before. Estelle was thrown off her guard by the suddenness of the meeting, and uttered a short, sharp cry of dismay which betrayed her. Poor child! She was little skilled in feigning. Ratcliff walked up to her and removed her hat.

I had seen men in a rage, but never had I witnessed such an infuriated expression as that which Ratcliff's features now exhibited. It was wolfish, beastly, in its ferocity. His smooth pink face grew livid. Seizing Estelle roughly by the arm, he — whatever he was about to do, the operation was cut short by a blow from my fist between his eyes which felled him senseless on the deck.

The spectacle of a rich planter knocked down by an Irishman was not a common one on board the Rigolette. We were taken in custody, Estelle and I, and confined together in a state-room.

Ratcliff was badly stunned, but cold water and brandy at length restored him. At Lorain the boat stopped till Van Buskirk and half a dozen low whites, his creatures and hangers-on, could be summoned to take me in charge. Ratcliff now recognized me as his acquaintance of the theatre, and a new paroxysm of fury convulsed his features. I was searched, deprived of my money, then handcuffed; then shackled by the legs, so that I could only move by taking short steps. Estelle's arms were pinioned behind her, and in that state she was forced into an open vehicle and conveyed to the house.

I was placed in an outbuilding near the stable, a sort of dungeon for refractory slaves. It was lighted from the roof, was unfloored, and contained neither chair nor log on which to sit. For two days and nights neither food nor drink was brought to me. With great difficulty, on account of my chain, I managed to get at a small piece of biscuit in my coat-pocket. This I ate, and, as the rain dripped through the roof, I was enabled to quench my thirst.

On the third day two men led me out to an adjoining building, and down-stairs into a cellar. As we entered, the first object I beheld sent such a shock of horror to my heart that I wonder how I survived it. Tied to a post, and stripped naked to her hips, her head drooping, her breast heaving, her back scored by the lash and bleeding, stood Estelle. Near by, leaning on a cotton-bale, was Ratcliff smoking a cigar. Seated on a block, his back resting against the wall, with one leg over the other, was a white man, holding a cowskin, and apparently resting from his arduous labors as woman-whipper. Forgetting my shackles, and uttering some inarticulate cry of anguish, I strove to rush upon Ratcliff, but fell to the ground, exciting his derision and that of his creatures, the miserable "mean" whites, the essence of whose manhood familiarity with slavery had unmoulded till they had become bestial in their feelings.

Estelle, roused by my voice, turned on me eyes lighted up by an affection which no bodily agony could for one moment enfeeble, and said, gaspingly: "My own husband! You see I keep my oath!"

"Husband indeed! We 'll see about that," sneered Ratcliff. "Fool! do you imagine that a marriage contracted by a slave without the consent of the master has any validity, moral or legal?"

I turned to him, and uttered — I know not what. The frenzy which seized me lifted me out of my normal state of thought, and by no effort of reminiscence have I ever since been able to recall what I said.

I only remember that Ratcliff, with mock applause, clapped his hands and cried, "Capital!" Then, lighting a fresh cigar, he remarked: "There is yet one little ceremony more to be gone through with. Bring in the bridegroom."

What new atrocity was this?

A moment afterwards a young, lusty, stout, and not ill-looking negro, fantastically dressed, was led in with mock ceremony, by one of the mean whites, a whiskey-wasted creature named Lovell. I looked eagerly in the face of the negro, who bowed and smirked in a manner to excite roars of laughter on the part of Ratcliff and his minions.

"Well, boy, are you ready to take her for better or for worse?" asked the haughty planter.

The negro bowed obsequiously, and, jerking off his hat, scratched his wool, and, with a laugh, replied: "'Scuze me, massa, but dis nigger can't see his wife dat is to be 'xposed in dis onhan'some mahnner to de eyes of de profane. If Massa Ratcliff hab no 'jection, I 'll jes' put de shawl on de bride's back. Yah, yah, yah!"

"O, make yourself as gallant as you please now," said the planter, laughing. "Let 's see you begin to play the bridegroom."

Gracious heavens! Was I right in my surmises? Under all his harlequin grimaces and foolery, this negro, to my quickened penetration, seemed to be crowding back, smothering, disguising, some intense emotion. His laugh was so extravagantly African, that it struck me as imitative in its exaggeration. I had heard a laugh much like it from the late Jim Crow Rice on the stage. Was the negro playing a part?

He approached Estelle, cut the thongs that bound her to the post, threw her shawl over her shoulders, and then, falling on one knee, put both hands on his heart, and rolled up his eyes much after the manner of Bombastes Furioso making love to Distaffina. The Ratcliffites were in ecstasies at the burlesque. Then, rising to his feet, the negro affectedly drew nearer to Estelle, and, putting up his hand, whispered, first in one of her ears, then in the other. I could see a change, sudden, but instantly checked, in her whole manner. Her lips moved. She must have murmured something in reply.

"Look here, Peek, you rascal," cried Ratcliff, "we must have the benefit of your soft words. What have you been saying to her?"

"I 'ze been tellin' her," said the negro, with tragic gesticulation, pointing to himself and then at me, "to look fust on dis yere pikter, den on dat. Wheugh!"

Still affecting the buffoon, he came up to me, presenting his person so that his face was visible only to myself. There was a divine pity in his eyes, and in the whole expression of his face the guaranty of a high and holy resolve. "She will trust me," he whispered. "Do you the same."

To the spectators he appeared to be mocking me with grimace. To me he seemed an angel of deliverance.

"Now, Peek, to business!" said Ratcliff. "You swear, do you, to make this woman your wife in fact as well as in name; do you understand me, Peek?"

"Yes, massa, I understan'."

"You swear to guard her well, and never to let that white scoundrel yonder come near or touch her?"

"Yes, massa, I swar ter all dat, an' ebber so much more. He 'll kotch what he can't carry if he goes fur to come nare my wife."

"Kiss the book on it," said Ratcliff, handing him a Bible.

"Yes, massa, as many books as you please," replied Peek, doing as he was bidden.

"Then, by my authority as owner of you two slaves, and as justice of the peace, I pronounce you, in presence of these witnesses, man and wife," said Ratcliff. "Why the hell, Peek, don't you kiss the bride?"

"O, you jes' leeb dis chile alone for dat air, Massa Ratcliff," replied the negro; and, concealing his mouth by both hands, he simulated a kiss.

"Now attend to Mrs. Peek while another little ceremony takes place," said Ratcliff.

At a given signal I was stripped of my coat, waistcoat, and shirt, then dragged to the whipping-post, and bound to it. I could see Estelle, her face of a mortal paleness, her body writhing as if in an agony. The first lash that descended on my bare flesh seemed to rive her very heart-strings, for she uttered a loud shriek, and was borne out senseless in the negro's arms.

"All right!" said Ratcliff. "We shall soon have half a dozen little Peeks toddling about. Proceed, Vickery."

A hundred lashes, each tearing or laying bare the flesh, were inflicted; but after the first, all sensibility to pain was lost in the intensity of my emotions. Had I been changed into a statue of bronze I could not have been more impenetrable to pain.

"Now, sir," said the slave lord, coming up to me, "you see what it is to cross the path of Carberry Ratcliff. The next time you venture on it, you won't get off so easy."

Then, turning to Vickery, he said: "I promised the boys they should have a frolic with him, and see him safely launched. They have been longing for a shy at an Abolitionist. So unshackle him, and let him slide."

My handcuffs and shackles were taken off. My first impulse on being freed, was to spring upon Ratcliff and strangle him. I could have done it. Though I stood in a pool of my own blood, a preternatural energy filled my veins, and I stepped forth as if just refreshed by sleep. But the thought of Estelle checked the vindictive impulse. A rope was now put about my neck, so that the two ends could be held by my conductors. In this state I was led up-stairs out of the building, and beyond the immediate enclosure of the grounds about the house to a sort of trivium, where some fifty or sixty "mean whites" and a troop of boys of all colors were assembled round a tent in which a negro was dealing out whiskey gratis to the company. Near by stood a kettle sending forth a strong odor of boiling tar. A large sack, the gaping mouth of which showed it was filled with feathers, lay on the ground.

There was a yell of delight from the assembly as soon as I appeared. Half naked as I was, I was dragged forward into their midst, and tied to a tree near the kettle. I could see, at a distance of about a quarter of a mile, Ratcliff promenading his piazza.

There was a dispute among the "chivalry" whether I should be stripped of the only remaining article of dress, my pantaloons, before being "fitted to a new suit." The consideration that there might be ladies among the distant spectators finally operated in my favor. A brush, similar to that used in white-washing, was now thrust into the bituminous liquid; and an illustration of one of "our institutions, sir," was entered upon with enthusiasm. Lovell was the chief operator. The brush was first thrust into my face till eyelids, eyebrows, and hair were glued by the nauseous adhesion. Then it was vigorously applied to the bleeding seams on my back, and the intolerable anguish almost made me faint. My entire person at length being thickly smeared, the bag of feathers was lifted over me by two men and its contents poured out over the tarred surface.

I will not pain you, my friends, by suggesting to your imagination all that there is of horrible, agonizing, and disgusting in this operation, which men, converted into fiends by the hardening influences of slavery, have inflicted on so many hundreds of imprudent or suspected persons from the Northern States. I see in it all now, so far as I was concerned, a Providential martyrdom to awake me to a sense of what slavery does for the education of white men.

O, ye palliators of the "institution"! — Northern men with Southern principles, — ministers of religion who search the Scriptures to find excuses for the Devil's own work, — and ye who think that any system under which money is made must be right, and of God's appointment, — who hate any agitation which is likely to diminish the dividends from your cotton-mills or the snug profits from your Southern trade, — come and learn what it is to be tarred and feathered for profaning, by thought or act, or by suspected thought or act, that holy of holies called slavery!

After the feathers had been applied, a wag among my tormentors fixed to my neck and arms pieces of an old sheet stretched on whalebone to imitate a pair of wings. This spectacle afforded to the spectators the climax of their exhilaration and delight. I was then led by a rope to the river's side and put on an old rickety raft where I had to use constant vigilance to keep the loose planks from disparting. Two men in a boat towed me out into the middle of the stream, and then, amid mock cheers, I was left to drift down with the current or drown, just as the chances might hold in regard to my strength.

Two thoughts sustained me; one Estelle, the other Ratcliff. But for these, with all my youth and power of endurance, I should have sunk and died under my sufferings. For nearly an hour I remained within sight of the mocking, hooting crowd, who were especially amused at my efforts to save myself from immersion by keeping the pieces of my raft together. At length it was floated against a shallow where some brushwood and loose sticks had formed a sort of dam. The sun was sinking through wild, ragged clouds in the west. My tormentors had all gradually disappeared. For the last thirty-six hours I had eaten nothing but a cracker. My eyes were clogged with tar. My efforts in keeping the raft together had been exhaustive. No sooner was I in a place of seeming safety than my strength failed me all at once. I could no longer sit upright. The wind freshened and the waves poured over me, almost drowning me at times. Thicker vapors began to darken the sky. A storm was rising. Night came down frowningly. The planks slipped from under me. I could not lift an arm to stop them. I tried to seize the brushwood heaped on the sand-bar, but it was easily detached, and offered me no security. I seemed to be sinking in the ooze of the river's bottom. The spray swept over me in ever-increasing volume. I was on the verge of unconsciousness.

Suddenly I roused myself, and grasped the last plank of my raft. I had heard a cry. I listened. The cry was repeated, — a loud halloo, as if from some one afloat in an approaching skiff. I could see nothing, but I lifted my head as well as I could, and cried out, "Here!" Again the halloo, and this time it sounded nearer. I threw my whole strength into one loud shriek of "Here!" and then sank exhausted. A rush of waves swept over me, and my consciousness was suspended.

When I came to my senses, I lay on a small cot-bedstead in a hut. A negro, whom I at once recognized as the man called Peek, was rubbing my face and limbs with oil and soap. A smell of alcohol and other volatile liquids pervaded the apartment. Much of my hair had been cut off in the effort to rid it of the tar.

"Estelle, — where is she?" were my first words.

"You shall see her soon," replied the negro. "But you must get a little strength first."

He spoke in the tones, and used the language, of an educated person. He brought me a little broth and rice, which I swallowed eagerly. I tried to rise, but the pain from the gashes left by the scourge on my back was excruciating.

"Take me to my wife," I murmured.

He lifted me in his arms and carried me to the open door of an adjoining cabin. Here on a mattress lay Estelle. A colored woman of remarkable aspect, and with straight black hair, was kneeling by her side. This woman Peek addressed as Esha. The little plain gold cross which Estelle used to wear on the ribbon round her neck was now made to serve as the emblem of one of the last sacraments of her religion. At her request, Esha held it, pinned to the ribbon, before her eyes. On a rude table near by, two candles were burning. Estelle's hands were clasped upon her bosom, and she lay intently regarding the cross, while her lips moved in prayer.

"Try to lib, darlin'," interrupted Esha; "try to lib, — dat 's a good darlin'! Only try, an' yer kn do it easy."

Estelle took the little cross in her hand and kissed it, then said to Esha, "Give this, with a lock of my hair, to —"

Before she could pronounce my name, I rallied my strength, and, with an irrepressible cry of grief, quitted Peek's support, and rushed to her side. I spoke her name. I took her dear head in my hands. She turned on me eyes beaming with an immortal affection. A celestial smile irradiated her face. Her lips pouted as if pleading for a kiss. I obeyed the invitation, and she acknowledged my compliance by an affirmative motion of the head; a motion that was playful even in that supreme moment.

"My own darling!" she murmured; "I knew you would come. O my poor, suffering darling!"

Then, with a sudden effort, she threw her arms about my neck, and, drawing me closer down to her bosom, said, in sweet, low tones of tenderness: "Love me still as among the living. I do not die. The body dies. I do not die. Love cannot die. Who believes in death, never loved. You may not see *me*, but I shall see *you*. So be a good boy. Do good to all. Love all; so shall you love me the better. I do not part with my love. I take it where it will grow and grow, so as to be all the more fit to welcome my darling. Carrying my love, I carry my heaven with me. It would not be heaven without my love. I have been with my father and mother. So beautiful they are! And such music I have heard! There! Lay your cheek on my bare bosom. So! You do not hurt me. Closer! closer! *Carissime Jesu, nunc libera me!*" *

Thus murmuring a line from a Latin poem which she had learnt in the convent where her childhood was passed, her pure spirit, without a struggle or a throe of pain, disentangled itself from its lovely mortal mould, and rose into the purer ether of the immortal life.

I afterwards learnt that Ratcliff, finding Estelle inexorable in her rejection of his foul proffers, was wrought to such a pitch of rage that he swore, unless she relented, she should be married to a negro slave. He told her he had a smart nigger

* The line is from the following prayer, attributed to Mary, Queen of Scots:—

"O domine Deus, speravi in Te;
Carissime Jesu, nunc libera me!
In dura catena, in misera pœna,
Desidero Te!
Languendo, gemendo, et genuflectendo
Adoro, imploro, ut liberes me."

he had recently bought in New Orleans, a fellow named Peek, who should be her husband. Goaded to desperation by his infamous threats, Estelle had replied, "Better even a negro than a Ratcliff!" This reply had stung him to a degree that was quite intolerable.

To be not only thwarted by a female slave, but insulted,— he, a South Carolinian, a man born to command, — a man with such a figure and such a face rejected for a strolling actor,— a vagabond, a fellow, too, who had knocked him down, — what slave-owner would tamely submit to such mortification! He brooded on the insult till his cruel purpose took shape and consistency in his mind; and it was finally carried out in the way I have described.

It may seem almost incredible to you who are from the North, that any man not insane should be guilty of such atrocities. But Mr. Onslow need not be told that slavery educates men — men, too, of a certain refinement — to deeds even more cowardly and fiendish. Do not imagine that the tyrant who would not scruple to put a black skin under the lash, would hesitate in regard to a white; and the note-book of many an overseer will show that of the whippings inflicted under slavery, more than one third are of women.*

For three weeks I was under Peek's care. Thanks to his tenderness and zeal, my wounds were healed, my strength was restored. Early in December I parted from him and returned to New Orleans. I went to my old friends, the Leroux. They did not recognize me at first, so wasted was I by suffering. Madame forgot her own troubles in mine, and welcomed me with a mother's affection. The grandchildren subdued their riotous mirth, and trod softly lest they should disturb me. The old Captain wept and raved over my story, and uttered more *sacr-r-r-rés* in a given time than I supposed even a Frenchman's volubility could accomplish. I bade these kind friends good by, and went northward.

In Cincinnati and other cities I resumed my old vocation as a play-actor. In two years, having laid up twenty-five hundred

* Some of these note-books have been brought to light by the civil war, and a quotation from one of them will be found on another page of this work.

dollars, I returned to the Red River country to secure the freedom of the slave to whom I owed my life. He had changed masters. It had got to Ratcliff's ears that Peek had cheated him in sparing Estelle and rescuing me. He questioned Peek on the subject. Peek, throwing aside all his habitual caution, had declared, in regard to Estelle, that if she had been the Virgin Mary he could not have treated her with more reverence; that he had saved my life, and restored me to her arms. Then, shaking his fist at Ratcliff, he denounced him as a murderer and a coward. The result was, that Peek, after having been put through such a scourging as few men could endure and survive, had been sold to a Mr. Barnwell in Texas.

I followed Peek to his new abode, and proposed either to buy and free him, or to aid him to escape. He bade me save my money for those who could not help themselves. He meant to be free, but did not mean to pay for that which was his by right. At that time he was investigating certain strange occurrences produced by some invisible agency that claimed to be spiritual. He must remain where he was a while longer. I was under no serious obligations to him, he said. He had simply done his duty.

We parted. I tried to find the woman Esha, who had been kind to my wife, but she had been sold no one knew to whom. I went to New Orleans, and assuming, by legislative permission, the name of William Vance, I entered into cotton speculations.

My features had been so changed by suffering, that few recognized me. My operations were bold and successful. In four years I had accumulated a little fortune. Occasionally I would meet Ratcliff. Once I had him completely in my power. He was in the passage-way leading to my office. I could have dragged him in and —

No! The revenge seemed too poor and narrow. I craved something huge and general. The mere punishing of an *individual* was too puny an expenditure of my hoarded vengeance. But to strike at the "institution" which had spawned this and similar monsters, that would be some small satisfaction.

Closing up my affairs in New Orleans, I entered upon that career which has gained me such notoriety in the Southwest.

I have run off many thousand slaves, worth in the aggregate many millions of dollars. My theatrical experience has made me a daring expert in disguising myself. At one time I am a mulatto with a gash across my face; at another time, an old man; at another, a mean whiskey-swilling hanger-on of the chivalry. My task is only just begun. It is not till we have given slavery its immedicable wound, or rather till it has itself committed suicide in the house of its friends, that I shall be ready to say, *Nunc dimittas, domi-ne!* *

* Should any person question the probability of the incidents in Vance's narrative, we would refer him to the "Letter to Thomas Carlyle" in the Atlantic Monthly for October, 1863. On page 501, we find the following: "Within the past year, a document has come into my hands. It is the private diary of a most eminent and respectable slaveholder, recently deceased. The chances of war threw it into the hands of our troops. . . . . . One item I must have the courage to suggest more definitely. Having bidden a young slave-girl (whose name, age, color, &c., with the shameless precision that marks the entire document, are given) to attend upon his brutal pleasure, and she silently remaining away, he writes, 'Next morning ordered her a dozen lashes for disobedience.'" In a foot-note to the above we are assured by Messrs. Ticknor and Fields that the author of the letter is "one whose word is not and cannot be called in question; and he pledges his word that the above is exact and *proven* fact."

CHAPTER XIII.

FIRE UP!

"What is the end and essence of life? It is to expand all our faculties and affections. It is to grow, to gain by exercise new energy, new intellect, new love. It is to hope, to strive, to bring out what is within us, to press towards what is above us. In other words, it is to be Free. Slavery is thus at war with the true life of human nature." — *Channing.*

AT the conclusion of Vance's narrative, Mr. Onslow rose, shook him by the hand, and walked away without making a remark.

Mrs. Berwick showed her appreciation by her tears.

"What a pity," said her husband, "that so fine a fellow as Peek did not accept your proposal to free him!"

"Peek freed himself," replied Vance. "He escaped to Canada, married, settled in New York, and was living happily, when a few days ago, rather than go before a United States Commissioner, he surrendered himself to that representative of the master race, Colonel Delancy Hyde, to whom you have had the honor to be introduced. Peek is now on board this boat, and handcuffed, lest he should jump overboard and swim ashore. If you will walk forward, I will show him to you."

Greatly surprised and interested, the Berwicks followed Vance to the railing, and looked down on Peek as he reclined in the sunshine reading a newspaper.

"But he must be freed. I will buy him," said Berwick.

"Don't trouble yourself," returned Vance. "Peek will be free without money and without price, and he knows it. Those iron wristbands you see are already filed apart."

"Are there many such as he among the negroes?"

"Not many, I fear, either among blacks or whites," replied Vance. "But, considering their social deprivations, there are more good men and true among the negroes — ay, among the slaves — than you of the North imagine. Your ideal of the negro is what you derive from the Ethiopian minstrels and from the books and plays written to ridicule him. His type is a low, ignorant trifler and buffoon, unfit to be other than a slave or an outcast. Thus, by your injurious estimate, you lend yourselves to the support and justification of slavery."

"Would you admit the black to a social equality?"

"I would admit him," replied Vance, "to all the civil rights of the white. There are many men whom I am willing to acknowledge my equals, whose society I may not covet. That does not at all affect the question of their rights. Let us give the black man a fair field. Let us not begin by declaring his inferiority in capacity, and then anxiously strive to prevent his finding a chance to prove our declaration untrue."

"But would you favor the amalgamation of the races?"

"That is a question for physiologists; or, perhaps, for individual instincts. Probably if all the slaves were emancipated in all the Cotton States, amalgamation would be much less than it is now. The French Quadroons are handsome and healthy, and are believed to be more vigorous than either of the parent races from which they are descended."

"Many of the most strenuous opponents of emancipation base their objections on their fears of amalgamation."

"To which," replied Vance, "I will reply in these words of one of your Northern divines, '*What a strange reason for oppressing a race of fellow-beings, that if we restore them to their rights we shall marry them!*' Many of these men who cry out the loudest against amalgamation keep colored mistresses, and practically confute their own protests. To marriage, but not to concubinage, they object."

"I see no way for emancipation," said Berwick, "except through the consent of the Slave States."

"God will find a way," returned Vance. "He infatuates before he destroys; and the infatuation which foreruns destruction has seized upon the leading men of the South. Plagiarizing from Satan, they have said to slavery, 'Evil, be thou our good!' They are bent on having a Southern Confederacy with power to extend slavery through Mexico into Central America. That can never be attempted without civil war, and civil war will be the end of slavery."

"Would you not," asked Berwick, "compensate those masters who are willing to emancipate their slaves?"

"I deny," said Vance, "that property in slaves can morally exist. No decision of the State can absolve me from the moral law. It is a sham and a lie to say that man can hold property in man. The right to make the black man a slave implies the right to make you or me a slave. No legislation can make such a claim valid. No vote of a majority can make an act of tyranny right, — can convert an innocent man into a chattel. All the world may cry out it is right, but they cannot make it so. The slaveholder, in emancipating his slave, merely surrenders what is not his own. I would be as liberal to him in the way of encouragement as the public means would justify. But the loss of the planter from emancipation is greatly over estimated. His land would soon double in value by the act; and the colored freedmen would be on the soil, candidates for wages, and with incentives to labor they never had before."

The bell for dinner broke in upon the conversation. It was not till evening that the parties met again on the upper deck.

"I have been talking with Peek," said Berwick, "and to my dismay I find he was betrayed by the husband of my step-mother. You must help me cancel this infernal wrong."

"I have laid my plans for taking all these negroes ashore at midnight at our next stopping-place," replied Vance. "I am to personate their owner. The keepers of the boat, who have seen me so much with Hyde, will offer no opposition. He is already so drunk that we have had to put him to bed. He begged me to look after his niggers. Whiskey had made him sentimental. He wept maudlin tears, and wanted to kiss me."

"Here's a check," said Berwick, "for twenty-five hundred dollars. Give it to Peek the moment he is free."

Vance placed it in a small water-proof wallet.

What's the matter?

A rush and a commotion on the deck! Captain Crane left the wheel-house, and jumped over the railing down to the lower deck forward, his mouth bubbling and foaming with oaths.

There had been a slackening of the fires, and the Champion was all at once found to be fast gaining on the Pontiac.

"Fire up!" yelled the Captain. "Pile on the turpentine splinters. Bring up the rosin. Blast yer all for a set of cowardly cusses! I'm bound to land yer either in Helena or hell, ahead of the Champion."

CHAPTER XIV.

WAITING FOR THE SUMMONER.

"So every spirit, as it is more pure,
And hath in it the more of heavenly light,
So it the fairer body doth procure,
To habit in, and it more fairly dight
With cheerful grace and amiable sight.
For of the soul the body form doth take,
For soul is form, and doth the body make."

Edmund Spenser.

IN the best chamber of the house of Pierre Toussaint in Franklin Street, looking out on blossoming grape-vines and a nectarine-tree in the area, sat Mrs. Charlton in an arm-chair, and propped by pillows. Her wasted features showed that disease had made rapid progress since the glance we had of her in the mirror.

A knock at the door was followed by the entrance of Toussaint.

"Well, Toussaint, what 's the news to-day?" asked the invalid.

Toussaint replied in French: "I do not find much of new in the morning papers, madame. Is madame ready for her breakfast?"

"Yes, any time now. I see my little Lulu is washing himself."

Lulu was the canary-bird. Toussaint quitted the room and returned in a few minutes, bringing in a tray, spread with the whitest of napkins, and holding a silver urn of boiling water, a pitcher of cream, and two little shining pots, one filled with coffee, the other with tea. The viands were a small roll, with butter, an omelette, and a piece of fresh-broiled salmon.

"Sit down and talk with me, Toussaint, while I eat," said the invalid. "Have you seen my husband lately?"

"Not, madame, since he called to recover the box."

"Has he sent to make inquiry in regard to my health?"

"Not once, to my knowledge."

"I cannot reconcile my husband's indifference with his fondness for money. He must know that my death will deprive him of twelve hundred a year. How do you account for it, Toussaint?"

"Pardon me, madame, but I would rather not say."

"And why not?"

"My surmise may be uncharitable, or it might give you pain."

"Do not fear that, Toussaint. I have surrendered what they say is the last thing a woman surrenders, — all personal vanity. So speak freely."

"Mr. Charlton is young and good-looking, madame, and he is probably well aware that, in the event of his being left a widower, it would not be difficult for him to form a marriage connection that would bring him a much larger income than that you supply."

"Nothing more likely, Toussaint. How strange that I can talk of these things so calmly, — eating my breakfast, thus! They say that a woman who has once truly loved must always love. What do you think, Toussaint?"

"This, madame, that if we love a thing because we think it good, and then find, on trial, that it is not good, but very bad, our love cannot continue the same."

"But do we not, in marriage, promise to love, honor, and obey?"

"Not by the Catholic form, madame. Try to force love, you kill it. It is like trying to force an appetite. You make yourself sick at the stomach in the attempt."

Here there was a ring at the door-bell, and Toussaint left the room. On his return he said: "The husband of madame is below. He wishes to speak with madame."

Surprised and disturbed, Mrs. Charlton said, "Take away the breakfast things."

"But madame has not touched the salmon nor the omelette, and only a poor little bit of the crust of this roll," murmured Toussaint.

"I have had enough, my good Toussaint. Take them away, and let Mr. Charlton come in."

Then, as if by way of contradicting what she had said a

moment before, she began smoothing her hair and arranging her shawl. The inconsistency between her practice and her profession seemed to suggest itself to her suddenly, for she smiled sadly, and murmured, "After all, I have not quite outlived my folly!"

Charlton entered unaccompanied. His manner was that of a man who has a big scheme in his head, which he is trying to disguise and undervalue. Moved by an unwonted excitement, he strove to appear calm and indifferent, but, like a bad actor, he overdid his part.

"I have come, Emily," said he, "to ask your pardon for the past."

"Indeed! Then you want something. What can I do for you?"

"You misapprehend me, my dear. Affairs have gone wrong with me of late; but my prospects are brightening now, and my wish is that you should have the benefit of the change."

"My time for this world's benefits is likely to be short," said the invalid.

"Not so, my dear! You are looking ten per cent better than when I saw you last."

"My glass tells me you do not speak truly in that. Come, deal frankly with me. What do you want?"

"As I was saying, my love," resumed Charlton, "my business is improving; but I need a somewhat more extended credit, and you can help me to it."

"I thought there was something wanted," returned the invalid, with a scornful smile; "but you overrate my ability. How can I help your credit? The annuity allowed by Mr. Berwick ends with my life. I have no property, real or personal, — except my canary-bird, and what few clothes you can find in yonder wardrobe."

"But, my dear," urged Charlton, "many persons imagine that you have property; and if I could only show them an authenticated instrument under which you bequeath, in the event of your death, all your estate, real and personal, to your husband, it would aid me materially in raising money."

"That, sir, would be raising money under false pretences. I shall lend myself to no such attempt. Why not tell the money-lenders the truth? Why not tell them your wife has nothing except what she receives from the charity of her step-son?"

Enraged at seeing how completely his victim had thrown off his influence, and at the same time indulging a vague hope that he might recover it, Charlton's lips began to work as if he were hesitating whether to try his old game of browbeating or to adopt a conciliatory course. A suspicion that the lady was disenchanted, and no longer subject to any spell he could throw upon her, led him to fall back on the more prudent policy; and he replied: "I have concealed nothing from the parties with whom I am negotiating. I have told them the precise situation of our affairs; but they have urged this contingency: your wife, it is true, is dependent, but her rich relatives may die and leave her a bequest. We will give you the money you want, if you will satisfy us that you are her heir."

"You fatigue me," said the invalid. "You wish me to make a will in your favor. You have the instruments all drawn up and ready for my signature in your pocket; and on the opposite side of the street you have three men in waiting who may serve as witnesses."

"But who told you this?" exclaimed Charlton, confounded.

"Your own brain by its motions told it," replied the wife. "I am rather sensitive to impressions, you see. Strike one of the chords of a musical instrument, and a corresponding chord in its duplicate near by will be agitated. Your drift is apparent. The allusions under which I have labored in regard to you have vanished, never, never to return! How I deferred the moment of final, irrevocable estrangement! How I strove, by meekness, love, and devotion, to win you to the better choice! How I shut my eyes to your sordid traits! But now the infatuation is ended. You are powerless to wound or to move me. The love you spurned has changed, not to hate, but to indifference. Free to choose between God and Mammon, you have chosen Mammon, and nothing I can say can make you reconsider your election."

"You do me injustice, my wife, my dearest —"

"Psha! Do not blaspheme. We understand each other at last. Now to business. You want me to sign a will in your favor, leaving you all the property I may be possessed of at the time of my death. Would you know when that time will be?"

"Do not speak so, Emily," said Charlton, in tones meant to be pathetic.

"It may be an agreeable surprise to you," continued the invalid, "to learn that my time in this world will be up the tenth of next month. I will sign the will, on one condition."

"Name it!" said Charlton, eagerly.

"The condition is, that you pay Toussaint a thousand dollars cash down as an indemnity for the expense he has been at on my account, and to cover the costs of my funeral."

With difficulty Charlton curbed his rage so far as to be content with the simple utterance, "Impossible!"

"Then please go," said the invalid, taking up a silver bell to ring it.

"Stop! stop!" cried Charlton. "Give me a minute to consider. Three hundred dollars will more than cover all the expenses,—medical attendance, undertaker's charges,—all. At least, I know an undertaker who charges less than half what such fellows as Brown of Grace pile on. Say three hundred dollars."

With a smile of indescribable scorn, the invalid touched the bell.

"Stop! We 'll call it five hundred," groaned the conveyancer.

A louder ring by the lady, and the old negro's step was heard on the stairs.

"Seven hundred,—eight hundred: O, I could n't possibly afford more than eight hundred!" said Charlton, in a tone the pathos of which was no longer feigned.

The invalid now rang the bell with energy.

"It shall be a thousand, then!" exclaimed Charlton, just as Toussaint entered the room.

"Toussaint," said the invalid, "Mr. Charlton has a paper he wishes me to sign. I have promised to do it on his paying you a thousand dollars. Accept it without demur. Do you understand?"

Toussaint bowed his assent; and Charlton, leaving the room,

returned with his three witnesses. The sum stipulated was paid to Toussaint, and the will was duly signed and witnessed. Possessed of the document, Charlton's first impulse was to vent his wrath upon his wife; but he discreetly remembered that, while life remained, it was in her power to revoke what she had done; so he dismissed his witnesses, and began to play the fawner once more. But he was checked abruptly.

"There! you weary me. Go, if you please," said she. "If I have occasion, I will send for you."

"May I not call daily to see how you are getting on?" whined Charlton.

"I really don't see any use in it," replied the invalid. "If you will look in the newspapers under the obituary head the eleventh or twelfth of next month, you will probably get all the information in regard to me that will be important."

"Cruel and unjust!" said the husband. "Have you no forgiveness in your heart?"

"Forgiveness? Trampled on, my heart has given out love and duty in the hope of finding some spot in your own heart which avarice and self-seeking had not yet petrified. But I despair of doing aught to change your nature. I must leave you to God and circumstance. Neither you nor any other offender shall lack my forgiveness, however; for in that I only give what I supremely need. Farewell."

"Good by, since you will not let me try to make amends for the past," said Charlton; and he quitted the room.

Half sorry for her own harshness, and thinking she might have misjudged her husband's present feelings, the invalid got Toussaint to help her into the next room, where she could look through the blinds. No sooner was Charlton in the street than he drew from his pocket the will, and walked slowly on as if feasting his eyes on its contents. With a gesture of exultation, he finally returned the paper to his pocket, and strode briskly up the street to Broadway.

"You see!" said the invalid, bitterly. "And I loved that man once! And there are worthy people who would say I ought to love him still. Love him? Tell my little Lulu to love a cat or a hawk. How can I love what I find on testing to be repugnant to my own nature? Tell me, Toussaint, does

God require we should love what we know to be impure, unjust, cruel?"

"Ah, madame, the good God, I suppose, would have us love the wicked so far as to help them to get rid of their wickedness."

"But there are some who will not be helped," said the invalid. "Take the wickedness out of some persons, and we should deprive them of their very individuality, and practically annihilate them."

"God knows," replied Toussaint; "time is short, and eternity is long, — long enough, perhaps, to bleach the filthiest nature, with Christ's help."

"Right, Toussaint. What claim have I to judge of the capacities for redemption in a human soul? But there is a terrible mystery to me in these false conjunctions of man and woman. Why should the loving be united to the unloving and the brutal?"

"Simply, madame, because this is earth, and not heaven. In the next life all masks must be dropped. What will the hypocrite and the impostor do then? Then the loving will find the loving, and the pure will find the pure. Then our bodies will be fair or ugly, black or white, according to our characters."

"I believe it!" exclaimed the invalid. "Yes, there is an infinite compassion over all. God lives, and the soul does not die, and the mistakes, the infelicities, the shortcomings of this life shall be as fuel to kindle our aspirations and illumine our path in another stage of being."

Here a clamorous newsboy stopped on the other side of the way to sell a gentleman an Extra.

"What is that boy crying?" asked the invalid.

"A great steamboat accident on the Mississippi," replied Toussaint.

CHAPTER XV.

WHO SHALL BE HEIR?

"I care not, Fortune, what you me deny,
You cannot rob me of free Nature's grace;
You cannot shut the windows of the sky,
Through which Aurora shows her brightening face."
Thomson.

WHEN we parted from Mr. Pompilard, he was trying to negotiate a mortgage for thirty thousand dollars on some real estate belonging to his wife. This mortgage was effected without recourse to the Berwicks, as was also a second mortgage of five thousand dollars, which left the property so encumbered that no further supply could be raised from it.

The money thus obtained Mr. Pompilard forthwith cast upon the waters of that great financial maelstrom in Wall Street which swallows so many fortunes. This time he lost; and our story now finds him and his family established in the poorer half of a double house, wooden, and of very humble pretensions, situated in Harlem, some seven or eight miles from the heart of the great metropolis. Compared with the princely seat he once occupied on the Hudson, what a poor little den it was!

A warm, almost sultry noon in May was brooding over the unpaved street. The peach-trees showed their pink blossoms, and the pear-trees their white, in the neighboring enclosures. All that Mr. Pompilard could look out upon in his poor, narrow little area was a clothes-line and a few tufts of grass with the bald soil interspersed. Yet there in his little back parlor he sat reading the last new novel.

Suddenly he heard cries of murder in the other half of his domicil. Throwing down his book, he went out through the open window, and, stepping on a little plank walk dignified with the name of a piazza, put his legs over a low railing and passed into his neighbor's house. That neighbor was an Irish tailor of the name of Pat Maloney, a little fellow with carroty whiskers and features intensely Hibernian.

On inquiring into the cause of the outcry, Pompilard learned that Maloney was only "larruping the ould woman with a bit of a leather strap, yer honor." Mrs. Maloney excused her husband, protesting that he was the best fellow in the world, except when he had been drinking, which was the case that day; "and not a bad excuse for it there was, your honor, for a band of Irish patriots had landed that blessed morning, and Pat had only helped wilcom them dacently, which was the cause of his taking a drap too much."

With an air of deference that he might have practised towards a grand-duchess, Pompilard begged pardon for his intrusion, and passed out, leaving poor Pat and his wife stunned by the imposing vision.

No sooner had Pompilard resumed his romance, than the dulcet strains of a hand-organ under the opposite window solicited his ear. Pompilard was a patron of hand-organs; he had a theory that they encouraged a taste for music among the humbler classes. The present organ was rich-toned, and was giving forth the then popular and always charming melody of "Love Not." Pompilard grew sentimental, and put his hand in his pocket for a quarter of a dollar; but no quarter responded to the touch of his fingers. He called his wife.

Enter a small middle-aged lady, dressed in white muslin over a blue under-robe, with ribbons streaming in all directions. She was followed by Antoinette, or Netty, as she was generally called, a little elfish-looking maiden, six or seven years old, with her hands thrust jauntily into the pockets of her apron, and her bright beady eyes glancing about as if in search of mischief.

"Lend me a quarter, my dear, for the organ-man," said Pompilard.

"Ah! there you have me at a disadvantage, husband," said the lady. "Do you know I don't believe ten cents could be raised in the whole house?"

And the lady laughed, as if she regarded the circumstance as an excellent joke. The child, taking her cue from the mother, screamed with delight. Then, imitating the sound of a bumble-bee, she made her father start up, afraid he was going to be stung. This put the climax to her merriment, and she threw herself on the sofa in a paroxysm.

"What a little devil it is!" exclaimed Pompilard, proudly smiling on his offspring. "Is it possible that no one in the house has so much as a quarter of a dollar? Where are the girls? Girls!"

His call brought down from up-stairs his two eldest, children of his first wife, — one, Angelica Ireton, a widow, whose perplexity was how to prevent herself from becoming fat, for she was already fair and forty; the other, Melissa (by Netty nicknamed Molasses), a sentimentalist of twenty-five, affianced, since her father's last financial downfall, to Mr. Cecil Purling, a gentleman five years her senior, who labored under the delusion that he was born to be an author, and who kept on ruining publishers by writing the most ingeniously unsalable books. Angelica had a son with the army in Mexico, and two little girls, Julia and Mary, older than Netty, but over whom she exercised absolute authority by keeping them constantly informed that she was their aunt.

Angelica was found to have in her purse the sum required for the organ-man. Pompilard took it, and started for the door, when a prolonged feline cry made him suppose he had trodden on the kitten. "Poor Puss!" he exclaimed; "where the deuce are you?" He looked under the sofa, and an outburst of impish laughter told him he had been tricked a second time by his little girl.

"That child will be kidnapped yet by the circus people," said Pompilard, complacently. "Where did she learn all these accomplishments?"

"Of the children in the next house, I believe," said Mrs. Pompilard; "or else of the sailors on the river, for she is constantly at the water-side watching the vessels, and trying to make pictures of them."

Pompilard went to the door, paid the organ-grinder, and re-entered the room with an "Extra" which the grateful itinerant had presented to him.

"What have we here?" said Pompilard; and he read from

the paper the announcement of a terrible steamboat accident, which had occurred on the night of the Wednesday previous, on the Mississippi.

"This is very surprising, — very surprising indeed," he exclaimed. "My dear, it appears from — "

The noise of a dog yelping, as if his leg had been suddenly broken by a stone, here interrupted him. He rushed to the window. No dog was there.

"Will that little goblin never be out of mischief? Take her away, Molasses," said the secretly delighted father. Then, resuming his seat, he continued: "It appears from this account, wife, that among the passengers killed by this great steamboat explosion were your niece Leonora Berwick, her husband, and child. Did she have more than one child?"

"Not that I know of," said Mrs. Pompilard. "Is poor Leonora blown up? That is very hard indeed. But I never set eyes on her, — though I have her photograph, — and I shall not pretend to grieve for one I never saw. My poor brother could never get over our elopement, you wicked Albert."

"Your poor brother thought I was cheating you, when I said I loved you to distraction. Now put your hand on your heart, Mrs. Pompilard, and say, if you can, that I have n't proved every day of my life that I fell short of the truth in my professions."

"I sha'n't complain," replied the lady, smiling; "but we were shockingly imprudent, both of us; and I tell Netty I shall disown her if she ever elopes."

"Of course Netty must n't take our example as a precedent."

Buoyed up on her husband's ever-sanguine and cheerful temperament, Mrs. Pompilard had looked upon their fluctuations from wealth to poverty as so many piquant variations in their way of life. This moving into a little mean house in Harlem, — what was it, after all, but playing poor? It would be only temporary, and was a very good joke while it lasted. Albert would soon have his palace on the Fifth Avenue once more. There was no doubt of it.

And so Mrs. Pompilard made the best of the present moment. Her step-daughters (she was the junior of one of them) used to treat her as they might a spoiled child, taking her in their laps, and petting her, and often rocking her to sleep.

The news Pompilard had been reading suggested to him a not improbable contingency, but he exhibited the calmness of the experienced gambler in considering it.

"My dear," said he, "if this news is true, it is not out of the range of possibilities that the extinction of this Berwick family may leave you the inheritrix of a million of dollars."

"That would be quite delightful," exclaimed Mrs. Pompilard; "for then that poor pining Purling could marry Melissa at once. Not that I wish my niece and her husband any harm. O no!"

"Yes, it would n't be an ill wind for Purling and Melissa, that 's a fact," said Pompilard. "The chances stand thus: If the mother died the last of the three, the property comes to you as her nearest heir. If the child died last, at least half, and perhaps all the property, must come to you. If the child died first (which is most probable), and then the father and the mother, or the mother and the father, still the property comes to you. If the father died first, then the child, and then the mother, the property comes to you. But if the mother died first, then the child, and then the father, the money all goes to Mrs. Charlton, by virtue of her kinship as aunt and nearest relative to Mr. Berwick. So you see the chances are largely in your favor. If the report is true that the family are all lost, I would bet fifteen thousand to five that you inherit the property. I shall go to the city to-morrow, and perhaps by that time we shall have further particulars."

Pompilard then plunged anew into his novel, and the wife returned to her task of trimming a bonnet, intended as a wedding present to a girl who had once been in her service, and who was now to occupy one of the houses opposite.

The next day, Pompilard, fresh, juvenile, and debonair, descended from the Harlem cars at Chambers Street, and strolled down Broadway, swinging his cane, and humming the Druidical chorus from Norma. Encountering Charlton walking in the same direction, he joined him with a "Good morning." Charlton turned, and, seeing Pompilard jubilant, drew from the spectacle an augury unfavorable to his own prospects. "Has the old fellow had private advices?" thought he.

Pompilard spoke of the opera, of Maretzek, the Dusseldorf gallery, and the Rochester rappings. At length Charlton interposed with an allusion to the great steamboat disaster. Pompilard seemed to dodge the subject; and this drove Charlton to the direct interrogatory, "Have you had any information in addition to what the newspapers give?"

"O nothing, — that is, nothing of consequence," said Pompilard. "Did you hear Grisi last night?"

"It appears," resumed Charlton, "that your wife's niece, Mrs. Berwick, was killed outright, that the child was subsequently drowned, and that Mr. Berwick survived till the next day at noon."

"Nothing more likely!" replied Pompilard, who had not yet seen the morning papers.

"Do you know any of the survivors?" asked Charlton.

"I have n't examined the list yet," said Pompilard.

And they parted at the head of Fulton Street.

Charlton built his hopes largely on the fact that Colonel Delancy Hyde was among the survivors. If, fortunately, the Colonel's memory should serve him the right way, he might turn out a very useful witness. At any rate, he (Charlton) would communicate with him by letter forthwith.

In one of the reports in the Memphis Avalanche, telegraphed to the morning papers, was the following extract: —

"Judge Onslow, late of Mississippi, and his son saved themselves by swimming. Among the bodies they identified was that of Mrs. Berwick of New York, wounded in the head. From the nature of the wound, her death must have been instantaneous. Her husband was badly scalded, and, on recognizing the body of his wife, and learning that his child was among the drowned, he became deeply agitated. He lingered till the next day at noon. The child had been in the keeping of a mulatto nurse. Mr. Burgess of St. Louis, who was saved, saw them both go overboard. It appears, however, that the nurse, with her charge in her arms, was seen holding on to a life-preserving stool; but they were both drowned, though every effort was made by Colonel Hyde, aided by Mr. Quattles of South Carolina, to save them.

"We regret to learn that Colonel Hyde is a large loser in slaves. One of these, a valuable negro, named Peek, is probably drowned, as he was handcuffed to prevent his escape. The other slaves may have perished, or may have made tracks for the underground railroad to Canada. The report that Mr. Vance of New Orleans was lost proves to be untrue. The night was dark, though not cloudy. The river is very deep, and the current rapid at the place of the explosion (a few miles above Helena), and it is feared that many persons have been drowned whose bodies it will be impossible to recover."

Pompilard read this account, and felt a million of dollars slipping away from his grasp. But not a muscle of his face betrayed emotion. Impenetrable fatalist, he still had faith in the culmination of his star.

"We must wait for further particulars," thought Pompilard; "there is hope still"; and, stopping at a stall to buy the new novel of "Monte Cristo" by Dumas, he made his way to the cars, and returned to Harlem.

Weeks glided by. Mrs. Charlton passed away on the day she had predicted, and Toussaint, after seeing her remains deposited at Greenwood, gave away in charity the thousand dollars which she had extorted for him from her husband.

Melissa Pompilard began to fear that the marriage-day would never come round. Cecil Purling, her betrothed, had made a descent on a young publisher, just starting in business, and had induced him to put forth a volume of "playful" essays, entitled "Skimmings and Skippings." The result was financial ruin to the publisher, and his rapid retreat back to the clerkship from which he had emerged.

But Purling was indomitable. He began forthwith to plan another publication, and to look round for another victim; comforting Melissa with the assurance that, though the critics were now in a league to keep him in obscurity, he should make his mark some day, when all his past works would turn out the most profitable investments he could possibly have found.

To whom should the Aylesford-Berwick property descend? That was now a question of moment, both in legal and financial circles. Pompilard read novels, made love to his wife, and romped with his daughters and grandchildren. Charlton groaned and grew thin under the horrible state of suspense in which the lawyers kept him.

CHAPTER XVI.

THE VENDUE.

"A queen on a scaffold is not so pitiful a sight as a woman on the auction-block." — *Charles Sumner.*

"Slavery gratifies at once the love of power, the love of money, and the love of ease; it finds a victim for anger who cannot smite back his oppressor, and it offers to all, without measure, the seductive privileges which the Mormon gospel reserves for the true believers on earth, and the Bible of Mahomet only dares promise to the saints in heaven." — *O. W. Holmes.*

ABOUT a month after the explosion of the Pontiac, a select company were assembled, one beautiful morning in June, under a stately palmetto-tree in front of the auction store of Messrs. Ripper & Co. in New Orleans, and on the shady side of the street. There was to be a sale of prime slaves that day. A chair with a table before it, flanked on either side by a bale of cotton, afforded accommodations for the ceremony. Mr. Ripper, the auctioneer, was a young man, rather handsome, and well dressed, but with that flushed complexion and telltale expression of the eyes which a habit of dissipation generally imparts to its victims.

The company numbered some fifty. They were lounging about in groups, and were nearly all of them smoking cigars. Some were attired in thin grass-cloth coats and pantaloons, some in the perpetual black broadcloth to which Americans adhere so pertinaciously, even when the thermometer is at ninety. There was but one woman present; and she was a strong-minded widow, a Mrs. Barkdale, who by the death of her husband had come into the possession of a plantation, and now, instead of sending her overseer, had come herself, to bid off a likely field-hand.

The negroes to be sold, about a dozen in number, were in the warehouse. Mr. Ripper paced the sidewalk, looking now and then impatiently at his watch. The sale was to begin at ten. Suddenly a tall, angular, ill-formed man, dressed in a light homespun suit, came up to Ripper and drew him aside to where a young man, dressed in black and wearing a white neckcloth, stood bracing his back up against a tree. His swarthy complexion, dark eyes, and long nose made it doubtful whether the Caucasian, the Jewish, or the African blood predominated in his veins. A general languor and unsteadiness of body showed that he had been indulging in the "ardent."

To this individual the tall man led up the auctioneer, and said: "The Reverend Quattles, Mr. Ripper; Mr. Ripper, the Reverend Quattles. Gemmlemen, yer both know *me*. I'm Delancy Hyde, — Virginia-born, be Gawd. ('Scuze me, Reverend sir.) None of your Puritan scum! My ahnces'tor, Delancy Hyde, kum over with Pocahontas and John Smith; my gra'fther owned more niggers nor 'ary other man in the county; my father was cheated and broke up by a damned Yankee judge, sir; that's why the family acres ain't mine."

"I've but five minutes more," interposed Mr. Ripper, impatiently.

"Wall, sir," continued the Colonel, "this gemmleman, as I war tellin' yer, is the Reverend Quattles of Alabamy."

The Reverend Quattles bowed, and, with fishy eyes and a maudlin smile, put his hand on his heart.

"The little nig I've brung yer ter sell, Mr. Ripper, b'longs ter the Reverend Quattles's brother, a high-tone gemmleman, who lives in Mobile, but has been unfortnit in business, and has had ter sell off his niggers. An' as I was goin' ter Noo Orleenz, he puts this little colored gal in my hands ter sell. The Reverend Quattles wanted ter buy her, but was too poor. He then said he'd go with me ter see she mowt fall inter the right hahnds. In puttin' her up, yer must say 't was a great 'fliction, and all that, ter part with her; that the Reverend Quattles, ruther nor see her fall inter the wrong hands, would sell his library, and so on; that she's the child of a quadroon as has been in the family all her life, and as is a sort of half-sister of the Reverend Quattles."

"O yes! I understand all that game," said Ripper, knocking with his little finger the ashes from his cigar.

The Colonel, in an *aside* to the auctioneer, now remarked: "The Reverend Quattles, in tryin' to stiddy his narves for the scene, has tuk too stiff a horn, yer see."

"Yes; take him where he can sleep it off. It's time for the sale to begin. Remember your lot is Number 12, and will be struck off last."

The auctioneer then made his way across the street, jumped on one of the cotton-bales, and thence into the chair placed near the table.

"Come, Quattles," said Hyde, "we've time for another horn afore we're wanted."

"No yer don't, Kunnle!" exclaimed Quattles, throwing off that worthy's arm from his shoulder. "I tell yer this is too cussed mean a business for any white man; I tell yer I won't give inter it."

"Hush! Don't bawl so," pleaded the Colonel.

"I *will* bawl. Yer think yer've got me so drunk I hain't no conscience left. But I tell yer, I woan't give in. I tell yer, I'll 'xpose the hull trick!"

"Hush! hush!" said the Colonel, patting him as he might a restive beast. "Arter the sale's over, we'll have a fust-rate dinner all by ou'selves at the St. Charles. Terrapin soup and pompinoe! Champagne and juleps! Ice-cream and jelly! A reg'lar blow-out! Think of that, Quattles! Think of that!"

"Cuss the vittles! O, I'm a poor, mis'able, used-up, good-for-northin' creetur, wuss nor a nigger! — yes, wuss nor a nigger!" said Quattles, bursting into maudlin sobs and weeping. The Colonel walked him away into a contiguous drinking-saloon.

"Brandy-smashes for two," said the Colonel.

The decoctions were brewed, and the tumblers slid along the marble counter, with the despatch of a man who takes pride in his vocation. They were as quickly emptied. Quattles gulped down his liquor eagerly. The Colonel then hired a room containing a sofa, and, seeing his companion safely bestowed there, made his own way back to the auction.

On one of the cotton-bales stood a prime article called a negro-wench. This was Lot Number 3. She was clad in an old faded and filthy calico dress that had apparently been made for a girl half her size. A small bundle containing the rest of her wardrobe lay at her feet. Her bare arms, neck, and breasts were conspicuously displayed, and her knees were hardly covered by the stinted skirt. Without shame she stood there, as if used to the scene, and rather flattered by the glib commendations of the auctioneer.

"Look at her, gentlemen!" said he. "All her pints good. Fust-rate stock to breed from. Only twenty-three years old, and has had five children already. And thar 's no reason why she should n't have a dozen more. I 'm only bid eight hunderd dollars for this most valubble brood-wench. Only eight hunderd dollars for this superior article. Thank you, sir; you 've an eye for good pints. I 'm offered eight hunderd and twenty-five. Only eight hunderd and twenty-five for this most useful hand. Jest look at her, sir. Limbs straight; teeth all sound; wool thick, though she has had five children. All livin', too; ain't they, Portia?"

"Yes, massa, all sole ter Massa Wade down thar in Texas. He 'm gwoin' ter raise de hull lot."

"You hear, gentlemen. Thar 's nothin' vicious about her. Makes no fuss because her young ones are carried off. Knows they 'll be taken good care of. A good, reasonable, pleasant-tempered wench as ever lived. And now I 'm offered only eight hunderd and — Did I hear fifty? Thank you, sir. Eight hunderd and fifty dollars is bid. Is thar nary a man har that knows the valoo of a prime article like this? Eight hunderd and fifty dollars. Goin' for eight hunderd and fifty! Goin'! Gone! For eight hunderd and fifty dollars. Gentlemen, you must be calculating on the opening of the slave-trade, if you 'll stand by and see niggers sacrificed in this way. Pass up the next lot."

The next "lot" was a man, a sulky, discontented-looking creature, but large, erect, and with shoulders that would have made his fortune as a hotel-porter. Laying down his bundle, he mounted the cotton-bale with a weary, desponding air, as if he had begun to think there was no good in reserve for him, either on the earth or in the heavens.

"Lot Number 4 is Ike," said the auctioneer. "A fust-rate field-hand. Will hoe more cotton in three hours than a common nigger will in ten. Ike is pious, and has been a famous exhorter among the niggers; belongs to the Baptist church. You all know, gentlemen, the advantage of piety in a nigger.

Ike's piety ought to add thirty per cent to his wuth. I 'm offered nine hunderd dollars for Ike. Nine hunderd dollars!"

Here a squinting, hatchet-faced fellow in a broad-brimmed straw hat, who had been making quite a puddle of tobacco-juice on the ground, leaped upon the bale, and lifted the slave's faded baize shirt so as to get a look at his back. Then, putting his finger on the side of his nose, the examiner winked at Ripper, and jumped down.

"Scored?" asked an anxious inquirer.

"Scored? Wall, stranger, he 's been scored, then put under a harrer, then paddled an' burnt. A hard ticket that."

The nine hundred dollar bid was as yet in the imagination of the auctioneer. But, with the quick penetration of his craft, he saw the strong-minded widow standing on tiptoe, her face eager with the excitement of bidding, and her words only checked by the desire to judge from the amount of competition whether the article were a desirable one.

"A thousand and ten! Thank you, sir, thank you!" said Ripper, bowing to a gentleman he had seen only in his mind's eye. Nobody could dispute the bid, all eyes being directed toward the auctioneer.

"A thousand and twenty-five," continued Ripper, turning in an opposite direction, and bowing to an equally imaginary bidder. Then, apparently catching the eye of the competing customer, "A thousand and forty!" he exclaimed; and so, see-sawing from one chimerical gentleman to the other, he carried the sham bidding up to a thousand and seventy-five.

At this point Mrs. Barkdale, pale, and following with swayings of her own body the motions of the auctioneer, her heart in her mouth almost depriving her of speech, waved her hand to attract his attention, and, rising on tiptoe, gasped forth, "A thousand and eighty!"

"Thank you, madam," said Ripper, politely touching his hat. Then, apparently catching the eye of his imaginary bidder on the right, "Monsieur Dupré," he said, "you won't allow such a bargain to slip through your hands, will you? *Voyez! Où trouverez-vous un mieux?* Thank you, sir; thank you! A thousand and ninety, — I 'm offered a thousand and ninety for this superior field-hand. Goin', — goin'. Thank you, madam.

Eleven hunderd dollars; only eleven hunderd dollars for this most valubble piece of property. I assure you, gentlemen, 't is not often you 've such a chance. Goin' for eleven hunderd dollars! Are you all done? Eleven hunderd dollars. Goin'! Gone! You were too late, sir. To Mrs. Barkdale for eleven hunderd dollars."

The widow, almost ready to faint, made her way to her carriage, and was driven off. Some of the company shrugged their shoulders, while others uttered a low, significant whistle. Ike, who maintained his dogged, sulky look, picked up his bundle, and was remanded to the warehouse, there to be kept till claimed.

"Now, gentlemen," said the auctioneer, "I have to call your attention to the primest fancy article that it has ever been my good fortin to put under the hammer. Lot Number 5 is the quadroon gal, Nelly. Bring her on."

Here a negro assistant led out, with his hand on her shoulder, a girl apparently not more than eighteen years of age, and helped her on the cotton-bale. She was modestly clad in an old but neatly-fitting black silk gown, and, notwithstanding the heat, wore round her shoulders a checked woollen shawl. Her hair was straight. Evidently she derived her blood chiefly from white ancestors. She was very pretty; and had a neat, compact figure, in which the tendency to plumpness, common among the quadroons, was not yet too marked for grace.

It was apparently the first time she had ever been put up for sale; for she had a scared, deprecatory look, strangely accompanied with a smile put on for the purpose of propitiating some well-disposed master, if such there might be among the crowd.

"Now, gentlemen," said Ripper, "here is Lot Number 5. It speaks for itself, and needs no puffin' from me. But thar is a little story connected with Nelly. She was the property of Miss Pettigrew, down in Plaquemine, and always thought she 'd be free as soon as her missis died. But her missis fell under conviction jest afore her death, and ordered in her will that Nelly should be sold, and the proceeds paid over to the fund for the support of indigent young men studyin' for the ministry. So, gentlemen, in biddin' lib'rally for this superior lot, you 'll have the satisfaction of forruding a most-er praiseworthy and pious objek."

"Make her drop her shawl," said a gray-haired man, with a blotched, unwholesome skin, and with dirty deposits of stale tobacco-juice at the corners of his mouth.

"Certainly, Mr. Tibbs," said Ripper, pulling off the girl's shawl as if he had been uncovering a sample of Sea-Island cotton.

"She has been a lady's maid, and nothin' else, I can assure you, gentlemen. Small hands and feet, yer see. Look at that neck and them shoulders! Her missis has kept her very strict; and the executor, by whose order she is sold, warrants you, gentlemen, she has never been *enceinte.* A very nice, good-natured, correct, and capable gal. Will never give her owner any trouble, and will ollerz do her best to please. Shall I start her at a thousand dollars?"

Here Mr. Tibbs and two other men jumped on the bale, and began to give a closer examination to the article. One pinched the flesh of its smooth and well-rounded shoulders. Another stretched its lips apart so as to get a sight of its teeth. Mr. Tibbs pulled at the bosom of its dress in order to draw certain physiological conclusions as to the truth of the auctioneer's warranty.

"Please don't," expostulated the girl, putting away his hand, and with her scared look trying hard to smile, but showing in the act a set of teeth that at once added twenty per cent to her value in the estimation of the beholder.

"You see her, gentlemen," said Ripper. "She 's just what she appears to be. No sham about her. No paddin'. All wholesome flesh and blood. What shall I have for Nelly?"

"A thousand dollars," said Tibbs.

"You hear the bid, gentlemen. I 'm offered a thousand dollars for this *very* superior article. Only a thousand dollars."

"Eleven hundred," said Jarvey, the well-known keeper of a gambling-saloon.

Tibbs glanced angrily at the audacious competitor, then nodded to the auctioneer.

"Eleven hundred and fifty is what I 'm offered for Lot Number 5. Gentlemen, bar in mind that you air servin' a pious cause in helpin' me to git the full valoo of this most-er excellent article. Remember the proceeds go to edicate indigent young men for the ministry. Mr. Jarvey, can't you do su'thin' for the church?"

"Twelve hundred," said Jarvey.

"Twelve fifty," exclaimed Tibbs, abruptly, in a tone sharp with exasperation and malevolence.

Nelly, seeing that the bidding was confined to these two, looked from the one to the other with an expression of deepest solicitude, as if scanning their countenances for some way of hope. Alas! there was not much to choose. To Jarvey, as the less ill-favored, she evidently inclined; but Tibbs had plainly made up his mind to "go his pile" on the purchase, and the article was finally knocked down to him for fifteen hundred dollars.

"You owt to be proud to bring sich a price as that, my gal," said Ripper, in a tone of congratulation. Nelly made a piteous, frightened attempt at a smile, then burst into tears, and got down from the bale, stumbling in her confusion so as to fall on her hands to the ground, much to the amusement of the spectators.

The lots from six to eleven inclusive did not excite much competition. They were mostly field-hands, coarse and stolid in feature, and showing a cerebral development of the most rudimental kind. They brought prices ranging from seven hundred to nine hundred dollars.

"Now, gentlemen," said Ripper, "I have one little fancy article to offer you, and then the sale will be closed. Bring on Number 12."

The colored assistant here issued from the warehouse and crossed the street, bearing a little quadroon girl and her bundle in his arms. Simultaneously a new and elegant barouche, drawn by two sleek horses, and having two blacks in livery on the driver's box, stopped in the rear of the crowd. The occupant got out, and strolled toward the stand. He was a middle-aged man, with well-formed features, a smooth, florid complexion, and a figure inclining to portliness. Apparently a gentleman, were it not for that imperious, aggressive air, which the habit of domineering from infancy over slaves generally imparts. He carried a riding-whip, with which he carelessly switched his legs.

As he drew near the stand, the auctioneer's assistant placed on the cotton-bale the little quadroon girl. She was almost an infant, evidently not three years old, with very black hair and eyebrows, though her eyes did not harmonize with the hue. She was naked even to her feet, with the exception of a little chemise that did not reach to her thighs. Her figure promised grace and health for the future. In the shape of her features there was no sign of the African intermixture indicated in the hue of her skin. With a wondering, anxious look she regarded the scene before her, and was making an obvious effort to keep from crying.

"Now here is Number 12, gentlemen," said Ripper. "Jest look at the little lady! Thar she is. Fust-rate stock. Look at her hands and feet. Belonged to the Quattles family of Mobile, and I'm charged by the Rev. Mr. Quattles to knock her down to himself (though he can't afford to buy her), rather than have her go into the wrong hands. She's the child of his half-sister, yer see, gentlemen. What am I offered for this little lady?"

"A hundred dollars," said a voice from the crowd.

"I'm offered two hunderd dollars for this little tidbit," said Ripper, pretending to have misunderstood the bid.

Colonel Delancy Hyde stepped forward, and, taking a position at the side of the auctioneer, addressed the crowd: "I know the Quattles family, gentlemen. It's an unfort'nit family, and they'd never have put this yere child under the hammer if so be they had n't been forced right up ter it by starn necessity."

"Who the hell are you?" asked a tall, lank, defiant-looking gentleman, who seemed to be disgusted at the Colonel's interference.

"Who am I? I'll tell yer who am I," cried the latter. "I'm Colonel Delancy Hyde. Anything to say agin that? Virginia-born, be Gawd! My father was Virginia-born afore me, and his father afore him, and they owned more niggers nor you ever looked at. Anything to say agin that, yer despisable corn-cracker, yer!"

"Hold yer tongue, Colonel; you're drivin' off a bidder," whispered Ripper. The Colonel collapsed at once, quelling his indignation.

"I 'm offered two hunderd dollars for Number 12," exclaimed the auctioneer, putting his hand on the little girl's head. "If there 's any good judge here of figger an' face, he won't see this article sacrificed for such a trifle."

"Two twenty-five," said Tibbs.

The gentleman who had descended from the barouche here drew nearer, and examined the form and features of the little girl with a closer scrutiny.

"Two fifty," said he, as the result of his inspection.

Tibbs, irritated by the competition, made his bid three hundred.

"Four hundred!" said the man with the riding-whip.

"Five hundred!" retorted Tibbs, ejecting the words with a vicious snort.

"Six hundred," returned his competitor, with perfect nonchalance.

"Seven hundred and fifty," shrieked Tibbs.

"A thousand," said the other, playing with his whip.

Tibbs did not venture further. Mortified and angry, he turned away, and consoled himself with an enormous cut of tobacco.

"Cash takes it," said the successful bidder, putting his finger to his lips by way of caution to the auctioneer, and then beckoning him to come down. Ripper exchanged a few words with him in a whisper, and told his assistant to put the little girl with her bundle into the barouche, and throw a carriage-shawl over her.

As the barouche drove off, Hyde asked, "Who is he?"

"Cash," replied Ripper. "Did n't you hear? I reckon you see more of overseers than of planters. You 've done amazin' well, Colonel, gittin' such a price fur that little concern."

"Yes," said Hyde; "Mr. Cash is a high-tone one, that 's a fak. I should know him agin 'mong a thousand."

The company dispersed, the auctioneer settled with his customers, and Hyde went to find Quattles, and give him the jackal's share of the spoils.

Let us follow the barouche. Leaving the business streets, it rolled on till, in about a quarter of an hour, it stopped before a respectable brick house, on the door of which was the sign, "Mrs. Gentry's Seminary for Young Ladies." Here the gentleman got out and rang the bell.

"Is Mrs. Gentry at home?"

"Yes, sir. Walk in. I will take your card."

He was ushered into a parlor. In five minutes the lady appeared, — a tall, erect person with prominent features, a sallow complexion, and dry puffs of iron-gray hair parted over her forehead. A Southern judge's daughter and a widow, Mrs. Gentry kept one of the best private schools in the city. On seeing the name of Carberry Ratcliff on the card, which Tarquin, the colored servant, had handed to her, she went with alacrity to her mirror, and, after a little pranking, descended to greet her distinguished visitor.

"Perhaps you have heard of me before," began Mr. Ratcliff.

"Often, sir. Be seated," said the lady, charmed at the idea of having a visit from the lord of a thousand slaves.

"I have in my barouche, madam, a little girl I wish to leave with you. She is my property, and I want her well taken care of. Can you receive her?"

Mrs. Gentry looked significantly at the gentleman, and he, as if anticipating her interrogatory, replied: "The child came into my possession only within this hour. I bought her quite accidentally at auction. She has none of my blood in her veins, I assure you."

"Can I see her?"

"Yes"; and, walking to the window, Ratcliff motioned to one of his negroes to bring the child in. This was done; and the infant was placed on the floor with her little bundle by her side, and nude as she was when exposed on the auction-block.

"A quadroon, I should think," said Mrs. Gentry.

"I really don't know what she is," replied Ratcliff. "I want you, however, to take her into your family, and raise her as carefully as if you knew her to be my daughter. You shall be liberally paid for your trouble."

"Is she to know that she is a slave?"

"As to that I can instruct you hereafter. Meanwhile keep the fact a secret, and mention my name to no one in connection with her. You can occasionally send me a daguerrotype, that I may see if her looks fulfil her promise. I wish you to be particular about her music and French, also her dancing. Let her understand all about dress too. You can draw upon me as often as you choose for the amount we fix upon; and the probability is, I shall not wish to see her till she reaches her fifteenth or sixteenth year. I rely upon you to keep her strictly, and, as she grows older, to guard her against making acquaintances with any of the other sex. Will seven hundred dollars a year pay you for your trouble?"

"Amply, sir," said the gratified lady. "I will do my best to carry out your wishes."

"You need not write me oftener than once a year," said Ratcliff.

"Not if she were dangerously ill?"

"No; not even then. You could take better care of her than I; and all my interest in her is *in futuro*."

"I think I understand, sir," said Mrs. Gentry; "and I will at once make a note of what you say."

"Here is payment for the first half-year in advance," said Ratcliff.

"Thank you, sir," returned the lady, quite overwhelmed at the great planter's munificence. "Shall I write you a receipt?"

"It is superfluous, madam."

All this while the child, with a seriousness strangely at variance with her infantile appearance, sat on the floor, looking intently first at the woman, then at the man, and evidently striving to understand what they were saying. Ratcliff now took his leave; but Mrs. Gentry called him back before he had reached the door.

"Excuse me, sir, there is something I wished to ask you? What was it? Oh! By what name shall we call the child?"

"Upon my word," said Ratcliff, "I have forgotten the name the auctioneer gave her. No matter! Call her anything you please."

"Well, then, Estelle is a pretty name. Shall I call her Estelle?"

Ratcliff started, came close up to Mrs. Gentry, looked her steadily in the face, and asked, "What put that name into your head?"

"I don't know. Probably I have seen it in some novel."

"Well, don't call her Estelle. Call her Ellen Murray."

"I will remember."

And the interview closed.

After the gentleman had gone, the child, with an anxious and grieved expression of face, tried to articulate an inquiry which Mrs. Gentry found it difficult to understand. At last she concluded it was an attempt to say, "Where 's Hatty?"

Mrs. Gentry rang the bell, and it was answered by a colored woman of large, stately figure, whose peculiar hue and straight black hair showed that she was descended from some tribe distinct from ordinary Africans.

"Where 's the chambermaid?" asked Mrs. Gentry.

"O missis, dat Deely 's neber on de spot when she 's wanted. De Lord lub us, what hab we here?"

"A new inmate of the family, Esha. I 've taken her to bring up."

"Some rich man's lub-child, I reckon, missis. But ain't she a little darlin'?" And Esha took her up from the floor, and kissed her. The child, feeling she had at last found a friend, threw its arms about the woman's neck, and broke into a low, plaintive sobbing, as if her little heart were overfull of long-suppressed grief.

"Thar! thar!" said Esha, soothing her; "she must n't greeb nebber no more. Ole Esha will lub her dearly!"

Mrs. Gentry opened the bundle, and was surprised to see several articles of clothing of a rich and fine texture, all neatly marked, though somewhat soiled.

"There, Esha," she said, "take the poor little thing and her bundle up-stairs, and dress her. To-morrow I 'll get her some new clothes."

Esha obeyed, and the child thenceforth clung to her as to a mother. To the servant's surprise, when she came to wash away the little one's tears, the skin parted with its tawny hue, and showed white and fair. On examining the child's hair, too, it was found to be dyed. What could be the object of this? It never occurred to Esha that the little waif might be a slave, and that a white slave was not so salable as a colored.

Mrs. Gentry communicated the phenomenon at once to Mr. Ratcliff, but he never alluded to it in any subsequent letter or conversation.

CHAPTER XVII.

SHALL THERE BE A WEDDING?

"Ah! spare your idol; think him human still;
Charms he may have, but he has frailties too!
Dote not too much, nor spoil what ye admire."
Young.

THE question as to the inheritance of the Aylesford-Berwick property was not decided without a lawsuit. The case was put into the courts, and kept there many months. The heavy legal expenses to which Charlton was subjected, and his reluctance to meet them, protracted the contest by alienating his lawyers. Pompilard went straight to the point by promising his counsel a fee of a hundred thousand dollars in the event of success; and thus he enlisted and kept active the best professional aid. Still the prospect was doubtful.

But even the *law's* delay must finally have an end. The hour of the final settlement of the great case by the ultimate court of appeal had come at last. The judges had entered and taken their seats. Charlton, pale and haggard, sat by the side of his lawyer, Detritch. Pompilard, still masking his age, entered airy as a maiden just stepping forth into Broadway in her new spring bonnet. He wore a paletot of light gray, a choker girt by a sky-blue silk ribbon, a white vest, checked pantaloons, and silk stockings under low-cut patent-leather shoes. Taking a seat at a little semicircular table near his lawyers, he exchanged repartees with them, and then tranquilly abided his fate. Charlton looked with anguish on the composure of his antagonist.

Just as the case was expected to come on, one of the judges was found to have left a certain document at home. They all retired, and a messenger was sent for the important paper. Hence a delay of an hour. Charlton could not conceal his agitation. Pompilard took up the morning journal, and read with sorrow of the death of an old friend.

"Poor old Toussaint! I see he has left us," said Pompilard.

"Yes," replied Girard, "All-Saint has gone. He was well named. He has never held up his head since he lost his wife."

"Toussaint was a gentleman, every inch of him," said Pompilard. "He believed in the elevation of the black man, not by that process of absorption or amalgamation which some of our noodles recommend, but by his showing in his life and character that a negro can be as worthy and capable of freedom as a white man. He was for keeping the blacks socially separate from the whites, though one before the law, and teaching them to be content with the color God had given them. A brave fellow was Toussaint. I remember — that was before your day — when the yellow fever prevailed here. Maiden Lane and the lower parts of the city were almost deserted. But Toussaint used to cross the barricades every day to tend on the sick and dying, and carry them food and medicine."

"Did you know him well?" asked Girard.

"Intimately, these thirty years. In his demeanor exquisitely courteous and respectful, there was never the slightest tinge of servility. You could not have known him as I did without forgetting his color and feeling honored in the companionship of a man so thoroughly generous, pious, and sincere. He would sometimes make playful allusions to his color. He seemed much amused once by my little Netty, who, when she was about three years old, said to him, after looking him steadily in the face for some time, 'Toussaint, do you live in a black house?' The other day, knowing he was quite ill, my wife called on him, and while by his bedside asked him if she should close a window, the light of which shone full in his face. 'O non, madam,' he replied, 'car alors je serai trop noir.'" *

Here Pompilard ceased, and looked up. There was a stir in the court-room. Their Honors had re-entered and taken seats. The messenger with the missing paper had returned. The presiding judge, after a long and tantalizing preamble, in the course of which Charlton was alternately elevated and depressed, at length summed up, in a few intelligible words, the final decision of the court. Charlton fainted.

Pompilard's lawyers bent down their heads, as if certain

* "O no, madam, for then I shall be too black." A Life of Toussaint, by Mrs. George Lee, was published in Boston some years since.

papers suddenly demanded their close scrutiny; but Pompilard himself was radiant. Everybody stared at him, and handsomely did he baffle everybody by his imperturbable good humor. It is not every day that one has an opportunity of seeing how a fellow-being is affected by the winning or the losing of a million of dollars. No one could have guessed from Pompilard's appearance whether he had won or lost. Unfortunately he had lost; and Charlton had reached the acme of his hopes, mortal or immortal,—he was a millionnaire.

Pompilard took the news home to his wife in the little old double house at Harlem; and her only comment was: "Poor dear Melissa! I had hoped to make her a present of a furnished cottage on the North River."

The conversation was immediately turned to the subject of Toussaint, and one would have thought, hearing these strange foolish people talk, that the old negro's exit saddened them far more than the loss of their fortune. Angelica, Pompilard's widowed daughter, entered. After her came Netty, the elf, now almost a young lady. She carried under her arm a portfolio, filled with such drawings of ships, beaches, and rocks as she could find in occasional excursions to Long Island, under the patronage of Mrs. Maloney, the tailor's wife.

Julia and Mary Ireton, daughters of Angelica, came in.

"Which of my little nieces will take my portfolio up-stairs?" asked Netty.

"I will, aunt," said the dutiful Mary; and off she ran with it.

"Poor Melissa! We shall now have to put off the wedding," sighed Angelica, on learning the result of the lawsuit.

"No such thing! It sha'n't be put off!" said Pompilard.

Netty threw her arms round the old man's neck, kissed him, and exclaimed: "Bravo, father of mine! Stick to that! It is n't half lively enough in this house. We want a few more here to make it jolly. Why can't we have such high times as they have in at the Maloneys'? There we made such a noise the other night that the police knocked at the door."

Maloney, by the way, be it recorded, had, under the pupilage of Pompilard, given up strong drink and wife-beating, and risen to be a tailor of some fashionable note. Pompilard had found out for him an excellent cutter,—had kept him posted in regard to the fashions, — and then had gone round the city to all the clubs, hotels, and opera-houses, blowing for Maloney with all his lungs. He did n't "hesitate to declare" that Maloney was the only man in the country who could fit you decently to pantaloons. Pantaloons were his *specialité*. His cutter was a born genius, — "an Englishman, sir, whose grandfather used to cut for the famous Brummel, — you 've heard of Brummel?" The results of all this persistent blowing were astonishing. Soon the superstition prevailed in Wall Street and along the Fifth Avenue, that if one wanted pantaloons he must go to Maloney. Haynes was excellent for dress-coats and sacks; but don't let him hope to compete with Maloney in pantaloons. You would hear young fops discussing the point with intensest earnestness and enthusiasm.

How many fortunes have a basis quite as airy and unsubstantial! Soon Maloney's little shop was crowded with customers. He was obliged to take a large and showy establishment in Broadway. Here prosperity insisted on following him. Wealth began to flow steadily in. He found himself on the plain, high road to fortune; and by whom but Pompilard had he been led there? The consequence was perpetual gratitude on the tailor's part, evinced in daily sending home, with his own marketing, enough for the other half of the house; evinced also in the determination to stick to Harlem till his benefactor would consent to leave.

While the Pompilards were discussing the matter of the wedding, Melissa and Purling entered from a walk. Melissa carried her years very well; though hope deferred had written anxiety on her amiable features. Purling was a slim, gentlemanly person, always affecting good spirits, though certain little silvery streaks in the side-locks over his ears showed that time and care were beginning their inevitable work. In aspiring to authorship he had not thought it essential that he should consume gin like Byron, or whiskey like Charles Lamb, or opium like De Quincey. But if there be an avenging deity presiding over the wrongs of undone publishers, Purling must be doomed to some unquiet nights. There was something sublime in the pertinacity with which he kept on writing after the public had snubbed him so repeatedly by utter neglect;

something still more sublime in the faith which led publishers to fall into the nets he so industriously wove for them.

The result of the lawsuit being made known to the new-comers, Melissa, hiding her face, at once left the room, and was followed by her sisters and step-mother.

Purling keenly felt the embarrassment of his position. Pompilard came to his relief. "We have concluded, my dear fellow," said he, "not to put off the wedding. Don't concern yourself about money-matters. You can come and occupy Melissa's room with her till I get on my legs once more. I shall go to work in earnest now this lawsuit is off my hands."

"My dear sir," said Purling, "you are very generous,— very indulgent. The moment my books begin to pay, what is mine shall be yours; and if you can conveniently accommodate me for a few months, till the work I'm now writing is —"

"Accommodate you? Of course we can! The more the merrier," interrupted Pompilard. "So it's settled. The wedding comes off next Wednesday."

And the wedding came off according to the programme. It took place in church. Pompilard was in his glory. Cards had been issued to all his friends of former days. Many had conveniently forgotten that such a person existed; but there were some noble exceptions, as there generally are in such cases. Presents of silver, of dresses, books, furniture, and pictures were sent in from friends both of the bride and bridegroom; so that the *trousseau* presented a very respectable appearance; but the prettiest gift of the occasion was a little porte-monnaie, containing a check for two thousand dollars signed by Pat Maloney.

As for Charlton, young in years, if not in heart, good-looking, a widower unencumbered with a child, what was there he might not aspire to with his twelve hundred thousand dollars?

He was taken in charge by the J——s, and the M——s, and the P——s, and introduced into "society." Yes, that is the proper name for "our set." A competition, outwardly calm, but internally bitter and intense, was entered upon by fashionable mothers having daughters to provide for. Charlton became the sensation man of the season. "Will he marry?" That was now the agitating question that convulsed all the maternal councils within a mile's radius of the new Fifth Avenue Hotel.

CHAPTER XVIII.

THE UNITIES DISREGARDED.

"Blessed are they who see, and yet believe not!
Yea, blest are they who look on graves, and still
Believe none dead; who see proud tyrants ruling,
And yet believe not in the strength of Evil."

Leopold Schefer.

THE admirers of Aristotle must bear with us while we take a little liberty: that, namely, of violating all the unities.

Fourteen years had slipped by since the great steamboat accident; fourteen years, pregnant with forces, and prolific of events, to the far-reaching influence of which no limit can be set.

In those years a mechanic named Marshall, while building a saw-mill for Captain Sutter in California, had noticed a glistening substance at the bottom of the sluice. Thence the beginning of the great exodus from the old States, which soon peopled the auriferous region, and in five years made San Francisco one of the world's great cities.

In those years the phenomena, by some called spiritual, of which our friend Peek had got an inkling, excited the attention of many thousand thinkers both in America and Europe. In France these manifestations attracted the investigation of the Emperor himself, and won many influential believers, among them Delamarre, editor of La Patrie. In England they found advocates among a small but educated class; while the Queen's consort, the good and great Prince Albert, was too far advanced on the same road to find even novelty in what Swedenborg and Wesley had long before prepared him to regard as among the irregular developments of spirit power.

"Humbug and idiocy!" cried the doctors.

"A cracking of the toe-joints!" said Conjurer Anderson.

"A scientific trick!" insisted Professor Faraday.

"Spirits are the last thing I 'll give into," said Sir David Brewster.

"O ye miserable mystics!" cried the eloquent Ferrier, "have ye bethought yourselves of the backward and downward course which ye are running into the pit of the bestial and the abhorred?"

"How very undignified for a spirit to rap on tables and talk commonplace!" objected the transcendentalists, who looked for Orphic sayings and Delphian profundities.

To all which the investigators replied: We merely take facts as we find them. The conjurers and the professors fail to account for what we see and hear. Sir David may give or refuse what name he pleases: the phenomena remain. Professor Ferrier may wax indignant; but his indignation does not explain why tables, guitars, and tumblers of water are lifted and carried about by invisible and impenetrable intelligent forces. We are sorry the manifestations do not please our transcendental friends. Could we have our own way, these spirits, forces, intelligences — call them what you will — should talk like Carlyle and deport themselves like Grandison. Could we have our own way, there should be no rattlesnakes, no copperheads, no mad dogs. 'T is a great puzzle to us why Infinite Power allows such things. We do not see the use of them, the *cui bono?* Still we accept the fact of their existence. And so we do of what, in the lack of a name less vague, we call *spirits*. There are many drunkards, imbeciles, thieves, hypocrites, and traitors, who quit this life. According to the transcendental theory, these ought to be converted at once, by some magical *presto-change!* into saints and sages, their identity wholly merged or obliterated. If the All-Wise One does not see it in that light, we cannot help it. If He can afford to wait, we shall not impatiently rave. It would seem that the Eternal chariot-wheels must continue to roll and flash on, however professors, conjurers, and quarterly reviewers may burn their poor little hands by trying to catch at the spokes.

"I did not bargain for this," grumbles the habitual novel-reader, resentfully throwing down our book.

Bear with us yet a moment longer, injured friend.

During these same fourteen years of which we have spoken,

the Slave Power of the South having, through the annexation of Texas, plunged the country into a war with Mexico for the extension of the area of slavery, met its first great rebuff in the establishment of California as a Free State of the Union.

The Fugitive-Slave Bill was given in 1850 to appease the slaveholding caste. Soon afterwards followed the repeal of that Missouri Compromise which had prohibited slavery north of a certain line. It was hoped that these two concessions would prove such a tub thrown to the whale as would divert him from mischief.

Then came the deadly struggle for supremacy in Kansas; pro-slavery ruffianism, on the one side, striving to dedicate the virgin soil to the uses of slavery; and the spirit of freedom, on the other side, resisting the profanation. The contest was long, doubtful, and bloody; but freedom, thank God! prevailed in the end. Slavery thus came to grief a second time; for the lords of the lash well knew that to circumscribe their system was to doom it, and that without ever new fields for extension it could not live and prosper.

One John Brown, of Ossawatomie in Kansas, during these years having learnt what it was to come under the ban of the Slave Power, — having been hunted, hounded, shot at, and had a son brutally murdered by the devilish hate, born of slavery, and engendering such dastardly butchers as Quantrell, — resolved to do what little service he could to God and man, by trying to wipe out an injustice that had long enough outraged heaven and earth. With less than fifty picked men he rashly seized on Harper's Ferry, held it for some days, and threw old Virginia into fits. He was seized and hung; and many good men approved the hanging; but in little more than a year afterwards, John Brown's soul was "marching on" in the song of the Northern soldiery going South to battle against rebellion, until the very Charlestown where his gallows was set up was made to ring with the terrible refrain in his honor, the echoes of which are now audible in every State, from Maine to Louisiana.

Slavery first showed its ungloved hand at the Democratic Convention at Charleston in 1860 for the nomination of President. Here it was that Stephen A. Douglas, the very man who had given to the South as a boon the repeal of the Missouri Compromise, was rejected by the Southern conspirators against the Union, and John C. Breckenridge, the potential and soon actual traitor, was put in nomination as the extreme pro-slavery candidate against Douglas. And thus the election of Abraham Lincoln, the candidate pledged against slavery extension, was secured.

This election " is not the cause of secession, but the opportunity," said Mr. Robert Barnwell Rhett of South Carolina. " Slavery shall be the corner-stone of our new Confederacy," said Mr. A. H. Stephens, Confederate Vice-President, who a few weeks before, namely, in January, 1861, had said in the Georgia Convention: " For you to attempt to overthrow such a government as this, under which we have lived for more than three quarters of a century, with unbounded prosperity and rights unassailed, is the height of madness, folly, and wickedness, to which I can neither lend my sanction nor my vote."

After raising armies for seizing Washington and for securing the Border States to slavery, Mr. Jefferson Davis, President of the improvised Confederacy, proclaimed to an amused and admiring world, " All we want is to be let alone."

Peaceful reader of the year 1875 (pardon the presumption that bids us hope such a reader will exist), bear with us for these digressions. In your better day let us hope all these terrible asperities will have passed away. But, while we write, our country's fate hangs poised. It is her great historic hour. Daily do our tears fall for the wounded or the slain. Daily do we regret that we, too, cannot give something better than words, thicker than tear-drops, to our country. But thus, through blood and anguish and purifying sufferings, is God leading us to that better future which you shall enjoy.

CHAPTER XIX.

THE WHITE SLAVE.

"Because immortal, therefore is indulged
This strange regard of deities to dust!
Hence, Heaven looks down on Earth with all her eyes;
Hence, the soul's mighty moment in her sight;
Hence, every soul has partisans above,
And every thought a critic in the skies."

Young.

"The creature is great, to whom it is allowed to imagine questions to which only a God can reply." — *Aimé Martin.*

NO one who has travelled largely through the Southern States will require to be told that the slave system sanctions the holding in slavery of persons who are undistinguishable in complexion from the whitest Anglo-Saxons. Several carefully authenticated cases, analogous to that developed in our story, though surpassing it in unspeakable baseness, have been recently brought to light. We need only hint at them at this stage of our narrative.

The reader has already divined that the little girl sold at the slave-auction, and placed under Mrs. Gentry's care, was no other than the unfortunate child whose parents were lost in the disaster of the Pontiac.

There is a class of minds which, either from inertness or lack of leisure, never revise the opinions they have received from others. If we might borrow a fresh illustration from Mrs. Gentry's copy-books, we might say that in her mental growth the tree was inclined precisely as the twig had been bent. She honestly believed that there was no appeal from what her sire, the judge, had once laid down as law or gospel. Having been bred in the belief that slavery was a wholesome and sacred institution, she would probably have seen her own sister dragged under it to the auction-block, and not have ventured to question the righteousness of the act.

There were only two passions which, should they ever come

in direct collision with her veneration for slavery, might possibly override it; but even on this there seemed to rest much uncertainty. Her acquisitiveness, as the phrenologists would have called it, was large; and then, although she was fast declining into the sere and yellow leaf, she had not surrendered all hope of one day finding a successor to the late Mr. Gentry in her affections.

Regarding poor little Clara Berwick (or Ellen Murray) as a slave, she could never be so far moved by the child's winning presence and ways as to look on her as entitled to the same atmosphere and sun as herself. No infantile grace, no solicitation of affection, could ever melt the icy barrier with which the pride and self-seeking, fostered by slavery, had encircled the heart, not naturally bad, of the schoolmistress. And yet she did her duty by the child to the best of her ability. Though not a highly educated person, Mrs. Gentry was shrewd enough to employ for her pupils the most accomplished teachers; and in respect to Clara she faithfully carried out Mr. Ratcliff's directions. True, she always exacted an obedience that was unquestioning and blind. She did not care to see that the child could have been led by a silken thread, only satisfy her reason or appeal to her affections. And so it was to Esha that Clara would always have to go for sympathy, both in her sorrows and her joys; and it was Esha whose influence was felt in the very depths of that fresh and sensitive nature.

From her third to her fourteenth year Clara gave little promise of beauty. Ratcliff, on receiving her photographs, used to throw them aside with a "Psha! After all, she 'll be fit only for a household drudge."

But as she emerged into her sixteenth year, and features and form began to develop the full meaning of their outlines, she all at once appeared in the new and startling phase of a rare model of incipient womanhood. Her hair, thick and flowing, was of a softened brown tint, which yet was distinct from that cognate hue, *abrun* (a-brown) or auburn, a shade suggestive of red. Her complexion was clear and pure, though not of that brilliant pink and white often associated with delicacy of constitution. A profile, delicately cut as if to be the despair of sculptors; a forehead not high, but high enough to show Mind enthroned there; eyes — it was not till you drew quite near that you marked the peculiarity already described in the infant of the Pontiac. The mouth and lips were small and passionate, the chin bold, yet not protrusive, the nostrils having that indescribable curve which often makes this feature surpass all the others in giving a character of decision to a face. A man of the turf would have summed up his whole description of the girl in the one word "blood."

Such a union of the sensuous nature with pure will and intellect might well have made a watchful parent tremble for her future.

Ratcliff had been for more than a year in South Carolina, helping to fire the Southern heart, and forward the secession movement. Early in January, 1861, he made a flying visit to New Orleans, and called on Mrs. Gentry.

After some conversation on public affairs, the lady asked, "Would you like to see my pupil?"

"Not if she resembles the photographs you 've sent me," replied Ratcliff. Then, looking at his watch, he added: "I leave for Charleston this afternoon, and have n't time to see her now. Early in March I shall be back, and will call then."

"You must see her a minute," said Mrs. Gentry. "I think you 'll admit she does no discredit to my bringing up." And she rang the bell.

"Tell Miss Murray, I desire her presence in the parlor."

Clara entered. She was attired in a plain robe of slate-colored muslin, exquisitely fitted, and had a book in her hand, as if just interrupted in study. She stood inquiringly before the schoolmistress, and seemed unconscious of another's presence.

"I wish you, Miss Murray, to play for this gentleman. Play the piece you last learnt."

Without the slightest shyness, Clara obeyed, seating herself at the piano, and performing Schubert's delectable "Lob der Throenen," (Eulogy of Tears,) with Liszt's arrangement. This she did with an executive facility and precision of touch that would have charmed a competent judge, which Ratcliff was not.

And yet astonishment made him speechless. He had expected an undeveloped, awkward, homely girl. Lo a beautiful young woman whose perfect composure and grace were such as few queens of society could exhibit! And all that youth and loveliness were his!

He looked at his watch. Not another moment could he remain. He drew near to Clara and took her hand, which she quickly withdrew. "Only maiden coyness," thought he, and said: "We must be better acquainted. But I must now hasten from your dangerous society, or I shall miss the steamer. Good by, my dear. Good by, Mrs. Gentry. You shall hear from me very soon."

And Mrs. Gentry rang the bell, and black Tarquin opened the door for Ratcliff. As it closed upon him, "Who is that old man?" asked Clara.

"Old? Why, he does n't look a year over forty," replied Mrs. Gentry. "That 's the rich Mr. Ratcliff."

"Well, I detest him," said Clara, emphatically.

"Detest!" exclaimed Mrs. Gentry, horror-stricken; for it was not often that Clara condescended to speak her mind so freely to that lady. "Detest? Is this the end of all my moral and religious teachings? O, but you 'll be *come up with*, if you go on in this way. Retire to your room, Miss."

Swiftly and gladly Clara obeyed.

Apropos of the aforesaid teachings, Ratcliff was very willing that his predestined victim should be piously inclined. It would rather add to the piquancy of her degradation. He wavered somewhat as to whether she should be a Protestant or a Catholic, but finally left the whole matter to Mrs. Gentry. That profound theologian had done her best to lead Clara into her own select fold, and, as she thought, had succeeded; but Clara was pretty sure to take up opinions the reverse of those held by her teacher. So, after sitting in weariness of spirit under the ministry of the Rev. Dr. Palmer in the morning, the perverse young lady would ventilate her religious conceptions by reading Fenelon, Madame Guyon, or Zschokke in the evening.

Mrs. Gentry believed in secession, and raved like a Pythoness against the cowardly Yankees. Clara, seeing a United States flag trampled on and torn in the street, secured a rag of it, secretly washed it, and placed it as a holy symbol on her bosom. Mrs. Gentry expatiated to her pupils on the righteousness and venerableness of slavery. Clara cut out from a pictorial paper a poor little dingy picture of Fremont, and concealed it between two leaves of her Bible, underlining on one of them these words: "Proclaim liberty throughout all the land unto all the inhabitants thereof."

Esha, the colored cook, a slave, was Clara's fast friend in all her youthful troubles. Esha had passed through all degrees of slavery,—from toiling in a cotton-field to serving as a lady's maid. Having had a child, a little girl, taken from her and sold, she ever afterwards refused to be again a mother. The straight hair, coppery hue, and somewhat Caucasian cast of features of this slave showed that she belonged to a race different from that of the ordinary negro. She had been named Ayesha, after one of Mahomet's wives. She generally wore a Madras handkerchief about her head, and showed a partiality for brilliant colors. Many were the stealthy interviews that she and Clara enjoyed together.

Said Esha, on one of these occasions: "Don't b'leeb 'em, darlin', whan dey say de slabe am berry happy, an' all dat. No slabe dat hab any sense am happy. He know, he do, dat suffn's tuk away from him dat God gabe him, and meant he sh'd hole on ter; and so he feel ollerz kind o' mean afore God an' man too; an' I 'fy anybody, white or black, to be happy who feel dat ar way."

"But it is n't the slave's fault, Esha, that he 's a slave."

"It 's de slabe's fault dat he stay a slabe, darlin'," said the old woman, with a strange kindling of the eyes. "But den de massa hab de raisin' ob him, an' so take good car' ter break down all dar am of de man in de poor slabe; an' de poor slabe hab no larnin', and dunno whar' to git a libbin' or how to sabe hisself from starvin'. An' if he run away, de people Norf send him back."

On studying Esha further, Clara discovered that she was half Mahometan, and could speak Arabic. Her mixed notions she had got partly from her father, Amri, who belonged to one of those African tribes who cultivate a pure deism, tempered only by faith in the mission of Mahomet as an inspired prophet. Amri had been captured by a hostile tribe and sold into slavery. He lived long enough to teach his little Esha some things which she remembered. She could repeat several Arabic poems, and Clara first became familiar with the Arabian Nights through this old household drudge. One of these poems had a mystical charm for Clara. Through the illiterate garb which the slave's English gave it, Clara detected a significance that led her to write out a paraphrase in the following words: —

"The sick man lay on his bed of pain. 'Allah!' he moaned; and his heart grew tender, and his eyes moist, with prayer.

"The next morning the tempter said to him: 'No answer comes from Allah. Call louder, still no Allah will hear thee or ease thy pain.'

"The sick man shuddered. His heart grew cold with doubt and inquietude; when suddenly before him stood Elias.

"'Child!' said Elias, 'why art thou sad? Dost think thy prayers are unheard and unanswered; that thy devotion is all in vain?'

"And the sick man replied: 'Ah! so often, and with such tears I have called on Allah! I call *Allah!* but never do I hear his "Here am I!"'

"And Elias left the sick man; but God said to Elias: 'Go to the tempted one; lift him up from his despair and unbelief.

"'Tell him that his very longing is its own fulfilment; that his very prayer, "Come, Allah!" is Allah's answer, "Here am I!"'

"Yes, every good aspiration is an angel straight from God. Say from the heart, 'O my Father!' and that very utterance is the Father's reply, 'Here, my child!'" *

Like many native Africans, Esha was fully assured of the existence of spirits, and of their power, in exceptional cases, to manifest themselves to mortals. And she related so many facts within her own experience, that Clara became a believer on human testimony, — the more readily because Esha's faith in demonism was unmixed with superstition.

"Tell me, Esha," said Clara, at one of their secret midnight conferences, "were you ever whipped?"

"Never badly, darlin'. It ain't de whippins and de suf'rins dat make de wrong ob slavery. De mos kindest thing dey could do de slabe would be ter treat him so he would n't stay a slabe no how. But dey know jes how fur to go, widout stirrin' up de man inside ob him. An' dat 's the cuss ob slabery."

"But, Esha, don't they generally treat the women well on the plantations?"

* By Dscheladeddin, a famous Mahometan mystic.

"De breedin' women dey treat well, — speshilly jes afore dar time,* — but I'ze known a pregnant woman whipped so she died de same night. O de poor bressed lily ob de world! O de angel from hebbn! O de sweet lubly chile! Nebber, no, nebber, nebber shall I disremember how I held de little gole cross afore dat chile's eyes, an' how she die wid de smile on her sweet face, and her own husband's head on her bosom."

And the old woman burst into a passion of tears, rocking herself to and fro, and living over again the sorrow of that death-bed scene to which she and Peek and one other, years before, had been witnesses.

Clara pacified her, and Esha said, "You jes stop one minute, darlin', and I'll show yer suff'n." She went to her garret-closet, and returned with a small silk bag, from which she took a package done up in fine linen. This she unpinned, and displayed a long strand of human hair, thick, silky, soft, and of a peculiarly beautiful color, hardly olive, yet reminding one of that hue. Holding it up, she said: "Dar! Dat's de hair I cut from de head of dat same bress-ed chile I jes tell yer 'bout."

"But that is the hair of a white woman," said Clara.

"Bress yer, darlin', she war jes as white as you am dis minute."

After some seconds of silence, Clara said, "Tell me of her."

And Esha related many, though not all, of the particulars already familiar to the reader in the story of Estelle.

"Esha, you must give me some of that hair," said Clara.

"Yes, darlin', I'll change half of it fur some ob yourn."

The exchange was made, Clara wrapping her portion in the little strip of bunting torn from the American flag.

On the subject of her birth Clara had put to Mrs. Gentry some searching questions, but had learnt simply that her parentage was unknown. For her concealed benefactor she had conceived a romantic attachment; and gratitude incited her to make the best of her opportunities, and to patiently bear her chagrins.

A month after the late interview with Ratcliff, Mrs. Gentry

* On the contrary, Mrs. Kemble says they are cruelly treated, and that the forms of suffering are "manifold and terrible" in consequence.

received a letter which caused Clara to be summoned to her presence.

"Sit down. I've something important to communicate," said the schoolmistress. "You 've often asked me to whom you are indebted for your support. Learn now that you belong to Mr. Carberry Ratcliff, whom you met here some weeks ago. He is the rich planter whose house and grounds in Lafayette you 've often admired."

"*Belong* to him?" cried Clara. "What do you mean? Am I his daughter? Am I in any way related?"

"No, you 're his slave. He bought you at auction."

Impulsive as her own mocking-bird by nature, Clara had learned that cruel lesson, which gifted children are often compelled to acquire when subjected to the rule of inferior minds, — the art, namely, of checking and disguising the emotions.

Excepting a quivering of her lips, a flushing of her brow, a slight heaving of her bosom, and a momentary expression as of deadly sickness in her face, she did not betray, by outward signs, the intensity of that feeling of disgust, hate, and indignation which Mrs. Gentry's communication had aroused.

"Did Mr. Ratcliff request you to inform me that he considered me his slave?" she asked, in a tone which, by a strenuous effort, she divested of all significance.

"Yes; he concluded you are now of an age to understand the responsibilities of your real situation. He not only paid a price for you when you were yet an infant, but he has maintained you ever since. But for him you might have been toiling in the sun on a plantation. But for him you might never have got an education. But for him you might never have heard of salvation through Christ. But for him you might never have had the privilege of attending the Rev. Dr. Palmer's Sunday school. Is there any sacrifice too great for you to make for such a master? Would it be too much for you to lay down your life for him? Speak!"

Mrs. Gentry, it will be seen, pursued the Socratic method of impressing truth upon her pupils. As Clara made no reply to her interrogatories, she continued: "As your instructress, it has been my object to make you feel sensibly the importance of doing your duty in whatever sphere you may be cast."

"And what, madame, may be the duty of a slave?" interposed Clara, stifling down and masking the rage of her heart.

"The duty of a slave," said Mrs. Gentry, "is to obey her master. Prompt and unhesitating obedience, that is her duty."

"Obedience to any and every command, — is that what you mean, madame?"

"Unquestionably, it is."

"And must I not exercise my reason as to what is right or wrong?"

"Your reason, under slavery, is subordinated to another's. You must not set up your own reason against your master's."

"Supposing my master should order me to stab or poison you, — ought I to do it?"

The judge's daughter, like all who venture to vindicate the leprous wrong on moral grounds, found herself nonplussed.

"You suppose a ridiculous and improbable case," she replied.

"Well, madame, let me state a fact. One of your pupils had a letter yesterday from a sister in Alabama, who wrote that a slave woman had killed herself under these circumstances: her master had compelled her to unite herself in so-called marriage with a black man, though she fully believed a former husband still lived. To escape the abhorred consequence, she put an end to her life. Was that woman right or wrong in opposing her master's will?"

"How can you ask?" returned Mrs. Gentry, reproachfully. "'T is the slave's duty to marry as the master orders."

"Even though her husband be living, do I understand you?"

"Undoubtedly. Ministers of the Gospel will tell you, if there 's wrong in it, the master, not the slave, is to blame." *

"I thank you for making the slave's duty so clear. You 're quite sure Dr. Palmer would approve your view?"

"Entirely. All his preaching on the subject convinces me of it."

"And the woman, you think, who killed herself rather than be false to her husband, went straight to hell?"

* The Savannah River Baptist Association of Ministers decreed (1836) that the slave, sold at a distance from his home, was not to be countenanced by the church in resisting his master's will that he should take a new wife.

"I can hope nothing better for her. She must have been a poor heathen creature, wholly ignorant of Scripture. Paul commands slaves to obey; and the woman who wilfully violates his injunction does it at the peril of her soul."

Clara was silent; and Mrs. Gentry, felicitating herself on the powerful moral lesson adapted to her pupil's "new sphere of duty," resumed, "By the way, your master — "

"Master!" shrieked Clara, running with upraised hands to Mrs. Gentry, as if to dash them down on her. Then suddenly checking herself, she said pleasantly: "You see I 'm a little unused to the name. What were you going to say?"

"Really, child, one would think you were out of your wits. It is n't as if you were going to be consigned to a master who 'd abuse you. There 's many a poor girl in our first society who 'd be glad to be taken care of as you 'll be. Only think of it! Here 's a beautiful diamond ring for you. And here 's a check for five hundred dollars for you to spend in dresses, and you 're to have the selecting of them all yourself, — think of that! — under my superintendence of course; but Madame Groux tells me your taste is excellent, and I shall not interfere. 'T is now nine o'clock. We 'll drive out this very forenoon to see what there is in the shops; for Mr. Ratcliff may be here any hour now. Run and get ready, that 's a good girl. The carriage shall be here at half past ten."

Without touching, or even looking at, the ring, Clara ran upstairs to her room, and, locking the door, knelt, with flushed, burning brow and brain, at a little *prie-dieu* in the corner. She did not try to put her prayer in words, for the emotions which swelled within her bosom were all unspeakable. Clara was intellectually a mystic, but the current of her individualism was too strong to be diverted from its course by ordinary influences, whether from spirits *in* or *out* of the flesh. She was too positive to be constrained by other impulses than those which her own will, enlightened by her own reason, had generated. So, while she felt assured that angelic witnesses were round about her, and that her every thought "had a critic in the skies," — and while she believed that, in one sense, nothing of mind or body was truly her own, — that she was but a vessel or recipient, — she keenly experienced the consciousness that she was a free, responsible agent. O mystery beyond all fathoming! O reconcilement of contrarieties which only Omnipotence could effect, and only Omnipotence can explain!

She paced the floor of her little room, — looked her situation unflinchingly in the face, — and resolved, with God's help, to gird herself for the strife. Her unknown benefactor, whom her imagination had so exalted, ah! how poor a thing, hollow and corrupt, he had proved! Could she ever forgive the man who had dared claim her as his slave?

And yet might she not misjudge him? Might he not be plotting some generous surprise? She recalled a single expression of his face, and felt satisfied she did him no injustice. How hateful now seemed all those accomplishments she had acquired! They were but the gilding of an abhorred chain.

In the midst of her whirling thoughts, her mocking-bird, which had been pecking at some crumbs in his cage, burst into such a wild *jubilate* of song, that Clara's attention was withdrawn for a moment even from her own great grief. Opening the door of the cage, she said: "Come, Dainty, you too shall be free. The window is open. Go find a pleasant home among the trees and on the plantations."

The bird flew about her head, and alighted on her forefinger, as it had been accustomed. Clara pressed the down of its neck to her cheek, and then, taking the little songster to the window, threw it off her finger. Dainty flew back into the room, and, alighting on Clara's head, pecked at her hair.

"Naughty Dainty! Good by, my pet! We must part. Freedom is best for both you and me." And, putting her head out of the window, Clara brushed Dainty off into the airy void, and closed the glass against the bird's return.

She now summoned Esha, and said: "Esha, we 've often wondered as to my true place in the world. The mystery is solved to-day. Mrs. Gentry informs me I 'm a slave."

"What! Wha-a-a-t! You? You, too, a slabe? My little darlin' a slabe? O, de good Lord in hebbn won't 'low dat!"

"We 've but a moment for talk, Esha. Help me to act. My owner (owner!) may be here any minute."

"Who am dat owner?"

"Mr. Carberry Ratcliff."

"No,—no,—no! Not dat man! Not him! De Lord help de dare chile if dat born debble wunst git hole ob her!"

"What do you know of him?"

"He war de cruel massa ob dat slabe gal whom you hab de hair ob in yer bosom."

"I 'm glad of it!" cried Clara, throwing her clenched hand in the air, and looking up as if to have the heavens hear her.

"O, darlin' chile, what am dar ole Esha kn do for her?"

Clara stopped short, and, pressing both hands on her forehead, stood as if calling her best thoughts to a council of war, and then said, "Can you get me a small valise, Esha?"

"Hab a carpet-bag I kn gib her. You jes wait one minute." And Esha returned with the desired article.

"Now help me pack it with the things I shall most need. Mrs. Gentry expects me soon to go a-shopping with her. When she calls for me, I shall be missing. I 've not yet made up my mind where to go. I shall think on that as I walk along. What 's the matter, Esha? What do you stare at?"

"Look dar! What yer see dar, darlin'?"

"A pair of little sleeve-buttons. How pretty! Gold with a setting of coral. And on the inside, in tiny letters, C. A. B."

"Wall, dat 's de 'stonishin'est ting I 'ze seen dis many a day. Ten—no, 'lebben—no, fourteen yars ago, as I war emptyin' suds out ob de wash-tub, I see dese little buttons shinin' on de groun'. 'T was de Monday arter you was browt here. Your little underclose had been in de wash. So what does I do but put de buttons in my pocket, tinkin' I 'd gib 'em ter missis ter keep fur yer. But whan I look for 'em, dey was clean gone,—could n't fine 'em nowhar. So I say noting t' all 'bout it. Jes now, as I tuk up fro' my trunk a little muslin collar dat de dare saint I tell yer 'bout used ter wear, what sh'd drop from de foles but dis same little pair ob buttons dat I hab'nt seen fur all dese yars. Take 'em, darlin', fur dey 'long ter you an' ter nobody else."

"Thank you, Esha. I 'll keep them with my other treasures"; and Clara fastened them with a pin to the piece of bunting in her bosom. "And now, good by. Pray for me, Esha."

"Night and day, darlin'. But Esha mus gib suffn more 'n

prayers. Take dese twenty dollars in gold, darlin'. Yer 'll want 'em, sure. Don't 'fuze 'em."

"How long have you been saving up this money, Esha?"

"Bress de chile, only tree muntz. Dat 's nuffn. You jes take 'em. Dar! Dat 's right. Tie 'em up safe in de corner ob yer hankerchy."

"But, Esha, you may not be paid back till you get to heaven." And Clara put on her bonnet, and spoke rapidly to choke down a sob.

"So much de better. Dar! Put 'em safe in yer pocket. Dat 's a good chile."

Fearing a refusal would only grieve the old woman, Clara received and put away the gold-pieces. Then, closing the spring of the carpet-bag, she kissed Esha, and said, "If they inquire for me, balk them as well as you can."

"Leeb me alone fur dat, darlin'. An' now yer mus' go. De Lord an' his proppet bless yer! Allah keep yer! De mudder ob God watch ober yer!"

In these ejaculations Esha would hardly have been held as orthodox either by a mufti or a D. D. But what if, in the balance of the All-Seeing, the sincere heart should outweigh the speculative head? Poor old Esha was Mahometan through reverence for her father; Catholic through influences from the family with whom she lived when a child; and Protestant through knowedge of many good men and women of that faith. She cared not how many saints there were in her calendar. The more the merrier. All goodness in man or woman, of whatever race or sect, was deified in her simple and semi-barbarous conceptions. Poor, ignorant, sinful, unregenerate creature!

"God bless you, Esha!" said Clara. "Look! There is poor Dainty perched on the window-sill. Plainly he is no Abolitionist. He prefers slavery. Take care of him."

"Dat I will, if only for your sake, darlin'."

And the old woman let the bird in and closed the window; and then — her bronzed face wet with tears — she conducted Clara to a back door of the house, from which the fugitive could issue, without being observed, into an obscure carriage-way.

CHAPTER XX.

ENCOUNTERS AT THE ST. CHARLES.

"Hail, year of God's farming! Hail, summer of an emancipated continent, which shall lay up in storehouse and barn the great truths that were worth the costly dressing of a people's blood!" — *Rev. John Weiss.*

IN one of the rooms of the St. Charles Hotel in New Orleans a man sat meditating. The windows looked out on a street where soldiers were going through their drill amid occasional shouts from by-standers. As the noise grew louder, the man rose and went to a window. He was hardly above the middle stature, slim and compact, but as lithe as if jointed like an eel. His hair was slightly streaked with gray. His features, though not full, spoke health, vigor, and pure habits of life; while his white, well-preserved teeth, neatly trimmed beard, and well-cut, well-adjusted clothes showed that, as he left his youth behind him, his attention to his personal appearance did not decrease. Fourteen years had made but little change in Vance. It had not tamed the fire of his eyes nor slackened the alertness of his tread.

As he caught sight of the "stars and bars" waving in the spring sunlight, an expression of scorn was emitted in his frown, and he exclaimed: "Detested rag! I shall yet live to trample you in the dirt on that very spot where you now flaunt so bravely. Shout on, poor fools! Continue, ye unreasoning cattle, to crop the flowery food, and lick the hand just raised to shed your blood. And you, too, leaders of the rank and file, led, in your turn, by South Carolina fire-eaters, go on and overtake that fate denounced by the prophet on evil-doers. Hug the strong delusion and believe the lie! Declare, with the smatterers of the Richmond press, that Christian civilization is a mistake, and that the new Confederacy is *a God-sent missionary to the nations* to teach them that pollution is purity, and incest a boon from heaven. The time is not far distant when you shall learn how far the Eternal Powers are the allies of human laziness, arrogance, and lust!"

Suddenly the soliloquist seemed struck by the appearance of some one in the crowd; for, taking from his pocket an opera-glass, and regulating the focus, he looked through it, then muttered: "Yes, it is he! Poor maggot! What haughtiness in his look!"

Just then a man on horseback, in the dress of a civilian, and followed by a slave, also mounted, rode forward nearer to where Vance sat at his window. A multitude gathered round the foremost equestrian, and called for a speech. "The Kunnle is jest frum South Kerlinay," exclaimed a swarthy inebriate, who seemed to be spokesman for the mob. "A speech frum Kunnle Ratcliff! Hoorray!"

Ratcliff, with a gesture of annoyance, rose in his stirrups, and said: "Friends, I 've nothing to tell you that you can't find better told in the newspapers. This is no time for talk. We want action now. All 's right at Charleston. Sumter has fallen. That 's the first great step. The Yankees may bluster, but they 'll never fight. The meanest white man at the South is more than a match for any five Yankees. We 'll have them begging to be let into our Southern Confederacy before Christmas. But we won't receive 'em. No! As Jeff Davis well says, sooner hyenas than Yankees! But we must whip them into decency. And so, before the next Fourth of July, we mean to have our flag flying over Faneuil Hall. We are the master race, my friends! We must show these nigger stealing, beggarly Yankees that they must stand cap in hand when they venture to come into our presence. Don't believe the croakers who tell you slavery will be weakened by secession. It 's going to be strengthened. So convinced am I of it, that I 've doubled my number of slaves; and if any of you wish to sell, bring on your niggers! Do you see that flag? Well, that flag has got to wave over all Mexico, Cuba, and Central America. In five years from now every man of you shall own his score of niggers and his hundred acres of land. So go ahead, and aim low when you sight a Yankee."

The speech was received with cheers, and Ratcliff started his horse; but the leading loafer of the crowd seized the reins, and said: "Can't let yer off so, Kunnle, — can't no how you kun fix it. We want a reg'lar game speech, sich as you kun make when you dam please. So fire up, and do your prettiest. Be n't we the master race?"

"Pshaw! Let go those reins," said Ratcliff, cutting the vagabond over his face with the but-end of a riding-whip.

The crowd laughed, and the loafer, astonished and sobered, dropped the reins, and put his hand to his eye, which had been badly hit. Ratcliff rode on, but a muttered curse went after him.

Seeing the loafer stand feeling of his eye as if had been hurt, Vance said to him from the window: "Go to the apothecary's, and tell him to give you something to bathe it in."

"Go ter the 'pothecary's! With nary a red in my pocket! Strannger, don't try to fool this child."

"Here 's money, if you want it."

"Money? I should like ter see the color of it, strannger."

"Hold your hat, then."

And Vance dropped into the hat something wrapped in a newspaper which the loafer incredulously unfolded. Finding in it a five-dollar gold-piece, he stared first at the money, then at Vance, and said: "Strannger, I'd say, God bless yer, if I did n't think, what a poor cuss like I could say would rayther harm than help. Have n't no influence with God A'mighty, strannger. But you 're a man, — you air, — not a sneakin' 'ristocrat as despises a poor white feller more 'n he does a nigger. I 've seen yer somewhar afore, but can 't say whar."

"Go and attend to your eye, my friend," said Vance.

"I will. An' if ever I kun do yer a good turn, jes call on ——"

Vance could not hear the name; but he bowed, and the loafer moved on. Looking in another direction, Vance saw Ratcliff dismount, throw the reins to his attendant, and disappear in a vestibule of the hotel. Vance rose and wildly paced the room. His whole frame quivered to the very tips of his fingers, which he stretched forth as if to clutch some invisible antagonist. He muttered incoherent words, and, smiting his brow as if to keep back thoughts that struggled too tumultuously for expression, cried: "O that I had him here, — here, face to face, — weaponless, both of us! Would I not — The merciless villain! The cowardly miscreant! To lash a woman! That moment of horror! Often as I 've lived it over, it is ever new. Can eternity make it fade? Again I see her, —

pale, very pale and bleeding, — and tied, — tied to the stake. O Ratcliff! When shall this bridled vengeance overtake thee? Pshaw! What is *he*, — an individual, — what is the sum of pain that *he* can suffer? Would that be a requital? Will not his own devices work better for me than aught *I* can do?"

Seating himself in an arm-chair, Vance calmed his vindictive thoughts. In memory he went back to that day when he first heard Estelle sing; then to their first evening in Mrs. Mallet's little house; then to the old magnolia-tree before it. That house he had bought and given in keeping to Mrs. Bernard, a married granddaughter of old Leroux, the Frenchman. Every tree and shrub in the area had been reverently cared for. Had not Estelle plucked blossoms from them all?

He thought of his marriage, — of his pleasant walks with Estelle in Jackson Square, — of their musical enjoyments, — of all her little devices to minister to his comfort and delight, — and then of the sudden clouding of this brief but most exquisite sunshine.

Vance took from the pocket of his vest a little circular box of rosewood. Unscrewing the cover, he revealed a photograph of Estelle, taken after her marriage. There was such a smile on the countenance as only the supreme happiness of a loving heart could have created. On the opposite circle was a curl of her hair of that strangely beautiful neutral tint which Vance had often admired. This he pressed to his lips. "Dear saint," he murmured, "I have not forgotten thy parting words. For thy sake will I wrestle with this spirit that would seek a *paltry* revenge. Thy smile, O my beloved! shall dispel the remembrance of thy agony, and thy love shall conquer all earth-born hate. For thy dear sake will I still calmly meet thy murderer. O, lend me of thy divine patience to endure his presence! Sweet child, affectionate and pure, I can dream of nothing in heaven more precious than thyself. If from thee, O my beloved! come this spiritual refreshing and reinforcement, — if from thee these tender influences, so bright and yet so gentle, — then must thy sphere be one within which the angels delight to come."

There was a knock at the door. Vance shut the box, replaced it in his pocket, and cried, "Come in!"

"Colored man down stars, sar, wants to see yer."

"Did he give his name?"

"Yes, sar, he say his name is Jacobs."

"Show him up."

A negro now entered wearing green spectacles, and a wig of gray wool. Across his cheek there was a scar. No sooner was the door closed upon the waiter, than Vance exclaimed: "Is it possible? Can this be you, Peek?"

Peek threw off his disguises, and Vance seized him by the hand as he might have seized a returning brother.

"What of your wife and child? Have you found 'em?"

"No, Mr. Vance, I'm still a wanderer over the earth in search of them. I shall find them in God's good time."

"Sit down, Peek."

"Excuse me, Mr. Vance, I'd rather stand."

"Very well. Then I'll stand too."

"Since you make it a point of politeness, sir, I'll sit."

"That's right. And now, my dear fellow, tell me what you've been about these many years. Surely you've discovered some traces of the lost ones?"

"None that have been of much use, Mr. Vance. I'm satisfied that Flora was lured on to Baltimore by some party who deceived her with the expectation of meeting me there. From Baltimore she and her child were taken to Richmond by the agent of her old master, and sold at auction to a dealer, who soon afterwards died. There the clew breaks."

"My poor Peek, your not finding her has probably saved you from a deeper disappointment."

"What do you mean, Mr. Vance?"

"The chance is, she has been forced to marry some other man."

"I know, sir, that would be the probability in the case of ninety-nine slave-women out of a hundred. But Flora once swore to me on the crucifix, she would be true to me or die. And I feel very certain she will keep her oath."

"Ah! slavery is so crafty and remorseless in working on human passions," sighed Vance. "But you are right, my dear Peek, in hoping on. Tell me of your adventures."

"When you and I parted at Memphis, Mr. Vance, I went to

Montreal. Flora had left there some weeks before. At New York I sought out Mr. Charlton; also the policemen. But I could get nothing out of them. At length a Canadian told me he had met Flora on board the Baltimore boat. I followed up the clew till it broke, as I 've told you. Since then I 've been seeking my wife and boy through all the Cotton States. The money you gave me from Mr. Berwick lasted me seven years; and then I had to work to get the means of continuing my search. There are not many counties in the Slave States which I have not visited."

"During your travels, Peek, you must have had opportunities of helping on the good cause."

"Yes, Mr. Vance. I needed some strong motive to send me far and wide among my poor brethren. Without it I might have led a selfish life, content with my own comforts. But God has ordered it all right. I bought a pass as an old slave preacher, and thus was able to visit the plantations, and establish secret societies in the cause of freedom. Give the slaves arms, treat them like men, and they will fight. But they will not rise unarmed in useless insurrection. As soon as the North will give them the means of defending their freedom, they will break their fetters. It is the North, and not the South, that now holds the slave in check."

"Yes, Peek; public sentiment is almost as much poisoned at the North as at the South, by this slavery virus."

"And what have *you*, sir, been about all these years?"

"Much of my time has been spent in Kansas. I 've been a border ruffian."

"A sham one, I suppose?"

"Well, Peek, so seriously did I play my part, that perhaps I shall go down in history as one of the pro-slavery leaders. John Brown of Ossawatomie would at one time have shot me on sight. He afterwards understood me better, — understood that, if I fraternized with the pro-slavery crew, it was to thwart their schemes. The rascals were continually astounded at finding their bloodiest secrets revealed to the Abolitionists, and little suspected that one of their most trusted advisers was the informer. Yes! I helped on the madness which God sends to those he means to destroy. Baffled in California, the devil of slavery set his heart on establishing his altars in Kansas. How effectually we have headed him off! And now the frenzied idiot wants secession and a slave empire. Heaven forbid I should arrest him in his fatuity! Let me rather help it on."

"Are you, then, a secessionist, Mr. Vance?"

"In one sense: I'm for secession from slavery by annihilating it, holding on to the Union. I was at the great Nashville convention. I've been the last few months watching things here in conservative Louisiana. She will have to follow South Carolina. That little vixen among States cracks the overseer's whip over our heads, and threatens us with her sovereign displeasure for our timidity. She has nearly frightened poor Governor Moore out of his boots."

"I've been thinking much lately," said Peek, "of our adventure on board the Pontiac. What ever became of Colonel Delancy Hyde?"

"The Colonel," replied Vance, "for a time wooed fortune in Kansas, but did n't win her. Since then I've lost him."

"The last I heard of him," said Peek, "he had quarrelled with a fellow at a cock-fight in Montgomery, and been wounded; and his sister, a decent woman, was tending on him."

"I confess I've a weakness for the Colonel," said Vance, "though unquestionably he's a great scoundrel."

"Did you ever learn, Mr. Vance, what became of that yellow girl he coveted?"

"She and the child were drowned," was the reply.

"What proof of that did you ever have?"

"My first endeavor, after the accident," said Vance, "was to serve the man to whom I had owed my own life; and it was not till I saw you secure from Hyde, and your scalds taken care of, I learnt from Judge Onslow that the Berwicks, husband and wife, had died from their wounds."

"Were their bodies ever recovered?"

"Those of the husband and wife I saw and recognized. But not half the bodies of the drowned were recovered, so strong was the current. It was not surprising, therefore, that the child and nurse should be of this number. Two of the passengers testified to seeing them in the river, — tried ineffectually to save them, and saw them go under."

"Did you ever learn who those passengers were?"

"No. But I satisfied myself, so far as I could from human testimony, that the child was not among the saved. Business called me suddenly to New Orleans. Why do you ask?"

"Excuse me. Were you never summoned as a witness on the trial which gave Mr. Charlton the Berwick property?"

"Never. Perhaps one of the inconveniences of my *aliases* is, that my friends do not often know where to find me, or how to address me. I was not aware there had been a trial."

"Nor was I," said Peek, "until a few weeks ago. At the Exchange Hotel in Montgomery, I waited on Captain Ireton of the army, who, learning that I had had dealings with Charlton, informed me that his (Ireton's) grandfather had been a party to a lawsuit growing out of the loss of the Pontiac, but that the case had been decided in Charlton's favor. When Captain Ireton learned that I, too, had been on the Pontiac, he put me many questions, in the course of which I learned that the evidence as to the death of the child and her nurse rested solely on the testimony of Colonel Delancy Hyde and his friend, Leonidas Quattles."

Vance started up and paced the floor, striking both palms against his forehead. "Dupe and fool that I 've been!" he exclaimed. "Deep as I thought myself, this thick-skulled Hyde has been deeper still. I 've been outwitted by a low rascal and blockhead. In all my talk with Hyde about the explosion, he never intimated to me that he had ever testified as a witness in a suit growing out of the accident. Never would he have kept silent on such a point if he had n't been guilty. He and Quattles and Charlton! What possible rascality might not have been hatched among the three! Of course there was knavery! What was the amount of property in suit?"

"More than a million of dollars, — so Ireton told me."

"A million? The father and mother dead, — then prove that the child — But stop. I 'm going too fast. *Hyde* could n't have been interested in having it supposed that the child was dead. How could he have known about the Berwick property?"

"But might he not have tried to kidnap the yellow girl?"

"There you hit it, Peek! Dolt that I 've been not to think of that! I remember now that Hyde once said to me, the yellow girl would bring sixteen hundred dollars in New Orleans. Well, supposing he took the yellow girl, what could he do with the white child?"

"Can you, of all men, Mr. Vance, not guess? He could sell the child as a slave. Or, if he wanted to make her bring a little better price, he could tinge her skin just enough to give it a slight golden hue."

Vance wet a towel in iced water, and pressed it on his forehead.

"But you pierce my heart, Peek, by the bare suggestion of such things," he said. "That poor child! Clara was her name,—a bright, affectionate little lady! Should Hyde have given false testimony in regard to her death, I shudder to think what may have become of her. She, born to affluence, may be at this moment a wretched menial, or worse, a trained Cyprian, polluted, body and soul. Why was I not more thorough in my investigations? But perhaps 't is not too late to prove the villany, if villany there has been."

"Hyde may be able to put you on the right track," suggested Peek.

Vance sat down, and for five minutes seemed lost in meditation. Then, starting up, he said: "Where would you next go in pursuit of your wife and child?"

"To Texas," replied Peek.

"To Texas you shall go. Would you venture to face Colonel Hyde?"

"With these green goggles I would face any of my old masters; and the scalds upon my face would alone prevent my being known."

"I can get you a pass from the Mayor himself, so that you 'd not be molested. Find Hyde, and bring him to me at any cost. Money will do it. When can you start?"

"By the next boat,—in half an hour."

"All right. Make your home at Bernard's when you return. The house is mine. Here 's the direction. Here 's a pass from the Mayor which I 've filled up for you. And here 's money, which you need n't stop to count. Good by!"

And, with a grasp of the hand, they parted, and Peek quitted the hotel to take the boat for Galveston.

He had no sooner gone than Vance went down-stairs to the dining-hall. Most of the guests had finished their dinners; but at a small table near that at which he took his seat were a company of four, lingering over the dessert.

Senator Wigman, a puffy, red-faced man, had been holding forth on the prospective glories of the Confederacy.

"Yes, sir," said he, refilling his glass with Burgundy, "with the rest of the world we'll trade, but never, never with the Yankees. Not one pound of cotton shall ever go from the South to their accursed cities; not one ounce of their steel or their manufactures shall ever cross our borders." And Wigman emptied his glass at a single gulp.

"Good for Wigman!" exclaimed Mr. Robson, a round, full-faced young man, rather fat, and wearing gold-rimmed spectacles. "But what about Yankee ice, Wigman? Will you deprive us of that also? And tell me, my Wigman, why is it that, since you despise these Yankees so intensely, you allow your children to remain at school in Massachusetts? Is n't that a little inconsistent, my Wigman?"

Wigman was obliged to refill his glass before he could summon his thoughts for a reply.

"Mr. Robson," he then said, "you're a scholar, and must be aware that the ancient Spartans, in order to disgust their children with intemperance, used to make their slaves drunk. If I send my children among the Yankees, it is that they may be struck by the superiority of the Southern character when they return home."

"So you've no faith in the old maxim touching evil communications," said Robson, taking a bottle of Champagne, and easing the cork so as to send it to the ceiling with a loud pop. "Now, gentlemen, bumpers all round! Onslow, let me fill your glass; Kenrick, yours. Drink to my sentiment. Here's confusion to the old concern!"

Vance was just lifting a spoonful to his lips; but he returned it to his plate as he heard the name of Onslow, and looked round. Yes, it was surely he! — the boy of the Pontiac, now a handsome youth of twenty-four. On his right sat the young man addressed as Kenrick. At the latter Vance hardly looked, so intent was he on Onslow's response.

Wigman spoke first. Holding up his glass, and amorously eyeing the salmon hue of the wine, he exclaimed: "Agreed! Here 's confusion to the old con-hiccup-concern!"

The Senator's unfortunate hiccup elicited inextinguishable laughter from the rest, until Robson rapped with the handle of his knife on the table, and cried: "Order! order! Gentlemen, I consider that man a sneaking traitor who 'll not get drunk in behalf of sentiments like those our friend the Senator has been uttering."

"Look here, young man, do you mean to insinuate that I 'm getting drunk," said Wigman, angrily.

"Far from it, Wigman. Any one can see you 're *not getting* drunk."

"I accept the apology," said Wigman, with maudlin dignity.

"Well, then, gentlemen," cried Robson, "now for the previous question! Confusion to the old concern!"

Wigman and Onslow drank to the sentiment, but Kenrick, calling a negro waiter, handed the glass to him, and said: "Throw that to the pigs, and bring me a fresh glass."

"Halloo! What the deuce do you mean by that?" cried Robson. "Have we a Bourbon among us? Have we a Yankee sympathizer among us? Is it possible? Does Mr. Charles Kenrick of Kenrick, son of Robert Kenrick, Esq., Confederate M. C., and heir to a thousand niggers, refuse to drink to the downfall of Abolitionism, and those other isms against which we 've drawn the sword and flung away the scabbard?"

"Yes, by Jove!" interposed Wigman. "And we 'll welcome our invaders with — with —"

"With bloody hands to hospitable graves," said Robson. "Speak quick, my Wigman. That 's the Southern formula, I believe, invented, like the new song of *Dixie*, by an impertinent Yankee. It 's devilish hard we have to import from these blasted Yankees the very slang and music we turn against them."

"Answer me, Mr. Charles Kenrick," said Wigman, assuming a front of judicial severity, "did you mean any offence to the Confederacy by dishonoring the sentiment of hostility to its enemy?"

"Damn the Confederacy!" said Kenrick.

"Hear him," said Robson. "Was there ever such blasphemy? Please write it down, Onslow, that he damns the Confederacy. And write Wigman down an — No matter for that part of it! We shall hear Kenrick blaspheming slavery by and by."

"Damn slavery!" said Kenrick.

"Kenrick is joking," said Onslow.

"Kenrick was never more serious in his life, Mr. Onslow!"

"Look here, my dear fellow," said Robson, "there *are* sanctities which must not be invaded, even under the privilege of Champagne. Insult the Virgin Mary, traduce the Holy Trinity, profane the Holy of holies, say that Jeff Davis is n't a remarkable man, as much as you please, but beware how you speak ill of the peculiar institution. We 'll twist the noose for you with a pleased alacrity unless you retract those wicked words, and do penance in two tumblers of Heidsieck drunk in expiation of your horrible levity."

"Damn slavery!" reiterated Kenrick.

"He 's a subject for the Committee of Safety," suggested Wigman.

"Kenrick is playing with us all this while," said Onslow. "Come! Confess it, old schoolfellow! You honor the new flag as much as I do."

"I 'll show you how much I honor it," said Kenrick; and, going to a table where a small Confederate flag was stuck in a leg of bacon, he tore off the silken emblem, ripped it in four parts, and, casting it on the floor, put his foot on the fragments and spat on them.

Wigman drew a small bowie-knife from a pocket inside of his vest, and, starting to his feet, kicked back his chair, and rushed with somewhat tortuous motion towards Kenrick; but, having miscalculated his powers of equilibrium, the Senator fell helplessly on the floor, and dropped his knife. Robson kicked it to a distant part of the room, and, helping Wigman to his feet, placed him in his chair, and counselled him not to try it again.

"It is to me that Mr. Kenrick must answer for this insult to the flag," said Onslow.

Kenrick bowed. Then, resuming his seat, he took a fresh glass, and, filling it till it overflowed with Champagne, rose and exclaimed: "The Union! not as it *was*, but as it *shall* be, with universal freedom, — from the St. Croix to the Rio Grande, — from Cape Cod to the Golden Gate!" Kenrick touched his lips reverently to the wine, then put it down, and, taking from his bosom a beautiful American flag made of silk, shook it out, and said, "Here, gentlemen, is *my* religion."

Onslow made a snatch at it, but Kenrick warded off his grip, and, folding and returning the flag to the inner pocket of his vest, calmly took his seat as if nothing had happened.

All this while Vance had been gazing on Kenrick intently, as if wrestling in thought with some inexplicable mystery. "Strange!" he murmured. "The very counterpart of my own person as I was at twenty-three! My very features! My very figure! The very color of my hair! And then, — what my mother often told me was a Carteret peculiarity, — when he smiles, that fan-like radiation of fine wrinkles under the temples from the outer corner of the eye! What does it all mean? I know of no relation of the name of Kenrick."

"I shall not sit at table with a traitor," cried Onslow.

"Then keep standing all the time," said Kenrick.

"Nonsense! I thought we were all philosophers in this company," interposed Robson, who, having had large commercial dealings with the elder Kenrick, was in no mood to see the son harmed. "Sit down, Onslow! Wigman, keep your seat. Now, waiter, green glasses all round, and a bottle of that sparkling Moselle. They 'll know at the bar what I mean."

Onslow resumed his seat. Wigman stiffened himself up and drew nearer to the table, fired at the prospect of a fresh bottle.

At this juncture Mr. George Sanderson, a Northern man with Southern principles, in person short, vulgar, and flashily dressed, the very *beau ideal* of a bar-room rowdy, having heard the clink of glasses, and sighted from the corridor an array of bottles, was seized with one of his half-hourly attacks of thirstiness, and entered to join the party, although Wigman was the only one he knew. The latter introduced him to the rest. Robson uncorked the Moselle, and asked, "Now that Sumter has fallen, what 's next on the programme?"

"Washington must be taken," said Sanderson.

"We must winter in Philadelphia," said Wigman.

"In what capacity? As conquerors or as captives?" said Kenrick.

"Is the gentleman at all shaky?" asked Sanderson.

"He has been shamming Abolitionism," replied Onslow.

"He damns slavery," cried the indignant Wigman.

"He 's sure to go to hell for that," said Robson; "intercession can't save him. He has committed the unpardonable sin. The Rev. Dr. Palmer has recently made researches in theology which satisfy himself and me and the rest of the saints, that the sin against the Holy Ghost is in truth nothing less than to be an Abolitionist."

"What is your private opinion of the Yankees, Mr. Sanderson?" asked Kenrick. "Do you think they 'll fight?"

"No, sir-r-r. Fifty thousand Confederates could walk through the Northern States, and plant their colors on every State capital north of Mason and Dixon's line. They could whip any army the Yankees could bring against them."

"Then you think the Yankees are cowards, eh?"

"Compared with the Southerners, — yes!" said Sanderson, holding up his glass for the waiter to refill.

"His opinion is that of an expert. He 's himself a Yankee!" cried Robson.

"I see Mr. Sanderson soars far above the spirit of the old proverb touching the bird that fouls its nest," said Kenrick.

"Order!" cried Robson. "Mr. Sanderson is a philosopher. He disdains vulgar prejudices. To him the old nest is straw and mud, and the old flag is a bit of bunting. Is n't it so, Sanderson?"

"Exactly so," said Sanderson, a little puzzled by Robson's persiflage, and seeking relief from it in another glass of wine. But, finding the Moselle bottle empty, he applied himself to a decanter labelled Old Monongahela.

A sudden snore from Wigman, who had fallen asleep in his chair, startled the party once more into laughter.

"Happy Wigman!" said Robson. "He smiles. He is dreaming of slavery extension into benighted, slaveless Mexico, — of Cuba annexed, and her stupidly mild slave-code reformed, — of tawny-hued houries, metifs, and quarteroons fanning him while he reposes, — of unnumbered Yankees howling over their lost trade, and kneeling vainly for help to him, — to Wigman! Profound Wigman! Behold the great man asleep! Happy Texas in having such a representative! Happy Jeff Davis in having such a counsellor! Gentlemen, my feelings grow too effusive. I must leave you. The dinner has been good. The wine has been good. I must make one criticism, however. The young gentlemen are degenerate. They do not drink. Look at them. They are perfectly sober. What is the world coming to? At our hotels, where twenty years ago we used to see fifty — yes, a hundred — champagne bottles on the dinner-table, we now don't see ten. And yet men talk of the progress of the age! 'T is all a delusion. The day of juleps has gone by. We are receding in civilization. Wigman is a type of the good old times, — a landmark, a pattern for the rising generation. To his immortal honor be it recorded, that after that most heroic achievement of this or any other age, the subjugation of Anderson's little starving garrison in Sumter by Beauregard, Wigman started in a small boat for the fort. Wigman landed. Wigman was the first to land. He entered one of the bomb-proofs. The first thought of a vulgar mind would have been to fly the victorious flag. Not so Wigman. On a shelf he saw a bottle. With a sublime self-abandonment he saw nothing else. He seized it; he uncorked it; he drank from it. And it was not till he had exhausted the last drop, that he learnt from the surgeon it was poison. O posterity! don't be ungrateful and forget this picture when you think of Sumter. Our Wigman was saved to us by an emetic. Hand him down, ye future Hildreths and Motleys of America. Unconscious Wigman! He responds with another rhoncus. Mr. Sanderson, I leave him to your generous care. Gentlemen, good by!" And without waiting for a reply, Robson received his hat from the attentive waiter, waved a bow to the party, and waddled out of the hall.

Mr. Sanderson, seeing that a bottle of Chateau Margaux

was but half emptied, sighed that he had not detected it sooner. Filling a goblet with the purple fluid, he drained it in long and appreciative draughts, rolling the smooth juice over his tongue, and carefully savoring the bouquet. Having emptied this bottle, he sighted another nearly two thirds full of champagne. Sanderson felt a pang at the thought that there was a limit to man's ability to quaff good liquor. He, however, went up to the attack bravely, and succeeded in disposing of two full tumblers. Then a spirit of meek content at his bibulous achievements seemed to come over him. He put his thumbs in the arm-holes of his vest, leaned back, and benignantly said, "This warm weather has made me a trifle thirsty."

Wigman suddenly started from his sleep, wakened by the cessation of noise. Sanderson rose, and assisted the Senator to his feet. "Come, my dear fellow," said he, "it 's time to adjourn. Good by, young gentlemen!" And arm in arm the two worthies staggered out of the hall, each under the impression that the other was the worse for liquor, and each affectionately counselling the other not to expose himself.

Vance still sat at his table, and from behind a newspaper glanced occasionally at the two young men who had so excited his interest.

"Now, Kenrick," said Onslow, "now that Robson the impenetrable, and Wigman the windy, and Sanderson the beastly, are out of the way, tell me what you mean by your incomprehensible conduct. When we met at table to-day, the first time for five years, I did not dream that you were other than you used to be, the enthusiastic champion of the South and its institutions."

"You wonder," replied Kenrick, "that I should express my detestation of the Rebellion and its cause, — of the Confederacy and its corner-stone, — that I should differ from my father, who believes in slavery. How much more reasonably might I wonder at *your* apostasy from truths which such a man as your father holds!"

"My father is an honorable man, — an excellent man," said Onslow; "but — "

"But," interrupted Kenrick, "if you were sincere just now in the epithet you flung at me, you consider him also a traitor.

Now a traitor is one who betrays a trust. What trust has your father betrayed?"

"He does not stand by his native State in her secession from the old Union," answered Onslow.

"But what if he holds that his duty to the central government is paramount to his duty to his State?" asked Kenrick.

"That I regard as an error," replied Onslow.

"Then by your own showing," said Kenrick, "all that you can fairly say is, that your father has erred in judgment, — not that he has been guilty of a base act of treason."

"No, I did n't mean that, Charles, — your pardon," said Onslow, holding out his hand.

Kenrick cordially accepted the proffered apology, and then asked: "May I speak frankly to you, Robert, — speak as I used to in the old times at William and Mary's?"

"Certainly. Proceed."

"Your father literally obeyed the Saviour's injunction. He gave up all he had, to follow where truth led. Convinced that slavery was a wrong, he ruined his fortunes in the attempt to substitute free labor for that of slaves. Through the hostility of the slave interest the experiment failed."

"I think," said Onslow, "my father acted unwisely in sacrificing his fortunes to an abstraction."

"An abstraction! The man who tries to undo a wrong is an abstractionist, is he? What a world this would be if all men would be guilty of similar abstractions. To such a one I would say, 'Master, lead on, and I will follow thee, to the last gasp, with truth and loyalty!' Strange! unaccountably strange, that his own son should have deserted him for the filthy flesh-pots of slavery!"

"May not good men differ as to slavery?" asked Onslow.

"Put that question," replied Kenrick, "to nine tenths of the slaveholders, — men in favor of lynching, torturing, murdering, those opposed to the institution. Put it to Mr. Carson, who, the other day, in his own house, shot down an unarmed and unsuspecting visitor, because he had freely expressed views opposed to slavery. Abolitionists don't hang men for not believing with them, — do they? But the whole code and temper of the South reply to you, that men may *not* differ, and *shall* not differ, on the subject of slavery. Onslow, give me but one thing, — and that a thing guaranteed by the Constitution of the United States, though never tolerated in the Slave States, — give me *liberty of the press* in those States, and I, as a friend of the Union, would say to the government at Washington, 'Put by the sword. Wait! I will put down this rebellion. I have the pen and the press! Therefore is slavery doomed, and its days are numbered.'"

"Why is it," asked Onslow, "if slavery is wrong, that you find all the intelligence, all the culture, at the South, and even in the Border States, on its side?"

"Ah! there," replied Kenrick, "there 's the sunken rock on which you and many other young men have made wreck of your very souls. Your æsthetic has superseded your moral natures. To work is in such shocking bad taste, when one can make others work for one!"

"Nine tenths of the men at the South of any social position," said Onslow, "are in favor of secession."

"I know it," returned Kenrick, "and the sadder for human nature that it should be so! In Missouri, in Kentucky, in Virginia, in Baltimore, all the young men who would be considered fashionable, all who thoughtlessly or heartlessly prize more their social *status* than they do justice and right, follow the lead of the pro-slavery aristocracy. I know from experience how hard it is to break loose from those social and family ties. But I thank God I 've succeeded. 'T was like emerging from mephitic vapors into the sweet oxygen of a clear, sun-bright atmosphere, that hour I resolved to take my lot with freedom and the right against slavery and the wrong!"

"How was your conversion effected?" asked Onslow. "Did you fall in love with some Yankee schoolmistress? I was n't aware you 'd been living at the North."

"I 've never set foot in a Free State," replied Kenrick. "My life has been passed here in Louisiana on my father's plantation. I was bred a slaveholder, and lived one after the most straitest sect of our religion until about six months ago. See at the trunkmaker's my learned papers in De Bow's Review. They 're entitled 'Slave Labor *versus* Free.' Unfortunately for my admirers and disciples, there was in my father's library a

10

little stray volume of Channing's writings on slavery. I read it at first contemptuously, then attentively, then respectfully, and at last lovingly and prayerfully. The truth, almost insufferably radiant, poured in upon me. Convictions were heaved up in my mind like volcanic islands out of the sea. I was spiritually magnetized and possessed."

"What said your father?"

"My father and I had always lived more as companions than as sire and son. There is only a difference of twenty-two years in our ages. My own mother, a very beautiful woman who died when I was five years old, was six years older than my father. From her I derived my intellectual peculiarities. Of course my father has cast me off, — disowned, disinherited me. He is sincere in his pro-slavery fanaticism. I wish I could say as much of all who fall in with the popular current."

"But what do you mean to do, Charles? 'T is unsafe for you to stay here in New Orleans, holding such sentiments."

"My plans are not yet matured," replied Kenrick. "I shall stand by the old flag, you may be sure of that. And I shall liberate all the slaves I can, beginning with my father's."

"You would not fight against your own State?"

"Incontinently I would if my own State should persist in rebellion against the Union; and so I would fight against my own county should that rebel against the State."

"Well, schoolfellow," said Onslow, with a fascinating frankness, "let us reserve our quarrels for the time when we shall cross swords in earnest. That time may come sooner than we dream of. The less can we afford to say bitter things to each other now. Come, and let me introduce you to a charming young lady. How long do you stay here?"

"Perhaps a week; perhaps a month."

"I shall watch over you while you remain, for I do not fancy seeing my old crony hung."

"Better so than be false to the light within me. Though worms destroy this body, yet in my flesh shall I see God."

Onslow made no reply, but affectionately, almost compassionately, took Kenrick by the arm and led him away.

Vance put down his newspaper, and then, immersed in meditation, slowly passed out of the dining-hall and up-stairs into his own room.

CHAPTER XXI.

A MONSTER OF INGRATITUDE.

"Faint hearts are usually false hearts, choosing sin rather than suffering." — *Argyle, before his execution.*

MRS. GENTRY had attired herself in her new spring costume, a feuillemorte silk, with a bonnet trimmed to match, of the frightful coal-hod shape, with sable roses and a bristling ruche. It was just such a bonnet as Proserpine, Queen of the Shades, might have chosen for a stroll with Pluto along the shore of Lake Avernus.

After many satisfactory glances in the mirror, Mrs. Gentry sat down and trotted her right foot impatiently. Tarquin, entering, announced the carriage.

"Well, go to Miss Ellen, and ask when she'll be ready."

Five minutes Mrs. Gentry waited, while the horses, pestered by stinging insects, dashed their hoofs against the pavements. At last Tarquin returned with the report that Miss Ellen's room was empty.

"Has Pauline looked for her?"

"Yes, missis."

"Ask Esha if she has seen her."

Pauline, standing at the head of the stairs, put the question, and Esha replied testily from the kitchen: "Don't know nuffin 'bout her. Hab suffin better ter do dan look af'r all de school-gals in dis house."

Pauline turned from the old heathen in despair, and suggested that perhaps Miss Ellen had stepped out to buy a ribbon or some hair-pins.

Mrs. Gentry waxed angry. "O, but she'll be come up with!" This was the teacher's favorite form of consolation. The *Abolitionists* would be come up with. Abe Lincoln would be come up with. General Scott would be come up with. Everybody who offended Mrs. Gentry would be come up with, — if not in this world, why then in some other.

An hour passed. She began to get seriously alarmed. She sent away the carriage. Hardly had it gone, when a second vehicle drew up before the door, and out of it stepped Mr. Ratcliff. She met him in the parlor, and, fearing to tell the truth, merely remarked, that Ellen was out making a few purchases.

"When will she be back?"

"Perhaps not till dinner-time."

"Then I'll call to-morrow at this hour."

Mrs. Gentry passed the day in a state of wretched anxiety. She sent out messengers. She interested a policeman in the search. But no trace of the fugitive! Mrs. Gentry was in despair. If Ellen had not been a slave, her disappearance would have been comparatively a small matter. If it had been somebody's free-born daughter who had absconded, it would n't have been half so bad. But here was a slave! One whose flight would lay open to suspicion the teacher's allegiance to *the* institution! Intolerable! Of course it was no concern of hers to what fate that slave was about to be consigned.

Ah! sister of the South, — (and I have known many, the charms of whose persons and manners I thought incomparable,) — a woman whose own virtue is not rooted in sand, cannot, if she thinks and reasons, fail to shudder at a system which sends other women, perhaps as innocent and pure as she herself, to be sold to brutal men at auctions. And yet, if any one had told Mrs. Gentry she was no better than a procuress, both she and the Rev. Dr. Palmer would have thought it an impious aspersion.

At the appointed hour Ratcliff appeared. Mrs. Gentry's toilet that day was appropriate to the calamitous occasion. She was dressed in a black silk robe intensely flounced, and decorated around the bust with a profluvium of black lace that might have melted the heart of a Border-ruffian. She entered the parlor, tragically shaking out a pocket handkerchief with an edging of black.

"O Mr. Ratcliff! Mr. Ratcliff!" she exclaimed, rushing forward, then checking herself melodramatically, and seizing the back of a chair, as if for support.

"Well, madam, what's the matter?"

"That heartless, — that ungrateful girl!"

"What of her?"

Mrs. Gentry answered by applying her handkerchief to her eyes very much as Mrs. Siddons used to do in Belvidera.

"Come, madam," interrupted Ratcliff, "my time is precious. No damned nonsense, if you please. To the point. What has happened?"

Rudely shocked into directness by these words, Mrs. Gentry replied: "She has disappeared, — r-r-run away!"

"Damnation!" was Ratcliff's concise and emphatic comment. He started up and paced the room. "This is a damned pretty return for my confidence, madam."

"O, she'll be come up with, — she'll be come up with!" sobbed Mrs. Gentry.

"Come up with, — where?"

"In the next world, if not in this."

"Pooh! When did she disappear?"

"Yesterday, while I was waiting for her to go out to buy her new dresses. O the ingratitude!"

"Have you made no search for her?"

"Yes, I've made every possible inquiry. I've paid ten dollars to a police-officer to look her up. O the ingratitude of the world! But she'll be come up with!"

"Did you let her know that I was her master?"

"Yes, 't was only yesterday I imparted the information."

"How did she receive it?"

"She was a little startled at first, but soon seemed reconciled, even pleased with the idea of her new wardrobe."

"Have you closely questioned your domestics?"

"Yes. They know nothing. She must have slipped unobserved out of the house."

"Is there any one among them with whom she was more familiar than with another?"

"She used to read the Bible to old Esha, by my direction."

"Call up old Esha. I would like to question her."

Esha soon appeared, her bronzed face glistening with perspiration from the kitchen fire, — the never-failing bright-colored Madras handkerchief on her head.

"Esha," said Mr. Ratcliff, "have you ever seen me before?"

"Yes, Massa Ratcliff, of'n. Lib'd on de nex' plantation to yourn. I 'longed to Massa Peters wunst. But he 'm dead and gone."

"Do you know what an oath is, Esha?"

"Yes, massa, it 's when one swar he know dis or dunno dat."

"Very well. Do you know what becomes of her who swears falsely?"

"O yes, massa; she go to de lake of brimstone and fire, whar' she hab bad time for eber and eber, Amen."

"Are you a Christian, Esha?"

"I 'ze notin' else, Massa Ratcliff."

"Well, Esha, here 's the Holy Bible. Take it in your left hand, kiss the book, and then hold up your right hand."

Esha went through the required form.

"You do solemnly swear, as you hope to be saved from the torments of hell through all eternity, that you will truly answer, to the best of your knowledge and belief, the questions I may put to you. And if you lie, may the Lord strike you dead. Now kiss the book again, to show you take the oath."

Esha kissed the book, and returned it to the table.

"Now, then, do you know anything of the disappearance of this girl, Ellen Murray?"

"Nuffin, massa, nuffin at all."

"Did she ever tell you she meant to leave this house?"

"Nebber, massa! She nebber tell me any sich ting."

"Did she have any talk with you yesterday?"

"Not a bressed word did dat chile say to me 'cep ter scole me 'cause I did n't do up her Organdy muslin nice as she 'spected. De little hateful she-debble! How can dis ole nig do eb'ry ting all at wunst, and do 't well, should like ter know? It 's cook an' wash an' iron, an' iron an' wash an' —"

"There! That will do, Esha. You can go."

"Yes, Massa Ratcliff."

Stealing into the next room, Esha listened at the folding-doors.

"She knows nothing, — that 's very clear," said Ratcliff. He went to the window, and looked out in silence a full minute; then, coming back, added: "Stop snivelling, madam. I 'm not a fool. I've seen women before now. This girl must be found, — found if it costs me ten thousand dollars. And you must aid in the search. If I find her, — well and good. If I don't find her, you shall suffer for it. This is what I mean to do: I shall have copies of her photograph put in the hands of the best detectives in the city. I shall pay them well in advance, and promise five hundred dollars to the one that finds her. They'll come to you. You must give them all the information you can, and lend them your servants to identify the girl. This old Esha plainly has a grudge against her, and may be made useful in hunting her up. Let her go out daily for that purpose. Tell all your pupils to be on the watch. I'll break up your school if she is n't found. Do you understand?"

"I'll do all I can, sir, to have her caught."

"That will be your most prudent course, madam."

And Ratcliff, with more exasperation in his face than his words had expressed, quitted the house.

"The brute!" muttered Mrs. Gentry, as through the blinds she saw him enter his barouche, and drive off. "He treated me as if I'd been a drab. But he'll be come up with, — he will!"

Esha crept down into the kitchen, with thoughts intent on what she had heard.

CHAPTER XXII.

THE YOUNG LADY WITH A CARPET-BAG.

"Pain has its own noble joy when it kindles a consciousness of life, before stagnant and torpid." — *John Sterling.*

CHILDREN are quick to detect flaws in the genealogy of their associates. School-girls are quite as exclusive in their notions as our grown-up leaders of society. Woe to the candidate for companionship on whose domestic record there hangs a doubt!

Mrs. Gentry having felt it her duty to inform her pupils that Clara was not a lady, the latter was thenceforth "left out in the cold" by the little Brahmins of the seminary. She would sit, like a criminal, apart from the rest, or in play-hours seek the company, either of Esha or the mocking-bird.

One circumstance puzzled the other young ladies. They could not understand why, in the more showy accomplishments of music, singing, and dancing, more expense should be bestowed on Clara's education than on theirs. The elegance and variety of her toilet excited at once their envy and their curiosity.

Clara, finding that she was held back from serious studies, gave her thoughts to them all the more resolutely, and excelled in them so far as to shock the conservative notions of Mrs. Gentry, who thought such acquisitions presumptuous in a slave. The pupils all tossed their little heads, and turned their backs, when Clara drew near. All but one. Laura Tremaine prized Clara's counsels on questions of dress, and defied the jeers and frowns that would deter her from cultivating the acquaintance of one suspected of ignoble birth. Something almost like a friendship grew up between the two. Laura was the only daughter of a wealthy cotton-broker who resided the greater part of the year in New Orleans, at the St. Charles Hotel.

The two girls used to stroll through the garden with arms about each other's waist. One day Clara, in a gush of candor, not only avowed herself an Abolitionist, but tried to convert Laura to the heresy. *Quelle horreur!* There was at once a cessation of the intimacy,—Laura exacting a recantation which the little infidel proudly refused.

The disagreement had occurred only a few days before that flight of Clara's in which we must now follow her. After parting from Esha, she walked for some distance, ignorant why she selected one direction rather than another, and having no clearly defined purpose as to her destination. She had promenaded thus about an hour, when she saw a barouche approaching. The occupant, a man, sat leaning lazily back with his feet up on the opposite cushions. A black driver and footman, both in livery, filled the lofty front seat. As the vehicle rolled on, Clara recognized Ratcliff. She shuddered and dropped her veil.

Fortunately he was half asleep, and did not see her.

Whither now? Of two streets she chose the more obscure. On she walked, and the carpet-bag began to be an encumbrance. The heat was oppressive. Occasionally a passer-by among the young men would say to an acquaintance, "Did you notice that figure?" One man offered to carry the bag. She declined his aid. On and on she walked. Whither and why? She could not explain. All at once it occurred to her she was wasting her strength in an objectless promenade.

Her utterly forlorn condition revealed itself in all its desolateness and danger. She stopped under the shade of a magnolia-tree, and, leaning against the trunk, put back her veil, and wiped the moisture from her face. She had been walking more than two hours, and was overheated and fatigued. What should she do? The tears began to flow at the thought that the question was one for which she had no reply.

Suddenly she looked round with the vague sense that some one was watching her. She encountered the gaze of a gentleman who, with an air of mingled curiosity and compassion, stood observing her grief. He wore a loose frock of buff nankin, with white vest and pantaloons; and on his head was a hat of very fine Panama straw. Whether he was young or old Clara did not remark. She only knew that a face beautiful from its compassion beamed on her, and that it was the face of a gentleman.

"Can I assist you?" he asked.

"No, thank you," replied Clara. "I'm fatigued, — that's all, — and am resting here a few minutes."

"Here's a little house that belongs to me," said the gentleman, pointing to a neat though small wooden tenement before which they were standing. "I do not live here, but the family who do will be pleased to receive you for my sake. You shall have a room all to yourself, and rest there till you are refreshed. Do you distrust me, my child?"

There are faces out of which Truth looks so unequivocally, that to distrust them seems like a profanation. Clara did not distrust, and yet she hesitated, and replied through her tears, "No, I do not distrust you, but I've no claim on your kindness."

"Ah! but you *have* a claim," said Vance (for it was he); "you are unhappy, and the unhappy are my brothers and my sisters. I've been unhappy myself. I knew one years ago, young like you, and like you unhappy, and through her also you have a claim. There! Let me relieve you of that bag. Now take my arm. Good! This way." Clara's tears gushed forth anew at these words, and yet less at the words than at the tone in which they were uttered. So musical and yet so melancholy was that tone.

He knocked at the door. It was opened by Madame Bernard, a spruce little Frenchwoman, who had married a journeyman printer, and who felt unbounded gratitude to Vance for his gift of the rent of the little house.

"Is it you, Mr. Vance? We've been wondering why you did n't come."

"Madame Bernard, this young lady is fatigued. I wish her to rest in my room."

"The room of Monsieur is always in order. Follow me, my dear."

And, taking the carpet-bag, Madame conducted her to the little chamber, then asked: "Now what will you have, my dear? A little claret and water? Some fruit or cake?"

"Nothing, thank you. I'll rest on the sofa awhile. You're very kind. The gentleman's name is Vance, is it?"

"Yes; is he not an acquaintance?"

"I never saw him till three minutes ago. He noticed me

resting, and, I fear, weeping in the street, and he asked me in here to rest."

"'T was just like him. He's so good, so generous! He gives me the rent of this house with the pretty garden attached. You can see it from the window. Look at the grapes. He reserves for himself this room, which I daily dust and keep in order. Poor man! 'T was here he passed the few months of his marriage, years ago. His wife died, and he bought the house, and has kept it in repair ever since. This used to be their sleeping-room. 'T was also their parlor, for they were poor. There's their little case of books. Here's the piano on which they used to play duets. 'T was a hired piano, and was returned to the owner; but Mr. Vance found it in an old warehouse, not long ago, had it put in order, and brought here. 'T is one of Chickering's best; a superb instrument. You should hear Mr. Vance play on it."

"Does he play well?" asked Clara, who had almost forgotten her own troubles in listening to the little woman's gossip.

"Ah! you never heard such playing! I know something of music. My family is musical. I flatter myself I'm a judge. I've heard Thalberg, Vieuxtemps, Jael, Gottschalk; and Mr. Vance plays better than any of them."

"Is he a professor?"

"No, merely an amateur. But he puts a soul into the notes. Do you play at all, my dear?"

"Yes, I began to learn so early that I cannot recollect the time when."

"I thought you must be musical. Just try this instrument, my dear, that is, if you're not too tired."

"Certainly, if 't will oblige you."

Seating herself at the piano, Clara played, from Donizetti's *Lucia*, Edgardo's melodious wail of abandonment and despair, "*L' universo intero e un deserto per me sensa Lucia.*"

Mrs. Bernard had opened the door that Vance might hear. At the conclusion he knocked and entered. "Is this the way you rest yourself, young pilgrim?" he asked. "You're a proficient, I see. You've been made to practise four hours a day."

"Yes, ever since I can remember."

"So I should think. Now let me hear something in a different vein."

Clara, while the blood mounted to her forehead, and her whole frame dilated, struck into the "Star-spangled Banner," playing it with her whole soul, and at the close singing the refrain,

> "And the Star-spangled Banner in triumph shall wave
> O'er the land of the free and the home of the brave."

"But that's treason!" cried Mrs. Bernard.

"Yes, Mrs. Bernard," said Vance, "run at once to the police-station. Tell them to send a file of soldiers. We must have her arrested."

"O no, no!" exclaimed Clara, deceived by Vance's grave acting. Then, seeing her mistake, she laughed, and said: "That's too bad. I thought for a moment you were in earnest."

"We will spare you this time," said Vance, with a smile that made his whole face luminous; "but should outsiders in the street hear you, they may not be so forbearing. They will tear our little house down if you're not careful."

"I'll not be so imprudent again," returned Clara. "Will you play for me, sir?" And she resumed her seat on the sofa.

Vance played some extemporized variations on the Carnival of Venice; and Clara, who had regarded Mrs. Bernard's praises as extravagant, now concluded they were the literal truth. "Oh!" she exclaimed, naively, "I never heard playing like that. Do not ask me to play before you again, sir."

Mrs. Bernard left to attend to the affairs of the *cuisine*.

"Now, mademoiselle," said Vance, "what can I do before I go?"

"All I want," replied Clara, "is time to arrange some plan. I left home so suddenly I'm quite at a loss."

"Do I understand you've left your parents?"

"I have no parents, sir."

"Then a near relation, or a guardian?"

"Neither, sir. I am independent of all ties."

"Have you no friend to whom you can go for advice?"

"I had a friend, but she gave me up because I'm an Abolitionist."

"My poor little lady! An Abolitionist? You? In times like these? When Sumter has fallen, too? No wonder your friend has cast you off. Who is she?"

"Miss Laura Tremaine. She lives at the St. Charles. Do you know her, sir?"

"Slightly. I met her in the drawing-room not long since. She does not appear unamiable. But why are you an Abolitionist?"

"Because I believe in God."

Vance felt that this was the summing-up of the whole matter. He looked with new interest on the "little lady." In height she was somewhat shorter than Estelle, — not much over five feet two and a half. Not from her features, but from the maturity of their expression, he judged she might have reached her eighteenth year. Somewhat more of a brunette than Estelle, and with fine abundant hair of a light brown. Eyes — he could not quite see their color; but they were vivid, penetrating, earnest. Features regular, and a profile even more striking in its beauty than her front face. A figure straight and slim, but exquisitely rounded, and every movement revealing some new grace. Where had he seen a face like it?

After a few moments of contemplation, he said: "Do not think me impertinently curious. You have been well educated. You have not had to labor for a living. Are the persons to whom you 've been indebted for support no longer your friends?"

"They are my worst enemies, and all that has been bestowed on me has been from hateful motives and calculations." — "Now I 'm going to ask a very delicate question. Are you provided with money?" — "O yes, sir, amply." — "How much have you?" — "Twenty dollars." — "Indeed! Are you so rich as that? What 's your name?" — "The name I 've been brought up under is Ellen Murray; but I hate it." — "Why so?" — "Because of a dream." — "A dream! And what was it?" — "Shall I relate it?" — "By all means."

"I dreamed that a beautiful lady led me by the hand into a spacious garden. On one side were fruits, and on the other side flowers, and in the middle a circle of brilliant verbenas from the centre of which rose a tall fountain, fed from a high hill in the neighborhood. And the lady said, 'This is your garden, and your name is not Ellen Murray.' Then she gave me a letter sealed with blue — no, gray — wax, and said, 'Put this letter on your eyes, and you shall find it there when you wake. Some one will open it, and your name will be seen written there, though you may not understand it at first.' 'But am I not awake?' I asked. 'O no,' said the lady. 'This is all a dream. But we can sometimes impress those we love in this way.' 'And who are you?' I asked. 'That you will know when you interpret the letter,' she said."

"And what resulted from the dream?" — "The moment I waked I put my hand on my eyes. Of course I found no letter. The next night the lady came again, and said, 'The seal cannot be broken by yourself. Your name is not Ellen Murray, — remember that.' A third night this dream beset me, and so forcibly that I resolved to get rid of the name as far as I could. And so I made my friends call me Darling."

"Well, Darling, as you — " — "O, but, sir! *you* must not call me Darling. That would never do!" — "What *can* I call you, then?" — "Call me Miss, or Mademoiselle." — "Well, Miss." — "No, I do not like the sibilation." — "Will *Ma'am* do any better?" — "Not till I'm more venerable. Call me Perdita." — "Perdita what?" — "Perdita Brown, — yes, I love the name of Brown."

"Well, Perdita, as you've not quite made up your mind to seek the protection of Miss Tremaine, my advice is that you remain here till to-morrow. Here is a little case filled with books; and on the shelf of the closet is plenty of old music, — works of Handel, Mozart, Beethoven, Mendelssohn, Schubert, and some of the Italian masters. Do you play Schubert's Sacred Song?" — "I never heard it." — "Learn it, then, by all means. 'T is in that book. Shall I tell Mrs. Bernard you'll pass the night here?" — "Do, sir. I'm very grateful for your kindness." — "Good by, Perdita! Should anything detain me to-morrow, wait till I come. Keep up your four hours' practice. Madame Bernard is amiable, but a little talkative. I shall tell her to allow you five hours for your studies. Adieu, Perdita!"

He held out his hand, and Clara gave hers, and cast down her eyes. "You've told me a true story?" said he. "Yes! I will trust you."

"Indeed, sir, I 've told you nothing but the truth."

Yes. She had told the truth, but unhappily not the *whole* truth. And yet how she longed to kneel at his feet and confess all! Various motives withheld her. She was not quite sure how he had received her antislavery confessions. He might be a friend of Mr. Ratcliff. There was dismay in the very possibility. And finally a certain pride or prudence restrained her from throwing herself on the protection of a stranger not of her own sex.

And so the golden opportunity was allowed to escape!

Vance lingered for a moment holding her hand, as if to invite her to a further confidence; but she said nothing, and he left the room. Clara opened the music-book at Schubert's piece, and commenced playing. Vance stopped on the stairs and listened, keeping time approvingly. "Good!" he said. Then telling the little landlady not to interrupt Miss Brown's studies, he quitted the house, walking in the direction of the hotel.

Clara practised till she could play from memory the charming composition commended by Vance. Then she threw herself on the bed and fell asleep. She had not remained thus an hour when there was a knock. Dinner! Mr. Bernard had come in; a dapper little man, so remarkably well satisfied with himself, his wife, and his bill of fare, that he repeatedly had to lay down knife and fork and rub his hands in glee.

"Are you related to Mr. Vance?" he asked Clara.

"Not at all. He saw me in the street, weary and distressed. The truth is, I had left my home for a good reason. I have no parents, you must consider. He asked me in here. From his looks I judged he was a man to trust. I gladly accepted his invitation."

"Truly he 's a friend in need, Mademoiselle. I saw him do another kind thing to-day."

"What was it?"

"It happened only an hour ago in Carondelet Street. A ragged fellow was haranguing a crowd. He spoke on the wrong side, — in short, in favor of the old flag. Some laughed, some hissed, some applauded. Suddenly a party of men, armed with swords and muskets, pushed through the crowd, and seized the speaker. They formed a court, Judge Lynch presiding, under a palmetto. They decided that the vagabond should be hung. He had already been badly pricked in the flank with a bayonet. And now a table was brought out, he was placed on it, and a rope put round his neck and tied to a bough. Decidedly they were going to string him up."

"Good heavens!" cried Clara, who, as the story proceeded, had turned pale and thrust away the plate of food from before her. "Did you make no effort to save him?"

"What could I do? They would merely have got another rope, and made me keep him company. Well, the mob were expecting an entertainment. They were about to knock away the table, when Monsieur Vance pushed through the crowd, hauled off the hangman, and, jumping on the table, cut the rope, and lifted the prisoner faint and bleeding to the ground. What a yell from Judge Lynch and the court! Monsieur Vance, his coat and vest all bloody from contact with —"

"What a shame!" interposed Mrs. Bernard. "A coat and vest he must have put on clean this morning! So nicely ironed and starched!"

"But my story agitates you, Mademoiselle," said the type-setter. "You look pale." And the little man, not regarding the inappropriateness of the act, rubbed his hands.

"Go on," replied Clara; and she sipped from a tumbler of cold water.

"There 's little more to say, Mademoiselle. Messieurs, the bullies, drew their swords on Monsieur Vance. He showed a revolver, and they fell back. Then he talked to them till they cooled down, gave him three cheers, and went off. I and old Mr. Winslow helped him to find a carriage. We put the wounded man into it. He was driven to the hospital, and his wound attended to. 'T is serious, I believe."

And Bernard again rubbed his hands.

"And was that the last you saw of Mr. Vance?" asked Clara.

"The last. Shall I help you to some pine-apple, Mademoiselle?"

"No, thank you. I 've finished my dinner. You will excuse me."

And she returned to the little room assigned to her use.

CHAPTER XXIII.

WILL YOU WALK INTO MY PARLOR?

" Sing again the song you sung
When we were together young ;
When there were but you and I
Underneath the summer sky.
Sing the song, and o'er and o'er,
Though I know that nevermore
Will it seem the song you sung
When we were together young."

George William Curtis.

VANCE passed on through the streets, wondering what could be the mystery which had driven his new acquaintance forth into the wide world without a protector. Should he speak of her to Miss Tremaine? Perhaps. But not unless he could do it without betrayal of confidence.

There was something in Perdita that reminded him of Estelle. Had a pressure of similar circumstances wrought the peculiarity which awakened the association? Yet he missed in Perdita that diaphanous simplicity, that uncalculating candor, which seemed to lead Estelle to unveil her whole nature before him. But Perdita had not wholly failed in frankness. Had she not glorified the old flag in her music? And had she not been outspoken on the one forbidden theme?

As these thoughts flitted through his mind, excluding for the moment those graver interests, involving a people's doom, he heard the shouts of a crowd, and saw a man, pale and bloody, standing on a table under a tree, from a branch of which a rope was dangling. Vance comprehended the meaning of it all in an instant. He darted toward the spot, gliding swift, agile, and flexuous through the compacted crowd. Yes! The victim was the same man to whom he had given the gold-piece, some days before. Vance put a summary stop to Judge Lynch's proceedings, breaking up the court precisely as Bernard had related. The wounded man was conveyed to the hospital. Here Vance saw his wound dressed, hired an extra attendant to nurse him, and then, in tones of warmest sympathy, asked the sufferer what more he could do for him.

The man opened his eyes. A swarthy, filthy, uncombed, unshaven wretch. He had been so blinded by blood that he had not recognized Vance. But now, seeing him, he started, and strove to raise himself on his elbow.

Vance and the surgeon prevented the movement. The patient stared, and said: "You 've done it agin, have yer? What 's yer name?"

"This is Mr. Vance," replied the surgeon.

"Vance! Vance!" said the patient, as if trying to force his memory to some particular point. Then he added: "Can't do it! And yit I 've seen him afore somewhar."

"Well, my poor fellow, I must leave you. Good by."

"Why, this hand is small and white as a woman's!" said the patient, touching Vance's fingers carefully as he might have touched some fragile flower. "Yer 'll come agin to see me, — woan't yer?"

"Yes, I 'll not forget it." — "Call to-morrow, will yer?" — "Yes, if I 'm alive I 'll call." — "Thahnk yer, strannger. Good by."

Giving a few dollars to the surgeon for the patient's benefit, Vance quitted the hospital. An hour afterwards, in his room at the St. Charles, he penned and sent this note: —

"To Perdita: I shall not be able to see you again to-day. Content yourself as well as you can in the company of Mozart and Beethoven, Bellini and Donizetti, Irving and Dickens, Tennyson and Longfellow. The company is not large, but you will find it select. Unless some very serious engagement should prevent, I will see you to-morrow. Vance."

This little note was read and re-read by Clara, till the darkness of night came on. She studied the forms of the letters, the curves and flourishes, all the peculiarities of the chirography, as if she could derive from them some new hints for her incipient hero-worship. Then, lighting the gas, she acted on the advice of the letter, by devoting herself to the performance of Beethoven's Fifth Symphony.

Vance meanwhile, after a frugal dinner, eliminated from

luxurious viands, rang the bell, and sent his card to Miss Tremaine. Laura's mother was an invalid, and Laura herself, relieved from maternal restraint, had been lately in the habit of receiving and entertaining company, much to her own satisfaction, as she now had an enlarged field for indulging a propensity not uncommon among young women who have been much admired and much indulged.

Laura was a predestined flirt. Had she been brought up between the walls of a nunnery, where the profane presence of a man had never been known, she would instinctively have launched into coquetry the first time the bishop or the gardener made his appearance.

Having heard Madame Brugière, the fashionable widow, speak of Mr. Vance as the handsomest man in New Orleans, Laura was possessed with the desire of bringing him into her circle of admirers. So, one day after dinner, she begged her father to stroll with her through a certain corridor of the hotel. She calculated that Vance would pass there on his way to his room. She was right. " Is that Mr. Vance, papa ? " — " Yes, my dear." — " O, do introduce him. They say he 's such a superb musician. We must have him to try our new piano." — " I 'm but slightly acquainted with him." — " No matter. He goes into the best society, you know." (The father did n't know it, — neither did the daughter, — but he took it for granted she spoke by authority.) " He 's very rich, too," added Laura. This was enough to satisfy the paternal conscience. " Good evening, Mr. Vance ! Lively times these ! Let me make you acquainted with my daughter, Miss Laura. We shall be happy to see you in our parlor, Mr. Vance." Vance bowed, and complimented the lady on a tea-rose she held in her hand. " Did you ever see anything more beautiful ? " she asked. — " Never till now," he replied. — " Ah ! The rose is yours. You 've fairly won it, Mr. Vance ; but there 's a condition attached : you must promise to call and try my new piano." — " Agreed. I 'll call at an early day." He bowed, and passed on. " A very charming person," said Laura. — " Yes, a gentleman evidently," said the father. — " And he is n't redolent of cigar-smoke and whiskey, as nine tenths of you ill-smelling men are," added Laura. — " Tut ! Don't abuse your future husband, my dear." — "How old should you take Mr. Vance to be?" — "About thirty-five." — "O no! Not a year over thirty." — "He 's too old to be caught by any chaff of yours, my dear!" — "Now, papa! I 'll not walk with you another minute!"

A few evenings afterwards, as Laura sat lonely in her private parlor, a waiter put into her hand a card on which was simply written in pencil, "MR. VANCE." She did not try to check the start of exultation with which she said, "Show him in."

Laura was now verging on her eighteenth year. A little above the Medicean height, her well-rounded shoulders and bust prefigured for her womanhood a voluptuous fulness. Nine men out of ten would have pronounced her beautiful. Had she been put up at a slave-vendue, the auctioneer, if a connoisseur, would have expatiated thus: "Let me call your attention, gentlemen, to this *very* superior article. Faultless, you see, every way. In limb and action perfect. Too showy, perhaps, for a field-hand, but excellent for the parlor. Look at that profile. The Grecian type in its perfection! Nose a little *retroussé*, but what piquancy in the expression! Hair dark, glossy, abundant. Cheeks, — do you notice that little dimple when she smiles? Teeth sound and white: open the mouth of the article and look, gentlemen. Just feel of those arms, gentlemen. Complexion smooth, brilliant, perfect. Did you ever see a head and neck more neatly set on the shoulders? — and such shoulders! What are you prepared to bid, gentlemen, for this very, very superior article?"

Laura was attired in a light checked foulard silk, trimmed with cherry-colored ribbons. Running to the mirror, she adjusted here and there a curl, and lowered the gauze over her shoulders. Then, resuming her seat, she took Tennyson's "In Memoriam" from the table, and became intensely absorbed in the perusal.

As Vance entered, Laura said to herself, "I know I 'm right as to his age!" Nor was her estimate surprising. During the last two lustrums of his nomadic life, he had rather reinvigorated than impaired his physical frame. He never counteracted the hygienic benefits of his Arab habits by vices of eating and drinking. Abjuring all liquids but water, sleeping often on the bare ground under the open sky, he so hardened and purified his constitution that those constantly recurring local inflammations which, under the name of "colds" of some sort, beset men in their ordinary lives in cities, were to him almost unknown. And so he was what the Creoles called *bien conservé*.

Laura, with a pretty affectation of surprise, threw down her book, and, with extended hand, rose to greet her visitor. To him the art he had first studied on the stage had become a second nature. Every movement was proportioned, graceful, harmonious. He fell into no inelegant posture. He did not sit down in a chair without naturally falling into the attitude that an artist would have thought right. That consummate ease and grace which play-goers used to admire in James Wallack were remarkable in Vance, whether in motion or in repose.

Taking Laura's proffered hand, he led her to the sofa, where they sat down. After some commonplaces in regard to the news of the day, he remarked: "By the way, do you know of any good school in the city for a young girl, say of fourteen?"

"Yes. Mrs. Gentry's school, which I 've just left, is one of the most select in the city. Here 's her card." — "But are her pupils all from the best families?" — "I believe so. Indeed, I know the families of all except one." — "And who is *she?*" — "Her name is Ellen Murray, but I call her Darling. I think she must be preparing either for the opera or the ballet; for in music, singing, and dancing she 's far beyond the rest of us." — "And behind you in the other branches, I suppose." — "I 'm afraid not. She won't be kept back. She must have given twice the time to study that any of the rest of us gave." — "Does she seem to be of gentle blood?" — "Yes; though Mrs. Gentry tells us she is low-born. For all that, she 's quite pretty, and knows more than Madame Groux herself about dress. And so Darling and I, in spite of Mrs. Gentry, were getting to be quite intimate, when we quarrelled on the slavery question, and separated." — "What! the little miss is a politician, is she?" — "Oh! she 's a downright Abolitionist! — talks like a little fury against the wrongs of slavery. I could n't endure it, and so cast her off." — "Bring her to me. I 'll convert her in five minutes." — "O you vain man! But I wish you could hear her sing. Such a voice!" — "Could n't you give me an opportunity? You should n't have quarrelled with her, Miss Tremaine! It rather amuses me that she should talk treason. Why not arrange a little musical party? I'll come and play for you a whole evening, if you 'll have Darling to sing." — "O, that would be so charming! But then Darling and I have separated. We don't speak." — "Nonsense! Miss Laura Tremaine can afford to offer the olive-branch to a poor little outcast." — "To be sure I can, Mr. Vance! And I 'll have her here, if I have to bring her by stratagem." — "Admirable! Just send for me as soon as you secure the bird. And keep her strictly caged till I can hear her sing." — "I 'll do it, Mr. Vance. Even the dragon Gentry shall not prevent it." — "Shall I try the new piano?" — "O, I 've been so longing to hear you!"

And Vance, seating himself at the instrument, exerted himself as he had rarely done to fascinate an audience. Laura, who had taste, if not diligence, in music, was charmed and bewildered. "How delightful! How very delightful!" she exclaimed. Vance was growing dangerous.

At that moment the servant entered with two cards.

"Did you tell them I 'm in?" — "Yes, Mahmzel."

"Well, then," said Laura, with an air of disappointment, "show them up." And handing the cards to Vance, she asked, "Shall I introduce them?"

"Mr. Robert Onslow, — Charles Kenrick. Certainly."

The young men entered, and were introduced.

Kenrick drew near, and said: "Mr. Vance, allow me the honor of taking you by the hand. I 've heard of the poor fellow you rescued from the halter of Judge Lynch. In the name of humanity, I thank you. That poor ragged declaimer merely spoke my own sentiments."

"Indeed! What did he say?"

"He said, according to the Delta's report, that this was the rich man's war; that the laboring man who should lift his arm in defence of slavery was a fool. All which I hold to be true."

"Pshaw, Charles! A truce to politics!" said Onslow. "Why will you thrust it into faces that frown on your wild notions?"

"Miss Tremaine reigns absolute in this room," rejoined Vance; "and from the slavery she imposes we have no desire, I presume, to be free."

"And her order is," cried Laura, "that you sink the shop. Thank you, Mr. Vance, for vindicating my authority."

There was no further jarring. Both the young men were personally fine specimens of the Southern chivalric race. Onslow was the larger and handsomer. He seemed to unite with a feminine gentleness the traits that make a man popular and beloved among men; a charming companion, sunny-tempered, amiable, social, ever finding a soul of goodness in things evil, and making even trivialities surrender enjoyments, where to other men all was barren. Life was to him a sort of grand picnic, and a man's true business was to make himself as agreeable as possible, first to himself, and then to others.

Far different seemed Kenrick. To him the important world was that of ideas. All else was unsubstantial. The thought that was uppermost must be uttered. Not to conciliate, not to please, even in the drawing-room, would he be an assentator, a flatterer. To him truth was the one thing needful, and therefore, in season and out of season, must error be combated whenever met. The times were of a character to intensify in him all his idiosyncrasies. He could not smile, and sing, and utter small-talk while his country was being weighed in the balance of the All-just, — and her institutions purged as by fire. And so to Laura he dwindled into insignificance.

Vance rose to go.

"One song. Indeed, I must have one," said Laura.

Vance complied with her request, singing a favorite song of Estelle's, Reichardt's

"Du liebes Aug', du lieber Stern,
Du bist mir nah', und doch so fern!"*

Then, pressing Laura's proffered hand, and bowing, he left.

"What a voice! what a touch!" said Onslow.

"It was enchanting!" cried Laura.

"I thought he was a different sort of man," sighed Kenrick.

* "Beloved eye, beloved star,
Thou art so near, and yet so far!"

CHAPTER XXIV.

CONFESSIONS OF A MEAN WHITE.

"Throw thyself on thy God, nor mock him with feeble denial;
Sure of his love, and O, sure of his mercy at last;
Bitter and deep though the draught, yet drain thou the cup of thy trial,
And in its healing effect smile at the bitterness past."
Lines composed by Sir John Herschel in a dream.

AFTER an early breakfast the following morning, Vance proceeded to the hospital. The patient had been expecting him.

"He has seemed to know just how near you 've been for the last hour," said the nurse. "He followed — "

"Sit down, Mr. Vance, please," interrupted the patient.

Vance drew a chair near to the pillow and sat down.

"It all kum ter me last night, Mr. Vance! Now I remember whar 't was I met yer. But fust lem me tell yer who an' what I be. My name 's Quattles. I was born in South Kerliny, not fur from Columby. I was what the niggers call a *mean white*, and my father he was a mean white afore me, and all my brothers they was mean whites, and my sisters they mahrrid mean whites. The one thing we was raised ter do fiust-rate, and what we tuk ter kindly from the start, was ter shirk labor. We was taught 't was degradin' ter do useful work like a nigger does, so we all tried hard ter find su'thin' that mowt be easy an' not useful."

"My dear fellow," interrupted Vance, who saw the man was suffering, "you 're fatiguing yourself too much. Rest awhile."

"No, Mr. Vance. You mus n't mind these twitchin's an' spazums like. They airn't quite as bahd as they look. Wall, as I war sayin', one cuss of slavery ar', it drives the poor whites away from honest labor; makes 'em think it 's mean-sperretid ter hoe corn an' plant 'taters. An' this feelin', yer see, ar' all ter the profit uv the rich men, — the Hammonds, Rhetts, an' Draytons, — 'cause why? 'cause it leaves ter the rich all the good land, an' drives the poor whites ter pickin' up a mean livin', any way they kin, outside uv hard work! Howsomever, I did n't see this; an' so, like other mis'rable fools, I thowt I war a sort uv a 'ristocrat myself, 'cause I could put on airs afore a nigger. An' this feelin' the slave-owners try to keep up in the mean whites; try to make 'em feel proud they 're not niggers, though the hull time the poor cusses fare wuss nor any nigger in a rice-swamp."

"My friend," said Vance, "you 've got at the truth at last, though I fear you 've been long about it."

"Yer may bet high on that, Mr. Vance! How I used ter cuss the Abolishuners, an' go ravin' mahd over the meddlin' Yankees! Wall, what d' yer think war the best thing South Kerliny could do fur me, after never off'rin' me a chance ter larn ter read an' write? I 'll tell yer what the *peculiar* prermoted me ter. I riz to be foreman uv of a rat-pit."

"Of a *what?*" interrogated Vance.

"Of a rat-pit. There war a feller in Charleston who kept a rat-pit, whar a little tareyer dog killed rats, so many a minute, to please the sportin' gentry an' other swells. Price uv admission one dollar. The swells would come an' bet how many rats the dog would kill in a minute, — 't was sometimes thirty, sometimes forty, and wunst 't was fifty. My bus'ness was ter throw the rats, one after another, inter the pit. We 'd a big cage with a hole in the top, an' I had ter put my bar hand in, an' throw out the rats fast as I could, one by one. The tareyer would spring an' break the backs uv the varmints with one jerk uv his teeth. Great bus'ness fur a white man, — war n't it? So much more genteel than plantin' an' hoein'! Wall, I kept at that pleasant trade five yars, an' then lost my place 'cause both hands got so badly bit I could n't pull out the rats no longer."

"You must have seen things from a bad stand-point, my friend."

"Bad as 't was, 't was better nor the slavery stand-pint I kum ter next. Yer 'v heerd tell uv Jeff McTavish? Wall, Jeff hahd an overseer who got shot in the leg by a runaway swamp nigger, an' so I was hired as a sort uv overseer's mate. I war n't brung up ter be very tender 'bout niggers, Mr.

Vance; but the way niggers was treated on that air plantation was too much even for my tough stomach. I 've seen niggers shot down dead by McTavish fur jest openin' thar big lips to answer him when he was mad. There war n't ten uv his slaves out uv a hunderd, that war n't scored all up an' down the back with marks uv the lash." *

"Did you whip them?" inquired Vance.

"I did n't do nothin' else; but I did it slack, an' McTavish he found it out, and begun jawin' me. An' I guv it to him back, and we hahd it thar purty steep, an' bymeby he outs with his revolver, but I war too spry for him. I tripped him up, an' he hahd ter ask pardon uv a mean white wunst in his life, an' no mistake. A little tahmrin' water, please."

Vance administered a spoonful, and the patient resumed his story.

"In coorse, I hahd ter leave McTavish. Then fur five years I 'd a tight time of it keepin' wooded up. What with huntin' and fishin', thimble-riggin' an' stealin', I got along somehow, an' riz ter be a sort uv steamboat gambler on the Misippy. 'T was thar I fust saw you, Mr. Vance."

"On the Mississippi! When and where?"

"Some fifteen yars ago, on boord the Pontiac, jest afore she blowed up."

"Indeed! I 've no recollection of meeting you."

"Don't yer remember Kunnle D'lancy Hyde?"

"Perfectly."

"Wall, I war his shadder. He could n't go nowhar I did n't foller. If he took snuff, I sneezed. If he got drunk, I staggered. Don't yer remember a darkish, long-haired feller, he called Quattles?"

"Are you that man?" exclaimed Vance, restraining his emotion.

"I'm nobody else, Mr. Vance, an' it ain't fur nothin' I 've

* General Ullmann writes from New Orleans, June 6, 1863, to Governor Andrew: "Every man (freed negro) presenting himself to be recruited, strips to the skin. My surgeons report to me that *not one in fifteen* is free from marks of severe lashing. More than one half are rejected because of disability from lashing with whips, and the biting of dogs on calves and thighs. It is frightful. Hundreds have welts on their backs as large as one of your largest fingers."

got yer here to har what I've ter tell. Ef I don't stop to say I'm sorry for the mean things I done, 't aint 'cause I hain't some shame 'bout it, but 'cause time's short. When the Pontiac blowed up, I an' the Kunnle (he's 'bout as much uv a kunnle as I'm uv a bishop), we found ou'selves on that part uv the boat whar least damage was did. We was purty well corned, for we'd been drinkin' some, but the smash-up sobered us. The Kunnle's fust thowt was fur his niggers. Says I: 'Let the niggers slide. We sh'll be almighty lucky ef we keep out of hell ou'selves.' 'T was ev'ry man for hisself, yer know."

"Were you on the forward part of the wreck?"

"Yes, Mr. Vance, an' it soon began ter sink. Poor critters, men an' women, some scalded, some strugglin' in the water, war cryin' for help. The Kunnle an' I —."

"Stop a moment," said Vance; and, drawing out paper and pencil, he made copious notes.

"As I war sayin', Mr. Vance, the Kunnle an' I got four life-presarvin' stools, lahshed 'em together, an' begun ter make off for the shore. Says I, 'We owt ter save one uv those women folks.' A yaller gal, with a white child in her arms, was screamin' out for us to take her an' the child. Jèst then she got a blow on the head from a block that fell from one uv the masts. It seemed ter make her wild, an' she dropped inter the water, but held on tight ter the young 'un. Says the Kunnle to me, says he, 'Now, Cappn, you take the gal, an' I'll take the bebby.' An' so we done it, and all got ashore safe. We lahnded on the Tennessee side. The sun hahd n't riz, but 't was jest light enough ter see. We made tracks away from the river till we kum ter a nigger's desarted hut, out of sight 'tween two hills. Thar we left the yaller gal and the bebby. The gal seemed kind o' crazy; so we fastened 'em in."

"And the child?" asked Vance. "Did you know whose it was?"

"O yes, I knowed it, 'cause I'd seen the yaller gal more 'n a dozen times, off an' on, leadin' the little thing about. The Berwicks, a North'n family, was the parrents. Wall, the Kunnle an' I, we went back ter the river to see what was goin' on. The sun was up now. The Champion hahd turned back to give help. Poor critters war dyin' all round from scalds and bruises. All at wunst the Kunnle an' I kum upon a crowd round Mr. Berwick, who lay thar on the ground bahdly wounded. His wife lay dead close by. He kept askin' fur his child. A feller named Burgess told him he seed the yaller gal an' child go overboord, an' that they must have drownded. Prehaps he did see 'em in the water, but he did n't see us pick 'em up. Old Onslow he said he an' his boy had sarched ev'ry-whar, but could n't find the child nowhar. They b'leeved she was drownded. A drop uv water, Mr. Vance."

"And did n't you undeceive them?" asked Vance, giving the water.

"No, Mr. Vance. The Kunnle seed a prize in that yaller gal, and the Devil put an idee inter his head. Says the Kunnle to me, says he, 'Now foller yer leader, Cappn.' (He used ter call me Cappn.) 'Swar jest as yer har me swar.' Then up he steps an' says to Mr. Onslow, 'Judge, it 's all true what Mr. Burgess says; the yaller gal, with the child in her arms, war crowded overboord. This gemmleman an' I tried ter save them. Ef we did n't, may I be shot. We throw'd the gal a life-presarver, but she could n't hold on, no how. Fust the child went under, an' we was so chilled we could n't save it. Then the gal let go her grip uv the stool an' sunk. 'T war as much as we could do ter git ashore ou'selves.'"

"Did the judge put you to your oaths?" asked Vance.

"Yes, Mr. Vance. He swar'd us both; then writ down all we said, read it over ter us, and we put our names ter it, an' 't was witnessed all right. The feller Burgess bahcked us up by sayin' he see us in the water jest afore the gal fell, which was all true. It seemed a plain case. The judge tell'd it all ter Mr. Berwick, an' he growed sort o' wild, an' died soon arter. What bekummed of *you* all that time, Mr. Vance?"

"I landed on the Arkansas side," said Vance. "I supposed the Berwick family all lost. The bodies of the parents I saw and identified, and Burgess told me he 'd talked with two men who saw the child go down."

"Wall, Mr. Vance. Thar ain't much more uv a story. We went ter Memphis. The Kunnle swelled round consid'rable, and got his name inter the newspapers. But the yuller gal she was sort o' cracked-brained. She war no use ter us or ter the child. The Kunnle got low-sperreted. He 'd made a bad spec, ahter all. He 'd lost his niggers ; an' the yuller gal, she as he hoped ter sell in Noo Orleenz fur sixteen hunderd dollars, she turned out a fool. Howzomever, he found a lightish, genteel sort uv a nigger, a quack doctor, who took her off our hands. He said as how she mowt be 'panned an' made as good as noo."

" And what did you do with the child ? "

" Wall, another bright idee hahd struck the Kunnle. Says he, ' Color this young 'un up a little, and she 'd bring risin' uv four hunderd dollars at a vahndoo. Any mahn, used ter buyin' niggers, would see at wunst she 'd grow up ter be a val'able fancy article. Ef I could afford it, I 'd hold her on spekilation till she war fifteen.' Wall, Mr. Vance, uv all the mean things I ever done, the meanest was to let the Kunnle, whan we got ter Noo Orleenz, take that poor little patient thing, as I had toted all the way down from Memphis, an' sell her ter the highest bidder."

With an irrepressible groan, Vance walked to the window. When he returned, he looked with pity on Quattles, and said, " Proceed ! "

" Yer see, Mr. Vance, I owed the Kunnle two hunderd dollars, he 'd won from me at euchre. He offered ter make it squar ef I 'd give up my int'rest in the child. Wall, I 'd got kind o' fond uv the little thing ; an' 't was n't till I got blind drunk on 't that I could bring my mind ter say yes. The thowt uv what I done that day has kept me drunk most ever sence. But the Kunnle, he tried to comfort me like. Says he, ' The child was fairly ourn, seein' as how we saved it from drownin'.' ' Don't take on so, old feller,' says he. ' Think yerself lucky ef yer hahv n't nothin' wuss nor that agin yerself.' But 't was no go. He never could make me hold up my head agin like as I used ter ; an' we two cut adrift, an' hain't kept 'count uv each other sence."

" How did he dispose of the child ? "

" He stained her skin till she looked like a half mulatter, an' then he jest got Ripper, the auctioneer, ter sell her."

" Who bought the child ? "

" Wall, Cash bowt her. That 's all I ever could find out. Ef Ripper knowed more, he would n't tell."

"To whom did you sell the yellow girl?"

"We did n't sell her at all. Was glad to git her off our hahnds at no price. The chap what took her called hisself Dr. Davy. He was a free nigger, a trav'lin' quack, — one of those fellers that 'tises to cure ev'ry thing."

"When did you last hear of him?"

"The last I heerd tell uv Davy, he war in Natchez, and that war five years ago."

"What became of the yellow girl?"

"Wall, thar 's a quar story 'bout that. Whan we fust saw that air gal on the wreck, she was callin' out ter us, 'Take me an' the child with yer!' She said it wunst, an' hahd jest begun ter say it again, an' hahd got as fur as *Take*, whan the block hit her on the head, an' she fell inter the water. Wall, six months ahter, Davy took that air gal ter a surgeon in Philadelphy, an' hahd her 'panned; an' jest as the crushed bone war lifted from the brain, that gal cried out, '— me an' the child with yer!' Shoot me ef she did n't finish the cry she 'd begun jest six months afore.* She got back her senses all straight, an' Davy made her his wife."

"Did you keep anything that belonged to the child?"

"Jest you feel in the pockets uv them pants under my piller, and git out my pus."

Vance obeyed, and drew forth a small bag of wash-leather. This he emptied on the coverlet, the contents being a few dimes and five-cent pieces, a tonga-bean, and a small pill-box covered with cotton-wool and tied round with twine.

"Thar! Open that ar' box," said the patient.

Vance opened it, and took out a pair of little sleeve-buttons, gold with a setting of coral. Examining them, he found on the under surface the inscription C. A. B. in diminutive characters.

"I 'll tell you how 't was," said the wounded man. "That night of the 'splosion the yuller gal an' the child must have gone ter bed without ondressin'; for they 'd thar cloze all on.

* Abercrombie relates an authenticated case of the same kind. A woodman, while employed with his axe, was hit on the head by a falling tree. He remained in a semi-comatose state for a whole year. On being trepanned, he uttered an exclamation which was found to be the completion of the sentence he had been in the act of uttering when struck twelve months before.

Most like the gal fell asleep an' forgot. Soon as we touched the shore, the Kunnle says ter me, says he, 'Cap'n, you cahrry the child, an' I 'll pilot the gal.' Wall; I took the child in my arms, an' as I cahrr'd her, I seed she wore gold buttons on the sleeves uv her little pelisse, — a pair on each; an', thinks I, the Kunnle will pocket them buttons sure. So I pocketed 'em myself; but whan it kum to partin' with the child, I jest took one pair uv the buttons, an sowd 'em on inside uv the bosom uv her little shirt whar they would n't be seen. The other pair is that thar. Take 'em an' keep 'em, Mr. Vance."

"Have you any article of clothing belonging to her?"

"Not a rag, Mr. Vance. They all went with her."

"Did you notice any mark on the clothes?"

"Yes, they was marked C. A. B., in letters worked in hahnsum with white silk."

"Was that the kind of letter?" asked Vance, who, having drawn the cipher in old English, held it before the patient's eyes.

"Yes, them 's um. I remember, 'cause I used ter ondress the child. An', now I think uv it, one uv her eyes was bluish, an' t' other grayish."

"What day was it you parted with the child?"

"The same day she was sold."

"When was that?"

"It must have been in May follerin' the 'splosion. Lem me see. 'T was that day I got the pill-box. I 'd been ter the doctor's fur some physickin' stuff. He give me a prescrip, an' I went an' got some pills in that air box, an' then throwed the pills away an' kept the box."

Vance glanced at the cover. The apothecary's name and the number of the prescription were legible. Vance put the box in his pocket.

"Can't yer think uv su'thin' else?" asked Quattles.

"Only this," replied Vance: "How shall I manage Hyde?"

"Wall, ef the Kunnle sh'd hold up his milk, you jest say ter him these eer words: 'Dorothy Rusk must be provided for. What kn I do fur her?' The widder Rusk is his sister, yer see, an' that 's the one soft spot the Kunnle's got."

Vance carefully recorded the mysterious words; then asked,

"Do you remember Peek, the runaway slave Hyde had in charge?"

"In coorse I do," said Quattles, twisting with pain from his wound. "Should you ever see that nigger, Mr. Vance, tell him that Amos Slink, St. Joseph Street, kn tell him su'thing' 'bout his wife. Amos wunst tell 'd me how he 'coyed her down from Montreal. 'T was through that same lawyer chap that kum it over Peek."

"Can Amos identify you as the Quattles of the Pontiac?"

"In coorse he can, for he knowed all 'bout me at the time."

"And now, my friend, I wish to have this testimony of yours sworn to and witnessed; but I 'm overtasking your strength."

"Do it, Mr. Vance. Help me ter lose my strength, ef yer think I kn do any good tellin' the truth."

"Can you get along without this opiate two hours longer?"

"Yes, Mr. Vance, I kn do without it altogether."

"Then I 'll leave you for two hours."

"One word, Mr. Vance."

"What is it?"

"Did yer ever pray?"

"Yes; every man prays who tries to do good or undo evil. You 've been praying for the last hour, my friend."

"How did yer know that? I 've been thinkin' of it, that 's a fak. But I 'm not up to it, Mr. Vance. Could you pray for me jest three minutes?"

"Willingly, my poor fellow."

And kneeling at the little cot, Vance, holding a hand of the sufferer, prayed for him so tenderly, so fervently, and so searchingly withal, that the poor dying outcast wept as he had never wept before. O precious tears, parting the mist that hung upon his future (even as clouds are parted that hide the sunset's glories), and revealing to his spiritual eyes new possibilities of being, fruits of repentance, through a mercy which (God be thanked!) is not measured by the mercy of men.

Leaving the hospital, Vance stepped into an office, and drew up, in the form of a deposition, all the facts elicited from Quattles. His next step was to find Amos Slink. That gentleman had settled down in the second-hand clothing business. Vance made a liberal purchase of hospital clothing; and then adverted to the past exploits of Amos in the "nigger-catching" line. Amos proudly produced letters to authenticate his prowess. They bore the signature of Charlton. "I want you to lend me those letters, Mr. Slink."

"Could n't do it, Mr. Vance. Them letters I mean to hand down to my children."

"Well, it's of no consequence. I'll go into the next store for the rest of my goods."

"Don't think of it. Here! take the letters. Only return 'em." Vance not only secured the letters, but got Mr. Slink to go with him to the hospital to identify Quattles.

Then, on his way, enlisting three friends who were good Union men, one of them being a justice of the peace, Vance led them where the wounded man lay. Slink, who was known to the parties, identified the patient as the Mr. Quattles of the Pontiac; and the identification was duly recorded and sworn to. Vance then read his notes aloud to Quattles, whose competency to listen and understand was formally attested by the surgeon. The justice administered the oath. Quattles put his name to the document, and the signature was duly witnessed by all present.

No sooner was the act completed than the patient sank into unconsciousness. "He'll not rally again," said the surgeon. A quick, heavy breathing, gradually growing faint and fainter, — and lo! there was a smile on the face, but the spirit that had left it there had fled!

Vance first went to the apothecary whose name was on the pill-box. "Did Mr. Gargle keep the books in which he pasted his prescriptions?"

"Yes, he had them for twenty years back."

"Would he look in the volume for 18—, for a certain number?"

"Willingly."

In two minutes the number was found, and the day of the prescription fixed. Vance then proceeded to the office of *L'Abeille*, turned to the newspaper of that day, and there, in the advertising columns, found a sale advertised by P. Ripper & Co., auctioneers. It was a sale of a "lot" of negroes; and as a sort of postscript to the specifications was the following: —

"Also, one very promising little girl, an orphan, two years old, almost white; can take care of herself; promises to be very pretty; has straight, brown hair, regular features, first-rate figure. Warranted sound and healthy. Amateurs who would like to train up a companion to their tastes will find this a rare opportunity to purchase."

Not pausing to indulge the emotions which these cruel words awoke, Vance went in search of Ripper & Co. The firm had been broken up more than ten years before. Not one of the partners was in the city. They had disappeared, and left no trace. Were any of their old account-books in the warehouse? No. The building had been burnt to the ground, and a new one erected on its site.

"Where next?" thought Vance. "Plainly to Natchez, to see if I can learn anything of Davy and his wife."

CHAPTER XXV.

MEETINGS AND PARTINGS.

"I hold it true, whate'er befall, —
I feel it when I sorrow most, —
'T is better to have loved and lost
Than never to have loved at all."
Tennyson.

IT being too late to take the boat for Natchez, Vance proceeded to the St. Charles. The gong for the five o'clock ordinary had sounded. Entering the dining-hall, he was about taking a seat, when he saw Miss Tremaine motioning to him to occupy one vacant by her side.

"Truly an enterprising young lady!" But what could he do?

"I'm so glad to see you, Mr. Vance! I've not forgotten my promise. I called to-day on Mrs. Gentry, — found her in the depths. Miss Murray has disappeared, — absconded, — nobody knows where!"

"Indeed! After what you've said of her singing, I'm very anxious to hear her. Do try to find her."

"I'll do what I can, Mr. Vance. There's a mystery. Of that much I'm persuaded from Mrs. Gentry's manner."

"You mustn't mind Darling's notions on slavery."

"O no, Mr. Vance, I shall turn her over to you for conversion."

"Should you succeed in entrapping her, detain her till I come back from Natchez, which will be before Sunday."

"Be sure I'll hold on to her."

Mr. Tremaine came in, and began to talk politics. Vance was sorry he had an engagement. The big clock of the hall pointed to seven o'clock. He rose, bowed, and left.

"Why," sighed Laura, "can't other gentlemen be as agreeable as this Mr. Vance? He knows all about the latest fashions; all about modes of fixing the hair; all about music and dancing; all about the opera and the theatre; in short, what is there the man does n't know?"

Papa was too absorbed in his terrapin soup to answer.

Let us follow Vance to the little house, scene of his brief, fugitive days of delight. He stood under the old magnolia in the tender moonlight. The gas was down in Clara's room. She was at the piano, extemporizing some low and plaintive variations on a melody by Moore, "When twilight dews are falling soft." Suddenly she stopped, and put up the gas. There was a knock at her door. She opened it, and saw Vance. They shook hands as if they were old friends.

"Where are the Bernards?"

"They are out promenading. I told them I was not afraid."

"How have you passed your time, Miss Perdita?"

"O, I 've not been idle. Such choice books as you have here! And then what a variety of music!"

"Have you studied any of the pieces?"

"Not many. That from Schubert."

"Please play it for me."

Tacitly accepting him as her teacher, she played it without embarrassment. Vance checked her here and there, and suggested a change. He uttered no other word of praise than to say: "If you 'll practise six years longer four hours a day, you 'll be a player."

"I shall do it!" said Clara.

"Have you heard that famous Hallelujah Chorus, which the Northern soldiers sing?"

"No, Mr. Vance."

"No? Why, 't is in honor of John Brown (any relation of Perdita?) You shall hear it."

And he played the well-known air, now appropriated by the hand-organs. Clara asked for a repetition, that she might remember it.

"Sing me something," he said.

Clara placed on the reading-frame the song of "Pestal."

"Not that, Perdita! What possessed you to study that?"

"It suited my mood. Will you not hear it?"

"No! . . . . Yes, Perdita. Pardon my abruptness. But that song was the first I ever heard from lips, O so fair and dear to me!"

Clara put aside the music, and walked away toward the window. Vance went up to her. He could see that she was with difficulty curbing her tears.

O, if this man whose very presence inspired such confidence and hope, — if it was sweeter to him to *remember* another than to *listen* to *her*, — where in the wide world should she find, in her desperate strait, a friend?

There was that in her attitude which reminded Vance of Estelle. Some lemon-blossoms in her hair intensified the association by their odors. For a moment it was as if he had thrown off the burden of twenty years, and was living over, in Clara's presence, that ambrosial hour of first love on the very spot of its birth. "For O, she stood beside him like his youth, — transformed for him the real to a dream, clothing the palpable and the familiar with golden exhalations of the dawn!" Be wary, Vance! One look, one tone amiss, and there 'll be danger!

"Let us talk over your affairs," he said. "To-morrow I must leave for Natchez. Will you remain here till I come back?"

Clara leaned out of the window a moment, as if to enjoy the balmy evening, and then, calmly taking a seat, replied: "I think 't will be best for me to lay my case before Miss Tremaine. True, we parted in a pet, but she may not be implacable. Yes, I will call on her. To you, a stranger, what return for your kindness can I make?"

"This return, Perdita: let me be your friend. As soon as 't is discovered you 've no money, your position may become a painful one. Let me supply you with funds. I 'm rich; and my only heir is my country."

"No, Mr. Vance! I 've no claim upon you, — none whatever. What I want for the moment is a shelter; and Laura will give me that, I 'm confident."

Vance reflected a moment, and then, as if a plan had occurred to him by which he could provide for her without her knowing it, he replied: "We shall probably meet at the St. Charles. You can easily send for me, should you require my help. Be generous, and say you 'll notify me, should there be an hour of need?"

"I 'll not fail to remember you in that event, Mr. Vance."

"Honor bright?"

"Honor bright, Mr. Vance!"

"Consider, Perdita, you can always find a home in this house. I shall give such directions to Mrs. Bernard as will make your presence welcome."

"Then I shall not feel utterly homeless. Thank you, Mr. Vance!"

"And by the way, Perdita, do not let Miss Tremaine know that we are acquainted."

"I 'll heed your caution, Mr. Vance."

"We shall meet again, my dear young lady. Of that I feel assured."

"I hope so, Mr. Vance."

"And now farewell! I 'll tell Bernard to order a carriage and attend to your baggage. Good by, Perdita!"

"Good by, Mr. Vance."

Again they shook hands, and parted. Vance gave his directions to the Bernards, and then strolled home to his hotel. As he traversed the corridor leading to his room, he encountered Kenrick. Their apartments were nearly opposite.

"I was not aware we were such near neighbors, Mr. Kenrick."

"To me also 't is a surprise, — and a pleasant one. Will you walk in, Mr. Vance?"

"Yes, if 't is not past your hour for visitors."

They went in, and Kenrick put up the gas. "I can't offer you either cigars or whiskey; but you can ring for what you want."

"Is it possible you eschew alcohol and tobacco?"

"Yes," replied Kenrick; "I once indulged in cigars. But I found the use so offensive in others that I myself abandoned it in disgust. One sits down to converse with a person disguised as a gentleman, and suddenly a fume, as if from the essence of old tobacco-pipes, mixed with odors from stale brandy-bottles, poisons the innocent air, and almost knocks one down. It 's a mystery that ladies endure the nuisance of such breaths. My sensitive nose has made me an anti-rum, anti-tobacco man."

"But I fear me you 're a come-outer, Mr. Kenrick! Is it conservative to abuse tobacco and whiskey? No wonder you are unsound on the slavery question!"

"Come up to the confessional," Mr. Vance! Admit that you 're as much of an antislavery man as I am."

"More, Mr. Kenrick! If I were not, I might be quite as imprudent as you. And then I should put a stop to my usefulness."

"You puzzle me, Mr. Vance."

"Not as much as you 've puzzled *me*, my young friend. Come here, and look in the mirror with me."

Vance took him by the hand and led him to a full-length looking-glass. There they stood looking at their reflections.

"What do you see?" asked Vance.

"Two rather personable fellows," replied Kenrick, laughing; "one of them ten or twelve years older than the other; height of the two, about the same; figures very much alike, inclining to slimness, but compact, erect, well-knit; hands and feet small; heads, — I have no fault to find with the shape or size of either; hair similar in color; eyes, — as near as I can see, the two pairs resemble each other, and the crow's-feet at the corners are the same in each; features, — nose, — brows — I see why you 've brought me here, Mr. Vance! We are enough alike to be brothers."

"Can you explain the mystery?" asked Vance, "for I can't. Can there be any family relationship? I had an aunt, now deceased, who was married to a Louisianian. But his name was not Kenrick."

"What was it?"

"Arthur Maclain."

"My father! Cousin, your hand! In order to inherit property, my father, after his marriage, procured a change of name. I can't tell you how pleasant to me it is to meet one of my mother's relations."

They had come together still more akin in spirit than in blood. The night was all too short for the confidences they now poured out to each other. Vance told his whole story, pausing occasionally to calm down the excitement which the narrative caused in his hearer.

When it was finished Kenrick said: "Cousin, count me your ally in compassing your revenge. May God do so to me, and more also, if I do not give this beastly Slave Power blood for blood."

"I can't help thinking, Charles," said Vance, "that your zeal has the purer origin. *Mine* sprang from a personal experience of wrong; yours, from an abstract conception of what is just; from those inner motives that point to righteousness and God."

"I almost wish sometimes," replied Kenrick, "that I had the spur of a great personal grievance to give body to my wrath. And yet Slavery, when it lays its foul hand on *the least of these little ones* ought to be felt by me also, and by all men! But now — now — I shall not lack the sting of a personal incentive. *Your* griefs, cousin, fall on my own heart, and shall not find the soil altogether barren. This Ratcliff, — I know him well. He has been more than once at our house. A perfect type of the sort of beast born of slavery, — moulded as in a matrix by slavery, — kept alive by slavery! Take away slavery, and he would perish of inanition. He would be, like the plesiosaur, a fossil monster, representative of an extinct genus."

"Cousin," said Vance, "all you lack is to join the serpent with the dove. Be content to bide your time. Here in Louisiana lies your work. We must make the whole western bank of the Mississippi free soil. Texas can be taken care of in due time. But with a belt of freedom surrounding the Cotton States, the doom of slavery is fixed. Give me to see that day, and I shall be ready to say, 'Now, Lord, dismiss thy servant!'"

"I had intended to go North, and join the army of freedom," said Kenrick; "but what you say gives me pause."

"We must not be seen together much," resumed Vance. "And now good night, or rather, good morning, for there's a glimmer in the east, premonitory of day. Ah, cousin, when I hear the braggarts around us, gassing about Confederate courage and Yankee cowardice, I can't help recalling an old couplet I used to spout, when an actor, from a play by Southern, —

'There is no courage but in innocence,
No constancy but in an honest cause!'"

CHAPTER XXVI.

CLARA MAKES AN IMPORTANT PURCHASE.

"Allow slavery to be ever so humane. Grant that the man who owns me is ever so kind. The wrong of him who presumes to talk of owning me is too unmeasured to be softened by kindness."

LAURA TREMAINE had just come in from a drive with her invalid mother, and stood in the drawing-room looking out on a company of soldiers. There was a knock at the door. A servant brought in a card. It said, "Will Laura see Darling?" The arrival, concurring so directly with Laura's wishes, caused a pleasurable shock. "Show her in," she said; and the next moment the maidens were locked in each other's embrace.

"O, you dear little good-for-nothing Darling," said Laura, after there had been a conflux of kisses. "Could anything be more *apropos*? What 's the meaning of all this? Have you really absconded? Is it a love affair? Tell me all about it. Rely on my secrecy. I 'll be close as bark to a tree."

"Will you solemnly promise," said Clara, "on your honor as a lady, not to reveal what I tell you?"

"As I hope to be saved, I promise," replied Laura.

"Then I will tell you the cause of my leaving Mrs. Gentry's. 'T was only day before yesterday she told me, — look at me, Laura, and say if I look like it! — she told me I was a slave."

"A slave? Impossible! Why, Darling, you 've a complexion whiter than mine."

"So have many slaves. The hue of my skin will not invalidate a claim."

"That 's true. But who presumes to claim you?"

"Mr. Carberry Ratcliff."

"A friend of my father's! He 's very rich. I 'll ask him to give you up. Let me go to him at once."

"No, Laura, I 've seen the man. 'T would be hopeless to try to melt him. You must help me to get away."

"But you do not mean,—surely you do not mean to—to —"

"To what, Laura? You seem gasping with horror at some frightful supposition. What is it?"

"You'd not think of running off, would you? You would n't ask me to harbor a fugitive slave?"

Clara looked at the door. The color flew to her cheek,—flamed up to her forehead. Her bosom heaved. Emotions of unutterable detestation and disgust struggled for expression. But had she not learnt the slave's first lesson, duplicity? Her secret had been confided to one who had forthwith showed herself untrustworthy. Bred in the heartless fanaticism which slavery engenders, Laura might give the alarm and have her stopped, should she rise suddenly to go. Farewell, then, white-robed Candor, and welcome Dissimulation!

After a pause, "What do you advise?" said Clara.

"Well, Darling, stay with me a week or two, then go quietly back to Mrs. Gentry's, and play the penitent."

"Had n't I better go at once?" asked Clara, simulating meekness.

"O no, Darling! I can't possibly permit that. Now I've got you, I shall hold on till I've done with you. Then we'll see if we can't persuade Mr. Ratcliff to free you. Who'd have thought of this little Darling being a slave!"

"But had n't I better write to Mrs. Gentry and tell her where I am?"

"No, no. She'll only be forcing you back. You shall do nothing but stay here till I tell you you may go. You shall play the lady for one week, at least. There's a Mr. Vance in the house, to whom I've spoken of your singing. He's wild to hear you. I've promised him he shall. I would n't disappoint him on any account."

Clara saw that, could she but command courage to fall in with Laura's selfish plans, it might, after all, be safer to come thus into the very focus of the city's life, than to seek some corner, penetrable to police-officers and slave-hunters.

"How will you manage?" asked Clara.

"What more simple?" replied Laura. "I'll take you right into my sleeping-room; you shall be my schoolmate, Miss

Brown, come to pass a few days with me before going to St. Louis. Papa will never think of questioning my story."

"But I 've no dresses with me."

"No matter. I 've a plenty I 've outgrown. They 'll fit you beautifully. Come here into my sleeping-room. It adjoins, you see. There! We 're about of a height, though I 'm a little stouter."

"It will not be safe for me to appear at the public table."

"Well, you shall be an invalid, and I 'll send your meals from the table when I send mother's. Miss Brown from St. Louis! Let me see. What shall be your first name?"

"Let it be Perdita."

"Perdita? The lost one! Good. How quick you are! Perdita Brown! It does not sound badly. Mr. Onslow, — Miss Brown, — Miss Perdita Brown from St. Louis! Then you 'll courtesy, and look so demure! Won't it be fun?"

Between grief and anger, Clara found disguise a terrible effort. So! Her fate so dark, so tragic, was to be Laura's pastime, not the subject of her grave and tender consideration!

Already had some of the traits, congenital with slavery, begun to develop themselves in Clara. Strategy now seemed to her as justifiable under the circumstances as it would be in escaping from a murderer, a lunatic, or a wild beast. Was not every pro-slavery man or woman her deadly foe, — to be cheated, circumvented, robbed, nay, if need be, slain, in defence of her own inalienable right of liberty? The thought that Laura was such a foe made Clara look on her with precisely the same feelings that the exposed sentinel might have toward the lurking picket-shooter.

An expression so strange flitted over Clara's face, that Laura asked: "What 's the matter? Don't you feel well?"

Checking the exasperation surging in her heart, Clara affected frivolity. "O, I feel well enough," she replied. "A little tired, — that 's all. What if this Mr. Onslow should fall in love with me?"

"O, but that would be too good!" exclaimed Laura. Between you and me, I owe him a spite. I 've just heard he once said, speaking of me, 'Handsome, — but no depth!' Hang the fellow! I 'd like to punish him. He 's proud as Lucifer.

Would n't it be a joke to let him fall in love with a poor little slave?"

"So, you don't mean to fall in love with him yourself?"

"O no! He's good-looking, but poor. Can you keep a secret?"

"Yes."

"Well, I mean to set my cap for Mr. Vance."

"Possible?"

"Yes, Perdita. He's fine-looking, of the right age, very rich, and so altogether fascinating! Father learnt yesterday that he pays an enormous tax on real estate."

"And is he the only string to your bow?"

"O no. But our best young men are in the army. Onslow is a captain. O, I must n't forget Charles Kenrick. Onslow is to bring him here. Kenrick's father owns a whole brigade of slaves. Hark! Dear me! That was two o'clock. Will you have luncheon?"

"No, thank you. I'm not hungry."

"Then I must leave you. I've an appointment with my dressmaker. In the lower drawers there you'll find some of my last year's dresses. I've outgrown them. Amuse yourself with choosing one for to-night. We shall have callers."

Laura hurried off. Clara, terrified at the wrathfulness of her own emotions, walked the room for a while, then dropped upon her knees in prayer. She prayed to be delivered from her own wild passions and from the toils of her enemies.

With softened heart, she rose and went to the window.

There, on the opposite sidewalk, stood Esha! Crumpling up some paper, Clara threw it out so as to arrest her attention, then beckoned to her to come up. Stifling a cry of surprise, Esha crossed the street, and entered the hotel. The next minute she and Clara had embraced.

"But how did you happen to be there, Esha?"

"Bress de chile, I'ze been stahndin' dar de last hour, but what for I knowed no more dan de stones. 'T warn't till I seed de chile hersef it 'curred ter me what for I'd been stahndin' dar."

"What happened after I left home?"

"Dar war all sort ob a fuss dat ebber you see, darlin'. Fust de ole woman war all struck ob a heap, like. Den Massa Ratcliff, he come, and he swar like de Debble hisself. He cuss'd de ole woman and set her off cryin', and den he swar at her all de more. Dar was a gen'ral break-down, darlin'. Massa Ratcliff he 'b goin' ter gib yer fortygraf ter all de policemen, an' pay five hundred dollar ter dat one as 'll find yer. He sends us niggers all off — me an' Tarquin an' de rest — ter hunt yer up. He swar he 'll hab yer, if it takes all he 's wuth. He come agin ter-day an' trow de ole woman inter de highstrikes. She say he 'll be come up wid, sure, an' you 'll be come up wid, an' eberybody else as does n't do like she wants 'em ter, am bound to be come up wid. Yah, yah, yah! Who 's afeard?"

"So the hounds are out in pursuit, are they?"

"Yes, darlin'. Look dar at dat man stahndin' at de corner. He 'm one ob 'em."

"He 's not dressed like a policeman."

"Bress yer heart, dese 'tektivs go dressed like de best gem'men about. Yer 'd nebber suspek dey was doin' de work ob hounds."

"Well, Esha, I 'm afraid to have you stay longer. I 'm here with Miss Tremaine. She may be back any minute. I can't trust her, and would n't for the world have her see you here."

"No more would I, darlin'! Nebber liked dat air gal. She 'm all fur self. But good by, darlin'! It 's sich a comfort ter hab seed you! Good by!"

Esha slipped into the corridor and out of the hotel. Clara put on her bonnet, threw a thick veil over it, and hurried through St. Charles Street to a well-known cutlery store. "Show me some of your daggers," said she; "one suitable as a present to a young soldier."

The shopkeeper displayed several varieties. She selected one with a sheath, and almost took away the breath of the man of iron by paying for it in gold. Dropping her veil, she passed into the street. As she left the shop, she saw a man affecting to look at some patent pistols in the window. He was well dressed, and sported a small cane.

"Hound number one!" thought Clara to herself, and, having walked slowly away in one direction, she suddenly turned, retraced her steps, then took a narrow cross-street that debouched into one of the principal business avenues. The individual had followed her, swinging his cane, and looking in at the shop-windows. But Clara did not let him see he was an object of suspicion. She slackened her pace, and pretended to be looking for an article of muslin, for she would stop and examine the fabrics that hung at the doors.

Suddenly she saw Esha approaching. Moment of peril! Should the old black woman recognize and accost her, she was lost. On came the old slave, her eyes wide open and her thoughts intent on detecting detectives. Suddenly, to her consternation, she saw Clara stop before a "magasin" and take up some muslin on the shelf outside the window; and almost in the same glance, she saw the gentleman of the cane, watching both her and Clara out of the corners of his eyes. A sideway glance, quick as lightning from Clara, and delivered without moving her head, was enough to enlighten Esha. She passed on without a perceptible pause, and soon appeared to stumble, as if by accident, almost into the arms of the detective. He caught her by the shoulder, and said, "Don't turn, but tell me if you noticed that woman there, — there by Delmar's, with a green veil over her face?"

"Yes, massa, I seed a woman in a green veil."

"Well, are you sure she may n't be the one?"

"Bress yer, massa, I owt to know de chile I 'ze seed grow up from a bebby. Reckon I could tell her widout seein' her face."

"Go back and take a look at her. There! she steps into the shop."

Glad of the opportunity of giving Clara a word of caution, Esha passed into Delmar's. Beckoning Clara into an alcove, she said: "De veil, darlin'! De veil! Dat ole rat would nebber hab suspek noting if 't hahd n't been fur de veil. His part ob de play am ter watch eb'ry woman in a veil."

"I see my mistake, Esha. I 've been buying a dagger. Look there!"

"De Lord save us!" said Esha, with a shudder, half of horror and half of sympathy. "Don't be in de street oftener dan yer kin help, darlin'? Remember de fotygrafs. Dar! I mus go."

Esha joined the detective. "Did you get a good sight of her?" he asked.

"Went right up an' spoke ter her," said Esha. "She 's jes as much dat gal as she 's Madame Beauregard."

The detective, his vision of a $ 500 *douceur* melting into thin air, pensively walked off to try fortune on a new beat.

Clara, now that the danger was over, began to tremble. Hitherto she had not quailed. Leaving the shop, she took the nearest way to the hotel. For the last twenty-four hours agitation and excitement had prevented her taking food. Wretchedly faint, she stopped and took hold of an iron lamp-post for support.

An officer in the Confederate uniform, seeing she was ill, said, "Mademoiselle, you need help. Allow me to escort you home."

Dreading lest she should fall, through feebleness, into worse hands, Clara thanked him and took his proffered arm. "To the St. Charles, sir, if you please."

"I myself stop at the St. Charles. Allow me to introduce myself: Robert Onslow, Captain in Company D, Wigman Regiment. May I ask whom I have the pleasure of assisting?"

"Miss Brown. I 'm stopping a few days with my friend, Miss Tremaine."

"Indeed! I was to call on her this evening. We may renew our acquaintance."

"Perhaps."

Clara suddenly put down her veil. Approaching slowly like a fate, rolled on the splendid barouche of Mr. Ratcliff. He sat with arms folded and was smoking a cigar. Clara fancied she saw arrogance, hate, disappointment, rage, all written in his countenance. Without moving his arms, he bowed carelessly to Onslow.

"That 's one of the prime managers of the secession movement."

"So I should think," said Clara; but Onslow detected nothing equivocal in the tone of the remark. Having escorted her to the door of Miss Tremaine's parlor, he bowed his farewell, and Clara went in. Laura had not yet returned.

CHAPTER XXVII.

DELIGHT AND DUTY.

"According to our living here, we shall hereafter, by a hidden concatenation of causes, be drawn to a condition answerable to the purity or impurity of our souls in this life: that silent Nemesis that passes through the whole contexture of the universe, ever fatally contriving us into such a state as we ourselves have fitted ourselves for by our accustomary actions. Of so great consequence is it, while we have opportunity, to aspire to the best things." — *Henry More*, A. D. 1659.

IT may seem strange that Onslow and Kenrick, differing so widely, should renew the friendship of their boyhood. We have seen that Onslow, allowing the æsthetic side of his nature to outgrow the moral, had departed from the teachings of his father on the subject of slavery. Kenrick, in whom the moral and devotional faculty asserted its supremacy over all inferior solicitings, also repudiated *his* paternal teachings; but they were directly contrary to those of his friend, and, in abandoning them, he gave up the prospect of a large inheritance.

To Onslow, these thick-lipped, woolly-headed negroes, — what were they fit for but to be hewers of wood and drawers of water to the gentle and refined? It was monstrous to suppose that between such and him there could be equality of any kind. The ethnological argument was conclusive. Had not Professor Moleschott said that the brain of the negro contains less phosphorus than that of the white man? Proof sufficient that Cuffee was expressly created to pull off my boots and hoe in my cotton-fields, while I make it a penal offence to teach him to read!

Onslow, too, had been fortunate in his intercourse with slaveholders. Young, handsome, and accomplished, he had felt the charm of their affectionate hospitality. He had found taste, culture, and piety in their abodes; all the graces and all the amenities of life. What wonder that he should narcotize his moral sense with the aroma of these social fascinations! Even at the North, where the glamour they cast ought not to distort the sight, and where men ought healthfully to look the abstract abomination full in the face, and testify to its deformity, — how many consciences were drugged, how many hearts shut to justice and to mercy!

With Kenrick, brought up on a plantation where slavery existed in its mildest form, meditation on God's law as written in the enlightened human conscience, completely reversed the views adopted from upholders of the institution. Thenceforth the elegances of his home became hateful. He felt like a robber in the midst of them.

The spectacle of some hideous, awkward, perhaps obscene and depraved black woman, hoeing in the corn-field, instead of awakening in his mind, as in Onslow's, the thought that she was in her proper place, did but move him to tears of bitter contrition and humiliation. How far there was sin or accountability on her part, or that of her progenitors, he could not say; but that there was deep, immeasurable sin on the part of those who, instead of helping that degraded nature to rise, made laws to crush it all the deeper in the mire, he could not fail to feel in anguish of spirit. Through all that there was in her of ugliness and depravity, making her less tolerable than the beast to his æsthetic sense, he could still detect those traits and possibilities that allied her with immortal natures, and in her he saw all her sex outraged, and universal womanhood nailed to the cross of Christ, and mocked by unbelievers!

The evening of the day of Clara's arrival at the St. Charles, Onslow and Kenrick met by agreement in the drawing-room of the Tremaines. Clara had told Laura, that, in going out to purchase a few hair-pins, she had been taken suddenly faint, and that a gentleman, who proved to be Captain Onslow, had escorted her home.

"Could anything be more apt for my little plot!" said Laura. "But consider! Here it is eight o'clock, and you 're not dressed! Do you know how long you 've been sleeping? This will never do!"

A servant knocked at the door, with the information that two gentlemen were in the drawing-room.

"Dear me! I must go in at once," said Laura. "Now tell me you 'll be quick and follow, Darling."

Clara gave the required pledge, and proceeded to arrange

her hair. Laura looked on for a minute envying her those thick brown tresses, and then darted into the next room where the visitors were waiting. Greeting them with her usual animation of manner, she asked Onslow for the news.

"The news is," said Onslow, "my friend Charles is undergoing conversion. We shall have him an out-and-out Secessionist before the Fourth of July."

"On what do you base your calculations?" asked Kenrick.

"On the fact that for the last twelve hours I have n't heard you call down maledictions on the Confederate cause."

"Perhaps I conclude that the better part of valor is discretion."

"No, Charles, yours is not the Falstaffian style of courage."

"Well, construe my mood as you please. Miss Tremaine, your piano stands open. Does it mean we 're to have music?"

"Yes. Has n't the Captain told you of his meeting a young lady, — Miss Perdita Brown?"

"I 'll do him the justice to say he *did* tell me he had escorted such a one."

"What did he say of her?"

"Nothing, good or bad."

"But that 's very suspicious."

"So it is."

"Pray who is Miss Perdita Brown?" asked Onslow.

"She 's a daughter of — of — why, of Mr. Brown, of course. He lives in St. Louis."

"Is she a good Secessionist?"

"On the contrary, she 's a desperate little Abolitionist."

"Look at Charles!" said Onslow. "He 's enamored already. I 'm sorry she is n't secesh."

"Think of the triumph of converting her!" said Laura.

"That indeed! Of course," said Onslow, "like all true women, she 'll take her politics from the man she loves."

And the Captain smoothed his moustache, and looked handsome as Phœbus Apollo.

"O the conceit!" exclaimed Laura. "Look at him, Mr. Kenrick! Is n't he charming? Where 's the woman who would n't turn Mormon, or even Yankee, for his sake? Surely one of us weak creatures could be content with one tenth or even one twentieth of the affections of so superb an Ali. Come, sir, promise me I shall be the fifteenth Mrs. Onslow when you emigrate to Utah."

Onslow was astounded at this fire of raillery. Could the lady have heard of any disparaging expression he had dropped?

"Spare me, Miss Laura," he said. "Don't deprive the Confederacy of my services by slaying me before I've smelt powder."

"Where's Miss Brown all this while?" asked Kenrick.

Laura went to the door, and called "Perdita!"

"In five minutes!" was the reply.

Clara was dressing. When, that morning, she came in from her walk, she thought intently on her situation, and at last determined on a new line of policy. Instead of playing the humble companion and shy recluse, she would now put forth all her powers to dazzle and to strike. She would, if possible, make friends, who should protest against any arbitrary claim that Ratcliff might set up. She would vindicate her own right to freedom by showing she was not born to be a slave. All who had known her should feel their own honor wounded in any attempt to injure hers.

Having once fixed before herself an object, she grew calm and firm. When her dinner was sent up, she ate it with a good appetite. Sleep, too, that had been a stranger to her so many hours, now came to repair her strength and revive her spirits.

No sooner had Laura left to attend to her visitors, than Clara plunged into the drawers containing the dresses for her choice. With the rapidity of instinct she selected the most becoming; then swiftly and deftly, with the hand of an adept and the eye of an artist, she arranged her toilet. A dexterous adaptation of pins speedily rectified any little defect in the fit. Where were the collars? Locked up. No matter! There was a frill of exquisite lace round the neck of the dress; and this little narrow band of maroon velvet would serve to relieve the bareness of the throat. What could she clasp it with? Laura had not left the key of her jewel-box. A common pin would hardly answer. Suddenly Clara bethought herself of the little coral sleeve-button, wrapped up in the strip of bunting. That would serve admirably. Yes. Nothing could be better.

It was her only article of jewelry; though round her right wrist she wore a hair-bracelet of her own braiding, made from that strand given her by Esha; and from a flower-vase she had taken a small cape-jasmine, white as alabaster, and fragrant as a garden of honeysuckles, and thrust it in her hair. A fan? Yes, here is one.

And thus accoutred she entered the room where the three expectants were seated.

On seeing her, Laura's first emotion was one of admiration, as at sight of an imposing *entrée* at the opera. She was suddenly made aware of the fact that Clara was the most beautiful young woman of her acquaintance; nay, not only the most beautiful, but the most stylish. So taken by surprise was she, so lost in looking, that it was nearly a third of a minute before she introduced the young gentlemen. Onslow claimed acquaintance, presented a chair, and took a seat at Clara's side. Kenrick stood mute and staring, as if a paradisic vision had dazed his senses. When he threw off his bewilderment, he quieted himself with the thought, "She can't be as beautiful as she looks, — that's one comfort. A shrew, perhaps, — or, what is worse, a coquette!"

"When were you last in St. Louis, Miss Brown?" asked Onslow.

"All questions for information must be addressed to Miss Tremaine," said Clara. "I shall be happy to talk with you on things I know nothing about. Shall we discuss the Dahlgren gun, or the Ericsson Monitor?"

"So! She sets up for an eccentric," thought Onslow. "Perhaps politics would suit you," he added aloud. "I hear you're an Abolitionist."

"Ask Miss Tremaine," said Clara.

"O, she has betrayed you already," replied Onslow.

"Then I've nothing to say. I'm in her hands."

"Is it possible," said Kenrick, who was irrepressible on the one theme nearest his heart, "is it possible Miss Brown can't see it, — can't see the loveliness of that divine cosmos which we call slavery? Poor deluded Miss Brown! I know not what other men may think, but as for me, give me slavery or give me death! Do you object to woman-whipping, Miss Brown?"

"I confess I've my prejudices against it," replied Clara. "But these charges of woman-whipping, you know, are Abolition lies."

"Yes, so Northern conservatives say; but we of the plantations know that nearly one half the whippings are of women." *

"Come! Sink the shop!" cried Laura. "Are we so dull we can't find anything but our horrible *bête noir* for our amusement? Let us have scandal, rather; nonsense, rather! Tell us a story, Mr. Kenrick."

"Well; once on a time — how would you like a ghost-story?"

"Above all things. Charming! Only ghosts have grown so common, they no longer thrill us."

"Yes," said Kenrick, — whose trivial thoughts ever seemed to call up his serious, — "yes; materialism has done a good work in its day and generation. It has taught us that the business of this world must go on just as if there were no ghosts. The supernatural is no longer an incubus and an oppression. Its phenomena no longer frighten and paralyze. Let us, then, since we are now freed from their terrors, welcome the great facts themselves as illumining and confirming all that there is in the past to comfort us with the assurance of continuous life issuing from seeming death."

"Dear Mr. Kenrick, is this a time for a lecture?" expostulated Laura. "Are n't you bored, Perdita?"

* Among the foul records the Rebellion has unearthed is one, found at Alexandria, La., being a stray leaf from the diary of an overseer in that vicinity, in the year 1847. It chronicles the whippings of slaves from April 20 to May 21. Of thirty-nine whippings during that period, *nineteen were of females*. We give a few extracts from this precious and authentic document: —

"April 20. Whipped Adam for cutting cotton too wide. Nat, for thinning cotton. — 21. Adaline and Clem, for being behind. — 24. Esther, for leaving child out in yard to let it cry. — 27. Adaline, for being slow getting out of quarters. — 28. Daniel, for not having cobs taken out of horse-trough. — May 1. Anna, Jo, Hannah, Sarah, Jim, and Jane, for not thinning corn right. Clem, for being too long thinning one row of corn. Esther, for not being out of quarters quick enough. — 10. Adaline, for being last one out with row. — 15. Esther, for leaving grass in cotton. — 17. Peggy, for not hoeing as much cane as she ought to last week. — 18. Polly, for not hoeing faster. — 20. Martha, Esther, and Sarah, for jawing about row, while I was gone. — 21. Polly, for not handling her hoe faster."

A United States officer from Cambridge, Mass., sent home this stray leaf, and it was originally published in the Cambridge Chronicle.

"On the contrary, I'm interested."

"What do you think of spiritualism, Miss Brown?"

"I've witnessed none of the phenomena, but I don't see why the testimony of these times, in regard to them, should n't be taken as readily as that of centuries back."

"My father is a believer," said Onslow; "and I have certainly seen some unaccountable things, — tables lifted into the air, — instruments of music floated about, and played on without visible touch, — human hands, palpable and warm, coming out from impalpable air: — all very queer and very inexplicable! But what do they prove? *Cui bono?* What of it all?"

"'Nothing in it!' as Sir Charles Coldstream says of the Vatican," interposed Laura.

"You demand the use of it all, — the *cui bono,* — do you?" retorted Kenrick. "Did it ever occur to you to make your own existence the subject of that terrible inquiry, *cui bono?*"

"Certainly," replied Onslow, laughing; "my *cui bono* is to fight for the independence of the new Confederacy."

"And for the propagation of slavery, eh?" returned Kenrick. "I don't see the *cui bono.* On the contrary, to my fallible vision, the world would be better off without than with you. But let us take a more extreme case. These youths — Tom, Dick, and Harry — who give their days and nights, not to the works of Addison, but to gambling, julep-drinking, and cigar-smoking, — who hate and shun all useful work, — and are no comfort to anybody, — only a shame and affliction to somebody, — can you explain to me the *cui bono* of their corrupt and unprofitable lives?"

"But how undignified in a spirit to push tables about and play on accordions!"

"Well, what authority have you for the supposition that there are no undignified spirits? We know there are weak and wicked spirits *in* the flesh; why not *out* of the flesh? A spirit, or an intelligence claiming to be one, writes an ungrammatical sentence or a pompous commonplace, and signs *Bacon* to it; and you forthwith exclaim, 'Pooh! this can't come from a spirit.' How do you know that? May n't lies be told in other worlds than this? Will the ignoramus at once be made a scholar, — the dullard a philosopher, — the blackguard a gentleman, — the sinner a saint, — the liar truthful, — by the simple process of elimination from this husk of flesh? Make me at once altogether other than what I am, and you annihilate me, and there is no immortality of the soul."

"But what has the ghost contributed to our knowledge during these fourteen years, since he appeared at Rochester? Of all he has brought us, we may say, with Shakespeare, 'There needs no ghost come from the grave to tell us that.'"

"I'll tell you what the ghost has contributed, not at Rochester merely, but everywhere, through the ages. He has contributed *himself*. You say, *cui bono?* And I might say of ten thousand mysteries about us, *cui bono?* The lightning strikes the church-steeple, — *cui bono?* An idiot is born into the world, — *cui bono?* It is absurd to demand as a condition of rational faith, that we should prove a *cui bono*. A good or a use may exist, and we be unable to see it. And yet grave men are continually thrusting into the faces of the investigators of these phenomena this preposterous *cui bono?*"

"Enough, my dear Mr. Kenrick!" exclaimed Laura.

But he was not to be stopped. He rose and paced the room, and continued: "The *cui bono* of phenomena must of course be found in the mind that regards them. 'I can't find you both arguments and brains,' said Dr. Johnson to a noodle who thought Milton trashy. One man sees an apple fall, and straightway thinks of the price of cider. Newton sees it, and its suggests gravitation. One man sees a table rise in the air, and cries: 'It can't be a spirit; 't is too undignified for a spirit!' Mountford sees it, and the immortality of the soul is thenceforth to him a fact as positive as any fact of science."

"Your story, dear Mr. Kenrick, your story!" urged Laura.

"My story is ended. The ghost has come and vanished."

"Is that all?" whined Laura. "Are n't we, then, to have a story?"

"In mercy give us some music, Miss Brown," said Onslow.

"Play Yankee Doodle, with variations," interposed Kenrick.

"Not unless you 'd have the windows smashed in," pleaded Onslow; and, giving his arm, he waited on Clara to the piano.

"She dashed into a medley of brilliant airs from operas, uniting them by extemporized links of melody to break the abruptness of the transitions. The young men were both connoisseurs; and they interchanged looks of gratified astonishment.

"And now for a song!" exclaimed Laura.

Clara paused a moment, and sat looking with clasped hands at the keys. Then, after a delicate prelude, she gave that song of Pestal, already quoted.* She gave it with her whole soul, as if a personal wrong were adding intensity to the defiance of her tones.

Kenrick, wrought to a state of sympathy which he could not disguise, had taken a seat where he could watch her features while she sang. When she had finished, she covered her face with her hands, then, finding her emotion uncontrollable, rose and passed out of the room.

"What do you think of that, Charles?" asked Onslow.

"It was terrible," said Kenrick. "I wanted to kill a slaveholder while she sang."

"But she has the powers of a *prima donna*," said Onslow, turning to Laura.

"Yes, one would think she had practised for the stage."

Clara now returned with a countenance placid and smiling.

"How long do you stay in New Orleans, Miss Brown?" inquired Onslow.

"How long, Laura?" asked Clara.

"A week or two."

"We shall have another opportunity, I hope, of hearing you sing."

"I hope so."

"I have an appointment now at the armory. Charles, are you ready to walk?"

"No, thank you. I prefer to remain."

Onslow left, and, immediately afterwards, Laura's mother being seized with a timely hemorrhage, Laura was called off to attend to her. Kenrick was alone with Clara. Charming opportunity! He drew from her still another and another song. He conversed with her on her studies, — on the books

* See Chapter XII. page 112.

she had read, — the pictures she had seen. He was roused by her intelligence and wit. He spoke of slavery. Deep as was his own detestation of it, she helped him to make it deeper. What delightful harmony of views! Kenrick felt that his time had come. The hours slipped by like minutes, yet there he sat chained by a fascination so new, so strange, so delightful, he marvelled that life had in it so much of untasted joy.

Kenrick was not accustomed to be critical in details. He looked at general effects. But the most trifling point in Clara's accoutrements was now a thing to be marked and remembered. The little sleeve-button dropped from the band round her throat. Kenrick picked it up, — examined it, — saw, in characters so fine as to be hardly legible, the letters C. A. B. upon it. ("B. stands for Brown," thought he.) And then, as Clara put out her hand to receive it, he noticed the bracelet she wore. "What beautiful hair!" he said. He looked up at Clara's to trace a resemblance. But his glance stopped midway at her eyes. "Blue and gray!" he murmured.

"Yes, can you read them?" asked Clara.

"What do you mean?"

"Only a dream I had. There 's a letter on them somebody is to open and read."

"O, that I were a Daniel to interpret!" said Kenrick.

At last Miss Tremaine returned. Her mother had been dangerously ill. It was an hour after midnight. Sincerely astounded at finding it so late, Kenrick took his leave. Heart and brain were full. "Thou art the wine whose drunkenness is all I can desire, O love!"

And how was it with Clara? Alas, the contrariety of the affections! Clara simply thought Kenrick a very agreeable young man: handsome, but not so handsome as Onslow; clever, but not so clever as Vance!

CHAPTER XXVIII.

A LETTER OF BUSINESS.

"This war's duration can be more surely calculated from the moral progress of the North than from the result of campaigns in the field. Were the whole North to-day as one man on the moral issues underlying the struggle, the Rebellion were this day crushed. God bids us, I think, *be just and let the oppressed go free*. Let us do his bidding, and the plagues cease." — *Letter from a native of Richmond, Va.*

THE following letter belongs chronologically to this stage in our history: —

From F. Macon Semmes, New York, to T. J. Semmes, New Orleans.

"Dear Brother: I have called, as you requested, on Mr. Charlton in regard to his real estate in New Orleans. Let me give you some account of this man. He is taxed for upwards of a million. He inherited a good part of this sum from his wife, and she inherited it from a nephew, the late Mr. Berwick, who inherited it from his infant daughter, and this last from her mother. Mother, child, and father — the whole Berwick family — were killed by a steamboat explosion on the Mississippi some fifteen or sixteen years ago.

"In the lawsuit which grew out of the conflicting claims of the relatives of the mother on the one side, and of the father on the other, it was made to appear that the mother must have been killed instantaneously, either by the inhalation of steam from the explosion, or by a blow on the head from a splinter; either cause being sufficient to produce immediate death. It was then proved that the child, having been seen with her nurse alive and struggling in the water, must have lived after the mother, — thus inheriting the mother's property. But it was further proved that the child was drowned, and that the father survived the child a few hours; and thus the father's heir became entitled to an estate amounting to upwards of a million of dollars, all of which was thus diverted from the Aylesford family (to whom the property ought to have gone), and bestowed on a man alien in blood and in every other respect to all the parties fairly interested.

"This fortunate man was Charlton. The scandal goes, that even the wife from whom he derived the estate (and who died before he got it) had received from him such treatment as to alienate her wholly. The nearest relative of Mrs. Berwick, *née* Aylesford, is a Mrs. Pompilard, now living with an aged husband and with dependent step-children and grandchildren, in a state of great impoverishment. To this aunt the large property derived from her brother, Mr. Aylesford, ought to have gone. But the law gave it to a stranger, this Charlton. I mention these facts, because you ask me to inform you what manner of man he is.

"Let one little anecdote illustrate. Mr. Albert Pompilard, now some eighty years old, has been in his day a great operator in Wall Street. He has made half a dozen large fortunes and lost them. Five years ago, by a series of bold and fortunate speculations, he placed himself once more on the top round of the financial ladder. He paid off all his debts with interest, pensioned off a widowed daughter, lifted up from the gutter several old, broken-down friends, and advanced a handsome sum to his literary son-in-law, Mr. Cecil Purling, who had found, as he thought, a short cut to fortune. Pompilard also bought a stylish place on the Hudson; and people supposed he would be content to keep aloof from the stormy fluctuations of Wall Street.

"But one day he read in the financial column of the newspaper certain facts that roused the old propensity. His near neighbor was a rich retired tailor, a Mr. Maloney, an Irishman, who used to come over to play billiards with the venerable stock-jobber. Pompilard had made a visit to Wall Street the day before. He had been fired with a grand scheme of buying up the whole of a certain stock (in which sellers at sixty days at a low figure were abundant) and then holding on for a grand rise. He did not find it difficult to kindle the financial enthusiasm of poor Snip.

"Brief, the two simpletons went into the speculation, and lost every cent they were worth in the world. Simultaneously with their break-down, Purling, the son-in-law, managed to lose all that had been confided to his hands. The widowed daughter, Mrs. Ireton, gave up all the little estate her father had settled on her. Poor Maloney had to go back to his goose; and Pompilard, now almost an octogenarian, has been obliged, he and his family, to take lodgings in the cottage of his late gardener.

"The other day Mr. Hicks, a friend of the family, learning

that they were actually pinched in their resources, ventured to call upon Charlton for a contribution for their relief. After an evident inward struggle, Charlton manfully pulled out his pocket-book, and tendered — what, think you? — why, a ten-dollar bill! Hicks affected to regard the tender as an insult, and slapped the donor's face. Charlton at first threatened a prosecution, but concluded it was too expensive a luxury. Thus you see he is a miser. It was with no little satisfaction, therefore, that I called to communicate the state of his affairs in New Orleans.

"He lives on one of the avenues in a neat freestone house, such as could be hired for twenty-five hundred a year. There is a stable attached, and he keeps a carriage. Soon after he burst upon the fashionable world as a millionnaire, there was a general competition among fashionable families to secure him for one of the daughters. But Charlton, with all his wealth, did not want a wife who was merely stylish, clever, and beautiful; she must be rich into the bargain. He at last encountered such a one (as he imagined) in Miss Dykvelt, a member of one of the old Dutch families. He proposed, was accepted, married, — and three weeks afterwards, to his consternation and horror, he received an application from old D., the father-in-law, for a loan of a hundred thousand dollars.

"Charlton, of course, indignantly refused it. He found that he had been, to use his own words, 'taken in and done for.' Old Dykvelt, while he kept up the style of a prince, was on the verge of bankruptcy. The persons to whom Charlton applied for information, knowing the object of the inquiry and the meanness of the inquirer, purposely cajoled him with stories of Dykvelt's wealth. Charlton fell into the trap. Charlotte Dykvelt, who was in love at the time with young Ireton (a Lieutenant in the army and a grandson of old Pompilard), yielded to the entreaties of her parents and married the man she detested. She was well versed in the history of his first wife, and resolved that her own heart, wrung by obedience to parental authority, should be iron and adamant to any attempt Charlton might make to wound it.

"He soon found himself overmatched. The bully and tyrant was helpless before the impassive frigidity and inexorable determination of that young and beautiful woman. He had a large iron safe in his house, in which he kept his securities and coupons, and often large sums of money. One day he discovered he had been robbed of thirty thousand dollars. He charged the theft upon his wife. She neither denied nor confessed it, but treated him with a glacial scorn before which he finally cowered and was dumb. Undoubtedly she had taken the money. She forced him against his inclination to move into a decent house, and keep a carriage; and at last, by a threat of leaving him, she made him settle on her a liberal allowance.

"A loveless home for him, as you may suppose! One daughter, Lucy Charlton, is the offspring of this ill-assorted marriage; a beautiful girl, I am told, but who shrinks from her father's presence as from something odious. Probably the mother's impressions during pregnancy gave direction to the antipathies of the child; so that before it came into the world it was fatherless.

"Well, I called on Charlton last Thursday. As I passed the little sitting-room of the basement, I saw a young and lovely girl putting her mouth filled with seed up to the bars of a cage, and a canary-bird picking the food from her lips. A cat, who seemed to be on excellent terms with the bird, was perched on the girl's shoulder, and superintending the operation. So, thought I, she exercises her affections in the society of these dumb pets rather than in that of her father.

"I found Charlton sitting lonely in a sort of library scantily furnished with books. A well-formed man, but with a face haggard and anxious as if his life-blood were ebbing irrecoverably with every penny that went from his pockets. On my mentioning your name, his eyes brightened; for he inferred I had come with your semiannual remittances. He was at once anxious to know if rents in New Orleans had been materially affected by the war. I told him his five houses near Lafayette Square, excepting that occupied on a long lease by Mr. Carberry Ratcliff, would not bring in half the amount they did last year. He groaned audibly. I then told him that your semiannual collections for him amounted to six thousand dollars, but that you were under the painful necessity of assuring him that the money would have to be paid all over to the Confederate government.

"Charlton, completely struck aghast, fell back in his chair, his face pale, and his lips quivering. I thought he had fainted.

"'Your brother would n't rob me, Mr. Semmes?' he gasped forth.

"'Certainly not,' I replied; 'but his obedience is due to the authorities that are uppermost. The Confederate flag waves over New Orleans, and will probably continue to wave. All your real estate has been or will be confiscated.'

"'But it is worth two hundred thousand dollars!' he exclaimed, in a tone that was almost a shriek.

"'So much the better for the Confederate treasury!' I replied.

"I then broached what you told me to in regard to his making a *bona fide* sale of the property to you. I offered him twenty thousand dollars in cash, if he would surrender all claim.

"'Never! never!' he exclaimed. 'I'll run my risk of the city's coming back into our possession. I see through your brother's trick.'

"'Please recall that word, sir,' I said, touching my wristbands.

"'Well, your brother's *plan*, sir. Will that suit you?'

"'That will do,' I replied. 'My brother will pay your ten thousand dollars over to the Confederacy. But I am authorized to pay you a tenth part of that sum for your receipt in full of all moneys due to you for rents up to this time.'

"'Ha! you Secessionists are not quite so positive, after all, as to your fortune!' he exclaimed. 'You're a little weak-kneed as to your ability to hold the place, — eh?'

"'The city will be burnt,' I replied, 'before the inhabitants will consent to have the old flag restored. You'd better make the most, Mr. Charlton, of your opportunity to compound for a fractional part of the value of your Southern property.'

"It was all in vain. I could n't make him see it. He hates the war and the Lincoln administration; but he won't sell or compound on the terms you propose. And, to be frank, I would n't if I were he. It would be a capital thing for us if he could be made to do it. But as he is in no immediate need of money, we cannot rely on the stimulus of absolute want to influence him as we wish. I took my leave, quite disgusted with his obstinacy.

"The fall of Sumter seems to have fired the Northern heart in earnest. I fear we are going to have serious work with these Yankees. Secretary Walker's cheerful promise of raising the Confederate flag over Faneuil Hall will not be realized for some time. Nevertheless, we are bound to prevail — I hope. Of course every Southern man will die in the last ditch rather than yield one foot of Southern soil to Yankee domination. We must have Maryland and the Chesapeake, Fortress Monroe, and all the Gulf forts, Western Virginia, Missouri, Kentucky, Delaware, — every square inch of them. Not a rood must we part with. We can whip, if we'll only think so. We're the master race, and can do it. Can hold on to our niggers into the bargain. At least, we'll talk as if we believed it. Perhaps the prediction will work its fulfilment. Who knows?

"Fraternally yours, F. M. S."

CHAPTER XXIX.

THE WOMAN WHO DELIBERATES IS LOST.

"O North-wind! blow strong with God's breath in twenty million men." — *Rev. John Weiss.*

"Loud wind, strong wind, sweeping o'er the mountains,
Fresh wind, free wind, blowing from the sea,
Pour forth thy vials like streams from airy fountains,
Draughts of life to me." — *Miss Muloch.*

ON coming down to the breakfast-table one morning, Kenrick was delighted to encounter Vance, and asked, "What success?"

"I found in Natchez," was the reply, "an old colored man who knew Davy and his wife. They removed to New York, it seems, some three years ago. I must push my inquiries further. The clew must not be dropped. The old man, my informant, was formerly a slave. He came into my room at the hotel, and showed me the scars on his back. Ah! I, too, could have showed scars, if I had deemed it prudent."

"Cousin William," said Kenrick, "I would n't take the testimony of our own humane overseer as to slavery. I have studied the usages on other plantations. Let me show you a photograph which I look at when my antislavery rage wants kindling, which is not often."

He produced the photograph of a young female, apparently a quarteroon, sitting with back exposed naked to the hips, — her face so turned as to show an intelligent and rather handsome profile. The flesh was all welted, seamed, furrowed, and scarred, as if both by fire and the scourge.

"There!" resumed Kenrick, "that I saw taken myself, and know it to be genuine. It is one out of many I have collected. The photograph cannot lie. It will be terrible as the recording angel in reflecting slavery as this civil war will unearth it. What will the Carlyles and the Gladstones say to this? Will it make them falter, think you, in their Sadducean hoot against a noble people who are manfully fighting the great battle of humanity against such infernalism as this?"

"They would probably fall back on the doubter's privilege."

"Yes, that's the most decent way of escape. But I would pin them with the sharp fact. That woman (her name was Margaret) belonged to the Widow Gillespie,* on the Black River. Margaret had a nursing child, and, out of maternal tenderness, had disobeyed Mrs. Gillespie's orders to wean it. For this she was subjected to *the punishment of the hand-saw*. She was laid on her face, her clothes stripped up to around her neck, her hands and feet held down, and Mrs. Gillespie, sitting by, then 'paddled,' or stippled the exposed body with the hand-saw. She then had Margaret turned over, and, with heated tongs, attempted to grasp her nipples. The writhings of the victim foiled her purpose; but between the breasts the skin and flesh were horribly burned."

"A favorite remark," said Vance, "with our smug apologists of slavery, is, that an owner's interests will make him treat a slave well. Undoubtedly in many cases so it is. But I have generally found that human malignity, anger, or revenge is more than a match for human avarice. A man will often gratify his spite even at the expense of his pocket."

Kenrick showed the photograph of a man with his back scarred as if by a shower of fire.

"This poor fellow," said Kenrick, "shows the effects of the *corn-husk punishment;* not an unusual one on some plantations. The victim is stretched out on the ground, with hands and feet held down. Dry corn-husks are then lighted, and the burning embers are whipped off with a stick so as to fall in showers of live sparks on the naked back. Such is the 'patriarchal' system! Such the tender mercies bestowed on 'our man-servants and our maid-servants,' as that artful dodger, Jeff Davis, calls our plantation slaves."

"And yet," remarked Vance, "horrible as these things are, how small a part of the wrong of slavery is in the mere *physical* suffering inflicted!"

"Yes, the crowning outrage is mental and moral."

"This war," resumed Vance, "is not sectional, nor geographi-

* The names and the facts are real. See Harper's Weekly, July 4, 1863.

cal, nor, in a party sense, political: it is a war of eternally antagonistic principles, — Belial against Gabriel."

"I took up a Northern paper to-day," said Kenrick, "in which the writer pleads the necessity of slavery, because, he says, 'white men can't work in the rice-swamps.' Truly, a staggering argument! The whole rice production of the United States is only worth some four millions of dollars per annum! A single factory in Lowell can beat that. And we are asked to base a national policy on such considerations!"

Here the approach of guests led to a change of topic.

"And how have *your* affairs prospered?" asked Vance.

"Ah! cousin," replied Kenrick, "I almost blush to tell you what an experience I've had."

"Not fallen in love, I hope?"

"If it isn't that, 't is something very near it. The lady is staying with Miss Tremaine. A Miss Perdita Brown. Onslow took me to see her."

"And which is the favored admirer?"

"Onslow, I fear. I'm not a lady's man, you see. Indeed, I never wished to be till now. Give me a few lessons, cousin. Teach me a little small-talk."

"I must know something of the lady first."

"To begin at the beginning," said Kenrick, "there can be no dispute as to her beauty. But there is a something in her manner that puzzles me. Is it lack of sincerity? Not that. Is it preoccupation of thought? Sometimes it seems that. And then some apt, flashing remark indicates that she has her wits on the alert. You must see her and help me read her. You visit Miss Laura?"

"Yes. I'll do your bidding, Charles. How often have you seen this enchantress?"

"Too often for my peace of mind: three times."

"Is she a coquette?"

"If one, she has the art to conceal art. There seems to be something on her mind more absorbing than the desire to fascinate. She's an unconscious beauty."

"Say a deep one. Shall we meet at Miss Tremaine's to-night?"

"Yes; the moth knows he'll get singed, but flutter he must."

"Take comfort, Charles, in that of thought of Tennyson's, who tells us,

> 'That not a moth with vain desire
> Is shrivelled in a fruitless fire.' "

The cousins parted. They had no sooner quitted the breakfast-room than Onslow entered. After a hasty meal, he took his sword-belt and military-cap, and walked forth out of the hotel. As he passed Wakeman's shop, near by, for the sale of books and periodicals, he was attracted by a photograph in a small walnut frame in the window. Stopping to examine it, he uttered an exclamation of surprise, stepped into the shop, and said to Wakeman, "Where did you get that photograph?"

"That was sent here with several others by the photographer. You'll find his name on the back."

"I see. What shall I pay you for it?"

"A dollar."

"There it is."

Onslow took the picture and left the shop, but did not notice that he was followed by a well-dressed gentleman with a cigar in his mouth. This individual had been for several days watching every passer-by who looked at that photograph. He now followed Onslow to the head-quarters of his regiment; put an inquiry to one of the members of the Captain's company, and then strolled away as if he had more leisure than he knew what to do with. But no sooner had he turned a corner, than he entered a carriage which was driven off at great speed.

Not an hour had passed when a black man in livery put into Onslow's hands this note: —

"Will you come and dine with me at five to-day without ceremony? Please reply by the bearer.

"Yours, C. Ratcliff."

What can he want? thought Onslow, somewhat gratified by such an attention from so important a leader. Presuming that the object merely was to ask some questions concerning military matters, the Captain turned to the man in livery, and said, "Tell Mr. Ratcliff I will come."

Punctually at the hour of five Onslow ascended the marble steps of Ratcliff's stately house, rang the bell, and was ushered into a large and elegantly furnished drawing-room, the windows of which were heavily curtained so as to keep out the glare of the too fervid sunlight. Pictures and statues were disposed about the apartment, but Onslow, who had a genuine taste for art, could find nothing that he would covet for a private gallery of his own.

Ratcliff entered, habited in a cool suit of grass-cloth. The light hues of his vest and neck-tie heightened the contrast of his somewhat florid complexion, which had now lost all the smoothness of youth. Self-indulgent habits had faithfully done their work in moulding his exterior. Portly and puffy, he looked much older than he really was. But in his manner of greeting Onslow there was much of that charm which renders the hospitality of a plantation lord so attractive. Throwing aside all that arrogance which would have made his overseers and tradespeople keep their distance, he welcomed Onslow like an old friend and an equal.

"You 've a superb house here," said the ingenuous Captain.

"'T will do, considering that I sometimes occupy it only a month in the year," replied Ratcliff. "I 'm glad to say I only hire it. The house belonged to a Miss Aylesford, a Yankee heiress; then passed into the possession of a New York man, one Charlton; but I pay the rent into the coffers of the Confederate government. The property is confiscate."

"Won't the Yankees retaliate?"

"We sha'n't allow them to."

"After we 've whipped Yankee-Doo-dle-dom, what then?"

"Then a strong military government. Having our slaves to work for us, we shall become the greatest martial nation in the world. Our poor whites, now a weakness and a burden, we will convert into soldiers and Cossacks; excepting the artisan and trading classes, and them we must disfranchise." *

"Can we expect aid from England?" asked Onslow.

"Not open aid, but substantial aid nevertheless. Exeter Hall may grumble. The *doctrinaires*, the Newmans, Brights,

* Mr. W. S. Grayson of Mississippi writes, in De Bow's Review (August, 1860): "Civil liberty has been the theme of praise among men, and most wrongfully. This is the infatuation of our age." And Mr. George Fitzhugh of Virginia writes: "Men are never efficient in military matters, or in industrial pursuits, until wholly deprived of their liberty. *Loss of liberty is no disgrace.*"

Mills, and Cobdens may protest and agitate. The English clodhoppers, mudsills, and workies of all kinds will sympathize of course with the low-born Yankees. But the master race of England, the non-producers, will favor the same class here. The disintegration of North America into warring States is what they long to see. Already the English government is swift to hail us as belligerents. Already it refuses what it once so eagerly proffered, — an international treaty making privateering piracy. Soon it will let us fit out privateers in English ports. Yes, England is all right."

Here a slave-boy announced dinner, and they entered a smaller but lofty apartment, looking out on a garden, and having its two open windows pleasantly latticed with grape-vines. A handsome, richly dressed quadroon lady sat at the table. In introducing his young guest, Ratcliff addressed her as Madame Volney.

Onslow, in his innocence, inquired after Mrs. Ratcliff.

"My wife is an invalid, and rarely quits her room," said the host.

The dinner was sumptuous, beginning with turtle-soup and ending with ices and fruits. The costliest Burgundies and Champagnes were uncorked, if only for a sip of their flavors. Madame Volney, half French, was gracious and talkative, occasionally checking Ratcliff in his eating, and warning him to be prudent. At last cigars were brought on, and she left the room. Ratcliff rose and listened at the door, as if to be sure she had gone up-stairs. Then, walking on tiptoe, he resumed his seat. He alluded to the opera, — to the ballet, — to the subject of pretty women.

"And *apropos* of pretty women," he exclaimed, "let me show you a photograph of one I have in my pocket."

As he spoke, there was a rustling in the grape-vines at a window. He turned, but saw nothing.

Onslow took the photograph, and exclaimed: "But this is astonishing! I 've a copy of the same in my pocket."

"You surprise me, Captain. Do you know the original?"

"Quite well; and I grant you she 's beautiful."

Onslow did not notice the expression of Ratcliff's face at this confession, but another did. Lifting a glass of Burgundy so as to help his affectation of indifference, "Confess now, Captain," said Ratcliff, "that you 're a favorite! That delicate mouth has been pressed by your lips; those ivory shoulders have known your touch."

"O never! never!" returned Onslow, with the emphasis of sincerity in his tone. "You misjudge the character of the lady. She 's a friend of Miss Tremaine, — is now passing a few days with her at the St. Charles. A lady wholly respectable. Miss Perdita Brown of St. Louis! That rascally photographer ought to be whipped for making money out of her beautiful picture."

"Has she admirers in her train?" asked Ratcliff.

"I know of but one beside myself."

"Indeed! And who is he?"

"Charles Kenrick has called on her with me."

"By the way, Wigman tells me that Charles insulted the flag the other day."

"Poh! Wigman was so drunk he could n't distinguish jest from earnest."

"So Robson told me. But touching this Miss Brown, — is she as pretty as her photograph would declare?"

"It hardly does her justice. But her sweet face is the least of her charms. She talks well, — sings well, — plays well, — and, young as she is, has the bearing, the dignity, the grace, of the consummate lady."

Here there was another rustling, as if the grape-vine were pulled. Ratcliff started, went to the window, looked out, but, seeing nothing, remarked, "The wind must be rising," and returned to his seat. "I 've omitted," said he, "to ask after your family; are they well?"

"Yes; they were in Austin when I heard from them last. My father, I grieve to say, goes with Hamilton and his set in opposition to the Southern movement. My brother, William Temple, is equally infatuated. My mother and sister of course acquiesce. So I 'm the only faithful one of my family."

"You deserve a colonelcy for that."

"Thank you. Is your clock right?"

"Yes."

"Then I must go. I 've an engagement."

"Sorry for it. Beware of Miss Brown. This is the day of Mars, not Venus. Good by."

When Onslow had gone, Ratcliff sat five minutes as if meditating on some plan. Then, drawing forth a pocket-book, he took out an envelope, — wrote on it, — reflected, — and wrote again. When he had finished, he ordered the carriage to be brought to the door. As he was passing through the hall, Madame Volney, from the stairs, asked where he was going.

"To the St. Charles, on political business."

"Don't be out late, dear," said Madame. "Let me see how you look. Your neck-tie is out of place. Let me fix it. There! And your vest needs buttoning. So!" And as her delicate hands passed around his person, they slid unperceived into a side-pocket of his coat, and drew forth what he had just deposited there.

"Bother! That will do, Josephine," grumbled Ratcliff. She released him with a kiss. He descended the marble steps of the house, entered a carriage, and drove off.

Madame passed into the dining-room, the brilliant gas-lights of which had not yet been lowered, and, opening the pocket-book, drew out several photographic cards, all containing one and the same likeness of a young and beautiful girl. As the quadroon scanned that fresh vernal countenance, that adorably innocent, but earnest and intelligent expression, those thick, wavy tresses, and that exquisitely moulded bust, her own handsome face grew grim and ugly by the transmuting power of anger and jealousy. "So, this is the game he's pursuing, is it?" she muttered. "This is what makes him restive! Not politics, as he pretends, but this smoothed-faced decoy! Deep as you've kept it, Ratcliff, I've fathomed you at last!"

Searching further among his papers, she found an envelope, on which certain memoranda were pencilled, and among them these: "*First see Tremaine. Arrange for seizure without scandal or noise. Early in morning call on Gentry, — have her prepared. Take Esha with us to help.*"

Hardly had Madame time to read this, when a carriage stopped before the door. Laying the pocket-book with its contents, as if undisturbed, on the table, she ran half-way up-stairs. Ratcliff re-entered, and, after looking about the hall, passed into the dining-room. "Ah! here it is!" she heard him say to the attendant; "I could have sworn I put it in my pocket." He then left the house, and the carriage again drove off, — drove to the St. Charles, where Ratcliff had a long private interview with the pliable Tremaine.

While it was going on, Laura and Clara sat in the drawing-room, waiting for company. Laura having disapproved of the costume in which Clara had first appeared, the latter now wore a plain robe of black silk; and around her too beautiful neck Laura had put a collar, large enough to be called a cape, fastening it in front with an old-fashioned cameo pin. But how provoking! This dress would insist on being more becoming even than the other!

Vance was the earliest of the visitors. On being introduced to Clara, he bowed as if they had never met before. Then, seating himself by Laura, he devoted himself assiduously to her entertainment. Clara turned over the leaves of a music-book, and took no part in the conversation. Yes! It was plain that Vance was deeply interested in the superficial, but showy Laura. Well, what better could be expected of a man?

Once more was Laura summoned to the bed-side of her mother. "How vexatious!" Regretfully she left the drawing-room. As soon as she had gone, Vance rose, and, taking a seat by Clara, offered her his hand. She returned its cordial pressure. "My dear young friend," he said, "tell me everything. What can I do for you?"

O, that she might fling herself on that strong arm and tender heart! That she might disclose to him her whole situation! Impulses, eager and tumultuous, urged her to do this. Then there was a struggle as if to keep down the ready confession. Pride battled with the feminine instinct that claimed a protector.

What! This man, on whom she had no more claim than on the veriest stranger, — should she put upon him the burden of her confidence? This man who in one minute had whispered more flattering things in the ear of Laura than he had said to Clara during the whole of their acquaintance, — should she ask favors from *him?* O, if he would, by look or word, but betray that he felt an interest in her beyond that of mere friendship! But then came the frightful thought, "I am a slave!" And

Clara shuddered to think that no honorable attachment between her and a gentleman could exist.

"What of that? Surely I may claim from him the help which any true man ought to lend to a woman threatened with outrage. Stop there! Does not the chivalry of the plantation reverse the notions of the old knight-errants, and give heed to no damsel in distress, unless she can show free papers? Nay, will not the representative of the blood of all the cavaliers look calmly on, and smoke his cigar, while a woman is bound naked to a tree and scourged?"

And then her mind ran rapidly over certain stories which a slave-girl, once temporarily hired by Mrs. Gentry, had told of the punishments of female slaves: how, for claiming too long a respite from work after childbirth, they had been "fastened up by their wrists to a beam, or to a branch of a tree, their feet barely touching the ground," and in that position horribly scourged with a leather thong; perhaps, the father, brother, or husband of the victim being compelled to officiate as the scourger! *

"But surely this man, whose very glance seems shelter and protection, — this true and generous *gentleman*, — must belong to a very different order of chivalry from that of the Davises, the Lees, and the Toombses. Yes! I 'll stake my life he 's another kind of cavalier from those foul, obscene, and dastardly woman-whipping miscreants and scoundrels. Yes! I 'll comply with that gracious entreaty of his, 'Tell me everything!' I 'll confess all."

Her heart throbbed. She was on the point of uttering that one name, *Ratcliff*, — a sound that would have inspired Vance with the power and wisdom of an archangel to rescue her, — when there were voices at the door, and Laura entered, followed by Onslow. They brought with them a noise of talking and laughing. Soon Kenrick joined the party.

The golden opportunity seemed to have slipped by!

To Kenrick's gaze Clara never appeared so transcendent. But there was an unwonted paleness on her cheeks; and what meant that thoughtful and serious air? For a sensitive moral barometer commend us to a lover's heart!

* Testimony of Mrs. Fanny Kemble to facts within her knowledge.

Of course there was music; and Clara sang.

"What do you think of her voice?" asked Laura of Vance.

"It justifies all your praises," was the reply; and then, seeing that Clara was not in the mood for display, he took her place at the piano, and rattled away just as Laura requested. Onslow tried to engage Clara in conversation; but a cloud, as if from some impending ill, was palpably over her.

Kenrick sat by in silence, deaf to the brilliant music. Clara's presence, with its subtle magnetism, had steeped his own thoughts in the prevailing hue of hers. Suddenly he turned to her, and whispered: "You want help. What is it? Grant me the privilege of a brother. What can I do for you?"

The glance Clara turned upon him was so full of thanks, so radiant with gratitude, that hope sprang in his heart. But before she could put her reply in words, Laura had come up, and taken her away to the piano for a concluding song. Clara gave them Longfellow's "Rainy Day" to Dempster's music.

The little gilt clock over the mantel tinkled eleven.

Vance rose to go, and said to Laura, "May I call on Miss Brown to-morrow with some new music?"

"I 'll answer for her, yes," replied Laura. "We shall be at home any time after twelve."

The gentlemen all took leave. Onslow made his exit the last. A rose that had been fastened in Clara's waist dropped on the floor. "May I have it?" he asked, picking it up.

"Why not? I wish it were fresher. Good night!" And she put out her hand. Onslow eagerly pressed it; but Clara, lifting his, said, "May this hand never strike except for justice and human freedom!"

"Amen to that!" replied Onslow, before he well took in the entire meaning of what she had said.

He hastened to rejoin his friends, following them through the corridor. He seemed to tread on air. "I was the only one she offered to shake hands with!" he exultingly soliloquized.

The three parted, after an interchange of good nights. Both Onslow and Kenrick betook themselves to their rooms, each with no desire for other companionship than his own rose-colored dreams.

CHAPTER XXX.

A FEMININE VAN AMBURGH.

"She who ne'er answers till a husband cools,
Or, if she rules him, never shows she rules." — *Pope.*

THE morning after the dinner, Madame Volney rose at sunrise, and was stealing on tiptoe into her dressing-room, when Ratcliff, always a late riser, grumbled, "What 's the matter?"

"There 's to be an early church-service," she replied.

"Bah! You 're always going to church!"

The quadroon made no reply, but gently retired, dressed, and glided out of the house into the open air. On through the yet deserted streets she swiftly passed. A white fog brooded over the city. Heavy-winged sea-birds were slowly making their way overhead to the marshes of Lake Ponchartrain, or still farther out to the beaches of the Gulf. The sound of drums and fifes in the distance occasionally broke the matutinal stillness. The walls of the streets were covered with placards of meetings of volunteer companies, — of the Wigman Rifles, the MacMahon Guards, the Beauregard Lancers, the Black Flag Invincibles.

After half an hour's walk, the quadroon paused before a house, on the door of which was a brass plate presenting the words, — "Mrs. Gentry's Seminary for Young Ladies." While she looked and hesitated, a black girl came up from some steps leading into the basement, and with a mop and pail of water proceeded to wash the sidewalk.

"Is Esha in?" asked the quadroon.

"Yes, missis, Esha am in. Jes you go down dem steps inter de kitchen, an' dar you 'll fine Esha, sure." And taking the direction pointed out, Madame found herself in the presence of a large, powerfully built mulatto woman, who was engaged in preparations for breakfast.

"Is this Esha?"

"Yes, missis, dis am nob'dy else."

"Esha, I want a few minutes' talk with you."

"Take a char, den, missis, and 'scuse my looks."

"You look like a good woman, Esha, so no matter for dress."

"Tahnk yer, missis. Esha 's like de res', — not too good, — but nebdeless dar 's wuss folks dan she."

"Esha, who is this young girl Mr. Ratcliff is after?"

Esha's eyes snapped, and she looked sharply at her visitor. "Why you want ter know?" she asked.

"Are you a slave, Esha?"

"Yes, missis, I 'se born a slabe, — hab libd a slabe, an' 'spek to die a slabe."

"I too am a slave, Esha. I belonged to old Etienne La Harpe, who died six years ago. Though I had had two children, one by him and one by his son, the old man's widow sent me to the auction-block. I was sold to the highest bidder. I was bought by Mr. Carberry Ratcliff."

"Ah! by him? by him?" muttered Esha.

"I was handsome. He made me his favorite. I 've been faithful to him. Even his wife, poor thing, blesses the day I came into the house. She would have died long ago but for my care. The slaves, too, come to me with their sorrows. I do what I can for their relief. I am not, by nature, a bad woman. I would continue to serve this man and his household."

"Do yer lub him, — dis Massa Ratcliff?"

"That 's a hard question, Esha. He has treated me like a lady. I am practically at the head of his house. I have a carriage at my command. He gives me all the money I ask for. He prizes me for my prudence and good temper. I love him so far as this: I should hate the woman who threatened to step between me and him. Now tell me who this girl is whose photograph he has."

"She, missis? She am a slabe too."

"She a slave? Whose slave?"

"She 'longs to Massa Ratcliff!"

"And he has kept it a secret from me!"

Esha, like most slaves, was a quick judge of character. She

had an almost intuitive perception of shams. Convinced of the quadroon's sincerity, she now threw a cushion on the floor, and, seating herself on it after the Oriental fashion, frankly told the whole story of the child Clara, and disclosed the true nature of her own relations to Ratcliff. When she had concluded, Madame Volney impulsively kissed her.

"And are you sure," she asked, "quite sure that little Darling, as you call her, will resist Ratcliff to the last?"

"Dat chile will sooner die dan gib up ter dat ole man. What you 'spose she went out ter buy dat day I met her last? Wall, missis, she buyed a dagger."

"Good! I love her!" cried Madame Volney, with flushed cheeks. "But. Esha, do you know where she is now?"

"Yes, missis; but I tink I better not tell eb'n you, — 'cause you see —"

"She's with Miss Tremaine, at the St. Charles!"

"De Lord help us! How yer know dat, missis?" cried Esha, alarmed. "Do Massa Ratcliff know 'bout it?"

"He knows it all, and has made his preparations for seizing the girl this very day. He'll be here this morning to give you your directions. Now, Esha, don't make a blunder. Don't let him see that you're the girl's friend. Say nothing of my visit. I'll tell you what I suspect: Ratcliff knows his wife can't live three months longer. He has never had a child by her. All his children are mulattoes and illegitimate. The desire of his heart is for a lawful heir. He means — Are you sure the girl is white?"

"I tell yer, missis, whoebber sold her, fust stained her skin to put up de price. Should n't be 'stonished if dat chile was kidnapped."

Madame Volney looked at her watch. "Esha," she said, "you'll be employed by Ratcliff to help secure her person. If, when he comes to you, the ribbon on his straw hat is *green*, do as he tells you. Should the ribbon be *black*, tell him to wait ten minutes. Then do you run round the corner to Aurora Street, where you'll see a carriage with a white handkerchief held out at the right-hand window. You'll find me there. We'll drive to the St. Charles, and take the girl with us somewhere out of Ratcliff's reach. Can you remember all I've told you?"

"Ebry word ob it, missis! Tahnk de Lord fur sendin' yer. Watch Massa Ratcliff sharp. Fix him sure, missis, — fix him sure!"

"Trust me, Esha! He seizes no young girl to-day, unless I let him. But be very prudent. You may need money."

"No, missis. No pay fur tellin' de troof."

"But you may need it for the child's sake."

"O yis, missis. I 'll take it fur de chile, sure."

Madame Volney placed in her hands thirty dollars in gold, then left the house, and, hailing a carriage at a neighboring stand, told the driver where to take her. "Double speed, double fare!" she added. In ten minutes she was at home.

Ratcliff had not yet come down. He had rung the bell, and given orders for an early breakfast. Madame went up to her dressing-room, and put on her most becoming morning attire. We have called her a quadroon; but her complexion was of that clear golden hue, mixed with olive and a dash of carnation, which so many Southern amateurs prefer to the pure red and white of a light-haired Anglo-Saxon.

When Ratcliff came down, he complimented her on her good looks, and kissed her.

"I 've been to confession," she said, as she touched the tap of a splendid silver urn, and let hot water into the cups.

"And what have you been confessing, Josy?"

"I 've been confessing how very foolish I 've been the last few months."

"Foolish in what, Josephine?"

"Foolish in my jealousy of *you*."

"Jealousy? What cause have I given you for jealousy? I 've been too much bothered about public matters to have time to think of any woman but you."

"That 's partly true. But don't I know what you most desire of earthly things?"

"Of course! You know I desire the success of the Southern Confederacy, corner-stone and all."

"No, not that. You covet one thing even more than that."

"Indeed! What is it?"

"A legitimate child who may inherit your wealth, and transmit your name."

"Yes, I'd like a child. But we must take things as they come along. You must n't be jealous because now and then I may have dropped a hint of regret that I've no direct heir to my estate."

"You've not confined yourself to hints. You've been provident in act as well as in thought."

"What the deuce do you mean?"

"Don't be angry when I tell you, you have n't planned a plan, the last three months, of which I have n't been aware."

"Well, I've always thought you the keenest woman of my acquaintance; but I'd like to have it put through my hair what you're exactly driving at now. What is it?"

"This: I know your scheme in regard to Miss Murray, and, what is more, I highly approve of it."

"You're the Devil!" exclaimed Ratcliff, starting up from his seat. Then, seeing Josephine's unaffected smile and evident good humor, he sat down.

"At first I was a little chagrined," she said, "especially when I found Mademoiselle so very pretty. But I've reflected much on it since, and talked with my confessor about it."

"The deuce you have! Talked with your confessor, eh?"

"Yes, with my confessor. And the result is, that, so far from opposing you in your plan, I've concluded to give it my support."

"And what do you understand to be my plan?"

"Perhaps 't is vague even in your own mind as yet. But I'll tell you what I mean. Your wife is not likely to live many weeks longer. You'll inherit from her a large estate. You'll wish to marry again, and this time with a view to offspring. Both taste and policy will lead you to choose a young and accomplished woman. Who more suitable than Miss Murray?"

"Why, Josephine, she's a slave!"

"A slave, is she? Look me in the face and tell me, if you can, you believe she has a drop of African blood in her veins. No! That child must have been kidnapped. And you have often suspected as much."

"Where the Devil — Confound the woman!" muttered Ratcliff, half frightened at what looked like clairvoyance.

"Yes," she continued, "her parents must have been of gentle blood. Look at her hands and feet. Hear her speak."

"What is there you don't find out, Josy?" exclaimed Ratcliff. "Here you tell me things that have been working in my mind, which I was hardly aware of myself till you mentioned them!"

"O, I 've known all about your search for the girl. 'T was not till after a struggle I could reconcile it to my mind to lend you my aid. But this was what I thought: He will soon be a widower. He will desire to marry; not that he does not love his Josy —"

"Yes, Josy, you 're right there; you 're a jewel of a woman. Such devilish good common sense! Go on."

"He would marry, not that he does not love his Josy, but because he wants a legitimate child of his own. That 's but natural and proper. Why should I oppose it, and thus give him cause to cast me out from his affections? Why not give him new reason for attachment, by showing him I am capable of a sacrifice for his sake? Yes, he will love me none the less for letting him see that without one jealous pang I can help him to a young and beautiful wife."

"But, Josy, would you really recommend my marrying this girl?"

"Why not? Where will you find her equal?"

"But just think of it, — she was sold to me at public auction as a slave."

"Yes, and the next day Mrs. Gentry wrote you that the coloring stuff had washed off from her skin, and she was whiter than any one in the school. You wrote not a word in reply. But did not the thought occur to you, the child has been kidnapped? Of course it did! In this great city of rogues and murderers, did you not consider there were plenty of men capable of such an act? Deny it if you can."

"Josy, you 're enough to unsteady a man's nerves. How did you discover there was such a being as Miss Murray? and how did you get out of my mind what I had thought about the kidnapping? and how, what I myself had hardly dreamed of, the idea, namely, of making her my wife?"

"When one loves," replied Josephine, "one is quick to

watch, and sharp to detect. At first, as I 've told you, I was disposed to be jealous. But reflection soon convinced me 't would be for your happiness to take this young person, now in the false position of a slave, and educate her for your wife. Even if the world should know her story, what would you care? You 're above all social criticism. Besides, would it not be comical for our swarthy Creole ladies to snuff at such a beautiful blonde, whose very presence would give the lie to all that malice could insinuate as to her birth?"

"O, I don't care for what society may say. I 'm out of the reach of its sneers. And what you urge, Josy, is reasonable, — very. Yes, she 's a remarkably fine girl, and I 've certainly taken a strong fancy to her. Some of our first young men are already deep in love with her. Of course she 'd be eternally grateful, if I were to emancipate her and make her my wife."

Josephine could hardly repress a smile of triumph to see this thorough-bred tyrant, who knew no law but his own will, thus falling into the snare she was so delicately spreading for him. Something of the satisfaction Van Amburgh might have felt when his tiger succumbed, spread its glow over her cheeks. Never in his coarse calculations had Ratcliff thought of showing Clara any further mercy than he had shown to the humblest of his concubines. And yet Josephine, by her apt suggestions, had half persuaded him, little given as he was to introspective analysis, that the idea of making the girl his wife had originated in his own mind!

"Did he keep the whole story from her because he supposed Josy would be jealous?" asked the quadroon, with a caress.

"Why, yes, Josy; to tell the truth, I thought there 'd have to be a scene sure, when you found out I 'd been educating such a girl with a view to her taking your place some time. So I kept dark. But you 're a trump, — you are! I should n't wonder if you could acquire the same influence over her that you now have over my wife."

"Easily!" said Josephine. "I 've seen her. I like her. I know we should agree. When she learns it was my wish you should emancipate and marry her, she will regard me as her friend. I can teach her not to be jealous of me."

"Capital!" exclaimed Ratcliff. "Josy can remain where

she is in the family. Josy will not have to abdicate. There 'll be no unpleasant row between the two women. The whole thing can be harmoniously managed."

"Why not, Carberry? And let me say 't would be folly to seize this girl rudely, wounding her pride and rousing her resentment. The true way is to decoy her gently till you get her into your possession, and then secure her by such means as I can suggest."

"Hang me, but you 're right again, Josy! I had thought of carrying her off this very day."

"Yes, I supposed so."

"Supposed so? Where in the name of all the devils did you get your information? For there 's but one person beside myself who knows anything about it."

"And that 's Mr. Tremaine!"

"So it is, by Jove! How did you know it?"

"I put this and that together, and drew an inference. You mean to place her again, for the present, at Mrs. Gentry's."

"True! That was my plan. But I had n't mentioned it to a soul."

"What of that? Where one loves, one has such insight! But is there any one at Mrs. Gentry's on whom you can rely to keep watch of the girl?"

"Yes, there 's an old slave-woman, — Esha. She has a grudge against the little miss, and is n't likely to be too indulgent."

"But why, Carberry, would you take the little miss to Mrs. Gentry's rather than to your own house? I see! You thought I would be in the way; that I would be jealous of her! Confess!"

"Yes, Josy, I did n't think anything else."

"Well, now, let me plan for you: first, I, with Esha, will call on her. Esha can easily persuade her that the best thing she can do will be to come with us to this house. We 'll have the blue room ready for her. It being between two other rooms, and having no other exit than through them, she will not have another chance to abscond. Esha would perhaps be a suitable person to keep guard. But then probably Mrs. Gentry would n't part with Esha."

"Bah! Gentry will have to do as I order, or see her school broken up as an Abolition concern. Your plan strikes me favorably, Josy; but what if the girl should refuse to accompany you?"

"We can have an officer close by to apply to in case of need."

"Of course! What a woman you are for plotting!"

"Yes, Carberry, give me *carte blanche* to act for you, and I'll have her here before one o'clock. But there's a condition, Carberry."

"Name it, Josy."

"It is, that so long as your present wife lives, you shall keep strictly aloof from the maiden, not even taking the liberty of a kiss. Don't you see why? She has been religiously brought up. She is pure, with affections disengaged. Would it be for your future interests as a husband to undo all that has been done for her moral education? Surely no! You mean to make her your wife; and the wife of Carberry Ratcliff must be intemerate!"

"Right! right! A thousand times right!" exclaimed the debauchee, his pride getting the ascendency.

"For the present, then," continued the quadroon, "you, a married man, must hardly look on her. Consent to this, and I'll take the whole trouble of the affair off your hands. I'll bring the girl here, and so mould her that she will be prepared to be your lawful wife as soon as decency may permit."

Ratcliff rose from the table, and paced the floor. Under Josephine's way of presenting the subject, what had seemed rather an embarrassing job began to assume a new and attractive aspect. How well-judged the whole arrangement! The idea of elevating Clara to the exalted position of successor to the present Mrs. Ratcliff was fast becoming more and more inviting to his contemplation. Wealth in a wife would be of no account. He would have enough of his own. Family rank was desirable; but did not the girl give every sign of high blood? It would not be surprising if, in fact, she were of a stock almost equal to his own in gentility. Besides, would not he, a Ratcliff, carry, lodged in his own person, sufficient dignity of pedigree to cover the genealogical shortcomings of a wife?

The fact that Onslow and Kenrick admired her did much to enhance the girl's value in his eyes; and he could readily see how it would be for Madame Volney's interests, since she knew he meant to marry again, to have the training, to a certain extent, of his future wife, and put her under a seeming obligation. And so the quadroon's protestations that she had conquered all jealousy on the subject seemed to him the most natural thing in the world.

"Well, Josy," said he, after a silence of some minutes, "I accept your condition; I give the promise you demand."

"Honor bright?"

"Yes; you 'll have me close under your eyes. I commit the girl entirely to your keeping. I will myself go at once and see Esha, and send her to you here. I 'll also see Tremaine, and shut up his mouth with a plug that will be effectual. The fellow owes me money. Then you can take Esha in the carriage, and go and put your plan in execution."

"Good! You 've decided wisely, Carberry. Shall I order the carriage for you?"

"Yes. I 'll send it back to you with Esha, and then myself go on foot to the St. Charles to see Tremaine."

Ratcliff passed out of the breakfast-room, and the quadroon went to the hat-closet in the hall, and removed the straw hat with a *black* ribbon on it, leaving the one distinguished by a *green* band. She then rang and ordered the carriage.

CHAPTER XXXI.

ONE OF THE INSTITUTIONS.

"Small service is true service while it lasts;
Of friends, however humble, scorn not one." — *Wordsworth.*

ON being bought at the auction-block by Ratcliff, and introduced into his household, Josephine Volney, the quadroon, had devoted herself to the health of his wife from purely selfish motives. But in natures not radically perverse, beneficence cannot long be divorced from benevolence. Josephine believed her interests lay in preventing as long as possible a second marriage: hence, at first, her sedulous care of the invalid wife.

Those who know anything of society in the Slave States are well aware that concubinage (one of the institutions of *the* institution) is there, in many conspicuous instances, as patiently acquiesced in by wives as polygamy is in Utah. Mrs. Ratcliff had, at first, almost adored her husband. Very unattractive, personally, she had yet an affectionate nature, and one of her most marked traits was gratitude for kindness. Soon Ratcliff dropped the mask by which he had won her; and she, instead of lamenting over her mistake, accepted as a necessary evil the fact of his relations to the handsome slave. The latter attempted no deception, but conducted herself as discreetly as any woman, so educated, could have done, under such compulsory circumstances.

Mrs. Ratcliff was soon touched by Josephine's obvious solicitude to minister to her happiness and health. The slave-girl's childlike frankness begot frankness on the part of the wife. Seeing that their interests were identical, each was gradually drawn to the other, till a sincere and tender attachment was the result. The wife was made aware of her husband's calculations in regard to a second marriage; and Josephine found in that wife a faithful and crafty ally, too deep, with all her shallowness, to be fathomed by the husband.

No sooner had Ratcliff quitted the house, on the morning of the breakfast described, than Josephine hurried to the invalid's room. A poor diminutive Creole lady, with wrinkled skin, darker even than the quadroon's, and with one shoulder higher than the other, she sat, with a white crape-shawl wrapped round her, in a large arm-chair. Her face, as Josephine entered, lighted up with a smile of welcome that for a moment seemed to transfigure even those withered and pain-stricken features. In half an hour Josephine had put her in possession of all the developments of the last two days, and of her own plans for controlling the movements of Ratcliff in regard to the young white woman supposed to be his slave.

With absorbed interest the invalid listened to the details, and approved warmly of what Josephine had planned. Her feminine curiosity was pleased with the idea of having, in her own house and under her own eye, this young person whom Ratcliff had presumed to think of as a second wife; while the thought of baffling him in his selfish schemes sent a shock of pleasure to her heart. Furthermore, the excitement seemed to brace up her frame anew, and to ruffle into breezy action the torpid tide of her monotonous existence.

Esha was announced and introduced. A new and refreshing incident for the invalid! And now, if Esha had needed any further confirmation of the quadroon's story, it was amply afforded. Josephine's project for the present security of Ratcliff's white slave was discussed and approved.

The carriage was waiting at the door. "Go now," said Mrs. Ratcliff, "and be sure you bring the girl right up to see me."

In less than twenty minutes afterwards, as Clara, lonely and anxious, sat in Tremaine's drawing-room, a servant entered and told her that a colored woman was in Number 13, waiting to see her. Supposing it could be no other than Esha, she followed the servant to the room, and, on entering, recoiled at sight of a stranger. For a moment the quadroon was so absorbed in scanning the girl's whole personal outline, that there was silence on both sides.

"What 's wanting?" asked Clara, half dreading some trick.

"Please close the door, and I 'll tell you," was the reply. Clara did as she was requested. "Have you any objections to locking the door?" continued the quadroon.

"None whatever," replied Clara, and she locked it.

"You fear I may be here as an agent of Mr. Ratcliff," said Josephine.

"Ah! am I betrayed?" cried Clara, instinctively carrying her hand to her bosom, where lay the weapon she had bought. The quadroon noticed the gesture, and smiled. "Sit down," she said, "and do not consider me an enemy until I have proved myself such. Listen to what I have to propose." Clara took a seat where she could be within reach of the door, and then pointed to the sofa.

"Yes, I will sit here," said the quadroon, complying with the tacit invitation. "Now, listen, dear young lady, to a proposition I am authorized to make. Mr. Ratcliff will very soon be a widower. His wife cannot survive three months. He has seen you, and likes you. He is willing to lift you from slavery to freedom, — from poverty to wealth, — from obscurity to grandeur, — on one very easy condition; this, namely: that, as soon after his wife's death as propriety will allow, you will yourself become Mrs. Ratcliff."

"Never!" exclaimed Clara, the blood flaming up like red auroras over neck, face, and brow.

"But consider, my dear. You will, in the first place, be forthwith treated with all the respect and consideration due to Mr. Ratcliff's future bride. As soon as he has you secure as his wife, he will emancipate you, — make you a free woman. Think of that! Mr. Ratcliff is supposed to be worth at least five millions. You will at once have such a purse as no other young woman in the city can boast. Now why not be reasonable? Why not say *yes* to the proposition?"

"Never! never!" cried Clara, carrying her hand again to her breast with a gesture she thought significant only to herself.

Josephine rose and felt of the bosom of Clara's dress till she distinguished the weapon of which Esha had spoken. Then a smile, so sincere as to forbid suspicion, broke over the quadroon's face, and she exclaimed: "Let me kiss you! Let me hug you!" And having given vent to her satisfaction in an embrace, she unlocked the door, and there stood Esha.

"What does it all mean, Esha?" asked Clara, bewildered.

"It mean, darlin', dat Massa Ratcliff hab tracked you to dis yere place, an' we two women mean to pull de wool ober his eyes, so he can't do yer no harm no how. You jes do what we want yer to, and we 'll bodder him so he sha'n't know his head 's his own."

Josephine then communicated all the facts that had come to her knowledge in regard to Ratcliff's pursuit of Clara, together with her own conversation with him that morning, and the plan she had contrived for his discomfiture. "As soon," she said, "as such an opportunity offers that I can be sure you can be put beyond his reach, I will supply you with money, and help you to escape."

Truth beamed from her looks, and made itself musical in her tones, and Clara gratefully pressed her hand.

"And shall I have Esha with me?" she asked.

"Yes; and Mrs. Ratcliff, though an invalid, will also befriend you. 'T will be strange indeed if we four women can't defeat one man."

"But I shall have all the slave-hunters in the Confederacy after me if I try to get away."

"Do not fear. We have golden keys that open many doors of escape."

Clara did not hesitate. She had faith in Esha's quickness, as well as in her own, to detect insincerity. And so she was persuaded that her safest present course would be to go boldly into the house of the very man she had most cause to dread!

It was agreed that the three should leave together at once. Clara went to her sleeping-room, and there, encountering the chambermaid, made her a present of two dollars, and sent her off. Laura was absent at the dressmaker's.

"I would like," said Clara, "to find out at the bar what charge has been made for my stay here, and pay it."

"Let me do it for you," suggested the quadroon.

"If you would be so kind!" replied Clara. "Here are fifteen dollars. I don't think it can come to more than that."

Without taking the money, Josephine left the room. In five minutes she returned with a receipted bill, made out against "Miss Tremaine's friend." This receipt Clara enclosed, together with a five-dollar gold-piece, in a letter to Laura, containing these words: —

"I thank you for all the hospitality I have received at your hands. Enclosed you will find my hotel bill receipted, also five dollars for the use of such dresses as I have worn. With best wishes for your mother's restoration to health and for your own welfare, I bid you good by. P. B."

The three women now passed through a side entrance to the street where the carriage was in waiting; and before half an hour had elapsed, Clara was established in the blue room of the house in Lafayette Square, — the invalid lady had seen her and approved, — and Esha, like a faithful hound, was following her steps, keeping watch, as Ratcliff had directed, though for other reasons than he had imagined.

Hardly had Clara left the hotel, before Vance called. He had come, fully resolved to wring from her, if possible, the secret of her trouble. Much to his disappointment, he learned she had gone and would not return. He called a second time, and saw Miss Tremaine. That young lady, warned and threatened by her father, now displayed such a ready and facile gift for lying, as would have highly distinguished her in diplomacy.

"Only think of it, Mr. Vance," said the intrepid Laura, "it turns out that Miss Brown has been having a love affair with one of her father's clerks, a low-born Yankee. He followed her to New Orleans, — managed to send a letter to her at Mrs. Gentry's, — Clara went forth to find him, but, failing in her search, came to claim hospitality of me. This morning her father — a very decent man he seems to be — arrived from Mobile and took her, fortunately before she had been able to meet her lover."

The story was plausible. Vance, however, looked the narrator sharply and searchingly in the face. She met his glance with an expression beaming with innocence and candor. It was irresistible. The strong man surrendered all suspicion, and gave in "beat."

CHAPTER XXXII.

A DOUBLE VICTORY.

"Whence it is manifest that the soul, speaking in a natural sense, loseth nothing by Death, but is a very considerable gainer thereby. For she does not only possess as much body as before, with as full and solid dimensions, but has that accession cast in, of having this body more invigorated with life and motion than it was formerly." — *Henry More*, A. D. 1659.

"No, sure, 't is ever youth there! Time and Death
Follow our flesh no more; and that forced opinion,
That spirits have no sexes, I believe not.
There *must* be love, — there *is* love!"
Beaumont and Fletcher.

"I SHALL be jealous of this little lady if you go on at this rate," said Madame Volney to Mrs. Ratcliff, a week after Clara had been established in the house.

"Never fear that I shall love you less, my dear Josephine," replied the invalid. Then, pointing to her heart, she added: "I 've a place here big enough for both of you. I only wish 't were in better repair."

"Have you had those sharp throbbings to-day?"

"Not badly. You warn me against excitement. I sometimes think I 'm better under it. Certainly I 've improved since Esha and Darling have been here. What should I do now without Darling to play and read to me? What a touch she has! And what a voice! And then her selection of music and of books is so good. By the way, she promised to translate a story for me from the German. I wonder if she has it finished. Go ask her."

The answer was brought by Clara herself, and Josephine left the two together. Yes, Clara had written out the story. It was called *Zu Spat*, or "Too Late," and was by an anonymous author. Clara read aloud from it. She had read about ten minutes, when the following passage occurred: —

"Selfish and superstitious, the Baroness put out of her mind the irksome thought of making her will; but now, struck speechless by disease, and paralyzed in her hands, she was impotent to communicate her wishes. Her agonized effort to say something in her last moments undoubtedly related to a will. But she died intestate, and all her large estate passed into the hands of a comparative stranger. And thus the humble friends whose kindness had saved and prolonged her life were left to struggle with the world for a meagre support. If in the new condition to which she had passed through death she could look back on her selfishness and its consequences, what poignant regrets must have been hers!"

"Read that passage again," said Mrs. Ratcliff; adding, after Clara had complied, "You need n't read any more now."

That evening the wife summoned the husband to an interview. Somewhat surprised at the unusual command, Ratcliff made his appearance and took a seat at her side. His manner was that of a man who thinks no woman can resist him, and that his transparent cajoleries are the proper pabulum for her weak intellect, — poor thing!

"Well, my peerless one, what is it?" he asked.

"I wish to talk with you, Ratcliff, about this white slave of yours. What do you think of her?"

"Think of her? Nothing! I've given no thought to the subject. I've hardly looked at her."

"Lie Number 1," thought the invalid, looking him in the face, but betraying no distrust in her expression.

The truth was, that Ratcliff, for the first time in his life, was under the power of a sentiment which, if not love, was all that there was in his nature akin to it. Even at political meetings his thoughts would stray from the public business, from the fulminations of "last-ditch" orators and curb-stone generals, and revert to that youthful and enchanting figure. True, Josephine rigidly exacted conformity to the conditions that kept him aloof from all communication with the girl. But Ratcliff, through the window-blinds, would now and then see her, in the pride of youth and beauty, walking with Esha in the garden. He would hear her songs, too. And once, — when he thought no one knew it, — though the quadroon had her eye on him, — he overheard Clara's conversation. "She has mind as well as beauty," thought he.

And that brilliant and dainty creature was *his*, — *his!* He could, if he chose, marry her to the blackest of his slaves. Of course he could! There was no indignity he could not put upon her, under the plea of upholding his rights as a master. Had he not once proved it in another case, on his own plantation? And who had ever dared raise a voice against the just assertion of his rights? Truly, any such rash malcontents, opening their lips, would have been in danger of being ducked as Abolitionists!

Patience! Yes, Josephine was right in her scheme of keeping the young girl secluded from his too fascinating society. Not a hint must the maiden have of the favor with which he regarded her, — not an intimation, until the present Mrs. Ratcliff should considerately "step out." Then — Well, what then? Why, then an end to hopes deferred and desires unfulfilled! Then an immediate private marriage, to be followed by a public one, after a decent interval.

Every secret device and cherished anticipation, meanwhile, of that imperious nature was understood and analyzed by the quadroon. She felt a vindictive satisfaction in seeing him riot in calculations which she would task her best energies to baffle. Esha's stories of his conduct to Estelle had withered the last bloom of affection which Josephine's heart had cherished towards him.

"I'm glad you're so indifferent to this white slave," said Mrs. Ratcliff to her husband.

"And why should you be glad, my pet?"

"Because, Ratcliff, I want you to give her to me."

Staggered by the suddenness of the request, and puzzled for an answer, he replied: "But she may prove a very valuable piece of property. There's many a man who would pay ten thousand dollars for her, two or three years hence."

"Well, if you don't want to *give* her, then *sell* her to me. I'll pay you twenty thousand dollars for her."

"You shall have her for nothing, my dear," said Ratcliff, after reflecting that the slave would still be virtually his, inasmuch as no conveyance of her could be made by his wife without his consent.

Detecting the trap, the wife at once replied: "Thank you, dear husband. This generosity is so like you! Can she be freed?"

"No. There are recent State laws against emancipation. It was found there were too many weak-minded persons, who, in their last moments, beginning to have scruples about slave-holding, would think to purchase heaven by emancipating their slaves. The example was bad, and productive of discontent among those left in bondage."

"Well, then, Ratcliff, there 's one little form you must consent to. The title-deed must be vested in Mr. Winslow."

Ratcliff started as if recoiling from a pitfall. The remark brought home to his mind the disagreeable consideration that there was nearly half a million of dollars which ought to come to his wife, but which was absolutely in the keeping and under the control of Simon Winslow. It happened in this wise: The father of Mrs. Ratcliff, old Kittler, not having that entire faith in his son-in-law which so distinguished a member of the chivalry as the South Carolinian ought to have commanded, gave into the hands of Winslow a large sum of money, relying solely upon his honor to use it *in loco parentis* for the benefit of the lady. But there were no legal restrictions imposed upon Simon as to the disposition of the property, and if he had chosen to give or throw it away, or keep it himself, he might have done it with impunity.

Winslow acted much as he would have done if Mrs. Ratcliff had been his own daughter. He invested the money solely for her ultimate benefit and disposal, seeing that her husband already had millions which she had brought him. Ratcliff, however, regarded as virtually his the money in Winslow's hands, and had several angry discussions with him on the subject. But Simon was impracticable. The only concession he would make was to say, that, in the event of Mrs. Ratcliff's death, he should respect any *requests* she might have made. There had consequently been an informal will, if *will* it could be called, made by her a year before, in Ratcliff's favor.

Wanting money now to carry out his speculations in slaves, Ratcliff had again applied to Winslow for this half a million, — had tried wheedlings and threats, both in vain. He had even threatened to denounce Simon before the Committee of Safety, — to denounce him as a "damned Yankee and Abolitionist." To which Simon had replied by taking a pinch of snuff.

Simon, though born somewhere in the vicinity of Plymouth Rock, was one of the oldest residents of New Orleans. He had helped General Jackson beat off Packenham. He had stood by him in his rough handling of the *habeas corpus* act. Simon had been a slaveholder, though rather as an experiment than for profit; for, finding that the State Legislature were going to pass a law against emancipation, he took time by the forelock, and not only made all his slaves free, but placed them where they could earn their living.

The invalid wife's proposal to vest the title to the white slave in Winslow caused in Ratcliff a visible embarrassment.

"You know, my dear," he replied, "I would do anything for your gratification; but there are particular reasons why —"

"Why what, husband?"

"Give me a few days to think the matter over. We 'll talk of it when I have n't so much on my mind. Meanwhile I 'll tell you what I *will* consent to: Josephine shall be yours to do with just as you please."

"Come, that 's something," said the wife. "What I ask, then, is, that you convey Josephine to Mr. Winslow to hold in trust for me. Will you do this the first thing in the morning?"

"I certainly will," replied Ratcliff, flattering himself that his ready compliance with one of his wife's morbid whims would more than content her for his evasion of the other.

"Well, then, good night," said she, pointing to the door.

She submitted, with a slight shudder, imperceptible to Ratcliff, to be kissed by him, and he went down-stairs. Josephine issued from behind a screen whither the wife had beckoned her to go on his first coming in. If there had been any remnant of affection for him in the quadroon's heart, she was well cured of it by what she had heard.

The invalid called for writing materials, and penned a note. "Take this, Josephine," she said, "early to-morrow to Mr. Winslow. In it I simply tell him of Ratcliff's proposition in regard to yourself, and ask him, the moment that affair is attended to, to come and see me."

The clock was striking twelve the next day when Mr. Winslow came, and Josephine ushered him into the invalid's presence.

"You may leave us alone for a while, Josephine," she said.

As soon as the quadroon had gone out and shut the door, the invalid motioned to Winslow to draw near. He was upwards of seventy, tall and erect, with venerable gray locks, and an expression of face at once brisk and gentle, benevolent and keen.

"What 's the state of the property you still hold for me, Mr. Winslow?"

"It is half invested in real estate in Northern cities, and half in special deposits of gold in Northern banks."

"Indeed! Then you must have sent it North long before these troubles began."

"Yes, more than four years ago, — soon after the Nashville Convention."

"What 's the amount in your hands?"

"Half a million; probably it will be seven hundred thousand, if gold should rise, as I think it will."

"And how much, Mr. Winslow, of the property my father left me has gone to Mr. Ratcliff?"

"More than three millions."

"Very well. I wish to revoke all previous requests I may have made as to the disposition of the property in your hands. Now take your pen and write as I shall dictate."

"Let me first explain, Mrs. Ratcliff, that any conveyance of personalty you might make would be null without your husband's consent. But in this case forms are of no account, and even witnesses are unnecessary. Everything is left to my individual honor and discretion."

"I 'm aware of that, Mr. Winslow. It is not so much a will as a series of requests I 've to make."

"I see you understand it, madam. The memoranda you give me I will embody in the form of a will of my own. Proceed!"

"Put down," said the invalid, "a hundred thousand for the Orphan Asylum."

"Excellent; but as the Secessionists are using that sacred fund for war purposes, I shall take the liberty of withholding the bequest for the present. Go on."

"A hundred thousand to the Lying-in Hospital."

"Nothing could be more proper. Proceed."

"A hundred thousand to the fund for the Sisters of Charity."

"Ah! those dear sisters! Bless you for remembering them, madam."

"A hundred thousand to be distributed in sums of five thousand severally to the persons whose names I have here written down."

She handed him a sheet of paper containing the names, and he transcribed them carefully.

"And now," resumed the invalid, "the remainder of the fund in your possession I wish paid over, when you can safely do it, one half to the slave Josephine, the other half to the white slave, Ellen Murray, of whom Josephine will tell you, and whom you must rescue from slavery. Both must be free before the money can be of any service to them."

"Of course. Their owner could at once appropriate any sum you might leave to them, even though it were a million of dollars."

"You have now heard all I have to say, Mr. Winslow."

"Then, madam, you will please write under these memoranda with your own hand something to this effect, and sign your name, with date, place, et cetera: '*This I declare to be my own spontaneous, unbiassed request to Mr. Winslow, to dispose of the property in his possession, in the manner hereinabove stated.*' The autograph will have no legal force, but it may serve to satisfy your husband."

The lady wrote, and handed back the paper.

"Good!" said Winslow. "Before taking another meal, I will draw up and sign a will by which your requests can be made effectual."

"Your hand, Mr. Winslow! My father trusted you as he did no other man, and I thank you for your loyalty to what you knew to be his wishes."

"The task he put upon me has been a very simple one, madam. Good by. We shall soon meet again, I hope."

"Yes. I shall be quite well of my heart-complaint *then*. Good by."

Hardly had Winslow left the house than Ratcliff drove up and entered. He was in a jubilant mood. News had just been received of the Confederate victory at Bull Run. He knocked at his wife's door. "Come in!" He entered. Josephine and Clara were present, trying to soothe the invalid. One was bathing her forehead with *eau de Cologne;* the other was kneeling, and rubbing her feet. She had been telling them what she had done. She had kissed first one and then the other, lavishing on them profuse tokens of affection. Her eyes gleamed with an unnatural brightness, and her cheeks were flushed with the glow of a great excitement.

As Ratcliff came in she rose, and, standing between Josephine and Clara, put an arm round the shoulder of each, and looked her husband steadily in the face. Her expression was that of one who cannot find words adequate to the utterance of some absorbing emotion. The look was compounded at once of defiance and of pity. Her lips moved, but no articulation followed. Then suddenly, with a gasped "Ah!" she convulsively bowed her body like a tree smitten by the tornado. The pain, if sharp, was but for a moment.

The motion was her last. She sank into the faithful arms that encircled her. The one attenuated chord that bound her to the mortal life had been snapped.

Ratcliff started forward, and satisfied himself that his wife was really dead. Then he looked up at Clara.

She caught the expression of his countenance, and instinctively comprehended it, even as the little bird understands the hawk, or the lamb the wolf. Josephine saw it too. What a triumph now to think that she was no longer *his* slave!

But Clara, — what of *her?* Mrs. Ratcliff's sudden death seemed to shatter the last barrier between her and danger.

Ratcliff did not affect to conceal his satisfaction. Here was a double victory! The Federals and his wife both disposed of in one day! Youth and beauty within his grasp! Truly, fortune seemed to be heaping her good things upon him. That half a million too, in Winslow's hands, would come very opportunely; for slaves could be bought cheap, dog-cheap, now that croakers were predicting ruin to the institution.

"Josephine," said he, "I must go at once to see Winslow, the late" — how readily he seized on that word! — "the late Mrs. Ratcliff's man of business. I may not be home to dinner.

You 'd better not take out the carriage. The horses would be frightened; for the streets are all in commotion with salvos for our great victory. Good by till I return."

Once more he turned on Clara that look from which she had twice before shrunk dismayed and exasperated.

After he had gone, "Help me to escape at once!" she exclaimed.

"No," replied Josephine. "This is our safest place for the present. The avenues of escape from the city are all closed; and we should find it difficult to go where we would not be tracked. The danger is not immediate. Do not look so wild, Darling. I swear to you that I will protect you to the last. Whither thou goest I will go, and where thou lodgest I will lodge."

CHAPTER XXXIII.

SATAN AMUSES HIMSELF.

"We can die;
And, dying nobly, though we leave behind us
These clods of flesh, that are too massy burdens,
Our living souls fly crowned with living conquests."
Beaumont and Fletcher.

VANCE sat in his room at the St. Charles. He seemed plunged in meditation. His fingers were playing with a little gold cross he wore round his neck; a trinket made very precious by the dying kiss and pious faith of Estelle. It recalled to him daily those memorable moments of their last earthly parting. And she now seemed so near to him, so truly alive to him, in all his perplexities, that he would hardly have been surprised to see her suddenly standing in immortal youth by his side. How could he, while thus possessed with her enchanting image, evoke from his heart any warmer sentiment than that of friendship for any other woman?

He thought of the so-called Perdita. He feared he would have to leave the city without getting any further light than Miss Tremaine had vouchsafed on the mystery that surrounded that interesting young person. One thing, on reconsideration, puzzled him and excited his distrust in Laura's story. Perdita had pretended that the name Brown was improvised for the occasion, — assumed while she was conversing with him. Could she have been deceiving?

There were still other reflections that brought anxiety. He had not yet heard from Peek. Could that faithful friend have failed in all his inquiries for Hyde?

The immediate matter for consideration, however, was the danger that began to darken over Vance's own path. It had been ascertained by leading Secessionists, interested in providing for the financial wants of the Rebellion, that Vance had drawn more than a hundred thousand dollars of special deposits of gold from the banks since the fall of Sumter. The question was now put to him by the usurpers, What had been done with that money? He was summoned to appear before the authorities with an explanation. A committee would be in session that very evening to hear his statement.

There was still another subject to awaken his concern. Kenrick had been called on to set at rest certain unfavorable reports, by appearing before that same committee, and accepting a captaincy in the confederate army. Onslow was to be presented with a colonel's commission.

Vance had made preparations for the escape of Kenrick and himself. A little steam-tug called the Artful Dodger, carrying the Confederate flag, lay in the river. Everybody supposed she was a sort of spy on United States cruisers. For two days she had lain there with steam all up, ready to start at a moment's warning. Her crew appeared to be all ashore, except the captain, mate, engineer, cook, and two stewards. The last three were black men. The other three, if they were not Yankees, had caught some peculiarities of pronunciation which the schoolmaster is vainly striving to extirpate at the North. These men said *beeyownd* for *bound*, and *neeyow* for *now*.

While Vance was meditating on his arrangements, a card was brought to him. It bore the name "Simon Winslow."

"Show him in," said Vance to the servant.

As Simon entered, Vance recognized him as the individual who had aided him the day of the rescue of Quattles from the mob.

"There 's a sort of freemasonry, Mr. Vance." said Winslow, "that assures me I may trust you. Your sympathies, sir, are with the Union."

Wary and suspicious, Vance bowed, but made no reply.

"Do not doubt me," continued Winslow. "True, I 've been a slaveholder. But 't is now several years since I owned a slave. Mr. Vance, I want your counsel, and, it may be, your aid. Still distrustful? How shall I satisfy you that I 'm not a traitor knave?"

"Enough, Mr. Winslow! I 'll trust your threescore years and your loyal face. Tell me what I can do for you. Be seated."

They sat down, and the old man resumed: "I have lived in this city more than forty years, Mr. Vance, but for some time I've foreseen that there would be little hope for a man of Northern birth unless he would consent to howl with the pack for secession and a slave confederacy. Now I'm too old to tune my bark to any such note. The consequence is, I am a marked man, liable at any moment to be seized and imprisoned. My property here is nearly all in real estate; so if that is confiscated, as it will be, I've no fear but Uncle Sam will soon come to give it back to me. The rest of my assets it will be hard for the keenest-scented inquisitor to find. To-day, by the death of Mrs. Ratcliff—"

"Of what Mrs. Ratcliff?" inquired Vance.

"Mrs. Carberry Ratcliff. By her death I become the legally irresponsible, and therefore all the more *morally* the responsible, manager of an estate of more than half a million, of which a considerable portion is to be used by me for the benefit of two women at present slaves."

"But her husband will never consent to it!" interposed Vance.

"Fortunately," replied Winslow, "all the property was some time since sent North and converted into gold. Well: I've just come from an interview with Ratcliff himself. He came to tell me of his wife's death. He brought with him a *quasi* will, signed a year ago, in which his wife requests me to hand over to him such property as I may consider at her disposal. He called on me to demand that I should forthwith surrender my trust; said he was in immediate need of three hundred thousand dollars. He did not dream of a rebuff. He was in high spirits. The news from Bull Run had greatly elated him. His wife's death he plainly regarded as a happy relief. Conceive of his wrath, when, in the midst of his lofty hopes and haughty demands, I handed him a copy of the memoranda, noted down by me this very day, in which Mrs. Ratcliff makes a very different disposition of the property."

"I know something of the man's temper," said Vance.

"He laughed a scornful laugh," resumed Winslow, "and, shaking his forefinger at me, said: 'You shall swing for this, you damned old Yankee! Your trusteeship is n't worth a straw. I'll have you compelled to disgorge, this very hour.' But when I told him that the whole half-million, left in my hands by his wife's father, was safely deposited in gold in a Northern city, the man actually grew livid with rage. He drew his Derringer on me, and would probably have shot me but for the sober second thought that told him he could make more out of me living than dead. In a frenzy he left my office. This was about half an hour ago. After reflection on our interview I concluded it would be prudent in me to escape from the city if possible, and I have come to ask if you can aid me in doing it."

"Nothing could be more opportune," replied Vance, "than your coming. I have laid all my plans to leave in a small steamer this very night. A young friend goes with me. You shall accompany us. Have you any preparations to make?"

"None, except to find some trustworthy person with whom I can leave an amount of money for the two slave-women of whom I spoke. For it would be dangerous, if not impracticable, to attempt to take them with us."

"Yes, use your golden keys to unlock their chains in this case," said Vance. "Do not show yourself again on the street. Ratcliff will at once have detectives at your heels. Hark! There's a knock at the door. Pass into my chamber, and lock yourself in, and open only to my rapping, thus, — one, two — one, two — one."

Winslow obeyed, and Vance, opening his parlor door, met Kenrick.

"Well, cousin," asked Vance, "are you all ready? You look pale, man! What's the matter?"

"Nothing," replied Kenrick; "that is, everything. I wish I'd never seen that Perdita Brown! Look here! They've got her photograph in the print-shops. Beautiful, is it not?"

"Yes; it almost does her justice. Could you draw out from the Tremaines no remark which would afford a further clew?"

"After you had failed, what could I hope to do? But I'll tell you what I ventured upon. All stratagems in love and war are venial, I suppose. Seeing that Miss Tremaine was deeply interested in your conquering self, I tried to pique her by making her think you were secretly enamored of Miss

Brown. She denied it warmly. I then said: 'Reflect! Has n't he been very inquisitive in trying to find out all he could about her?' She was obliged to confess that you had; and at last, after considerable skirmishing between us, she dropped this remark: 'Those who would fall in love with her had better first find out whether she 's a lady.' 'She certainly appears one,' I replied. 'Yes,' said Miss Tremaine, 'and so does many a Creole who has African blood in her veins.'"

"Ah! what could that mean?" exclaimed Vance, thoughtfully. "Can that story of a paternal Brown be all a lie?"

Here there was a low knock at the door. Vance opened it, and there stood Peek.

"Come in!" said Vance, grasping him by the hand, drawing him in, and closing the door. "What news?"

And then, seeing the negro's hesitation, Vance turned to Kenrick, and said: "Cousin, this is the man to whom you need no introduction. He was christened Peculiar Institution; but, for brevity, we call him Peek."

Kenrick put out his hand with a face so glowing with a cordial respect that Peek could not resist the proffer.

"Now, Peek," said Vance, "pull off that hot wig and those green spectacles, and, unless you would keep us standing, sit down and be at ease. There! That 's right. Now, first of all, did you hit upon any trace of your wife and boy?"

"None, Mr. Vance. I think they cannot be in Texas."

"Then what of Colonel Delancy Hyde?"

"The Colonel was said to have attached himself to the fortunes of General Van Dorn. That 's all I could find out about Hyde."

"Pity! I must unearth the fellow somehow. The fate of that poor little girl of the Pontiac haunts me night and day. My suspicions of foul play have been fully confirmed. When you have time, read this letter which I had written to send you. It will tell you of all I learnt from Quattles and Amos Slink. But you have something to ask. What is it?"

"Where shall I find Captain Onslow of the Confederate army?"

Vance pointed to Kenrick, who replied: "I know him well. He is probably now in this house. 'T is his usual time for dressing for dinner."

"I've terrible news for him," said Peek.

"What has happened?"

"On my way from Austin to Fort Duncan on the Rio Grande I passed through San Antonio. You have heard something of the persecutions of Union men in Western Texas?"

"Yes. Good Heavens! Is old Onslow among the victims?"

"He and his whole family — wife, son, and daughter — have been slain by the Confederate agents."

The cousins looked at each other, and each grew paler as he read the other's thought. Vance spoke first. "Go on, Peek," he said. "Tell us what you know."

"The old man, you see," said Peek, "has been trying for some time to do without slave labor. He has employed a good many Germans on his lands. The slaveholders have n't liked this. At the beginning of the Rebellion he went with old Houston and others against secession; but when Houston caved in, Onslow remained firm and plucky. He kept quiet, however, and did nothing that the Secesh authorities could find fault with. But what they wanted was an excuse for murdering him and seizing his lands. They employed three scoundrels, a broken-down lawyer, a planter, and a horse-jockey, to visit him under the pretence that they were good Union and antislavery men, trying to escape the conscription. The old man fell into the trap. Thinking he was among friends, he freely declared, that 'he meant to keep true to the old flag; that only one of his family had turned traitor; the rest (thank God!) including the women, were thoroughly loyal; that secession would prove a failure, and end (thank God always!) in the breaking up of slavery.' At the same time he told them he should make no resistance, either open or clandestine, to the laws of the State. The scoundrels tried to implicate him in some secret plot, but failed. They had drawn out of him enough, however, for their purposes. They left him, and straightway denounced him as an Abolitionist. A gang of cutthroats, set on by the Rebel leaders, came to hang him. Well knowing he could expect no mercy, the old man barricaded his doors, armed his household, and prepared to resist. The women loaded the guns while the men fired. Several of the assailants were wounded. The rest grew furious, and at last made an entrance by a back door, rushed in, and overpowered William Onslow, the son, who had received a ball in his neck. They dragged him out and hung him to a tree. The daughter they tried to pinion and lash to the floor, but she fought so desperately that a ruffian, whose hair she had torn out by the roots, shot her dead. The mother, in a frantic attempt to save the daughter, received a blow on the head from which she died. The old man, exhausted and fatally wounded, was disarmed, and placed under guard in the room from which he had been firing. It was not till the women and the son were dead that I arrived on the spot. I claimed to be a Secesh nigger, and the passes Mr. Vance had given me confirmed my story. The Rebels regarded me as a friend and helper. I lurked round the room where the old man was confined, and at last, through whiskey, I persuaded his guard to lie down and go to sleep. I then made myself known to the sufferer. I helped him write a letter to his surviving son. Here it is, stained as you see by the writer's blood. You can read it, Mr. Vance. It contains no secrets. Hardly had I concealed it in my pocket, when some of the Rebels came in, seized the old man, helpless and dying as he was, and, dragging him out, hung him on a tree by the side of his son."

Peek ended his narrative, and Vance, taking the proffered letter, slowly drew it from the envelope and unfolded it. There dropped out four strands of hair: one white, one iron-gray, one a fine and thick flaxen, and one a rich brown-black.

"I cut off those strands of hair, thinking that Captain Onslow might prize them," said Peek.

"You did well," remarked Vance. "And since you have authority to permit it, I will read this letter."

He then read aloud as follows: —

"Stricken down by a death-wound, I write this. When it reaches you, my son, you will be the last survivor of your family. The faithful negro who bears this letter will tell you all. You may rely on what he says. This crafty, this Satanic Slave Power has — I can use the pen no longer. But I can dictate. The negro must be my amanuensis."

And then, in a different handwriting, the letter proceeded: —

"This Slave Power, which, for many weeks past, has been hunting down and hanging Union men, has at last laid its bloody hand on our innocent household. Should you meet Colonel A. J. Hamilton,* he will tell you something of what the pro-slavery butchers have been doing.

"Yesterday three men called on me. They brought forged letters from one I knew to be my friend. The trick succeeded. I admitted them to my confidence. They left and denounced me to the Confederate leaders. My only crime was a secret sympathy with the Union cause. Not a finger had I lifted or threatened to lift against the ruling powers of the State. But I did not love slavery, — that was the crime of crimes in the eyes of Jeff Davis's immediate partisans and friends.

"To-day they came with ropes to hang us, — to hang us, remember, not for resistance to authority, however usurped, not for one imprudent act or threat against slavery, but simply because we were known at heart to disapprove of slavery, and consequently to love the old flag. And many hundreds have been hung here for no other offence. We knew we could expect no better fate than our neighbors had bravely encountered; and we resolved, men and women, to sell our lives dearly. Your brother fell wounded, and was hung; then your sister, resisting outrage, was slain; then your mother, striving to protect Emily, received a mortal blow. And I am lying here wounded, soon to be dragged forth and hung — for what? — for unbelief, not in a God, but in the Southern Confederacy and its corner-stone!

"And this is slavery! All these brutalities and wrongs spring from slavery as naturally as the fruit from the blossom. That which is inherently wrong must, by eternal laws, still produce and reproduce wrong. The right to hold one innocent

* Late member of Congress from Texas. In his speech in New York (1862) he said: "I know that the loyalists of Texas have died deaths not heard of since the dark ages until now; not only hunted and shot, murdered upon their own thresholds, but tied up and scalded to death with boiling water; torn asunder by wild horses fastened to their feet; whole neighborhoods of men exterminated, and their wives and children driven away."

It is estimated by a writer in the New Orleans Crescent (June, 1863), that at least *twenty-five hundred* persons had been hung in Texas during the preceding two years *for fidelity to the Union.*

The San Antonio (Texas) Herald, a Rebel sheet of November 13th, 1862, taunted the Unionists with the havoc that had been made among them! It says: "They (Union men) are known and will be remembered. Their numbers were small at first, and they are becoming every day less. In the mountains near Fort Clark and along the Rio Grande *their bones are bleaching in the sun,* and in the counties of Wire and Denton *their bodies are suspended by scores* from black-jacks."

Such are the shameless butchers and hangmen that Slavery spawns!

man a slave, implies the right to enslave or murder any other man! There is no such right. It is a lie born in the inmost brain of hell. No laws can make it a right. No clamor of majorities can give it a sanction. In slavery, Satan once more scales the heavenly heights.

"Jeff Davis, I hear, has just joined the church. Would he be pardoned, and *retain* the offence? If so, not prayers nor sacraments can save his trembling and perjured soul from the guilt of such wrongs as I and mine, and hundreds of other true men and women, here in Texas have fallen under because of slavery. God is not to be cheated by any such flattering unction as Davis is laying to his heart. The more he seeks to cover profane with holy things, the deeper will be his damnation in that world where all shams and self-delusions are dissolved, and the true man stands revealed, to be judged by his fidelity to Christ's golden rule, — to the cause of justice and humanity on earth.

"Our national agony is the old conflict of the Divine with the Satanic principle. Believe in God, my son, and you cannot doubt the result. Do you suppose Eternal Justice will be patient much longer? Think of the atrocities to which this American slave system has reconciled us! A free white man can, in any of the Slave States, go into a negro's house and beat or kill any of the inmates, and not be prosecuted by law, except a free white man sees him do it; because *a negro's testimony is not taken against a white man.* As for the *marriage* of slaves, you well know what a mere farce — what a subject for ribaldry and laughter — it is among the masters. No tie, whether of affection, of blood, or of form, is respected.*

"The originators of this rebellion saw that *by inevitable laws of population* slavery must go down under a republican form of government. Their fears and their jealousies of freedom grew intolerable. The very word *free* became hateful. They saw that their property in slaves depended for its duration on the action of political forces slumbering in the mass of their white population, which population, though now densely ignorant, would gradually learn that slavery is adverse to the interests of nine tenths of the whites. And so this war was originated *even less to separate from the North than to crush into hopeless subjection, through that separation, the white masses at*

* "Marriage," says a Catholic Bishop of a Southern State, quoted in the Cincinnati Catholic Telegraph, "is scarcely known amongst them (the slaves); the masters *attach no importance to it.* In some States those who teach them (the slaves) to read *are punished with death.*"

the South. The slave barons dreaded lest this drugged and stupefied giant should rouse from his ignoble slumber, and, learning his strength, and opening his eyes to the truth, should, Samson-like, seize the pillars of their system. To prevent this, a grand oligarchy of slaveholders must be created, and the liberties of the whites destroyed!

"You will see all this now, my son. Yes, I have this comfort in my extremity: my son will be converted from wrong; the stubborn head will be reached through the stricken heart; we shall not have died in vain. And his conversion will be instantaneous. But be prudent, my son. Let not passion betray you. These Rebel leaders are as remorseless as they are crafty. All the bad energies of the very prince of devils are ranged on their side, and will help them to temporary success.

"Let them see that higher and more persistent energies can spring from the right. What I most fear for the North is the paralyzing effect of its prosperity. It will go on thriving on the war, while the South is learning the wholesome training of adversity. Young men at the North will be tempted by money-making to stay at home. The voice of Mammon will be louder than the voice of God in their hearts. This will be their tremendous peril. But God will not be thwarted. If prosperity will not make the North do God's work, then adversity must be called in.

"Set your heart on no private vengeance, my son. Take this as my dying entreaty. Let your revenge be the restoration of the old flag. All the rest must follow as the night the day. . . . . And now, farewell! May God bless and guide you. I go to join your mother, brother, and sister. Their spirits are round me while I speak. Their love goes forth to you with mine, and my prayer for you is their prayer also. Adieu!"

There was silence for a full minute after the reading.

"I'll wait," said Kenrick, "till he gets through dinner before I tell him the news. He'll need all his strength, poor fellow!"

"I foresee," said Vance, "that Onslow will be of our party of escape this night." And then, turning to Peek, he remarked: "Your coming, Peculiar, is timely. I want the help of a trustworthy driver. You are the man for us. Can you, without exciting suspicion, get the control of a carriage and two fast, fresh horses?"

Peek reflected a moment, and then said: "Yes; I know a

colored man, Antoine Lafour, who has the care of two of the best horses in the city. His master really thinks Antoine would fight any Abolitionist who might come to free him; but Antoine and I laugh at the old man's credulity."

"There 's yet another service you can render," said Vance; and he gave five raps on the door of his chamber.

The lock was turned from the inside, and Winslow appeared.

"You 're among friends," said Vance. "This is my cousin, Mr. Kenrick; and this is Peculiar Institution, otherwise called Peek. Notwithstanding his inauspicious name, you may trust him as you would your own right hand."

"But I want an agent who can write and keep accounts."

"Then Peek is just the man for you. Of his ability you can satisfy yourself in five minutes. For his *honesty* I will vouch."

"But will he remain in New Orleans the next six months?"

"I hope so," replied Vance. "This is my plan for you, Peek: that you should still occupy that little house of mine with the Bernards. I 've spoken to them about it; and they will treat you well for my sake. I want some one here with whom I may freely communicate; and more, I want you to pursue your search for Colonel Delancy Hyde, and to secure him when found, which you can easily do with money. Will you remain?"

"You know how it is with me, Mr. Vance," said Peek. "I have two objects in life: One is to find my wife and child; the other is to help on the great cause. For both these objects I can have no better head-quarters than New Orleans."

"Good! He will remain, Mr. Winslow. Go now both of you into the next room. You 'll find writing materials on the table."

The old man and the negro withdrew. Kenrick paced the floor, thinking one moment of Clara, and the next of the dreadful communication he must make to Onslow. Vance sat down and leaned his head on his hands to consider if there was anything he had left undone.

"I hear some one knocking at the door of my room," said Kenrick. He went into the corridor, and a servant handed him a card. It was from Onslow, and pencilled on it was the following: —

"Come to the dinner-table, Kenrick. Where are you? Dreaming of Perdita? Or planning impracticable victories for your Yankee friends? Come and join me in a bottle of claret. It may be our last together. Only think of it, my dear fellow, I am to be made a Colonel! But that will not please you. Sink politics! We will ignore all that is disagreeable. There shall be no slavery, — no Rebeldom, — no Yankeedom. All shall be Arcadian. We will talk over old times, and compare notes in regard to Perdita. I don't believe you are a tenth part as much in love as I am. Where has the enchantress gone? 'O matchless sweetness! whither art thou vanished? O thou fair soul of all thy sex! what paradise hast thou enriched and blessed?' Come, Kenrick, come; if only for auld lang syne, come and chat with me; for the day of action draws near, when there shall be no more chatting!"

Sick at heart, Kenrick handed the card to Vance, who read it, and said: "The sooner a disagreeable duty is discharged, the better. Go, cousin, and let him know the character of that fell Power which he would serve. Let him know what reason he, of all men, has to love it!"

"I 'd rather face a battery than do it; but it must be done."

At the same moment Winslow and the negro entered.

"I 've arranged everything with Peek," said the old man. "I 've placed in his hands funds which I think will be sufficient."

"That reminds me that I must do the same," said Vance; and, taking a large sum in bank-bills from his pocket-book, he gave it to Peek to use as he might see fit, first for the common cause, and secondly for prosecuting inquiries in regard to the kidnapped child of the Pontiac, and his own family.

Peek carefully noted down dates and amounts in a memorandum-book, and then remarked, "Now I must see Captain Onslow."

"Give me that letter from his father, and I will myself deliver it," said Kenrick.

"But I promised to see him."

"That you can do this evening."

Peek gave up the letter, and Kenrick darted out of the room.

Turning to Vance and Winslow, Peek remarked: "I thank

you for your confidence, gentlemen. I 'll do my best to deserve it."

"I wish our banks deserved it as well," said Vance; then he added: "And now, Peek, make your arrangements carefully, and be with the carriage at the door just under my window at nine o'clock precisely."

Peek compared watches with Vance, promised to be punctual, and took his leave.

Vance rang the bell, and ordered a private dinner for two. Unlocking a drawer, he took from it two revolvers and handed one to Winslow, with the remark, "You are skilled in the use of the pistol, I suppose?"

"Though I 've been a planter and owned slaves, I must say *no*."

"Then a revolver would rather be a danger than a security."

And Vance thrust the pistols into the side pockets of his own coat.

Dinner was brought in.

"Come," said Vance, "we must eat. My way of life has compelled me to suffer no excitement to impair my appetite. Indeed, I have passed through the one supreme excitement, after which all others, even the prospect of immediate death, are quite tame. Happy the man, Mr. Winslow, who can say, I cling to this life no longer for myself, but for others and for humanity!"

"Such a sentiment would better become a man of my age than of yours," replied Winslow.

"Here 's the dinner," said Vance. "Now let us talk nothing but nonsense. Let us think of nothing that requires the effort of a serious thought."

"Well then," replied Winslow. "Suppose we discuss the last number of De Bow's Review, or that charlatan Maury's last lying letter in the London Times."

"Excellent!" said Vance. "For reaching the very sublime of the superficial, commend me to De Bow or to the Chevalier Maury."

Before the dinner was over, each man felt that the day had not been unprofitable, since he had earned a friend.

CHAPTER XXXIV.

LIGHT FROM THE PIT.

"There 's not a breathing of the common wind
That will forget thee; thou hast great allies;
Thy friends are exultations, agonies,
And love, and Man's unconquerable mind." — *Wordsworth.*

KENRICK found Onslow seated at one of the tables of the large dining-hall and expecting his coming. The chair on his right was tipped over on its fore legs against the table as a signal that the seat was engaged. On Onslow's right sat the scoffer, Robson.

As Kenrick advanced, Onslow rose, took him by the hand, and placed him in the reserved seat. Robson bowed, and filled three glasses with claret.

"But how grave and pale you look, Charles!" said Onslow. "What the deuce is the matter? Come on! *Absit atra cura!* Begone, dull care! Toss off that glass of claret, or Robson will scorn you as a skulker."

"The wine is not bad," said Robson, "but there should have been ice in the cooler. May the universal Yankee nation be eternally and immitigably consigned to perdition for depriving us of our ice. Every time I am thirsty, — and that is fifty times a day, — my temper is tried, and I wish I had a plenipotentiary power of cursing. With the thermometer at ninety, 't is a lie to say Cotton is king. Ice is king. The glory of our juleps has departed. For my own part, I would grovel at old Abe's feet if he would give us ice."

Kenrick could not force a smile. He touched his lips with the claret.

"You will take soup?" inquired Onslow. "It is tomato, and very good."

"What you please, I 'm not hungry."

Onslow ordered the servant to bring a plate of soup. Kenrick stirred it a moment, tasted, then pushed it from him. Its color reminded him of the precious blood, dear to his friend, which had been so ruthlessly shed.

"A plate of pompinoe," said Onslow.

The dainty fish was put before Kenrick, and he broke it into morsels with his fork, then told the servant to take it away.

"But you 've no appetite," complained Onslow. "Is it the Perdita?"

Kenrick shook his head mournfully.

"Is it Bull Run?"

"No. Had not somebody been afraid of hurting slavery, and so played the laggard, the United States forces would have carried the day; and that would have been the worst thing for the country that could have happened!"

"Did I not promise there should be no politics? Nevertheless, expound."

"He laughs best who laughs last. Let that suffice. It is not time yet for the Union to gain decisive victories; nor will it be time till the conscience of the people of the North is right and ripe for the uprooting of slavery. Their conservative politicians, — their Seymours and Pughs, — who complain of the 'irrepressible negro,' — must find out it is the irrepressible God Almighty, and give up kicking against the pricks. Then when the North as one man shall say, 'Thy kingdom come,' — Thy kingdom of justice and compassion, — then, O then! we may look for the glorious day-star that shall herald the dawn. God reigns. Therefore shall slavery not reign. I believe in the moral government of the world."

"Is n't it a pity, Robson, that so good a fellow as Charles should be so bitter an Abolitionist?"

"Wait till he 's tempted with a colonelcy in the Confederate army," sneered Robson. "Ah! Mr. Kenrick, when you see Onslow charging into Philadelphia, at the head of his troop of horse, sacking that plethoric old city of rectangles, — leering at the pretty Quakeresses, — knocking down his own men for unsoldierly familiarities, — walking into those Chestnut Street jewelry stores and pocketing the diamond rings, — when you see all that, you 'll wish you 'd gone with the winning side."

"As I live," cried Onslow, "there 's a tear in his eye! What does it mean, Charley?"

"If it is a tear, respect its sanctity," replied Kenrick, gravely.

"Gentlemen, I must go," said Robson, who found the atmosphere getting to be unjoyous and uncongenial. "Good by! I 've a polite invitation to be present at a meeting to raise money for the outfit of a new regiment. Between ourselves, if it were a proposition to supply the alligators in our bayous with gutta-percha tails, I would contribute my money much more cheerfully, assured that it would do much more good, and be a far more profitable investment. Addio!"

No sooner had he gone than Kenrick said: "Let us adjourn to your room. I have something to say to you."

In silence the friends passed out of the hall and up-stairs into Onslow's sleeping apartment.

"Kenrick," said he, "your manner is inexplicable. It chills and distresses me. If I can do anything for you before I go North to fight for the stars and bars —"

"Never will you lift the arm for that false flag!" interrupted Kenrick. "You will join me this very hour in cursing it and spurning it."

"Charles, your hate of the Confederacy grows morbid. Let it not make us private as well as public enemies."

"No, Robert, we shall be faster friends than ever."

And Kenrick affectionately threw his arms round his friend and pressed him to his breast.

"But what does this mean, Charles?" cried Onslow. "There 's a terrible pity in your eyes. Explain it, I beseech you."

Kenrick drew from his pocket a letter-envelope, and, taking from it four strands of hair, placed them on the white marble of the bureau before Onslow's eyes. The Captain looked at them wonderingly; took up one after another, examined it, and laid it down. His breast began to heave, and his cheek to pale. He looked at Kenrick, then turned quickly away, as if dreading some foreshadowing of an evil not to be uttered. For five minutes he walked the room, and said nothing. Then he again went to the bureau and regarded the strands of hair.

"Well," said he, speaking tremulously and quickly, and not daring to look at Kenrick, "I recognize these locks of hair. This white hair is my father's; this half gray is my mother's;

this beautiful flaxen is my sister Emily's; and this brownish black is my brother's. Why do you put these before me? A sentimental way of telling me, I suppose, that they all send their love, and beg I would turn Abolitionist!"

"Yes," sighed Kenrick. "From their graves they beg it."

With a look of unspeakable horror, his hands pressed on the top of his head as if to keep down some volcanic throe, his mouth open, his tongue lolling out, idiot-like, Onslow stood speechless staring at his friend.

Kenrick led him gently to the sofa, forced him to sit down, and then, with a tenderness almost womanly in its delicacy, removed the sufferer's hands from his head, and smoothed back his thick fine hair from his brow, and away from his ears. Onslow's inward groanings began to grow audible. Suddenly he rose, as if resolved to master his weakness. Then, sinking down, he exclaimed, "God of heaven, can it be?" And then groans piteous but tearless succeeded.

At last, as if bracing himself to an effort that tore his very heart-strings, he rose and said, "Now, Charles, tell me all."

Kenrick handed him the letter which Peek had brought. "Let me leave you while you read," he said. Onslow did not object; and Kenrick went into the corridor, and walked there to and fro for nearly half an hour. Then he re-entered the chamber. Onslow was on his knees by the sofa; his father's letter, smeared with his father's life-blood, in his hand. The young man had been praying. And his eyes showed that prayer had so softened his heart that he could weep. He rose, calm, though very pale.

"Where can I see this negro?" he asked.

"He will be here at the hotel this evening," replied Kenrick.

"And what, — what," said Onslow hesitatingly, "what did they do with my father?"

"They hung him on the same tree with your brother."

"Yes," said Onslow, with a calmness more terrible than a frantic grief. "Yes! Of course his gray hairs were no protection."

There was a pause; and then, "What do you mean to do?" said Kenrick.

"Can you doubt?" exclaimed Onslow.

A servant knocked at the door and left a package. It contained a complimentary letter and a Colonel's commission, signed by the Confederate authorities. "You see these," said Onslow, handing them to Kenrick. Then, taking them, he contemptuously tore them, and madly threw the pieces on the floor.

"Yes, my father is right," he cried. "It is Slavery that has done this horror. On the head of Slavery lies the guilt. O the blind fool, the abject fawner, that I 've been! Instead of being by the side of my brave brother, here I was wearing the detested livery of the brutal Power that smote down a whole family because they would not kneel at its bloody footstool! Who ever heard of a man being harmed at the North for *defending* Slavery? No! 't is a foul lie to say that aught but Slavery can prompt and lend itself to such barbarities! The cowardly butchers! O, damn them! damn them!"

And he tore from his shoulders the badges of his military rank, and, spurning them with his foot, continued: "My noble father! the good, the devout, the heroic old man! How, even under his mortal agony, his belief in God, in right, in immortality, shines forth! Did ever an outcast creature apply to him in vain for help? Quick to resent, how much quicker he was to forgive! The soul of rectitude and truth! Did you ever see his seal, Charles? A straight line, with the motto *Omnium brevissima recta!* But he could not bow to Slavery as the supreme good. For that he and his must be slaughtered! And William, the brave and gentle! And Emily, the tenderly-bred and beautiful! And my sainted — "

He knelt, and, raising both arms to heaven, cried: "Hear me, O God! Eternal Justice, hear me! If ever again, in thought or act, I show mercy to this merciless Slave Power, — if ever again I palliate its crimes or utter a word in extenuation of its horrors, — that moment annihilate me as a wretch unfit either for this world or any other!"

Then, rising, he said, "Kenrick, your hand!"

"Not yet," said Kenrick. "My friend, Slavery is no worse to-day than it was yesterday. You have known for the last three months that these minions and hirelings of the slave aristocracy were hounding, hanging, and torturing men throughout Slavedom, for the crime of being true to their country's flag."

"I knew it, Kenrick; but my heart was hardened, and therefore have God's hammers smitten it thrice, — nay, four times, terribly! I saw these things, but turned away from them! Idle and false to say, Slavery is not responsible for them! They are the very spawn of its filthy loins. I know it, — I, who have been behind the scenes, know what the leaders say as to the means of treading out every spark of Union fire. And I — heedless idiot that I was! — never once thought that the bloody instructions might return to plague *me*, — that my own father's family might be among the foremost victims! I acknowledge the hand of God in this stroke! A voice cries to me, as of old to Saul, 'Why persecutest thou me?' And now there fall from my eyes as it were scales, and I arise and am baptized!"

"My dear friend," said Kenrick, "I want your conversion to be, not the result of mere passion, but of calm conviction. I have been asking myself, What if a party of Unionists should outrage and murder those who are nearest and dearest to myself, — would I, therefore, embrace the pro-slavery cause? And from the very depths of my soul, I can cry *No!* Not through passion, — though I have enough of that, — but through the persuasion of my intellect, added to the affirmation of my heart, do I array myself against this hideous Moloch of slavery. By a terrible law of affinity, wrongs and crimes cannot stand alone. They must summon other wrongs and crimes to their support; and so does murder as naturally follow in the train of slavery, as the little parasite fish follows the shark. It is fallacy to say that the best men among slaveholders do not approve of these outrages; for these outrages are now the necessary and inseparable attendants of the system."

"I believe it," said Onslow. "O the wickedness of my apostasy from my father's faith! O the sin, and O the punishment! It needed a terrible blow to reach me, and it has come. Kenrick, do not withhold your hand. Trust me, my conversion is radical. The 'institution' shall henceforth find in me its deadliest foe. '*Delenda est!*' is now and henceforth my motto!"

Kenrick clasped his proffered hand, and, looking up, said, "So prosper us, Almighty Disposer, as we are true to the promises of this hour!"

"Charles," said Onslow, "I did not think that Perdita would so soon have her prayer granted."

"What do you mean?"

"Her last words to me were, 'May this arm never be lifted except in the cause of right!' I feel that God has heard her."

It jarred on Kenrick's heart for the moment to see that Onslow, in the midst of his troubles, still thought of Perdita; but soon, stilling the selfish tremor, he said: "What we would do we must do quickly. Will you go North with me and join the armies of the Union?"

"Yes, the first opportunity."

"That opportunity will be this very night."

"So much the better! I'm ready. I had but one tie to bind me here; and that was Perdita. And she has fled. And what would I be to her, were she here? Nothing! Charles, this day's news has made me ten years older already. O for an army with banners, to go down into that bloody region of the Rio Grande, and right the wrongs of the persecuted!"

"Be patient. We shall live to see the old flag wave resplendent over free and regenerated Texas."

"Amen! Good heavens, Charles! — it appalls me, when I think what a different man I am from what I was when I crossed this threshold, one little hour ago!"

"In these volcanic days," said Kenrick, "such changes are not surprising. These terrible eruptions, 'painting hell on the sky,' uptear many old convictions, and illumine many benighted minds."

"Yes," rejoined Onslow, "in that infernal flash, coming from my own violated home, I see slavery as it is, — monstrous, bestial, devilish! — no longer the graceful, genteel, hospitable, and fascinating embodiment which I — fond fool that I was! — have been wont to think it. The Republicans of the North were right in declaring that not one inch more of national soil should be surrendered to the pollutions of slavery."

"Time flies," said Kenrick. "Have you any preparations to make?"

"Yes, a few bills to pay and a few letters to write."

"Can you despatch all your work by quarter to nine?"

"Sooner, if need be."

"That will answer. Have your baggage ready, and let it be compact as possible. I'll call for you at your room at quarter to nine. Vance goes with us."

"Is it possible? I supposed him an ultra Secessionist."

"He has a stronger personal cause than even you to strike at slavery."

"Can that be? Well, he shall find me no tame ally. Do you know, Charles, you resemble him personally?"

"Yes, there's good reason for it. We are cousins."

Onslow's heart was too full to comment on the reply. He took up the strands of hair, kissed them fervently, and placed them with his father's letter in a little silk watch-bag, which he pinned inside of his vest just over his heart.

"If ever my new faith should falter," he said, "here are the mementos that will revive it. God! Did I need all this for my reformation?"

"Be firm, — be prudent, my friend," said Kenrick. "And now good by till we meet again."

Onslow pressed Kenrick's proffered hand, and replied, "You shall find me punctual."

CHAPTER XXXV.

THE COMMITTEE ADJOURNS.

"Why now, blow, wind; swell, billow; and swim, bark!
The storm is up, and all is on the hazard." — *Shakspeare.*

VANCE'S plan was to escape down the river in his little steam-tug, and join some one of the blockading fleet of the United States, either at Pass à l'Outre or at the Balize. The unexpected accession of two fellow-fugitives led him to postpone his departure from the St. Charles to nine o'clock. His own and Kenrick's baggage had been providently put on board the Artful Dodger the day before. Winslow, in order not to jeopard any of the proceedings, had accepted Vance's offer to get from the latter's supply whatever articles of apparel he might need.

At ten minutes before nine, the four fugitives met in Vance's room. Vance and Onslow grasped each other by the hand. That silent pressure conveyed to each more than words could ever have told. The sympathy between them was at once profound and complete.

"The negro who is to drive us," said Vance, "is the man to whom your father confided his last messages."

"Ah!" exclaimed Onslow; "let me be with him. Let me learn from him all I can!"

Vance told him he should ride on the outside with Peek. Then turning to Winslow, he said: "Those white locks of yours are somewhat too conspicuous. Do me the favor to hide them under this black wig."

The disguise was promptly carried into effect. At nine o'clock Vance put his head out of the window. A rain-storm had set in, but he could see by the gas-lights the glistening top of a carriage, and he could hear the stamping of horses.

"All right," said he. "Peek is punctually on the spot. Does that carpet-bag contain all your baggage, Mr. Onslow?"

"Yes, and I can dispense with even this, if you desire it."

"You have learnt one of the first arts of the soldier, I see," said Vance. "There can be no harm in your taking that amount. Now let me frankly tell you what I conceive to be our chief, if not our only hazard. My venerable friend, here, Winslow, was compelled, a few hours since, in the discharge of his duty, to give very dire offence to Mr. Carberry Ratcliff, of whom we all have heard. Knowing the man as I do, I am of opinion that his first step on parting with our friend would be to put spies on his track, with the view of preventing his departure or concealment. Mr. Winslow thinks Ratcliff could not have had time to do this. Perhaps; but there's a chance my venerable friend is mistaken, and against that contingency I wish to be on my guard. You see I take in my hand this lasso, and this small cylindrical piece of wood, padded with india-rubber at either end. Three of us, I presume, have revolvers; but I hope we shall have no present use for them. You, Mr. Winslow, will go first and enter the carriage; Kenrick and I will follow at ten or a dozen paces, and you, Onslow, will bring up the rear. In your soldier's overcoat, and with your carpet-bag, it will be supposed you are merely going out to pass the night at the armory."

While this conversation was going on, Peek had dismounted from the driver's seat. He had taken the precaution to cover both the horses and the carriage with oil-cloth, apparently as a protection against the rain, but really to prevent an identification. No sooner had his feet touched the side-walk, than a man carrying a bludgeon stepped up to him and said, "Whose turn-out have you here, darkey?"

"Dis am massa's turn-out, an' nobody else's, sure," said Peek, disguising his voice.

"Well, who's massa?"

"Massa's de owner ob dis carriage. Thar, yer'v got it. So dry up, ole feller!"

The inquirer tried to roll up the oil-cloth to get a sight of the panel. Peek interposed, telling him to stand off. The man raised his bludgeon and threatened to strike. Peek's first impulse was to disarm him and choke him into silence, but, fearing the least noise might bring other officers to the spot, he prudently abstained. Just at this moment, Winslow issued from the side door of the hotel, and was about to enter the carriage, when the detective who had succeeded in rolling up the covering of the panel till he could see the coat-of-arms, politely stopped the old man, and begged permission to look at him closely by the gaslight, remarking that he had orders from head-quarters to arrest a certain suspected party.

"Pooh! Everybody in New Orleans knows me," said Winslow.

"I can't help that, sir," said the detective, laying his hand on the old man's shoulder, "I must insist on your letting—"

Before the speaker could finish his sentence, his arms were pinioned from behind by a lasso, and he was jerked back so as to lose his balance. But one articulation escaped from his lips, and that was half smothered in his throat. "O'Gorman!" he cried, calling to one of his companions; but before he could repeat the cry, a gag was inserted in his mouth, and he was lifted into the carriage and there held with a power that speedily taught him how useless was resistance.

Kenrick made Peek and Onslow acquainted, and these two sprang on to the driver's seat. The rest of the party took their places inside.

"Down! down!" cried Peek, thrusting Onslow down on his knees and starting the horses. The next moment a pistol was discharged, and there was the whiz of a bullet over their heads. But the horses had now found out what was wanted of them, and they showed their blood by trotting at a two-fifty speed along St. Charles Street.

Peek was an accomplished driver. That very afternoon he had learnt where the steam-tug lay, and had gone over the route in order to be sure of no obstructions. He now at first took a direction away from the river to deceive pursuit. Then winding through several obscure streets, he came upon the avenue running parallel with the Levee, and proceeded for nearly two miles till he drew near that part of the river where the Artful Dodger, with steam all up, was moored against the extensive embankment, from the top of which you can look down on the floor of the Crescent City, lying several feet below the river's level.

The rain continued to pour furiously, each drop swelling to the size of a big arrow-head before reaching the earth. It was not unusual to see carriages driven at great speed through the streets during such an elementary turmoil: else the policemen or soldiers would have tried to stop Peek in his headlong career. Probably they had most of them got under some shelter, and did not care to come out to expose themselves to a drenching. On and on rolled the carriage. The rain seemed to drown all noises, so that the occupants could not tell whether or no there was a trampling of horses in pursuit.

As the carriage passed on to a macadmized section of the road, "Tell me," said Onslow, "what happened after my father gave you the letter?"

"I hardly had time to conceal it," replied Peek, "when six of the ruffians entered the room, and I was ordered out. I pleaded hard to stay, but 't was no use. The house was entirely surrounded by armed men, ready to shoot down any one attempting to escape. Your father had enjoined it upon me that I should leave him to die rather than myself run the risk of not reaching you with his letter and his messages."

"*Did* he?" cried Onslow. "Was he, then, more anxious that I should know all, than that he himself should escape?"

"He feared life more than death after what had happened," said Peek. "The six ruffians tried to get out of him words to implicate certain supposed Union men in the neighborhood; but he would tell no secrets. He obstinately resisted their orders and threats, and at last their leader, in a rage, thrust his sword into the old man's lungs. The wound did not immediately kill; but the loss of blood seemed likely to make him faint. Fearing he would balk them in their last revenge, the ruffians dragged him out to a tree and hung him."

"Did you see it done?"

"I saw him the moment after it was done. I had been trying to satisfy myself that there was no life in your mother's body; and it was not till I heard the shouts of the crowd that I learnt what was going on below. I ran out, but your father was already dead. He died, I learnt, without a struggle, much to the disappointment of the Rebels."

"And my mother," asked Onslow. "Was there any hope?"

"None whatever, sir. She was undoubtedly dead."

"Peek, you have a claim upon me henceforth. At present I 've but little money with me, but what I have you must take."

"Not a penny, sir! You 'll need it more than I. Mr. Vance and Mr. Winslow have supplied me with ten times as much as I shall require."

Onslow said no more. For the first time in his life he felt that a negro could be a gentleman and his equal.

"Peek," said he, "you may refuse my money, but you must not refuse my friendship and respect. Promise me you will seek me if I can ever aid you. Nay, promise me you will visit me when you can."

"That I do cheerfully, sir. Here we are close by the steam-tug."

Peek pulled up the horses, and he and Onslow jumped to the ground. The door was opened, and those inside got out. The detective, who was the principal man of his order in New Orleans (Myers himself), and whose mortification at being overreached by a non-professional person was extreme, made a desperate effort to escape. Vance was ready for it. He simply twisted the lasso till Myers cried out with pain and promised to submit. Then pitching him on board the steam-tug, Vance left him under the guard of Kenrick and the Captain. Winslow followed them on board; and Vance, turning to Peek, said: "Now, Peek, drive for dear life, and take back your horses. Our danger is almost over; but yours is just beginning."

"Never fear for me, Mr. Vance. I could leave the horses and run, in case of need. Do not forget the telegraph wires."

"Well thought of, Peek! Farewell!"

They interchanged a quick, strong grasp of the hand, and Peek jumped on the box and drove off.

Vance saw a telegraph-pole close by, the wires of which communicated with the forts on the river below. Climbing to the top of it, he took from his pocket a knife, having a file on one of its blades, and in half a minute severed the wire, then tied it by a string to the pole so that the place of the disconnection might not be at once discovered.

The next moment he cast off the hawser and leaped on

board the tug. Everything was in readiness. Captain Payson was in his glory. The pipes began to snort steam, the engines to move, and the little tug staggered off into the river. Hardly were they ten rods from the levee, however, when a carriage drove up, and a man issued from it who cried: "Boat ahoy! Stop that boat! Every man of you shall be hung if you don't stop that boat."

Captain Payson took up his speaking-trumpet, and replied: "Come and stop it yourself, you blasted bawler!"

"By order of the Confederate authorities I call on you to stop that boat," screamed the officer.

"The Confederate authorities may go to hell!" returned old Payson.

The retort of the officer was lost in the mingled uproar of winds and waves.

Confounded at the steam-tug's defiance, the officer, O'Gorman by name, stood for a minute gesticulating and calling out wildly, and then, re-entering the carriage, told the driver to make his best speed to Number 17 Diana Street.

Let us precede him by a few minutes and look in upon the select company there assembled. In a stately apartment some dozen of the principal Confederate managers sat in conclave. Prominent among them were Ratcliff, and by his side his lawyer, Semmes, an attenuated figure, sharp-faced and eager-eyed. Complacent, but inwardly cursing the Rebellion, sat Robson with his little puffed eyes twinkling through gold-rimmed spectacles, and his fat cheeks indicating good cheer. It was with difficulty he could repress the sarcasms that constantly rose to his lips. Wigman and Sanderson were of the company; and the rest of the members were nearly all earnest Secessionists and gentlemen of position.

Ratcliff had communicated his grievances, and it had been decided to send a messenger to bring Winslow before the conclave to answer certain questions as to his disposition of the funds confided to him by the late Mrs. Ratcliff. The messenger having returned once with the information that Winslow was not at home, had been sent a second time with orders to wait for him till ten o'clock.

It had been also resolved to summon Charles Kenrick before

the conclave, and an officer had been sent to the hotel for that purpose.

There was now a discussion as to Vance. Who knew him? No one intimately. Several had a mere bowing acquaintance with him. Ratcliff could not remember that he had ever seen him. Had Vance contributed to the cause? Yes. He had paid a thousand dollars for the relief of the suffering at the hospital. Did anybody know what he was worth? A cotton-broker present knew of his making "thirty thousand dollars clean" in one operation in the winter of 1858. Did he own any real estate in the city? His name was not down in the published list of holders. If he owned any, it was probably held under some other person's name. Among tax-payers he was rated at only fifty thousand dollars; but he might have an income from property in other places, perhaps at the North, on which he ought to pay his quota in this hour of common danger. It was decided to send to see why Vance did not come; and a third officer was despatched to find him.

"Does any one know," asked Semmes, "whether Captain Onslow has yet got the news of this terrible disaster to his family in Texas?"

"The intelligence has but just reached us at head-quarters," replied Mr. Ferrand, a wealthy Creole. "I hope it will not shake the Captain's loyalty to the good cause."

"Why should it?" inquired Ratcliff.

"He must be a spooney to let it make any difference," said Sanderson.

"Some people are so weak and prejudiced!" replied Robson. "Tell them the good of the institution requires that their whole family should be disembowelled, and they can't see it. Tell them that though their sister was outraged, yet 't was in the holy cause of slavery, and it does n't satisfy 'em. Such sordid souls, incapable of grand sacrifices, are too common."

"That 's a fact," responded George Sanderson, who was getting thirsty, and adhered to Robson as to the genius of good liquor.

"Old Onslow deserved his fate," said Mr. Curry, a fiery little man, resembling Vice-President Stephens.

"To be sure he deserved it!" returned Robson. "And so

did that heretical young girl, his daughter, deserve hers. Why, it 's asserted, on good authority, that she had been heard to repeat Patrick Henry's remark, that slavery is inconsistent with the Christian religion!"

Mr. Polk, who, being related to a bishop, thought it was incumbent on him to rebuke extreme sentiments, here mildly remarked: "We do not make war on young girls and women. I 'm sorry our friends in Texas should resort to such violent practices."

"Let us have no half-way measures!" exclaimed Robson. "We can't check feminine treason by sprinkling rose-water."

"The rankest Abolitionists are among the women," interposed Ratcliff.

"No doubt of it," replied Robson. "Or if a woman is n't an Abolitionist herself, she may become the mother of one. An ounce of precaution is worth a pound of cure."

"Gentlemen," said Mr. Polk, "I base my support of slavery on evangelical principles, and they teach me to look upon rape and murder as crimes."

"It will do very well for you and the bishops," replied Robson, "to tell the *hoi polloi*, — the people, — that slavery is evangelical; but here in this snug little coterie, we must n't try to fool each other, — 't would n't be civil. We 'll take it for granted there are no greenhorns among us. We can therefore afford to speak plainly. Slavery is based on the principle that *might makes right*, and on no other."

"That 's the talk," said Ratcliff.

"That being the talk," continued Robson, "let us face the music without dodging. The object of this war is to make the slaveholding interest, more than it has ever been before, the ruling interest of America; to propagate, extend, and at the same time consolidate slavery; to take away all governing power from the people and vest it in the hands of a committee of slaveholders, who will regard the wealth and power of their order as paramount to all other considerations and laws, human or divine. I presume there 's nobody here who will deny this."

"Is it quite prudent to make such declarations?" asked Mr. Polk, in a deprecatory tone.

"Is there any one here, sir, you want to hoodwink?" returned Robson.

"O no, no!" replied Mr. Polk. "I presume we are all qualified to understand the esoteric meaning of the Rebellion."

"It is no longer esoteric," said Robson. "The doctrine is openly proclaimed. What says Spratt of South Carolina? What says Toombs? What De Bow, Fitzhugh, Grayson, the Richmond papers, Trescott, Cobb? They are openly in favor of an aristocracy, and against popular rights."

Before any reply was made, there was a knock at the door, and Ratcliff was called out. In three minutes he returned, his face distorted with anger and excitement. "Gentlemen," said he, "we are the victims of an infernal Yankee trick. I have reason to believe that Winslow, aided perhaps by other suspected parties, has made his escape this very night in a little steam-tug that has been lying for some days in the river, ready for a start."

"Which way has it gone?" asked Semmes.

"Down the river. Probably to Pass à l'Outre."

"Telegraph to the forts to intercept her," said Semmes.

"A good idea!" exclaimed Ratcliff. "I'd do it at once." He joined O'Gorman outside, and the next moment a carriage was heard rolling over the pavements.

"Gentlemen," said Robson, "if we expect to see any of the parties we have summoned here to-night, there is something so touching and amiable in our credulity that I grieve to harshly dispel it. But let me say that Mr. Kenrick would see us all in the profoundest depths before he would put himself in our power or acknowledge our jurisdiction; Mr. Vance can keep his own counsel and will not brook dictation, or I'm no judge of physiognomy; Captain Onslow has a foolish sensitiveness which leads him to resent murder and outrage when practised against his own family; and as for old Winslow, he has n't lived seventy years not to know better than to place himself within reach of a tiger's claws. I think we may as well adjourn, and muse over the mutability of human affairs."

Before Robson's proposition was carried into effect, an errand-boy from the telegraph-office brought Semmes this letter: —

"The scoundrels have cut the telegraph wires, and we can't communicate with the forts. I leave here at once to engage a boat for the pursuit. Shall go in her myself. You must do this one thing for me without fail: Take up your abode at once, this very night, in my house, and stay there till I come back. Use every possible precaution to prevent another escape of that young person of whom I spoke to you. Do not let her move a step out of doors without you or your agents know precisely where she is. I shall hold you responsible for her security. I may not be back for a day or two, in which case you must have my wife's interment properly attended to.

"Yours, RATCLIFF."

"I agree with Mr. Robson," said Semmes, "that we may as well adjourn. The telegraph wires are cut, and I should not wonder if all the summoned parties were among the fugitives. Ratcliff pursues."

The select assemblage broke up, and above the curses, freely uttered, rang the sardonic laugh of Robson. "Two to one that Ratcliff does n't catch them!" said he; but no one took up the bet, though it should be remembered, in defence of Wigman and Sanderson, that they were too busy in the liquor-closet to heed the offer.

"Ah! my pious friends, — still at it, I see!" exclaimed Robson, coming in upon them. "You remind me of a French hymn I learnt in my youth:

'Tous les méchants sont buveurs d'eau;
C'est bien prouvé par le déluge!'

Which, for Sanderson's benefit, I will translate:

'Who are the wicked? Why, water-drinkers!
The deluge proves it to all right thinkers.'"

Leaving the trio over their cups, let us follow the enraged Ratcliff in his adventures subsequent to his letter to Semmes.

The Rebel was a boat armed with a one-hundred-pound rifled gun, and used for occasional reconnoitring expeditions down the river. Ratcliff had no difficulty in inducing the captain to put her on the chase; but an hour was spent hunting up the engineer and getting ready. At last the Rebel was started in pursuit. The rain had ceased, and the moon, bursting occasionally from dark drifting clouds, shed a fitful light. Ratcliff paced the deck, smoking cigars, and nursing his rage.

It was nearly sunrise before they reached Forts Jackson and St. Philip, thirty-three miles above the Balize. Nothing could yet be seen of the steam-tug; but there was a telltale pillar of smoke in the distance. "We shall have her!" said Ratcliff, exultingly.

Following in the trail of the Rebel were numerous sea-gulls whom the storm had driven up the river. The boat now entered that long canal-like section where the great river flows between narrow banks, which, including the swamps behind them, are each not more than two or three hundred yards wide, running out into the Gulf of Mexico. Here and there among the dead reeds and scattered willows a tall white crane might be seen feeding. Over these narrow fringes of swampy land you could see the dark-green waters of the Gulf just beginning to be incarnadined by the rising sun. With the salt-water so near on either side that you could shoot an arrow into it, you saw the river holding its way through the same deep, unbroken channel, keeping unmixed its powerful body of fresh water, except when hurricanes sweep the briny spray over these long ribbons of land into the Mississippi.

Vance had abandoned his original intention of trying the Pass à l'Outre. Having learned from a pilot that the Brooklyn, carrying the Stars and Stripes, was cruising off the Southwest Pass, he resolved to steer in that direction. But when within five miles of the head of the Passes, one of those capricious fogs, not uncommon on the river, came down, shrouding the banks on either side. The Artful Dodger crept along at an abated speed through the sticky vapor. Soon the throb of a steamer close in the rear could be distinctly heard. The Artful had but one gun, and that was a 5-inch rifled one; but it could be run out over her after bulwarks.

All at once the fog lifted, and the sun came out sharp and dazzling, scattering the white banks of vapor. The Rebel might be seen not a third of a mile off. A shot came from her as a signal to the Artful to heave to. Vance ordered the Stars and Stripes to be run up, and the engines to be reversed. The Rebel, as if astounded at the audacity of the act on the part of her contemptible adversary, swayed a little in the current so as to present a good part of her side. Vance saw his oppor-

15 *

tunity, and, with the quickness of one accustomed to dead-shots, decided on his range. The next moment, and before the Rebel could recover herself, he fired, the shock racking every joint in the little tug.

The effect of the shot was speedily visible and audible in the issuing of steam and in cries of suffering on board the Rebel. The boiler had been hit, and she was helpless. Vance fired a second shot, but this time over her, as a summons for surrender. The confederate flag at once disappeared. The next moment a small boat, containing half a dozen persons, put out from the Rebel as if they intended to gain the bank and escape among the low willows and dead reeds of the marshy deposits. But before this could be done, two cutters bearing United States flags, were seen to issue from a diminutive bayou in the neighborhood, and intercept the boat, which was taken in tow by the larger cutter. The Artful Dodger then steamed up to the disabled Rebel and took possession.

At the mouth of the Southwest Pass they met the Brooklyn. Vance went on board, found in the Commodore an old acquaintance, and after recounting the adventures of the last twelve hours, gave up the two steamers for government use. It was then arranged that he and his companions should take passage on board the store-ship Catawba, which was to sail for New York within the hour; while all the persons captured on board the Rebel, together with the detective carried off by Vance, should be detained as prisoners and sent North in an armed steamer, to leave the next day.

"There 's one man," said Vance, — "his name is Ratcliff, — who will try by all possible arts and pleadings to get away. Hold on to him, Commodore, as you would to a detected incendiary. 'T is all the requital I ask for my little present to Uncle Sam."

"He shall be safe in Fort Lafayette before the month is out," replied the Commodore. "I 'll take your word for it, Vance, that he is n't to be trusted."

"One word more, Commodore. My crew on board the little tug are all good men and true. Old Skipper Payson, whom you see yonder, goes into this fight, not for wages, but for love. He has but one fault!"

"What 's that? Drinks, I suppose!"

"No. He 's a terrible Abolitionist."

"So much the better! We shall all be Abolitionists before this war is ended. 'T is the only way to end it."

"Good, my Commodore! Such sentiments from men in your position will do as much as rifled cannon for the cause."

"More, Mr. Vance, more! And now duty calls me off. Your men, sir, shall be provided for. Good by."

Vance and the Commodore shook hands and parted. Vance was rowed back to the Artful Dodger. On his way, looking through his opera-glass, he could see Ratcliff in the cutter, gnawing his rage, and looking the incarnation of chagrin.

The Catawba was making her toilet ready for a start. She lay at a short distance from the Artful. Vance, Winslow, Kenrick, and Onslow went on board, where the orders of the Commodore had secured for them excellent accommodations. Before noon a northeasterly breeze had sprung up, and they took their leave of the mouths of the Mississippi.

Ratcliff no sooner touched the deck of the Brooklyn, than, conquering with an effort his haughtiness, he took off his hat, and, approaching the Commodore, asked for an interview.

The Commodore was an old weather-beaten sailor, not far from his threescore and ten years. He kept no "circumlocution office" on board his ship, and as he valued his time, he could not tolerate any tortuous delays in coming to the point.

"Commodore," said Ratcliff, "'t is important I should have a few words with you immediately."

"Well, sir, be quick about it."

"Commodore, I have long known you by reputation as a man of honor. I have often heard Commodore Tatnall —"

"The damned old traitor! Well sir?"

"I beg pardon; I supposed you and Tatnall were intimate."

"So we were! Loved him once as my own brother. He and I and Percival have had many a jolly time together. But now, damn him! The man who could trample on the old flag that had protected and honored and enriched him all his life is no better than a beast. So damn him! Don't let me hear his name again."

"I beg pardon, Commodore. As I was saying, we know you to be a gentleman —"

"Stop! I'm an officer in the United States service. That's the only capacity I shall allow you to address me in. Your salvy compliments make me sick. What do you want?"

"It's necessary I should return at once to New Orleans."

"Indeed! How do you propose to get there?"

"When you hear my story, you'll give me the facilities."

"Don't flatter yourself. I shall do no such thing."

"But, Commodore, I came out in pursuit of an unfaithful agent, who was running off with my property."

"Hark you, sir, when you speak in those terms of Simon Winslow, you lie, and deserve the cat."

Ratcliff grew purple in the struggle to suppress an outburst of wrath. But, after nearly a minute of silence, he said: "Commodore, my wife died only a few hours ago. Her unburied remains lie in my house. Surely you'll let me return to attend her funeral. You'll not be so cruel as to refuse me."

"Pah! Does your dead wife need your care any more than my live wife needs mine? 'T is your infernal treason keeps me here. Can you count the broken hearts and ruined constitutions you have already made, — the thousands you have sent to untimely graves, — in this attempt to carry out your beastly nigger-breeding, slavery-spreading speculation? And now you presume to whine because I'll not let you slip back to hatch more treason, under the pretence that you want to go to a funeral! As if you had n't made funerals enough already in the land! Curse your impudence, sir! Be thankful I don't string you up to the yard-arm. Here, Mr. Buttons, see that this fellow is placed among the prisoners and strictly guarded. I hold you responsible for him, sir!"

The Commodore turned on his heel and left Ratcliff panting with an intolerable fury that he dared not vent. Big drops of perspiration came out on his face. The Midshipman, playfully addressed as Mr. Buttons, was a very stern-looking gentleman, of the name of Adams, who wore on his coat a very conspicuous row of buttons, and whose fourteenth birthday had been celebrated one week before. Motioning to Ratcliff, and frowning imperiously, he stamped his foot and exclaimed, "Follow me!" The slave-lord, with an internal half-smothered groan of rage and despair, saw that there was no help, and obeyed.

CHAPTER XXXVI.

THE OCCUPANT OF THE WHITE HOUSE.

"They forbore to break the chain
 Which bound the dusky tribe,
Checked by the owner's fierce disdain,
 Lured by 'Union' as the bribe.
Destiny sat by and said,
 'Pang for pang your seed shall pay;
Hide in false peace your coward head, —
 I bring round the harvest-day.'"

R. W. Emerson.

IN one of the smaller parlors of the White House in Washington sat two men of rather marked appearance. One of them sat leaning back in his tipped chair, with his thumbs in the arm-holes of his vest, and his right ancle resting on his left knee. His figure, though now flaccid and relaxed, would evidently be a tall one if pulled out like the sliding joints of a spy-glass; but gaunt, lean, and ungainly, with harsh angles and stooping shoulders. He was dressed in a suit of black, with a black satin vest, and round his neck a black silk kerchief tied carelessly in a knot, and passing under a shirt-collar turned down and revealing a neck brawny, sinewy, and tanned.

The face that belonged to this figure was in keeping with it, and yet attractive from a certain charm of expression. Nose prominent and assertive; cheek-bones rather obtrusive, and under them the flesh sallow and browned, though partially covered by thick bristling black whiskers; eyes dark and deeply set; mouth and lips large; and crowning all these features a shock of stiff profuse black hair carelessly put aside from his irregularly developed forehead, as if by no other comb than that which he could make of his long lank fingers.

This man was not only the foremost citizen of the Republic, officially considered, but he had a reputation, exaggerated beyond his deserts, for homeliness. By the Rebel press he was frequently spoken of as "the ape" or the "gorilla." From the rowdy George Sanderson to the stiff, if not stately Jefferson Davis (himself far from being an Adonis), the pro-slavery champions took a harmless satisfaction, in their public addresses, in alluding, in some contemptuous epithet, to the man's personal shortcomings. So far from being disturbed, the object of all these revilings would himself sometimes playfully refer to his personal attractions, unconscious how much there was in that face to redeem it from being truly characterized either as ugly or commonplace.

As he sat now, with eyes bent on vacancy, and his mind revolving the arguments or facts which had been presented by his visitor, his countenance assumed an expression which was pathetic in its indication of sincere and patient effort to grasp the truth and see clearly the way before him. The expression redeemed the whole countenance, for it was almost tender in its anxious yet resigned thoughtfulness; in its profound sense of the enormous and unparalleled responsibilities resting on that one brain, perplexing it in the extreme.

The other party to the interview was a man whose personal appearance was in marked contrast. Although he had numbered in his life nearly as many years as the President, he looked some ten years younger. His figure was strikingly handsome, compact, and graceful; and his clothes were nicely adapted to it, both in color and cut. Every feature of his face was finely outlined and proportioned; and the whole expression indicated at once refinement and energy, habits of intellectual culture and of robust physical exercise and endurance. This man was he who has passed so long in this story under the adopted name of Vance.

There had been silence between the two for nearly a minute. Suddenly the President turned his mild dark eyes on his visitor, and said: "Well, sir, what would you have me do?"

"I would have you lead public opinion, Mr. President, instead of waiting for public opinion to lead you."

"Make this allowance for me, Mr. Vance: I have many conflicting interests to reconcile; many conflicting facts and assertions to sift and weigh. Remember I am bound to listen, not merely to the men of New England, but to those of Kentucky, Maryland, and Eastern Tennessee."

"Mr. President, you are bound to listen to no man who is not ready to say, Down with slavery if it stands in the way of the Republic! You should at once infuse into every branch of the public service this determination to tear up the bitter root of all our woes. Why not give me the necessary authority to raise a black regiment?"

"Impossible! The public are not ripe for any such extreme measure."

"There it is! You mean that the public shall be the responsible President instead of Abraham Lincoln. O, sir, knowing you are on the side of right, have faith in your own power to mould and quicken public opinion. When last August in Missouri, Fremont declared the slaves of Rebels free, one word of approval from you would have won the assent of every loyal man. But, instead of believing in the inherent force of a great idea to work its own way, you were biased by the semi-loyal men who were lobbying for slavery, and you countermanded the righteous order, thus throwing us back a whole year. Do I give offence?"

"No, sir, speak your mind freely. I love sincerity."

"We know very well, Mr. President, that you will do what is right eventually. But O, why not do it at once, and forestall the issue? We know that you will one of these days remove Buell and other generals, the singleness of whose devotion to the Union as against slavery is at least questionable. We know that you will put an end to the atrocious pro-slavery favoritism of many of our officers. We know you will issue a proclamation of emancipation."

"I think not, Mr. Vance."

"Pardon me, you will do it before next October. You will do it because the pressure of an advanced public opinion will force you to do it, and because God Almighty will interpose checks and defeats to our arms in order that we of the North may, in the fermentation of ideas, throw off this foul scum, redolent of the bottomless pit, which apathy or sympathy in regard to slavery engenders. Yes, you will give us an emancipation proclamation, and then you will give us permission to raise black regiments, and then, after being pricked, and urged, and pricked again, by public opinion, you will offset the Rebel threats of massacre by issuing a war bulletin declaring that the United States will protect her fighting men of whatever color, and that there must be life for life for every black soldier killed in violation of the laws of war."

"But are you a prophet, Mr. Vance?"

"It requires no gift of prophecy, Mr. President, to foretell these things. It needs but full faith in the operation of Divine laws to anticipate all that I have prefigured. You refuse now to let me raise a black regiment. In less than ten months you will give me a *carte blanche* to enlist as many negroes as I can for the war."

"Perhaps, — but I don't see my way clear to do it yet."

"A great man," said Vance, "ought to lead and fashion public opinion in stupendous emergencies like this, — ought to throw himself boldly on some great principle having its root in eternal justice, — ought to grapple it, cling to it, stake everything upon it, and make everything give way to it."

"But I am not a great man, Mr. Vance," said the President, with unaffected *naïveté*.

"I believe your intentions are good and great, Mr. President," was the reply; "for what you supremely desire is, to do your duty."

"Yes, I claim that much. Thank you."

"Well, your duty is to take the most energetic measures for conquering a peace. Under the Constitution, the war power is committed to your hands. That power is not defined by the Constitution, for it is imprescriptible; regulated by international usage. That usage authorizes you to free the slaves of an enemy. Why not do it?"

"Would not a proclamation of emancipation from Abraham Lincoln be much like the Pope's bull against the comet?"

"There is this difference: in the latter case, the fulmination is against what we have no reason to suppose is an evil; in the former case, you would attack with moral weapons what you know to be a wrong and an injustice immediately under your eyes and within your reach. If it could be proved that the comet is an evil, the Pope's bull would not seem to me an absurdity; for I have faith in the operation of ideas, and in the triumph of truth and good *throughout the universe.* But the emancipation proclamation would not be futile; for it would give body and impulse to an *idea*, and that idea one friendly to right and to progress."

The President rose, and, walking to the window, drummed a moment with his fingers abstractedly on the glass, then, returning to his chair, reseated himself and said: "As Chief Magistrate of the Republic, my first duty is to save it. If I can best do that by tolerating slavery, slavery shall be tolerated. If I can best do it by abolishing slavery, you may be sure I will try to abolish it. But I must n't be biased by my feelings or my sentiments."

"Why not?" asked Vance. "Do not all great moral truths originate in the feelings and the sentiments? The heart's policy is often the safest. Is not cruelty wrong because the heart proclaims it? Is not despotism to be opposed because the heart detests it?"

"Mr. Vance, you eager philanthropists little know how hard it often is for less impulsive and more conservative men to withstand the urgency of those feelings that you give way to at once. But you have read history to little purpose if you do not know that the best cause may be jeoparded by the premature and too radical movements of its friends. I have been blamed for listening to the counsels of Kentucky politicians and Missouri conservatives; and yet if we had not held back Kentucky from the secession madness, she might have contributed the straw that would have broken the camel's back."

"O Kentucky!" exclaimed Vance, "I know thy works, that thou art neither cold nor hot. I would thou wert cold or hot. So then, because thou art lukewarm, and neither cold nor hot, I will spue thee out of my mouth! Mr. President, the ruling powers in Kentucky would hand her over bound to Jeff Davis to-morrow, *if they dared;* but they dare not do it. In the first place, they fear Uncle Sam and his gunboats; in the next place, they fear Kentuckians, of whom, thank God! there are enough who do not believe in slavery; and, lastly, they fear the nineteenth century and the spirit of the age. Better take counsel from the Rhetts and Spratts of South Carolina than from the selfish politicians of Kentucky! They will moor you to the platform of a false conservatism till the golden opportunity slips by, and new thousands must be slaughtered before it can be recovered."

"Well, what would be your programme?"

"This, Mr. President: accept it as a foregone conclusion that slavery *must* be exterminated; and then bend all your energies on accelerating its extermination. We sometimes hear it said, 'What! do you expect such a vast system — so interwoven with the institutions of the South — to be uprooted and overthrown all at once?' To which I reply, 'Yes! *The price paid has been already proportionate to the magnitude of the overthrow.*' Before the war is over, upwards of a million of men will have lost their lives in order that Slavery might try its experiment of establishing an independent slave empire. A million of men! And there are not four millions of slaves in the country! We will not take into account the treasure expended, — the lands desolated, — the taxes heaped upon the people, — the ruin and anguish inflicted. It strikes me the price we have paid is big enough to offset the vastness of the social change. And, after all, it is not such a formidable job when you consider that there are not forty thousand men in the whole country who severally own as many as ten slaves. Why, in a single campaign we lose more soldiers than there are slaveholders having any considerable stake in the institution. Experience has proved that there could be universal emancipation to-morrow without bad results to either master or slave, — with advantage, on the contrary, to both."*

"Well, Mr. Vance, we will suppose the Mississippi opened; New Orleans, Mobile, Charleston, and Richmond captured, — the Rebellion on its last legs; — what then?"

"With the capture of New Orleans and Vicksburg, and the opening of the Mississippi, you have Secessia on the hip, and her utter subjugation is merely a question of time. When she cries *peccavi*, and offers to give in, I would say to the people of the Rebel States: '*First*, Slavery, the cause of this war, must be surrendered, to be disposed of at the discretion of the victors. *Secondly*, you must so modify your constitutions that Slavery can never be re-established among you. *Thirdly*,

* Our experience in South Carolina and Louisiana proves that there would be no danger, but, on the contrary, great good in instant emancipation.

every anti-republican feature in your State governments must be abandoned. *Fourthly*, every loyal man must be restored to the property and the rights you may have robbed him of. *Fifthly*, no man offensively implicated in the Rebellion must represent any State in Congress. *Sixthly*, no man must be taxed against his will for any debt incurred through rebellion against the United States. Under these easy and honorable terms, I would readmit the seceded States to the Union; and if these terms are refused, I would occupy and hold the States as conquered territory."

"And could we reconcile such a course with a due regard to law?"

"Surely yes; for the people in rebellion are at once subjects and belligerents. They are public enemies, and as such are entitled only to such privileges as we may choose to concede. They are subjects, and as such must fulfil their obligations to the Republic."

"But you say nothing of confiscation," Mr. Vance.

"I would be as generous as possible in this respect, Mr. President. Loyal men who have been robbed by the secession fury must of course be reimbursed, and the families of those who have been hung for their loyalty must be provided for. I see no fairer way of doing this than by making the robbers give up their plunder, and by compelling the murderers to contribute to the wants of those they have orphaned. But beyond this I would be governed by circumstances as they might develop themselves. I would practice all the clemency and forbearance consistent with justice. Those landholders who should lend themselves fairly and earnestly to the work of substituting a system of paid labor for slavery should be entitled to the most generous consideration and encouragement, whatever their antecedents might have been. I would do nothing for vengeance and humiliation; everything for the benefit of the Southern people themselves and their posterity. Questions of indemnification should not stand in the way of a restored Union."

"Undoubtedly, Mr. Vance, the interests of the masses, North and South, are identical."

"That is true, Mr. President, but it is what the Rebel leaders try to conceal from their dupes. The most damnable effect of slavery has been the engendering at the South of that large class of mean whites, proud, ignorant, lazy, squalid, and brutally degraded, who yet feel that they are a sort of aristocracy because they are not niggers. Having produced this class, Slavery now sees it must rob them of all political rights. Hence the avowed plan of the Secession leaders to have either a close oligarchical or a monarchical government. The thick skulls of these mean whites (or if not of them, of their children) we must reach by help of the schoolmaster, and let them see that their interests lie in the elevation of labor and in opposition to the theories of the shallow *dilettanti* of the South, who, claiming to be great political thinkers and philosophers, maintain that capital ought to own labor, and that there must be a hereditary servile race, if not black, then white, in whom all mental aspiration and development shall be discouraged and kept down, in order that they may be content to be hewers of wood and drawers of water. As if God's world-process were kept up in order that a few Epicurean gentlemen may have a good time of it, and send their sons to Paris to eat sumptuous dinners and attend model-artist entertainments, while thousands are toiling to supply the means for their base pleasures. As if a Frederick Douglas must be brutified into a slave in order that a Slidell may give Sybarite banquets and drive his neat span through the Champs Elysées!"

"What should we do with the blacks after we had freed them?"

"Let them alone! Let them do for themselves. The difficulties in the way are all those of the imagination."

"I like the moderation of your views as to confiscation."

"When the mass of the people at the South," continued Vance, "come to see, as they will eventually, that we have been fighting the great battle of humanity and of freedom, for the South even more than for the North, for the white man even more than for the black, there will be such a reaction as will obliterate every trace of rancor that internecine war has begotten. But I have talked too much. I have occupied too much of your time."

"O no! I delight to meet with men who come to me,

thinking how they may benefit, not themselves, but their country. The steam-tugs you gave us off the mouths of the Mississippi we would gladly have paid thirty thousand dollars for. I wish I could meet your views in regard to the enlistment of black troops; but — but — that pear is n't yet ripe. Failing that, you shall have any place you want in the Butler and Farragut expedition against New Orleans. As for your young friends, — what did you say their names are?"

"Robert Onslow and Charles Kenrick."

"O yes! Onslow, you say, has been a captain in the Rebel service. Both the young men shall be honorably placed where they can distinguish themselves. I 'll speak to Stanton about them this very day. Let me make a note of it."

The President drew from his pocket a memorandum-book and hastily wrote a line or two. Vance rose to take his leave.

"Mr. President," said he, "I thank you for this interview. But there 's one thing in which you 've disappointed me."

"Ah! you think me rather a slow coach, eh?"

"Yes; but that was n't what I alluded to."

"What then?"

"From what I 've read about you in the newspapers, I expected to have to hear one of your stories."

A smile full of sweetness and *bonhommie* broke over the President's care-worn face as he replied: "Really! Is it possible? Have you been here all this time without my telling you a story? Sit down, Mr. Vance, and let me make up for my remissness."

Vance resumed his seat.

The President ran his fingers through his long, carelessly disposed hair, pushing it aside from his forehead, and said: "Once on a time the king of beasts, the lion, took it into his head he would travel into foreign parts. But before leaving his kingdom he installed an old 'coon as viceroy. The lion was absent just four months to a day; and on his return he called all the principal beasts to hear their reports as to the way in which affairs had been managed in his absence. Said the fox, 'You left an old imbecile to rule us, sire. No sooner were you gone than a rebellion broke out, and he appointed for our leader a low-born mule, whose cardinal maxim in military matters was to put off till to-morrow whatever could be just as well done to-day; whose policy was a masterly inactivity instead of a straightforward movement on the enemy's works.' Said the sheep, 'The 'coon could have had peace if he had listened to me and others who wanted to draw it mild and to compromise. Such a bloodthirsty wretch as the 'coon ought to be expelled from civilized society.' Said the horse, 'He is too slow.' Said the ox, 'He is too fast.' Said the jackass, 'He does n't know how to bray; he can't utter an inspiring note.' Said the pig, 'He is too full of his jokes and stories.' Said the magpie, 'He is a liar and a thief.' Said the owl, 'He is no diplomatist.' Said the tiger, 'He is too conservative.' Said the beaver, 'He is too radical.' 'Stop!' roared the king,—'shut up, every beast of you!' At once there was silence in the assembly. Then, turning to his viceroy, the lion said, 'Old 'coon, I wish no better proof that you have been faithful than all this abuse from opposite parties. You have done so well, that you shall be reinstalled for another term of four months!'"

"And what did the old 'coon say to that?" asked Vance.

"The old 'coon begged to be excused, protesting that he had experienced quite enough of the charms of office."

The President held out his hand. Vance pressed it with a respectful cordiality, and withdrew from the White House.

CHAPTER XXXVII.

COMPARING NOTES.

"But thou art fled, ...
Like some frail exhalation which the dawn
Robes in its golden beams, — ah ! thou hast fled ;
The brave, the gentle, and the beautiful,
The child of grace and genius ! "
Shelley.

NOT many weeks after the conversation (not altogether imaginary) at the White House, a young man in the uniform of a captain lay on the sofa in a room at Willard's Hotel in Washington. He lay reading a newspaper, but the paleness of his face showed that he had been suffering either from illness or a serious wound. This young man was Onslow. In a cavalry skirmish at Winchester, in which the Rebels had been handsomely routed, he had been shot through the lungs, the ball coming out at his back. There was one chance in a thousand that the direction taken by the ball would be such that the wound should not prove fatal; and this thousandth chance happened in his favor. Thanks to a naturally vigorous constitution, he was rapidly convalescing. He began to be impatient once more for action.

There was a knock at the door, and Vance entered.

"How is our cavalry captain to-day?" he asked cheerily.

"Better and better, my dear Mr. Vance."

"Let me feel of his pulse. Excellent! Firm, regular! Appetite?"

"Improving daily. He ate two boiled eggs and a lamb chop for breakfast, not to speak of a slice of aerated bread."

"Come now, — that will do. He will be ready soon for a bullet through his other lung. But he must not get restless. There 's plenty of fighting in store for him."

"Mr. Vance, I 've been pondering the strange story of your life; your interview with my father on board the Pontiac; the loss of the Berwicks; the supposed loss of their child; the developments by which you were led to suspect that the child was kidnapped; Peek's unavailing search for the rascal Hyde; the interview with Quattles, confirming your suspicion of foul play; and finally your interview last week in New York with the mulatto woman, Hattie Davy. Let me ask if Hattie thinks she could still identify the lost child."

"Yes, by certain marks on her person. She at once recognized the little sleeve-button I got from Quattles."

"Please let me look at it."

Vance took from his pocket a small circular box which he unscrewed, and there, in the centre of a circle of hair, lay the button. He handed the box to the wounded soldier. At this moment Kenrick entered the room.

"Ha, Lieutenant! What 's the news?" exclaimed Vance.

"Ask any one but me," returned Kenrick. "Have I not been all the morning trying guns at the navy-yard? What have you there, Robert! A lock of hair? Ah! I have seen that hair before."

"Impossible!" said Vance.

"Not at all!" replied Kenrick. "The color is too peculiar to be confounded. Miss Perdita Brown wore a bracelet of that hair the last evening we met her at the St. Charles."

"Again I say, impossible," quoth Vance. "Something like it perhaps, but not this. How could she have come by it?"

"Cousin," replied Kenrick, "I 'm quick to detect slight differences of color, and in this case I 'm sure."

Suddenly the Lieutenant noticed the little sleeve-button in Onslow's hand, and, while the blood mounted to his forehead, turning to him said, "How did you come by *this*, Robert?"

"Why do you ask with so much interest?" inquired Vance.

"Because that same button I 've seen worn by Perdita."

"Now I know you 're raving," said Vance; "for, till now, it has n't been out of my pocket since Quattles gave it me."

"Do you mean to say," exclaimed Kenrick, "that this is the jewel of which you told me; that which belonged to the lost infant of the Pontiac?"

"Yes; her nurse identifies it. Undoubtedly it is one of a pair worn by poor little Clara."

"Then," said Kenrick, with the emphasis of sudden conviction, "Clara and Perdita are one and the same!"

Startling as a severe blow was this declaration to Vance. It forced upon his consideration a possibility so new, so strange, so distressing, that he felt crushed by the thought that there was even a chance of its truth. Such an opportunity, thrust, as it were, by Fate under his eyes, had it been allowed to escape him? His emotions were those of a blind man, who being suddenly restored to sight, learns that he has passed by a treasure which another has picked up. He paced the room. He struck his arms out wildly. He pushed up the sleeves of his coat with an objectless energy, and then pulled them down.

"O blind mole!" he groaned, "too intent on thy own little burrow to see the stars out-shining! O beast with blinders! looking neither on the right nor on the left, but only straight before thy nose!"

And then, as if ashamed of his ranting, he sat down and said: "How strange that this possibility should never have occurred to me! I saw there was a mystery in the poor girl's fate, and I tried to make her disclose it. Had I only seen her that last day I called, I should have extorted her confidence. Once or twice during our interviews she seemed on the point of telling me something. Then she would check herself, as if from some prompting of delicacy or of caution. To think that I should have been so inconsiderate! To think, too, that I should have been duped by that heartless lay-figure for dressmakers and milliners, Miss Tremaine! Yes! I almost dread to look further lest I should be convinced that Charles is right, and that Clara Berwick and Perdita Brown are one and the same person. If so, the poor girl we all so admired is a slave!"

"A slave!" gasped Kenrick, struck to the heart by the cruel word, and turning pale.

"I'd like to see the man who'd venture to style himself her master in my presence!" cried Onslow, forgetting his wound, and half rising from the sofa.

"Soft!" said Vance. "We may be too hasty in our conclusion. There may be sleeve-buttons by the gross, precisely of this pattern, in the shops."

"No!" replied Kenrick. "Coral of that color is what you

do not often meet with. Such a delicate flesh tint is unusual. You cannot convince me that the mate of this button is not the one worn by the young lady we knew as Perdita. Perhaps, too, it is marked like the other pair. If so, it ought to have on it the letters —"

"What letters?" exclaimed Vance, fiercely, arresting Kenrick's hand so he could not examine the button.

"The letters C. A. B.," replied Kenrick.

"Good heavens, yes!" ejaculated Vance, releasing him, and sinking into an arm-chair. And then, after several seconds of profound sighing, he drew forth from his pocket-book an envelope, and said: "This contains the testimony of Hattie Davy in regard to certain personal marks that would go far to prove identity. One of these marks I distinctly remember as striking my attention in Clara, the child, and yet I never noticed it in the person we knew as Perdita. Could I have failed to remark it, had it existed?"

"Why not?" answered Kenrick. "Your thoughts are too intent on public business for you to apply them very closely to an examination of the personal graces or defects of any young woman, however charming."

"Tell me, Captain," said Vance to Onslow, "did you ever notice in Perdita any physical peculiarity, in which she differed from most other persons?"

"I merely noticed she was peculiarly beautiful," replied Onslow; "that she wore her own fine, rich, profuse hair exclusively, instead of borrowing tresses from the wig-maker, as nine tenths of our young ladies do now-a-days; that her features were not only handsome in themselves by those laws which a sculptor would acknowledge, but lovely from the expression that made them luminous; that her form was the most symmetrical; her —"

"Enough, Captain!" interrupted Vance. "I see you did not detect the peculiarity to which I allude. Now tell me, cousin, how was it with *you*? Were you more penetrating?"

"I think I know to what you refer," replied Kenrick. "Her eyes were of different colors; one a rich dark blue, the other gray."

"Fate! yes!" exclaimed Vance, dashing one hand against the other. "Can you tell me which was blue?"

"Yes, the left was blue."

Vance took from the envelope a paper, and unfolding it pointed to these lines which Onslow and Kenrick perused together: —

Vance. "You tell me one of her eyes was dark blue, the other dark gray. Can you tell me which was blue?"

Hattie. "Yes; for I remember a talk about it between the father and the mother. The father had blue eyes, the mother gray. The mother playfully boasted that the eye of *her* color was the child's *right* eye; to which the father replied, 'But the *left* is nearest the heart.' And so, sir, remembering that conversation, I can swear positively that the child's left eye was the blue one."

"Rather a striking concurrence of testimony!" said Onslow. "I wonder I should never have detected the oddity."

"Let me remark," replied Kenrick, "that it required a near observation to note the difference in the hue of the eyes. Three feet off you would hardly discriminate. The depth of shade is nearly equal in both. You might be acquainted with Perdita a twelvemonth and never heed the peculiarity. So do not, cousin, take blame to yourself for inattention."

"Do you remember, Charles," said Vance, "our visit to the hospital the day after our landing in New York?"

"Yes, I shall never forget the scene," replied Kenrick.

"Do you remember," continued Vance, "among the nurses quite a young girl, who, while carrying a salver of food to a wounded soldier, was asked by you if you should not relieve her of the burden?"

"Yes; and her reply was, 'Where are your shoulder-straps?' And she eyed me from head to foot with provoking coolness. 'I'm on my way to Washington for them,' answered I. 'Then you may take the salver,' said the little woman, graciously thrusting it into my hands."

"Well, Charles, when I was in New York last week, I saw that same little woman again, and found out who she is. How strangely, in this kaleidoscope of events which we call the world, we are brought in conjunction with those persons between whose fate and our own Chance or Providence seems to tender a significance which it would have us heed and solve!

This girl was a Miss Charlton, the daughter of that same Ralph Charlton who holds the immense estate that rightfully belongs to our lost Clara."

"Would he be disposed to surrender it?" asked Onslow.

"Probably not. I took pains while in New York to make inquiries. I learnt that his domestic *status* is far from enviable. He himself, could he follow his heart's proclivities, would be a miser. Then he could be happy and contented — in his way. But this his wife will not allow. She forces him by the power of a superior will into expenses at which his heart revolts, although they do not absorb a fifth part of his income. The daughter shrinks from him with an innate aversion which she cannot overcome. And so, unloving and unloved, he finds in his own base avarice the instrument that scourges him and keeps him wretched."

"I should not feel much compunction in compelling such a man to unclutch his riches," remarked Onslow.

"It will be very difficult to do that, I fear," said Vance, "even supposing we can find and identify the true heir."

"We must find her, cost what it may!" cried Kenrick. "Cousin, take me to New Orleans with you."

"No, Charles. You are wanted here on the Potomac. Your reputation in gunnery is already high. The country needs more officers of your stamp. You cannot be spared. The Captain here can go with me to the Gulf. He is wounded and entitled to a furlough. A trip to New Orleans by sea will do him good."

With a look of grave disappointment Kenrick took up a newspaper and kept his face concealed by it for a moment. Then putting it down, and turning to Vance, he said, with a sweet sincerity in his tone: "Cousin, where my wishes are so strongly enlisted, you can judge better than I of my duty. I yield to your judgment, and, if you persist in it, will make no effort to get from government the permission I covet."

"Truly I think your place is here," said Vance.

A servant entered with a letter. It was for Vance. He opened it, and finding it was from Peek, read as follows: —

"New Orleans, February, 1862.

"Dear Mr. Vance: On leaving you at the Levee I drove straight for the stable where my horses belonged. I passed the night with my friend Antoine, the coachman. The next day I went to your house, where I have stayed with those kind people, the Bernards, ever since.

"Please inform Mr. Winslow I duly attended to his commissions. What will seem strange to you is the fact that in attending to his affairs I am attending to yours. Two days after your departure the newspapers contained flaming accounts of the treacherous seizure of the Artful Dodger by Messrs. Vance, Winslow, & Co., — their pursuit by the Rebel, the encounter, the Rebel's discomfiture, the 'abduction' of Mr. Ratcliff, the funeral of his poor wife, etc. Seeing that Mr. Ratcliff was absent, I thought the opportunity favorable for me to call at his house on the quadroon lady, Madame Volney, to whom Mr. Winslow had commended me. I went and found in the servant who opened the door an old acquaintance, Esha, whom years ago you sought for in vain. She was here keeping watch over a white slave.

"And who is the white slave? you will ask. Ah! there 's the mystery. Who *is* she indeed! In the first place, she is claimed by Ratcliff; in the next, she and Madame Volney are the residuary legatees of the late Mrs. Ratcliff; in the next, she is the young lady who has been staying with Miss Tremaine at the St. Charles."

Here there was a cry of pain from Vance, so sharp and sudden that Kenrick started forward to his relief.

"What 's the matter? Is it bad news?" inquired Onslow.

"I 'll finish reading the letter by myself," replied Vance, taking his departure without ceremony.

Seated in his own apartment, he continued the reading: —

"Do not think me fanciful, Mr. Vance, but the moment I set eyes on this young woman the conviction struck me, She is the lost Clara for whom we are seeking. The coincidence of age and the fact that I have had the search of her on my mind, may fully explain the impression. *May.* But you know I believe in the phenomena of Spiritualism. *Belief* is not the right word. *Knowledge* would be nearer the truth.

"There is here in New Orleans a young man named Bender who calls himself a *medium.* He is a worthless fellow, and I have several times caught him cheating. But he nevertheless gives me glimpses of spiritual powers. There are some plain cases in which cheating is impossible. For instance, if without throwing out any previous hint, however remote, I think of twenty different persons in succession, my knowledge of whom is a secret in my own brain, and if I say to a medium, 'Of what person am I thinking now?' and if the medium instantly, without hesitation or inquiry, gives me the right reply twenty times in succession, I may reasonably conclude — may I not? — that the power is what it appears to be, and that the medium gets his knowledge through a faculty which, if not preternatural, is very rare, and is denied as possible by science. Well, this test has been fulfilled, not once only, but more than fifty different times.*

"I got Madame Volney's consent to bring Bender to the house. After he had showed her his wonderful powers of thought-reading, we put the hand of the white slave in his, and bade him tell us her name. He wrote with great rapidity, *Clara Aylesford Berwick.* We asked her father's name. In a moment the medium's limbs twitched and writhed, his eyeballs rolled up so that their natural expression was lost, and he extended his arm as if in pain. Then suddenly dropping the girl's hand he drew up the sleeve from his right arm, and there, in crimson letters on the white skin were the words *Henry Berwick.*†

"Now whether this is the right name or not I do not know. I presume that it is; though it is rarely safe to trust a medium in such cases. The child's name I have heard you say was Clara Berwick. I have never spoken or written it except to yourself. Still Bender may have got the father's name, — the surname at least, — from my mind. But if the name *Henry* is right, where did he get *that?* I am not aware of ever having known the father's name. The check he once gave you for me you never showed me, but cashed it yourself. Still I shall not too positively claim that the name was communicated preternaturally; for experience has convinced me it may have been in my mind without my knowing it. Every thought of our lives is probably photographed on our brains, never to be obliterated. Let me study, then, to multiply my good thoughts. But in whatever way Bender got the name, whether from my mind or from a spirit, the fact is interesting and important in either case.

"The effect upon Clara (for so we now all call her) of this singular event was such as to convince her instantaneously that

* The writer has fully tested it in repeated instances; and there are probably several hundred thousand persons at this moment in the United States, to whom the same species of test is a *certainty*, not merely a *belief*.

† The parallel facts are too numerous and notorious to need specification.

the name was right, and that she is the child of Henry Berwick. As soon as the medium had gone, she asked me if I could not find out who Mr. Berwick was. I then told her the story of the Pontiac, down to the recent confession of Quattles, and my own search for Colonel Delancy Hyde. All my little group of hearers — Madame Volney, Esha, and Clara — were deeply interested, as you may suppose, in the narrative. Clara was much moved when she learnt that the same Mr. Vance, whose acquaintance she had made, was the one who had known the parents, and was now seeking for their daughter. She has a serene conviction that she is the identical child. When I read what you had written about different colored eyes, she simply said, 'Look, Peek!' And there they were, — blue and gray!

"Mr. Ratcliff's house is in the charge of his lawyer, Mr. Semmes, who keeps a very strict eye over all outgoings and incomings. Esha has his confidence, but he distrusts both Clara and Madame Volney. By pretending that I am her half-brother, Esha enables me to come and go unsuspected. The medium, Bender, was introduced as a chiropedist. Clara never goes out without a driver and footman, who are agents and spies of Semmes. It does not matter at present; for it would be difficult in the existing state of affairs to remove Clara out of the city without running great risk of detection and pursuit. I have sometimes thought of putting her in a boat and rowing down the river to Pass à l'Outre; but the hazard would be serious.

"As it is important to collect all the proofs possible for Clara's identification, it was at first agreed among the women that Esha should call, as if in the interests of Mr. Ratcliff, on Mrs. Gentry, the teacher, and get from that lady all the facts, dates, and memorials that may have a bearing on Clara's history. But, on reflection, I concluded it would be better to put the matter in the hands of a lawyer who could take down in legal form, with the proper attestation, all that Mrs. Gentry might have to communicate. Mr. Winslow had given me a letter of introduction to Mr. Jasper, his confidential adviser, and a loyal man. To him I went and explained what I wanted. He at once gave the business his attention. With two suitable witnesses he called on Mrs. Gentry and took down her deposition. I had told him to procure, if possible, some articles of dress that belonged to the child when first brought to the house. This he succeeded in doing. A little undershirt and frock, — a child's petticoat and pocket-handkerchief, — were among the articles, and they were all marked in white silk, C. A. B. Mrs. Gentry said that her own oath as to the clothes could be confirmed by Esha's. Esha was accordingly sent for, and she came, and, being duly sworn, identified the clothes as those the child had on when first left at the house; which clothes Esha had washed, and the child had subsequently worn. This testimony being duly recorded, the clothes were done up carefully in a paper package, to which the seals of all the gentlemen present were attached; and then the package was placed in a small leather trunk which was locked.

"I should mention one circumstance that adds fresh confirmation. In telling Miss Clara what Quattles had confessed (the details of which you give in that important letter you handed me) I alluded to the pair of sleeve-buttons. 'Was there any mark upon them?' she asked. 'Yes, the initials C. A. B.' She instantly drew forth from her bosom another pair, the counterpart probably of that described in your letter, and on one of the buttons were the same characters! Can we resist such evidences?

"Let me mention another extraordinary development. Madame Volney does not scruple to resort to all the stratagems justifiable in war to get information from the enemy. Mr. Semmes is an old fox, but not so cunning as to guard against an inspection of his papers by means of duplicate keys. In one of the drawers of the library he deposits his letters. In looking them over the other day, Madame V. found one from Mr. Semmes's brother in New York, in which the fact is disclosed that this house, hired by Mr. Ratcliff, belonged to Miss Clara's father, and ought, if the inheritance had not been fraudulently intercepted, to be now her property! Said Miss Clara to me when she learnt the fact, 'Peek, if I am ever rich, you shall have a nice little cottage overlooking my garden.' Ah! Mr. Vance, I thought of Naomi, and wondered if she would be living to share the promised fortune.

"I have a vague fear of this Mr. Semmes. Under the affectation of great frankness, he seems to me one of those men who make it a rule to suspect everybody. I have warned the women to take heed to their conversation; to remember that walls have ears. I rely much on Esha. She has, thus far, been too deep for him. He has several times tried to throw her off her guard; but has not yet succeeded. He is evidently distrustful and disposed to lay traps for us.

"It appears that Mr. Ratcliff's plan, at the time you intercepted him in his career, and had him sent North, was to offer marriage to this young girl he claims to hold as a slave. Marriage with him would plainly be as hateful to her as any other species of relation; and my present wish is to put her as soon as possible beyond his reach, lest he should any time unexpectedly return. Madame Volney is so confident in her power to save her, that Clara's anxieties seem to be much allayed; and now that she fully believes she is no slave, but the legitimate child of honorable parents, she cultivates an assurance as to her safety, which I hope is not the precursor of misfortune. The money which Mr. Winslow left in my hands for her use would be sufficient to enable us to carry out some effectual scheme of escape; but Madame Volney does not agree with me as to the importance of an immediate attempt. Will Ratcliff come back? That is the question I now daily ask myself.

"I recognized on Clara's wrist the other day a bracelet of your wife's hair. How did she come by it? The reply was simple. Esha gave it to her. Clara is very fond of questioning me about you. She has learnt from me all the particulars of your wife's tragical fate, and of the debt you yourself owe to the Slave Power. She takes the intensest interest in the war. Learning from me that my friend Cailloux was forming a secret league among the blacks in aid of the Union cause, she made me take five hundred dollars of the money left by Mr. Winslow for her in my possession, and this she sent to Cailloux with a letter. He wrote her in reply, that he wished no better end than to die fighting for the Union and for the elevation of his race.*

"I have not forgotten the importance of getting hold of Colonel Hyde. I have searched for him daily in the principal drinking-saloons, but have found no trace of him as yet. I have also kept up my search for my wife, having sent out two agents, who, I trust, may be more fortunate than I myself have been; for I sometimes think my own over-anxiety may have defeated my purpose. In making these searches I have availed myself of the means you have so generously placed at my disposal.

"The few Union men who are here are looking hopefully to the promised expedition of Farragut and Butler. But the Rebels are defiant and even contemptuous in their incredulity.

* Captain Andre Cailloux, a negro, was a well-educated and accomplished gentleman. He belonged to the First Louisiana regiment, and perished nobly at Port Hudson, May 17, 1863, leading on his men in the thickest of the fight. His body was recovered the latter part of July, and interred with great ceremony at New Orleans.

They say our fleet can never pass Forts Jackson and St. Philip. And then they have an iron ram, on the efficacy of which they largely count. Furthermore, they mean to welcome us with bloody hands, &c.; die in the last ditch, &c. We shall see. This prayer suffices for me: *God help the right!* Adieu!

"Faithfully, PEEK."

We have seen with what profound emotion Vance received the information, that the man whose formidable power was enclosing Clara in its folds was the same whose brutality had killed Estelle. Vance could no longer doubt that Clara and Perdita were identical. He looked in his memorandum-book to assure himself of the name of Clara's father. Yes! Bender was right. There were the words: *Henry Berwick.*

Then putting on his hat Vance hurried to the War Office. Would the Secretary have the goodness to address a question to the officer commanding at Fort Lafayette? Certainly: it could be done instantly by telegraph. Have the goodness to ask if Mr. Ratcliff, of New Orleans, is still under secure confinement.

The click of the telegraph apparatus in the War Office was speedily heard, putting the desired interrogatory.

"Expect a reply in half an hour," said the operator.

Vance looked at his watch, and then passed out into the paved corridor and walked up and down. He thought of Clara, — of the bracelet of his wife's hair on her wrist. It moved him to tears. Was there not something in the identity in the position of these two young and lovely women that seemed to draw him by the subtle meshes of an overruling fate to Clara's side? Could it be that Estelle herself, a guardian angel, was favoring the conjunction?

For an instant that gracious image which had so long been the light of his waking and his sleeping dreams, seemed to retire, and another to take her place; another, different, yet hardly less lovely.

For an instant, and for the second time, visions of a new domestic paradise, — of beautiful children who should call him father, — of a daughter whose name should be Estelle, — of life's evening spent amid the amenities of a refined and happy home,

— flitted before his imagination, and importuned desire. But they speedily vanished, and that other transcendent image returned and resumed its place.

Ah! it was so life-like, so real, so near and positive in its presence, that no other could be its substitute! For no other could his heart's chalice overflow with immortal love. Had she not said, —

> "And dear as sacramental wine
> To dying lips was all she said,"—

had she not said, "I shall see you, though you may not see me?" Vance took the words into his believing heart, and thenceforth they were a reality from the sense of which he could not withdraw himself, and would not have withdrawn himself if he could.

He looked again at his watch, and re-entered that inner office of the War Department, to which none but those high in government confidence were often admitted.

"We have just received a reply to your inquiry," said the clerk. "Mr. Ratcliff of New Orleans made his escape from Fort Lafayette ten days ago. The Department has taken active measures to have him rearrested."

CHAPTER XXXVIII.

THE LAWYER AND THE LADY.

"The Devil is an ass." — *Old Proverb.*

PEEK'S apprehensions in regard to Ratcliff's agent, Semmes, were not imaginary. Semmes was of the school in politics and policy of old Mr. Slidell. He did not believe in the vitality and absoluteness of right and goodness. His life maxim was, while bowing and smirking to all the world, to hold all the world as cheats. To his mind, slavery was right, because it was profitable; and inwardly he pooh-poohed at every attempt to vindicate or to condemn it from a moral or religious point of view. He laid it down as an axiom, that slavery must exist just so long as it paid.

"Worthy souls, sir, these philanthropists, — but they want the virile element, — the practical element, sir! Like women and poets, they are led by their emotions. If the world were in the hands of such softs, the old machine would be smashed up in universal anarchy."

Ah, thou blind guide! These tender souls thou scornest are they who always prevail in the long run. They prevail, because God rules through them, and because he does not withdraw himself utterly from human affairs! They prevail because Christ's doctrine of self-abnegation, and of justice and love, is the very central principle of progress, whether in the heavens or on the earth; because it is the keystone of the arch by which all things are upheld and saved from chaos. Yes, Divine duty, Charity! "Thou dost preserve the stars from wrong, — and the most ancient heavens, through thee, are fresh and strong!"

Benjamin Constant remarked of conservative Talleyrand, that had he been present at the creation of all things, he would have exclaimed, "Good God! chaos will be destroyed!" Beware of the conservatism that would impede God's work of justice and of love!

Ratcliff, in his last confidential interview with Semmes, had communicated to the lawyer all the facts which he himself was in possession of in regard to the White Slave. In the quiet of Ratcliff's library, Semmes now carefully revolved and weighed all these particulars. The fact that Clara might be wrongfully held as a slave made little impression upon him, his proper business being to conform to his client's wishes and to make his client's claim as strong as possible, without regard to any other considerations. What puzzled him greatly was Madam Volney's apparent interest in Clara; and as for Esha, she was a perfect sphinx in her impenetrability. As he pondered the question of her fidelity, the thought occurred to him, Why not learn something of her antecedents from Mrs. Gentry? A good idea!

That very evening he knocked at the door of the "select establishment." A bright-faced black boy had run up the steps in advance of him, and asked who it was he wanted to see. "Mrs. Gentry." "Well, sir, she 's in. Just give the bell a good pull." And the officious boy disappeared. A minute afterwards the lawyer was seated in the lady's presence in her little parlor.

"And have you heard from poor Mr. Ratcliff?" she asked.

"He is still in confinement, I believe, in Fort Lafayette."

"Ah! is he, poor man?" returned the lady; and it was on her mind to add: "I knew he would be come up with! I said he would be come up with!" But she repressed the exulting exclamation, and simply added: "Those horrid Yankees! Do you think, Mr. Semmes, we are in any danger from this down-east general, known as Picayune Butler?"

"Don't be under concern, Madam. He may be a sharp lawyer, but if he ever comes to New Orleans, it will be as a prisoner."

"And how is Miss Murray?"

"Never better, or handsomer. And by the way, I wish to make some inquiries respecting the colored woman Esha, who, I believe, lived some time in your family."

"Yes, Esha lived with me fifteen years. A capital cook,

and good washer and ironer. I would n't have parted with her if Mr. Ratcliff had n't been so set on borrowing her. She was here some days ago about that deposition business."

"O yes," said Semmes, thoroughly startled, yet concealing every sign of surprise, and remarking: "By the way, how did you get through with that business?"

"O, very well. Mr. Jasper and the other gentlemen were very polite and considerate."

Jasper! He was the counsel in the great case of Winslow *versus* Burrows. Probably he was now Winslow's confidential agent and adviser. Semmes's thin, wiry hands closed together, as if grasping a clew that would lead him to hidden treasures.

"I hope," said he, carefully trying his ground, "you were n't incommoded by the application."

"Not at all. I only had to refer to my account-books, which gave me all the necessary dates. And as for the child's clothes, they were in an old trunk in the garret, where they had n't been touched for fifteen years. I had forgotten all about them till Mr. Jasper asked me whether I had any such articles."

Semmes was still in the dark.

"And was Esha's testimony taken?"

"Yes, though I don't see of what use it can be, seeing that she 's a slave, and her deposition is worthless under our laws."

"To what did Esha depose?"

"Have n't you seen the depositions?"

"O yes! But not having read them carefully as yet, I should like the benefit of your recollections."

"O, Esha merely identified the girl's clothes and the initials marked upon them, — for she knows the alphabet. She also remembered seeing Mr. Ratcliff lift the child out of the barouche the day he first called here. All which was taken down."

"Could you let me see the clothes and the account-books?"

"I gave them all up to Mr. Jasper. Did n't he tell you so?"

"Perhaps. I may have forgotten."

Semmes bade Mrs. Gentry good evening.

"Headed off by all that 's unfortunate!" muttered he, as he walked away. "And by that smooth Churchman, Jasper!

Why did n't I think to hermetically seal up this Mrs. Gentry's clack, and take away all her traps and books? And Esha, — if she were n't playing false, she would have reported all this to me at once. But I 'll let the old hag see that, deep as she is, she is n't beyond the reach of my plummet. That pretended brother of hers, too! He must be looked after. I should n't wonder if he were a spy of Winslow's. I must venture upon a *coup d'état* at once, if I would defeat their plottings. How shall I manage it?"

Semmes had on his books heavy charges against Ratcliff for professional services, and did not care to jeopard their payment by any slackness in attending to that gentleman's parting injunctions. He saw he would be justified in any act of precaution, however extreme, that was undertaken in good faith towards his client. And so he resolved on two steps: one was to arrest Esha's pretended brother, and the other to withdraw Clara from the surveillance of Esha and Madame Volney.

Peek had not been idle meanwhile. For several weeks he had employed a boy to dog Semmes's footsteps; and when that enterprising lad brought word of the lawyer's visit to Mrs. Gentry's, Peek saw that his own communications with the women at Ratcliff's were cut off. He immediately sent word of the fact to Esha, and told her to redouble her caution.

Semmes waited three days in the hope that Peek would make his appearance; but at length growing impatient, took occasion to accost the impracticable Esha.

"Esha, can that brother of yours drive a carriage?"

"O yes, massa, he can do eb'ry ting."

"Well, Jim wants to go up to Baton Rouge to see his wife, and I 've no objection to hiring your brother awhile in his place."

"Dar 's noting Jake would like quite so well, massa; but how unfortnit it am! — Jake 's gone to Natchez."

"Where does Jake live when he 's here?"

"Yah, yah! Dat 's a good joke. Whar does he lib? He lib all 'bout in spots. Jake 's got more wives nor ole Brigham Young."

Finding he could make nothing out of Esha, Semmes resolved on his second precaution; for he felt that, with two plotting women against him, his charge was likely any moment to be abstracted from under his eyes. He had the letting of several vacant houses, some of them furnished. If he could secretly transfer Clara to one of these, he could guard and hold her there without being in momentary dread of her escape. He thought long and anxiously, and finally nodded his head as if the right scheme had been hit upon at last.

Clara was an early riser. Every morning, in company with Esha, she took a promenade in the little garden in the rear of the house. One morning as they were thus engaged, and Clara was noticing the indications of spring among the early buds and blossoms (though it was yet March), a woman, newly employed as a seamstress in the family, called out from the kitchen window, "O Esha! Come quick! Black Susy is trying to catch Minnie, to kill her for stealing cream." Minnie was a favorite cat, petted by Madame Volney.

"Don't let her do it, Esha!" exclaimed Clara. "Run quick, and prevent it!"

Esha ran. But no sooner had she disappeared over the threshold than Clara, who stood admiring an almond-tree in full bloom, felt a hood thrown over her face from behind, while both her hands were seized to prevent resistance. The hood was so strongly saturated with chloroform, that almost before she could utter a cry she was insensible.

When Clara returned to consciousness, she found herself lying on a bed in a large and elegant apartment. The rich Parisian furniture, the Turkish carpet, and the amber-colored silk curtains told of wealth and sumptuous tastes. Her first movement was to feel for the little dagger which she carried in a sheath in a hidden pocket. She found it was safe. The windows were open, and the pleasant morning breeze came in soft and cool.

As she raised herself on her elbow and looked about, a woman wearing the white starched linen bonnet of a Sister of Charity rose from a chair and stood before her. The face of this woman had a tender and serious expression, but the head showed a deficiency in the intellectual regions. Indeed, Sister Agatha was at once a saint and a simpleton; credulous as a child, though pious as Ignatius himself. She was not in truth a recognized member of the intelligent order whose garb she wore. She had been rejected because of those very traits she now revealed; but being regarded as harmless, she was suffered to play the Sister on her own account, procuring alms from the charitable, and often using them discreetly. Having called at Semmes's office on a begging visit, he had recognized in her a fitting tool, and had secured her confidence by a liberal contribution and an affectation of rare piety.

"How do you feel now, my dear?" asked Agatha.

"What has happened?" said Clara, trying to recall the circumstances which had led to her present position. "Who are you? Where 's Esha? Why is not Josephine here?"

"There! don't get excited," said the sister. "Your poor brain has been in a whirl, — that 's all."

"Please tell me who you are, and why I am here, and what has happened."

"I am Sister Agatha. I have been engaged by Mr. Semmes to take care of you. What has happened is, — you have had one of your bad turns, that 's all."

Clara pondered the past silently for a full minute; then, turning to the woman, said: "You would not knowingly do a bad act. I get that assurance from your face. Have they told you I was insane?"

"There, dear, be quiet! Lie down, and don't distress yourself," said Sister Agatha. "We 'll have some breakfast for you soon."

"You speak of my having had a bad turn," resumed Clara. "What sort of a bad turn? A fit?"

"Yes, dear, a fit."

"Come nearer to me, Sister Agatha. Don't you perceive an odor of chloroform on my clothes?"

"Why not? They gave it for your relief."

"No; they gave it to render me powerless, that they might bring me without a struggle to this place out of the reach of the two friends with whom I have been living. Sister Agatha, don't let them deceive you. Do I talk or look like an insane person? Do not fear to answer me. I shall not be offended."

"Yes, child, you both talk and look as if you were not in your right mind. So be a good girl and compose yourself."

Clara stepped on the floor, walked to the window, and saw that she was in the third story of a spacious house. She tried the doors. They were all locked, with the exception of one which communicated by a little entry, occupied by closets, with a corresponding room which looked out on the street from the front.

"I am a prisoner within these rooms, am I?" asked Clara.

"Yes, there 's no way by which you can get out. But here is everything comfortable, you see. In the front room you will find a piano and a case of pious books. Here is a bathing-room, where you can have hot water or cold. This door on my right leads to a billiard-table, where you can go and play, if you are good. You need not lack for air or exercise."

"When can I see Mr. Semmes?"

"He promised to be here by ten o'clock."

"Do not fail to let me see him when he comes. Sister Agatha, is there any way by which I can prove to you I am not insane?"

"No; because the more shrewd and sensible you are, the more I shall think you are out of your head. Insane people are always cunning. You have showed great cunning in all you have said and done."

"Then if I turn simple, you will think I am recovering, eh?"

"No; I shall think you are feigning. Why, I once passed a whole day with a crazy woman, and never one moment suspected she was crazy till I was told so."

"Who told you I am crazy?"

"The gentleman who engaged me to attend you, — Mr. Semmes."

"Am I crazy only on one point or on many?"

"You ought to know best. I believe you are what they call a monomaniac. You are crazy on the subject of freedom. You want to be free."

"But, Sister Agatha, if you were shut up in a house against your will, would n't you desire to be free?"

"There it is! I knew you would put things cunningly. But I 'm prepared for it. You must n't think to deceive me, child, Why not be honest, and confess your wits are wandering?"

The door of the communicating room was here unlocked.

"What 's that?" asked Clara.

"They are bringing in your breakfast," said the sister. "I hope you have an appetite."

Though faint and sick at heart, Clara resolved to conceal her emotions. So she sat down and made a show of eating.

"I will leave you awhile," said the sister. "If you want anything, you can ring."

Left to herself, Clara rose and promenaded the apartment, her thoughts intently turned inward to a survey of her position. Why had she been removed to this new abode? Plainly because Semmes feared she would be aided by her companions in baffling his vigilance and effecting her escape. Clara knelt by the bedside and prayed for light and guidance; and an inward voice seemed to say to her: "You talk of trusting God, and yet you only half trust him."

What could it mean? Clara meditated upon it long and anxiously. What had been her motive in procuring the dagger! A mixed motive and vague. Perhaps it was to take her own life, perhaps another's. Had she not reached that point of faith that she could believe God would save her from both these alternatives? Yes; she would doubt no longer. Walking to the back window she drew the dagger from its sheath and threw it far out into a clump of rose-bushes that grew rank in the centre of the area.

The key turned in the door, and Sister Agatha appeared.

"Mr. Semmes is here. Can he come in?"

"Yes. I 've been waiting for him."

The sister withdrew and the gentleman entered.

"Sit down," said Clara. "For what purpose am I confined here?"

"My dear young lady, you desire to be treated with frankness. You are sensible, — you are well educated, — you are altogether charming; but you are a slave."

"Stop there, sir! How do you know I 'm a slave?"

"Of course I am bound to take the testimony of my client, an honorable gentleman, on that point."

"Have you examined the record! Can Mr. Ratcliff produce any evidence that the child he bought was white? Look at me. Look at this arm. Do you believe my parentage is other than pure Saxon? If that does n't shake your belief, let me tell you that I have proofs that I am the only surviving child of that same Mr. and Mrs. Berwick who were lost more than fourteen years ago in a steamboat explosion on the Mississippi."

"Proofs? You have proofs? Impossible! What are they?"

"That I do not choose to tell you. Only I warn you that the proofs exist, and that you are lending yourself to a fraud in helping your client to hold me as a slave."

"My dear young lady, don't encourage such wild, romantic dreams. Some one, for a wicked purpose, has put them into your head. The only child of Mr. and Mrs. Berwick was lost with them, as was clearly proved on the trial that grew out of the disaster, and their large property passed into the possession of a distant connection."

"But what if the story of the child's loss was a lie, — what if she was saved, — then kidnapped, — then sold as a slave? What if she now stands before you?"

"As a lawyer I must say, I don't see it. And even if it were all true, what an incalculable advantage the man who has millions in possession will have over any claimant who can't offer a respectable fee in advance! Who holds the purse-strings, wins. 'T is an invariable rule, my child."

"God will defend the right, Mr. Semmes; and I advise you to range yourself on his side forthwith."

"It would n't do for me to desert my client. That would be grossly unprofessional."

"Even if satisfied your client was in the wrong?"

"My dear young lady, that 's just the predicament where a lawyer's services are most needed. What can I do for you?"

"Nothing, for I 'm not in the wrong. My cause is that of justice and humanity. You cannot serve it."

"In that remark you wound my *amour propre*. Now let me put the case for my client: Accidentally attending an auction he buys an infant slave. He brings her up tenderly and well. He spares no expense in her education. No sooner does she reach a marriageable age, than, discarding all gratitude for his kindness, she runs away. He discovers her, and she is brought to his house. His wife dying, he proposes to marry and emancipate this ungrateful young woman. Instead of being touched by his generosity, she plots to baffle and disappoint him. Who could blame him if he were to put her up at auction to-morrow and sell her to the highest bidder?"

"If you speak in sincerity, sir, then you are, morally considered, blind as an owl; if in raillery, then you are cruel as a wolf."

"My dear young lady, you show in your every remark that you are a cultivated person; that you are naturally clever, and that education has added its polish. How charming it would be to see one so gifted and accomplished placed in that position of wealth and rank which she would so well adorn! There must never be unpleasant words between me and the future Mrs. Ratcliff, — never!"

"Then, sir, you 're safe, however angrily I may speak."

"Your pin-money alone, my dear young lady, will be enough to support half a dozen ordinary families."

Clara made no reply, and Semmes continued: "Think of it! First, the tour of Europe in princely style; then a return to the most splendid establishment in Louisiana!"

"Well, sir, if your eloquence is exhausted, you can do me a favor."

"What is it, my dear young lady?"

"Leave the room."

"Certainly. By the way, I expect Mr. Ratcliff any hour now."

"I thought he was in Fort Lafayette!" replied Clara, trying to steady her voice and conceal her agitation.

"No. He succeeded in escaping. His letter is dated Richmond."

Clara made no reply, and the old lawyer passed out, muttering: "Poor little simpleton. 'T is only a freak. No woman in her senses could resist such an offer. She 'll thank me one of these days for my anæsthetic practice."

CHAPTER XXXIX.

SEEING IS BELIEVING.

"It is a very obvious principle, although often forgotten in the pride of prejudice and of controversy, that what has been seen *by one pair of human eyes* is of force to countervail all that has been reasoned or guessed at by a thousand human understandings." — *Rev. Thomas Chalmers.*

WHEN, after some detention, Esha returned to the garden, and could not see Clara, she ran up-stairs and sought her in all the rooms. Then returning to the garden she looked in the summer-house, in the grape-arbor, everywhere without avail. Suddenly she caught sight of a small black girl, a sort of under-drudge in the kitchen, who was standing with mouth distended, showing her white teeth, and grinning at Esha's discomfiture. It was the work of a moment for Esha to seize the hussy, drag her into the wash-house, and by the aid of certain squeezings, liberally applied to her cervical vertebræ, to compel her to extrude the fact that Missie Clara had been forcibly carried off by two men, and placed in a carriage, which had been driven fast away.

When Esha communicated this startling information to Madame Volney, the wrath of the latter was terrible to behold. It was well for Lawyer Semmes that his good stars kept him that moment from encountering the quadroon lady, else a sudden stop might have been put to his professional usefulness.

After she had recovered from her first shock of anger, she asked: "Why has n't Peek been here these five days?"

"'Cause he 'cluded 't wan't safe," replied Esha. "He seed ole Semmes war up ter su'thin, an' so he keep dark."

"Well, Esha, we must see Peek. You know where he lives?"

"Yes, Missis, but we mus' be car'ful 'bout lettin' anybody foller us."

"We can look out for that. Come! Let us start at once."

The two women sallied forth into the street, and proceeded

some distance, Esha looking frequently behind with a caution that proved to be not ill-timed. Suddenly she darted across the street, and going up to a negro-boy who stood looking with an air of profound interest at some snuff-boxes and pipes in the window of a tobacconist, seized him by the wool of his head and pulled him towards a carriage-stand, where she accosted a colored driver of her acquaintance, and said: "Look har, Jube, you jes put dis little debble ob a spy on de box wid yer, and gib him a twenty minutes' dribe, an' den take him to Massa Ratcliff's, open de door, an' pitch him in, an' I 'll gib yer half a dollar ef yer 'll do it right off an' ahx no questions; an' ef he dars ter make a noise you jes put yer fingers har, — dy'e see, — and pinch his win'pipe tight. Doan let him git away on no account whatsomebber."

"Seein' as how jobs air scarss, Esha, doan' car ef I do; so hahnd him up."

Esha lifted the boy so that Jube could seize him by the slack of his breeches and pull him howling on to the driver's seat. Then promising a faithful compliance with Esha's orders, he received the half-dollar with a grin, and drove off. Rejoining Madame Volney, Esha conducted her through lanes and by-streets till they stopped before the house occupied by Peek. He was at home, and asked them in.

"Are you sure you were n't followed?" was his first inquiry. Esha replied by narrating the summary proceedings she had taken to get rid of the youth who had evidently been put as a spy on her track.

"That was well done, Esha," said Peek. "Remember you 've got the sharpest kind of an old lawyer to deal with; and you must skin your eyes tight if you 'spect to 'scape being tripped."

"Wish I 'd thowt ob dat dis mornin', Peek; for ole Semmes has jes done his wustest, — carried off dat darlin' chile, Miss Clara."

Peek could hardly suppress a groan at the news.

"Now what 's to be done?" said Madame Volney. "Think of something quickly, or I shall go mad. That smooth-tongued Semmes, — O that I had the old scoundrel here in my grip! Can't you find out where he has taken that dear child?"

"That will be difficult, I fear," said Peek; "difficult for the reason that Semmes will be on the alert to baffle us. He will of course conclude that some of us will be on his track. He would turn any efforts we might make to dog him directly against us, arresting us when we thought ourselves most secure, just as the boy-detective was arrested by Esha."

"But what if Ratcliff should return?"

"That 's what disturbs me; for the papers say he has escaped."

"Then he may be here any moment?"

"For that we must be prepared."

"But that is horrible! I pledged my word — my very life — that the poor child should be saved from his clutches. She *must* be saved! Money can do it, — can't it?"

"Brains can do it better."

"Let both be used. Is not this a case where some medium can help us? Why not consult Bender?"

"There is, perhaps, one chance in a hundred that he might guide us aright," said Peek. "That chance I will try, but I have little hope he will find her. During the years I have been searching for my wife I have now and then sought information about her from clairvoyants; but always without success. The kingdom of God cometh not with observation. So with these spiritual doings. Look for them, and you don't find them. Don't look, and they come. I once knew a colored boy, a medium, who was lifted to the ceiling before my eyes in the clear moonlight. A white man offered him a hundred dollars if he would show him the same thing; but it could n't be. No sooner had the white man gone than the boy was lifted, while the rest of us were not expecting it, and carried backward and forward through the air for a full minute. Seeing is believing."

"But we 've no time for talking, Peek. We must act. *How* shall we act?"

"Can you give me any article of apparel which Miss Clara has recently worn, — a glove, for instance?"

"Yes, that can easily be got."

"Send it to me at once. Send also a glove which the lawyer has worn. Do not let the two come in contact. And be careful your messenger is not tracked."

" Do you mean to take the gloves to a clairvoyant ? "

" Not to a clear-see'er, but to a clear-smeller, — in short, to a four-footed medium, a bloodhound of my acquaintance."

" O, but what hound can keep the scent through our streets ? "

" If any one can, Victor can."

" Well, only do something, and that quickly, for I 'm distracted," said Madame Volney, her tears flowing profusely. " Come, Esha, we 'll take a carriage at the corner, and drive home."

" Not at the corner ! " interposed Peek. " Go to some more distant stand. Move always as if a spy were at your heels."

The two women passed into the street. Half an hour afterwards Esha returned with the glove. There was a noise of firing.

" Dem guns am fur de great vict'ry down below," said Esha. " De Yankees, dey say, hab been beat off han'some at Fort Jackson ; an' ole Farragut he 's backed out ; fines he can't come it. But, jes you wait, Peek. Dese Yankees hab an awful way of holdin' on. Dey doan know when dey air fair beat. Dey crow loudest jes when dey owt ter shut up and gib in."

Esha slipped out of the house, looking up and down the street to see if she were watched, and Peek soon afterwards passed out and walked rapidly in the direction of St. Genevieve Street. The great thoroughfares were filled with crowds of excited people. The stars and bars, emblem of the perpetuity of slavery, were flaunted in his face at every crossing. The newspapers that morning had boasted how impregnable were the defences. The hated enemy — the mean and cowardly Yankees — had received their most humiliating rebuff. Forts Jackson and St. Philip and the Confederate ram had proved too much for them.

Peek stopped at a small three-story brick house of rather shabby exterior and rang the bell. The door was opened by an obese black woman with a flaming red and yellow handkerchief on her head. In the entry-way a penetrating odor of fried sausages rushed upward from the kitchen and took him by the throat.

" Does Mr. Bender board here ? "

"Yes, sar, go up two pair ob stairs, an' knock at de fust door yer see, an' he 'll come."

Peek did as he was directed. "*J. Bender, Consulting Medium*," appeared and asked him in. A young and not ill-looking man, in shabby-genteel attire. Shirt dirty, but the bosom ornamented with gold studs. Vest of silk worked with sprigs of flowers in all the colors of the rainbow. His coat had been thrown off. His pantaloons were of the light-blue material which the war was making fashionable. He was smoking a cigar, and his breath exhaled a suspicion of whiskey.

"How is business, Mr. Bender?" asked Peek.

"Very slim just now," said Bender. "This war fills people's minds. Can I do anything for you to-day?"

"Yes. You remember the young woman at the house I took you to the other day, — the one whose name you said was Clara?"

"I remember. She paid me handsomely. Much obliged to you for taking me. Will you have a sip of Bourbon?"

"No, thank you. I don't believe in anything stronger than water. I want to know if you can tell me where in the city that young lady now is."

Bender put down his cigar, clasped his hands, laid them on the table, and closed his eyes. In a minute his whole face seemed transfigured. A certain sensual expression it had worn was displaced by one of rapt and tender interest. The lids of the eyes hung loosely over the uprolled balls. He looked five years younger. He sighed several times heavily, moved his lips and throat as if laboring to speak, and then seemed absorbed as if witnessing unspeakable things. He remained thus four or five minutes, and then put out his hands and placed them on one of Peek's.

"Ah! this is a good hand," said the young seer; "I like the feel of it. I wish his would speak as well of him."

"Of whom do you mean?"

"Of this one whose hands are on yours. Ah! he is weak and you are strong. He knows the right, but he will not do the right. He knows there is a heaven, and yet he walks hellward."

"Can we not save him?" asked Peek.

"No. His own bitter experiences must be his tutor."

"Why will he try to deceive," asked Peek; — "to deceive sometimes even in these manifestations of his wonderful gift?"

"You see it is the very condition of that gift that he should be impressible to influences whether good or bad. He takes his color from the society which encamps around him. Sometimes, as now, the good ones come, and then so bitterly he bewails his faults! Sometimes the bad get full possession of him, and he is what they will, — a drunkard, a liar, a thief, a scoffer. Yes! I have known him to scoff at these great facts which make spirit existence to him a certainty."

"Can I help him in any way? Will money aid him to throw off the bad influences?"

"No. Poor as he is, he has too much money. He does n't know the true uses of it. He must learn them through suffering. Leave him to the discipline of the earth-life. You know what that is. How much you have passed through! How sad, and yet how brave and cheerful you have been! It all comes to me as I press the palm of your hand. Ah! you have sought her so long and earnestly! And you cannot find her! And you think she is faithful to you still!"

"Yes, and neither mortal nor spirit could make me think otherwise. But tell me where I shall look for her."

The young man lifted the black hand to his white forehead and pressed the palm there for a moment, and then, with a sigh, laid it gently on the table, and said: "It is of no use. I get confused impressions, — nothing clear and forcible. Why have you not consulted me before about your wife?"

"Because, first, I wished to leave it to you to find out what I wanted; and this you have done at last. Secondly, I did not think I could trust you, or rather the intelligences that might speak through you. But you have been more candid than I expected. You have not pretended, as you often do, to more knowledge than you really possess."

"The reason is, that I am now admitted into a state where I can look down on myself as from a higher plane; so that I feel like a different being from myself, and must distinguish between *me*, as I now *am*, and *him* as he usually *is*. Do you know what is truly the hell of evil-doers? *It is to see them-*

*selves as they are, and God as he is.** These tame preachers rave about hell-fire and lakes of sulphur. What poor, feeble, halting imaginations they have Better beds of brimstone than a couch of down on which one lies seeing what he might have been, but is n't, — then seeing what he *is!* But pardon me; your mind is preoccupied with the business on which you came. You are anxious and impatient."

"Can you tell me," asked Peek, "what it is about?"

The clairvoyant folded his arms, and, bending down his head, seemed for a minute lost in contemplation. Then looking up (if that can be said of him while his external eyes were closed), he remarked: "The bloodhound will put you through. Only persevere."

"And is that all you can tell me?" inquired Peek.

"Yes. Why do you seem disappointed?"

"Because you merely give me the reflection of what is in my own mind. You offer me no information which may not have come straight from your own power of thought-reading. You show me no proof that your promise may not be simply the product of my own sanguine calculations."

"I cannot tell you how it is," replied the clairvoyant; "I say what I am impressed to say. I cannot argue the point with you, for I have no reasons to give."

"Then I must go. What shall I pay?"

"Pay him his usual fee, two dollars. Not a cent more."

The clairvoyant sighed heavily, and leaning his elbows on the table, covered his face with his hands. He remained in this posture for nearly a minute. Suddenly he dropped his hands, shook himself, and started up. His eyes were open. He stared wildly about, then seemed to slip back into his old self. The former unctuous, villanous expression returned to his face. He looked round for his half-smoked cigar, which he took up and relighted.

Peek drew two dollars from a purse, and offered them to him.

"I reckon you can afford more than that," said Mr. Bender.

"That 's your regular fee," replied Peek. "I have n't been here half an hour."

* The actual definition given by E. A., one of the Rev. Chauncy Hare Townshend's mesmerized subjects.

"O well, we won't dispute about it," said the medium, thrusting the rags into a pocket of his vest.

Peek left the house, the dinner-bell sounding as he passed out, and another whiff from the breath of the sausage-fiend that presided over that household pursuing him into the street.

The course he now took was through stately streets occupied by large and showy houses. He stopped before one, on the door-plate of which was the name, Lovell. Here his friend Lafour lived as coachman. For two weeks they had not met. Peek was about to pass round and ring at the servant's door on the basement story of the side, when an orange was thrown from an upper window and fell near his feet. He looked up. An old black woman was gesticulating to him to go away. Peek was quick to take a hint. He strolled away as far as he could get without losing sight of the house. Soon he saw the old woman hobble out and approach him. He slipped into an arched passage-way, and she joined him.

"What 's the matter, mother?"

"Matter enough. De debble's own time, and all troo you, Peek. I 'se been watchin' fur yer all de time dese five days."

"Explain yourself. How have I brought trouble on Antoine?"

"Dat night you borrid de ole man's carriage, — dat was de mischief. Policeman come las' week, an' take Antoine off ter de calaboose. Tree times dey lash him ter make him tell whar dey can find you; but he tell 'em, so help him God, he dun know noting 'bout yer."

Peek reflected for a moment, and then recalled the fact that Myers, the detective, had got sight of the coat-of-arms on the carriage. Yes! the clew was slight, but it was sufficient.

"My poor Antoine!" said Peek. "Must he, then, suffer for me? Tell me, mother, what has become of Victor, his dog?"

"Goramity! dat dog know more'n half de niggers. He would n't stay in dat house ahfer Antoine lef; could n't make him do it, no how."

"Where shall I be likely to find the dog?"

"'Bout de streets somewhar, huntin' fur Antoine. Ef dat dumb critter could talk, he 'd 'stonish us all."

"Well, mother, thank you for all your trouble. Here 's a dollar to buy a pair of shoes with. Good by."

The old woman's eyes snapped as she clutched the money, and with a "Bress yer, Peek!" hobbled away.

The rest of that day Peek devoted to a search for Victor. He sought him near the stable, — in the blacksmith's shop, — in the market, — at the few houses which Antoine frequented; but no Victor could be found. At last, late at night, weary and desponding, Peek retraced his steps homeward; and as he took out the door-key to enter the house, the dog he had been looking for rose from the upper step, and came down wagging his tail, and uttering a low squealing note of satisfaction.

"Why, Victor, is this you? I 've been looking for you all day."

The dog, as if he fully understood the remark, wagged his tail with increased vigor, and then checked himself in a bark which tapered off into a confidential whine, as if he were afraid of being heard by some detective.

Victor was a cross between a Scotch terrier and a thorough-bread Cuba bloodhound, imported for hunting runaway slaves. He combined the good traits of both breeds. He had the accurate scent, the large size and black color of the hound, the wiry hair, the tenacity, and the affectionate nature of the terrier. In the delicate action of his expressive nose, you saw keenness of scent in its most subtle inquisitions.

Late as was the hour, Peek (who, in the event of being stopped, had the mayor's pass for his protection) determined on an instant trial of the dog's powers, for the exercise of which perhaps the night would in this instance be the most favorable time. He took him to Semmes's office, and making him scent the lawyer's glove, indicated a wish to have him find out his trail. Victor either would not or could not understand what was wanted. He threw up his nose as if in contempt, and turned away from the glove as if he desired to have nothing to do with it. Then he would run away a short distance, and come back, and rise with his fore feet on Peek's breast. He repeated this several times, and at last Peek said: "Well, have your own way. Go ahead, old fellow."

Victor thanked him in another low whine, uttered as if addressed exclusively to his private ears, and then trotted off, assured that Peek was following. In half an hour's time, he stopped before a square whitewashed building with iron-grated windows.

"Confound you, Victor!" muttered Peek. "You 've told me nothing new, bringing me here. I was already aware your master was in jail. I can do nothing for him. Can't you do better than that? Come along!"

Returning to Semmes's office, Peek tried once more to interest the dog in the glove; but Victor tossed his nose away as if in a pet. He would have nothing to do with it.

"Come along, then, you rascal," said Peek. "We can do nothing further to-night. Come and share my room with me."

He reached home as the clock struck one. Victor followed him into the house, and eagerly disposed of a supper of bones and milk. Peek then went up to bed and threw down a mat by the open window, upon which the dog stretched himself as if he were quite as tired as his human companion.

CHAPTER XL.

THE REMARKABLE MAN AT RICHMOND.

> "Let me have men about me that are fat;
> Sleek-headed men, and such as sleep o' nights:
> Yond' Cassius has a lean and hungry look."
>
> *Shakespeare.*

YES, Ratcliff had escaped. His temper had not been sweetened by his forced visit to the North. In Fort Lafayette he had for a while given way to the sulks. Then he changed his tactics. Finding that Surgeon Mooney, though a Northern man, had conservative notions on the subject of the "nigger," he addressed himself to the work of befooling that functionary. Inasmuch as Nature had already half done it to his hands, he did not find the task a difficult one.

In his imprisonment Ratcliff had ample time for indulging in day-dreams. He grew almost maudlin over that photograph of Clara. Yes! By his splendid generosity he would bind to him forever that beautiful young girl.

He must transmit his proud name to legitimate children. He must be the founder of a noble house; for the Confederacy, when triumphant, would undoubtedly have its orders of nobility. A few years in Europe with such a wife would suit him admirably. Slidell and Mason, having been released from Fort Warren in Boston harbor, would be proud to take him by the hand and introduce him and his to the best society.

These visions came to soften his chagrin and mitigate the tediousness of imprisonment. But he now grew impatient for the fulfilment of his schemes. Delay had its dangers. True, he confided much in the vigilance of Semmes, but Semmes was an old man, and might drop off any day. A beautiful white slave was a very hazardous piece of property.

It was not difficult for Ratcliff to persuade Surgeon Mooney that his health required greater liberty of movement. At a time when, under the Davis *régime*, sick and wounded United

States soldiers, imprisoned at Richmond in filthy tobacco-warehouses, were, in repeated instances, brutally and against all civilized usages shot dead for going to the windows to inhale a little fresh air, the National authorities were tender to a degree, almost ludicrous in contrast, of the health and rights of Rebel prisoners. If any of these were troubled with a bowel complaint or a touch of lumbago, the "central despotism at Washington" was denounced, by journals hostile to the war, as responsible for the affliction, and the people were called on to rescue violated Freedom from the clutches of an insidious tyrant, even from plain, scrupulous "old Abe," son of a poor Kentuckian who could show no pedigree, like Colonel Delancy Hyde and Jefferson Davis.

A pathetic paragraph appeared in one of the newspapers, giving a piteous story of a "loyal citizen of New Orleans," who, for no namable offence, was made to pine in a foul dungeon to satisfy the personal pique of Mr. Secretary Stanton. Soon afterwards a remonstrance in behalf of this victim of oppression was signed by Surgeon Mooney. Ratcliff, whom the public sympathy had been led to picture as in the last stage of a mortal malady, was forthwith admitted to extraordinary privileges. He was enabled to communicate clandestinely with friends in New York. He soon managed to get on board a Nova Scotia coasting schooner. A week afterwards, he succeeded in running the blockade, and in disembarking safely at Wilmington, N. C.

Anxious as he was to get home, he must first go to Richmond to pay his respects to "President" Davis, of whom everybody at the South used to say to Mr. W. H. Russell of the London Times, "Don't you think our President is a remarkable man?" Ratcliff was not unknown to Davis, and sent up his card. It drew forth an immediate "Show him in." The "remarkable man" sat in his library at a small table strewn with letters and manuscripts. A thin, Cassius-like, care-burdened figure, slightly above the middle height. What some persons called dignity in his manner was in truth merely ungracious stiffness; while his *hauteur* was the unquiet arrogance that fears it shall not get its due. His face was not that of a man who could prudently afford to sneer (as he had publicly done) at Abraham Lincoln's homeliness. But before him lay letters on which the postage-stamp was an absurdly flattered likeness of himself, — as like him as the starved apothecary is like Jupiter Tonans.

In the original the cheeks were shrunken and sallow, leaving the bones high and salient. The jaws were thin and hollow; the forehead wrinkled and out of all proportion with the lower part of the face; the eyes deep-set, and one of them dulled by a severe neuralgic affection. The lips were too thin, and there was no sweetness in the mouth. The whole expression was that of one whose besetting characteristic is an intense self-consciousness.

This man could not be betrayed into the ease and *abandon* of one of nature's noblemen, for he was never thinking so much of others as of himself. The absence in him of all geniality of manner was not the reserve of a gentleman, but the frigidity of an unsympathetic and unassured heart. There was little in him of the Southern type of manhood. It is not to be wondered that bluff General Taylor could not overcome his repugnance to him as a son-in-law.

Although at the head of the Rebellion, this man had no vital faith in it; no enthusiasm that could magnetize others by a noble contagion. He was not a fanatic, like Stonewall Jackson. And yet, just previously to Ratcliff's call, he had been exercised in mind about joining the church, — a step he finally took.

He had few of the qualities of a statesman. His petty malignities overcame all sense of the proprieties becoming his station; for he would give way, even in his public official addresses, to scurrilities which had the meanness without the virility of the slang of George Sanderson, and which showed a lack of the primary elements of a heroic nature.

A man greatly overrated as to abilities. A repudiator of the sacred obligations assumed by his State, it was his added infelicity to be defended by John Slidell. Never respected for truthfulness by those who knew him best. Future historians will contrast him with President Lincoln, and will show that, while the latter surpassed him immeasurably in high moral attributes, he was also his superior in intellectual pith.

The interview between Ratcliff and Davis began with an

interchange of views on the subject of New Orleans. Each cheered the other with assurances of the impracticability of the Federal attack. After public affairs had been discussed, the so-called President said: "Excuse me for not having asked after Mrs. Ratcliff. Is she well?"

"She died some time since," replied Ratcliff.

"Indeed! In these times of general bereavement we find it impossible to keep account of our friends."

"It is my purpose, Mr. President, to marry soon again. You have yourself set the example of second nuptials, and I believe the experiment has been a happy one."

"Yes; may yours be as fortunate! Who is the lady?"

"A young person not known in society, but highly respectable and well educated. I shall have the pleasure to present her to you here in Richmond in the course of the summer."

"Mrs. Davis will be charmed to make her acquaintance. Come and help us celebrate Lee's next great victory."

"Thank you. If I can get my affairs into position, I may wish to pass the next year in Europe with my new wife. It would not be difficult, I suppose, for you to give me some diplomatic stamp that would make me pass current."

"The government will be disposed, no doubt, to meet your views. We are likely to want some accredited agent in Spain. A post that would enable you to fluctuate between Madrid and Paris would be not an unpleasant one."

"It would suit me entirely, Mr. President."

"You may rely on my friendly consideration."

"Thank you. How about foreign recognition?"

"Slidell writes favorably as to the Emperor's predispositions In England, the aristocracy and gentry, with most of the trading classes, undoubtedly favor our cause. They desire to see the Union permanently broken up, and will help us all they can. But they must do this *indirectly*, seeing that the mass of the English people, the rabble rout, even the artisans, thrown out of employment by this war, sympathize with the plebeians of the North rather than with us, the true master race of this continent, the patricians of the South."

"I'm glad to see, Mr. President, you characterize the Northern scum as they deserve, — descendants of the refuse sent over by Cromwell."

"Yes, Mr. Ratcliff, you and I who are gentlemen by birth and education, — and whose ancestors, further back than the Norman Conquest, were all gentlemen,*— can poorly disguise our disgust at any association with Yankees."

"Gladstone says you 've created a nation, Mr. President."

"Yes; Gladstone is a high-toned gentleman. His ancestors made their fortunes in the Liverpool slave-trade."

"Have you any assurances yet from Mason?"

"Nothing decisive. But the eagerness of the Ministry to humble the North in the Trent affair shows the real *animus* of the ruling classes in England. Lord John disappoints me occasionally. Bad blood there. But the rest are all right."

"A pity they could n't put their peasantry into the condition of our slaves!"

"A thousand pities! But the new Confederacy must be a Missionary to the Nations,† to teach the ruling classes throughout the world, that slavery is the normal *status* for the mechanic and the laborer. Meanwhile the friends of monarchy in Europe must foresee that such a triumph as republicanism would have in the restoration of the old Union, with slavery no longer a power in the land, and with an army and navy the first in the world, would be an appalling spectacle."

"What do you hear from Washington, Mr. President?"

"The last I heard of the gorilla, he was investigating the so-called spiritual phenomena. The letter-writers tell of a *medium* having been entertained at the White House."

Here Mr. Memminger came in to talk over the state of the Rebel exchequer, — a subject which Mr. Davis generally disposed of by ignoring; his old experience in repudiation teaching him that the best mode of fancy financiering was, — if we may descend to the vernacular, — to "go it blind."

"I 'll intrude no longer on your precious time," said Ratcliff. "I go home to send you word that the renegade Tennessean, Farragut, and that peddling lawyer from Lowell, Picayune Butler, have been spued out of the mouths of the Mississippi."

The "President" rose, pressed Ratcliff's proffered hand, and, with a stiff, angular bow, parted from him at the door.

* Mr. Davis's father was a "cavalier." He dealt in horses.

† "Reverently, we feel that our Confederacy is a God-sent missionary to the nations, with great truths to preach." —*Richmond Enquirer*.

CHAPTER XLI.

HOPES AND FEARS.

"In the same brook none ever bathed him twice:
To the same life none ever twice awoke."
Young.

THREE days after his interview with the "remarkable man," Ratcliff was at Montgomery, Ala. There he telegraphed to Semmes, and received these words in reply: "All safe. On your arrival, go first to my office for directions." Ratcliff obeyed, and found a letter telling him not to go home, but to meet Semmes immediately at the house to which the latter had transferred the white slave. Half an hour did not elapse before lawyer and client sat in the curtained drawing-room of this house, discussing their affairs.

"I cannot believe," said Ratcliff, "that Josephine intended to have the girl escape. She was the first to plan this marriage."

"I did not act on light grounds of suspicion," replied Semmes. "I had myself overheard remarks which convinced me that Madame was playing a double game. Either she or some one else has put it into the girl's head that she is not lawfully a slave, but the kidnapped child of respectable parents."

As he spoke these words Semmes looked narrowly at Ratcliff, who blenched as if at an unexpected thrust. Following up his advantage, Semmes continued: "And, by the way, there is one awkward circumstance which, if known, might make trouble. I see by examining the notary's books, that, in the record of your proprietorship, you speak of the child as a *quadroon.* Now plainly she has no sign of African blood in her veins."

Ratcliff gnawed his lips a moment, and then remarked: "The fact that the record speaks of the child as a quadroon does not amount to much. She may have been born of a quadroon mother, and may have been tanned while an infant so as to appear herself like a quadroon; and subsequently her skin may have turned fair. All that will be of little account. Half of the white slaves in the city would not be suspected of having African blood in their veins, but for the record. Who would think of disputing my claim to a slave, — one, too, that had been held by me for some fifteen years?"

Well might Ratcliff ask the question. It is true that the laws of Louisiana had some ameliorated features that seemed to throw a sort of protection round the slave; and one of these was the law preventing the separation of young children from their mothers under the hammer; and making ownership in slaves transferable, not by a mere bill of sale, like a bale of goods, but by deed formally recorded by a notary. But it is none the less true that such are the necessities of slavery that the law was often a dead letter. There was always large room for evasion and injustice; and the man who should look too curiously into transactions, involving simply the rights of the slave, would be pretty sure to have his usefulness cut short by being denounced as an Abolitionist.

The ignominious expulsion of Mr. Hoar who went to South Carolina, not to look after the rights of slaves, but of colored freemen, was a standing warning against any philanthropy that had in view the enforcement or testing of laws friendly to the blacks.

"I should not be surprised," remarked Semmes, "if this young woman either has, or believes she has, some proofs invalidating your claim to hold her as a chattel."

"Bah! I've no fear of that. Who, in the name of all the fairies, does the little woman imagine she is?"

"She cherishes the notion that she is the daughter of that same Henry Berwick who was lost in the Pontiac. Should that be so, the house you live in is hers. That would be odd, would n't it? You seem surprised. Is there any probability in the tale?"

"None whatever!" exclaimed Ratcliff, affecting to laugh, but evidently preoccupied in mind, and intent on following out some vague reminiscence.

He remembered that the infant he had bought as a slave and taken into his barouche wore a chemise on which were initial letters marked in silk. He was struck at the time by the fineness of the work and of the fabric. He now tried to recall those initial letters. By their mnemonic association with a certain word, he had fixed them in his mind. He strove to recall that word. Suddenly he started up. The word had come back to him. It was *cab*. The initials were C. A. B. Semmes detected his emotion, and drew his own inferences accordingly.

"By the way," said he, "having a little leisure last night, I looked back through an old file of the Bee newspaper, and there hit upon a letter from the pen of a passenger, written a few days after the explosion of the Pontiac."

"Indeed! One would think, judging from the trouble you take about it, you attached some degree of credence to this fanciful story."

"No. 'T is quite incredible. But a lawyer, you know, ought to be prepared on all points, however trivial, affecting his client's interests."

"Did you find anything to repay you for your search?"

"I will read you a passage from the letter; which letter, by the way, bears the initials A. L., undoubtedly, as I infer from the context, those of Arthur Laborie, whose authority no one in New Orleans will question. Here is the passage. The letter is in French. I will translate as I read:—

"'Among the mortally wounded was a Mr. Berwick of New York, a gentleman of large wealth. They had pointed him out to me the day before, as, with a wife and infant child, the latter in the arms of a nurse, a colored woman, he stood on the hurricane-deck. The wife was killed, probably by the inhalation of steam. I saw and identified the body. The child, they said, was drowned; if so, the body was not recovered. A colored boy reported, that the day after the accident he had seen a white child and a mulatto woman, probably from the wreck, in the care of two white men; that the men told him the woman was crazy, and that the child belonged to a friend of theirs who had been drowned. I give this report, in the hope it may reach the eyes of some friend of the Berwicks, though it did not seem to make much impression on the officials who conducted the investigation. Probably they had good reason for dismissing the testimony; for Mr. Berwick died in the full belief that his wife and child had already passed away.'"

"I don't see anything in all that," said Ratcliff, impatiently.

"Perhaps not," replied Semmes; "but an interested lawyer would see a good deal to set him thinking and inquiring. The letter, having been published in French, may not have met the eyes of any one to whom the information would have been suggestive."

"Really, Semmes, you seem to be trying to make out a case."

"The force of habit. 'Tis second nature for a lawyer to revolve such questions. Many big cases are built on narrower foundations."

"Psha! The incident might do very well in a romance, but 'tis not one of a kind known to actual life."

"Pardon me. Incidents resembling it are not infrequent. There was the famous Burrows case, where a child stolen by Indians was recovered and identified in time to prevent the diversion of a large property. There was the case of Aubert, where a quadroon concubine managed to substitute her own child in the place of the legitimate heir. Indeed, I could mention quite a number of cases, not at all dissimilar, and some of them having much more of the quality of romance."

"Damn it, Semmes, what are you driving at? Do you want to take a chance in that lottery?"

"Have I ever deserted a client? We must not shrink — we lawyers — from looking a case square in the face."

"Nonsense! The art how *not* to see is that which the prudent lawyer is most solicitous to learn. It is not by looking a case square in the face, but by looking only at *his* side of it, that he wins."

"On the contrary, the man of nerve looks boldly at the danger, and fends off accordingly. Should you marry this young lady, it may be a very pleasant thing to know that she's the true heir to a million."

"Curse me, but I did n't think of that!" cried Ratcliff, rubbing his hands, and then patting the lawyer on the shoulder. "Go on with your investigations, Semmes! Hunt up more information about the Pontiac. Go and see Laborie. Question Ripper, the auctioneer. I left him in Montgomery, but he will be at the St. Charles to-morrow. Find out who Quattles was;

and who the Colonel was who acted as Quattles's friend, but whose name I forget. 'T is barely possible there *may* have been some little irregularities practised; and if so, so much the better for me! What fat pickings for you, Semmes, if we could make it out that this little girl is the rightful heir! All this New Orleans property can be saved from Confederate confiscation. And then, as soon as the war is ended, we can go and establish her rights in New York."

Semmes took a pinch of snuff, and replied: "You remember Mrs. Glass's well-worn receipt for cooking a hare: 'First, catch your hare.' So I say, first make sure that the young girl will say *yes* to your proposition."

"What! do you entertain a doubt? A slave? One I could send to the auction-block to-morrow? Do you imagine she will decline an alliance with Carberry Ratcliff? Look you, Semmes! I've set my heart on this marriage more than I ever did on any other scheme in my whole life. The chance — for 't is only a remote chance — that she is of gentle blood, — well-born, the rightful heir to a million, — this enhances the prize, and gives new piquancy to an acquisition already sufficiently tempting to my eyes. There must be no such word as *fail* in this business, Mr. Lawyer. You must help me to bring it to a prosperous conclusion instantly."

"No: do not say *instantly*. Beware being precipitate. Remember what the poet says, — 'A woman's *No* is but a crooked path unto a woman's *Yes*.' Do not mind a first rebuff. Do not play the master. Be distant and respectful. Attempt no liberties. You will only shock and exasperate. By a gentle, insinuating course, you may win."

"*May* win? I *must* win, Semmes! There must be no *if* about it."

"I want to see you win, Ratcliff; but show her you assume there 's no *if* in the case, and you repel and alienate her."

"I don't know that. Most women like a man the better for being truly, as well as nominally, the lord and master. The more imperious he is, the more readily and tenaciously they cling to him. I don't believe in letting a woman suppose that she can seize the reins when she pleases."

The lawyer shrugged his shoulders, then replied: "The

tyrant is hated by every person of sense, whether man or woman. I grant you there are many women who have n't much sense. But this little lady of yours is the last in the world on whom you can safely try the experiment of compulsion. Take my word for it, the true course is to let her suppose she is free to act. You must rule her by not seeming to rule."

"Well, let me see the girl, and I can judge better then as to the fit policy. I 've encountered women before in my day. You don't speak to a novice in woman-taming. I never met but one yet who ventured to hold out against me, — and she got the worst of it, I reckon." And a grim smile passed over Ratcliff's face as he thought of Estelle.

"You will find the young lady in the room corresponding with this, on the third story," said the lawyer. "The door is locked, but the key is on the outside. Please consider that my supervision ends here. I leave the servants in the house subject to your command. The Sister Agatha in immediate attendance is a pious fool, who believes her charge is insane. She will obey you implicitly. Sam will attend to the marketing. My own affairs now claim my attention. I 've suffered largely from their neglect during your absence. Be careful not to be seen coming in or going out of this house. I have used extreme precautions, and have thus far baffled those who would help the young woman to escape."

"I shall not be less vigilant," replied Ratcliff. "I accept the keys and the responsibility. Good by. I go to let the young woman know that her master has returned."

Ratcliff seized his hat and passed out of the room up-stairs as fast as his somewhat pursy habit of body would allow.

"There goes a man who puts his hat on the head of a fool," muttered the old lawyer. "Confound him! If he were n't so deep in my books, I would leave him to his own destruction, and join the enemy. I 'm not sure this would n't be the best policy as it is."

Thus venting his anger in soliloquy Mr. Semmes quitted the house, and walked in meditative mood to his office.

Ratcliff paused at the uppermost stair on the third story. From the room came the sound of a piano-forte, with a vocal accompaniment. Clara was singing "While Thee I seek, protecting Power," — a hymn which, though written by Helen Maria Williams when she thought herself a deist, is used by thousands of Christian congregations to interpret their highest mood of devout trust and pious resignation. As the clear, out-swelling notes fell on Ratcliff's ears, he drew back as if a flaming sword had been waved menacingly before his face.

He walked down into the room below and waited till the music was over; then he boldly proceeded up-stairs again, knocked at the door, unlocked it, and entered. Clara looked round from turning the leaves of a music-book, rose, and bent upon her visitor a penetrating glance as if she would fathom the full depth of his intents. Ratcliff advanced and put out his hand. She did not take it, but courtesied and motioned him to a seat.

She was dressed in a flowing gauze-like robe of azure over white, appropriate to the warmth of the season. Her hair was combed back from her forehead and temples, showing the full symmetry of her head. Her lips, of a delicate coral, parted just enough to show the white perfection of her teeth. Rarely had she looked so dangerously beautiful. Ratcliff was swift to notice all these points.

Assuming that a compliment on her personal appearance could never come amiss to a woman, young or old, he said: "Upon my word, you are growing more beautiful every day, Miss Murray. I had thought there was no room for improvement. I find my mistake."

Ratcliff looked narrowly to see if there were any expression of pleasure on her face, but it did not relax from its impenetrability.

"Will you not be seated?" he asked.

She sat down, and he followed her example. There was silence for a moment. The master felt almost embarrassed before the young girl he had so long regarded as a slave. Something like a genuine emotion began to stir in his heart as he said: "Miss Murray, you are well aware that I am the only person to whom you are entitled to look for protection and support. From an infant you have been under my charge, and I hope you will admit that I have not been ungenerous in providing for you."

"One word, sir, at the outset, on that point," interposed Clara. "All the expense you have been at for me shall be repaid and overpaid at once with interest. You are aware I have the means to reimburse you fully."

"Excuse me, Miss Murray; without meaning to taunt you, — simply to set you right in your notions, — let me remark, that, being my slave, you can hold no property independent of me. All you have is legally mine."

"How can that be, sir, when what I have is entirely out of your power; safely deposited in the vaults of Northern banks, where your claim not only is not recognized, but where you could not go to enforce it without being liable to be arrested as a traitor?"

A dark, savage expression flitted over Ratcliff's face as he thought of the turn which his wife, aided by Winslow, had served him; but he checked the ire which was rising to his lips, and replied: "Let me beg you not to cherish an unprofitable delusion, my dear Miss Murray. When this war terminates, as it inevitably will, in the triumph of the South, one of the conditions of peace which we shall impose on the North will be, that all claims resulting out of slavery, either through the abduction of slaves or the transfer of property held as theirs, shall be settled by the fullest indemnification to masters. In that event your little property, which Mr. Winslow thinks he has hid safely away beyond my recovery, will be surely reached and returned to me, the lawful owner."

"Well, sir," replied Clara, forcing a calmness at which she herself was surprised, "supposing, what I do not regard as probable, that the South will have its own way in this war, and that my title to all property will be set aside as superseded by yours, let me inform you that I have a friend who will come to my aid, and make you the fullest compensation for all the expense you have been at on my account."

"Indeed! Is there any objection to my knowing to what friend you allude?"

"None at all, sir. Madame Volney is that friend."

"Well, we will not discuss that point now," said Ratcliff, smiling incredulously as he thought how speedily a few blandishments from him would overcome any resolution which the lady referred to might form. "My plans for you, Miss Murray, are all honorable, and such as neither you nor the world can regard as other than generous. Consider what I might do if I were so disposed! I could put you up at auction to-morrow and sell you to some brute of a fellow who would degrade and misuse you. Instead of that, what do I propose? First let me speak a few words of myself. I am, it is true, considerably your senior, but not old, and not ill-looking, if I may believe my glass. My property, already large, will be enormous the moment the war is over. I have bought within the last six months, at prices almost nominal, over a thousand slaves, whose value will be increased twenty-fold with the return of peace. My position in the new Confederacy will be among the foremost. Already President Davis has assured me that whatever I may ask in the way of a new foreign mission I can have. Thus the lady who may link her fate with mine will be a welcome guest at all the courts of Europe. If she is beautiful, her beauty will be admired by princes, kings, and emperors. If she is intellectual, all the wits and great men of London and Paris will be ambitious to make her acquaintance. Now what do you think I propose for you?"

"Let me not disguise my knowledge," replied Clara, looking him in the face till he dropped his eyelids. "You propose that I should be your wife."

"Ah! Josephine has told you, then, has she? And what did you say to it?"

"I said I could never say *yes* to such a proposition from a man who claimed me as a slave."

"But what if I forego my claim, and give you free papers?"

"Try it," said Clara, sternly.

"Can you then give me any encouragement?"

The idea was so hideous to her, and so strong her disinclination to deceive, or to allow him to deceive himself, that she could not restrain the outburst of a hearty and emphatic "*No!*"

Ratcliff's eyes swam a moment with their old glitter that meant mischief; but the recollection of his lawyer's warning restored him to good humor. He resolved to bear with her waywardness at that first interview, and to let her say *no* as much as she pleased.

"You say *no* now, but by and by you will say *yes*," he replied.

Clara had risen and was pacing the floor. Suddenly she stopped and said: "My desire is to disabuse you wholly of any expectation, even the most remote, that I can ever change my mind on this point. Under no conceivable circumstances could I depart from my determination."

"Tell me one thing," replied Ratcliff. "Do you speak thus because your affections are pre-engaged?"

"I do not," said Clara; "and for that reason I can make my refusal all the more final and irrevocable; for it is not biased by passion. I beg you seriously to dismiss all expectation of ever being able to change my purpose; and I propose you should receive for my release such a sum as may be a complete compensation for what you have expended on me."

Ratcliff had it in his heart to reply, "Slave! do your master's bidding"; but he discreetly curbed his choler, and said, "Can you give me any good reason for your refusal?"

"Yes," answered Clara, "the best of reasons: one which no gentleman would wish to contend against: my inclinations will not let me accept your proposal."

"Inclinations may change," suggested Ratcliff.

"In this case mine can only grow more and more adverse," replied Clara.

Ratcliff found it difficult to restrain himself from assuming the tone that chimes so well with the snap of the plantation scourge; and so he resolved to withdraw from the field for the present. He rose and said: "As we grow better acquainted, my dear, I am persuaded your feelings will change. I have no wish to force your affections. That would be unchivalrous towards one I propose to place in the relation of a *wife*."

He laid a significant emphasis on this last word, *wife;* and Clara started as at some hideous object in her path. Was there, then, another relation in which he might seek to place her, if she persisted in her course? And then she recollected Estelle; and the flush of an angry disgust mounted to her brow. But she made no reply; and Ratcliff, with his hateful gaze devouring her beauties to the last, passed out of the room.

On the whole he felicitated himself on the interview. He

thought he had kept his temper remarkably well, and had not allowed this privileged beauty to irritate him beyond the prudent point. He believed she could not resist so much suavity and generosity on his part. She had confessed she was heart-free: surely that was in his favor. It was rather provoking to have a slave put on such airs; but then, by Jove, she was worth enduring a little humiliation for. Possibly, too, it might be high blood that told in her. Possibly she might be that last scion of the Berwick stock which an untoward fate had swept far from all signs of parentage.

These considerations, while they disposed Ratcliff to leniency in judging of her waywardness, did but aggravate the importunity of his desires for the proposed alliance. Although hitherto his tastes had led him to admire the coarser types of feminine beauty, there was that in the very difference of Clara from all other women with whom he had been intimate, which gave novelty and freshness and an absorbing fascination to his present pursuit. The possession of her now was the prime necessity of his nature. That prize hung uppermost. Even Confederate victories were secondary. Politics were forgotten. He did not ask to see the newspapers; he did not seek to go abroad to confer with his political associates, and tell them all that he had seen and heard at Richmond. Semmes's caution in regard to the danger of his being tracked had something to do with keeping him in the house; but apart from this motive, the mere wish to be under the same roof with Clara, till he had secured her his beyond all hazard, would have been sufficient to keep him within doors.

Ratcliff went down into the dining-room. The table was set for one. He thought it time to inquire into the arrangements of the household. He rang the bell, and it was answered by a slim, delicate looking mulatto man, having on the white apron of a waiter.

"What's your name, and whose boy are you?" asked Ratcliff.

"My name is Sam, sir, and I belong to lawyer Semmes," replied the man, smoothing the table-cloth, and removing a pitcher from the sideboard.

"What directions did he leave for you?"

"He told me to stay and wait upon you, sir, just as I had upon him, till you saw fit to dismiss me."

"What other servants are there in the house?"

"One colored woman, sir, and one, a negro; Manda the cook, and Agnes the chambermaid."

"Any other persons?"

"Only the young woman that's crazy, and the Sister of Charity that attends her. They are on the third floor."

Ratcliff looked sharply at the mulatto, but could detect in his face no sign that he mistrusted the story of the insane woman.

"Send up the chambermaid," said Ratcliff.

"Yes, sir. When will you have your dinner, sir?"

"In half an hour. Have you any wines in the house?"

"Yes, sir; Sherry, Madeira, Port, Burgundy, Hock, Champagne."

"Put on Port and Champagne."

Sam's departure was followed by the chamber-maid's appearance.

"Are my rooms all ready, Agnes?"

"Yes, massa. Front room, second story, all ready. Sheets fresh and aired. Floor swept dis mornin'. All clean an' sweet, massa."

There was something in the forward and assured air of this negro woman that was satisfactory to Ratcliff. Some little coquetries of dress suggested that she had a weakness through which she might be won to be his unquestioning ally in any designs he might adopt. He threw out a compliment on her good looks, and this time he found his compliment was not thrown away. He gave her money, telling her to buy a new dress with it, and promised her a silk shawl if she would be a good girl. To all of which she replied with simpers of delight.

"Now, Agnes," said he, "tell me what you think of the little crazy lady up-stairs?"

"I'se of 'pinion, sar, dat gal am no more crazy nor I'm crazy."

"I'm glad to hear you say so, for I intend to make her my wife; and want you to help me all you can in bringing it about."

"Should n't tink massa would need no help, wid all his money. Wheugh! What 's de matter? Am she offish?"

"A little obstinate, that 's all. But she 'll come round in good time. Only you stand by me close, Agnes, and you shall have a hundred dollars the day I 'm married."

"I nebber 'fuse a good offer, massa. You may count on dis chile, sure!"

"Now go and send up dinner," said Ratcliff, confident he had secured one confederate who would not stick at trifles.

The dinner was brought up hot and carefully served.

"Curse me but this does credit to old Semmes," soliloquized Ratcliff, as course after course came on. "The wines, too, are not to be impeached. I wonder if his Burgundy is equal to his Champagne."

Ratcliff pressed his foot on the brass mushroom under the table and rang the bell.

"A bottle of Burgundy, Sam."

The mulatto brought on a bottle, and drew the cork gently and skilfully, so as not to shake the precious contents.

"Ah! this will do," said Ratcliff; "it must be of the famous vintage of eighteen hundred and — confound the date! Sam, you sly nigger, try a glass of this."

"Thank you, sir, I never drink."

"Nigger, you lie! Hand me that goblet."

Sam did as he was bid. Ratcliff filled the glass with the dark ruby liquid, and said, "Now toss it off, you rascal. Don't pretend you don't like it."

Sam meekly obeyed, and put down the emptied goblet. Ratcliff skirmished feebly among the bottles a few minutes longer, then rose, and made his way unsteadily to the sofa.

"Sam, you solemn nigger, what 's o'clock?" said he.

"The clock is just striking ten, sir."

"Possible? Have I been three — hiccup — hours at the table? Sam, see me up-stairs and put me to bed."

Half an hour afterwards Ratcliff lay in the heavy, stertorous slumber which wine, more than fatigue, had engendered.

He was habitually a late sleeper. It wanted but a few minutes to eleven o'clock the next morning when Sam started to answer his bell. Ratcliff called for soda-water. Sam had taken the precaution to put a couple of bottles under his arm, foreseeing that it would be needed.

It took a full hour for Ratcliff to accomplish the duties of his toilet. Then he went down to breakfast. And still the one thought that pursued him was how best to extort compliance from that beautiful maiden up-stairs.

A brilliant idea occurred to him. He would go and exert his powers of fascination. Without importunately urging his suit, he would deal out his treasure of small-talk: he would read poetry to her; he would try all the most approved means of making love.

Again he knocked at her door. It was opened by Sister Agatha, who at a sign from him withdrew into the adjoining room. Clara was busy with her needle.

"Have you any objection to playing a tune for me?" he asked, with the timid air of a Corydon.

Clara seated herself at the piano and began playing Beethoven's Sonatas, commencing with the first. Ratcliff was horribly bored. After he had listened for what seemed to him an intolerable period, he interrupted the performance by saying, "All that is very fine, but I fear it is fatiguing to you."

"Not at all. I can go through the whole book without fatigue."

"Don't think of it! What have you here? 'Willis's Poems.' Are you fond of poetry, Miss Murray?"

"I *am* fond of poetry; but my name is not Murray."

"Indeed! What may it then be?"

"My name is Berwick. I am no slave, though kidnapped and sold as such while an infant. You bought me. But you would not lend yourself to a fraud, would you? I must be free. You shall be paid with interest for all your outlays in my behalf. Is not that fair?"

"I am too much interested in your welfare, my dear young lady, to consent to giving you up. You will find it impossible to prove this fanciful story which some unfriendly person has put into your head. Even if it were true, you could never recover your rights. But it is all chimerical. Don't indulge so illusory a hope. What I offer, on the other hand, is substantial, solid, certain. As my wife you would be lifted at once to a position second to that of no lady in the land."

Clara inadvertently gave way to a shudder of dislike. Ratcliff noticed it, and rising, drew nearer to her and asked, "Have I ever given you any cause for aversion?"

"Yes," she replied, starting up from the music-chair, — "the cause which the master must always give the slave."

"But if I were to remove that objection, could you not like me?"

"Impossible!"

"Have I ever done anything to prevent it?"

"Yes, much."

"Surely not toward you; and if not toward you, toward whom?"

"Toward Estelle!" said Clara, roused to an intrepid scorn, which carried her beyond the bounds at once of prudence and of fear.

Had Ratcliff seen Estelle rise bodily before him, he could not have been struck more to the heart with an emotion partaking at once of awe and of rage. The habitually florid hue of his cheeks faded to a pale purple. He swung his arms awkwardly, as if at a loss what to do with them. He paced the floor wildly, and finally gasping forth, "Young woman, you shall — you shall repent this," left the room.

He did not make his appearance in Clara's parlor again that day. It was already late in the afternoon. Dinner was nearly ready. The consideration that such serious excitement would be bad for his appetite gradually calmed him down; and by the time he was called to the table he had thrown off the effects of the shock which a single word had given him. The dinner was a repetition of that of the day before, varied by the production of new dishes and wines. Sam was evidently doing his best as a caterer. Again Ratcliff sat late, and again Sam saw him safe up-stairs and helped him to undress. And again the slave-lord slept late into the hours of the forenoon.

After breakfast on the third day of his return he paced the back piazza for some two hours, smoking cigars. He had no thought but for the one scheme before him. To be baffled in that was to lose all. Public affairs sank into insignificance. Sam handed him a newspaper, but without glancing at it he threw it over the balustrade into the area. "She's but a wayward girl, after all! I must be patient with her," thought he, one moment. And the next his mood varied, and he muttered to himself: "A slave! Damnation! To be treated so by a slave, — one I could force to drudge instead of letting her play the lady!"

Suddenly he went up-stairs and paid her a third visit. His manner and speech were abrupt.

"I wish to deal with you gently and generously," said he; "and I beseech you not to compel me to resort to harshness. You are legally my slave, whatever fancies you may entertain as to your origin or as to a flaw in my title. You can prove nothing, or if you could, it would avail you nothing, against the power which I can exert in this community. I tell you I could this very day, in the mere exercise of my legal rights, consign you to the ownership of those who would look upon your delicate nurture, your assured manners, and your airs of a lady, merely as so many baits enhancing the wages of your infamy; who would subject you to gross companionship with the brutal and the merciless; who would scourge you into compliance with any base uses to which they might choose to put you. Fair-faced slaves are forced to such things every day. Instead of surrendering yourself to liabilities like these, you have it in your power to take the honorable position of my wife, — a position where you could dispense good to others while having every luxury that heart could covet for yourself. Now decide, and decide quickly; for I can no longer endure this torturing suspense in which you have kept me. Will you accede to my wishes, or will you not?"

"I will not!" said Clara, in a firm and steady tone.

"Then remember," replied Ratcliff, "it is your own hands that have made the foul bed in which you prefer to lie."

And with these terrible words he quitted the room.

Frightened at her own temerity, Clara at once sank upon her knees, and called with earnest supplication on the Supreme Father for protection. Blending with her own words those immortal formulas which the inspired David wrote down for the help and refreshing of devout souls throughout all time, she exclaimed: "Thou art my hiding-place and my shield: I hope in thy word. Seven times a day do I praise thee because of thy righteous judgments. Wonderfully hast thou led me heretofore: forsake me not in this extreme. Save now, I beseech thee, O Lord; *send now prosperity!* Let thine hand help me. Deliver my soul from death, mine eyes from tears, and my feet from falling. Out of the depth I cry unto thee. O Lord, hear my voice, and be attentive unto my supplications."

As she remained with head bent and arms crossed upon her bosom, motionless as some sculptured saint, she suddenly felt the touch of a hand on her head, and started up. It was Sister Agatha, who had come to bid her good by.

"But you 're not going to leave me!" cried Clara.

"Yes; I 've been told to go."

"By whom have you been told to go?"

"By the gentleman who now takes charge of you, — Mr. Ratcliff."

"But he 's a bad man! Look at him, study him, and you 'll be convinced."

"O no! he has given me fifty dollars to distribute among the poor. If you were in your senses, my child, you would not call him bad. He is your best earthly friend. You must heed all he says. Agnes will remain to wait on you."

"Agnes? I 've no faith in that girl. I fear she is corrupt; that money could tempt her to much that is wrong."

"What fancies! Poor child! But this is one of the signs of your disease, — this disposition to see enemies in those around you. There! you must let me go. The Lord help and cure you! Farewell!"

Sister Agatha withdrew herself from Clara's despairing grasp and eager pleadings, and, passing into the sleeping-room, opened the farther door which led into the billiard-room, of the door of which, communicating with the entry, she had the key.

For the moment Hope seemed to vanish from Clara's heart with the departing form of the Sister; for, simple as she was, she was still a protection against outrage. No shame could come while Sister Agatha was present.

Suddenly the idea occurred to Clara that she had not tested all the possibilities of escape. She ran and tried the doors. They were all locked. We have seen that she had the range of a suite of three large rooms: a front room serving as a parlor and connected by a corridor, having closets and doors at either end, with the sleeping-room looking out on the garden in the rear. This sleeping-room, as you looked from the windows, communicated with the billiard-room on the left, and had one door, also on the left, communicating with the entry on which you came from the stairs. This door was locked on the outside. The parlor also communicated with this entry or hall by a door on the left, locked on the outside. The house was built very much after the style of most modern city houses, so that it is not difficult to form a clear idea of Clara's position.

Finding the doors were secure against any effort of hers to force them, it occurred to her to throw into the street a letter containing an appeal for succor to the person who might pick it up. She hastily wrote a few lines describing her situation, the room where she was confined, the fraud by which she was held a slave, and giving the name of the street, the number of the house, &c. This she signed *Clara A. Berwick.* Then rolling it up in a handkerchief with a paper-weight she threw it out of the window far into the street. Ah! It went beyond the opposite sidewalk, over the fence, and into the tall grass of the little ornamented park in front of the house!

She could have wept at the disappointment. Should she write another letter and try again? While she was considering the matter, she saw a well-dressed lady and gentleman promenading. She cried out "Help!" But before she could repeat the cry a hand was put upon her mouth, and the window was shut down.

"No, Missis, can't 'low dat," said the chuckling voice of Agnes.

Clara took the girl by the hand, made her sit down, and then, with all the persuasiveness she could summon, tried to reach her better nature, and induce her to aid in her escape. Failing in the effort to move the girl's heart, Clara appealed to her acquisitiveness, promising a large reward in money for such help as she could give. But the girl had been pre-persuaded by Ratcliff that Clara's promises were not to be relied upon; and so, disbelieving them utterly, she simply shook her head and simpered. How could Agnes, a slave, presume to disobey a great man like Massa Ratcliff? Besides, he meant the young missis no harm. He only wanted to make her his wife. Why should she be so obstinate about it? Agnes could n't see the sense of it.

During the rest of the day, Clara felt for the first time that her every movement was watched. If she went to the window, Agnes was by her side. If she took up a bodkin, Agnes seemed ready to spring upon her and snatch it from her hand.

Terrible reflections brought their gloom. Clara recalled the case of a slave-girl which she had heard only the day before her last walk with Esha. It was the case of a girl quite white belonging to a Madame Coutreil, residing just below the city. This girl, for attempting to run away, had been placed in a filthy dungeon, and a thick, heavy iron ring or yoke, surmounted by three prongs, fastened about her neck.* If a *mistress* could do

* This yoke was on exhibition several months at Williams and Everett's, Washington Street, Boston, it having been sent by Governor Andrew with a letter, the original of which we have before us while we write. It bears date September 10th, 1863. It says of this yoke (which we have held in our hands), that it "was cut from the neck of a slave girl" who had worn it "for three weary months. An officer of Massachusetts Volunteers, whose letter I enclose to you, sent me this memento," &c. That officer's original letter, signed S. Tyler Read, Captain Third Massachusetts Cavalry, is also before us. He writes to the Governor of Massachusetts, that, having been sent with a detachment of troops down the river to search suspected premises on the plantation of Madame Coutreil, his attention was attracted by a small house, closed tightly, and about nine or ten feet square. "I demanded," writes Captain Read, "the keys, and after unlocking double doors found myself in the entrance of a dark and loathsome dungeon. 'In Heaven's name, what have you here?' I exclaimed to the slave mistress. 'O, only a little girl, — *she runned away!*' I peered into the darkness, and was able to discover, sitting at one end of the room upon a low stool, a girl about eighteen years of age. *She had this iron torture riveted about her neck, where it had rusted through the skin, and lay corroding apparently upon the flesh.* Her head was bowed upon her hands, and she was almost insensible from emaciation and immersion in the foul air of her dungeon. She was quite white. . . . . I had the girl taken to the city, where this torture was removed from her neck by a blacksmith, who cut the rivet, and she was subsequently made free by military authority."

See in the Atlantic Monthly (July, 1863) a paper entitled "Our General," from the pen of one who served as Deputy Provost Marshal in New Orleans. His facts are corroborated both by General Butler and Governor Shepley, who took pains to authenticate them. A girl, "a perfect blonde, her hair of a very pretty, light shade of brown, and perfectly straight," had been publicly whipped by her master (who was also her father), and then "forced to marry a colored man." We spare our readers the mention of the most loathsome fact in the narrative.

Another case is stated by the same writer. A mulatto girl, the slave of such things, what barbarity might not a *master* like Ratcliff attempt?

And where was Ratcliff all this while?

Still keeping in the house, brooding on the one scheme on which he had set his heart. He smoked cigars, stretched himself on sofas, cursed the perversity of the sex, and theorized as to the efficacy of extreme measures in taming certain feminine tempers. Was not a woman, after all, something like a horse? Had he not seen Rarey tame the most furious mare by a simple process which did not involve beating or cruelty? The consideration was curious, — a matter for philosophy to ruminate.

Ratcliff dined late that day. It was almost dark enough for the gas to be lighted when he sat down to the table. The viands were the choicest of the season, but he hardly did them justice. All the best wines were on the sideboard. Sam filled three glasses with hock, champagne, and burgundy; but, to his surprise and secret disappointment, Ratcliff did not empty one of them. "Mr. Semmes used to praise this Rudesheimer very highly," said Sam, insinuatingly. Ratcliff simply raised his hand imperiously with a gesture imposing silence. He sipped half a glass of the red wine, then drank a cup of coffee, then lit a cigar, and resumed his walk on the piazza.

It was now nine o'clock in the evening. Without taking off any of her clothes, Clara had laid down on the bed. Agnes sat sewing at a table near by. The room was brilliantly illuminated by two gas-burners. Light also came through the corridor from a burner in the parlor. Every few minutes the chambermaid would look round searchingly, as if to see whether the young "missis" were asleep. In order to learn what effect it would have, Clara shut her eyes and breathed as

one Landry, was brought to General Butler. She had been brutally scourged by her master. He confessed to the castigation, but pleaded that she had tried to get her freedom. The poor girl's back had been flayed "until the quivering flesh resembled a fresh beefsteak scorched on a gridiron." It was declared by influential citizens, who interceded for him, that Landry was (we quote the recorded words) "not only *a high-toned gentleman*, but a person of unusual amiability of character." General Butler freed the girl, and compelled the high-toned Landry to pay over to her the sum of five hundred dollars.

if lost in slumber. Agnes put down her work, moved stealthily to the bed, and gently felt around the maiden's waist and bosom, as if to satisfy herself there was no weapon concealed about her person.

While the negro woman was thus engaged, there was a sound as if a key had dropped on the billiard-room floor, which was of oak and uncarpeted. Agnes stopped and listened as if puzzled. There was then a sound as if the outer door of the billiard-room communicating with the entry were unlocked and opened. Agnes went up to the mantel-piece and looked at the clock, and then listened again intently.

There was now a low knock from the billiard-room at the chamber-door, which was locked on the inside, and the key of which was left in while Agnes was present, but which she was accustomed to take out and leave on the billiard-room side when she quitted the apartments to go down-stairs.

Before unlocking the door on this occasion she asked in a whisper, "Who 's dar?"

The reply came, "Sam."

"What 's de matter?"

"I want to speak with you a minute. Open the door."

"Can't do it, Sam. It 's agin orders."

"Well, no matter. I only thought you 'd like to tell me what sort of a shawl to get."

"What? — what 's dat you say 'bout a shawl?"

"The Massa has given me ten dollars to buy a silk shawl for you. What color do you want?"

Clara heard every word of this little dialogue. It was followed by the chambermaid's unlocking the door, taking out the key and entering the billiard-room. Clara started from the bed, and went and listened. The only words she could distinguish were, "I 'll jes run up-stairs an' git a pattern fur yer." Clara tried the door, but found it locked. She listened yet more intently. There was no further sound. She waited five minutes, then went back to the bed and sat down.

A sense of something incommunicable and mysterious weighed upon her brain and agitated her thoughts. It was as if she were enclosed by an atmosphere impenetrable to intelligences that were trying to reach her brain. For a week she had seen no newspaper. What had happened during that time? Great events were impending. What shape had they taken? The terror of the Vague and the Unknown dilated her eyes and thrilled her heart.

As she sat there breathless, she heard through the window, open at the top, the distant beat of music. The tune was distinguishable rather by the vibrations of the air than by audible notes. But it seemed to Clara as if a full band were playing the Star-Spangled Banner. What could it mean? Nothing. The tune was claimed both by Rebels and Loyalists.

Hark! It had changed. What was it now? Surely that must be the air of "Hail Columbia." Never before, since the breaking out of the Rebellion, had she heard that tune. As the wind now and then capriciously favored the music, it came more distinct to her ears. There could be no mistake.

And now the motion of the sounds was brisk, rapid, and lively. Could it be? Yes! These rash serenaders, whoever they were, had actually ventured to play "Yankee Doodle." Was it possible the authorities allowed such outrages on Rebel sensibilities?

And now the sounds ceased, but only for a moment. A slower, a grand and majestic strain, succeeded. It arrested her closest attention. What was it? What? She had heard it before, but where? When? What association, strange yet tender, did it have for her? Why did it thrill and rouse her as none of the other tunes had done? Suddenly she remembered it was that fearful "John Brown Hallelujah Chorus," which Vance had played and sung for her the first evening of their acquaintance.

The music ceased; and she listened vainly for its renewal. All at once a harsh sound, that chilled her heart, and seemed to concentrate all her senses in one, smote on her ears. The key of the parlor door was slowly turned. There was a step, and it seemed to be the step of a man.

Clara started up and pressed both hands on her bosom, to keep down the flutterings of her heart, which beat till a sense of suffocation came over her.

The awe and suspense of that moment seemed to protract it into a whole hour of suffering. "God help me!" was all she could murmur. Her terror grew insupportable. The steps came over the carpet, — they fell on the tessellated marble of the little closet-passage, — they drew near the half-open door which now alone intervened.

Then there was a knock on the wood-work. She wanted to say, "Who's there?" but her tongue refused its office. The strength seemed ebbing from every limb. Horror at the thought of her helplessness came over her. Then a form — the form of a man — stood before her. She uttered one cry, — a simple "Oh!" — and sinking at his feet, put her arms about his knees and pressed against them her head.

There are times when a brief, hardly articulate utterance, — a simple intonation, — seems to carry in it whole volumes of meaning. That single *Oh!* — how much of heart-history it conveyed! In its expression of transition from mortal terror to entire trustfulness and delight, it was almost childlike. It spoke of unexpected relief, — of a joyful surprise, — of a gratitude without bounds, — of an awful sense of angelic guardianship, — of an inward faith vindicated and fulfilled against a tumultuous crowd of selfish external fears and misgivings.

The man whose appearance had called forth this intensified utterance wore the military cap and insignia of a Colonel in the United States service. His figure seemed made for endurance, though remarkable for neatness and symmetry. His face was that of one past the middle stage, — one to whom life had not been one unvaried holiday. The cheeks were bronzed; the eyes mobile and penetrating, the mouth singularly sweet and firm. Clara knew the face. It was that of Vance.

He lifted her flaccid form from the posture in which she had thrown herself, — lifted and supported it against his breast as if to give her the full assurance of safety and protection. She opened her eyes upon him as thus they stood, — eyes now beaming with reverential gratitude and transport. He looked at them closely.

"Yes," said he, "there they are! the blue and the gray! Why did I not notice them before?"

"Ah!" she cried. "Here is my dream fulfilled. You have at last taken from them that letter which lay there."

There was the sound of footsteps on the landing in the upper hall. Clara instinctively threw an arm over Vance's shoulder. The key of the chamber-door was turned, and Ratcliff entered.

He had been pacing the piazza and smoking uncounted cigars. The distant music, which to Clara's aroused senses had been so audible, had not been heard by him. He had not dreamed of any interruption of his plans. Was he not dealing with a slave in a house occupied by slaves? What possible service was there he could not claim of a slave? Were not slaves made every day to scourge slaves, even their own wives and children, till the backs of the sufferers were seamed and bloody? Besides, he had fortified the fidelity of one of them — of Agnes — by presents and by flatteries. Even the revolver he usually carried with him was laid aside in one of the drawers of his dressing-room as not likely to be wanted.

On entering the chamber, Ratcliff, before perceiving that there was an unexpected occupant, turned and relocked the door on the inside.

Was it some vision, the product of an incantation, that now rose before his eyes? For there stood the maiden on whose compliance he had so wreaked all the energy of his tyrannical will, — his own purchased slave and thrall, — creature bound to serve either his brute desires or his most menial exactions, — there she stood, in the attitude of entire trust and affection, folded in the arms of a man!

Instantly Ratcliff reflected that he was unarmed, and he turned and unlocked the door to rush down-stairs after his revolver. But Vance was too swift for him. Placing Clara in a chair, quick as the tiger-cat springs on his prey, he darted upon Ratcliff, and before the latter could pass out on to the landing, relocked the door and took the key. Then dragging him into the middle of the room, he held him by a terrible grip on the shoulders at arm's length, face to face.

"Now look at me well," said Vance. "You have seen me before. Do you recognize me now?"

Wild with a rage to which all other experiences of wrath were as a zephyr to a tornado, Ratcliff yet had the curiosity to look, and that look brought in a new emotion which made even his wrath subordinate. For the first time in more than twenty years he recognized the man who had once offended him at the theatre, — who had once knocked him down on board a steamboat in the eyes of neighbors and vassals, — who had robbed him of one beautiful slave girl, and was now robbing him of another. Yes, it never once occurred to Ratcliff that he, a South Carolinian, a man born to command, was not the aggrieved and injured party!

Vance stood with a look like that of St. George spearing the dragon. The past, with all its horrors, surged up on his recollection. He thought of that day of Estelle's abduction, — of the escape and recapture, — of that scene at the whipping-post, — of the celestial smile she bent on him through her agony, — of the scourging he himself underwent, the scars of which he yet bore, — of those dreadful hours when he clung to the loosened raft in the river, — of the death-scene, the euthanasia of Estelle, of his own despair and madness.

And here, before him, within his grasp, was the author of all these barbarities and indignities! Here was the man who had ordered and superintended the scourging of one in whom all the goodness and grace that ever made womanhood lovely and adorable had met! Here was the haughty scoundrel who had thought to bind her in marriage with one of his own slaves! Here was the insolent ruffian! Here the dastard murderer! What punishment could be equal to his crimes? Death? His life so worthless for hers so precious beyond all reckoning? Oh! that would go but a small way toward paying the enormous debt!

Vance carried in a secret pocket a pistol, and wore a small sword at his side. This last weapon Ratcliff tried to grasp, but failed. Vance looked inquiringly about the room. Ratcliff felt his danger, and struggled with the energy of despair. Vance, with the easy knack of an adroit wrestler, threw him on the floor, then dragging him toward the closet, pulled from a nail a thick leather strap which hung there, having been detached from a trunk. Then hurling Ratcliff into the middle of the room, he collared him before he could rise, and brought down the blows, sharp, quick, vigorous, on face, back, shoulders, till a shriek of "murder" was wrung from the proud lips of the humbled adversary.

Suddenly, in the midst of these inflictions, Vance felt his

arm arrested by a firm grasp. He disengaged himself with a start that was feline in its instant evasiveness, turned, and before him stood Peek, interposing between him and the prostrate Ratcliff.

"Stand aside, Peek," said Vance; "I have hardly begun yet. You are the last man to intercede for this wretch."

"Not one more blow, Mr. Vance."

"Stand aside, I say! Come not between me and my mortal foe. Have I not for long years looked forward to this hour? Have I not toiled for it, dreamed of it, hungered for it?"

"No, Mr. Vance, I'll not think so poorly of you as to believe you 've done any such thing. It was to right a great wrong that you have toiled, — not to wreak a poor revenge on flesh and blood."

"No preaching, Peek! Stand out of the way! I'd sooner forego my hope of heaven than be balked now. Away!"

"Have I ever done that which entitles me to ask a favor of you, Mr. Vance?"

"Yes; for that reason I will requite the scars you yourself bear. The scourger shall be scourged."

"Would you not do *her* bidding, could you hear it; and can you doubt that she would say, Forgive?"

Vance recoiled for a moment, then replied: "You have used the last appeal; but 't will not serve. *My* wrongs I can forgive. *Yours* I can forgive. But *hers*, never! Once more I say, Stand aside!"

"You *shall* not give him another blow," said Peek.

"Shall not?"

And before he could offer any resistance Peek had been thrown to the other side of the room so as to fall backward on his hands.

Then, in a moment, Vance seemed to regret the act. He jumped forward, helped the negro up, begged his pardon, saying: "Forgive me, my dear, dear Peek! Have your own way. Do with this man as you like. Have n't you the right? Did n't you once save my life? Are you hurt? Do you forgive me?" And the tears sprang to Vance's eyes.

"No harm done, Mr. Vance! But you are quick as lightning."

"Look at me, Peek. Let me see from your face that I 'm forgiven."

And Peek turned on him such an expression, at once tender and benignant, that Vance, seeing they understood each other, was reassured.

Clara had sat all this time intently watching every movement, but too weak from agitation to interfere, even if she had been so disposed.

Ratcliff, recovering from the confusion of brain produced by the rapid blows he had endured, looked to see to whom he had been indebted for help. In all the whims of Fate, could it be there was one like this in reserve? Yes! that negro was the same he, Ratcliff, had once caused to be scourged till three men were wearied out in the labor of lashing. The fellow's back must be all furrowed and criss-crossed with the marks got from him, Ratcliff. Yet here was the nigger, coming to the succor of his old master! The instinct of servility was stronger in him even than revenge. Who would deny, after this, what he, Ratcliff, had often asserted, "Niggers will be niggers?"

And so, instead of recognizing a godlike generosity in the act, the slave-driver saw in it only the habit of a base spirit, and the wholesome effect, upon an inferior, of that imposing quality in his, Ratcliff's, own nature and bearing, which showed he was of the master race, and justified all his assumptions.

Watching his opportunity Ratcliff crawled toward the billiard-room door, and, suddenly starting up, pulled it open, thinking to escape. To his dismay he encountered a large black dog of the bloodhound species, who growled and showed his teeth so viciously that Ratcliff sprang back. Following the dog appeared a young soldier, who, casting round his eyes, saw Clara, and darting to her side, seized and warmly pressed her extended hand. Overcome with amazement, Ratcliff reeled backward and sank into an arm-chair, for in the soldier he recognized Captain Onslow.

Voices were now heard on the stairs, and two men appeared. One of them was of a compact, well-built figure, and apparently about fifty years old. He was clad in a military dress, and his aspect spoke courage and decision. The individual at his side, and who seemed to be paying court to him, was a tall, gaunt figure, in the coarse uniform of the prison. He carried his cap in his hand, showing that half of his head was entirely bald, while the other half was covered with a matted mass of reddish-gray hair.

This last man, as he mounted the stairs and stood on the landing, might have been heard to say: "Kunnle Blake, you 're a high-tone gemmleman, ef you air a Yankee. You see in me, Kunnle, a victim of the damdest ongratitood. These Noo-Orleenz 'ristocrats could n't huv treated a nigger or an abolitioner wuss nor they 've treated *me.* I told 'em I wuz Virginia-born; told 'em what I 'd done fur thar damned Confed'racy; told 'em what a blasted good friend I 'd been to the institootion; but — will you believe it? — they tuk me up on a low charge of 'propriatin' to private use the money they giv me ter raise a company with; — they hahd me up afore a committee of close-fisted old fogies, an' may I be shot ef they did n't order me to be jugged, an' half of my head to be shaved! An' 't was did. Damned ef it warnt! But I 'll be even with 'em, damn 'em! Ef I don't, may I be kept ter work in a rice-swamp the rest of my days. I 'll let 'em see what it is to treat one of the Hyde blood in this 'ere way, as if he war a low-lived corn-cracker. I 'll let 'em see what thar rotten institootion 's wuth. Ef they kn afford ter make out of a born gemmleman a scarecrow like I am now, with my half-shaved scalp, jes fur 'propriatin' a few of thar damned rags, well and good. They 'll hahv ter look round lively afore they kn find sich another friend as Delancey Hyde has been ter King Cotton, — damn him! They shall find Delancy Hyde kn unmake as well as make."

To these wrathful words, Blake replied: "Perhaps you don't remember me, Colonel Hyde."

"Cuss me ef I do. Ef ever I seed you afore, 't was so long ago that it 's clean gone out of my head."

"Don't you remember the policeman who made you give up the fugitive slave, Peek, that day in the lawyer's office in New York?"

"I don't remember nobody else!" exclaimed Hyde, jubilant

at the thought of claiming one respectable man as an old acquaintance, and quite forgetting the fact that they had parted as foes. "Kunnle Blake, we must liquor together the fust chance we kn git. As for Peek, I don't want to see a higher-toned gemmleman than Peek is, though he *is* blacker than my boot. Will you believe it, Kunnle? That ar nigger, findin' as how I wuz out of money, arter Kunnle Vance had tuk me out of jail, what does he do but give me twenty dollars! In good greenbacks, too! None of your sham Confed'rate trash! Ef that ain't bein' a high-tone gemmleman, what is? He done it too in the most-er delicate manner, — off-hand, like a born prince."

By this time the interlocutors had entered the billiard-room. After them came a colored man and a negro. One of these was Sam, the house-servant, the other Antoine, the owner of the dog. Immediately after them came Esha and Madame Josephine. They passed Ratcliff without noticing him, and went to Clara, and almost devoured her with their kisses.

No sooner had these two moved away in this terrible procession than an oldish lady, hanging coquettishly on the arm of a man somewhat younger than herself, of a rather red face, and highly dressed, entered the room, and, apparently too much absorbed in each other to notice Ratcliff, walked on until the lady, encountering Clara, rushed at her hysterically, and shrieking, "My own precious child!" fell into her arms in the most approved melodramatic style. This lady was Mrs. Gentry, who had recently retired from school-keeping with "something handsome," which the Vigilance Committee had been trying to get hold of for Confederate wants, but which she had managed to withhold from their grasp, until that "blessed Butler" coming, relieved her fears, and secured her in her own. The gentleman attending her was Mr. Ripper, ex-auctioneer, who, in his mellow days, finding that Jordan was a hard road to travel, had concluded to sign the temperance pledge, reform, and take care of himself. With this view, what could he do better than find some staid, respectable woman, with "a little something of her own," with whom he could join hands on the downhill of life? As luck would have it, he was introduced to Mrs. Gentry that very evening, and he was now paying his first devoirs.

After the appearance of this couple, steps heavy and slow were heard ascending the stairs into the billiard-room; and the next moment Mr. Winslow appeared, followed by Lawyer Semmes. And, bringing up the rear of the party, and presenting in himself a fitting climax to these stunning surprises, came a large and powerful negro in military rig, bearing a musket with bayonet fixed, and displaying a small United States flag. This man was Decazes, an escaped slave belonging to Ratcliff, and for whom he had offered a reward of five hundred dollars.

Ratcliff had half-risen from his chair, holding on to the arms with both hands for support. His countenance, laced by the leathern blows he had received, his left eye blue and swollen, every feature distorted with consternation, rage, and astonishment, he presented such a picture of baffled tyranny as photography alone could do justice to. Was it delirium, — was it some harrowing dream, — under which he was suffering? That flag! What did it mean?

"Semmes!" he exclaimed, "what has happened? Where do these Yankees come from?"

"Possible? Have n't you heard the news?" returned the lawyer. "Farragut and Butler have possession of New Orleans. What have you been doing with yourself the last three days?"

"Butler?" exclaimed Ratcliff, astounded and incredulous, — "Picayune Butler? — the contemptible swell-head, — the pettifogging — "

Semmes walked away, as if choosing not to be implicated in any treasonable talk.

Suddenly recognizing Winslow, Ratcliff impotently shook his fists and darted at him an expression of malignant and vindictive hate.

Could it be? New Orleans in the hands of the Vandals, — the "miserable miscreants," — the "hyenas," as President Davis and Robert Toombs were wont to stigmatize the whole people of the North? Where was the great ram that was to work such wonders? Where were the Confederate gunboats? Were not Forts Jackson and St. Philip impregnable? Could not the Chalamette batteries sink any Yankee fleet that floated? Had not the fire-eaters, — the last-ditch men, — resolved that New Orleans should be laid in ashes before the detested flag, emblematic of Yankee rule, should wave from the public buildings? And here was a black rascal in uniform, flaunting that flag in the very face of one of the foremost of the chivalry! Let the universe slide after this! Let chaos return!

The company drifted in groups of two and three through the suite of rooms. Sam disappeared suddenly. The women were in the front room. Ratcliff, supposing that he was unnoticed, rose to escape. But Victor the hound, was on hand. He had been lying partly under the bed, with his muzzle out and resting on his fore paws, affecting to be asleep, but really watching the man whom his subtle instincts had told him was the game for which he was responsible; and now the beast darted up with an imperious bark, and Ratcliff, furious, but helpless, sank back on his seat.

Colonel Delancy Hyde approached, with the view of making himself agreeable.

"Squire Ratcliff," said he, "you seem to be in a dam bad way. Kin I do anything fur yer? Any niggers you want kotched, Squire? Niggers is mighty onsartin property jes now, Squire. Gen'ral Butler swars he 'll have a black regiment all uniformed afore the Fourth of July comes round. Would n't give much fer yer Red River gangs jes now, Squire! Reckon they 'll be findin' thar way to Gen'ral Butler's head-quarters, sure."

Ratcliff cowered and groaned in spirit as he thought of the immense sums which, in his confidence in the success of the Rebellion, he had been investing in slaves. Unless he could run his gangs off to Texas, he would be ruined.

"Look at me, Squire," continued the Colonel; "I 'm Kunnle Delancy Hyde, — Virginia born, be Gawd; but, fur all that, I might jest as well been born in hell, fur any gratitude you cust 'ristocrats would show me. Yes, you 're one on 'em. Here I 've been drudgin' the last thirty years in the nigger-ketchin' business, and see my reward, — a half-shaved scalp, an' be damned to yer! But my time 's comin'. Now Kunnle Delancy Hyde tries a new tack. Instead of ketchin' niggers, he 's goin' to free 'em; and whar he kotched one he 'll free a thousand. Lou'siana 's bound to be a free State. All Cottondom 's bound to be free. Uncle Sam shall have black regiments afore Sumter soon. Only the freedom of every nigger in the land kn wipe out the wrongs of Delancy Hyde, — kn avenge his half-shaved scalp!"

Here the appearance of Sam, the house-servant, with a large salver containing a pitcher, a sugar-bowl, a decanter, tumblers, and several bottles, put a stop to the Colonel's eloquence, and drew him away as the loadstone draws the needle.

Onslow came near to Ratcliff, looked him in the face contemptuously, and turned away without acknowledging the acquaintance. After him reappeared Ripper and Mrs. Gentry, arm-in-arm, the lady with her hands clasped girlishly, and her shoulder pressed closely up against that of the auctioneer. It was evident she was going, going, if not already gone. Ripper put up his eye-glass, and, carelessly nodding, remarked, "Such is life, Ratcliff!" (Ratcliff! The beggar presumed to call him Ratcliff!) The couple passed on, the lady exclaiming so that the observation should not be lost on the ears for which it was intended, — "I always said he would be come up with!"

Semmes now happening to pass by, Ratcliff, deeply agitated, but affecting equanimity, said: "How is it, Semmes? Are you going to help me out of this miserable scrape?"

"Our relations must end here, Mr. Ratcliff," replied the lawyer.

"So much the better," said Ratcliff; "it will spare my standing the swindle you call professional charges on your books."

"Don't be under a misapprehension, my poor friend," returned Semmes. "I have laid an attachment on your deposits in the Lafayette Bank. They will just satisfy my claim."

And taking a pinch of snuff the lawyer walked unconcernedly away. "O that I had my revolver here!" thought Ratcliff, with an inward groan.

But here was Madame Josephine. Here was at least *one* friend left to him. Of her attachment, under any change of fortune, he felt assured. Her own means, not insignificant, might now suffice for the rehabilitation of his affairs. She drew near, her face radiant with the satisfaction she had felt in the recovery of Clara. She drew near, and Ratcliff caught her eye, and rising and putting out his hands, as if for an embrace, murmured, in a confidential whisper, "Josephine, dearest, come to me!"

She frowned indignantly, threw back her arm with one scornful and repelling sweep, and simply ejaculating, "No more!" moved away from him, and took the proffered arm of the trustee of her funds, the venerable Winslow.

The party now passed away from Ratcliff, and out of the two rooms; most of them going down-stairs to the carriages that waited in the street to bear them to the St. Charles Hotel, over whose cupola the Stars and Stripes were gloriously fluttering in the starlight.

Ratcliff found himself alone with the ever-watchful bloodhound. Suddenly a whistle was heard, and Victor started up and trotted down-stairs. Ratcliff rose to quit the apartment. All at once the stalwart negro, lately his slave, in uniform, and bearing a musket, with the old flag, stood before him.

"Follow me," said the man, with the dignity of a true soldier.

"Where to?"

"To the lock-up, to wait General Butler's orders."

On a pallet of straw that night Ratcliff had an opportunity of revolving in solitude the events of the day. In the miscarriage of his schemes, in the downfall of his hopes, and in the humbling of his pride, he experienced a hell worse than the imagination of the theologian ever conceived. What pangs can equal those of the merciless tyrant when he tumbles into the place of his victims and has to endure, in unstinted measure, the stripes and indignities he has been wont to inflict so unsparingly on others!

CHAPTER XLII.

HOW IT WAS DONE.

"From Thee is all that soothes the life of man,
His high endeavor and his glad success,
His strength to suffer and his will to serve:
But O, thou bounteous Giver of all good,
Thou art of all thy gifts thyself the crown!
Give what thou canst, without thee we are poor,
And with thee rich, take what thou wilt away!" — *Cowper.*

ALL the efforts of Peculiar to induce the bloodhound, Victor, to take the scent of either of the gloves, had proved unavailing. At every trial Victor persisted in going straight to the jail where his master, Antoine, was confined. Peek began to despair of discovering any trace of the abducted maiden.

Were dumb animals ever guided by spirit influence? There were many curious facts showing that birds were sometimes used to convey impressions, apparently from higher intelligences. At sea, not long ago, a bird had flown repeatedly in the helmsman's face, till the latter was induced to change his course. The consequence was, his encounter with a ship's crew in a boat, who must have perished that night in the storm, had they not been picked up. There were also instances in which dogs would seem to have been the mere instruments of a super human and supercanine sagacity. But Victor plainly was not thus impressible. His instincts led him to his master, but beyond that point they would not or could not be made to exert themselves.

Had not Peek's faith in the triumph of the right been large, he would have despaired of any help from the coming of the United States forces. For weeks the newspapers had teemed with paragraphs, some scientific and some rhetorical, showing that New Orleans must not and could not be taken. They all overflowed with bitterness toward the always "cowardly and base-born" Yankees. The Mayor of the city wrote, in the true magniloquent and grandiose style affected by the Rebel leaders: "As for hoisting any flag not of our own adoption, the man lives not in our midst whose hand and heart *would not be paralyzed at the mere thought of such an act!*"

A well-known physician, who had simply expressed the opinion that possibly the city might have to surrender, had been waited on by a Vigilance Committee and warned. Taking the hint, the man of rhubarb forthwith handed over a contribution of five hundred dollars, in expiation of his offence.

All at once the confident heart of Rebeldom was stunned by the news that two of the Yankee steamers had passed Forts Jackson and St. Philip. The great ram had been powerless to prevent it. Then followed the announcement that seven, — then thirteen, — then twenty, — then the whole of Farragut's fleet, excepting the Varuna, were coming. Yes, the Hartford and the Brooklyn and the Mississippi and the Pensacola and the Richmond, and the Lord knew how many more, were on their way up the great river. They would soon be at English Bend; nay, they would soon be at the Levee, and have the haughty city entirely at their mercy!

No sooner was the terrible news confirmed than the Rebel authorities ordered the destruction of all the cotton-bales stored on the Levee. The rage, the bitterness, the anguish of the pro-slavery chiefs was indescribable. Several attempts were made to fire the city, and they would probably have succeeded, but for a timely fall of rain. On the landing of the United States forces, the frenzy of the Secessionists passed all bounds; and one poor fellow, a physician, was hung by them for simply telling a United States officer where to find the British Consulate.

But if some hearts were sick and crushed at the spectacle, there were many thousands in that great metropolis to whom the sight of the old flag carried a joy and exultation transcending the power of words to express; and one of these hearts beat under the black skin of Peek. Followed by Victor, he ran to the Levee where United States troops were landing, and there — O joy unspeakable! — standing on the upper deck of one of the smaller steamers, and almost one of the first persons he saw, was Mr. Vance.

Peek shouted his name, and Vance, leaping on shore, threw

his arms impulsively round the brawny negro, and pressed him to his breast. Brief the time for explanations. In a few clear words, Peek made Vance comprehend the precise state of affairs, and in five minutes the latter, at the head of a couple of hundred soldiers, and with Peek walking at his side, was on his way to the jail. Victor, the bloodhound, evidently understood it all. He saw, at length, that he was going to carry his point.

Arrived at the jail, a large, square, whitewashed building, with barred windows, they encountered at the outer door three men smoking cigars. The foremost of them, a stern-looking, middle-aged man, with fierce, red whiskers, and who was in his shirt-sleeves, came forward, evidently boiling over with a wrath he was vainly trying to conceal, and asked what was wanted.

"There is a black man, Antoine Lafour, confined here. Produce him at once."

"But, sir," said the deputy, "this is altogether against civilized usage. This is a place for —"

"I can't stop to parley with you. Produce the man instantly."

"I shall do no such thing."

Vance turned to an orderly, and said, "Arrest this man." At once the deputy was seized on either side by two soldiers. "Now, sir," said Vance, cocking his pistol and taking out his watch, "Produce Antoine Lafour in five minutes, or I will shoot you dead."

The bloodhound, who had been scenting with curious nose the man's person, now seconded the menace by a savage growl, which seemed to have more effect even than the pistol, for the deputy, turning to one of the men in attendance, said sulkily, "Bring out the nigger, and be quick about it."

In three minutes Antoine appeared, and the dog leaped bodily into his arms, the negro talking to him much as he would to a human being. "I knowed you 'd do it, ole feller! Thar! Down! Down, I say, ole Vic! It takes you, — don't it? Down! Behave yourself afore folk. Why, Peek, is this you?"

"Yes, Antoine, and this is Mr. Vance, and here 's the old flag, and you 're no longer a slave."

"What? I no longer a — No! Say them words agin, Peek! Free? Owner of my own flesh an' blood? Dis arm mine? Dis head mine? Bress de Lord, Peek! Bress him for all his mercies! Amen! Hallelujah!"

The released negro could not forego a few wild antics expressive of his rapture. Peek checked him, and bade him remember the company he was in; and Antoine bowed to Vance and said: "'Scuze me, Kunnle. I don't perfess to be sich a high-tone gemmleman as Peek here, but —"

"Stop!" cried Peek; "where did you get those last words?"

"What words?" asked Antoine, showing the whites of his eyes with an expression of concern at Peek's suddenly serious manner.

"Those words, — 'high-tone gemmleman.' Whom did you ever hear use them?"

"Yah, yah! Wall, Peek, those words I got from Kunnle Delancy Hyde."

"Where, — where and when did you get them?"

"Bress yer, Peek, jes now, — not two minutes ago, — dar in the gallery whar the Kunnle's walkin' up and down."

Peek smiled significantly at Vance, and the latter, approaching the deputy who had not yet been released from custody, remarked: "You have a man named Hyde confined there."

"Yes, Delancy Hyde. The scoundrel stole the funds given to him to pay recruiting expenses."

"For which I desire to thank him. Bring him out."

"But, sir, you would n't —"

"Five minutes, Mr. Deputy, I give you, a second time, in which to obey my orders. If Mr. Delancy Hyde is n't forthcoming before this second-hand goes round five times, one of your friends here shall have the opportunity of succeeding you in office, and you shall be deposited where the wicked cease from troubling."

The deputy was far from being agreeably struck at the prospect of quitting the company of the wicked. But for them his vocation would be wanting. And so he nodded to a subordinate, and in three minutes out stalked the astonishing figure of Colonel Delancy Hyde, wearing a dirty woollen Scotch cap, and attired in the coarsest costume of the jail.

Ignorant of the great event of the day, not perceiving the old flag, and supposing that he had been called out to be shot, Hyde walked up to Vance, and said: "Kunnle, you look like a high-tone gemmleman, and afore I 'm shot I want ter make a confidential request."

"Well, sir, what is it?" said Vance, shading his face with his cap so as not to be recognized. "Speak quick. I can't spare you three minutes."

"Wall, Kunnle, it 's jes this: I 've a sister, yer see, in Alabamy, jest out of Montgomery; her name 's Dorothy Rusk. She 's a widder with six childern; one on 'em an idiot, one a cripple, and the eldest gal in a consumption. Dorothy has had a cruel hard time on it, as you may reckon, an' I 've ollerz paid her rent and a leetle over till this cussed war broke out, since when I 've been so hard up I 've had ter scratch gravel thunderin' lively to git my own grub. Them Confed'rate rags that I 'propriated, I meant to send to Dorothy; but the fogies, they war too quick for me. Wall, ter come ter the pint: I want you ter write a letter ter Dorothy, jes tellin' her that the reason why Delancy can't remit is that Delancy has been shot; and tellin' her he sent his love and all that — whar you can't come it too strong, Kunnle, for yer see Dorothy an' I, we was 'bout the same age, and used ter make mud-pies together, and sail our boats together down thar in the old duck-pond, when we was childern; an' so yer see —"

Vance looked into his face. Yes, the battered old reprobate was trying to gulp down his agitation, and there were tears rolling down his cheeks. Vance was touched.

"Hyde, don't you know me?" he said.

"What! Mr. Vance? Mr. Vance!"

"Nobody else, Hyde. He comes here a United States officer, you see. New Orleans has surrendered to Uncle Sam. Look at that flag. Instead of being shot, you are set at liberty. Here 's your old friend, Peek."

The knees of Colonel Delancy Hyde smote each other, and his florid face grew pale. Flesh and blood he could encounter well as any man, but a ghost was a piling on of something he had n't bargained for. Yet there palpably before him stood Peek, the identical Peek he believed to have been drowned in the Mississippi some fifteen years back.

"Wall, how in creation —"

"It 's all right, Hyde," interrupted Vance. "And now if you want that sister of yours provided for, you just keep as close to my shadow as you can."

Hyde was too confounded and stupefied to make any reply. These revelations coming upon him like successive shocks from a galvanic-battery, were too much for his equanimity. Awe-struck and stunned, he stared stupidly, first at Vance, then at the flag, and finally at Peek.

The roll of the drum, accompanied by Vance's orders to the soldiers, roused him, and then attaching himself to Peek, he marched on with the rest, Peek beguiling the way with much useful and enlightening information.

They had not marched farther than the next carriage-stand when Vance, leaving Captain Onslow in command, with orders to bivouac in Canal Street, slipped out of the ranks, and beckoning to Peek and his companions, they all, including Antoine and Hyde, entered a vehicle which drove off with the faithful Victor running at its side.

Behold them now in Vance's old room at the St. Charles. The immediate matter of concern was, how to find Clara? How was the search to be commenced?

Antoine, a bright, well-formed negro of cheerful aspect, after scratching his wool thoughtfully for a moment, said: "Peek, you jes gib me them two glubs you say you 've got."

Antoine then took the gloves, and, throwing them on the floor, called Victor's attention to them, and said: "Now, Vic, I want yer to show these gemmen your broughten up. Ob dem two glubs, you jes bring me de one dat you tink you kn fine de owner ob right off straight, widout any mistake. Now, be car'ful."

Victor snuffed at the large glove, and instantly kicked it aside with contempt. Then, after a thoughtful scenting of the small glove, he took it up in his mouth and carried it to Antoine.

"Berry well," said Antoine. "Dat 's your choice, is it? Now tell me, Vic, hab yer had yer dinner?"

The dog barked affirmatively.

"Berry well. Now take a good drink." And, filling a

washbowl with water, Antoine gave it to the dog, who lapped from it greedily.

"Hab yer had enough?" asked Antoine.

Victor uttered an affirmative bark.

"Wall, now," said Antoine, "you jes take dis ere glub, an' don't yer come back till you fine out su'thin' 'bout de owner ob it. Understan'?"

The dog again barked assent, and Antoine, escorting him down-stairs and out-of-doors, gave him the glove. Victor at once seized it between his teeth and trotted off at "double-quick," up St. Charles Street.

During the interval of waiting for Victor's return, "Tell me now, Peek," said Vance, "of your own affairs. Have you been able to get any clew from Amos Slink to guide you in your search for your wife?"

"All that he could do," replied Peek, "was merely to confirm what I already suspected as to Charlton's agency in luring her back into the clutch of Slavery."

"I must make the acquaintance of that Charlton," said Vance. "And by the way, Hyde, you must know something of the man."

"I know more nor I wish I did," replied Hyde. "I could scar' up some old letters of his'n, I'm thinkin', ef I was ter sarch in an old trunk in the house of the Widder Rusk (her as is my sister) in Montgomery."

"Those letters we must have, Hyde," said Vance. "You must lay your plans to get them. 'T would be hardly safe for you to trust yourself among the Rebels. They 've an awkward fashion of hanging up without ceremony all who profane the sanctity of Confederate scrip. But you might send for the letters."

"That 's a fak, Kunnle Vance. I 'm gittin' over my taste for low society. I want nothin' more ter do with the Rebels. But I've a nephew at Montgomery, —Delancy Hyde Rusk, —who can smuggle them letters through the Rebel lines easy as a snake kn cahrry a toad through a stump-fence. He 'll go his death for his Uncle Delancy. He 's got the raal Hyde blood in him, — he has, — an' no mistake."

"Can he read and write?"

"I'm proud to say he kin, Kunnle. I towt his mother, and she towt him and the rest of the childern."

"Well, Hyde, go into the next room and write a letter to your nephew, telling him to start at once for New York city, and report himself to Mr. William C. Vance, Astor House. I'll give you a couple of hundred dollars to enclose for him to pay his expenses, and a couple of hundred more for your sister."

Four hundred dollars! What an epoch would it be in their domestic history, when that stupendous sum should fall into the hands of Mrs. Rusk! Colonel Hyde moved with alacrity to comply with Vance's bidding.

Mr. Winslow and Captain Onslow now entered, followed by Colonel Blake, between whom and Vance a friendship had sprung up during the voyage from New York. Suddenly Peek, who had been looking from the window, exclaimed: "There goes the man who could tell us, if he would, what we want."

"Who is it?" cried Vance.

"Ratcliff's lawyer, Semmes. See him crossing the street!"

"Captain Onslow," said Vance, "arrest the man at once."

Five minutes did not elapse before Semmes, bland and suave, and accompanied by Peek and Onslow, entered the room.

"Ha! my dear friend Winslow!" cried the old lawyer, putting out his hand, "I'm delighted to see you. Make me acquainted with your friends."

Winslow introduced him to all, not omitting Peek, to whom Semmes bowed graciously, as if they had never met before, and as if the negro were the whitest of Anglo-Saxons.

"Sit down, Mr. Semmes," said Vance; "I have a few questions to put to you. Please answer them categorically. Are you acquainted with a young lady, claimed by Mr. Carberry Ratcliff as a slave, educated by him at Mrs. Gentry's school, and recently abducted by parties unknown from his house near Lafayette Square?"

"I do know such a young person," replied Semmes; "I had her in my charge after Mr. Ratcliff's compulsory departure from the city."

"Well. And do you know where she now is?"

"I certainly do not."

"Have you seen her since she left Ratcliff's house?"

Happily for Semmes, before he could perjure himself irretrievably, there was a knock at the door, and Antoine entered, followed by the bloodhound, bearing something tied in a white handkerchief, in his mouth.

A general sensation and uprising! For all except the lawyer had been made acquainted with the nature of the dog's search. Semmes glanced at the bloodhound, — then at the negroes, — and then at the other persons present, with their looks of absorbed attention. Surely, there was a *dénouement* expected; and might it not be fatal to him, if he left it to be supposed that he was colluding with Ratcliff in what would be stigmatized as rascality by low, cowardly, base-born Yankees, though, after all, it was only the act of a slave-owner enforcing his legal rights in a legitimate way?

Darting forward, just as Vance received from Antoine the little bundle the dog had been carrying, the lawyer exclaimed: "Colonel Vance, I do not *know*, but I can *conjecture* where the girl is. Seek her at Number 21 Camelia Place."

Vance paused, and looked the old lawyer straight in the eyes till the latter withdrew his glance, and resorted to his snuff-box to cover his discomfiture. Deep as he was, he saw that he had been fathomed. But Vance bowed politely, and said: "We will see, sir, if your information agrees with that of the dog."

He untied the handkerchief, took out the paper-weight, and underneath it found Clara's note, which he opened and read. Then turning to the lawyer, he said: "I congratulate you, Mr. Semmes. You *were* right in your *conjecture*."

None but Semmes and Peek noticed the slightly sarcastic stress which Vance put on this last word from his lips.

Vance now knelt on one knee, and resting on the other the fore-legs of the bloodhound, patted his head and praised him in a manner which Victor, by his low, gratified whine, seemed fully to comprehend and appreciate.

Peek, who had been restless ever since the words "21 Camelia Place" had fallen on his ears, here said: "Lend me your revolver, Mr. Vance, and don't leave till I come back. I promise not to rob you of your share in this work."

"I will trust you with the preliminary reconnoissance, Peek," said Vance, giving up the weapon. "Be quick about it."

Peek beckoned to Antoine, and the two went out, followed by the bloodhound.

Mr. Semmes, now realizing that by some display of zeal, even if it were superserviceable, he might get rid of the ill odor which would follow from lending himself to Ratcliff's schemes, approached Vance and said: "Colonel, it was only quite recently that I heard of the suspicions that were entertained of foul play in the case of that little girl claimed by Ratcliff as a slave. Immediately I looked into the notary's record, and I there found that the slave-child is set down as a quadroon; a misstatement which clearly invalidates the title. I have also discovered a letter, written in French, and published in L'Abeille, in which some important facts relative to the loss of the Pontiac are given. The writer, Monsieur Laboulie, is now in the city. Finally, I have to inform you that Mr. Ripper, the auctioneer who sold the child, is now in this house. I would suggest that both he and the Mrs. Gentry, who brought her up, should be secured this very evening, as witnesses."

"I like your suggestion, Mr. Semmes," said Vance, in a tone which quite reassured the lawyer; "go on and make all the investigations in your power bearing on this case. Get the proper affidavit from Monsieur Laboulie. Secure the parties you recommend as witnesses. I employ you professionally."

In his rapid and penetrating judgments of men, Vance rarely went astray; and when Semmes, who was thinking of a little private business of his own with the President of the Lafayette Bank, remarked, "If you can dismiss me now, Colonel, I will meet you an hour hence at any place you name," Vance knew the old lawyer would keep his promise, and replied: "Certainly, Mr. Semmes. You will find me at 21 Camelia Place."

Peek and Antoine, taking a carriage, drove at full speed to the house designated. Here they found to their surprise in the mulatto Sam, a member of a secret society of men of African descent, bound together by faith in the speedy advent of the United States forces, and by the resolve to demand emancipation. Peek at once satisfied himself that Clara was in no immediate danger. He found that Sam had withdrawn the bullets from Ratcliff's revolver, and was himself well armed, having determined to shoot down Ratcliff, if necessary, in liberating Clara. In pursuance of his plan he had lured the negrowoman, Agnes, up-stairs, under the pretence already mentioned. Here he had gagged, bound, and confined her securely. Hardly had he finished this job, when, looking out of the window, he had seen Peek and Antoine get out of a carriage and reconnoitre the house. Instantly he had run down-stairs, opened the front door, and made himself known.

It was arranged that Antoine and Sam, well armed, and supported by the bloodhound, should remain and look after Ratcliff, not precipitating action, however, and not communicating with Clara, whose relief Peek had generously resolved should first come from the hands of Vance.

Then jumping into the carriage, Peek drove to Lafayette Square, and taking in Madame Josephine and Esha, returned to the St. Charles Hotel. Here he told Vance all he had done, and introduced the two women, — Vance greeting Esha with much emotion, as he recognized in her that attendant at his wife's death-bed for whom he had often sought.

Four carriages were now drawn up on Gravier Street. Into one stepped Winslow, Hyde, and Vance; into another Semmes, Blake, Onslow, and Blake's trusty servant, Sergeant Decazes, the escaped slave. Into the third carriage stepped Madame Josephine, Esha, and Peek; and into the fourth, Mrs. Gentry and Mr. Ripper.

This last vehicle must be regarded as the centre of interest, for over it the Loves and Graces languishingly hovered.

In introducing Ripper to Mrs. Gentry, Semmes had remarked, in an aside to the former: "A retired schoolma'am: some money there!" Here was a shaft that went straight to the auctioneer's heart. In three minutes he drew from the lady the fact that, ten days before, she had received a visit from a Vigilance Committee, who had warned her, if she did not pay over to them five thousand dollars within a week, her house would be confiscated, sold, and the proceeds paid over to the Confederate treasury. "Five thousand dollars indeed!" said the lady, in relating the interview; "a whole year's income! O, have n't they been nicely come up with!"

The Confederate highwaymen had done what Satan recommended the Lord to do in the case of Job: they had tried Mrs. Gentry in her substance, and she had not stood the test. It had wrought a very sudden and radical change in her political notions. Even slavery was no longer the august and unapproachable thing which she had hitherto imagined; and she threw out a sentiment which savored so much of the abolition heresy, that Ripper, thinking to advance himself in her good opinion, avowed himself boldly an emancipationist, and declared that slavery was "played out." These words, strange to say, did not make him less charming in Mrs. Gentry's eyes.

The drive in the carriage soon offered an opportunity for tenderer topics, and before they reached Camelia Street, the enterprising auctioneer had declared that he really believed he had at last, after a life-long search, found his "affinity." And from that he ventured to glide an arm round the lady's waist, — a familiarity at which her indignation was so feebly simulated, that it only added new fuel to hope.

But Camelia Place was now reached, and the carriages stopped. The whole party were noiselessly introduced into the house. Vance darted up to the room where Clara's note had instructed him he could find her. Seeing the key on the outside, he turned it, opened the door, and presented himself to Clara in the manner already related. The unsuspecting Ratcliff soon followed, and then followed the scenes upon which the curtain has already been raised.

As Vance left the house, with Clara on his arm, several of Ratcliff's slaves gathered round them. To all these Vance promised immediate freedom and help. An old black hostler, named Juba, or Jube, who was also a theologian and a strenuous preacher, was spokesman for the freedmen. He proposed "tree chares for Massa Vance." They were given with a will.

"An' now, Massa Vance," said the Reverend Jube, "may de Lord bress yer fur comin' down har from de Norf ter free an' help we. De Lord bress yer an' de young Missis likewise. An' when yer labors am all ended, an' yer 'v chewed all de hard bones, an' swollerd de bitter pill, may yer go ober Jordan wid a tight hold on de Lord, an' not leeb go till yer git clar inter de city ob Zion." *

* Actual words of a negro preacher, taken down on the spot by a hearer.

CHAPTER XLIII.

MAKING THE BEST OF IT.

"O, blest with temper whose unclouded ray
Can make to-morrow cheerful as to-day!" — *Pope.*

A SOUND of the prompter's whistle, sharp and stridulous.

The scenes move, — they dispart. The Crescent City, with its squares and gardens filled with verdure, its stately steeples, and its streets lying lower than the river, and protected only by the great Levee from being converted into a bed for fishes, — the Crescent City, under the swift touch of our fairy scene-shifters, divides, slides, and disappears.

A new scene simultaneously takes its place. It represents a street in New York. Not one of the clean, broad, well-kept avenues, lined on either side with mansions, beautiful and spacious. It is a trans-Bowery Street, narrow and noisome, dirty and dismal. There the market-man stops his cart and haggles for the price of a cabbage with the care-worn housewife, who has a baby in her arms and a two-year-old child tugging at her gown. Poor woman! She tries to cover her bosom as the wayfarer, redolent of bad tobacco, passes by with a grin at her shyness. There the milkman rouses you at daylight by his fiendish yell, a nuisance not yet abated in the more barbarous parts of the city. There the soap-man and the fish-man and the rag-man stop their carts, presenting in their visits the chief incidents that vary the monotony of life in Lavinia Street, if we except an occasional dog-fight.

One of the tenements is a small, two-story brick house, with a basement beneath the street-level, and a dormer window in the attic. A family moved in only the day before yesterday. They have hardly yet got settled. Nevertheless, let us avail ourselves of the author's privilege (universal "dead-head" that he is!) and enter.

We stand in a little hall, the customary flight of stairs being in front, while a door leads into the front sitting-room or parlor on the left. Entering this room, the first figure we notice is an apparently young man, rather stout, with black whiskers and hair, and dressed in a loose sack and pantaloons, in the size and cut of which the liberal fashion of the day is somewhat exaggerated. He stands in low-cut shoes and flesh-colored silk stockings. About his neck he wears a choker of the most advanced style, and tied with a narrow lustring ribbon, gay with red and purple. As his back is partly turned to us, we cannot yet see who he is.

A woman, in age perhaps not far from fifty, with a pleasant, well-rounded face, and attired in a white cambric wrapper, richly embroidered, her hair prudently hidden under a brown chenille net, stands holding a framed picture, waiting for it to be hung. It is Marshall's new engraving of Washington. The lady is Mrs. Pompilard, *born* Aylesford; and the youth on the chair is her husband, the old, yet vernal, the venerable yet blooming, Albert himself. It is more than ten years since he celebrated his seventieth birthday.

Having hung the picture, Pompilard stepped down, and said: "There! Show me the place in the whole city where that picture would show to more advantage than just there in that one spot. The color of the wall, the light from the window are just what they ought to be to bring out all the beauties. Let us not envy Belmont and Roberts and Stewart and Aspinwall their picture-galleries, — let us be guilty of no such folly, Mrs. Pompilard, — while we can show an effect like that!"

"Who spoke of envying them, Albert? Not I, I 'm sure! The house will do famously for our temporary use. Yet it puzzles me a little to know where I am to stow these two children of Melissa's."

"Pooh! That can be easily managed. Leonora can have a mattress put down for her in the upper entry; and as for the five-year-old, Albert, my namesake, he can throw himself down anywhere, — in the wood-shed, if need be. Indeed, his mother tells me she found him, the other night, sleeping on the boards of the piazza, in order, as he said, to harden himself to be a soldier. How is poor Purling this morning?"

"His wound seems to be healing, but he 's deplorably low-spirited; so Melissa tells me."

"Low-spirited? But we must n't allow it! The man who could fight as he did at Fair Oaks ought to be jolly for the rest of his life, even though he had to leave an arm behind him on the battle-field."

"It is n't his wound, I suspect, that troubles him, but the state of his affairs. The truth is, Purling is fearfully poor, and he 's too honest to run in debt. His castles in the air have all tumbled in ruins. Nobody will buy his books, and his publishers have all failed."

"But he can't help that. The poor fellow has done his best, and I maintain that he has talents of a certain sort."

"Perhaps so, but his forte is not imaginative writing."

"Then let him try history."

"But I repeat it, my dear Albert, imaginative writing is not his forte."

"Ah! true. You are getting satirical, Mrs. Pompilard. Our historians, you think, are prone to exercise the novelist's privilege. Let us go up and see the Major."

They mounted one flight of stairs to the door of the front chamber, and knocked. It was opened by Mrs. Purling, once the sentimental Melissa, now a very matronly figure, but still training a few flaxen, maiden-like curls over her temples, and shedding an air of youth and summer from her sky-blue calico robe, with its straw-colored facings. She inherited much of the paternal temperament; and, were it not that her husband's desponding state of mind had clouded her spirits, she would have shown her customary aspect of cheerful serenity.

"Is the Major awake?"

"O yes! Walk in."

"Ah! Cecil, my hearty," exclaimed Pompilard, "how are you getting on?"

"Pretty well, sir. The wound 's healing, I believe. I 'm afraid we 're inconveniencing you shockingly, coming here, all of us, bag and baggage."

"Don't speak of it, Major. Even if we *are* inconvenienced (which I deny), what then? Ought n't *we*, too, to do something for our country? If *you* can afford to contribute an arm, ought n't we to contribute a few trifling conveniences? For my part, I never see a maimed or crippled soldier in the street, that I don't take off my hat to him; and if he is poor, I give him what I can afford. Was he not wounded fighting for the great idea of national honor, integrity, freedom, — fighting for me and my children? The cold-blooded indifference with which people who stay snugly and safely at home pass by these noble relics from the battle-field, and pursue their selfish amusements and occupations while thousands of their countrymen are periling life and health in their behalf, is to me inexplicable. If we can't give anything else, let us at least give our sympathy and respect, our little word of cheer and of honor, to those who have sacrificed so much in order that we might be undisturbed in our comforts!"

"I'm afraid, sir," continued the Major, "that your good feelings blind you to the gravity, in a domestic point of view, of this incursion into your household of the whole Purling race. But the truth is, I expected a remittance, about this time, from my Philadelphia publisher. It does n't come. I wonder what can be the matter?"

Yes! The insatiable Purling, having exhausted New York, had gone to Philadelphia with his literary wares, and had found another victim whose organ of marvellousness was larger than his bump of caution.

"Don't bother yourself about remittances, Major," said Pompilard. "Don't be under any concern. You must n't suppose that because, in an eccentric freak, Mrs. Pompilard has chosen to occupy this little out-of-the-way establishment, the exchequer is therefore exhausted. Some persons might complain of the air of this neighborhood. True, the piny odors of the forest are more agreeable than the exhalations one gets from the desiccating gutters under our noses. True, the song of the thrush is more entrancing than the barbaric yell of that lazy milkman who sits in his cart and shrieks till some one shall come with a pitcher. But in all probability we sha'n't occupy these quarters longer than the summer months. Why it was that Mrs. Pompilard should select them, more especially for the *summer* months, has mystified me a little; but the ladies know best. Am sorry we could n't welcome you at Redcliff or Thrushwood, or some other of our old country-seats ; but — the fact is, we 've disposed of them all. To what we have, my dear Cecil, consider yourself as welcome as votes to a candidate or a contract to an alderman. So don't let me hear you utter the word *remittances* again."

"Ah ! my dear father, we men can make light of these household inconveniences, but they fall heavy on the women."

"Not on my wife, bless her silly heart ! Why, she 'll be going round bragging that she has a wounded Major in her house. She 's proud of you, my hero of ten battles ! Did n't I hear her just now boasting to the water-rate collector, that she had a son in the house who had lost an arm at Fair Oaks ? A son, Major ! Ha, ha, ha ! Was n't it laughable ? She 's trying to make people think you 're her *son !* I tell you, Cecil, while Albert Pompilard has a crust to eat or a kennel to creep into, the brave volunteer, wounded in his country's cause, shall not want for food or shelter."

The Major looked wistfully at Mrs. Pompilard, and said : "He does n't make allowance for a housekeeper's troubles, — does he, mother ? So long as the burden does n't fall on *him*, he does n't realize what a bore it is to have an extra family on one's hands when one barely has accommodations for one's own."

"What *he* says, *I* say, Cecil !" replied Madame, kissing the invalid's pale forehead. "You 're a thousand times welcome, my dear boy, — you and Melissa and the children ; and where will you find two better children, or who give less trouble ? No fear but we can accommodate you all. And if you 've any wounded companion who wants to be taken care of, just send him on. For your sake, Cecil, and for the sake of the old flag, we 'll take him in, and do our best by him."

"Hear her ! Hear the darling little woman !" exclaimed Pompilard, lifting her in his arms, and kissing her with a genuine admiration. "Bravo, wife ! Give me the woman whose house is like a Bowery omnibus, always ready for one more. While this war lasts, every true lady in the land ought to be willing to give up her best room, if wanted, for a hospital."

The hero of Fair Oaks was suddenly found to be snivelling. He made a movement with his right shoulder as if to get a handkerchief, but remembering that his arm was gone, he used his left hand to wipe away his tears. "You 're responsible, between you, for this break-down," said the lachrymose Major. "I 'm sure I thank you. You 've given me two good starts in life already, father, and both times I 've gone under. With such advantages as I 've had, I ought to be a rich man, and here I am a pauper. Poor Melissa and the children are bound to be dependent on their friends. I 'm afraid I 'm an incompetent, a ne'er-do-well."

Pompilard flourished a large white silk handkerchief, and, blowing his nose sonorously, replied: "Bah! 'T was no fault of yours, Cecil, that your operations out West proved a failure. 'T was the fortune of war. I despise the man who never made a blunder. How the deuce could you know that a great financial revulsion was coming on, just after you had bought? Let the spilt milk sink into the sand. Don't fret about it. We 'll have you hearty as a buck in a week or two. You shall rejoin your regiment in time for the next great fight."

The Major smiled faintly, and, shaking his head incredulously, replied: "The fact is, what makes me so low is, that, at the time I went into that last fight, I was just recovering from a fever got in the swamps of the Chickahominy."

"I know all about it, my brave boy! I 've just got a letter, Mrs. Pompilard, from his surgeon. He writes me, he forbade Cecil's moving from his bed; told him 't would be at the risk of his life. Like a gallant soldier, Cecil rose up, pale and wasted as he was, and went into the thick of the frolic. A Minie bullet in the right arm at last checked his activity. Faint from exhaustion and loss of blood, he sank insensible on the damp field, and there lay twenty-four hours without succor, without food, the cold night-dews aggravating his disease."

"Well, father," said the Major, "between you and me, superadded to the fever I got a rheumatic affection, which I 'm afraid will prevent my doing service very soon again in the field."

"So much the better!" returned Pompilard. "Then, my boy, we can keep you at home, — have you with us all the time. You can sit in your library and write books, while Molasses sits by and works slippers for *old blow-hard*, as the boys here in Lavinia Street have begun to call me."

"My books don't sell, sir," sighed the ex-author, with another incredulous shake of the head. "Either there 's a conspiracy among the critics to keep me down, or else I 'm grossly mistaken in my vocation. Besides, I 've lost my right arm, and can't write. "Do you know," he continued, wiping away a tear, — "do you know what one of the newspapers said on receiving the news of my wound? Well, it said, 'This will be a happy dispensation for publishers and the public, if it shall have the effect of keeping the Major from again using the pen!'"

"The unclean reptile!" exclaimed Pompilard, grinding his heel on the floor as if he would crush something. "Don't mind such ribaldry, Major."

"I would n't, if I were n't afraid there 's some truth in it," sighed the unsuccessful author.

"It 's an entire lie!" exclaimed Pompilard; "your books are good books, — excellent books, — and people will find it out some of these days. You shall write another. You don't need an arm, do you, to help you do brain-work? Did n't Sir Walter employ an amanuensis? Why can't Major Purling do the same? Why can't he dictate his *magnum opus*, — the crowning achievement of his literary life, — his history of the Great Rebellion, — why can't he dictate it as well without as with an arm?"

The Major's lips began to work and his eyes to brighten. Ominous of disaster to the race of publishers, the old spirit began to be roused in him, bringing animation and high resolve. The passion of authorship, long repressed, was threatening to rekindle in that bosom. He tried to rub his forehead with his right hand, but finding it gone, he resorted to his left. His hair (just beginning to get crisp and grayish over his ears) he pushed carelessly away from his brow. He jerked himself up from his pillow, and exclaimed: "Upon my word, father-in-law, that 's not a bad idea of yours, — that idea of tackling myself to a history of the war. Let me see. How large a work ought it to be? Could it be compressed into six volumes of the size of Irving's Washington? I think it might. At any rate, I could try. 'A History of the Great Rebellion: its Rise and Fall. By Cecil Purling, late Major of Volunteers.'

Motto: 'All which I saw and part of which I was.' Come, now! That would n't sound badly."

"It would be a trump card for any publisher," said Pompilard, growing to be sincerely sanguine. "Get up the right kind of a Prospectus, and publish the work by subscription. I could procure a thousand subscribers myself. There 's no reason why we should n't get twenty thousand. We might all make our fortunes by it."

"So we might!" exclaimed the excited Major, forgetting that there were ladies present, and that he had on only his drawers, and leaping out of bed, then suddenly leaping back again, and begging everybody's pardon. "It can be easily calculated," continued he. "Just hand me a slip of paper and a pencil, Melissa. Thank you. Look now, father-in-law; twenty thousand copies at two dollars a volume for six volumes would give a hundred and forty thousand dollars clear. Throw off fifty per cent of that for expenses, commissions, printing, binding, et cetera, and we have left for our profit *seventy thousand dollars!*

"Nothing can be plainer," said Pompilard.

"But the publisher would want the lion's share of that," interposed Melissa.

"Pooh! What do *you* know about it?" retorted Pompilard. "If we get up the work by subscription, we can take an office and do our own publishing."

"To be sure we can!" exclaimed the Major, reassured.

Here Pompilard's eldest daughter, Angelica Ireton, long a widow, and old enough to be a grandmother, entered the room with a newspaper.

"What is it, Jelly?" asked the paternal voice.

"News of the surrender of Memphis! And, only think of it! Frederick is highly complimented in the despatch."

"Good for Fred!" said Pompilard. "Make a note of it, Major, for the new history."

A knock at the door now introduced the once elfish and imitative Netty, or Antoinette, grown up into a dignified young lady of striking appearance, who, if not handsome, had a face beaming with intelligence and the cheerfulness of an earnest purpose. She wore, not a Bloomer, but a sort of blouse, which looked well on her erect and slender figure; and her hair, as if to be put out of harm's way in working hours, was combed back into a careless though graceful knot.

"Walk in, Netty!" said the wounded man.

"Here 's our great *artiste*, — our American Rosa Bonheur!" cried Pompilard, patting her on the head.

"Why, father, I never painted a horse or a cow in my life," expostulated Netty. "Remember, I 'm a marine painter. I deal in ships, shipwrecks, calms, squalls, and sea-washed rocks; not in cattle."

"Yes, Cecil, she 's engaged on a bit of beach scenery, which will make a sensation when 't is hung in the Academy. Better sea-water has n't been painted since Vernet; and she beats Vernet in rigging her ships."

"Hear him," said the artistic Netty. "All his geese are swans. What a ridiculous papa it is!"

"Go back to your easel, girl," exclaimed Pompilard. "Cecil and I are talking business."

"And that reminds me," said Netty, "I came to say that Mr. Maloney is in the parlor, and wants to see you."

"Has the rascal found me out so soon?" muttered Pompilard. "I supposed I had dodged him."

"Dodged Mr. Maloney, dear? What harm has he ever committed?" asked Mrs. Pompilard, in surprise.

"No harm, perhaps; but he 's the most persistent of duns."

"Is he dunning you now, my love?"

"Yes, all the time."

"Do you owe him much?"

"Not a cent, confound him!"

"Then what is he dunning you for?"

"O, he 's dunning me to get me to borrow money of him, and I know he can't afford to lend it."

"Go and see him, my dear, and treat him civilly at least."

Pompilard turned to the Major, who was now deep in his Prospectus, and fired with the thought of a grand success that should make amends for all his past failures in authorship. Seeing that the invalid was thoroughly cured of his attack of the blues, Pompilard remarked, "Strike while the iron 's hot, Major," and passed out to meet the visitor who was waiting for him below.

Pat Maloney was pacing the parlor in a great rage; and he exploded in these words, as Pompilard presented himself: "Arn't ye ashamed to look an honest man in the face, yer desateful ould sinner?"

"What 's the bother now, Pat? Whose mare 's dead?" said Pompilard.

"Whose mare 's dead, yer wicked ould man? Is that the kind o' triflin' ye think is goin' down wid Pat Maloney? Look at that wall."

"Well, what of it?"

"What of it? See the cracks of it, bedad, and the dirt of it, and the damp of it, and hearken to the rats of it, yer wicked ould man! What of it? See that baste of a cock-roach comin' out as confidint as ye plaze, and straddlin' across the floor. Smell that smell up there in the corner. Dead rats, by jabbers! And this is the entertainment, is it, ye bring a dacent family to, that was n't born to stenches and filthiness! Typhus and small-pox in every plank under the feet of ye! And a sick sodger ye 've got in the house too; and because he was n't quite kilt down in them swamps on the Chickahominy, ye think ye 'll stink him to death in this hole of all the nastiness!"

"Mr. Maloney, this is my house, sir, such as it is, and I must request you either to walk out of it or to keep a civil tongue in your head."

"Hoo! Ye think to come the dignified over me, do ye, yer silly ould man! I 'm not to be scaret by any such airs. I tell ye it 's bastely to bring dacent women and children inter sich a cesspool as this. By jabbers, I shall have to stop at Barker's, as I go back, and take a bath."

"Maloney, leave the house."

"Lave the house, is it? Not till I 'm ready, will I lave the house on the biddin' of the likes of a man who has n't more regard for the mother that bore him nor to do what you 've been doin', yer ould barbarryan."

"Quit the house, I say! If you think I 'm going to borrow money of a beggarly Irish tailor, you 'll find yourself mistaken, Mr. Pat Maloney!"

"O, it 's that game yez thinkin' to come on me, is it? Ha!

By jabbers, I 'm ready for yer there too. He 's a beggarly Irish tailor, is he? Then why did ye have the likes o' him at all yer grand parties at Redcliff? Why did ye have him and his at all yer little family hops? Why could n't ye git through a forenoon, yer ould hyppercrit, widout the beggarly Irish tailor, to play billiards wid yer, or go a fishin' wid yer, or a sailin' wid yer?"

"I don't choose to keep up the acquaintance, Mr. Maloney, now that you are poor."

"That 's the biggest lie ye iver tould in yer life, yer ould chate!"

"Do you tell me I lie? Out of my house! Pay your own debts, you blackguard Paddy, before you come playing flush of your money to a gentleman like me."

"A jintleman! Ye call yerself a jintleman, do ye, — ye onnateral ould simpleton? Ye bring born ladies inter a foul, unreputable house like this is, in a foul, unreputable street, wid a house of ill-fame on both sides of yer, and another oppersit, and then ye call yerself a jintleman. A jintleman, bedad! Ha, ha!"

"You lie, Pat Maloney. My next-door neighbors are decent folks, — much decenter than you are, you foul-mouthed Paddy."

"And thin ye tell me to pay my debts, do yer? Find the debt of Pat Maloney's that 's unpaid, and he 'll pay it double, yer unprincipled ould calumniator. If 't warrent for yer eighty yares, I 'd larrup yer on the spot."

"I claim no privilege of age, you cowardly tailor. That 's a dodge of yours that won't serve. Come on, you ninth part of a man, if you have even that much of a man left in you. Come on, or I 'll pound your head against the wall."

"Ye 'd knock the house down, bedad, if ye tried it. I 'd like no better sport nor to polish ye off wid these two fists of mine, yer aggrawatin' superannuated ould haythen."

"You shall find what my eighty years can do, you ranting Paddy. Since you won't go quietly out of the house, I 'll put you out."

And Pompilard began pulling up his sleeves, as if for action. Maloney was not behind him in his pugilistic demonstrations.

"If ye want to have the wind knocked out of yer," said he, "jist try it, yer quarrelsome ould bully, — gittin' up a disturbance like this at your time of life!"

Here Angelica, who had been listening at the door, burst into the room, and interposed between the disputants. By the aid of some mysterious signs and winks addressed to Maloney, she succeeded in pacifying him so far that he took up his hat, and shaking his head indignantly at Pompilard, followed her out of the room. The front door was heard to open and close. Then there was a slight creaking on the basement stairs, followed by a coughing from Angelica, and a minute afterwards she re-entered the parlor.

She found her father with his fists doubled, and his breast thrown back, knocking down an imaginary Irishman in dumb show.

"Has that brute left the house?" he asked.

"Yes, father. What did he want?"

"He has been dunning me to borrow a couple of thousand dollars of him, — the improvident old fool. He needs every cent of his money in his business. He knows it. He merely wants to put me under an obligation, knowing I may never pay him back. He can't dupe me."

"If 't would gratify poor Maloney, why not humor him?" said Angelica. "He feels eternally grateful to you for having made a man of him. You helped him to a fortune. He has often said he owed it to you that he was n't a sot about the streets."

"If I helped him to a fortune, I showed him how to lose it, Jelly. So there we 're just even. I tell you I won't get in debt again, if I can help it. You, Jelly, are the only one I 've borrowed from since the last great crash."

"And in borrowing from me, you merely take back your own," interposed Angelica.

"I 've paid everything in the way of a debt, principal and interest," said Pompilard. "And I don't want to break the charm again at my time of life. Debt is the Devil's own snare. I know it from sad experience. I 've two good schemes on foot for retrieving my affairs, without having to risk much money in the operation. If you can let me have five hundred dollars, I think 't will be the only nest-egg I shall need."

"Certainly, father," said Angelica; and going down-stairs into the basement, she found the persevering Maloney waiting her coming.

"Mr. Maloney," said she, "let me propose a compromise. My father wants five hundred dollars of me. I have n't it to give him. But if you 'll lend it on my receipt, I 'll take it and be very thankful."

"Make it a thousand, and I 'll say yes," said Pat.

"Well, I 'll not haggle with you, Mr. Maloney," replied Angelica.

Maloney handed her the money, and, refusing to take a receipt, seized his hat, and quitted the house by the back area, looking round suspiciously, and snuffing contemptuously at the surroundings, as he emerged into the alley-way which conducted him to one of the streets leading into the Bowery.

Angelica put five hundred dollars in her port-monnaie, and handed the like amount to her sire. He thrust it into his vest-pocket, brushed his hat, and arranged his choker. Mrs. Pompilard came down with the Prospectus that was to be the etymon of a new fortune. He took it, kissed wife and daughter, and issued from the house.

As he passed up Lavinia Street, many a curious eye from behind curtains and blinds looked out admiringly on the imposing figure. One boy on the sidewalk remarked to another: "I say, Ike, who is that old swell as has come into our street? I 've a mind to shy this dead kitten at him."

"Don't do it, Peter Craig!" exclaimed Ike; "father says that man 's a detective, — a feller as sees you when you think he ain't looking. We 'd better mind how we call arter him again, 'Old blow-hard!'"

CHAPTER XLIV.

A DOMESTIC RECONNOISSANCE.

"O Spirit of the Summer time!
  Bring back the roses to the dells;
The swallow from her distant clime,
  The honey-bee from drowsy cells.
Bring back the singing and the scent
  Of meadow-lands at dewy prime; —
O, bring again my heart's content,
  Thou Spirit of the Summer time!"
W. Allingham.

THE following Wednesday, Pompilard returned rather earlier than usual from his diurnal visit to Wall Street. He brought home a printed copy of the Prospectus, and sent it up-stairs to the wounded author. Then taking from the book-case a yellow-covered pamphlet, he composed himself in an arm-chair, and, resting his legs on an ottoman, began reading that most thrilling production of the season, "The Guerilla's Bride, or the Temptation and the Triumph, by Carrie Cameron."

Mrs. Pompilard glided into the room, and, putting her hands over his eyes from behind, said, "What 's the matter, my love?"

"Matter? Nothing, wife! Leave me to my novel."

"Always of late," she replied, "when I see you with one of these sensation novels, I know that something has gone wrong with you."

"Nonsense, you silly woman! I know what you want. It 's a kiss. There! Take it and go."

"You 've lost money!" said Madam, receiving the kiss, then shaking her finger at him, and returning to her household tasks.

She was right in her surmise. Pompilard, hopeful of Union victories on the Peninsula of Virginia, had been selling gold in expectation of a fall. There had been a large rise, and his five hundred dollars had been swallowed up in the great maw of

Wall Street like a straw in Niagara. He passed the rest of that day in the house, reading his novel, or playing backgammon with the Major.

The next morning, putting the Prospectus and his pride with it in his pocket, he issued forth, resolved to see what could be done in furtherance of the grand literary scheme which was to immortalize and enrich his son-in-law. Entering Broadway he walked up to Union Park, then along Fourteenth Street to the Fifth Avenue. And now, every square or two, he would pass door-plates that displayed some familiar name. Frequently he would be tempted to stop, but he passed on and on, until he came to one which bore in large black walnut letters the name CHARLTON.

With this gentleman he had not had any intercourse since the termination of that great lawsuit in which they had been opposed. Charlton, having put the greater part of his property into gold just before the war, had made enormous sums by the rise in the precious metal. It was noticed in Wall Street, that he was growing fat; that he had lost his anxious, eager look. War was not such a bad thing after all. Surely he would be glad of the opportunity of subscribing for five or ten copies of the wounded Purling's great work.

These considerations encouraged the credulous Pompilard to call. A respectable private carriage stood before the house, and in it sat a young lady, probably Miss Charlton, playing with a pet spaniel. Pompilard rang the door-bell, and a dapper footman in white gloves ushered him up-stairs into the library. Here Charlton sat computing his profits on the rates of exchange as given in that day's report.

He rose on Pompilard's entrance, and with a profuse politeness that contrasted somewhat with his manner on previous occasions, shook hands with him, and placed him in a seat. Excessive prosperity had at last taught Charlton to temper his refusals with gracious speech. It was so much cheaper to give smooth words than solid coin!

"Am delighted to see you, Mr. Pompilard!" quoth he. "How fresh and young you 're looking! Your family are all well, I trust."

"All save my son-in-law, Major Purling. He, having been

thrown on his back by a bad wound and by sickness got in camp, now proposes to occupy himself with preparing a history of the war. Here is his Prospectus, and we want your name to head the subscription."

"A most laudable project! Excellent! I don't doubt the Major's ability to produce a most authentic and admirable work. I shall take great pleasure in commending it to my friends."

Here Charlton, who had received one of the papers from Pompilard, and glanced at it, handed it back to the old man.

"I want your autograph, Mr. Charlton. The work, you perceive, will be in six volumes at only two dollars a volume. For how many copies will you put down your name?"

"Excuse me, Mr. Pompilard, but the demands on my purse for objects, public and private, are so incessant just now, that I must decline subscribing. Probably when the work is published I shall desire to procure a copy for my library. I have heard of Major Purling as a gallant officer and a distinguished writer. I can't doubt he will succeed splendidly. Make my compliments to your estimable family."

Here a lady elegantly dressed, as if for a promenade, entered the room, and asked for the morning paper. She looked searchingly at Pompilard, and then went up to him, and putting out her hand, said, "Have you forgotten Charlotte Dykvelt?"

"Impossible! Who could have believed it? And you are now Mrs. Charlton!"

The lady's lip curled a little, as if no gracious emotion came with the reminder. Then taking from the old man's hand the printed sheet which Charlton had returned to him, she exclaimed: "What have we here? A Prospectus! Is not Major Purling your son-in-law? To be sure he is! A brave officer! He must be encouraged in his project. And how is your daughter, Mrs. Ireton? I see," continued Mrs. Charlton, laying down the Prospectus and pulling away nervously at her gloves, — "I see that your grandson, Captain Ireton, has been highly complimented for gallant behavior on the Mississippi."

"Yes, he 's a good boy, is Fred. Do you know he was a great admirer of yours?"

The lady was suddenly absorbed in looking for a certain advertisement of a Soldier's Relief Meeting. Pompilard took up his Prospectus, began folding it, and rose from his chair as if to go.

"Let me look at that Prospectus a moment," said Mrs. Charlton, taking up a pen.

"Certainly," he replied, handing her the paper. While she read it, he examined what appeared a bronze vase that stood on one side of the table. He undertook to lift it, and drew out from a socket, which extended beneath the surface of the wood, a polished steel tube.

"Take care, Mr. Pompilard!" said Charlton; "'t is loaded. No one would suppose 't was a revolver, eh? I got it the day after old Van Wyck was robbed, sitting in his library. Please don't mention the fact that I have such a weapon within my reach."

"I have put down my name for thirty copies," said Mrs. Charlton, returning to Pompilard his Prospectus.

"But this is munificent, Madam!" exclaimed the old man.

Charlton gnawed his lips in helpless anger.

Madam had played her cards so well, that it was a stipulation she and her daughter should have each a large allowance, in the spending of which they were to be independent. Drawing forth her purse, she took from it three one hundred dollar bills, a fifty, and a ten, and handed them to Pompilard.

"Do you wish to pay in advance, Madam?" he asked.

"I wish that money to be paid directly to the author, to aid him in his patriotic labors," she replied. "There need be no receipt, and there need be no delivery of books."

Pompilard took the bills and looked her in the face. He felt that words would be impertinent in conveying his thanks. She gave him one sad, sweet smile of acknowledgment of his silent gratitude. "Major Purling," said he, in a tone that trembled a little, "will be greatly encouraged by your liberality. I will bid you good morning, Madam. Good morning, Mr. Charlton!"

Husband and wife were left alone.

"That 's the way you fool away my money, is it, Mrs. Charlton? Three hundred and sixty dollars disposed of already! A nice morning's work!"

"You speak of the money as yours, sir. You forget. By

contract it is mine. I shall spend it as I choose. Does not our agreement say that my allowance and my daughter's shall be absolutely at our disposal?"

"Those allowances, Mrs. Charlton, must be cut down to meet the state of the times. I can't afford them any longer."

"Sir, you say what you know to be untrue. Your profits from the rise in exchange alone, since the war began, have already been two hundred thousand dollars. The rise in your securities generally has been enormous. And yet you talk of not *affording* the miserable pittance you allow me and my daughter!"

"A miserable pittance! O yes! Ten thousand a year for pin-money is a very miserable pittance."

"So it is, when one lays by five times that amount of superfluous income. Thank me that I don't force you to double the allowance. Do you think to juggle *me* with your groans about family expenses and the hard times? Am I so easily duped, think you, as not to see through the miserly sham?"

"This is the woman that promised to love, honor, and obey!"

"Do you twit me with that? Go back, Charlton, to that first day you pressed me to be your wife. I frankly told you I could not love you, — that I loved another. You made light of all that. You enlisted the influence of my parents against me. You drove me into the toils. No sooner was I married than I found that you, with all your wealth, had chosen me merely because you thought I was rich. What a satisfaction it was to me when I heard of my father's failure! What was your disappointment, — your rage! But there was no help for it. And so we settled down to a loveless life, in which we have thus far been thoroughly consistent. You go your way, and I mine. You find your rapture in your coupons and dividends; I seek such distraction as I can in my little charities, my Sanitary Aid Societies, and my Seaman's Relief. If you think to cut me off from these resources, the worst will probably be your own."

Charlton was cowed and nonplussed, as usual in these altercations. "There, go!" said he. "Go and make ducks and drakes of your money in your own way. That old Pomposity has left his damned Prospectus here on the table."

Mrs. Charlton passed out and down-stairs. On a slab in the hall was a bouquet which a neighboring greenhouse man she had befriended had just left. She stooped to smell of it. What was there in the odors which brought back associations that made her bow her head while the tears gushed forth? Conspicuous among the flowers was a bunch of English violets,—just such a little bunch as Frederick Ireton used to bring her in those far-off days, when the present and the future seemed so flooded with rose-hues.

"Miss Lucy wants to know if you 're ever coming?" said a servant.

"Yes!" replied Mrs. Charlton. "'T is too bad to keep her waiting so!" And the next moment she joined her daughter in the carriage.

Meanwhile Charlton, as his wife left him, had groaned out, in soliloquy, "What a devil of a woman! How different from my first wife!" Then he sought consolation in the quotations of stock. While he read and chuckled, there was a knock. It was only Pompilard returned for his Prospectus. As the old man was folding it up, the white-gloved footman laid a card before Charlton. "Vance!" exclaimed the latter: "I 'm acquainted with no such person. Show him up."

Vance had donned his citizen's dress. He wore a blue frock, fastened by a single black silk button at the top, a buff vest, white pantaloons, and summer shoes. Without a shoulder-strap, he looked at once the soldier and the gentleman. Rapidly and keenly he took Charlton's physiognomical measure, then glanced at Pompilard. The latter having folded up his Prospectus, was turning to quit the room. As he bowed on departing, Charlton remarked, "Good day to you, Mr. Pompilard."

"Did I hear the name Pompilard?" inquired Vance.

"That is my name, sir," replied the old man.

"Is it he whose wife was a Miss Aylesford?"

"The same, sir."

"Mr. Pompilard, I have been trying to find you. My carriage is at the door. Will you do me the favor to wait in it five minutes for me till I come down?"

"Certainly, sir." And Pompilard went out.

"Now, Mr. Charlton," said Vance, "what I have to say is, that I am called Colonel Vance; that I am recently from New Orleans; that while there it became a part of my official duty to look at certain property held in your name, but claimed by another party."

"Claimed by a rebel and a traitor, Colonel Vance. I'm delighted to see you, sir. Will you be seated?"

"No, thank you. Let me propose to you, that, as preliminary to other proceedings, I introduce to you to-night certain parties who came with me from New Orleans, and whose testimony may be at once interesting and useful."

"I shall be obliged to you for the interview, Colonel Vance."

"It would be proper that your confidential lawyer should be present; for it may be well to cross-question some of the witnesses."

"Thank you for the suggestion, Colonel Vance. I shall avail myself of it."

"As there will be ladies in the party, I hope your wife and daughter will be present."

"I will give them your message."

"Tell them we have a young officer with us who was shot through the lungs in battle not long since. Shall we make the hour half-past eight; — place, the Astor House?"

"That would suit me precisely, Colonel Vance."

"Then I will bid you good day, sir, for the present."

Charlton put out his hand, but Vance bowed without seeming to notice it, and passed out of the house into the carriage.

"Mr. Pompilard," said he, as the carriage moved on, "are you willing to take me on trust, say for the next hour, as a gentleman, and comply with my reasonable requests without compelling me to explain myself further? Call me, if you please, Mr. Vance."

"Truly, Mr. Vance," replied Pompilard, "I do not see how I risk much in acceding to your proposition. If you were an impostor, you would hardly think of fleecing *me*, for I am shorn close already. Besides, you carry the right signet on your front. Yes, I *will* trust you, Mr. Vance."

"Thank you, sir. Your wife is living?"

"I left her alive and well some two hours ago."

"Has she any children of her own?"

"One, — a daughter, Antoinette. We call her Netty. A most extraordinary creature! An artist, sir! Paints sea-pieces better than Lane, Bradford, or Church himself. A girl of decided genius."

"Well, Mr. Pompilard, if your house is not far from here, I wish to drive to it at once, and have your wife and daughter do us the honor to take seats in this carriage."

"That we can do, Mr. Vance. Driver, 27 Lavinia Street! The day is pleasant. They will enjoy a drive. I must make you acquainted with my son-in-law, Major Purling. A noble fellow, sir! Had an arm shot off at Fair Oaks. Used up, too, by fever. Brave as Julius Cæsar! And, like Julius Cæsar, writes as well as he fights. He proposes getting up a history of the war. Here 's his Prospectus."

Vance looked at it. "I must n't be outdone," said he, "by a lady. Put me down also for thirty copies. Put down Mr. Winslow and Madame Volney each for as many more."

"But that is astounding, sir!" cried Pompilard. "A hundred and twenty copies disposed of already! The Major will jump out of his bed at the news!"

As the carriage crossed the Bowery and bowled into Lavinia Street, Pompilard remarked: "There are some advantages, Mr. Vance, in being on the East River side. We get a purer sea air in summer, sir."

At that moment an unfortunate stench of decayed vegetables was blown in upon them, by way of comment, and Pompilard added: "You see, sir, we are very particular about removing all noxious rubbish. Health, sir, is our first consideration. We have the dirt-carts busy all the time."

Here the carriage stopped. "A modest little place we have taken for the summer, Mr. Vance. Small, but convenient and retired. Most worthy and quiet people, our neighbors. Walk in, sir."

They entered the parlor. "Take a seat, Mr. Vance. If you 've a taste for art, let me commend to your examination that fine engraving between the windows. Here 's a new book, if you are literary, — Miss Carrie Cameron's famous novel. Amuse yourself."

And having handed him "The Guerilla's Bride," Pompilard rushed up-stairs. Instantly a great tumult was heard in the room over Vance's head. It was accompanied with poundings, jumpings, and exultant shouts. Three hundred and sixty dollars had been placed on the coverlid beneath which lay the wounded Purling. It was the first money his literary efforts had ever brought him. The spell was broken. Thenceforth the thousands would pour in upon him in an uninterrupted flood. Can it be wondered that there was much jubilation over the news?

Vance was of course introduced to all the inmates, and made a partaker in their good spirits. At last Mrs. Pompilard and Netty were dressed and ready. Vance handed them into the carriage. He and Pompilard took the back seat. As they drove off they encountered a crowd before an adjoining door. It was composed of some of those "most worthy and quiet neighbors" of whom Pompilard had recently spoken. They were gathering, amid a Babel of voices, round a cart where an ancient virago, Milesian by birth, was berating a butcher whom she charged with having sold her a stale leg of mutton the week before.

"One misses these bustling little scenes in the rural districts," quoth Pompilard. "They serve to give color and movement, life and sparkle, to our modest neighborhood."

"Mrs. Pompilard," said Vance, "we are on our way to the Astor House, where I propose to introduce to you a young lady. I wish you and your daughter to scrutinize her closely, and to tell me if you see in her a likeness to any one you have ever known."

CHAPTER XLV.

ANOTHER DESCENDANT OF THE CAVALIERS.

"Those flashes of marvellous light point to the existence of dormant faculties, which, unless God can be supposed to have *over-furnished* the soul for its appointed field of action, seem only to be awaiting more favorable circumstances, to awaken and disclose themselves." —*John James Tayler.*

WHILE the carriage is rolling on, and the occupants are getting better acquainted, let us hurry forward and clear the way by a few explanations.

Vance and his party had now been several days in New York, occupying contiguous suites of rooms at the Astor House. The ladies consisted of Clara, Madam Volney, and Mrs. Ripper (late Mrs. Gentry). Esha was, of course, of the party. She had found her long-lost daughter in Hattie, or Mrs. Davy, now a widow, whose testimony came in to fortify the proofs that seemed accumulating to place Clara's identity beyond dispute. Hattie joyfully resumed her place as Clara's *femme de chambre*, though the post was also claimed by the unyielding Esha.

The gentlemen of the party included Mr. Winslow, Mr. Semmes, Mr. Ripper, Captain Onslow, Colonel Delancy Hyde, and a youth not yet introduced.

Never had Vance showed his influence in so marked a degree as in the change he had wrought in Hyde. Detecting in the rascal's affection for a widowed sister the one available spot in his character, Vance, like a great moral engineer, had mounted on that vantage-ground the guns which were to batter down the citadels of ignorance, profligacy, and pride, in which all the regenerative capabilities of Hyde's nature had been imprisoned so long. The idea of having that poor toiling sister — her who had "fust taught him to make dirt-pies, down thar by the old duck-pond" — rescued with her children from poverty and suffering, placed in a situation of comfort and respectability, was so overpowering to the Colonel, that it enabled Vance to lead him like a child even to the abjuring of strong drink and profanity. Cut off from bragging of his Virginia birth and his descent from the Cavaliers, — made to see the false and senseless nature of the slang which he had been taught to expectorate against the "Yankees," — Hyde might have lost his identity in the mental metamorphosis he was undergoing, were it not that a most timely substitute presented itself as a subject for the expenditure of his surplus gas.

Vance had collected and arranged a body of proofs for the establishment of Clara's identification as the daughter of Henry Berwick; but, if Colonel Hyde's memory did not mislead him, there was collateral evidence of the highest importance in those old letters from Charlton, which might be found in a certain trunk in the keeping of the Widow Rusk in Alabama. With deep anxiety, therefore, did they await the coming of that youthful representative of the Hyde family, Master Delancy Hyde Rusk.

The Colonel stood on the steps of the Astor House from early morn till dewy eve, day after day, scrutinizing every boy who came along. Clad in a respectable suit of broadcloth, and concealing the shorn state of his scalp under a brown wig, he did no discredit to the character of Mr. Stetson's guests. His patience was at length rewarded. A boy, travel-soiled and dusty, apparently fifteen years old, dressed in a butternut-colored suit, wearing a small military cap marked C. S. A., and bearing a knapsack on his back, suddenly accosted Colonel Hyde with the inquiry, "Does Mr. William C. Vance live here?" In figure, face, and even the hue of his eyebrows, the youth was a miniature repetition of the Colonel himself; but the latter, in his wig and his new suit, was not recognized till the exclamation, "Delancy!" broke in astonishment from his lips.

"What, uncle? Uncle Delancy?" cried the boy; and the two forgot the proprieties, and embraced in the very eyes of Broadway. Then the Colonel led the way to his room.

"Is this 'ere room yourn, Uncle D'lancy? An' is this 'ere trunk yourn? And this 'ere umbrel? Crikee! What a fine trunk! And do you and the damned Yankees bet now on the same pile, Uncle D'lancy?"

"Delancy Hyde Rusk," said the Colonel solemnly, "stahnd up thar afore me. So! That 'll do! Now look me straight in the face, and mind what I say."

"Yes, uncle," said Delancy junior, deeply impressed.

"Fust, have yer got them air letters?"

"Yes, uncle, they 're sewed inter my side-pocket, right here."

"Wal an' good. Now tell me how 's yer mother an' all the family."

"Mother 's middlin' bright now; but Malviny, she died in a fit last March, and Tom, the innocent, he died too; and Charlotte Ann, she was buried the week afore your letter cum; and mother, she had about gi'n up; for we had n't a shinplaster left after payin' for the buryin', and we thowt as how we should have ter starve, sure; and lame Andrew Jackson and the two young 'uns, they wahr lookin' pretty considerable peakid, I kn tell yer, when all at wunst your letter cum with four hunderd dollars in it. Crikee! Did n't the old woman scream for joy? Did n't she hug the childern, and cry, and laugh, and take on, till we all thowt she was crazy-like? And did n't she jounce down on her knees, and pray, jest like a minister does?"

"Did she? Did she, Delancy? Tell it over to me again. Did she raally pray?"

"I reckon she did n't do nothin' else."

"Try ter think what she said, Delancy. Try ter think. It 's important."

"Wal, 't was all about the Lord Jesus, and Brother D'lancy, and not forsakin' the righteous, and bless the Lord, O my soul, and the dear angels that was took away, and then about Brother D'lancy again, and might the Lord put his everlastin' arms about him, and might the Lord save his soul alive, and all that wild sort of talk, yer know. Why, uncle! Uncle D'lancy! What 's the matter with yer?"

Yes! the old sinner had boo-hooed outright; and then, coving his face with his hands, he wept as if he were making up for a long period of drought in the lachrymal line.

We have spoken of the influence which Vance had applied to this stony nature. We should have spoken of other influences, perhaps more potent still, that had reached it through

Peek. Before the exodus from New Orleans, Peek had introduced him to certain phenomena which had shaken the Colonel's very soul, by the proofs they gave him of powers transcending those usually ascribed to mortals, or admitted as possible by science. The proofs were irresistible to his common sense, *First*, That there was a power outside of himself that could read, not only his inmost nature, but his individual thoughts, as they arose, and this without any aid from him by look, word, or act.

Here was a test in which there was no room left for deception. The *savans* can only explain it by denying it; and there are in America more than three millions of men and women who *know* what the denial amounts to. Given a belief in clairvoyance, and that in spirits and immortality follows. The motto of the ancient Pagan theists was, "*Si divinatio est, dii sunt.*" *

Secondly, Hyde saw heavy physical objects moved about, floated in the air, made to perform intelligent offices, and all without the intervention of any agencies recognized as material.

The hard, cold atheism of the man's heart was smitten, rent, and displaced. For the first time, he was made to feel that the body's death is but a process of transition in the soul's life; that our trials here have reference to a future world; that what we love we become; that heavenly thoughts must be entertained and relished even here, if we would not have heaven's occupations a weariness and a perplexity to us hereafter. For the first time, the awful consciousness came over him as a reality, that all his acts and thoughts were under the possible scrutiny of myriads of spiritual eyes, and, above them all, those Supreme eyes in whose sight even the stars are not pure,—how much less, then, man that is a worm! For the first time, he could read the Bible, and catch from its mystic words rich gleams of comforting truth. For the first time, he could feel the meaning of that abused and uncomprehended word, *pardon;* and he could dimly see the preciousness of Christ's revelations of the Father's compassion.

Return we to the interview between uncle and nephew.

* If there is divination (clairvoyance), there must be gods (spirits).

Having wiped his eyes and steadied his voice, the Colonel said: "Delancy Hyde Rusk, yer 've got ter larn some things, and unlarn others. Fust of all, you 're not to swar, never no more."

"What, Uncle D'lancy! Can't I swar when I grow up? *You* swar, Uncle D'lancy!"

"I 'm clean cured of it, nevvy. Ef ever you har me swar again, Delancy Hyde Rusk, you jes tell me of 't, an' I 'll put myself through a month's course of hard-tack an' water."

"Can't I say *hell*, Uncle D'lancy, nor *damn*?"

"You 're not ter use them words profanely, nevvy, unless you want that air back of yourn colored up with a rope's end. Now look me straight in the face, Delancy Hyde Rusk, an' tell me ef yer ever drink sperrits?"

"Wall, Uncle D'lancy, I promised the old woman —"

"Stop! Say you promised mother."

"Wall, I promised mother I would n't drink, and I have n't."

"Good! Now, nevvy, yer spoke jest now of the Yankees. What do yer mean by Yankees?"

"I mean, uncle, ev'ry man born in a State whar they hain't no niggers to wallop. Yankees are sneaks and cowards. Can't one Suth'n-born man whip any five Yankees?"

"I reckon not."

"What! Not ef the Suth'n man 's Virginia-born?"

"I reckon not. Delancy Hyde Rusk, that 's the decoy the 'ristocrats down South have been humbuggin' us poor whites with tell the common sense is all eat clean out of our brains. They stuff us up with that air fool's brag so we may help 'em hold on ter thar niggers. Whar did the Yankees come from? They camed from England like we did. They speak English like we do. Thar ahnces'tors an' our ahnces'tors war countrymen. Now don't be sich a lout as ter suppose that 'cause a man lives North, and hain't no niggers ter wallop, he must be either a sneak or a coward, or what Jeff Davis calls a hyena."

"Ain't we down South the master race, Uncle D'lancy?"

"Wall, nevvy, in some respects we air; in some respects not. In dirt an' vermin, ignorance an' sloth, our poor folks kn giv thar poor folks half the game, an' beat 'em all holler. In brag an' swagger our rich folks kn beat thars. But I 'll tell yer what it is, nevvy: ef, as the slaveholders try to make us think, it 's slavery that makes us the master race, then we must be powerful poor cattle to owe it to niggers and not to ou'selves that we 're better nor the Yankees. Now mind what I 'm goin' ter say: the best thing for the hull Suth'n people would be to set ev'ry slave free right off at wunst."

"What, Uncle D'lancy! Make a nigger free as a white man? Can't I, when I 'm a man, own niggers like gra'f'ther Hyde done? What 's the use of growin' up ef I can't have a nigger to wallop when I want ter, I sh'd like ter know?"

"Delancy Hyde Rusk, them sentiments must be nipped in the bud."

The Colonel went to the door and locked it, then cast his eyes round the room as if in search of something. The boy followed his movements with a curiosity in which alarm began to be painfully mingled. Finally, the Colonel pulled a strap from his trunk, and, approaching Delancy junior, who was now uttering a noise between a whimper and a howl, seized him by the nape of the neck, bent him down face foremost on to the bed, and administered a succession of smart blows on the most exposed part of his person. The boy yelled lustily; but after the punishment was over, he quickly subsided into a subdued snuffling.

"Thar, Delancy Hyde Rusk! yer 'll thahnk me fur that air latherin' all the days of yer life. Ef I 'd a-had somebody to do as much for me, forty yars ago, I should n't have been the beast that Slavery brung me up ter be. Never you talk no more of keepin' niggers or wallopin' niggers. They 've jest as much right ter wallop you as you have ter wallop them. Slavery 's gone up, sure. That game 's played out. Thank the Lord! Jest you bar in mind, Delancy Hyde Rusk, that the Lord made the black man as well as the white, and that ef you go fur to throw contempt on the Lord's work, he 'll bring yer up with a short turn, sure. Will you bar that in mind fur the rest of yer life, Delancy Hyde Rusk?"

"Yes, Uncle D'lancy. I woan't do nothin' else."

"An' ef anybody goes fur to ask yer what you air, jest you speak up bright an' tell him you 're fust a Union man, an' then an out-an'-out Abolitionist. Speak it out bold as ef you meant it, — *Ab-o-litionist!*"

"What, uncle! a d-d-da —"

The boy's utterance subsided into a whimper of expostulation as he saw the Colonel take up the strap.

But he was spared a second application. Having given him his first lesson in morals and politics, Colonel Hyde made him wash his face, and then took him down-stairs and introduced him to Vance. The latter received with eagerness the precious letters of which the boy was the bearer; at once opened them, and having read them, said to Hyde: "I would not have failed getting these for many thousand dollars. Still there 's no knowing what trap the lawyers may spring upon us."

Turning to Delancy junior, Vance, who had opened all the windows when the youth came in, questioned him as to his adventures on his journey. The boy showed cleverness in his replies. It was a proud day for the elated Hyde when Vance said: "That nephew of yours shall be rewarded. He 's an uncommonly shrewd, observing lad. Now take him down-stairs and give him a hot bath. Soak him well; then scrub him well with soap and sand. Let him put on an entire new rig, — shirt, stockings, everything. You can buy them while he 's rinsing himself in a second water. Also take him to the barber's and have his hair cut close, combed with a fine-tooth comb, and shampooed. Do this, and then bring him up to my room to dinner. Here 's a fifty-dollar bill for you to spend on him."

Three hours afterwards Delancy junior reappeared, too much astonished to recognize his own figure in the glass. Colonel Hyde had thenceforth a new and abounding theme for gasconade in describing the way "that air bi, sir, trahv'ld the hull distance from Montgomery ter New York, goin' through the lines of both armies, sir, an' bringin' val'able letters better nor a grown man could have did."

A dinner at Vance's private table, with ladies and gentlemen present, put the apex to the splendid excitements of the day in the minds of both uncle and nephew.

CHAPTER XLVI.

THE NIGHT COMETH.

"How swift the shuttle flies that weaves thy shroud!" — *Young.*

ON the evening of the day of the encounter in Charlton's library, some of the principal persons of our story were assembled in one of the private parlors of the Astor House in New York.

Some hours previously, Vance had introduced Clara to her nearest relatives, the Pompilards; but before telling them her true name he had asked them to trace a resemblance. Instantly Netty had exclaimed: "Why, mother, it is the face you have at home in the portrait of Aunt Leonora." And Aunt Leonora was the grandmother of Clara!

Vance then briefly presented his proofs of the relationship. Who could resist them? Pompilard, in a high state of excitement, put his hands under Clara's arms, lifted her to a level with his lips, and kissed her on both cheeks. His wife, her grand-aunt, greeted her not less affectionately; and in embracing "Cousin Netty," Clara was charmed to find a congenial associate.

Pompilard all at once recollected the gold casket which old Toussaint had committed to his charge for Miss Berwick. Writing an order, he got Clara to sign it, and then strode out of the room, delighted with himself for remembering the trust. Half an hour afterwards he returned and presented to his grand-niece the beautiful jewel-box, the gift of her father's step-mother, Mrs. Charlton. Clara received it with emotion, and divesting it of the cotton-wool in which it had been kept wrapped and untouched so many years, she unlocked it, and drew forth this letter: —

"MY DEAR LITTLE GRANDDAUGHTER: This comes to you from one to whom you seem nearer than any other she leaves behind. She wishes she could make you wise through her experience. Since her heart is full of it, let her speak it. In that event, so important to your happiness, your marriage, may you be warned by her example, and neither let your affections blind your reason, nor your reason underrate the value of the affections. Be sure not only that you love, but that you are loved. Choose cautiously, my dear child, if you choose at all; and may your choice be so felicitous that it will serve for the next world as well as this. E. B. C."

The Pompilards remained of course to dinner; and then to the expected interview of the evening. They were introduced to the highly-dressed bride, Mrs. Ripper, formerly Clara's teacher; also to the quadroon lady, Madame Volney. And then the gentlemen — Captain Onslow, Messrs. Winslow, Semmes, and Ripper, and last, not least, Colonel Delancy Hyde and his nephew — were all severally and formally presented to the Pompilards.

"Does it appear from Charlton's letters to Hyde that Charlton knew of Hyde's villany in kidnapping the child?" asked Mr. Semmes of Vance.

"No, Charlton was unquestionably ignorant, and is so to this day, of the fact that the true heir survives. All that he expected Hyde to do was to so shape his testimony as to make it appear that the child died *after* the mother and *before* the father. On this nice point all Charlton's chances hung. And the letters are of the highest importance in showing that it was intimated by the writer to Hyde, that, in case his testimony should turn out to be of a certain nature, he, Hyde, besides having his and Quattles's expenses to New York all paid, should receive a thousand dollars."

"That is certainly a tremendous point against Charlton. Is it possible that Hyde did not see that he held a rod over Charlton in those letters?"

"Both he and Quattles appear to have been very shallow villains. Probably they did not comprehend the legal points at issue, and never realized the vital importance of their testimony."

"Let me suggest," said Semmes, "the importance of having Charlton recognize Hyde in the presence of witnesses."

"Yes, I had thought of that, and arranged for it."

Here there was a stir in the little unoccupied anteroom adjoining. The Charltons and Charlton's lawyer, Mr. Detritch, had arrived. The ladies were removing their bonnets and shawls. Hyde drew near to Vance, and the latter threw open the door. Charlton entered first. The prospect of recovering his New Orleans property had put him in the most gracious of humors. His dyed hair, his white, well-starched vest, his glossy black dress-coat and pantaloons, showed that his personal appearance was receiving more than usual attention. He would have been called a handsome man by those who did not look deep as Lavater.

After saluting Vance, Charlton started on recognizing the gaunt figure of Delancy Hyde. Concluding at once that the Colonel had come as a friend, Charlton exclaimed: "What! My old friend, Colonel Delancy Hyde? Is it possible?"

And there was a vehement shaking of hands between them.

Detritch and the ladies having entered, all the parties were formally introduced to one another. The mention of Miss Berwick's name excited no surprise on the part of any one.

The company at once disposed themselves in separate groups for conversation. Captain Onslow gave his arm to Miss Charlton, and they strolled through the room to talk of ambulances, sanitary commissions, hospitals, and bullets through the lungs. Pompilard, who declared he felt only eighteen years old while looking at his niece, divided his delightful attentions between Madame Volney and Mrs. Ripper. Clara invited Colonel Hyde to take a seat near her, and gave him such comfort as might best confirm him in the good path he was treading. Hyde junior looked at the war pictures in Harper's Weekly. Winslow and Mrs. Charlton found they had met five years before at Saratoga, and were soon deep in their recollections. Semmes and Detritch skirmished like two old roosters, each afraid of the other. Ripper made himself agreeable to Mrs. Pompilard and Netty, by talking of paintings, of which he knew something, having sold them at auction. Vance took soundings of Charlton's character, and found that rumor, for once, had not been unjust in her disparagement. The man's heart, what there was of it, was in his iron safe with his coupons and his certificates of deposit.

Suddenly Vance went to the piano, and, striking some of the loud keys, attracted the attention of the company, and then begged them to be silent while he made a few remarks. The hum of conversation was instantly hushed.

"We are assembled, ladies and gentlemen," he said, "on business in which Mr. Charlton here present is deeply interested."

Mr. Charlton, who occupied an arm-chair, and had Detritch on his right, bowed his acknowledgments.

"If," continued Vance, "I have not communicated privately to Mr. Charlton, or his respectable counsel, all the startling and important facts bearing on the case, I hope they will understand that it was not through any failure of respect for them, and especially for Mrs. and Miss Charlton, but simply because I have thought it right to choose the course which seemed to me the most proper in serving the cause of justice and of the party whose interests I represent."

Charlton and Detritch looked at each other inquiringly, and the look said, "What is he driving at?"

The amiable bride (Mrs. Ripper) touched Pompilard coquettishly with her fan, and, pointing to Charlton, whispered, "O, won't he be come up with?"

"No innocent man," continued Vance, "will think it ever untimely to be told that he is holding what does not belong to him; that he has it in his power to rectify a great wrong; to make just restitution. On the table here under my hand are certain documents. This which I hold up is a certified printed copy of the great Trial, by the issue of which Mr. Charlton, here present, came into possession of upwards of a million of dollars, derived from the estate of the brother of one of the ladies now before me. It appears from the judge's printed charge (see page 127) on the Trial, that the essential testimony in the case was that given by one Delancy Hyde and one Leonidas Quattles. With the former, Mr. Charlton has here renewed his acquaintance. Mr. Quattles died some months since, but we here have his deposition, duly attested, taken just before his death."

"What has all this to do with my property in New Orleans?" exclaimed Charlton, thoroughly mystified.

" Be patient, sir, and you will see. The verdict, ladies and gentlemen, turned upon the question whether, on the occasion of the explosion of the Pontiac, the child, Clara, or her father, Henry Berwick, died first. The testimony of Messrs. Hyde and Quattles was to the effect that the child died first. But it now appears that the father died — "

" A lie and a trick ! " shouted Charlton, starting up with features pale and convulsed at once with terror and with rage. " A trick for extorting money. Any simpleton might see through it. Have we been brought here to be insulted, sir ? You shall be indicted for a conspiracy. 'T is a case for the grand jury, — eh, Detritch ? "

" My advice to you, Mr. Charlton," said Detritch, " is to turn this gentleman over to me, and to refuse to listen yourself to anything further he may have to say."

In this advice Charlton snuffed, as he thought, the bad odor of a fee, and he determined not to be guided by it. Laughing scornfully, he said, resuming his seat : " Let the gentleman play out his farce. He hopes to show, does he, that the child died *after* the father ! "

" No, ladies and gentleman," said Vance, crossing the room, taking Clara by the hand, and leading her forth, " what I have to show is, that she did n't die at all, and that Clara Aylesford Berwick now stands before you."

Charlton rose half-way from his chair, the arms of which he grasped as if to keep himself from sinking. His features were ghastly in their expression of mingled amazement and indignation, coupled with a horrible misgiving of the truth of the disclosure, to which Vance's assured manner and the affirmative presence of Colonel Hyde gave their dreadful support. Charlton struggled to speak, but failed, and sank back in his chair, while Detritch, after having tried to compose his client, rose and said : " In my legal capacity I must protest against this most irregular and insidious proceeding, intended as it obviously is to throw my client and myself off our guard, and to produce an alarm which may be used to our disadvantage."

" Sir," replied Vance, " you entirely misapprehend my object. It is not to your fears, but to your manhood and your sense of justice that I have thought it right to make my first appeal. I propose to prove to you by facts, which no sane man can resist, that the young lady whose hand I hold is the veritable Miss Berwick, to whom her mother's estate belonged, and to whom it must now be restored, with interest."

"With interest! Ha, ha, ha!" cried Charlton, with a frightful attempt at a merriment which his pale cheeks belied.

"There will be time," continued Vance, "for the scrutiny of the law hereafter. I court it to the fullest extent. But I have thought it due to Mr. Charlton, to give him the opportunity to show his disposition to right a great wrong, in the event of my proving, as I can and will, that this lady is the person I proclaim her to be, the veritable Miss Berwick."

Moved by that same infatuation which compels a giddy man to look over the precipice which is luring him to jump, Charlton, with a deplorable affectation of composure, wiped the perspiration from his brow, and said: "Well, sir, bring on these proofs that you pretend are so irresistible. I think we can afford to hear them, — eh, Detritch?"

"First," said Vance, "I produce the confession of Hyde, here present, and of Quattles, deceased, that the infant child of Mr. Berwick was saved by them from the wreck of the Pontiac, taken to New Orleans, and sold at auction as a slave. The auctioneer, Mr. Richard Ripper, is here present, and will testify that he sold the child to Carberry Ratcliff, whose late attorney, T. J. Semmes, Esq., is here present, and can identify Miss Berwick as the child bought, according to Ratcliff's own admission, from the said Ripper. Then we have the testimony of Mrs. Ripper, lately Mrs. Gentry, by whom the child was brought up, and of Esha, her housemaid, both of whom are now in this house. We have further strong collateral testimony from Hattie Davy, now in this house, the nurse who had the child in charge at the time of the accident, and who identifies her by the marks on her person, especially by her different colored eyes, — a mark which I also can corroborate. We have articles of clothing and jewels bearing the child's initials, to the reception and keeping of which Mrs. Ripper and Esha will testify, and which, when unsealed, will no doubt be sworn to by Mrs. Davy as having belonged to the child at the time of the explosion."

"Well, sir," said Mr. Detritch, with a sarcastic smile, "I think Brother Semmes will admit that all this does n't make out a case. Unless you can bring some proof (which I know you cannot) of improper influences being applied by my client to induce his chief witnesses to give the testimony they did, you can make little headway in a court of law against a party who is fortified in what he holds by more than fourteen years of possession."

"Even on this point, sir," replied Vance, "we are not weak. Here are five original letters, with their envelopes, postage-marks, &c., all complete, from Mr. Charlton to Colonel Delancy Hyde, offering him and his accomplice their expenses and a thousand dollars if they will come on to New York and testify in a certain way. Here also are letters showing that, in the case of a colored woman named Jacobs, decoyed from Montreal back into slavery, the writer conducted himself in a manner which will afford corroborative proof that he was capable of doing what these other letters show that he did or attempted."

As Vance spoke, he held one of the letters so that Charlton could read it. The latter, while affecting not to look, read enough to be made aware of its purport. His fingers worked so to clutch it, that Detritch pulled him by the coat; and then Charlton, starting up, exclaimed: "I 'll not stay here another moment to be insulted. This is a conspiracy to swindle. Come along, Detritch. Come, Mrs. Charlton and Lucy."

He passed out. Detritch offered his arm to Mrs. Charlton. She declined it, and he left the room. There was an interval of silence. Every one felt sympathy for the two ladies. Mrs. Charlton approached Vance, and said, "Will you allow me to examine those letters?"

"Certainly, madam," he replied.

She took them one by one, scrutinized the handwriting, read them carefully, and returned them to Vance. She then asked the privilege of a private conference with Hyde, and the Colonel accompanied her into the anteroom. This interview was followed by one, first with Mrs. Ripper, then with Mr. Winslow, then with Esha and Mrs. Davy, and finally with Clara. During the day Pompilard had sent home for a photograph-book containing likenesses of Clara's father, mother, and maternal grandmother. These were placed in Mrs. Charlton's hands. A glance satisfied her of the family resemblance to the supposed child.

Re-entering the parlor Mrs. Charlton said: "Friends, there is no escape that I can see from the proofs you offer that this young lady is indeed Clara Aylesford Berwick. Be sure it will not be my fault if she is not at once instated in her rights. I bid you all good evening."

And then, escorted by Captain Onslow, she and her daughter took their leave, and the company broke up.

Charlton, impatient, had quitted the hotel with Detritch and sent back the carriage. They were closeted in the library when Mrs. Charlton and Lucy returned. The unloving and unloved wife, but tender mother, kissed her daughter for good-night and retired to her own sleeping-room. She undressed and went to bed; but not being able to sleep, rose, put on a light *robe de chambre*, and sat down to read. About two o'clock in the morning she heard the front door close and a carriage drive off. Detritch had then gone at last!

Charlton's sleeping-room was on the other side of the entry-way opposite to his wife's. She threw open her door to hear him when he should come up to bed. She waited anxiously a full hour. She began to grow nervous. Void as her heart was of affection for her husband, something like pity crept in as she recalled his look of anguish and alarm at Vance's disclosures. Ah! is it not sad when one has to despise while one pities! "Shall I not go, and try to cheer him?" she asked herself. Hopeless task! What cheer could she give unless she went with a lie, telling him that Vance's startling revelation was all a trick!

The laggard moments crept on. Though the gas was put up bright and flaring, she could not have so shivered with a nameless horror if she had been alone in some charnel-house, lighted only by pale, phosphoric gleams from dead men's bones.

But why did not Charlton come up?

The wind, which had been rising, blew back a blind, and swept with a mournful whistle through the trees in the area. Then it throbbed at the casement like a living heart that had something to reveal.

Why does he not come up?

Why not go down and see?

Though the entry-ways and the stairs were lighted, it seemed a frightful undertaking to traverse them as far as the library. Still she would do it. She darted out, placed her hand on the broad black-walnut balustrade, and stepped slowly down, — down, — down the broad, low, thickly carpeted stairs.

At last she stood on one of the spacious square landings.

What terrible silence! Not even the rattle of an early milk-cart through the streets! Heavenly Powers! Why this unaccountable pressure, as of some horrid incubus, upon her mind, so that every thought as it wandered, try as she might to control it, would stop short at a tomb? She recoiled. She drew back a step or two up, — up the stairs. And then, at that very moment, there was a dull, smothered, explosive sound which smote like a hand on her heart. She sank powerless on the stairs, and sat there for some minutes, gasping, horror-stricken, helpless.

Then rallying her strength she rushed up three flights to the room of Fletcher, the man-servant, and bade him dress quickly and come to her. He obeyed, and the two descended to the library.

Through the glass window of the door the gas shone brightly. Fletcher entered first; and his cry of alarm told the whole tragic tale. Mrs. Charlton followed, gave one look, and fell senseless on the floor.

Leaning back in his arm-chair, — his head erect, — his eyes open and staring, — sat Charlton. On his white vest a crimson stain was beginning to spread and spread, and, higher up, the cloth was blackened as if by fire. The vase-like ornament which had attracted Pompilard's attention on the library table had been drawn forth from its socket, and the pistol it concealed having been discharged, it lay on the floor, while Charlton's right hand, as it hung over the arm of the chair, pointed to the deadly weapon as if in mute accusation of its instrumentality.

CHAPTER XLVII.

AN AUTUMNAL VISIT.

"Why linger, why turn back, why shrink, my heart?
Thy hopes have gone before: from all things here
They have departed; thou shouldst now depart." — *Shelley.*

THE defunct having left no will, administrators of his estate were appointed. These deemed it proper to be guided by the wishes of the widow and the daughter, notwithstanding the latter was still a minor. Those wishes were, that the identification of Miss Berwick, conclusive as it was, should be frankly admitted, and her property, with its accumulated interest, restored to her without a contest.

There was a friendly hearing in chambers, before the probate and other judges. The witnesses were all carefully examined; the contents of the sealed package in the little trunk were identified; and at last, in accordance with high legal and judicial approval, the vast estate, constituting nearly two-thirds of the amount left by Charlton, was transferred to trustees to be held till Clara should be of age. And thus finally did Vance carry his point, and establish the rights of the orphan of the Pontiac.

It was on a warm, pleasant day in the last week of September, 1862, that he called to take leave of her.

Little more than an hour's drive beyond the Central Park brought him to a private avenue, at the stately gate of which he found children playing. One of these was a cripple, who, as he darted round on his little crutch, chasing or being chased, seemed the embodiment of Joy exercising under difficulties. His name was Andrew Rusk. An old colored woman who was carrying a basket of fruit to some invalid in the neighborhood, stopped and begged Andrew not to break his neck. Vance, recognizing Esha, asked if Clara was at home.

"Yes, Massa Vance; she 'll be powerful glad to see yer."

While Vance is waiting in a large and lofty drawing-room

for her appearance, let us review some of the incidents that have transpired since we encountered her last.

One of Clara's first acts, on being put in partial possession of her ancestral estate, had been to present her aunt Pompilard with a furnished house, retaining for herself the freedom of a few rooms. The house stood on a broad, picturesque semicircle of rocky table-land, that protruded like a huge bracket from a pleasant declivity, partly wooded, in view of the Palisades of the Hudson. The grounds included acres enough to satisfy the most aspiring member of the Horticultural Society. The house, also, was sufficiently spacious, not only for present, but for prospective grandchildren of the Pompilard stock. To the young Iretons and Purlings it was a blessed change from Lavinia Street to this new place.

Amid these sylvan scenes, — these green declivities and dimpling hollows, — these gardens beautiful, and groves and orchards, — the wounded Major and aspiring author, Cecil Purling, grew rapidly convalescent. The moment it was understood in fashionable circles that, through Clara's access to fortune, he stood no longer in need of help, subscribers to his history poured in not merely by dozens, but by hundreds. He soon had confirmation made doubly sure that he should have the glorious privilege of being independent through his own unaided efforts. This time there is no danger that he will ruin a publisher. The work proceeds. On your library shelf, O friendly reader, please leave a vacant space for six full-sized duodecimos!

Pompilard's first great dinner, on being settled in his new home, was given in honor of the Maloneys. In reply to the written invitation, Maloney wrote, "The beggarly Irish tailor accepts for himself and family." On entering the house, he asked a private interview with Pompilard, and thereupon bullied him so far, that the old man signed a solemn pledge abjuring Wall Street, and all financial operations of a speculative character thenceforth forever.

The dinner was graced by the presence of Mr. and Mrs. Ripper, both of them now furious Abolitionists, and proud of the name. The lady was at last emphatically of the opinion that "Slavery will be come up with."

Clara had Esha and Hattie to wait on her, though rather in the capacity of friends than of servants. Having got from Mrs. Ripper a careful estimate of the amount paid by Ratcliff for the support and education of his putative slave, Clara had it repaid with interest. The money came to him most acceptably. His large investments in slaves had ruined him. His "maid-servants and man-servants"* had flocked to the old flag and found freedom. A piteous communication from him appeared on the occasion in the Richmond Whig. We quote from it a single passage.

"What contributed most to my mortification was, that in my whole gang of slaves, among whom there were any amount of Aarons, Abrahams, Isaacs, and Jacobs, there was not one Abdiel, — not one remained loyal to the Rebel."

The philosophical editor, in his comments, endeavored to shield his beloved slavery from inferential prejudice, and said:

"The escaped slave is ungrateful; therefore, slavery is wrong! Children are often ungrateful; does it follow that the relation of parent and child is wrong?" †

Could even Mr. Carlyle have put it more cogently?

The money received by Clara from Mrs. Ratcliff's private estate was all appropriated to the establishment of an institution in New Orleans for the education of the children of freed slaves. To this fund Madame Volney not only added from her own legacy, but she went back to New Orleans to superintend the initiation of the humane and important enterprise.

"Into each life some rain must fall." The day after the dinner to the Maloneys intelligence came of the death of Captain Ireton. He had been hung by the fierce slaveocracy at Richmond as a spy. It was asserted that he had joined the Rebel Engineer Corps, at Island Number Ten, to obtain information for the United States. However this may have been, it is certain *he was not captured in the capacity of a spy;* and every one acquainted with the usages of civilized warfare will recognize the atrocity of hanging a man on the ground that he had *formerly* acted as a spy. The Richmond papers palliated

* See Mr. Jefferson Davis's proclamation for a fast, March, 1863.

† These quotations are genuine, as many newspaper readers will recollect.

the murder by saying Ireton had "*confessed* himself to be a spy." As if any judicial tribunal would hang a man on his own confession! "Would you make me bear testimony against myself?" said Joan of Arc to her judges.

Much to the disgust of the pro-slavery leaders, who had counted on a display of that cowardice which they had taught the Southern people to regard as inseparable from Yankee blood, Ireton met his death cheerily, as a bridegroom would go forth to take the hand of his beloved.* It reminded them unpleasantly of old John Brown.

"Whether on the gallows high
Or in the battle's van,
The fittest place for man to die
Is where he dies for man."

The news of Ireton's death was mentioned by Captain Onslow while making a morning call on Miss Charlton. Her mother had dressed herself to drive out on some visits of charity. As she was passing through the hall to her carriage, Lucy called her into the drawing-room and communicated the report. The widow turned deadly pale, and left the room without speaking. She gave up her drive for that day, and commissioned Lucy to fulfil the beneficent errands she had planned. Captain Onslow begged so hard to be permitted to accompany Lucy, that, after a brief consultation between mother and daughter, consent was given.

Thus are Nature and Human Life ever offering their tragic contrasts! Here the withered leaf; and there, under the decaying mould, the green germ! Here Grief, finding its home in the stricken heart; and there thou, O Hope, with eyes so fair!

* The case seems to have been precisely parallel to that of Spencer Kellogg Brown, hung in Richmond, September 25th, 1863, as a spy. On the 18th of that month, Brown told the Rev. William G. Scandlin of Massachusetts (see the latter's published letter), that they had kept him there in prison "*until all his evidence had been sent away, allowed him but fifteen hours to prepare for his defence, and denied him the privilege of counsel.*" Brown was captured by guerillas, not while he was acting as a spy, but while returning from destroying a rebel ferry-boat near Port Hudson, which he had done under the order of Captain Porter. The hanging of this man was as shameless a murder as was ever perpetrated by Thugs. But Slavery, disappointed in the hanging of Captains Sawyer and Flynn, was yelling lustily for a Yankee to hang; and Jeff Davis was not man enough to say "No."

Colonel Delancy Hyde speedily had an opportunity of showing the sincerity of his conversion, political and moral. He went into the fight at South Mountain, and was by the side of General Reno when that loyal and noble officer (Virginia-born) fell mortally wounded. For gallant conduct on that occasion Hyde was put on General Mansfield's staff, and saw him, too, fall, three days after Reno, in the great fight at Antietam. On this occasion Hyde lost a leg, but had the satisfaction of seeing his nephew, Delancy junior, come out unscathed, and with the promise of promotion for gallantry in carrying the colors of the regiment after three successive bearers had been shot dead.

Hyde was presented with a wooden leg, of which he was quite proud. But the great event of his life was the establishment of his sister, the Widow Rusk, with her children, in a comfortable cottage on the outskirts of Pompilard's grounds, where the family were well provided for by Clara. Here on the piazza, looking out on the river, the Colonel played with the children, watched the boats, and read the newspapers. Perhaps one of the profoundest of his emotions was experienced the day he saw in one of the pictorial papers a picture of Delancy junior, bearing a flag riddled by bullets. But the Colonel's heart felt a redoubled thrill when he read the following paragraph: —

"This young and gallant color-bearer is, we learn, a descendant of an illustrious Virginia family, his ancestor, Delancy Hyde, having come over with the first settlers. Nobly has the youth adhered to the traditions of the Washingtons and the Madisons. His uncle, the brave Colonel Hyde, was one of the severely wounded in the late battle."

The Colonel did not faint, but he came nearer to it than ever before in his life.

Can the Ethiopian change his skin? It has generally been thought not. But there was certainly an element of grace in Hyde which now promised to bleach the whole moral complexion of the man; and that element, though but as a grain of mustard-seed, was love for his sister and her offspring.

Mr. Semmes was glad to receive, as the recompense for his services, the exemption of certain property from confiscation.

At their parting interview Vance ingenuously told him he considered him a scoundrel. Semmes did n't see it in that light, and entered into a long argument to prove that he had done no wrong. Vance listened patiently, and said in reply, "Do you perceive an ill odor of dead rats in the wall?" Semmes snuffed, and then answered, "Indeed I don't perceive any bad smell." "I *do*," said Vance; "good by, sir!" And that was the end of their acquaintance.

But it is in the track of Vance and Clara that we promised to conduct the reader. Clara had proposed a ramble over the grounds. Never had she appeared so radiant in Vance's eyes. It was not her dress, for that was rather plain, though perfect in its adaptedness to the season and the scene. It was not that jaunty little hat, hiding not too much of her soft, thick hair. But the climate of her ancestral North seemed to have added a new sparkle and gloss to her beauty. And then the pleasure of seeing Vance showed itself so unreservedly in her face!

They strolled through the well-appointed garden, and Vance was glad to see that Clara had a genuine love of flowers and fruits, and could name all the varieties, distinguishing with quick perception the slightest differences of form and hue. In the summer-house, overlooking the majestic river, and surrounded, though not too much shaded, by birches, oaks, and pines, indigenous to the soil, they found Miss Netty Pompilard engaged in sketching. She ran away as they approached, presuming, like a sensible young person, that she could be spared. Even the mocking-bird, Clara's old friend Dainty, who pecked at a peach in his cage, seemed to understand that his noisy voluntaries must now be hushed.

The promenaders sat down on a rustic bench.

"Well, Clara," said Vance, "I have heard to-day great and inspiring news. It almost made me feel as if I could afford to stop short in my work, and to be content, should I, like Moses, be suffered only to *see* the promised land with my eyes, but not to 'go over thither.'"

"To what do you allude?"

"To-morrow President Lincoln issues a proclamation of prospective emancipation to the slaves of the Rebel States."

" Good!" cried Clara, giving him her hand for a grasp of congratulation.

" But I foresee," said Vance, " that there is much yet to be done before it can be effective, and I 've come to bid you a long, perhaps a last farewell."

Clara said not a word, but ran out of the summer-house below the bank into a little thicket that hid her entirely from view. Here she caught at the white trunk of a birch, and leaning her forehead against it, wept passionately for some time. Vance sat wondering at her disappearance. Ten minutes passed, and she did not return. He rose to seek her, when suddenly he saw her climbing leisurely up the bank, a few wild-flowers in her hand. There was no vestige of emotion in her face.

" You wondered at my quitting you so abruptly," she said. " I thought of some fringed gentians in bloom below there, and I ran to gather them for you. Are they not of a lovely blue?"

" Thank you," said Vance, not wholly deceived by her calm, assured manner.

" So you really mean to leave us?" she said, smiling and looking him full in the face. " I 'm very sorry for it."

" So am I, Clara, for it would be very delightful to settle down amid scenes like these and lead a life of meditative leisure. But not yet can I hope for my discharge. My country needs every able-bodied son. I must do what I best can to serve her. But first let me give you a few words of advice. Your Trustees tell me you have been spending money at such a fearful rate, that they have been compelled to refuse your calls. To this you object. Let me beg you to asquiesce with cheerfulness. They are gentlemen, liberal and patriotic. They have consented to your giving your aunt this splendid estate and the means of supporting it. They have allowed you to bestow portentous sums in charity, and for the relief of sick and wounded soldiers. I hear, too, that Miss Tremaine has sent to you for aid."

" Yes; her mother is dead, and her father has failed. They are quite poor."

" So you 've sent her a couple of thousand dollars. The first pauper you shall meet will have as much claim on you as she.

Would I check that divine propensity of your nature, — the desire to bestow? O never, never! Far from it! Cherish it, my dear child. Believe in it. Find your constant delight in it. But be reasonable. Consider your own future. A little computation will show you that, at the present rate, it will not take you ten years to get rid of all your money. You will soon have suitors in plenty. Indeed, I hear that some very formidable ones are already making reconnoissances, although they find to their despair that the porter forbids them entrance unless they come on crutches; and I hear you send word to your serenaders, to take their music to the banks of the Potomac. But your time will soon come, Clara. You will be married. (Please not pull that fringed gentian to pieces in that barbarous way!) You will have your own tasteful, munificent, and hospitable home. Reserve to yourself the power to make it all that, and do not be wise too late."

"And is there nothing I can do, Mr. Vance, to let you see I have some little gratitude for all that you have done for me?"

"Ah! I shall quote Rochefoucault against you, if you say that. 'Too great eagerness to requite an obligation is a species of ingratitude.' All that I 've done is but a partial repayment of the debt I owed your mother's father; for I owed him my life. Besides, you pay me every time you help the brave fellow whose wound or whose malady was got in risking all for country and for justice."

"We must think of each other often," sighed Clara.

"That we cannot fail to do," said Vance. "There are incidents in our past that will compel a frequent interchange of remembrances; and to me they will be very dear. Besides, from every soul of a good man or woman, with whom I have ever been brought in communication (either by visible presence or through letters or books), I unwind a subtile filament which keeps us united, and never fails. I meet one whose society I would court, but cannot, — we part, — one thinks of the other, 'How indifferent he or she seemed!' or 'Why did we not grow more intimate?' And yet a friendship that shall outlast the sun may have been unconsciously formed."

"You must write me," said Clara.

"I 'm a poor correspondent," replied Vance; "but I shall

obey. And now my watch tells me I must go. I start in a few hours for Washington."

They strolled back to the house. Vance took leave of all the inmates, not forgetting Esha. He went to Hyde's cottage, and had an affectionate parting with that worthy; and then drove to a curve in the road where Clara stood waiting solitary to exchange the final farewell.

It was on an avenue through the primeval forest, having on either side a strip of greensward edged by pine-trees, odorous and thick, which had carpeted the ground here and there with their leafy needles of the last years growth, now brown and dry.

The mild, post-equinoctial sunshine was flooding the middle of the road, but Clara stood on the sward in the shade. Vance dismounted from his carriage and drew near. All Clara's beauty seemed to culminate for that trial. A smile adorably tender lighted up her features. Vance felt that he was treading on enchanted ground, and that the atmosphere swam with the rose-hues of young romance. The gates of Paradise seemed opening, while a Peri, with hand extended, offered to be his guide. Youth and glad Desire rushed back into that inner chamber of his heart sacred to a love ineffably precious.

Clara put out her hand; but why was it that this time it was her right hand, when heretofore, ever since her rescue in New Orleans, she had always given the left?

Rather high up on the wrist of the right was a bracelet; a bracelet of that soft, fine hair familiar to Vance. He recognized it now, and the tears threatened to overflow. Lifting the wrist to his lips he kissed it, and then, with a "God keep you!" entered the carriage, and was whirled away.

"It was the bracelet, not the wrist, he kissed," sighed Clara.

CHAPTER XLVIII.

TIME DISCOVERS AND COVERS.

"*Crito.* How and where shall we bury you?

"*Socrates.* Bury me in any way you please, if you can catch me to bury. Crito obstinately thinks, my friends, I am that which he shall shortly behold dead. Say rather, Crito, — say if you love me, 'Where shall I bury your body'; and I will answer you, 'Bury it in any manner and in any place you please.'" — *Plato.*

ON rolled the months, nor slackened their speed because of the sufferings and the sighings with which they went freighted. Almost every day brought its battle or its skirmish. Almost every day men, — sometimes many hundreds, — would be shot dead, or be wounded and borne away in ambulances or on stretchers, not grudging the sacrifices they had made.

O precious blood, not vainly shed! O bereaved hearts, not unprofitably stricken! Do not doubt there shall be compensation. Do not doubt that every smallest effort, though seemingly fruitless, rendered to the right, shall be an imperishable good both to yourselves and others.

On rolled the months, bringing alternate triumph and disaster, radiance and gloom, to souls waiting the salvation of the Lord. The summer of 1863 had come. There had been laurels for Murfreesboro' and crape for Chancellorville. Vicksburg and Port Hudson yet trembled in the balance. Pennsylvania was threatened with a Rebel invasion. The Emancipation Proclamation, gradual as the great processes of nature, was working its way, though not in the earthquake nor in the fire. Black regiments had been enlisted, and were beginning to answer the question, Will the negro fight?

On the sixth of June, 1863, a cavalry force of Rebels made their appearance some four miles from Milliken's Bend on the Mississippi, and attacked and drove a greatly inferior Union force, composed mainly of the Tenth Illinois cavalry.

Suddenly there rose up in their path, as if from the soil, two hundred and fifty black soldiers. They belonged to the Eleventh Louisiana African regiment, and were under the command of Colonel Lieb. They had never been in a fight before. The "chivalry" came on, expecting to see their former bondsmen crouch and tremble at the first imperious word; but, to the dismay of the Rebels, they were met with such splendid bravery, that they turned and fled, and the Illinois men were saved.

The next day nine hundred and forty-one troops of African descent had a hand-to-hand engagement with a Texan brigade, commanded by McCulloch, which numbered eighteen hundred and sixty-five. Three hundred and forty-five of the colored troops were killed or wounded, though not till they had put *hors de combat* twice that number of Rebels. The gunboat Choctaw finally came up to drive off the enemy.

Conspicuous for intrepid conduct on both these occasions was a black man, slightly above the middle height, but broad-shouldered, well-formed, and athletic. Across his left cheek was a scar as if from a sabre-cut. This man had received the name of Peculiar Institution, but he was familiarly called Peek. On the second day his words and his example had inspired the men of his company with an almost superhuman courage. Bravely they stood their ground, and nowhere else on the field did so many of the enemy's dead attest the valor of these undrilled Africans.

One youth, apparently not seventeen, had fought by Peek's side and under his eye with heroic defiance of danger. At last, venturing too far from the ranks, he got engaged with two Rebel officers in a hand-to-hand encounter, and was wounded. Peek saw his danger, rushed to his aid, parried a blow aimed at the lad's life, and shot one of the infuriate officers; but as he was bearing the youth back into the ranks, he was himself wounded in the side, and fell with his burden.

The boy's wound was not serious. He and Peek were borne within the protection of the guns of the Choctaw. They lay in the shade cast by the Levee. The surgeon looked at Peek's wound, and shook his head. Then turning to the boy he exclaimed, "Why, Sterling, is this you?"

At the name of Sterling, Peek had roused himself and turned a gaze, at once of awe and curiosity, on the youth; then sending the surgeon to another sufferer, had beckoned to the boy to draw near.

"Is your name Sterling?"

"Yes, sir."

"Where were you born?"

"In Montreal."

"And your mother's name was Flora Jacobs, and your father's — Sterling! *I* am your father!"

Profoundly overcome by the disclosure, the boy was speechless for a time with agitation. But Peek pressed him to tell of his mother. "And be quick, Sterling; for my time is short."

We need not give the boy's narrative in his own words, interrupted as it was by the inquiries put by Peek, while his life-blood was ebbing. The story which Clara Berwick had heard at school, and communicated to Mrs. Gentry, was the story of Flora Jacobs. Those who hate to think ill of slavery sneer at such reports as the exaggerations of romance; but the great heart of humanity will need no testimony to show that, in the nature of things, they must be too often true.

Flora and Sterling, mother and son, were held as slaves by one Floyd in Alabama. Flora had religiously kept her oath of fidelity to Peek, much to the chagrin and indignation of her master, who saw that he was losing at least fifty per cent on his investment, through her stubborn resistance to his demands that she should increase and multiply after the fashion of his Alderneys and Durhams. At last it happened that Sterling, who had been inspired by his mother with the desire to seek his father, ran away, was retaken, and tied up for a whipping. Ten lashes had been given, and had drawn blood. And there were to be one hundred and ninety more! The mother, in an agony, interceded. There was only one way by which she could save him. She must marry coachman George. She consented. But a month afterwards Floyd learnt that Flora had made the marriage practically null, and had not suffered coachman George to touch even the hem of her robe. Floyd was enraged. He wrought upon the evil passions of George. There were first threats, and then an attempt at violence. The attempt was baffled by Flora's inflicting upon herself a mortal stab. As she fell on the floor she marked upon it with her own blood a cross, and kissed it with her last breath.

"'T is all right, — all just as it should be," murmured Peek.

"God knew best. Bless him always for this meeting, Sterling. Hold the napkin closer to the wound. There! I knew she would be true! So! Take the belt from under my vest. Easy! It contains a hundred dollars. 'T is yours. Take the watch from the pocket. So! A handsome gold one, you see. 'T was given me by Mr. Vance. The name 's engraved on it. Can you write? Good. Your mother taught you. Write by the next mail to William C. Vance, Washington, D. C. Tell him what has happened. Tell him how your mother died. He 'll be your friend. You fought bravely, my son. What sweetness God puts into this moment! Take no trouble about the body I leave behind. Any trench will do for it. Fight on for freedom and the right. Slavery must die. All wrong must die. You can't wrong even a worm without wronging yourself more than it. Remember that. Holy living makes holy believing. Charity first. Think to shut out others from heaven, and the danger is great you 'll shut yourself out. Don't strike for revenge. Slay because 't is God's cause on earth you defend; and don't fight unless you see and believe that much, let who may command. Love life. 'T is God's gift and opportunity. The more you suffer, the more, my dear boy, you can show you prize life, not for the world's goods, but for that love of God, which is heaven, — Christ's heaven. Think. Not to think is to be a brute. Learn something every day. Love all that 's good and fair. Love music. Love flowers. Don't be so childish as to suppose that because you don't hear or see spirits, they don't hear and see *you*. Remember that your mother and I can watch you, — can know your every thought. You 'll grieve us if you do wrong. You 'll make us very happy if you do right. Ah! The napkin has slipped. No matter. There! Let the blood ooze. See! Sterling! Look! There! Do you not see? They come. The angels! *Your* mother — *my* mother — and beyond there, high up there — one — Ah, God! Tell Mr. Vance — tell him — his — his —"

Peek stood up erect, lifted his clasped hands above his head, looked beyond them as if watching some beatific vision, then dropped his mortal body dead upon the earth.

CHAPTER XLIX.

EYES TO THE BLIND.

" Farewell ! The passion of long years I pour
Into that word ! " — *Mrs. Hemans.*

" Heureux l'homme qu'un doux hymen unira avec elle ! il n'aura à craindre que de la perdre et de lui survivre." — *Fenelon.*

IT was that Fourth of July, 1863, when every sincere friend of the Great Republic felt his heart beat high with mingled hope and apprehension. Tremendous issues, which must affect the people of the American continent through all coming time, were in the balance of Fate, and the capricious chances of war might turn the scale on either side. Gettysburg, Vicksburg, Port Hudson, Helena! The great struggles that were to make these places memorable had reached their culminating and critical point, but were as yet undecided.

Lee's Rebel army of invasion, highly disciplined, and numbering nearly a hundred thousand men, was marching into Pennsylvania. General Lee assured his friends he should remain North just as long as he wished; that there was no earthly power strong enough to drive him back across the Potomac. He expected "to march on Baltimore and occupy it; then to march on Washington and dictate terms of peace."

Such was Lee's plan. Its success depended on his defeating the Union army; and of that he felt certain.

The loyal North was unusually reticent and grave; "troubled on every side, yet not distressed; perplexed, but not in despair." A change of commanders in the army of the Potomac, when just on the eve of the decisive contest, added to the general seriousness.

Clara, since her parting from Vance, had addressed herself thoughtfully to the business of life. Duties actively discharged had brought with them their reward in a diffusive cheerfulness.

On the morning of that eventful Fourth of July, the ringing of bells and the firing of cannon roused her from slumber somewhat earlier than usual. On the piazza she met Netty Pompilard, and Mary and Julia Ireton, and Master and Miss Purling, and they all strolled to the river's side, — then home to breakfast, — then out to the mown field by the orchard, where a mammoth tent had been erected, and servants were spreading tables for the day's entertainment, to be given by Clara to all the poor and rich of the neighborhood. Colonel Hyde, having been commissioned to superintend the arrangements, was here in his glory, and not a little of his importance was reflected on the busy cripple, his nephew.

Clara's thoughts, however, were at Gettysburg, where brave men were giving up their lives and exposing themselves to terrible, life-wasting wounds, in order that we at home might live in peace and have a country, free and undishonored. She thought of Vance. She knew he had resigned his colonelcy, and was now employed in the important and hazardous, though untrumpeted labors of a scout or spy, for which he felt that his old practice as an actor had given him some aptitude. We subjoin a few fragmentary extracts from the last letter she had received from him: —

"Poor Peek, — rather let me say fortunate Peek! He fell nobly, as he always desired to fall, in the cause of freedom and humanity. His son, Sterling, is now with me; a bright, brave little fellow, who is already a great comfort and help."

"Until the North are as much in earnest for the right as the South are for the wrong, we must not expect to see an end to this war. It is not enough to say, 'Our cause is just. Providence will put it through.' If we don't think the right and the just worth making great sacrifices for, — worth risking life and fortune for, — we repel that aid from Heaven which we lazily claim as our due. God gives Satan power to try the nations as he once tried Job. 'Skin for skin,' says Satan; 'yea, all that a man hath will he give for his life.' Unless we have pluck enough to disprove the Satanic imputation, and to show we prize God's kingdom on earth more than we do life or limb or worldly store, then it is not a good cause that will save us, but a sordid spirit that will ruin us. O for a return of that inspiration which filled us when the first bombardment of Sumter smote on our ears!"

"The President will soon call for three hundred thousand more volunteers. O women of the North! — ye whose heart-wisdom foreruns the slow processes of our masculine reason, — lend yourselves forthwith to the great work of raising this force and sending it to fill up our depleted armies."

"This Upas-tree of slavery is now girdled, they tell us. 'Why not leave it to the winds of heaven to blow down?' But if this whirlwind of civil war can't do it, don't trust to the zephyrs of peace. No! The President's proclamation must be carried into effect on every plantation, in every dungeon, where a slave exists. Better that this generation should go down with harness on to its grave, and that war should be the normal state of the next generation, than that we should fail in our pledged faith to the poor victims of oppression whose masters have brought the sword."

The grand entertainment under the tent lasted late into the afternoon. An excellent band of music was present, and as the tunes were selected by Clara, they were all good. Pompilard was, of course, a prominent figure at the table. He was toast-master, speech-maker, and general entertainer. He said pleasant things to the women and found amusements for the children. He complimented "the gallant Colonel Hyde" on his "very admirable arrangements" for their comfort; and the Colonel replied in a speech, in which he declared that much of the honor belonged to his sister Dorothy, and his nephew, Andrew Jackson.

In a high-flown tribute to the Emerald Isle, "the land of the Emmetts and of that brave hater of slavery, O'Connell," Pompilard called up Maloney, who, in a fiery little harangue, showed that he did not lack that gift of extemporaneous eloquence which the Currans and the Grattans used so lavishly to exhibit. The band played "Rory O'More."

A compliment to "the historian of the war" called up Purling, who, in the lack of one arm, made the other do double duty in gesticulating. He was cheered to his heart's content. The band played "Hail Columbia."

A compliment to the absent Captain Delancy Hyde Rusk drew from his uncle this sentiment: "The poor whites of the South! may the Lord open their eyes and send them plenty of soap!" The band played "Dixie."

A venerable clergyman present, the Rev. Mr. Beitler, now rose and gave "The memory of our fallen brave!" This was drunk standing in solemn silence, with heads uncovered. But Mrs. Ireton and Clara vainly put their handkerchiefs to their faces to keep back their sobs. By a secret sympathy they sought each other, and sat down under a tree where they could be somewhat retired from the rest. Esha drew near, but had too much tact to disturb them.

It was four o'clock when a courier was seen running toward the assembled company. He came with an "Extra," containing that telegraphic despatch from the President of the United States, flashed over the wires that day, giving comforting assurances from Gettysburg. Pompilard stood on a chair and proposed a succession of cheers, which were vociferously delivered. Clara and Mrs. Ireton dried their tears and partook of the general joy. Then rapping on the table, Pompilard obtained profound silence; and the old clergyman, kneeling, addressed the Throne of Grace in words of thankfulness that found a response in every heart. The day's amusements ended in a stroll of the company through the beautiful grounds.

After the glory the grief. No sooner was it known that Lee, whipped and crestfallen, was retreating, than there was a call for succor to the wounded and the dying. Clara, under the escort of Major Purling (who was eager to glean materials for the great history) went immediately to Gettysburg. She visited the churches (converted into hospitals), where wounded men, close as they could lie, were heroically enduring the sharpest sufferings. She labored to increase their accommodations. If families would n't give up their houses for love, then they must for money. Yes, money can do it. She drew on her trustees till they were frightened at the repetition of big figures in her drafts. She soothed the dying; she made provision for the wounded; she ordered the wholesomest viands for those who could eat.

On the third day she met Mrs. Charlton and her daughter, and they affectionately renewed their acquaintance. As they walked together through a hospital they had not till then entered, Clara suddenly started back with emotion and turned deadly pale. But for Major Purling's support she would have fallen. Tears came to her relief, and she rallied.

What was the matter?

On one of the iron beds lay a captain of artillery. He did not appear to be wounded. He lay, as if suffering more from exhaustion than from physical pain. And yet, on looking closer, you saw from the glassy unconsciousness of his eyes that the poor man was blind. But O that expression of sweet resignation and patient submission! It was better than a prayer to look on it. It touched deeper than any exhortation from holiest lips. It spoke of an inward reign of divinest repose; of a land more beautiful than any the external vision ever looked on; of that peace of God which passeth all understanding.

Clara recognized in it the face of Clarles Kenrick. A cannon-ball had passed before his eyes, and the shock from the concussion of air had paralyzed the optic nerves. The surgeons gave him little hope of ever recovering his sight.

For some private reason, best known to herself, Clara did not make herself known to Kenrick. She did not even inform any one that she knew him. She induced Lucy Charlton to minister to his wants. On Lucy's asking him what she could do (for she did not know he was Onslow's friend), he said, "If you can pen a letter for me, I shall be much obliged."

"Certainly," said she; "and my friend here shall hold the ink while I write."

She received from the hands of her maid in attendance a portfolio with which she had come provided, anticipating such requests. She then took a seat by his side, while Clara sat at the foot of the cot, where she could look in his blind, unconscious face, and wipe away her tears unseen.

"I 'm ready," said Lucy. And he dictated as follows: —

"My dear Cousin: I received last night your letter from Meade's headquarters. 'T was a comfort to be assured you escaped unharmed amid your many exposures.

"You tell me I am put down in the reports as among the slightly wounded, and you desire to know all the particulars. Alas! I may say with the tragic poet, 'My wound is great because it is so small.' Don't add, as Johnson once did, 'Then 't would be greater, were it none at all.' A cannon-ball, my dear fellow, passed before my eyes, and the sight thereof is extinguished utterly. The handwriting of this letter, you will perceive, is not my own.

"What you say of Onslow delights me. So he has behaved nobly before Vicksburg, and is to be made a Colonel! The one hope of his heart is to be with the army of liberation that shall go down into Texas. Onslow will not rest till he has redeemed that bloody soil to freedom, and put an end to the rule of the miscreant hangmen of the State.

"I said the *one* hope of his heart. But what you insinuate leads me to suspect there may be still another, — a tender hope. Can it be? Poor fellow! He deserves it.

"You bid me take courage and call on Perdita. You tell me she is free as air, — that the bloom is on the plum as yet untouched, unbreathed upon. My own dear cousin, if I was hopeless before I lost my eyesight, what must I be now? But, since a thing of beauty is a joy forever, was I not lucky in making her acquaintance before that cannon-ball swept away my optic sense? Now, as I rest here on my couch, I can call up her charming image, — nay, I can hear the very tones of her singing. She is worthy of the brilliant inheritance you were instrumental in restoring to her. I shall always be the happier for having known her, even though the knowing should continue to be my disquietude.

"I have just heard from my father. He and his young wife are in Richmond. His pecuniary fortunes are at a very low ebb. His slaves were all liberated last month by Banks, who has anticipated the work I expected to do myself. My father begins to be disenchanted in regard to the Rebellion. He even admits that Davis is n't quite so remarkable a man as he had supposed. How gladly I would help my father if I could! May the opportunity be some day mine. All I have ('t is only five thousand dollars) shall be his.

"What can I do, my dear cousin, if I can't get back my eyesight? God knows and cares; and I am content in that belief. 'There is a special providence in the falling of a sparrow.' Am not I better than many sparrows? 'Hence have I genial seasons!' 'T is all as it should be; and though He slay me, yet will I trust in him.

"Farewell,

"CHARLES KENRICK.

"TO WILLIAM C. VANCE."

Several times during the dictating of this letter, Lucy (especially when Onslow's name was mentioned) would have betrayed both herself and Clara, had not the latter in dumb show dissuaded her. The next day Clara made herself known, and introduced Major Purling; but she did not allow the blind man to suspect that she was that friend of his unknown amanuensis, who had "held the ink."

Her own persuasions, added to those of the Major, forced Kenrick at last to consent to be removed to Onarock. Here, in the society of cheerful Old Age and congenial Youth, he rapidly recovered strength. But to his visual orbs there returned no light. There it was still "dark, dark, dark, amid the blaze of noon."

He did not murmur at the dispensation. In all Clara's studies, readings, and exercises he was made the partaker. Even the beautiful landscapes on all sides were brought vividly before his inner eyes by her graphic words. Along the river's bank, and through the forest aisles, and along the garden borders she would lead him, and not a flower was beautiful that he was not made to know it.

It was the 18th of October, 1863, — that lovely Sabbath which seemed to have come down out of heaven, — so beautiful it was, — so calm, so bright, — so soft and yet so exhilarating. The forest-trees had begun to put on their autumnal drapery of many colors. The maple was already of a fiery scarlet; the beech-leaves, the birch, and the witch-hazel, of a pale yellow; and there were all gradations of purple and orange among the hickories, the elms, and the ashes. The varnished leaves of the oak for the most part retained their greenness, forming mirrors for the light to reflect from, and flashing and glistening, as if for very joy, under the bland, indolent breeze. It was such weather as this that drew from Emerson that note, we can all respond to, in our higher moments of intenser life, "Give me health and a day, and I will make the pomp of emperors ridiculous."

With Kenrick, even to his blindness there came a sense of the beauty and the glow. He could enjoy the balmy air, the blest power of sunshine, the odors from the falling leaves and the grateful earth. And what need of external vision, since Clara could so well supply its want? He walked forth with her, and they stopped near a rustic bench overlooking the Hudson, and sat down.

"Indeed I must leave you to-morrow," said he, in continuation of some previous remark: "I 've got an excellent situation as sub-teacher of French at West Point."

"O, you 've got a situation, have you?" returned Clara.

The tears sprang to her eyes; but, alas for human frailty! this time they were tears of vexation.

There was silence for almost a minute. Then Kenrick said, "Do you know I 've been with you more than three months?"

"Well," replied Clara, pettishly, "is there anything so very surprising or disagreeable in that?"

"But I fear Onarock will prove my Capua, — that it will unfit me for the sterner warfare of life."

"O, go to your sterner warfare, since you desire it!"

And with a desperate effort at nonchalance she swung her hat by its ribbon, and sang that little air from "La Bayadère" by Auber, — "Je suis content, — je suis heureux."

"Clara, dear friend, you seem displeased with me. What have I done?"

"You want to humiliate me!" exclaimed Clara, reproachfully, and bursting into a passion of tears.

"Want to humiliate you? I can't see how."

"I suppose not," returned Clara, ironically. "There are none so blind as those who don't choose to see."

"What do you mean, dear friend?"

"Dear *friend* indeed!" sobbed Clara. "Is he as blind as he would have me think? Have n't I given hints enough, intimations enough, opportunities enough? Would the man force me to offer myself outright?"

There was another interval of silence, and this time it lasted full ten minutes. And then Kenrick, his breath coming quick, his breast heaving, unable longer to keep back his tears, drew forth his handkerchief, and covering his face, wept heartily.

He rose and put out his hand. Clara seized it. He folded her in his arms; and their first kiss, — a kiss of betrothal, — was exchanged.

THE END.

Cambridge: Stereotyped and Printed by Welch, Bigelow, & Co.

www.ingramcontent.com/pod-product-compliance
Lightning Source LLC
LaVergne TN
LVHW021321110826
845150LV00003B/637

* 9 7 8 1 4 2 5 5 5 6 5 4 9 *